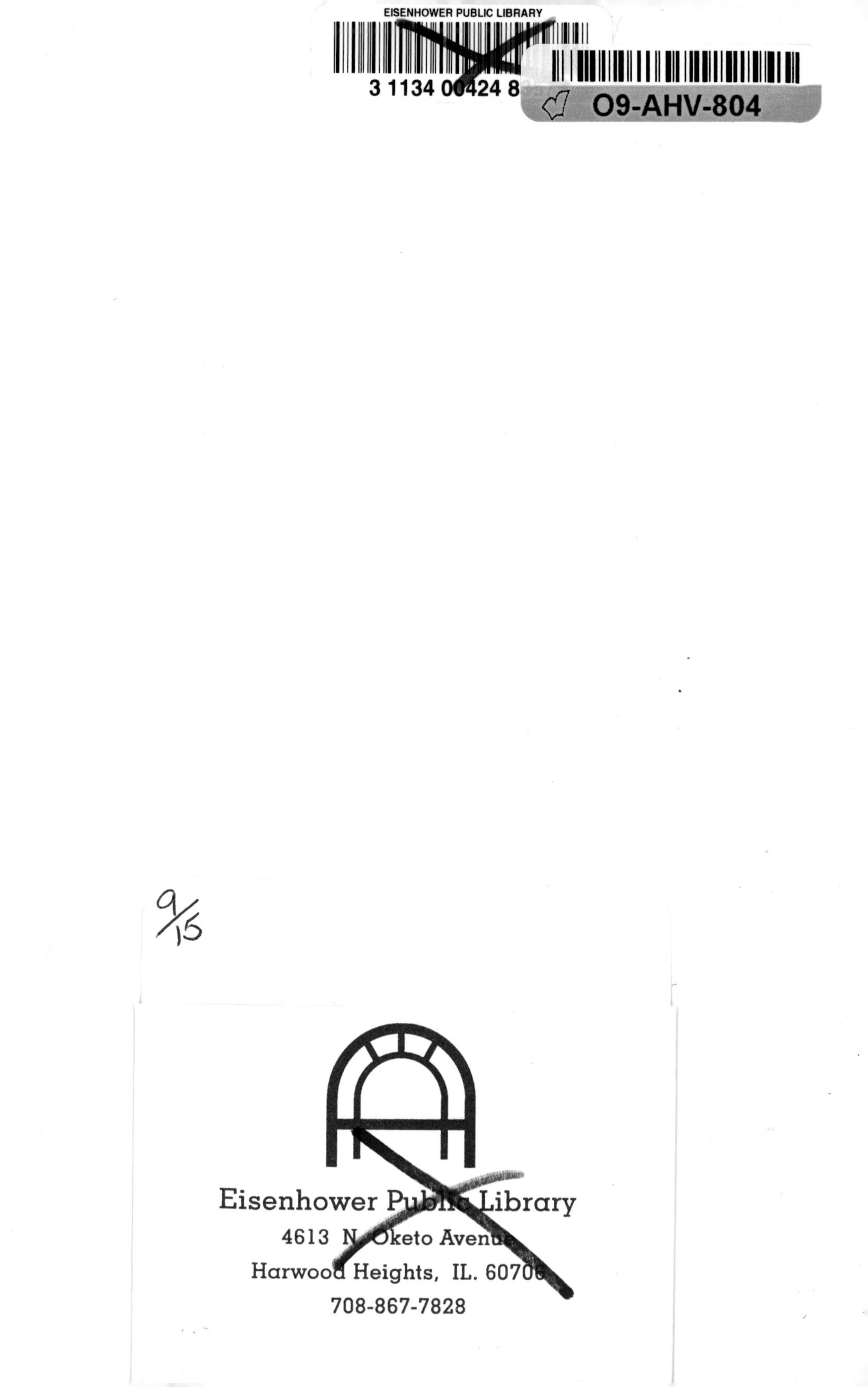

The Desert and the Blade

ALSO BY S. M. STIRLING

NOVELS OF THE CHANGE

Island in the Sea of Time

Against the Tide of Years

On the Oceans of Eternity

Dies the Fire

The Protector's War

A Meeting at Corvallis

The Sunrise Lands

The Scourge of God

The Sword of the Lady

The High King of Montival

The Tears of the Sun

Lord of Mountains

The Given Sacrifice

The Golden Princess

NOVELS OF THE SHADOWSPAWN

A Taint in the Blood

The Council of Shadows

Shadows of Falling Night

OTHER NOVELS BY S. M. STIRLING

The Peshawar Lancers

Conquistador

The Desert and the Blade

A NOVEL OF THE CHANGE

S. M. STIRLING

A ROC BOOK

ROC
Published by New American Library,
an imprint of Penguin Random House LLC
375 Hudson Street, New York, New York 10014

This book is an original publication of New American Library.

First Printing, September 2015

LIBRARY OF CONGRESS CATALOGING-IN-PUBLICATION DATA:

Stirling, S. M.
The desert and the blade: a novel of the Change / S. M. Stirling.
pages cm.—(Change series)
ISBN 978-0-451-41735-0 (hardcover)
1. Regression (Civilization)—Fiction. 2. Quests (Expeditions)—Fiction. 3. Princesses—Fiction. 4. Swords—Fiction. I. Title.
PS3569.T543D47 2015
813'.54—dc23 2015013752

Printed in the United States of America
10 9 8 7 6 5 4 3 2 1

Set in Weiss Medium

PUBLISHER'S NOTE
This is a work of fiction. Names, characters, places, and incidents either are the product of the author's imagination or are used fictitiously, and any resemblance to actual persons, living or dead, business establishments, events, or locales is entirely coincidental.

Penguin
Random
House

To Jan, forever

ACKNOWLEDGMENTS

To Harry Turtledove, for the loan of Topanga and the Chatsworth Lancers, with which he did things so intriguing I had to play with his toys. And very useful they turned out to be!

Thanks to Kier Salmon, unindicted co-conspirator, who has been my advisor and helper on the Change since the first. This was a big complex book and she helped immensely.

To Gina Tacconi-Moore, my niece, flower-girl at my wedding twenty-seven years ago, Queen of Physical Fitness and owner of CrossFit Lowell, who gave me some precise data on what a *really fit* young woman, such as herself, could do.

To Steve Brady, native guide to Alba, for assistance with dialects and British background, and also natural history of all sorts.

Pete Sartucci, knowledgeable in many aspects of Western geography and ecology, including the Mojave and Topanga, and convincing me that one scene went on too long and pointing out an embarrassingly large distance I hadn't noticed.

To Miho Lipton and Chris Hinkle, for help with Japanese idiom; and to Stuart Drucker, for assistance with Hebrew.

Diana L. Paxson, for help and advice, and for writing the beautiful Westria books, among many others. If you liked the Change novels, you'll probably enjoy the hell out of the Westria books—I certainly did, and they were one of the inspirations for this series; and her "Essential Asatru" and recommendation of "Our Troth" were extremely helpful . . . and fascinating reading. The appearance of the name Westria in the book is no coincidence whatsoever. And many thanks for the loan of Deor Wide-Faring and Thora Garwood.

To Dale Price, help with Catholic organization, theology and praxis.

To John Birmingham, aka that silver-tongued old rogue, King Birmo of Capricornia, most republican of monarchs.

To Cara Shulz, for help with Hellenic bits, including stuff I could not have found on my own.

To: Walter Jon Williams, John Miller, Vic Milan, Jan Stirling, Matt Reiten, Lauren Teffeau, and Shirl Sayzinski of Critical Mass, for constant help and advice as the book was under construction.

Thanks to John Miller, good friend, writer and scholar, for many useful discussions, for lending me some great books, and for some really, really cool old movies.

Special thanks to Heather Alexander, bard and balladeer, for permission to use the lyrics from her beautiful songs which can be—and should be!—ordered at http://faerietaleminstrel.com/inside. Run, do not walk, to do so.

To Alexander James Adams, http://faerietaleminstrel.com/inside, for cool music, likewise.

Thanks again to William Pint and Felicia Dale, for permission to use their music, which can be found at www.pintndale.com and should be, for anyone with an ear and salt-water in their veins.

And to Three Weird Sisters—Gwen Knighton, Mary Crowell, Brenda Sutton, and Teresa Powell—whose alternately funny and beautiful music can be found at http://www.threeweirdsisters.com.

And to Heather Dale for permission to quote the lyrics of her songs, whose beautiful (and strangely appropriate!) music can be found at www.HeatherDale.com, and is highly recommended. The lyrics are wonderful and the tunes make it even better.

To S.J. Tucker for permission to use the lyrics of her beautiful songs, which can be found at http://sjtucker.com, and should be.

And to Lael Whitehead of Jaiya, http://www.broadjam.com/jaiya, for permission to quote the lyrics of her beautiful songs.

Thanks again to Russell Galen, my agent, who has been an invaluable help, advisor and friend for more than a decade now, and never more than in these difficult times.

All mistakes, infelicities and errors are of course my own.

The Desert and the Blade

HIGH KINGDOM OF MONTIVAL
C. Y. 46

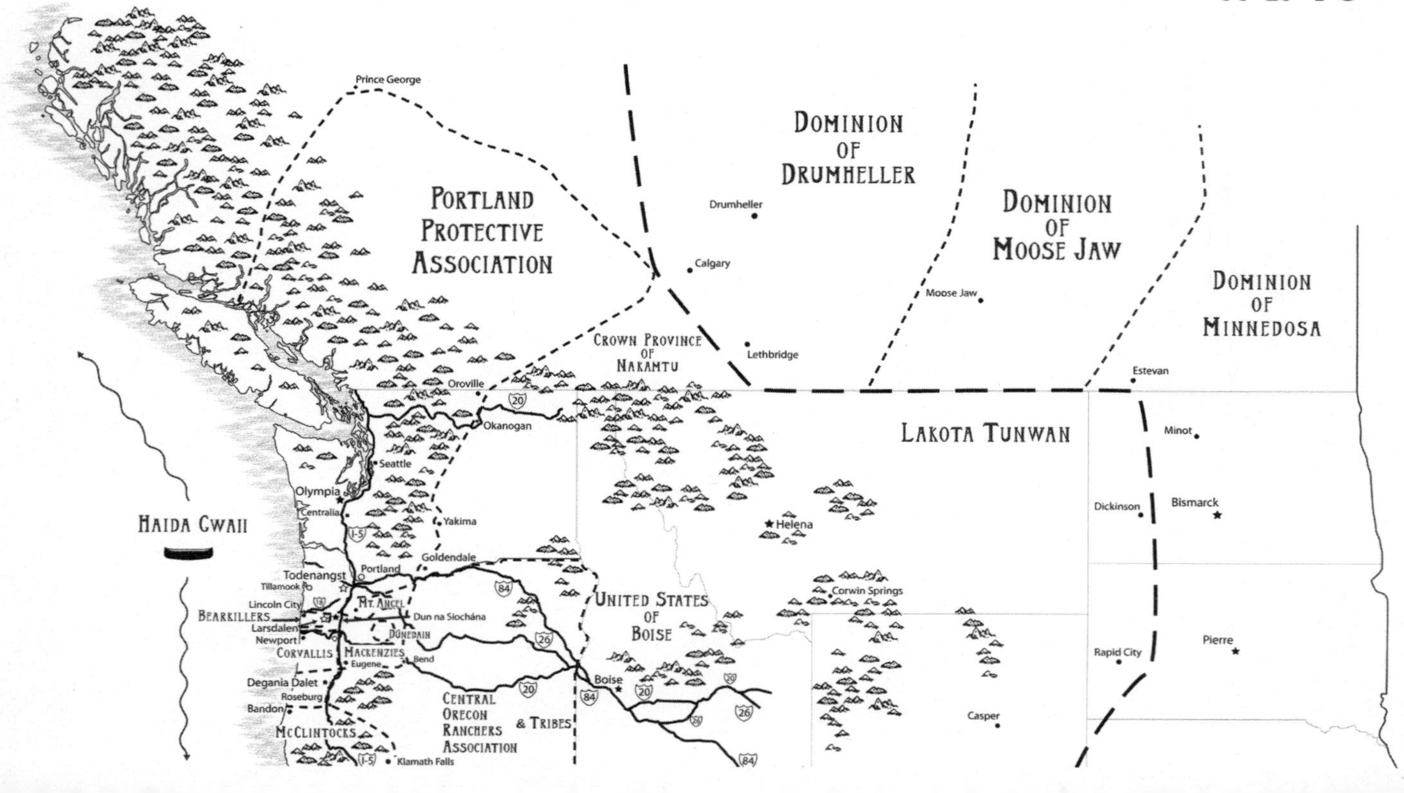
Prince George
PORTLAND PROTECTIVE ASSOCIATION
DOMINION OF DRUMHELLER
Drumheller
Calgary
Lethbridge
DOMINION OF MOOSE JAW
Moose Jaw
DOMINION OF MINNEDOSA
Estevan
Minot
Bismarck
Dickinson
Pierre
Rapid City
LAKOTA TUNWAN
CROWN PROVINCE OF NAKAMTU
Oroville
Okanogan
Seattle
Olympia
Centralia
Yakima
Goldendale
Helena
Corwin Springs
Casper
HAIDA GWAII
Todenangst
Portland
Tillamook
Lincoln City
BEARKILLERS
Larsdalen
Newport
CORVALLIS
MT. ANGEL
Dun na Siochána
DUNEDAIN
MACKENZIES
Eugene
Bend
Degania Dalet
Roseburg
Bandon
MCCLINTOCKS
Klamath Falls
CENTRAL OREGON RANCHERS & TRIBES ASSOCIATION
UNITED STATES OF BOISE
Boise
I-5
20
84
26

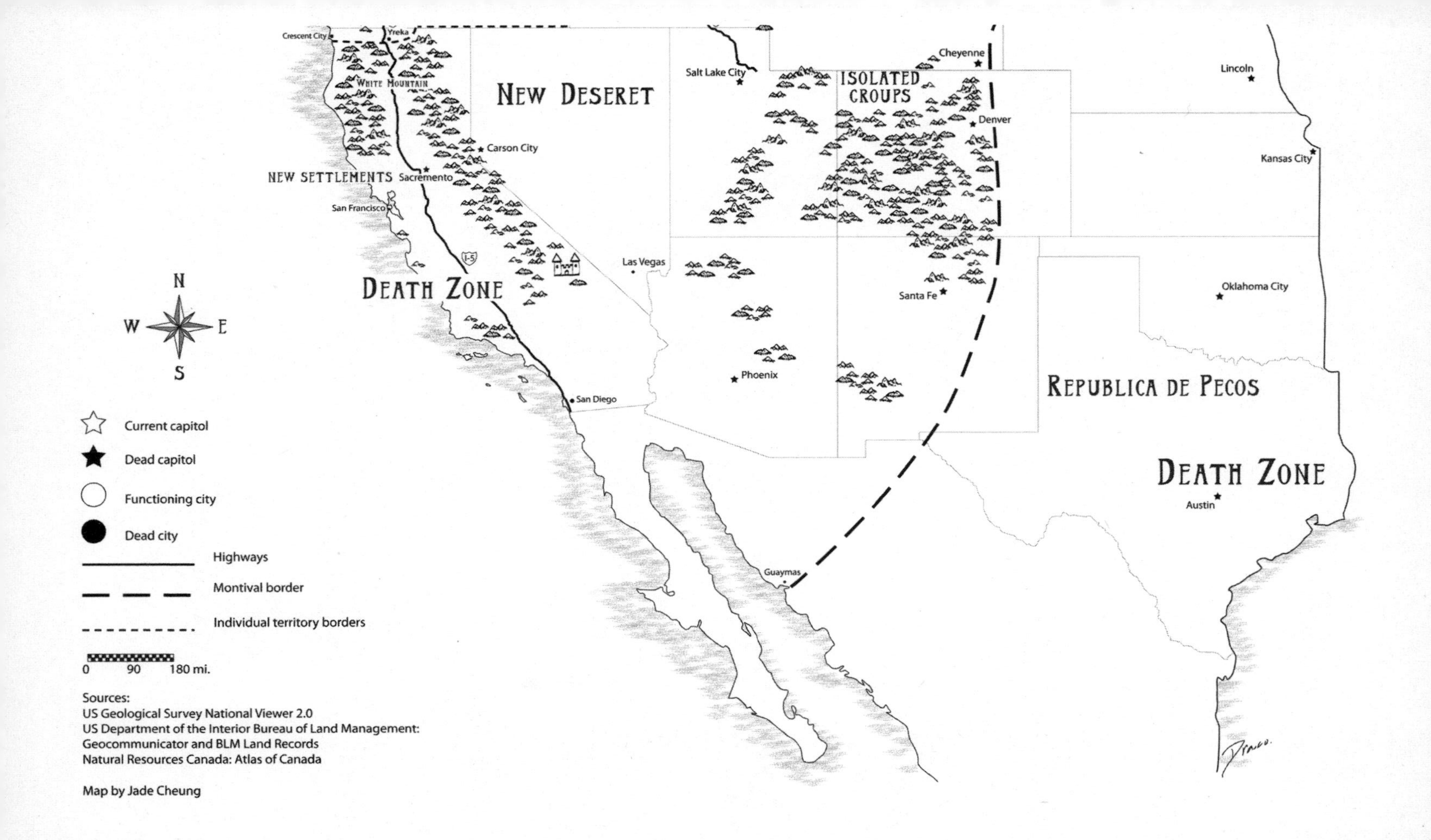
Crescent City
Yreka
White Mountain
New Deseret
Salt Lake City
Cheyenne
Isolated Croups
Lincoln
Denver
Carson City
Kansas City
New Settlements
Sacramento
San Francisco
I-5
Las Vegas
Death Zone
Oklahoma City
Santa Fe
N
W
E
S
Phoenix
Republica de Pecos
San Diego
Current capitol
Dead capitol
Death Zone
Functioning city
Austin
Dead city
Highways
Guaymas
Montival border
Individual territory borders
0 90 180 mi.
Sources:
US Geological Survey National Viewer 2.0
US Department of the Interior Bureau of Land Management:
Geocommunicator and BLM Land Records
Natural Resources Canada: Atlas of Canada
Map by Jade Cheung

PROLOGUE

David the Gutter—in the dialect of the Cut-Nose tribe of Loz'altos it sounded more like *Daf'teh-Gutrr*—wasn't insane, strictly speaking; not in the common run of things, that was. But right now his thoughts weren't as clear as usual while he stared at the bottom of the canoe and waited for the time to attack. He listened to the buzz of insects and the breathing of so many fighters, smelling their stink and the heavy silt-and-decay scent of the salt marsh.

His parents and grandparents *had* been mad, until his father met a Mud Hair band who flayed and ate him over days, and his mother stepped out from the fifteenth story of the ruined Palo Alto Office Tower because she heard voices telling her to. Daf' had taken Mud Hair heads to stand on spears and watch his father's funeral feast, though their meat had been rather stringy, even baked underground in a pit full of embers and heated stones and lavishly dressed with one of the last precious sealed jars of scavenged BBQ spice rub. Apart from the bloodpower, he actually preferred venison or wild pig. He had buried his mother's body by collapsing a leaning wall over a hole in the cracked concrete, and squatted brooding for hours, inchoate thoughts for which he had no words trickling through his mind. He'd gripped the haft of his axe hard enough to make his fingers ache, wishing there was an enemy he could smash down, and then he'd howled and slashed the air until the feral macaques had fled chittering up the vine-grown ruins.

The squat, heavily-muscled Cut-Nose was at home in the world the Change had left him, and he'd never believed much of the stories of the Old Time. Partly that was the fact that the thick gobbling variety of English he'd grown up with had a severely limited vocabulary; the founders of his folk had deliberately avoided thought as much as they could, to keep despair and self-loathing at bay. Mostly it was because *his* world was the overgrown ruins of what had once been Palo Alto and its neighbors, the little clans of the Cut-Noses, and the endless game of stalking and feasting that gave their lives meaning.

He was the most feared of all the chiefs, the one who'd extended the sway of those who bore the three horizontal scars on their noses over all the southeastern part of the peninsula. It was he who'd seen that the new enemies north of the Bridge, the ones with the stars and tree on their frighteningly subtle gear and the dirt-pushers they guarded, were not just a new tribe. They were a threat to *all* the tribes. It was he—puzzling endlessly over a captured Ranger bow—who'd whittled out a duplicate from lumps of wood and the tips of skis. His people valued him so highly they'd nursed him through the injuries he'd sustained when he avenged his father, tempting him with morsels of grilled Mud Hair liver during his illness.

As he waited bent over in the ancient aluminum canoe he was still puzzling over why he'd listened to the talks-in-head Meat who'd led them here; his dialect also used the same word for *outsider* and *food*. He was silent and still; all his folk could be silent and still, or they would have died young. Even children who cried out of season had to be killed, despite the constant, desperate need for more fighters and mothers. It was not good to talk much.

It had just seemed . . . *good* to do what the Meat who could walk in your head told them to do. The way it felt good to rut and eat and kill and sleep and wake. The way things should be, always would be. But when he tried to think *why* it was good his mind stuttered, like his step did now in cold weather, or when he was very tired.

One reason he'd stayed a chief was that he could think himself inside the heads of others, imagine how they spoke to themselves in the place behind the eyes where they lived. He could remember when he was a Little how he'd started to do that, and the realization that most couldn't, that they were slow and stupid and like dandelion fuzz inside their heads, while he was sharp like the edge of a carefully honed knife.

Now he felt that way himself when he tried to think about why he obeyed the Meat.

Feel . . . *dumb,* he thought.

Almost he whimpered, there in the dappled shade of the tall reeds. A flush of fear-sweat trickled down his flanks. He was the most feared of the Cut-Noses, but a half-dozen blades would have pierced his hide if he'd lost control on an ambush.

A ripple broke the surface of the water in the little inlet. Not a Fur, not the big flipper-foot kinds or the fine meat kind or any of the others. Heads turned towards it, eyes glaring in utter quiet. It was one of the Sharp Teeth. The man raised his face a little out of the water and spoke in their nasty hissing way, tongue flickering between the blackened filed points:

"They come," he said, and swam away again through the dozen or so canoes in this inlet to the next, where more waited.

Daf' raised his eyes. Not long after sunup. Hideously exposed if they attacked now; fighting was for the dark, or where there was dense cover. But they *must.*

"Gegown," he said softly, and dipped his paddle. "Mowv."

All around him the warriors of the Eater tribes of the Bay followed suit.

CHAPTER ONE

GOLDEN GATE/GLORANNON
(FORMERLY SAN FRANCISCO BAY)
CROWN PROVINCE OF WESTRIA
(FORMERLY CALIFORNIA)
HIGH KINGDOM OF MONTIVAL
(FORMERLY WESTERN NORTH AMERICA)
JULY/FUMIZUKI/CERWETH 14TH
CHANGE YEAR 46/FIFTH AGE 46/SHŌHEI 1/2044 AD

Crown Princess Órlaith Arminger Mackenzie put her right hand to a stay and shaded her eyes with her left, looking landward as the fog-shrouded Golden Gate loomed before the *Tarshish Queen*'s bow. Behind her the booms of the big merchant schooner's three gaff mainsails swung out to starboard, with a thump and twang she could feel as a shiver through her feet as well as her fingers when the travelers reached the end of their play and the foot of the forestaysail swept by overhead. They were beating back and forth until the fogbank lifted enough for the tricky passage into the Bay.

Her father had died there beyond the bridge, on the northern shore of the great inland water, at the hands of men who'd come this very path not three months gone.

Don't remember his death every moment, she told herself.

Which was wise, but hard, hard to do. Grandmother Juniper had once said to her that if wisdom was easy any fool would be able to do it. Then she'd thumped down the beater on her big loom with fingers age-gnarled but still deft and Órlaith had pinched out the lamp-wicks and both of them laughed. They'd been laughing still as they went down the stairs to sit by the hearth in the hall below, to watch winter cider simmering on the hob and listen to Aunt Fiorbhinn patiently leading her latest apprentice through a piece on the harp and breathe in the strong fir-sap scent of the Yule Tree.

It wasn't as funny now, though she probably understood it a lot better than she had at seventeen. Perhaps when she too was past seventy she'd be able to laugh at the thought again.

Though I'm not likely to see threescore and ten either. The ending completes our lives, it doesn't undo them, whenever it comes. Da died as he lived, as a warrior and a father and a King. As an enemy of the enemies of human kind.

He'd died because he put himself between her and a blade, a sneak attack by a prisoner with a pair of holdout throwing knives. After the battle was supposedly over, no time for anything but pure action without thought of consequence . . . She didn't feel guilty about it, or doubt for an instant that he'd have done exactly the same thing with a week to ponder it. Rudi Mackenzie would have been the first to say that it was the way of nature for a parent to fall defending his child—and then he'd have laughed and advised her to leave guilt to the Christians.

No, what she felt was *loss*, sorrow sharp as steel biting her flesh. Not just at his death, the ache that would have followed whenever he went to the Guardians of the Western Gate, but at the time and manner of it. A gripping bitterness that she'd never see him as an old man sitting in the sun and watching children play with a mug near his elbow and a cat curled in his lap and a smile on his face. That he would never spin tales of his wars and his wanderings and the wonders he'd seen and done with *her* children around him before the hearth with their faces rapt, or have them there to close his eyes and keen him to the pyre. Tired and ready for his rest, this life drained to the dregs and welcoming the shadow of the raven wings like cooling shade.

And she felt *rage* at those who had denied him that. Rage enough to boil the blood, rage that came back to choke her when she was halfway through a swallow of food or admiring a spray of flowers against a whitewashed wall or letting her eyelids drift downward after a hard day's ride.

Revenge you will take, but don't brood on it; that's a sharp knife you have to grasp by the blade—the tales are full of it warping even heroes. Da walked to the Dark Mother smiling, with open eyes, meeting the King's fate unflinching. Your fate too, one day. For the lord and the land and the folk are one, *and we of the Royal kin are the sacrifice that gives itself, dying that our people may live. Even when you were a little lass, he never hid from you that death comes for us all. Think of his life instead.*

She remembered when her first dog Maccon had been very old and the great shaggy beast had taken his last sickness, growing gaunt and thin and trembling, groaning sometimes in his basket at the foot of her bed. Until the healers shook their heads at her demands, Princess or no, and told her that things could only grow worse, and that quickly. Soon the pain would be more than the drugs could keep at bay.

Hold his head in your lap, so he can't see the knife, Rudi Mackenzie had said gently. *Maccon cannot know the* why *of things, but he knows the* what *well enough.*

The shade of the tree fell across them both and the bees hummed in the blossoms, that week after Beltane and the season of beginnings. This cherry tree had been the spot she and her dog had liked best to halt when they rambled through the woods about Dun Juniper in the summer season. She would lie and doze and dream with her head on his flank as she watched the west wind move across the valley below, cloud shadow across the rippling fields of gold like a tale told from far away. Until Maccon absently reached around and began to groom her head and she laughed and a single summer stretched out forever alike for both of them. . . .

Da had carried him there for this in his arms, at her asking, and a shovel he'd matter-of-factly had her bring leaned against the gnarled bark; she'd been still young enough that it was fitting for him to help.

Maccon had whimpered and feebly licked her as she stroked his ears and ruff, seeking to comfort the grief that he sensed in her even then, heedless of its cause. Da had smiled sadly at the sight, and said:

Of all the Kindreds, only we of the human-kind see time as a thing apart from us. And in it see always our own mortality, walking a step towards us with every dawn.

That is our special burden, to live with the shadow of the Crow Goddess' wings always before our eyes. Maccon is spared that. Just a little sting, and he will sleep without fear or hurt.

Will we meet again, Da? she'd asked, as she obeyed through her tears.

She took the dirk in her right hand while she cradled the big dog's gruesome graying muzzle against her with her left. Her father's voice had been warmly kind, but implacable:

Of course, pulse of my heart: we pass through the Western Gate, and rest in the Land of Summer once again with those dear to us, before the forgetting and the return. But dying still hurts, and grief is hard for those left behind. Maccon doesn't know that an ending and a parting comes now. Just that you who are his friend and his lord are with him, as you have been since the both of you were pups. Let that be his last memory here. He will roam those blessed hills where no sorrow comes in gladness, and greet you once more.

Why does he have to die? she'd said, choking back a shout that might have frightened the ailing beast. *Why does* anyone *have to die?*

That we don't know, darling girl, any more than Maccon knows why you cannot heal his hurt. As the Lord and the Lady are to us, so are you to him, and we can no more know the mind of the Goddess in its fullness than he can yours. But we do know that the Powers mean us to know of joy and loyalty and love: and the dog-kind they gave into our hands to show us how to take and give those precious things without stinting, in wholeness of heart.

She blinked at the light on the waves, in two times at once. "And how to bear grief, Da," she whispered. "That too."

A gentle kiss on the forehead, and: *Now a swift end to pain is the last gift you can give Maccon for his long loving service,* mo chroí, *until we all meet again. Place the point so. Now, call upon the Mother and bid him farewell.*

"Bear it, and do what must be done."

His big battered long-fingered hand had closed around hers on the bone hilt of the razor-edged knife with a terrifying restrained strength, and then—

The ship heeled until the deck slanted like a shallow roof, and she blinked, feeling him gone once more. Water purled and chuckled in twin curves, throwing rooster-tails of spray as the bowsprit dipped and rose, the sharp prow digging rhythmically into the blue swell and leaving a taste of salt on her lips as the cool droplets struck, like the taste of tears. It was only a few hours past the early summer dawn, and the light on the water was bright as they turned towards the rising sun, shining over and through the fogbanks ahead. Strands of her long yellow hair wavered across her face, blown forward by the steady breeze from the northeast and following the white curve of the sails like golden serpents.

From the quarterdeck the captain spoke crisply:

"Mr. Mate, stand by to strike sail, topsails only, on the fore, on the main."

"Aye aye, Cap'n."

"Then make it so, Mr. Mate."

The first mate's voice boomed out through a speaking-trumpet in a volley of musically accented nauticalese ending with:

"Lay aloft and furl!"

The ratlines thrummed as sailors ran up them to the spars of the square topsails on the fore and main and out along the manropes, fisting the canvas up and tying it off with the gaskets sewn into the sails as the deck crew hauled on the buntlines to help them. For the work ahead, precision was more important than speed. The shanty rang out as the teams on the ropes gripped and bent and threw their weight back in rhythmic unison:

"O wake her, O shake her,
O shake that girl
With—her—blue—pants—on!
O Johnny come to Hilo;
Poor—old—man!"

The slant of the deck eased slightly as pressure came off the top of the masts, and the wind seemed to pick up as the ship slowed. That cool moving air smelled only of a third of a planet of clean ocean behind them, crisp enough even in high summer and even this far south to make the padded arming doublet of fleece-stuffed canvas she wore under the back-

and-breast welcome, but somehow she thought she could detect the brackish scent of the Bay ahead and the huge tidal flats and wetlands about it. Off to the south the ruined towers of lost San Francisco reared on their hills, rust-red and stained-concrete brown above the mass of honeysuckle and scrub and renascent forest between and around them, or the stark white where the sand-dunes had emerged once more from under the works and plantings of human-kind.

Her liege knight Heuradys d'Ath came up behind her, walking so lightly that the sound of her rubber-tread boots on the deck was lost in the rattle and snap, creak and thutter and groan of a ship under sail, a symphony of wood and cordage and canvas dancing with the vast forces of the winds and the Mother Ocean.

No cheap commonplace hobnails for milady d'Ath! Órlaith thought. *A relief for the bosun. She grinds her teeth every time some man-at-arms puts gouges in her deck planking.*

"That hair looks untidy in this breeze, Orrey," the knight said, the staccato accents of the north in her voice.

Órlaith smiled affectionately. She knew Heuradys had given her a space to be alone, which was a difficult thing to find on a crowded ship where even the leaders were bunking four to a cabin, and would be even harder after today when they picked up the rest of their party who'd come overland to join them here. Then with beautiful timing she'd come up to the bow to keep her liege from turning her alone time into another inward replay of her father's death. The enemy ships had come along this very path, chasing Reiko's party on the end of a pursuit that had begun in the Sea of Japan, to meet what had been a routine, enjoyable progress by the High King and his heir through the new settlements on this southern frontier.

Her tone was deliberately light when she replied in the soft Mackenzie lilt; if a close friend was going to take the trouble to cheer you up, you should at least try to help.

"Oh, sure and I was just giving Johnnie a nice romantic image, the princess with her golden hair floatin' about her face as she stands in the bow, brooding deep and melancholy."

"Yet stern and noble as well. So put a foot up on the rail too, for Apollon's sake! Head up . . . left hand on the hilt of the Sword . . . do it right! Your little brother needs you to fulfill his artistic destiny, woman!"

Órlaith did as she bid for a moment, chuckling. "I think he's already working on a *chanson* about this whole thing—the "Song of Órlaith," maybe? Though really it should be "The Song of Reiko," since it's her ancestral sword we're after seeking, the wonder and amazement of the world. Fair breaking out all over, it is!"

She laid her palm on the moon-crystal hilt of the Sword of the Lady where it rode in the buckled blade-sling of her arming belt.

"Though I haven't heard if they've found Excalibur off in Greater Britain," she added sardonically. "Or if they have, the King-Emperor in Winchester is keeping it secret the now."

Heuradys grinned. "Arthur chucked *his* sacred snickersnee back to the watery tart when he went to snooze in Avalon against the hour of Britain's need. . . ."

"And he didn't wake up at the Change? Deep sleeper," Órlaith said.

"Well, maybe it disabled his alarm clock's bell. Or maybe he was the one inspiring Mad King Charles?" Heuradys said.

"They could have done much worse. Most did, in that part of the world."

"And we can let the Japanese equivalent of the troubadours take care of Reiko's epic."

"*Biwa hōshi* would be the closest they have, which is not very close to either troubadours or bards to our way of thinking. *Hōshi* being sort of a . . . hmmm, wandering priest-performer? And they do their epics in prose, though they recite them to music, so, their poetry mostly being short and . . . punchy," Órlaith said absently.

"*Biwa?*"

"Biwa . . . is something like a lute."

"Johnnie will do yours in classic *chantaire* style, don't worry. But is a line in one of his poems worth the tangles and snarls?"

"Poetry lasts longer than bad hair days, that it does."

That brought a snort and a roll of the eyes. Órlaith knew her friend liked her younger brother a good deal—John and she had been lovers once, briefly—but they were too much alike to be entirely compatible. They'd both had a Protectorate noble's training, martial and otherwise, in which music was just as essential a social skill as heraldry and falconry. But while Heuradys sang very well and was outright beautiful with a lute, Prince John had perfect pitch, played half a dozen instruments with casual skill and was genuinely talented at composition as well. Which the princess suspected made her knight slightly jealous.

On the other hand, she's better with the sword, so it balances; that's where Johnnie's just very good.

"I admit Johnnie will probably do a good job," Heuradys said grudgingly. "Flowing golden locks and all. He may even find a way to make *Kusanagi-no-Tsurugi* scan in English."

"My golden locks are indeed golden . . . just a very slight tinge of copper . . . and they do flow, when loose," she said aloud. "And get in my eyes and mouth and even up my *nose* sometimes, Brigit the Bright witness."

"It looks like it's dry by now. Want me to braid it?" Heuradys asked.

That was like putting on plate armor, you really couldn't do it well by yourself.

"Thanks, Herry. Clubbed fighting braid . . . Do it Dúnedain-style, why don't you? Then I'll do yours in the same. That's . . . tactful since we're landing in County Ithilien and meeting my Ranger cousins."

"You mean the Dúnedain will be flattered that you agree they're the only people who know how to do things with style."

"It's powerfully set on style and grace the Rangers are, for all that they're bonny fighters and fine wilderness scouts."

"You're being *diplomatic* again, Orrey."

"It's a habit, so."

"Thank the Grey-Eyed I wasn't born to be a politician," the noblewoman said cheerfully.

They were both tall long-limbed young women with the cat-grace that came of training to the war-arts and the dancing floor from childhood. And considerably heavier than their lean athletic builds suggested at first glance, simply because their bone and muscle were so dense. Heuradys was two years older and an inch shorter than her liege's five-eleven, with amber eyes and dark-auburn hair and comely regular features a little blunter than the chiseled looks the Crown Princess had inherited from Rudi Mackenzie and by repute from *his* father. Herry's sire, Rigobert de Stafford, Count of Campscapell and Baron Forest Grove, was a big blue-eyed ruggedly handsome man who'd been blond before he went gray; Delia de Stafford was still a dark-haired beauty in her fifties. Heuradys and the other three children they'd had via a pre-Change kitchen appliance had all inherited their looks in varying degree.

Her liege knight went on: "I can piss people off if I want to, and the only worry I have is that they'll try to kill me. Which is fair enough when you think about it. Sit."

Órlaith sank back against the slanted steel shield of the bow-chaser catapult, more leaning than sitting, as the sailors tied off aloft and slid down the shrouds to the deck behind them with soft barefoot thumps. Heuradys stood behind her, partially blocking the breeze, and began to do her hair in what the ancient world would have called a four-strand Dutch braid, her fingers very deft with the complex weave. Playing stringed instruments kept your hands and fingers nimble and supple and precise.

"You're well-mannered enough, I'd have thought," Órlaith said. "More courtly than I, at seventh and last. I've a hot temper betimes, I know, but you smiled and bowed just before you belted Sir Ymbolet across the chops with your gauntlet that time."

The suppleness and delicacy of touch was fortunate for her hair, because year after year of constant sparring in armor with longsword and kite-shield also made you very strong; and it made your hands strong in a way that surprised even peasants or sailors and shocked most others. It was why both of them had forearms that flowed smoothly into their hands without more than a slight dimpling at the wrist. Knights had a reputation for carelessness with fragile objects, but part of that was that many of them just broke things without meaning to.

"I didn't kill him, either," Heuradys replied.

"That too. *And* you sent him flowers in the infirmary. It was remarked on as an example of *courtesie* throughout the Association, so."

The comb Heuradys used and her sword-callused fingers tugged at knots occasionally nevertheless, but Órlaith ignored the slight stabs of pain. The wind and the long rolling pitch of the deck made that inevitable anyway. As her hand rested on the crystal pommel of the Sword of the Lady at her side she felt an indefinable tension. As if a voice were speaking urgently, but far away and blurred and vanishing when she turned her mind inward on it like the memory of a dream after waking.

The knight went on: "Courteous and courtly? Well, of course! But that's my general shining wonderfulness and near-goddesslike perfection, not politics."

She touched a forefinger to the back of Órlaith's skull: "Tilt your head forward."

I haven't been to the Kingmaking at Lost Lake yet, the princess thought as she did; that probably wouldn't happen until she came of Crown age, in five years. *I can bear Da's sword, but I don't get the full effect until then, the link to all the land of Montival.*

Since she had nothing serious to say beyond *I'm nervous but can't say why* or *I just miss Da something fierce* she spoke lightly instead:

"Herry, your father's Count of Campscapell, your birth mother's a Countess *and* Châtelaine of Ath and your second mother's a former Grand Constable, she's Baroness of Ath in her own right, and she's been High Marshal of Montival since you were ten, to boot. If that isn't being born to politics, I'd be curious what is!"

Heuradys mumbled a little around the horn-and-silver comb she was holding in her teeth as she spoke and made the final tucks:

"But I'm not the heir to anything the way you are, thank the Olympians each and every one. *And* the Fates."

"You've manors of your own you'll inherit out east."

Heuradys finished with the braid, and doubled it twice to club it tight at the nape of Órlaith's neck where it would be out of the way under the flare of a helm and nearly un-grabbable even without.

"Doesn't count compared to being a baron . . . or even more, to a Count," she said. "Diomede and Lioncel have to wear those hats, and very welcome my beloved brothers are to it. Here I am, off on an adventure with my liege-lady while they're under the Argus eyes of our parents, sitting in the Court Baron listening to endless variations on *who stole who's pig*, and trying to find the money to fix bridges and smiling and nodding while red-faced country knights punish the punchbowl at after-tournament buffets and detail every point of every ancestor of their favorite destrier since the Change. Poor babies."

"That doesn't sound so very bad," Órlaith laughed. "And they're staid settled married men in their thirties the now, with offspring so numerous . . ."

". . . that they swarm like vermin upon the earth," said Heuradys.

Who in fact delighted in being an aunt and was hero-worshipped in turn when she swept in bearing presents and glamour and stories from Court. She went on:

"*Bor*-ing! *And* I don't have to consider the political impact of how I do my hair, either."

That bit a little too close to the bone. Órlaith had absorbed the skills and necessities of kingcraft from her parents through her pores all her twenty-one years as well as from formal instruction, and had seen how it consumed their lives. Sometimes when you stepped back a little it was daunting to think of living that way until you died in harness . . . though of course most people *did* take up their parents' trade, willy-nilly.

And I'm slightly guilty at how much of a relief it is to run off like this. Ah, well, guilt . . . the Catholic half of the family can carry the burden for all of us.

"Adventure? Isn't that someone else, neck-deep in the shit with no shovel, and that far away from me?" she replied, and felt the new braid to make sure it was firm. "Your turn."

Heuradys handed her the comb and they traded positions. The knight's thick locks fell well past her armored shoulders, and were naturally wavy-to-curly as opposed to her liege's dense straight mane. They'd been rinsing in salt-water on shipboard, too, which made it harder to bring them to order. She started with the ends, teasing them out a handful at a time.

"People are always *saying* that to sound cynical and worldly-wise, but it doesn't mean they don't have adventures—witness us!" Heuradys said.

"Well, yes," Órlaith admitted.

This was, without dispute, an adventure of the most adventurous sort. It was an actual capital-Q *Quest*, like something out of what the Dúnedain called their *Histories*, or the ancient *chansons*. Or what her father had done. Slightly defensive, she went on:

"But we're not doing it just to be doing it, it isn't hunting tigers . . . and even that needs to be done, they being given to snacking on livestock and the farmers too."

I remember that first time I was allowed on a tiger hunt. . . .

"You've got a point . . . ouch!" Heuradys yelped.

She smiled and made her hands fall back into their rhythm. That first hunt had been when she was eighteen. Reeds moving against the wind, mud clutching at the soles of her boots, hand clenching on the riser of the bow hard enough to hurt. Her father loose-taut-alert like a cat himself, with the sun glittering on the broad base-winged blade of his great hunting-spear and Mother raising her crossbow in a smooth economical motion. The huntsman's horn, the hysterical baying of the hounds and a moaning grunting snarl loud enough to make your guts shiver . . .

"You tug, too," she said aloud. "I just don't moan about it. *And* you've got wiry hair, so hush a bit and keep still."

"It's not wiry, it's . . . it's pre-Raphaelite."

"A pre-Raphaelite painting it is!" Órlaith agreed teasingly. "Couldn't have found a better word myself!"

Heuradys didn't move her head, but she did roll her eyes around suspiciously.

That school of painters had always been very influential in the northrealm, once folk had time again for art. The Crown Princess' maternal grandmother Sandra had added dozens more of them to her collection not long before she died, part of a gift from the Bossman of Iowa on his accession. Though one of those paintings had been put on the gift list immediately, after a muttered *oh, my* and a pained expression on Sandra's part . . .

"*La Bella Mano*, by Dante Gabriel Rossetti, to be specific about it, so," Órlaith added, after just the right pause.

Which had enough accuracy, mostly in the shade of the hair, to strike home. *La Bella Mano* wasn't Rossetti's best work; more of a self-caricature, in fact.

"Now that's just *cruel*," Heuradys said with a chuckle. "I so do *not* have a neck like a camel and a little tiny head on the end of it."

Órlaith and her knight-to-be had been doing each other's hair on journeys since they were little girls, and the princess found the small shared ritual rather soothing.

They were both in half-armor for the landing, back-and-breast of overlapping riveted lames and vambraces on their forearms, partly as precaution, partly ceremony, and partly just because you had to wear armor frequently to keep accustomed to the weight and constriction. If you didn't exhaustion could cripple you too soon when you really, really needed to be at your best. Órlaith's suit of plate was in the standard form for a knight or man-at-arms, but made of the rare, costly and hard-to-work titanium alloy rather than common steel, lighter and stronger and immune to rust. She'd given Heuradys another as a Yule-present last year; it was literally a princessly gift, since only a monarch or their close kin could afford it. Even Órlaith herself hadn't had one until she was sure she'd gotten her full growth, and her brother Prince John was a year or two away from being fitted.

Normally Órlaith preferred the kilt and plaid of her father's people, the Clan Mackenzie, for everyday wear, though she was in breeks today.

Forbye, besides being Mackenzie fashion, long hair is just prettier, which is why Herry wears it so too, the dear girl being more than a bit of a fop, and I say it who loves her like a sister. Somehow the foppery isn't nearly as irritating with her as it is with Johnnie, who I love because he is *my brother but who is annoying and endearing in equal parts.*

Her fingers moved automatically as she thought. You could always say long hair made extra padding inside a helmet, to those who had no aesthetic sense; and in the Protectorate it was most definitely a woman's style, which slightly lessened her offensiveness to the unfortunately still fairly common fanatical variety of Catholic up there in the north-realm.

Twist, over under, tuck, plait . . . She stopped the train of political calculation and faction-balancing with an effort of will, a little appalled once she stopped to think about it:

Sure and Herry's right; I do always have to think about the politics, even of my hairstyles and what clothes I wear!

And to think that there were people who truly, seriously believed that being a monarch or a high noble meant a life spent doing just as you pleased. . . .

"Done," she said, tucking the last strand away, doubling the braid twice and tying it with a thong in a neat bow knot. She returned the comb: "Let's get back to the quarterdeck."

"This thing isn't steered from the same end as a horse," the knight agreed.

They turned and walked down the length of the schooner towards the stern, ducking occasional parties of sailors moving around doing sailorish things. The two young women exchanged a glance as they saw the crew begin to strip the protective tarpaulins from the catapults that crouched eight to a side and knock the locking-pins out of the ports in the four-foot bulwark through which they shot.

Órlaith's highly-unofficial expedition had hired the ship from Feldman & Sons—paying in promises, implicit promises as much of future Royal obligations as of money—but the merchant had made plain right at the beginning that she didn't command his ship or people. She could tell Captain Feldman the destination, but he, *he*, would give the orders that took them there.

Sailors unfolded and extended the pump levers behind the machines and worked them up and down to a brisk shanty; this one had a chorus about screwing cotton every day in a moveable bay, which probably wasn't as bizarre as it seemed at first hearing.

"Those always sound better in a dockside tavern," she said.

Heuradys nodded with a very slight wince; she had a much better ear than her liege, or was considerably more finicky, or both.

"That's because in a sailor's tavern they're usually just drunk when they sing, not grunting like pigs at the end of every line."

Beneath the voices ran the *bang*-crink-*bang*-crink-*bang*-crink sound of the hydraulic bottle jacks bending the throwing arms that jutted out to either side of each machine back against springs that had been part of the suspensions of mining trucks before the Change. Then the very final-sounding *chink-chack* of the locking mechanisms engaging. Chests were thrown open to reveal eight-pound cast round shot, sinister-looking tubular canister rounds bristling with finger-length darts of forged steel or half-inch shot for close work, glass napalm shells and four-foot finned javelins with points like chisels or cutting sickles or the menacing containers for thermite incendiary warheads. The crew-captains worked the elevating and traversing screws to check that the motion was smooth.

There was no fuss or angry shouting and few first-voyage chawbacons being shoved and cursed into unfamiliar tasks; they might not have the snap of a naval crew but they were at least as quick and skilled and showing no more nerves. Feldman & Sons went on long risky voyages to dangerous places, but they also paid first-rate wages and had a profit-sharing arrangement and the big crew meant the watch below could get a solid night's sleep instead of doing four hours on and four off every day.

The merchantman's First Mate caught their glance; this *was* supposed to be a peaceful meeting halfway along their journey to the mega-necropolis of Los Angeles, picking up a few more friends to accompany them from the southernmost outposts of living Montival. His grin was white against his thin dark-brown face as he opened the arms-locker and the bosun and her mates began handing out cutlasses and boarding-axes, crossbows and knock-down pikes to be racked where they could be seized instantly. Sailors were shrugging into jerkins of thick but supple oil-tanned walrus hide and fastening their quick-release clips when they had a moment to spare. Plain bowl helmets and light bucklers hung by rings next to the weapons.

"Cap'n Feldman doesn't believe in taking chances, Your Highness," he said.

With a musical singsong accent to his version of Montival's common English, and a way of stressing the syllables that showed his native tongue was something else altogether; she gathered he came from some place one of Feldman's ships had touched far abroad.

"Glad to see it, Mr. Radavindraban," Órlaith said gravely.

Because I am *feeling nervous about* something. *I think. And I didn't like that*

CHAPTER TWO

GOLDEN GATE/GLORANNON
(FORMERLY SAN FRANCISCO BAY)
CROWN PROVINCE OF WESTRIA
(FORMERLY CALIFORNIA)
HIGH KINGDOM OF MONTIVAL
(FORMERLY WESTERN NORTH AMERICA)
JULY/FUMIZUKI/CERWETH 14TH
CHANGE YEAR 46/FIFTH AGE 46/SHŌHEI 1/2044 AD

The *Tennō Heika*—Heavenly Sovereign Majesty—of Japan stood by the stern-chaser catapult of the *Tarshish Queen* and composed herself against the memories that flooded in as the ship approached the Golden Gate. Her left hand rested on the scabbard of the katana thrust through her sash with the thumb against the guard in a gesture as automatic as the movements of walking.

Her title was *Empress* in English, though in Nihongo the word for a ruler as opposed to that for a consort had no gender. Ruling empresses were nonetheless very rare. Her grandmother had been the first in more than two hundred years, for all her brief life—the last survivor of the dynasty, brought by the Seventy Loyal Men across the firestorm chaos of Change-stricken Honshū to the offshore refuge of Sado-ga-shima, that the line of *Amaterasu-ōmikami* be preserved. It had been, in the son she had born too young and died of bearing, and through him to her and her sisters.

The cool damp sea-wind cuffed at her tightly braided hair as she stood and remembered the last time she had passed here, on the *Red Dragon*. Brief months ago, with her father alive and the enemy close behind, that final battle on the shore only hours ahead. It had been . . .

A blur. Glimpses. Blood running from under someone's fingernails as they heaved at the pumps and the water jetted overboard. Atsuko sharpening a nick out of her naginata *with the shaft braced across her knee. Captain Ishikawa showing his teeth as he took the wheel in his own hands and called out to his ship as if it were a lover. Father holding a dying man's hand for a moment.*

Thirst, hunger, fear, weariness worse than all. The consciousness of hideous death or worse close at hand, close as the shriek of catapult bolts overhead, the sluggish heaving movement of the leaking waterlogged ship, the crackle of gathering flame in the rigging. Playing out what she must do at the last to avoid capture in her mind over and over, to settle her spirit to it: the dagger in her hand, point towards her throat, and . . .

She shook herself mentally, coming back to the moment, to the present, to loss and to hope and to *giri*. Her given name was Reiko, which had a number of meanings of which *Courteous Lady* was the most common nowadays. Members of the Imperial House of the Yamato Dynasty had no family name in the usual sense, and with them the use of the personal name was still more restricted than with most of her folk. Even as a small child few but her siblings and parents had ever called her Reiko, and now that her father was dead she would seldom hear it again at home unless from her mother and sisters in strict privacy. For the rest of her life to others she would be *Tennō Heika*, or in informal circumstances simply *Heika*, Majesty. When she died, she would be known as *Shōhei Tennō* after the era-name she had chosen on the day of her father's cremation: Empress of Victorious Peace.

Perhaps that is why it is so . . . comforting . . . to be on . . . what do they call it here . . . first-name terms with Órlaith and her brother. They are my peers in a way nobody in Dai-Nippon can be. And are also outside our system altogether, neh? *Nobody at home will know as yet what has happened. We were the first ship to reach this continent from the homeland since the Change. They do not expect us back for many months, at the very least. To them, Father is still alive, still our* Tennō Heika *and I his heir. I will have to take the news to Mother and Setsuko and Toshi and Yōko, and present the urn.*

Her younger sisters had called her *Stork Girl* sometimes when they played together. She was five foot six inches: or five shaku five *sen*, in the terms her people now used once again, carrying herself with easy grace on the swaying deck. That made her a very tall young woman for a Nihonjin of her generation, the first born to those themselves born after the Change; as tall as most samurai men and taller than all but a few commoners. The Imperial family of course fed as well as anyone did, but in modern Nihon even the wealthy and powerful ate a spare lean diet of rice and soy and vegetables supplemented by fish and a little chicken, with red meat—the odd *tonkatsu*, sliced batter-crusted pork cutlet, or the like—as a treat on special occasions. To rise from a meal ever so slightly hungry was good manners.

In years that were very bad many peasants thought *rice* a treat, and had porridge of boiled millet stretched with wild greens for their staple.

With an unexpectedly delicate courtesy the family of nobles where the Nihonjin party had been quartered near Portland, at Montinore on the Barony of Ath, had tried to supply them with familiar provisions, and had found cooks who could turn out dishes often fairly similar to what she'd grown up with. But it had been like one elaborate feast after another rather than the sort of food you actually ate day to day even in the Palace. They'd had to gently hint that plain noodles and pickled vegetables and a bit of fish would be a relief. One of the shocking things about Montival had been the sheer, almost gross, abundance of *food*. They'd had only the pre-Change books about ancient America to prepare them for what they found here, and that was just about the only thing in them that was still true.

Her five-foot-six height was lean whipcord, and she stood with a stillness that was always ready to explode into deadly movement. Everyone in Japan these days trained to arms to some extent, the upper classes more so, and since her brother Yoshihito's ship had been lost six years ago . . .

Grief made you more vulnerable to grief; for a moment the pain she'd felt during the long months of waiting and growing despair returned. She banished it with an effort of will, and instead thought of his last smile when he'd promised to bring her a *saru* monkey home from his expedition to Kyushu.

Since then she'd received a prince's education herself. Some had accounted that at least a little scandalous. Some had even whispered that her father was driven to distraction by the loss of his only son and eldest child. But he had insisted, which settled the matter.

Settled it in these times, at least, Reiko thought.

She knew that for much of her nation's history Emperors had been cloistered symbols rather than rulers, recluses whose role was mainly to exist as a link between the world and the spirits. Revered, godlike, theoretically omnipotent but practically powerless, seldom glimpsed by ordinary folk. And very separate from the aristocracy of the sword, the *bushi* whose warlord masters had held the powers of State in their iron fists. Sometimes peacefully for a while, sometimes rending each other in civil wars that passed over the land like burning tsunamis of destruction.

This was not such a time; her father had *ruled* the much-diminished realm that called itself *Dai-Nippon Teikoku*—the Empire of Great Japan—as a matter of aspiration. Egawa Katashi, leader of the Seventy Loyal Men, had been utterly honorable about that, despite his enormous prestige and years of exercising near-absolute power in the name of the child-Empress and then the young Tennō: his slogan had been *Revere the Emperor, Reclaim the Homeland,* and he'd punctiliously stepped aside to become an advisor and elder statesman as soon as her father had come to what the modern era considered an adult's years. She remembered that grim cold-eyed old man slightly, though he'd died when she was only six; he'd also been the sort who could utterly dominate a room without moving or speaking a word, though his—rare—angers had also been legendary.

And I too will rule, *and we* will *restore our country. We will make that hope of greatness real. But what we in truth govern from the Imperial Palace on Sado-ga-shima now is merely . . .*

When the Change flashed around the world in the spring of Heisei 10 and the machines went still there had been a hundred and twenty-five million human beings in Japan, numbers vast beyond all comprehension—the Montivallans thought that probably the whole planet didn't have more than four times that now. A year later somewhere around one in a thousand of those hundred and twenty-five million was still among the living, give or take. As far as the officials had been able to reconstruct; nobody had been keeping precise accounts just then. In the forty-five years since the number had grown, just a little. *Only* a little, to less than a third of a million at the last count, despite enough food in most years, if only just, and four or five or six children now being a normal family once more.

The war accounted for that.

Less than a decade after the Change the *jinnikukaburi* raids from across the Sea of Japan had begun, sometimes a single ship, sometimes small fleets, leaving nothing behind but burnt bone split for the marrow when they caught the dwellers unaware or won the fight that followed. Reiko had been born into the second generation of that merciless grinding conflict; had grown to adulthood with its inexorable demands.

Her battle garb of *hitatare* jacket and *hakama* were covered by a *Môgami Dô* armor, red-lacquered steel lames laced together with blue silk cord, save for the leg protection; her head bore a white headband with a single scarlet circle over the brows. The broad-tailed twelve-plate *kabuto* helmet under one arm had the stylized chrysanthemum *kamon* of her House on its brow. Two samurai of the Imperial Guard stood behind her, motionless but alert as tigers, their right hands on the hilts of their swords and their eyes never still. One had her bow over his back, a seven-foot *higoyumi*, ready to hand it to her on command, and the other her *naginata*.

"So little time since we were here last, and so much has happened," she said softly in her own language.

Guard commander Egawa Noboru ducked his head wordlessly at her side. His face showed little expression at the best of times. At the reminder that his Emperor had died while he lived it became more a thing of stone and silence than ever.

Since then I have put the Water of the Last Moment on my father's lips and filled his funeral urn.

She let the raw pain of loss flow through her without holding on to it with the fingers of attention. Pain hurt, grief perhaps worst of all, but it wasn't *important*. Her father had told her and shown her by example that the key to sanity in their position was to keep in mind that the role and the human being, the mask and the face beneath, were both real, but not to confuse the two. Her *role* was important, critically so; that was *giri*, duty and obligation. The person inside it and the emotions that person felt, the yearnings and desires and sufferings, the *ninjō*, not so very much. Not compared to persistence and doing what was necessary. You went on as long as you could and then a little more, that was all.

Instead of tears, she continued steadily: "The world has Changed yet again. Or perhaps that started when my father first saw the Grass-Cutting Sword in his dreams."

"Majesty, many apologies, I am ashamed to admit that I did not truly grasp *Saisei Tennō*'s great visions," the commander of the Imperial Guard said. "I beg the Heavenly Sovereign Majesty's pardon for my stupidity, my inexcusable blindness."

The general bowed as he spoke, his full set of armor creaking and clattering a little, and he used her father's posthumous era-name: Emperor of Rebirth. He was in his forties, more than two decades older than she. Older than her father had been as well, a short thick man built like something carved out of seasoned *kuri* wood, his weathered face and hands seamed with scars. The one that pierced his left hand from palm to back was the freshest, where he'd moved with desperate speed to put his own flesh between her and one of a pair of throwing-knives a *bakachon* prisoner had hidden just long enough. The other blade had been aimed at Princess Órlaith, and killed her father when he thrust her behind him.

"Yet you followed, and you were the key to putting aside those who opposed or obeyed unwillingly," she said gently. "Without your service, we would not be here now."

And I would be dead, she thought but did not say.

That was something that only had to be brought up once.

Egawa Noboru fulfilled his duty, and nobody who knows him would be surprised.

"I followed because he was our *Tennō*. I knew that without discipline and unity we would be truly and utterly lost, Majesty. And—so sorry—because *Saisei Tennō* had been right so often before. And because nothing more . . . more ordinary . . . had any real prospect of long-term success, only of slower defeat. Now . . ."

"None of us *truly* grasped his vision, General," she said, making a gesture of pardon with her folded steel *tessen* war-fan.

Nor do you now, she thought. *Though you are my most loyal retainer.*

All of them were loyal in an abstract sense, to the concept of the Chrysanthemum Throne, to the dynasty and the nation it embodied and symbolized. But Egawa was loyal to *her.* He'd overseen the martial part of her education, administering painful and stressful parts of it personally. And he respected her as an individual in a way that the peculiar distant closeness of teacher and disciple made possible, for in the dojo you learned another to the core, without many words being necessary. That was why he was here, and why Grand Steward Koyama Akira had been left behind at Montinore Manor, with only a letter to tell him what she had chosen when he awoke that morning.

Koyama had been born a little before the Change, and he had a tendency to think of her as still a wayward, headstrong child to be guided and restrained . . . albeit a clever, promising child to be restrained with exquisite deferential courtesy. The quiet but real rivalry between the two men hadn't hurt in bringing Egawa into the plot, either, of course.

And your father led the Seventy Loyal Men who saved my grandmother's life at the cost of so many of their own. Loyalty beyond all powers of human endurance, beyond all mere human reason, runs in your blood. No, you do not grasp, *my* bushi, *but now you truly* believe, *at least. As your father and his men did not flinch from the wrath of the Great Kami in a world become fire and death, so you will not turn back from this.*

She glanced forward. Órlaith and her *hatamoto* Heuradys d'Ath were walking back towards the quarterdeck as the crew prepared; she suppressed an impulse to smile and wave. The occasion was too public and too grave. There were many differences of detail, but the essential form was still quite like that of an Imperial Navy ship preparing for battle. Not that they *expected* a fight, not yet, but . . .

"Good to be prepared for the unexpected, Majesty," Egawa said.

A grudging approval was in his hoarse gravelly voice, and a bit of surprise that a mere *gaijin* merchant captain had earned it.

"Our men are ready to come on deck at a moment's notice," he added in the clipped impersonal tones of a report. "Their state of readiness is high and morale is excellent."

"And the Montivallans seem reasonably alert as well," Egawa added.

The rest of the Imperial Guard samurai were below with Órlaith's men-at-arms. Though communication was very limited, mostly by written message, both groups had achieved a certain wary mutual respect since the High King's party rescued the Nihonjin from the overwhelmingly superior force of *bakachon* marines and Haida pirates. It helped very much that they had a common enemy, and that of all Montivallans the member-realm called the Portland Protective Association seemed paradoxically closest to her own Empire in its approach to life. And . . .

She looked at the Sword of the Lady by Órlaith's side. Much of the time it seemed only a sword, recognizably of superlative quality despite being of the alien Western form, straight and double-edged with a curved bar guard and moonstone-crystal pommel clutched in antlers.

Reiko's fingers stroked the black lacquered scabbard of the weapon thrust through her own sash, an ancient masterwork of the legendary swordsmith Masamune, a *shoshu kitai* of seven laminations. It even had a name of its own: *Kotegiri,* steel-cutter, from a famous incident of battle in the Genkō War more than seven centuries ago. Great warriors, *daimyo* and rulers had borne this sword, and handed it down through the generations by inheritance or as spoils of war or as a treasured gift meant to bestow great honor, until it had passed into the collection of her five-times-grandfather Meiji *Tennō* in the twelfth year of his reign.

The leader of the Seventy Loyal Men had taken it from its display-case to carve a path to survival for her grandmother and rally the tattered remnants of the nation. Then he had presented it to her father when he came of age. It had been the sword of the *Saisei Tennō*—Emperor of Rebirth—in a dozen desperate fights against the *jinnikukaburi* enemy, until he fell three months ago with this very katana in his hands and an arrow in his breast . . .

And now to me.

When you drew this creation of jewel steel and subtle human art and deep time . . . felt its balance in your grasp as sweetly sure and true as the flight of a hawk down the slope of Ōjisan . . . then all the long, long history of her people became a living presence. A tale written in beauty and blood, glory and tears.

The tranquility of rice bowing before the sickle, she thought. *And deeds like skies full of storm.*

The Sword of the Lady was something else entirely. No mortal smith had ever smelted its metal from the bones of earth or laid it across his anvil beneath the hammer. Órlaith had said she thought it might not be matter at all, as humans defined the term, but instead a thought in the mind of her Goddess embodied in the world of human kind without being wholly *of* it. Certainly it had taken no hurt from resting on the High King's breast when he was on his funeral pyre . . . and she had seen it standing hilt-upright when the towering flames subsided, enclosed for a moment in sparks like moving coils of golden light.

When you came closer the eye was drawn, inward and inward, into depths beyond depths until you had to wrench your gaze away. Despite her burning curiosity she had never felt the slightest impulse to *touch* it, though. Something prevented her; not hostility, but a feeling of friendly apartness like a cat looking at you and then glancing away, or a glimpse into another's home in the evening dusk as a sliding door was opened and shut and spilled lamplight for an instant. There was a welcome there, but not for you.

Which is entirely fitting. As Kusanagi-no-Tsurugi *is ours, so this is theirs. To each land and people their own spirits and the mysteries woven into the fabric of their being. To be sure that blade is a very* young *mystery, but every story must have a beginning . . . and Father once said that the Change did more than end the era of the machines. It reopened a doorway in the world. One that had slowly closed over many thousands of years, a passage to the time of legends, so that they walk among us once more. And there is no doubting that it is a* powerful *mystery, a true shintai, the dwelling-place of* kami.

When it was unsheathed, even for practice, the world *flexed,* as if the very underlying fabric of reality was like the skin of a great *ō-daiko* drum struck by the player's club.

Once you have seen an actual magic sword, searching for one of your own becomes more credible! Even if you have not seen what Father saw. What I have now seen myself. And more.

"General . . ." she said quietly. "You know that I have seen what my father saw in my own dreams; the desert, the castle, the eight heads; but his vision was . . . abstract. He saw these things. I see *myself* amid these things, as does our ally."

She moved her eyes towards Órlaith for an instant. Egawa nodded, a little grudgingly. He would have very much preferred that they handle this business altogether by themselves. But he was pragmatist enough to see that they had no choice, and Órlaith's dogged, courteous insistence that she was merely *helping* the Nihonjin party on its mission soothed his honor.

She continued: "And on the voyage south, I saw something else. I saw the Grass-Cutting Sword itself."

He nodded stolidly; if they were to follow visions seen in dreams, he would use them as he would a scout's report.

"In the place we seek it, Majesty? That is good to hear. Intelligence is always helpful."

She shook her head, very slightly, and made a small curve through the air with her fan. "No. Nothing so . . . reassuring. I saw it in the hands of Yamato Takeru himself, as he fought his battle in the sea of grass. Wielding it like a whip of fire and air."

Egawa blinked. Even by Japanese standards that was extremely long ago. The *Brave of Yamato* had lived in the reign of his father the twelfth *Tennō*, according to records indistinguishable from legend, first written down in times much later but themselves very ancient. She was the one hundred and twenty-eighth ruler of the same dynasty.

"And no. I did not merely dream, even a true dream. I was . . . I was *there*. And he saw me also. Saw me as the Sun Goddess Herself. For a light shone through me like none other than Hers, and it filled *him* with fire, made him certain of victory. I saw a myth being born from the womb of time, General: and I was part of it, for a moment a *kamigakari*, the vessel of She who is my ancestress and his. The years coiled on themselves like a serpent, from today to our beginnings and back."

His face changed slightly. It was an expression she'd never seen, not even when they made their last stand in the ruins on the north of this bay expecting utter and final defeat. It took a moment to recognize fear. Or perhaps an awe deep enough to daunt even his rock-strong spirit.

She smiled with a small quirk of the lips. "This is very disturbing, my faithful *bushi*. To me, particularly! But it is in no way misfortune. We know that wicked *akuma* fight for the enemy, neh?"

"Yes, Majesty," he replied.

Of that there was no doubt whatsoever. The *bakachon* were led and ruled, or more accurately tormented and driven, by the descendants of the man who had ruled part of Korea before the Change. In its aftermath he had claimed to be a *kangshinmu*, a sorcerer-prophet empowered by superior beings to make cattle of all who were not pure followers of his doctrine. And more than claimed; he and his elite votaries could do things no normal man could. The one who had tried to kill her and the Montivallan princess had done so, surviving wounds that should have left him instantly dead. Surviving just long enough, and his eyes like pools of tar, windows into a nonexistence very far indeed from the *mu* of the Buddha.

Some *thing* had burrowed through the soul of the man that had once been, like a wasp larva inside a grub, leaving a gateway into a nothingness that *hated*, negation as an active principle.

Active. And hungry. Hungry for all that is.

Firmly but calmly she went on: "Should we not then be glad that the *kami* fight for *us*? Is ours not the Land of the Gods, and we their descendants?"

She saw his face settle again, into the familiar grim mask that might have served for an image of a *kami* itself: if there was a spirit that embodied *ganbaru*, the quality of absolute determination to overcome and accomplish whether it was possible or not, it would look much like that. It felt a little odd to hearten *him*, since he did that for her every time she looked at him.

"What then, Majesty?" he asked.

Her smile grew a little broader, and she touched the war-fan to his armored shoulder for an instant.

"Why, then we will go forward, General, I the foremost and you at my right hand. If men oppose us, we will cut them down; if evil spirits assail us, we will call on our guardian *kami* and defy them; if deserts and mountains and hardship lie in our path we will endure and overcome them. I will take up the sword my divine Ancestress gave us and the Brave of Yamato wielded, and with that and our allies and our own good steel and warrior hearts we will free our people of the terror from the sea and reclaim our homeland. We will have . . . victorious peace."

Egawa's face worked slightly, and for a moment she thought he would drop to his knees and bend his forehead to the deck. Instead he saved them both embarrassment by going to one knee only and bowing at a slight incline with his sword-hand fist to the ground—the warrior's gesture to his lord on the field of battle.

No words were necessary.

CHAPTER THREE

HRAEFNBEORG, BARONY OF MIST HILLS
(FORMERLY MENDOCINO COUNTY)
CROWN PROVINCE OF WESTRIA
(FORMERLY CALIFORNIA)
HIGH KINGDOM OF MONTIVAL
(FORMERLY WESTERN NORTH AMERICA)
JULY/MÆDMŌNAÞ 7TH
CHANGE YEAR 46/2044 AD

Deor *Wid-ferende*—which meant *Wide-farer* in the old tongue, the language his folk used for matters of name and lore and ritual—was glad to be home for a visit, sitting on the dais in the middle of his long-dead father's hall as the long summer day fell towards evening. Here, though, he was Deor Godulfson, son to the first Baron and brother to Lord Godric, the current holder of the title. It had been five years since he had seen his kin.

More or less glad, anyway, he thought, remembering his father, and the mother who hadn't long outlived him. *I'd forgotten quite how . . . rustic . . . Mist Hills is. Well, most places are; but most of them aren't places you nearly spent your entire life in. Back then we didn't know there was anything else but ruins and bones and savages.*

He was a lean man of medium height with pale gray eyes and a harpist's long deft hands, dark hair gathered in a queue at the back of his neck through a worked silver tie, wiry and fit in his thirty-second summer, his skin tanned and weathered by strange strong suns.

It was hard to remember *being* that desperately earnest, naive boy yearning for a world beyond the hills he knew; desperate for knowledge, for beauty, for music . . . full of longings that hadn't had names.

Longing to see the things I've seen, he thought. *Courts and kings and castles, beaches fringed with palms and the sun making the ocean a lake of crimson as it sank in the southern seas . . . and home again, to wonder if home is still a word you can speak. Are all journeys a circle, like Time itself? Didn't Woden Himself say something like that to High King in a dream? But you couldn't really come home again, because by the time you did, both you and home would have changed.*

That must be why he felt as if he were not quite at home in his skin, despite his pleasure in the sharp, sweet bite of Gowan's cider that filled his mug, and a belly still stretched by the feast his sister-in-law had put together the day of his return—a runner had taken the message to her as soon as a longboat from the ship had put them ashore.

Thora Garwood leaned towards him from her seat to the left and said softly:

"Is it all smaller than you remembered?"

They were of an age, and about the same in height, though his oath-sister was a little thicker-built than he, sprawling at her ease in the carved redwood chair, like a good-natured lynx. She had a graze across the knuckles of her left hand, and a slight mouse under one hazel eye. It had been just long enough since their last visit here for a new crop of eager young idiots to grow up discounting tales of the Bearkiller war-skills marked by the A-list brand between her brows, not to mention her own personal reputation. Eager to make a name for themselves by taking her genial offer of an all-in wrestle, and a little friendly bet on the side. They hadn't realized what the grins of their older relatives meant until too late, until they were sorry and sore and somewhat lighter of purse. Thora took what he considered a slightly childish glee in winning a bet, just for the sake of the thing and regardless of the stakes.

"No, not really," Deor said.

Up north in the Association lands this barony his father had built from the wreck of a world would be accounted a rather modest knight's fee bearing a too-grand title. But he'd built it with his own hands, and the willing help of those he'd saved when all else failed them, even the very fabric of things itself.

"Just . . . feeling . . . I'm not sure. A dream last night, but it fades when I try to bring it into focus."

The great timber-and-stone feasting hall was much as his father had finished it just a few years before he died; a long rectangle a hundred feet by fifty, with a ceiling of double hammer-beam timbers high above, the interior lit by windows at each end and set into the dormers over the doors at the sides. Wrought-iron holders for candles and lanterns could be lowered from above after dark. It smelled faintly of old woodsmoke and the sun's heat on the shingles of the roof. More of horse and hay drifting in from the outside, and warm wool on human skin, good food and the drowsy warmth of a long hot summer's day.

The chatter of voices as folk came in and sat down to dinner tended to be lost, though the acoustics were quite good for song. Two rows of log pillars ran lengthwise to support the upper part of the roof; the uprights were carved and painted with bands and chevrons of black, red, yellow and green. The long hearth down the center was swept and garnished with dried wildflowers and aromatic herbs in this summer season; cooking was done in a separate building, and in any case winters here were chilly and wet rather than really cold . . .

And now he knew what *really cold* meant, since he'd spent a February in a Lakota *ger* on the high eastern plains, and seen the *norðrljós* glittering and dancing and crackling in curtains of icy fire across the sky, reflecting on the berg-ice floating in the Trondheimsfjord.

Frankly, this place is a bit of a barn, though I love it.

He felt a tug of annoyance in the flow of welcome at the edge of his consciousness and his lips twitched in amusement.

I didn't mean to insult you—he sent a thought toward the hearth wight. *Your coals kept me warm many a winter's night, and I saw the world in the colors that licked over them.*

He drew the rune *Wynn*, for joy, over the cider in the turned oak mug before him, dipped out a drop and flicked it in offering toward the long hearth that ran down the center of the hall.

Though certainly Mist Hills is less *rustic now than it was then.*

The hangings on the wall included tapestries from northern workshops, bright with images of lords and ladies hawking or knights breaking lances at tournaments, a sport he had now seen and thought thunderously dull for the most part. Though there were the shields and spears and mail-coats and the skins of grizzly, cheetah, tiger and lion he remembered. There had been coffee for breakfast, albeit treated as a rare luxury trotted out for the returning prodigal. The floor had been re-laid with smooth tile, which was easier to clean than the original rough flagstones.

The saffron-robed, shaven-headed monk from the monastery of the Ten Thousand Buddhas near what used to be Ukiah might have been here in the old days, and the Pomo chief with beadwork and an abalone pendant on his butter-soft doeskin shirt. But the elegant dark man with the curled black mustachios was from Rancho Sotoyome, which was the new settlement established by the ex-thralls after the fall of the bandit and self-proclaimed Duke Morgruen, just after the first Montivallans had come to Mist Hills.

Deor's lips tightened; his father had died at Morgruen's hands, while he lay a bound prisoner. But he'd avenged him, in his own way. Morgruen might not have died on his blade, but he'd died still—and would not have, save for what Deor had done.

And there were two young Rangers with the White Tree and Seven Stars and Crown on their jerkins, whispering to each other in Sindarin, which would have been a mad dream back then . . .

His gaze sharpened with appreciation of the male of the Dúnedain pair—who was about the age he'd been when he first left home.

Faramir, that was the name.

Curly yellow hair like pale gold falling down his neck and framing blue-gray eyes and a snub nose, a spray of freckles across his high cheekbones. A lithely supple build too, and a tragic air that sat oddly on one so young; his companion was outright brooding, and had a nasty and barely-healed scar across her face.

His cousin, Morfind.

They'd ridden in with dispatches, and only the fact that it would cause grave offense without a good and stated reason had kept them from riding right out again, he judged.

Wait . . . I met them long ago, when the Dúnedain first came south to Eryn Muir. They were small children then, of course.

Thora raised a brow at him with a pursing of the lips and a sideways twist of her head that made her thick red hair toss.

Not bad, I agree! the gesture meant, as she flicked her eyes towards the comely Ranger youth.

She and Deor had been comrades for a long time, and had a compressed mutual wordless language for some things. A slight waggle of the hand.

But just a bit too young for either of us. Pity.

His own smile and movement of the brows said: *True, but no harm in looking.*

He'd never had any interest in those younger than full manhood, not since he'd been a gawky youth himself. And even then the ideal of his soul's desire had been the hard beauty of a warrior; as his mind saw Sigurd facing Fafnir, or Beowulf as he strode into Hrothgar's hall in the first iron pride of his flowering strength. But now full manhood's earliest years were getting to be younger than himself by a sometimes uncomfortable margin.

"Were *we* ever that young?" he added quietly.

"Just as young as that handsome lad when we met at Albion Cove, brother," she replied, and they both laughed softly. "Though we were both drenched with rain and I was expecting to drown, until we saw your signal-fire and *Ark*'s anchor held."

Deor's brother Godric came in, his hair wet and slicked back from washing off the sweat worked up breaking horses to harness, and wearing a clean blue tunic with gold embroidered hems and neck, and indoor shoes. Everyone rose in respect—the meal didn't begin until the Baron was seated. He was a stocky broad-shouldered man in his forties now, big-nosed and with a thrusting chin under his neatly trimmed dark-brown beard.

In fact he was the image of their father as Deor recalled him from his earliest memories. More so than last time. Enough so that it was a little startling, even to the streaks of gray in his beard and the way his forelock looked more pointed at the front as his hair receded on either side.

That passed. So too will this, he quoted to himself. *When you're my age or Thora's, the world seems to go on and on and you don't change, always strong and in command of hard-won powers that you lay up like a chest full of golden arm-rings. But coming back after five years you see that the worm never stops gnawing at the root of the World-Tree. Even more so that my nephew Leofric is a man grown with a wife and a little daughter of his own! I remember him making his first steps. And . . . the High King dead! Killed not a week's journey from this very spot!*

The shock of that blow was still echoing in his mind and heart, the more so that the others had had months to come to terms with it. He could remember his first meeting with Artos . . . Rudi Mackenzie . . . as if it were yesterday, the *aliveness* of the man, the chiseled face and steady blue-gray eyes . . .

After that there would always be something of him in my words when I sang of heroes.

And the way he'd been patiently kind with Deor's adolescent awkwardness at Court, arranged that he be unobtrusively protected, and seen potentials in the stranger from the little out-of-the-way settlement that Deor himself had only wistfully dreamed might be his. It had been Artos' word that won Deor a hearing from his half-sister Fiorbhinn at Dun Juniper, and she the foremost bard of their time; yes, and other lessons from his mother Lady Juniper that set his footsteps on a path deep and shadowy.

That passed, he thought. And of his grief: *So too will this.*

"*Wilcuma!* Be welcome!" Godric said as he stepped onto the dais and took his seat.

This was a casual family meal, not a formal feast, but there were guests. His wife Aerlene brought him his horn, this one full of beer with the foam visible over the silver-bound rim. Deor had drunk several tall mugs of Hraefnbeorg's good cool spring water before he asked for cider with his meal; especially in the warm season you didn't want to sit down still thirsty with the spirit of the grape, or the apple, before you. Beer was different, of course.

It did a man no harm to get drunk now and then, but only now and then.

"Hail the hall!" She turned to face her husband. "Hail Godric Eorl! This drink I bear to bless the land-father, wine and wynn for the boar of battle!"

The Eorl hammer-signed the horn and lifted it before his strong deep voice filled the space; for a moment Deor's vision blurred, as if he was watching his mother and father make the same familiar well-loved homely rite:

"Hail to the Gods, hail to the Goddesses, hail to the fathers and mothers of our folk! Hail to the *sele-aelf*, to *mund-aelfen* and *aecere-aelfen*, hail the wights that ward us all!"

He took a long swallow. "*Wuton wesan wel!* Let us be well!" and handed the horn back to his lady.

Once more she faced the hall. "To all our guests a host of welcomes!"

Her face shone. "Far have they fared! And none more so than my lord's brother Deor Godulfson, justly called the Wide-Farer, and his comrade and oath-sister Thora Garwood, called Swiftsword! Welcome among us once more!"

She signed, and the servers—her own younger children and those of the housecarls—brought out the food before they sat farther down the trestle tables to either side of the dais themselves. The meal was lighter in this season than it would be in cooler weather, though hearty enough for folk who'd been working with their hands all day, which everyone who dwelt here did, rank or no. Fertile soil and hard skilled work meant nobody in Mist Hills had gone hungry in a long time. Not since before he'd been born, not since the first terrible years after the Change when they struggled to get the tools and seed and knowledge they needed, and came to a good understanding with the landwights and the Gods of soil and weather and field.

So there were steaming platters of the first corn from the garden with its rows of white and yellow kernels to burst sweet on the tongue; big bowls of green salads with sharp white goat-cheese and walnuts crumbled in, plates of sliced tomatoes and onions, steamed peas, fried potatoes, hard-boiled eggs, platters heaped with cold sliced roast pork and venison garnished with pickles, chunks of hard yellow cheese with knives stuck in their tops, round loaves of coarse wholemeal bread and pottery crocks of yellow summer butter cool from the spring-house.

All good, but the real treat would be the fruits that followed; bowls of blueberries, boysenberries and strawberries and blackberries with thick cream, and baskets—mostly fine-woven Pomo work bought in trade—of peaches and cherries and nectarines, apricots blushing yellow-crimson and the first crisp yellow-green-red apples.

"Good to see you're up, brother," Godric said, a little teasing in his voice. "You were too weary last night for us to get much out of you."

"After the way your good lady fed us, it's a wonder I didn't sleep for a week!" Deor said politely.

"We spent some time today sparring with a few of your youngsters, lord," Thora said cheerfully. "Sweating the ale out, so to say, and earning dinner."

That too was needful work, and as hard as any. It had actually been a bit of a relief to face relative beginners, rather than his usual session with Thora's merciless perfectionism. He'd said more than once that stepping into a practice ring with her was like learning the harp from Lady Fiorbhinn . . . except that he enjoyed playing the harp and was naturally good at it, and he didn't try to make Thora learn *that*. Whereupon Thora would retort that the audience for a bad composition with the sword was likely to be far more hostile . . . and you couldn't choose whether or not to put on a performance.

Then they would both laugh. . . .

She broke a loaf from the basket at her elbow and handed part of it to Deor; the interior was still warm, since a big household like this had the need and the labor and equipment to bake nearly every day rather than the more common once or twice a week. Some very thrifty farm-wives didn't let their households eat bread new-baked lest they gorge on it for the taste alone.

"Your latest crop of fighters is promising, very promising, but they need seasoning," she said. "They're a little . . . academic. I'd drill them more in rough country, if I were you, lord Baron."

"We've had a peaceful time, since I swore to the High Kingdom," Godric said. "Nothing more than the odd bandit, or a duel between the white wands now and then; and a Haida raid four years ago, but that was only a skirmish."

He looked at the young Dúnedain woman with the axe-mark on her face. "The Rangers guard us well. Even the youngsters we send south to help them now and then rarely see real fighting . . . though that may change. Will change, from what I'm told. The Kingdom will call, and we will answer."

Deor could see his elder brother put aside care for the moment as he looked at him.

"So you still pick up that fine sword you brought home now and then?"

Deor began to bridle at the teasing tone; his brother had always protected him as a lad, but that time was past. His sister-in-law smiled and leaned forward and touched a short white mark on his chin.

"That wasn't taken in a battle of scops," she said.

"Oh, that was just a brawl in a harbor tavern." Deor shrugged.

And blinked as the rank-sweet smells of the hot alien night came back, and himself showing his teeth in a smile that hid a cold anticipation of sudden shocking unexpected death a world away from home.

"The knives came out. That was in . . . Zanzibar, I think . . . yes, Zanzibar."

Thora laughed, finished her mouthful of salad, picked a handful of olives out of a bowl, and spoke:

"Knives a foot long, curved, and shaving-sharp," she said. "And there were three of them, and two with swords, while the rest of the room hid under the tables or leapt out the windows screaming for the Sultan's men. It isn't easy to hide under a table there, they sit on the floor and the little stands holding the brass tops are only two feet high. There were more than a few white-robed backsides on display, and no time to kick them."

"It was a misunderstanding," Deor said into the laughter.

"No, I understood that churl perfectly when he grabbed at my ass uninvited," she said. "That's why I broke his arm—"

She smiled reminiscently, and Deor winced. She'd grabbed the man's wrist, twisted to lock the joint and then jerked the limb down over her rising knee, all as quick and fluid as an otter slipping into the water. The sound of bone and tendon and cartilage ripping was one he'd remember until his dying day; far from the worst thing he'd ever heard, but unpleasantly . . . primal. Not that the outlander hadn't deserved it, but if he lived it would be a long time before he got much use out of the limb.

"—and kicked his balls up around his ears."

Which was no joke either, no matter that everyone was laughing. With Thora's leg behind even a hasty snap kick . . . there were other things the man wouldn't be doing anytime soon, if ever.

"His *friends* misunderstood how a free woman of the Bearkillers expects to be treated," she finished. "Misunderstood *very badly*."

She turned to Godric and Aerlene; folk leaned forward from the benches to either side to hear.

"One of them hit me from behind with a teapot while I was dealing with the first, and next I knew I was lying on the floor blinking with blood and hot tea running over my face. While Deor stood over me with sword in his right hand and seax in the left screaming *Hraefnbeorg* and *Woden!*"

Deor shrugged at the looks he got. "Needs must, when men won't listen to reason," he said, and drank more cider. "I think it was a long time since anyone called on Victory-Father in Zanzibar. And perhaps the first time ever for Hraefnbeorg."

"One to four is long odds, with none standing to cover your back," Godric said respectfully.

"They couldn't all get at me at the same time, and it was half-dark," Deor said. "There was a lot of jostling and staggering. And they were hesitant at first. I think it had all gotten more serious than they expected very quickly."

Not to mention how one was curled in a ball and screaming like a rabbit in a trap.

"And the ones who could get close weren't glad of it," Thora said cheerfully. "He cut two, one badly, before I wobbled back to my feet and got my own blade out. We gave them a little more trouble to rock them back on their heels, put ourselves back-to-back, with them snapping around us, and ran for the ship as soon as we got outside. Twisty streets there! And we crossed steel with them again at the foot of the gangplank, backing up side-by-side, until the deck-watch showed the business end of their crossbows . . . and started shouting for the Sultan's men too."

"We'd have been in real trouble if the brawlers had been Zanzibaris themselves," Deor explained. "But they were foreigners there too, and not popular ones—*Omani*, their tribe is called, from a desert land north of there across the monsoon seas. Handsome brown men, good sailors and fine craftsmen and far-ranging traders, but they have some odd customs. I wish I had enough of their language to understand their poetry and songs, but . . . well, that's one of the curses of traveling. You drink of many springs, but none very deeply. The world is too wide for any man to learn."

He nodded to his brother's wife. Aerlene was a deep-bosomed woman with barley-colored hair and kind green eyes.

"Zanzibar is off the east coast of Africa; it's where those cloves I gave you came from. They grow them as we do apples, in orchards. Vast stretches of them, too; ships come from all over the world to buy them nowadays, so it's a good port to find a berth to wherever you want."

"They smell wonderful! We'll mull cider with them this winter, and they'll be fine indeed with the Yule hams. There's an old recipe my mother had from *her* mother, and I've never been able to use it before. Is the scent as good where they grow?"

"It is when they pick the flower-buds and dry them on mats across the orchards, and that's the season we arrived," Deor said and smiled reminiscently. "You can smell that scent miles offshore there, making the sea-breeze a wave of perfume as you approach. Then the surf, cream-white on the silver sand, with the long trunks and rustling leaves of the coconut palms swaying above, and the whitewashed buildings and minarets. They carve their doors from this hard dark wood as beautiful as jet, too, with worked silver studs. I wish I could have brought you one of *those*."

Thora grinned. "And they make this stuff from palm sap there . . . what did they call it . . ."

"*Chang'aa*," Deor said; he had a musician and poet's ear for words.

"White and sweet and strong!" she said, smacking her lips and taking a pull at her beer. "It's against their religion, but that doesn't keep them from drinking it, by the ale of Aegir!"

"The word means *kill-me-quick*," Deor added.

Everyone chuckled, and his sister Gytha touched the broad bracelet of worked gold coiled thrice high up on Deor's left arm.

Widowed sister, he reminded himself with another shock.

Like running down stairs in the dark and thinking there was one more when there wasn't. Her man had gone out in the middle of the night to check on why his dogs were going loudly mad and found it was a lion trying to kill his best Angus bull in the paddock. He'd had a spear with him, of course, and the lion hadn't survived the encounter, but neither had he in the end—lion-claws and fangs were filthy and the wounds they made always grew infected. That had happened three years ago, and the grass already grew thick and long on his barrow, dense with goldenrod and aster.

A place doesn't stop in time when you leave, he thought ruefully.

His arm-ring showed clearly. He was in a short-sleeved tunic of fine cotton dyed deep blue and embroidered at hem and neck, and green breeks cross-gartered below the knee. There were silver-and-turquoise plaques on the belt that held his seax—long weapons were hung on the wall—and a silver-and-gold valknut on a chain around his neck, showing his allegiance to Woden who sent the mead of poetry to men. A scop, a wandering bard of the sort who sang praise-songs for kings and drighten chiefs, wore the rewards of his craft as a badge of honor. He admitted to himself that besides custom, it was a pleasure to peacock a bit before his family.

"And where did this come from?" she asked. "Those are runes"—she did healing work, which needed runecraft as well as herblore and anatomy—"but not quite like ours."

"Ah, that was from King Bjarni in Norrheim," Deor said; the ancient world had called the heart of that realm northern Maine. "For the song I made and sang in his hall, and bearing him a word from our High King, his blood-brother and battle comrade."

For a moment it was as if a cloud had dimmed the sun.

"May he feast in Woden's hall!" murmured Godric, and raised his horn in salute.

Then he shook his head and looked at his brother again, smiling. Their folk held there was no better way for a man to die than for land and kin, and so their lord Artos had fallen, blade in hand and face to the foe. They would show courage in the face of grief, as he had in the face of peril, and go on about the lives his sacrifice had helped buy for them. His voice was steady as he went on:

"You traveled to Norrheim *twice*? Even our High King only went once! How do they fare?"

The Norrheimers were heathen like most of the folk of Mist Hills, though they used the *Norski* names for the old Gods, not the Saxon ones Deor's people followed. So did a fair number of the Bearkillers, Thora's folk, up in the Willamette; and in Boise many had followed the lead of the ruler's family, the Thurstons, who now offered to the Aesir. Which was natural enough, since the very name of their House meant *Stone of Thunor.*

It gave them all something in common. Followers of the White Christ weren't nearly as dominant on this continent as they'd been in the ancient days, but pagans were still a minority, albeit a considerable one. Heathen were a minority among pagans in turn. They tended to follow each other's fortunes with interest.

"King Bjarni is older, of course, but still strong in might and main. His eldest son Eric is a likely lad . . . young man! . . . of twenty-four, a wide-faring sailor and already his father's right hand with a son of his own; everyone says the Althing will hail him with no dispute. Norrheim grows in numbers and wealth and arts every year; their lands stretch north to the Royal Mountain now, and westward they're probing into the Great Lakes country. Rich soil waiting for the plow, the dead cities for mining, woods and rivers beyond end thick with timber and game and fish. And they're subduing the wild men, bringing them back to the world of human kind and building their own strength by it."

"We climbed the Sea-End Tower in the lost city of Toronto as the High King and his comrades did on the Quest. It's still standing, our lake-boat touched there on our way east," Thora said. "There's a little trade on the Lakes now, mostly Norrheimers, and they have an outpost near there."

Deor nodded. "Two thousand feet into the sky, step by step! Then to Eriksgarth where King Bjarni dwells when he's not visiting his jarls and outposts, and then we took ship over the eastern sea."

"With Ketil Ormsson, a Norrheimer merchant out of Kalksthorpe who trades grain and timber and metals to Iceland for their salt fish and fine wool cloaks," Thora said.

Everyone was rapt at the word; Iceland figured much in the old stories. Deor's eyes went distant, remembering the fuming smoke of the hot-springs as they stood into the bay and the ruins of Reykjavik stretched along the shore, and the flowering turf-roofs of the low-built modern longhouses in contrast.

"Most of those who lived in Iceland moved to England in the five years after the Change and became part of that folk. Not enough food at home, they were just about to starve, and the English needed hands and had good land to offer as they resettled from their refuges. But the ones who stayed are increasing once more, and they offer to the old Gods too nowadays. Some of their young folk leave for Norrheim each year. They've fine poets and scops . . . skálds they call them . . . but by the Gods, it's bleak there! Beautiful in a grand bare way, but . . ."

"Like Jotunheim in the old stories," Thora said, and drank with a shudder and smiled at the awestruck girl who refilled her horn. "Driftwood is a treasure and their sheep are thin because they have to travel at a run from one blade of grass to the next, or they'd starve to death between."

Everyone chuckled, and Thora went on:

"We didn't want to stay the winter, for all their poetry."

Godric raised brows gone a little shaggy. "That doesn't sound like Deor."

Deor laughed, and Thora jerked a thumb at him: "He didn't want to stay either, not after we tasted what they consider a fine delicacy—rotten shark buried underground and then hung in the wind for months!"

There were groans of incredulity, but Deor nodded with a wince.

Thora pulled out the silver hammer that hung around her neck and touched it to her lips.

"No," she said. "I swear it by almighty Thor! It smells worse than it tastes, and it tastes worse than anything I've ever willingly put in my mouth . . . and I've eaten ship's biscuit that crawled away if you put it down."

"That's why they serve it with Brennivín—" Deor put in as she banished the memory with cider and a bite of herbed roast pork. "A kind of vodka. Enough of that and you no longer care about the taste."

She cocked an eye at him and winked. "I got it down and kept it, just barely. *You* ran outside with a hand clapped over your mouth."

"We took a Norrlander ship from there to the Trondheimsfjord," he said, ignoring her loftily. "Norrland is a strong kingdom now, if loose-knit, and there are folk along the fjord, prosperous enough now though the city died. We spent the winter there, traveling by ski and hunting bear and moose."

"Though they call them elk—they don't have what *we* call elk, though they have red deer," Thora said.

"Do they offer to the Aesir too?" someone asked.

"Some do; more are Christians; and they're not what you'd call a pious folk in general," Deor said. "We had good guesting at the yeomen's steadings for song and tales—they were eager to show hospitality and hear our news of foreign lands; this part of the world is just fable to them now. In the spring we set out to England. Well, the Empire of Greater Britain, but England's still the heart of it."

"How do *they* fare?" Godric asked eagerly.

Their father had raised them on tales of the Anglo-Saxons, whose ways and faith he'd practiced in the Society for Creative Anachronism because they spoke to his soul, and then in deadly earnest after the Change.

"They fare well, though it's much changed from the old days of the stories, of course—they're Christians, to start with. Well, most of them. But rich, rich—well-tilled land, strong yeomen and wealthy thegns and eorls, knights and bowmen and castles, cities and trade, roads and railways and canals, ships . . . Full of ancient buildings, layer on layer whenever a man so much as digs a well, and many housing the living once more as their numbers grow and they clear the dead lands. We saw the White Horse of Uffington—"

"Hengest's banner!" someone murmured.

"—and the King-Emperor's court in Winchester—"

"Uintancæstir," Godric said, the same name in the old tongue from which the modern descended.

"—and William the Bastard's tower with its feet in the water in the ruins of London, all swamp and forest and monstrous overgrown works of the ancients. Nobody lives there save for a small garrison, but Winchester's a city as great as Portland or Darwin now, or greater; seventy-five thousand folk, they said. Not counting us travelers!"

There were murmurs of astonishment; it *was* a very large number, though he'd seen much bigger later in Asia. Sambalpur had five times that . . .

"The King-Emperor rules all the west of Europe to the Rhine and the Middle Sea, and even beyond that, though most of it's still empty from the Change and the great dying. Still, there are nearly two million in England now, and as many again in their other possessions. As many as in all Montival, or nearly."

Thora held up her left hand. If you looked closely, you could see that a divot was missing from the little finger at the tip.

"Speaking of *beyond*, I got this—and Deor got one on his leg you'll see in the bathhouse—off Agadir, in the southern province the English call Volublis."

"After a city the Rome-folk built there in their great days," Deor said. "It's much like our Westria, in parts. The English hold the lowlands, though very thinly—they're empty from the Change. Wild folk lair in the mountains inland, and in the deserts to the south. There are raids and skirmishes every year."

Thora nodded. "The fight off Agadir wasn't a brawl, it was proper sea-battle. Saloum rovers, Moorish corsairs from the Emirate of Dakar, attacking a British trade convoy we'd taken passage in. And we barely out of sight of the Union Jack flying from the fort's battlements. One of them nipped in and tried to board our merchant ship while the others kept the escort in play."

She clenched the hand into a fist. "They fought well when they came over the rail. Not as well as us, though!"

"Corsairs? Like the Haida here?" someone said.

Deor shrugged. "No, not as bitter a blood-feud as that. Just the contentions of kings; they don't like the Empire, there's an old grudge. The emirs think they should have got Volublis because their kinsfolk once held it. They're a hard folk and fierce, by what we heard, though that was from their foes. Sometimes they're at war with the Empire, sometimes they trade. They make some lovely things, I saw that, and it's a pity we couldn't stop in Dakar, which I heard was a great city for arts and learning now and well worth seeing."

"You sighed and looked like a boy who'd been told *no honey tart for you,*" Thora said. "And that at being denied a stop in the place the people who tried to kill us came from."

Deor shrugged acknowledgment and turned to his kin: "Traveling to see new lands carries a deal of staring at the same old ship with it!"

He drew the bulging coast of West Africa with a finger on the table, indicating where it turned east for a long way.

"The convoy scattered not far from here. Our ship went south and east, a long green coast edged with surf, to the land of the Ashanti where the King's Throne is a stool of pure gold and his courtiers cover their robes with gold beaten thin. They have their own tongue, but many of them speak English as well, at their port of Takoradi. We went inland from there through the jungle hills to the King's court in Kumasi, where there are new splendors amid the old ruins."

"And they make *chocolate.*" Thora sighed. "Caught a nasty fever there that Deor nursed me through, but it was almost worth it."

There were other sighs at that; he'd brought a little chocolate as gifts too, and a bit trickled in as trade now and then, just enough to tantalize. The tale went on, lubricated by more of the cider—a catalogue of wonders, around the tip of Africa, Madagascar, the troubled stay in Zanzibar and then on to Sri Lanka and the splendors of Hinduraj on the Bay of Bengal—until at last he said:

"And from there to Darwin in Capricornia, in the north of what the old maps call Australia—the King there is a wonderful old rogue with a silver tongue for a tale himself, and has some strange and powerful musicians at his court."

"But by Surt and all the fire giants, it's hot there!" Thora put in. "Hot all the time, day and night, and wet as a sauna half the year including the time we were there. The cloth rots off your back and the boots off your feet and the roaches are the size of mice and *hiss* at you, and I'm not drawing the long bow there either."

"Half the world trades there, though. From Darwin we took ship to Bali, which is beautiful as a dream and has the finest dancers I've ever seen, and from there to Hawaii, and from there back to Montival on a ship stopping in the Bay to pick up salvage . . . and some of our good Mist Hills cider and applejack, to be sure . . . and so here we are."

That was where they'd had the news about the High King. He was still mentally stuttering at it. It was like coming home and finding a mountain peak missing.

Instead of dwelling on that he scooped the last of the blueberries, blackberries and sliced peaches and nuts out of the bowl before him and drank the fruit-steeped cream.

"And though we traveled the world around, we never found fruit better than this. The taste makes me feel like a boy again."

"Around the world," Gytha whispered. "Around the *world*! My brother!"

Deor opened his mouth, then closed it again, looking around at the eyes staring at him. It struck him with a sudden shock that probably nobody here but she and his brother and their escort had even gone as far as Portland. Most would never leave this valley and the hills and woods about it, a day's journey on foot from the farmhouses where they'd been born.

Thora's hazel eyes were laughing, as if to say:

Well, what did you expect, with your head full of dreams again? That's why the world keeps surprising you!

He'd been years on ships and in the parts of port-cities full of rootless travelers, all strangers to each other, and it had come to seem as natural a way of life as any other. These people were flesh of his flesh and bone of his bone, this earth had borne and fed him, here his father and grandfather and kin from back even before the Change were laid in their graves . . . but looking at their glances now, for a moment he felt a whirling disorientation that made them as alien as any foreigner he'd met.

The silence echoed for a minute, and then his brother cleared his throat:

"We'll hear more of this!" he said. "What do you plan next?"

Thora was pouring more cream from a brown clay jug over another bowl of berries. "These are very fine. Mind, the Willamette's are as good, but these are fine indeed . . . well, we were thinking of settling down. If not right away, then soon."

There was sharp surprise in the glances his family gave him.

"When you've chased the rising sun until it sets, what more is there to do?" he said, spreading his long-fingered musician's hands. "There's a time to stop cutting timber and start building your house."

I've seen the sea turn silver and flash with winged fish leaping into a dawn like dancing fire, and beheld the ruins of London and Roma-beorg and Florence, and watched the white bears wrestle on glaciers. I've heard Niagara pour in torrents that sound like Thunor's hammer with the spray on my face. I've smelled the cloves off the coast of Zanzibar, and had a turbaned king throw me sapphires for my songs in the jungle hills of Taprobane, and stood by the roadside while elephants clothed in jeweled mail bore a Maharaja through the streets of Sambalpur, past temples like carved mountains. But I have no home. I've made songs that will live, but I need more time to compose, or so much of this will be lost when I die. Lost like tears in rain.

"And children need a home," Thora said.

At looks of blank surprise, she leaned across the table and prodded a finger into Deor's shoulder.

"He'd make a fine man to help raise 'em, even if he doesn't like the making part. I can handle that, though. With a little temporary help from some long lad."

That brought a startled laugh. "We've a good house in Portland, the High King's gift," he said. "And gold enough."

In fact mostly jewels, which they'd sent on to Corvallis to be converted into arcane entries in the ledgers of the First National Bank. Something else that would have been a fable from a tale when he was a boy . . .

"But they're strong Christians in Portland mostly, and neither of us is a city dweller in our hearts. Perhaps some land, somewhere . . ."

"With space for horses," Thora said, picking up a handful of raisins and tossing a few into her mouth; her hazel eyes looked dreamy for an instant. "And a vineyard. And plenty of space for Deor to talk to the landwights. He's the luckiest man that way I know, though they walk in his dreams more than *I* would like, by the Gods."

Deor's gaze went distant, and his fingers moved as if he were playing the harp that the High King's sister had given him, though Golden Singer was in his room in her case of oak and lacquered bison-hide. A dream had haunted his sleep, and they were meaningful to a scop—songsmith—and to a runemaster as well.

"To walk off some of this fine food myself is what I need now . . ."

He cast an apologetic look at his brother's wife, who smiled. She did not quite know how to react to him, he could see; she never had, and the more so when he came home so changed. There was a mix of pride and bewilderment there.

Thora's raised eyebrow said, *You're in one of your moods. What now?*

"Do you want company?" she added aloud.

He shook his head. "I'm just going up to the ridge—settle my head as well as my belly."

It's not just the dream, Deor thought as he stepped out along the trail into the long shadows, absently settling the weight of his sword with a shrug of the hips.

Hraefnbeorg had been built on the knob where a run of higher ground ended in a steep rocky spot. To the west, the trail dipped down and then up a slope and along the ridge. The trees within a quarter-mile of the berg had been cut back to provide a clear field of fire, though the chaparral that was growing up now would have to be cut soon if the goats couldn't cope.

Things have been too peaceful.

He felt a sense of presence as he passed the graveyard, the weathered slabs that honored his kin from before the Change dominated by the mound they had raised for Godulf.

"Are you pleased with me, Father?" he asked softly.

He stopped for a moment before the stone set in the barrow's side, carved with ravens and bearing the inscription:

Baron Godric Godulfson raised this barrow for his father Godulf the Wise, who saved his folk and died for them, undaunted. Thunor hallow these runes.

Then: "Are you surprised?" he whispered.

He stopped, surprised himself to realize that he still harbored that uncertainty. He had wandered the world with the High King's leave—almost a command, to bring him a word of all the lands and a sense of how the great globe fared now that two generations had passed since the old world's fall and human kind had begun to find its balance once again. But right now he felt as if that voyage had been an escape from responsibility. Why had his wanderings led him home? And on this day?

Overhead, a raven called and was answered by another. At sunset it was normal for mated pairs to check in as they winged home, but he shivered suddenly. Ravens warded his line, and their cries could bring warning, and sometimes, what looked like a pair of common ravens were something more. . . .

Leaving the cleared slope he passed beneath the Western Maple and oak and fir trees that crowned the ridge and continued on. Below him the slopes fell away in golden grass mixed with the deep green of little shaws of trees; beyond lay the meadows and patchwork fields of the farms, punctuated by the curving lines of carefully pruned grapevines. Now that trade had been established, Mist Hills was exporting their white wines, and he could see that some of the abandoned fields had been put into production once more. Horses dozed, and a herd of dairy cows was heading back towards its barn in single-file, needing no direction.

Beyond the river, the thickly forested southern hills rose in dark folds. For a moment the angle of one of the peaks reminded him of the shape of Mount Tamalpais, or Amon Tam, as they were calling it now, and suddenly an image from his dream leaped vividly into memory.

He remembered how King Artos had once tried to describe the messages he got from the Sword of the Lady. It had sounded a lot like the frustrating confusion of images that came to Deor when he was gestating a new poem. He frowned, trying to move from the image of the Mountain to the rest of his dream. There had been boats, and fighting on the shore. The clang of metal and shouts and screams . . .

Were these the first stirrings of a poem about the death of the High King? But that had happened at Beltane, when the hills would still have been green, whereas the slopes behind the battling warriors he saw had glowed with ripe Midsummer gold.

But now that he was remembering, what he felt was not grief or rage, but urgency. He had to know more. A little ways ahead, he remembered, was an ancient live-oak with a hollowed base that had cradled him through many dreaming hours. It was time to try *utiseta,* the old Norse practice of sitting out that he had learned in Norrheim. With no folk to distract him, perhaps he could untangle his dream.

Deor unrolled his cloak and slung it around his shoulders, for the cold sea-wind had sprung up with the setting of the sun, leaching the last of the day's heat—they were closer to the coast than you'd think here. In the east the moon was rising but the coastal hills were already wreathed with fog. Sweeping the hollow clear of debris, he settled himself against the trunk. With a sigh he let out his breath, allowing his awareness to flow with it, joining with that of the tree.

Ac-faeder, *Oak-father, hail,* he sent a silent message. *Since I last sat here I have seen many lands and many trees, but none so noble as thee . . .*

He smiled a little as a whisper of welcome passed through the prickle-edged leaves. *Guard me, old friend, for I have a journey to go . . .*

He adjusted his folded legs a little more comfortably, then closed his eyes, counting ever more slowly as he drew breath and let it out again. Awareness arrowed inward, then expanded, noting the rich earthy scent of the leaf mold, the small scufflings as ground squirrels sought shelter. A branch cracked as a doe led her half-grown fawn from cover. Farther still, a gray fox began his evening hunt. The raven called to his mate again, and was answered from the forest down the hill.

He took a deeper breath, and sent a greeting to the crusty old wight who ruled the ridge. He could sense the curiosity of other spirits as a feather-touch against his inner senses, and oddly, the same mix of excitement and security he had always felt in the presence of the High King. But this time it was mingled with the urgency that had throbbed in his dream. King Artos' blood had blessed the land, *his* land, this land of valleys and mountains north of the Bay. That sacrifice made it truly part of Montival. It was no surprise if the High King's spirit had joined the gathering of power he was feeling now. But what did Artos want him to *do*?

Then a two-note whistle and warble pierced his awareness as Meadowlark, his gold breast marked with black like the Hraefnbeorg banner, swooped and landed on his shoulder.

"Láwerce . . ." he breathed. *"Will you show me the meaning of my dream?"*

"Rad . . ." came his ally's answer, and the rune for riding shaped itself in his mind. *"Fly with me . . ."*

With a dizzying lurch his spirit slipped free.

Vision reoriented to a bird's view as they flew through the night. Looking down he saw dark shapes moving along the pale line of the old highway that ran north and south through the coastal lands. But something was different—the moon, which had been nearly full, was beginning to wane.

"It is the future, then, that you are showing me?"

Deor dipped lower to inspect the riders and recognized the Saxon helmets of Hraefnbeorg men. Each rider trailed a remount behind him. As he watched they jolted into a canter once more, and there was a cold glitter on the edges of their spears and in their set eyes and stern faces.

He followed Láwerce southward as the rising sun flamed on the great bay. In moments it was full day, and they were dropping downward past the remains of San Rafael, swooping toward the water's edge where a receding tide left mudflats shining in the sun. He recognized the odd tufted island just offshore; they must be nearing Círbann Rómenadrim, the ancient fishing village that the Dúnedain had restored as a way-station for scavenging forays.

Nearer still, he saw a ship he recognized—Moishe Feldman's *Tarshish Queen*—and an RMN frigate fighting off two Haida orcas and another that reminded him of a captured Korean warship he had seen in Capricornia. Bolts and round shot and flaming shells arced between them, and the sails bent as the ships made their deadly, stately wheeling dance.

But it was the activity on shore that caught his eye. On the slope between the village and the road Montivallan knights and a group that looked for all the world like warriors of Nihon battled an Eater horde. Individually, the savages were outmatched, but there were so many! Smoke rose into the sky, half-obscuring the vision.

A flare of light caught his eye and he focused on a tall knight who fought with a flowing grace. Deor had only once seen the Sword of the Lady unsheathed, but as the great blade rose and fell he felt a shock of recognition like a trumpet call, like a hot clean wind through the soul. But it was impossible! The High King's last fight had been in Napa, to the east, not here in San Pablo Bay.

The Eaters retreated, leaving the ground between them and the Montival band littered with the dying and the dead. He could half-see, half-sense presences, vast shadowy Powers at work . . . A robed figure swirling in rays of blinding light and heat before the entrance to a cave, her sleeves making giant arcs of flame larger than the sky as she danced love and danger and defiance. Another surrounded by a whirling raven-feathered cloud, at one moment a fair maiden with a bow, then a wrathful dark-haired warrior queen with sword in hand, next a grim sooty crone wielding a great scythe, all beautiful and all terrible beyond imagining.

And over the enemy, a flat darkness that loured and drew and drank . . .

Deor dropped closer as the knight eased off his, no, *her* helm, he realized as he saw the woman's fighting braid.

Órlaith! The Princess!

It was years since he had seen her, but all the strength and beauty that had been just showing like new leaves in spring was there now, honed by grief and a grim fury. The warrior behind her spoke, and with a quick glance at her foes she jammed the helmet on again.

The Eaters were gathering for another charge, dancing, screaming, pounding their bare feet on the ground until it shuddered, shaking bows and spears and notched blades in the air. Arrows began to whistle and hum.

"No!" shouted Deor. *"Not* her, *not again!"* But what came out was a bird's cry.

"Fly!" shrilled the Meadowlark. *"Fly home, and sing the men of Hraefnbeorg a battle song!"*

CHAPTER FOUR

GOLDEN GATE/GLORANNON
(FORMERLY SAN FRANCISCO BAY)
CROWN PROVINCE OF WESTRIA
(FORMERLY CALIFORNIA)
HIGH KINGDOM OF MONTIVAL
(FORMERLY WESTERN NORTH AMERICA)
JULY/FUMIZUKI/CERWETH 14TH
CHANGE YEAR 46/FIFTH AGE 46/SHŌHEI 1/2044 AD

When they'd walked a little farther down the hundred-and-sixty-foot length of the deck, Heuradys added sotto voce:

"He doesn't believe in taking risks? But your brother signed Captain Feldman up to take us on this crazed escapade, didn't he?" she murmured. "Either Prince John's grown inhumanly persuasive—"

"I've been told he *is* very persuasive," Órlaith said, cocking an ironic eye at her knight.

"Feldman isn't a girl he's charmed onto her back and besides *I* was the one who put the make on *him*, though granted a teenage boy doesn't need much persuasion. Still, listening to John's sales pitch shows our good Captain *does* take chances."

"But not *careless* chances. There are things his father did for Grandmother Juniper, during the Protector's War, I don't know the details, and vice versa. Though it should be safe enough here in the Bay," Órlaith answered. "It's later on things will be getting a bit hairy, probably."

"Oh, not the Eaters and Haida and Koreans; though some of all three *were* operating here after we left this spring."

Órlaith nodded. "That's how my cousin Malfind of the Rangers died. I haven't forgotten. Still, that was a skirmish with a small group."

"Yes, but what I was thinking of was your mother, or more precisely our sovereign lady the High Queen, now sole ruler, and what *she* might do to Feldman," Heuradys said. "She's not going to be pleased with anyone who helped us, you know that as well as I do. Better, probably."

Órlaith gave a slight mental wince. John and she had promised Feldman their protection, for him and his. That might require something drastic if their mother was stubborn enough to press a treason charge. The Great Charter specified that the Crown wouldn't pass to her as heir until she was twenty-six, which was still years away. Until then her mother was monarch of all Montival, as well as Lady Protector of the Association in her own right; the Protectorate would pass to John when she died. Órlaith's would be the first hereditary succession to the High Kingdom, and much of the great law of State was still unsettled; the Kingdom was very young as yet.

About a year older than I am, as something proclaimed abroad and seen like a banner against the sky to draw the dreams and hearts of our folk. Younger, as a thing my mother and father and their comrades built with sweat and their heart's blood.

All the humor went out of Heuradys' voice. "Orrey, she's your mother, she's always been good to me too and she's my High Queen . . . and she's a good one, she always thinks of the realm, but she *is* an Arminger. Now that you're not her little towhaired moppet anymore you need to start remembering that side of your heritage. Not just about the way your axe-crazy granddad used to have heads off right in the Throne room and you can still see the stains on the floor forty years later when the light's just right. *My* second mother spent decades working for *your* grandmother Sandra, and . . . well."

Órlaith nodded. Lady Tiphaine d'Ath had fourteen silver-filled notches in the dimpled black bone of her sword-hilt. That was just the formal death-duels, most of them in the Crown's interest. It didn't count the ones she simply made disappear, and spec-ops work in wartime. There was a reason her title had been pronounced *Lady Death* long before her second career as a field commander.

"And that was all the Queen Mother, your Nonni. *My* mother was just the dagger in her hand."

Órlaith nodded again. Baroness d'Ath had handled a good deal of her own martial education, and she'd taught the High King much a generation before that, so that what his daughter got from him was partly her doing. Lady Death was what Nonni Sandra had summoned experts to forge, from a Change-scarred youngster with potentials only the woman who would later be called the Spider of the Silver Tower had seen. You could feel the hand of the maker in the cool perfection of the instrument, all the more remarkable when you considered that Sandra had never been any sort of warrior herself. Fortunately Lady Death was sixty and retired from hands-on wetwork . . .

"So you may *really need* to protect Feldman," Heuradys warned; she was as careful of her liege's honor as of her person. "Even if it means things getting bruising and damage being done."

Órlaith nodded a third time, more slowly and reluctantly.

Though Mother won't . . . I greatly hope. It would create too much of a problem with Corvallis.

Captain Moishe Feldman was a prominent and wealthy citizen of that wealthy and powerful city-state, sailing out of Newport, its window on the Pacific. He and his firm were rising powers in the Economics Faculty of the University—which was what Corvallans called their Guild Merchant, in their eccentric and old-fashioned way.

Corvallis is as tender about its autonomy as any of the other realms of the High Kingdom, or a bit more so.

She'd experienced that first-hand, studying there.

Surely mother wouldn't . . .

With a sudden chill, she realized she *wasn't* absolutely sure, only . . .

Surely she wouldn't, unless I'm killed. Then . . . I'm not sure what she'd do. I should have thought that through better . . . maybe I didn't want to think about it? But I have to make sure the Feldmans come through unscathed even if I do *die on this.*

"I will if I have to. But Herry, mother ran off with Da on the Quest when she was our age," Órlaith said stoutly, hiding her sudden disquiet—which was with herself, mostly. "And she's . . . well, much more moderate in her angers than Nonni Sandra was."

"No," Heuradys said flatly. "That's not the right way to think of it. Queen Mother Sandra didn't *get* angry, not so you'd notice. Certainly not the way her husband did before his . . . early death. Even her loves and hates were . . . cool."

"Well, there you are then," Órlaith said.

Her maternal grandfather Norman Arminger, the first Lord Protector, had died when Órlaith's mother Mathilda was ten, long before her own birth. Killed by her father's father Mike Havel, the first Bear Lord, in a fight in which both died: the family history got complex about then.

"But people were just as afraid of Sandra as they were of him while he was alive. And more so, sometimes, after he was out of the way. You know what they called *her*."

The Spider of the Silver Tower, whose invisible webs ran throughout the Protectorate and beyond. Binding men of the sword in nets of intrigue and obligation and fear they couldn't cut with steel.

Heuradys was just a bit older, enough to have known Nonni Sandra from something less like a child's perspective. Not to mention that she wasn't an adored granddaughter. And Sandra Arminger had been political patron to all three of Heuradys' parents, so a lot of dirty linen must have come up around the dinner table. There was knowledgeable conviction in her voice when she went on:

"When Sandra was running things in the Protectorate back in the day, after the Protector's War, she just killed you . . . had someone like my second mother kill you . . . if she thought it was necessary. With a secret trial in Star Chamber, or a smile and a wink and a hint in the right quarters, or even with a sigh and a *pity about that*. Or you just . . . died of excruciatingly convenient natural causes. And that was all she wrote."

Órlaith winced a bit; that was brutal, but not really unfair. As she learned more of the history, she couldn't even say definitely if there had been any other way to tame the realm her grandfather had founded.

"Well, then let's say my mother shows her anger more but she's less ruthless about it than my Nonni was."

"I certainly *hope* she is," Heuradys said dryly. "At seventh and last."

When it's really hard, Órlaith added to herself, the thought that hung between them.

"She's . . . she's more under law than either of her parents. Not just the Kingdom's law, but in her soul."

They exchanged a glance and put aside things they couldn't affect right now.

"The High Queen will have found out what we've done by now . . . days ago . . . I'd have liked to be a fly on the wall at *that,*" Heuradys said more lightly.

"Oh, no, you wouldn't," Órlaith said with conviction. "I said Mother rules her anger. But when there's no innocent bystander . . . like you . . . it can rattle the cage pretty hard. Especially when someone pokes a stick between the bars to tickle the dragon, and by the Dagda's club, I've done that now, eh?"

Her da had been a man who seldom raged, even in battle; when he fought with his own hands it was with the calm focus of a craftsman doing hard skilled work, or sometimes in an exaltation of joy like possession by the Power that watched over him, the triune Crow Goddess called the *Morrigú,* the Shadow Queen. In fact for someone who was famous as a conquering hero-king he'd been gentle to a fault when he felt he could be; sometimes his calm reasonableness drove Mother crazy when they were having one of their infrequent arguments. And he'd never signed a death warrant or denied a petition for clemency without much thought and careful study of the details; she could remember him frowning over each, sometimes late into the night. It was only the knowledge that mercy to the guilty was cruelty to the innocent that had kept him from always sparing the axe and noose.

The other side of the family, however . . . *I can feel that anger in me, even if I control it.*

"You *really* wouldn't have wanted to be there. Even as a crow flying overhead, much less a bug on the wall."

"Point," Heuradys said. "But frankly I keep expecting to hear a scream like a tigress with her tail under a wagon-wheel, echoing all the way from Castle Todenangst."

"I'm sure she'll get over it," Órlaith replied confidently.

I hope.

CHAPTER FIVE

CASTLE TODENANGST, CROWN DEMESNE
PORTLAND PROTECTIVE ASSOCIATION
(FORMERLY NORTHERN OREGON)
HIGH KINGDOM OF MONTIVAL
(FORMERLY WESTERN NORTH AMERICA)
JULY 7TH, CHANGE YEAR 46/2044 AD

"Your Majesty, if you do not master your anger—" Lord Chancellor Ignatius began.

"Then my anger will master me, priest!" she said, whirling and pointing one finger at his face for a moment. "That's what you were going to say, *isn't* it?"

The silence that followed the shout stretched as High Queen Mathilda went pacing like a caged tigress through the chamber high in the Onyx Tower, while he and two select advisors sat at the conference table looking at her with . . .

With absolutely infuriating patience!

The stacks of documents at either side of each man were as untouched as the carafes of water and wine and the bowls of nuts and dried apricots and figs and cinnamon-flavored wafers. There were no clerks or secretaries in this great room with its curved outer wall and pointed-arch windows, though they could be called by the bell at the Chancellor's right hand. The loudest sound was the swish of her skirts and the scuff of her slippers on tile and carpet, and the hammering of blood in her ears. And very faintly in the distance the tolling of a church-bell. A cathedral was built into Todenangst, and other chapels as well.

It did not help when Ignatius tucked his hands into the sleeves of his plain Benedictine monk's robe and bowed his tonsured head in rueful acknowledgment and quite genuine humility. She felt as if the silk and jewels of the headdress that covered her coiled brown hair and framed her face were choking her, tighter than the mail coif under a helmet.

Then the priest-brother spoke, bolder than the two soldiers: "Yes, my child, that *was* what I was about to say. How well you know me, after all these years! Was I really that much of a sanctimonious prig just now?"

"My daughter—the *heir* to the *Throne of Montival*—and my son John who is *heir* to the *Protectorate*—abscond into the wild, not three months after their father was assassinated, and I should be *calm*?"

She paced in and out of the pools of light that shone through the Venetian-gothic tracery of the windows with her strong hands clasped behind her back and her gold-embroidered slippers scuffing on tile and fringed carpets. In middle age and after four children she was solidly built, her face square and rather heavy-featured, but the leonine brown eyes and the vigor of her stride were reminders that she had been a knight herself in her day, and a good one. The heavy furniture seemed to need its solid carved bulk to be safe around the controlled fury that crackled from her at the news that her two eldest children had slipped away and taken ship without permission.

Today she wore a dark-green kirtle over a long-sleeved tunic of royal-blue silk and a wimple of the same hue, bound with a gold chain and with a similar woven belt that bore her jeweled Associate's dagger. A black mourning band and a pinned-back veil of filmy black gauze marked her recent widowhood. The lines of grief new-graven into her face marked it more clearly still. She wasn't much past the prime of life and she was carrying a child even now, but the lineaments of her deep age could be glimpsed, a visage that would daunt the boldest.

"It's just now that you *do* need to be calm," one of the other advisors said. "And it's cruel hard on the pretty rugs you're being, grinding them underfoot so, Matti."

She scowled at Edain Aylward Mackenzie; the commander of the High King's Archers looked back steadily, with the familiarity of lifelong friendship and the Clan Mackenzie's indifference to hereditary rank. She flushed a little at the irony in the level gray eyes and the soft lilting Mackenzie accent.

"Don't tell me you abetted this, Edain!" Mathilda said.

"I had no knowledge of it, at all, at all, Matti," he said. "No suspicion, either—and I would have liked it the more if my mother or my wife had sent a wee message about it. But then, I've been tied up here."

Mathilda winced. *While you let the reins slip in your grief* went unspoken. *And being pregnant always gave me mood swings. By the Saints and Holy Mary, that's not it now! I've got* good reason *to be furious!*

With her husband Rudi Mackenzie—High King Artos to the rest of Montival—so recently dead by shocking treachery, killed by a prisoner he'd spared . . .

"He should have put them all to the sword, or hanged them as pirates taken in the act!" she burst out.

Edain spread his scarred strong hands. "In strict law, yes, he could have."

They'd landed in Montival unannounced, weapons bare. Fighting in company with Haida reavers who were outlaws by definition and their own choice, long since proclaimed as among the enemies-general of human kind to be slain on sight.

"But we knew nothing of the rights and wrongs of it, and Rudi wasn't ever the sort who'd kill without thought just because he could or because it was easier to bury the problem under bodies. Else he wouldn't have been the man we loved."

"You have a right to grief and anger, Your Majesty," Ignatius said gently. "But not to endanger the realm."

The words were like a wet towel slapped into the face. The more so for the restraint and sympathy. The realm came first. *That* was unavoidable even in the middle of a rage.

True enough, she thought, checking herself for an instant; there was a momentary surge of nausea, but that *was* the pregnancy, and she suppressed it with an effort of will.

At least I'm not far enough along for the baby to imitate a porpoise or get the hiccups, she thought. *Now,* that's *distracting!*

"How in the name of God, the Virgin and the Saints did she manage to do this with nobody the wiser?" she asked aloud.

"Very quickly, carefully and skillfully," Ignatius said. "I've pieced a little of it together."

"I'll tan her hide quickly too!" Mathilda burst out.

Edain gave a grim chuckle. "It's also true my first thought was to wallop your Órlaith, and my Karl and Mathun for haring off to the south after her," he said. "But on second thoughts, aren't they both a bit along in years for a swat on the backside? The pack of them are about the same age as you and I and the good Father here were on a certain day about twenty-three years ago, eh?"

He nodded to the other soldier present, Lord Maugis de Grimmond, Grand Constable of the Association and Baron of Tucannon.

"And the lord Baron's son is not much older," he added.

"That was different," Mathilda said.

She was conscious of how weak it sounded even as the words came out; she'd joined Rudi on the Quest eastward without a second thought, despite knowing how furious her mother would be.

And that defiance is literally famed in song and story and no doubt encouraged Órlaith and John to do the same to me. The biter bit!

Grand Constable Maugis was a shortish grim-looking jug-eared man in his forties with graying dark-red hair and a beak of a nose in the middle of a hard, scarred, seamed face that had been rather ugly to start with. He looked a little shocked at the Clansman's irreverence, but also stolidly determined to endure whatever his ruler chose to do.

And that's just as effective in getting me to calm down, she decided. *And come to think of it, he and I and Edain are all of an age, a few years more or less are nothing once you're past forty summers, and Ignatius is only a decade older. We've been running things since we were in our twenties, we Changelings . . . but our children are nearly grown now, itching to do. Think, Mathilda, think . . .*

Her mother had always said that self-command was half the secret of ruling well, not to mention more than half the secret of a ruler dying in power, old, and of natural causes; it was as close as she came to a direct criticism of her long-dead spouse.

The Quest had stayed a winter at Chenrezi Monastery, up in the high Rockies, while Rudi healed from an envenomed wound.

Mathilda's lips tightened as she remembered his fever-drawn face at the worst, in the cave before the monks found them. Hot and thin, the strong bones looking out from the wasting flesh, and the stink of death from the finger-deep hole in his right shoulder where the High Seeker's arrow had struck. She had known with cold certainty that he was dying then, like an abyss before her feet. *Something* had changed it, they'd all felt the change as his body relaxed and sweat broke out all over him and his eyes opened. He'd recovered over the months at Chenrezi, with careful nursing, but that right shoulder had never been quite the same—after that he'd fought with his blade in his left. It had killed him in the end, from what Órlaith and Edain said, slowing his shield-arm just a fraction of a second the way it did increasingly over the years when he was tired or cold.

She took a deep breath. The monks of the Noble Eightfold Path had taught them many things during the short days and long dark nights. She thought of a still pond, and her anger like the ripples from a stone tossed into it.

Let the ripples fade, let them pass through you and only the quiet waters remain.

She took another deep breath and turned her attention outward, grounding herself. The tapestries of war and the hunt and Catholic ritual that hung from the high ceiling of carved-plaster tracery to the tiled floor between the windows glittered with threads of precious metals and inset jewels, seeming to stir in the wind of her passage as much as the languorous drifts of summer air from outside. Bouquets on tables and in the hearth swept for summer scented the air with flowers, beneath the smell of furniture oil and polish and the lavender-infused wax of the unlit candles.

"Your Majesty, whatever decisions we make, we had best make them quickly," Maugis said.

Ignatius nodded. "Forgive me, but the death of the High King and the manner of it will render opinion more . . . malleable. For a while, at least."

Rudi Mackenzie had been widely loved and even more widely respected, the hero-king who'd turned back the Prophet's hordes and founded Montival, herself at his side. It hurt to trade on it, but he'd have been the first to tell her that kingcraft required you to think like that. It was what they were *for.*

And so would Mother. They were alike in that, at least. I'll have *to trade on that love, and the horror and anger at his death, to balance against the problems I'm going to have, ruling without him and being the child of my parents. Oh, Rudi!*

Her father Norman Arminger, the first Lord Protector, had lived here in the Onyx Tower for a few years, between the completion of Castle Todenangst and his death in the Protector's War when she was still a girl. The Arminger line had avoided it since, and the memories of blood and terror it evoked.

"Your Majesty . . ." the Knight-Brother who'd been Montival's Lord Chancellor since its inception said, " . . .consider that part of your anger is that you now have a focus for the rage we all feel at the High King's death. But however reckless and irresponsible their actions, Crown Princess Órlaith and her brother do not deserve that. They too are driven by anger and by grief. That is more pardonable in a woman so newly come to an adult's years or a young man . . . barely more than a boy of nineteen . . . than in us, who are charged by God with the welfare of millions."

Grudgingly, she nodded. She'd seen strong men, tried scarred knights gone white-haired and wrinkled in the Crown's service, glance at the famous portrait of her father peering out from under his brows that hung in her mother's quarters in the Silver Tower on the west side of Todenangst's keep. And seen them blanch and turn pale around the lips as they met that glowering gaze, even when the man portrayed was more than three decades dead. That anger was there in her too. She could feel it.

And now that Rudi's gone they'll remember it even more. I am *his daughter and I* am *an Associate. I have to keep things together until Órlaith comes of Throne age . . . and now she's run off into the Wild!*

As if reading her mind, which wasn't surprising after a generation of working together, Ignatius added:

"You have always been the face the High Kingdom turned to the Protectorate, Your Majesty."

"And Rudi was the High King who showed everyone *else* that the High Kingdom was *not* the north-realm writ large," she replied. "Yes, and Órlaith will continue that, while John gives the barons here a Lord Protector who's one of their own, an Associate and a Catholic . . . but one who can be relied on to back her up without disputing her authority. *But they've both left.*"

She sat at the head of the table, and slapped the dark oak with a hand that still had sword-calluses.

"I am not going to let them abandon their duty!"

CHAPTER SIX

GOLDEN GATE/GLORANNON
CROWN PROVINCE OF WESTRIA
(FORMERLY CALIFORNIA)
HIGH KINGDOM OF MONTIVAL
(FORMERLY WESTERN NORTH AMERICA)
JULY/FUMIZUKI/CERWETH 14TH
CHANGE YEAR 46/FIFTH AGE 46/SHŌHEI 1/2044 AD

Órlaith nodded respectfully in return to Captain Feldman's salute as she and Heuradys trotted up the ladder to the low poop-deck—sailors insisted on calling it a ladder, at least. They were as attached to the jargon of their trade as the College of Heralds, and that was saying a great deal.

Reiko stood by the stern-chaser catapult, giving a shallow bow that Órlaith returned to exactly the same degree, though she and the Empress of the much-diminished modern Japan also shared a small smile. Nobody back there would know that she *was* the Empress yet, which was odd when you thought of it, as if time passed more and more slowly as places grew more distant.

The smile lit up a face delicate yet strong, albeit usually rather somber in the time Órlaith had known her.

Though that's *no surprise. I've not been in much of a mood for song, dancing and dalliance myself, of late, and it would have been worse for the both of us if we hadn't found a way to strike back. Reiko's excellent company when she relaxes, clever and with a sly sense of humor.*

The commanders of Órlaith's men-at-arms, Sir Aleaume de Grimmond and Squire Droyn Jones de Molalla gave her actual salutes Association-style, right fist to breastplate, as they followed her up the ladder. She returned them punctiliously. They'd both sworn personal allegiance to her and risked the anger of her mother, and not so incidentally that of their own parents, to come along on what many would think a crazed escapade. At their level, family and politics were inseparable.

And gestures are important. How do we of human-kind deal with each other, if not with gestures and symbols? And doubly so, if you're royal. I don't think you can do this properly at all, if you don't realize that.

Her brother John was leaning against the stern rail trying out a *shakuhachi* bamboo flute he'd borrowed from one of Reiko's samurai. Making friends was one of his gifts. He lowered it and waved with a broad grin; he was two years younger than his sister and an inch shorter and in full armor, carrying it off well with his lean and broad-shouldered build. He favored their mother's side of the family, with green-flecked hazel eyes and wavy hair of a warm brown.

In fact he favored their mother's father, but with enough of Rudi Mackenzie to fine down the brutal bluntness to a lazy handsomeness, and laughter in the gaze rather than the hot throttled fury you saw in portraits of their famous, wicked maternal grandfather.

"We'll be heading in shortly, Your Highness," Feldman said to Órlaith, without taking the telescope from his eye as he scanned the fog-shrouded headlands to the east. "But I want good visibility for this."

She nodded silently; her parents had told and, more important, shown her that the mark of a good commander or ruler was to pick capable and trustworthy subordinates, see that they had whatever resources they needed, tell them very clearly *what* you wanted done . . . and then mostly stand back and let them do it. That was why judging character was the single most important skill a monarch needed. They'd also told her that it was surprisingly hard *not* to try and do someone else's work when things were tense and you had nothing to do but wait.

Alas, it's true, I'm finding, she thought. *Bad as an itch under your breastplate.*

Feldman struck her as extremely capable, trim and mentally and physically tough, and he knew perfectly well that speed was important. He was a wiry olive-skinned man in his mid-thirties, a few inches shorter than she, with black hair and dark-brown eyes and a close-cropped beard the color of raven-feathers except for a white streak that covered a scar. There were brass buttons on his blue nautical coat, a cutlass at his belt, and a flat peaked cap on his head that covered the kippah skullcap of his faith.

Reiko's Imperial Guard commander Egawa Noboru stood in his usual position at her elbow, short and thickset and strong in a full suit of the same *Môgami Dô* armor, save for the gauntlets in the upended helmet he had under one arm. Apparently he was simply ignoring the thought of falling overboard. The gear was lighter than a Montivallan knight's suit of plate, but not enough to matter if you were trying to swim. A healing scar on his left hand . . .

The same prisoner . . .

Luanne Salander nodded towards Egawa and spoke sotto voce to Órlaith:

"I think if Reiko's personal troll did go over the side, he'd just walk ashore along the bottom and come up on the beach dragging a disemboweled shark for sushi."

At barely nineteen Luanne was the youngest of their core of conspirators, a Bearkiller by origin and a cousin of hers and John's by courtesy, since she was the grand-niece of the woman who'd married their father's father Mike Havel. *After* he'd sired Rudi Mackenzie in a brief encounter with Lady Juniper, back in the first Change Year. There had been bad blood on his wife's side about it back then, and she'd been ruler of the Bearkillers for quite a while after Havel had died in the War of the Eye, but it had never quite come to blows, and it hadn't passed down to their generation.

"Tsk!" Órlaith said, a little sharply, but she half-welcomed the distraction.

Egawa still didn't speak much English, but she suspected that by now he *understood* far more. He looked like a blunt, no-nonsense fighting man. And largely was, but that didn't mean he was at all stupid, and he probably used his appearance and natural temperament as a conscious tool. Fighting meant breaking heads from the *inside* too, particularly at the higher levels.

I would wager any sum that underestimating Egawa-san's wits was the very last mistake a number of men ever made.

"That's a *compliment*, cousin," the Bearkiller said, her handsome full-lipped olive face and gray eyes smiling as she bowed slightly towards him. "Hey, I owe him one. And he's scary enough that I'm glad he's on our side."

Heuradys gave a very slight snort, and Órlaith nodded to her.

He isn't on our side, Luey, she thought. *Though it would be tactless to say anything of the sort aloud. He's on his ruler's side, and his nation's, and none other whatsoever. And for the present, that means he works with us, so. But if his duty demanded it he'd turn on us in an instant. So would Reiko, though she'd genuinely mourn such a necessity afterwards. Not that it's likely any such thing will happen—very unlikely indeed—but it's something to keep in mind. Also he does not tolerate disorder in his ranks.*

One of Egawa's Imperial Guard samurai had misinterpreted Luanne's reason for hopping their hippomotive-drawn train at the Larsdalen station in an unpleasantly personal way that might well have turned into something worse. The Japanese commander had administered discipline, also personally, with a series of open-handed blows to one side of the face and then the other until the man fell down semiconscious and bleeding from eyes, ears, nose and mouth, all delivered while the recipient stood at rigid attention. The bruises were still fairly spectacular; that was apparently the standard punishment drill in the Imperial Guard, equivalent to a Montivallan doing forced-march maneuvers with a sack full of sixty pounds of wet sand held across their shoulders. The subtle but definite mockery he received from his comrades probably hurt worse still.

The general's heavily scarred middle-aged face was impassive beneath the distinctive haircut with the pate shaved back towards the topknot; she'd rarely seen any expression on it except a slight scowl, but the almost imperceptible flick of his eyes towards Luanne confirmed Órlaith's guess.

That stone face is partly because he's a natural stoic, she thought. *And partly because he's feeling so out of place. He never dealt with foreigners much at other than sword's-point before he came here, and he can't really speak the language. Also . . .*

Órlaith grinned to herself. Reiko, who was much more mentally flexible than her guard-commander, had confessed in private that it had taken her concentration and time to learn how to distinguish one non-Japanese face from another beyond things like male or female and hair color. And that for weeks she'd been frightened that she'd commit some gross rudeness because to her eye Montivallans all looked alike.

"How are we placed, Captain?" Órlaith asked formally when Feldman snapped his telescope shut and nodded as if to himself.

"No new obstacles that I can see, Your Highness. The wind's favorable, right abaft the beam, which is the *Queen*'s best point of sailing," he said, cocking an eye skyward with a navigator's reflex and studying the flags at the main and mizzen. "Best of all, it's steady and it feels in a mood to stay that way for the next few hours at least. We'll make our run under the bridge as soon as the fog lifts enough for safety's sake."

He grinned. "Or as much safety as you can expect, at sea," he qualified.

There was a feeling through the Sword like a bronze bell ringing—truth, or at least conviction; when someone tried to lie to her now she could feel it like metal foil clenched between the back teeth. She frowned. Somehow the Sword-born certainty made her feel as if she was being unjustly mistrustful. There was no logic in that, but emotions didn't work by rule.

"The first time I came into these waters was my first voyage far-foreign when I was in my teens. As an apprentice supercargo on the old *Ark*, with my father Daniel, taking a load of metals and dried fruit and wine to Hawaii to trade for rum and indigo and Kona Gold. We made landfall not far north of here on our way back."

The Japanese naval captain Ishikawa Goru had studied the Montivallan marine maps very carefully. "Why make land so far south?" he said. "So sorry, but wind and current run south here, I think? Harder to beat back to your home port."

He'd been commander of the *Red Dragon*, the ship that brought the

Japanese party here; a man of around thirty with a more lively expression than most of his countrymen. He wore a light *kikko* tunic of small hexagonal steel plates joined by fine mail and sewn to a cloth backing, practical for a sailor and something you could shrug out of in seconds.

"Into the teeth of the winds and currents from here to Newport, yes," Feldman said.

His hand caressed the hilt of his cutlass. "But we were jumped by pirates. Three ships, Suluk corsairs out of Mindanao, they came in at dawn while we still had the peak of Mauna Loa in sight. Two of them chased us all the way back, keeping to north of us to head us off from waters the Navy patrolled. We'd have been wrecked on this coast if we hadn't stumbled on people from the Mist Hills barony, and they saved our lives again later."

Aside to Órlaith: "If you think civilization is thin on the ground here in Westria now, Your Highness, you should have seen it then! The Mist Hills people were afraid they were the last real human beings left."

And what is safety? she thought grimly as she nodded to him.

She knew the bones of that story. Mist Hills was yet another case of the pre-Change brotherhood known as the Society for Creative Anachronism preparing folk in ways that proved to be life-saving afterwards. The High King had confirmed Baron Godric in his land and title, and said the man was a strong lord and fine warrior, shrewd and just and well-liked by the folk in the little out-of-the-way valley *his* father had brought through the Change. She didn't recall him, but his younger brother Deor the bard had been much more at court.

Yet Da died here this very spring, where we thought *there was no threat, and Reiko's father—two monarchs on a single day. And my cousin Malfind of the Dúnedain near here only a little later, which proves we didn't make as clean a sweep of the strangers as we thought at the time. This is a very large land, and we Montivallans few yet so far south. Things can still brew without attracting notice.*

"How did the *gaijin* merchant deal with the *kaizoku*, Captain?" Egawa asked in his own language.

Ishikawa translated the question and was obviously interested himself. Órlaith hid her amusement at the tactful way he rendered it. *Gaijin* wasn't formally an insult; it translated fairly literally as *foreign country person* more or less, or *someone from another country*. As opposed to *ketōjin*, which was the alternative for non-Japanese of her type or Feldman's and meant something like *hairy savage* or *smelly barbarian monkey*.

Gaijin wasn't exactly a compliment, either, though; she didn't think there was a favorable or even neutral way to say "foreigner" in Japanese unless you tacked on some honorifics. The word for merchant he'd used, *shō*, wasn't particularly flattering either, but Órlaith wasn't surprised. Plenty of Associate nobles looked down their noses at traders too. The raised-hackle rivalry between those who lived by the sword and those who sought exchange was as old as the feud between dog and wolf, and unlikely ever to end.

"*Kaizoku* . . . that is, sea-bandit, pirate," Ishikawa said to Feldman. "You sink? Or escape?"

"We beat off boarders from one that first morning," he said.

"They not act together?"

"Not so you'd notice; more like dogs with a bone."

Ishikawa grinned. "Except bone not bite dog. How you do?"

"We dropped a sea-anchor to starboard where they couldn't see it and cracked on with every inch of canvas, had the crew run around to give a convincing imitation of absolute panic, let them get close without suspecting it was a broken wing trick . . . and then caught them point-blank with a broadside of case-shot just as they were rising to leap," Feldman said, his eyes distant for a second, his hand touching the hilt of his cutlass again.

"Need good timing, Feldman-san," the Japanese sailor said approvingly. "Risky, but . . . *ichiban* if it work."

Órlaith and her companions nodded grimly, the image of what those words meant when metal met flesh and bone flashing instantly into their minds. They were all young—Sir Aleaume was the oldest at twenty-six—but in their various ways they were all from families born to the sword and raised in the arts of war. Bulwarks or heavy shields or plate armor would stop the half-inch round balls, and they lost velocity quickly with distance. If you shot too soon the boarders would swarm over you before the catapults could be reloaded, and a pirate or warship could carry far more blades than a trader.

But right into the faces of half-naked men crowded tight together and jumping to the railing to leap between ships . . .

"My father was always good at picking the right moment, ashore or afloat," Feldman said. "He said it was the key to the deal. *That* one decided to go look for an easier prize."

Softly: "You could see the blood running out of her scuppers in streams, I remember that. That and the screaming."

He shook himself slightly and went on: "Then we cut the cable on the sea-anchor before the others could come up, and just ran. We traded bolts and round shot with the other two for weeks off and on, never quite managed to shake them though we tried every trick in the book at night and in bad weather—they're nasty bastards, Suluk corsairs, but they're good seamen with good ships, and no cowards. We had the advantage that they *didn't* want to burn or sink us, of course, there's no profit on a scatter of flaming splinters. They kept trying for our masts and rigging, or the rudder."

Ishikawa thought hard. "Why sea-thief so . . . *ganbaru* . . . so determined? I think not—"

Órlaith translated the word he used next: "Not cost-effective."

"I think they hung on so hard because they wanted our catapults, more than our hull or cargo—coffee and sugar aren't hard to come by in the tropic islands, nor ship-timber," Feldman said. "But war-catapults are scarce where they come from, and they can't exactly send an order in to Donaldson Foundry & Machine in Corvallis. And they were prepared to work and bleed for it."

"Life would be easier if only good and honest men were brave or skillful or determined," Egawa observed, and everyone chuckled when it was translated. "For *we* are good and honest altogether."

"Of course, General Egawa," Órlaith said dryly, and got a very brief glance of acknowledgment in return.

The captain of the *Tarshish Queen* went on: "Then we got lucky with a napalm shell that burst just short of the sails on another one and sprayed their canvas with flame. They dropped away to fight the fire, we didn't see them again, for which the name of the Lord be sanctified and blessed."

Another universal nod; wooden sailing ships were floating tinderboxes of dry wood, cloth and rope liberally smeared with tar.

"And we smashed the bowsprit off the third a week later. In a storm not long before we made landfall, they may have foundered or just given up. The *Ark* was in bad shape by then too. One mast was damaged by round shot, it went overboard in the blow despite all we could do with capstan bars and wolding, and we had half a dozen patched holes below the waterline, but we brought her in. Then we did emergency repairs and limped home to our families . . . and the drydock in the Newport repair yards."

"*Ganbaru*, Feldman-san," Reiko said, as Egawa grunted thoughtfully.

"*Ganbaru* means . . . ummmm, *working hard*," Órlaith said to the merchant sailor. "Or persistence *and* hard work . . . doing your best. It's by way of being a proverb, and a compliment, so, being a quality our Nihonjin friends think very highly of."

The fog thinned again, and Órlaith's lips shaped a soundless whistle into the cool salt breeze as her eyes adjusted. She'd seen the great bridge from the northern end on land once years ago, but never from the western sea until now. Never from the water at all, in fact. Her father had wanted to show it to her so and take a sailboat around the great Bay together . . .

There was stab of pain like a hand squeezing at her lungs and heart, and then she pushed it aside.

Da wouldn't want me to pass over something like this because of him.

Just the opposite; he'd always taken a boy's wholehearted laughing delight in wonders. She could remember the time he'd showed her one of the buffalo herds of the high plains on the eastern border of Montival, the land of the Seven Council Fires. Stampeding past four hundred thousand strong, and he sharing her whooping excitement as they galloped their horses less than half bowshot from the endless wall of moving flesh, the thunder and the dust and the grinning brown faces and streaming feather headdresses of their Lakota escort. She'd been eleven then, a decade ago.

And he would have kept that joy into the years of his deep age, she thought. *All that was taken from him! But I will see it for both of us.*

"And this is a wonder of the world, so it is," she said aloud.

To Reiko: "My father said that it was made during the reign of the ancient ruler of the Americans called Roosevelt."

She knew that the old America had been a republic, but it was more natural to use the modern terms. And few in Montival studied that part of history very closely; it grew more and more alien, less and less relevant to the contemporary world, as you approached the day of the Change. Often it was just incomprehensible by anyone but the rare scholar who immersed themselves in it; there were whole rows of dusty books in the university library in Corvallis about literary theories nobody could make heads or tails of and sciences that just didn't function anymore, if they ever had. Apparently the Japanese felt the same way about their history, if anything more strongly.

"I know the name," Reiko said neutrally, and Egawa frowned more emphatically.

Oooops, Órlaith thought. *Yes, he was the one who ruled here during that war the old Americans fought with Nihon back a century ago, when they were allied with the ruler of Deutschland—the one Reiko's folk call the Pacific War. Ah, well, even I can't be diplomatic* all *the time!*

Her eyes rested on the bridge. Its beauty tugged at the heart, but her mind was still working. How fast they could make the landing stage in Ithilien was one thing; whether the allies she'd summoned would be there . . . there was no way to tell.

Or to tell precisely how her mother had been reacting to that summons.

Or overreacting, *to be sure.*

Or for that matter, how the other effects were rippling out, and what the enemy was doing in response—it wouldn't do to forget that. When you cast words out into the world, you could neither recall them nor predict exactly where they would land. Rather like an arrow, except that words multiplied with compound interest.

CHAPTER SEVEN

CASTLE TODENANGST, CROWN DEMESNE
PORTLAND PROTECTIVE ASSOCIATION
(FORMERLY NORTHERN OREGON)
HIGH KINGDOM OF MONTIVAL
(FORMERLY WESTERN NORTH AMERICA)
JULY 7TH, CHANGE YEAR 46/2044 AD

The High Queen sighed and made a gesture of acknowledgement behind her back as she looked out the window, still collecting herself before she resumed the conference.

"That's a point, Father. You have a damnable habit of being reasonable and making *me* be reasonable when I don't want to be, you know that?"

"We all have our cross to bear, my daughter. I am part of yours, it seems."

And you are the crossbeam of mine. She felt her lips quirk unwillingly as she turned back.

The décor here was antique in the literal sense; the desks and tables and chairs were heavy dark carved Victorian neo-Gothic from some mansion or museum, salvaged not long after the Change by her mother's teams and stored until the castle needed them. There was a scent of wax and polish about them, and of upholstery covered in red doeskin, probably not changed much since her father's time—the Onyx Tower had been his particular lair, which accounted for much of its ill reputation.

Lord Chancellor Ignatius—brother of the Order of the Shield of St. Benedict, and priest as well—could have offices here without unpleasant political consequences; his Order had been among the leaders of the resistance against the Association in the old days. Though Ignatius had been a child then—he was less than a decade older than Mathilda, who had been conceived and born in the first Change Year.

Then Ignatius chuckled; his hair and beard were more than half white, but even as it deepened the lines at the corners of his eyes the expression made him look much younger. Though his baptismal name had been Karl Bergfried, his eyes were slanted and of a blue so midnight-dark it could easily be taken for black. That shape was the legacy of a Vietnamese grandmother, a bride brought back from some long-forgotten war of the ancient world. The old Americans had gotten around and about, on a scale inconceivable in modern times.

"Perhaps we should just devise a code, Your Majesty, with letters to fill in conversations we've had so often before? You say *'A,'* I reply with *'X,'* and we both save time and effort."

Maugis looked very slightly shocked again, and the Mackenzie was amused as he ran a hand over his oak-brown curls. This time Mathilda had to work at little harder at keeping the smile away. She and Ignatius . . . and Rudi . . . had worked together for a very long time. She knew the Chancellor had often longed to return to the peace and beauty of his warrior order's mother-house at Mt. Angel and its ancient round of toil and prayer. He never had, except for the odd retreat to refresh his soul. As he'd put it once, the Shield of St. Benedict weren't the Cistercians and he'd known that when he took his first vows as a novice.

God gave you a cross to carry—the weight precisely tailored to your capacity if you called on Him in your heart—and told you to drag it up to Heaven's gate. Ignatius had never faltered.

"Sure, and I think better of Christians in general when I hear you say something of that order, Father," he chuckled.

She stopped for a moment, pressing the palms of her hands together and touching the fingers to her chin. "And we're exhibiting our internal divisions before these . . . Japanese."

And without them, Rudi would still be alive! her heart cried.

She took a moment to force the thought away. Grief was natural, and it paid no account to fairness. She couldn't control what her heart felt, but she could control what she said and did. The thoughts came unbidden; that didn't mean she had to welcome them in and give them a home.

I'm an Arminger. That doesn't mean I have to . . . That is, the honor of House Artos is in my hands.

She was Lady Protector in her own right, and High Queen Regnant of all Montival until Órlaith came of age. She couldn't afford to act on resentment or angry impulse, not when she had to account for her actions to her conscience, her people, and to God and the Virgin who was her particular patron. Too much depended on a calm mind and considered decisions.

I saw Her at the Kingmaking, bringing mercy to Father in Purgatory. Remember those eyes, that voice. Holy Mary pierced with sorrows, intercede for a mother now!

And the visitors' Emperor had died only moments before Montival's High King, and left his daughter and heir in charge of their party. Apparently this Reiko and Órlaith had become partners in crime, or close friends, or both.

Órlaith . . . Órlaith is like her father that way. People—most people—like her. They trust her. They look into her eyes and see her smile and . . . something happens. Some people like me, but it isn't the same. I have to work at things.

"And they show their disputes before us," Ignatius said thoughtfully. At her expression of surprise:

"Your Majesty, the senior man left at Montinore manor on Barony Ath was Koyama Akira, the Grand Steward of the Imperial Household. Roughly comparable to my office, I gather. Marshal d'Ath thinks, and from my own flying visit I concur, that he was utterly flabbergasted when he woke and found his Empress and her escort gone and only he, a few of his staff members, and several other officials left. Astonished and, under a very tight control, furious with an anger born of fear for her as he read her note to him. Which indicates why their Empress acted as she did. She is young, very much Órlaith's age, her succession irregular and recent, and her authority possibly precarious."

"She took her guard commander and his samurai, plus her ship captain and his remaining sailors. You think the others aren't loyal?"

"Not necessarily, but in the Grand Steward's case there is the perhaps natural feeling of men long experienced in government that they know better than a young woman recently bereaved of her father. It was all very quietly managed."

"Just how deeply is Marshal d'Ath implicated in all this?" Maugis said, the lines deepening in his face.

Technically she was his superior; he was Grand Constable of the Association, but the Baroness of Ath was Marshal of the High King's Host, supreme commander of all Montival's soldiery under the Crown. In point of fact the High King had very little in the way of troops under arms in peacetime, apart from the guard regiments. Most of what force the High Kingdom did keep was off patrolling distant wilderness or afloat against the menace of Haida pirates from the far north. The Navy rarely came south of Puget Sound and very rarely south of Astoria at the mouth of the Columbia.

The Portland Protective Association's sheer size and feudal structure meant that it could muster more strength and do it much more quickly than any other part of Montival save perhaps Boise, and Boise was far away over the mountains. The sword had been in the sheath since her early adulthood, but neither her mother nor she herself nor the servants they had chosen had let it rust there.

Any display of Associate might had to be done very carefully, to avoid arousing old fears and feuds. The Prophet's War and the founding of the High Kingdom had brought them all together, in theory. Keeping it that way in fact took kingcraft. It would be harder now, just when they needed unity more than they had since the dark days of the kingdom's birth.

Ignatius shrugged. "My lord, the Marshal issued that do-what-the-bearer-orders order, but if the Crown Princess requested it, it's only a venial sin for Lady d'Ath to sign it without prior reference to Todenangst. She did submit a duplicate in the usual report through the usual channels. . . ."

"Without flagging it for attention," Maugis said dryly. "So that it disappeared into the routine to-be-read stack in your office, my Lord Chancellor."

"Yes, and I have been paying less attention to my routine correspondence than I should. Her communication indicates that she did not ask what the prerogative mandamus was for . . . Granted, probably she deliberately did not ask."

"My mother was fond of those," Mathilda said. "She used to call them a *get out of jail free card*, for some reason. Like a lettre de cachet."

Ignatius nodded; neither of them mentioned that a lettre de cachet from the first Lord Protector or his wife and successor Sandra Arminger had been mostly used when someone—someone like Tiphaine d'Ath in her dreadful deadly prime, for example—was sent out to make a third party disappear, visibly or otherwise, disappear into death or a dungeon or just nonexistence.

Most of those had read: *The bearer has done what has been done by my authority, and for the good of the State.*

"A pre-Change reference of some sort," he said.

And went on in an utterly neutral tone: "Your Majesty may of course dismiss Baroness d'Ath, since High Marshal is an office held at the Crown's pleasure."

"I don't think so," Mathilda said . . . feeling her own reluctance at the words.

She forced detachment and suppressed the feeling of betrayal and went on judiciously: "D'Ath has built up quite a fund of credit with the Crown, dating back to my parents' time."

She winced inwardly; it was only a decade later that she'd realized those services included saving Rudi's life on her mother's orders . . . when her father had tried to have him killed. It wasn't something they publicized, even now.

Which meant . . .

"And this doesn't exhaust it, not yet, not unless it turns to a complete disaster, however annoyed I am with Tiph for abetting this nonsense. And she's due to retire in a few years anyway. Plus . . . she's close to Órlaith, she tutored her a great deal, as she did me when I was a girl."

"Lady Heuradys d'Ath seems to have been deeply involved," Ignatius said.

Mathilda shrugged and flipped a hand in a dismissive gesture; that was precisely what she'd have expected of the Marshal's adopted daughter. She'd known the girl . . .

Don't get too middle-aged, Mathilda, she scolded herself. *Heuradys d'Ath's twenty-three and a belted knight and about as dangerous as Tiphaine was at the same age. Not as cold and not nearly as angry at the world as Tiph was when she was Mom's living stiletto, but . . . Heuradys is certainly not that wide-eyed page of ten you used to sneak treats to or find giggling in corners with* your *daughter. Not anymore.*

. . . known the *young woman* since she'd been born, and had nearly as much to do with her as her own mothers for the last decade and more.

"She's been Órlaith's best friend since they were little girls, and she's her sworn liege knight," she said. "It's not even *technically* illegal for her under Association law, she's an officer of Orrey's household, not mine or of the Crown."

And even if I wanted *to punish her, every Associate noble would be up in arms, possibly quite literally, if I did that to a vassal for obeying her oath of fealty.*

"And Prince John apparently arranged the charter of the ship in Newport," Ignatius said. "My informants—"

He ran the High Kingdom's intelligence network, among other duties.

"—say that a knight matching the Prince's description, but bearing arms that aren't in the College of Herald's records, was closeted with the head of Feldman & Sons several times. Then he wasn't seen again until the ship left."

"I thought his valet was supposed to keep an eye on him?" she said sharply.

"Goodman Evrouin is supposed to keep him *safe,*" the cleric said. "Your Majesty, he couldn't do that effectively if he was simply a spy fastened on your son against his will. As it is, at least he's *with* him. Prince John is no fool, and not easily overborne, for all that he's only nineteen. Consider his parentage!"

Mathilda slumped into a chair and put a hand to her forehead. "I never thought I'd feel so sympathetic to the way Mother reacted when I went off to join Rudi on the Quest. Still, we can't let this go on. Lord Maugis, Edain, what are our options?"

"Your Majesty, Feldman's *Tarshish Queen* is a fast ship, the Navy people tell me—it's on the auxiliary reserve list, of course—and this merchant Moishe Feldman a good sailor with a crack crew, one of the best in Newport," Maugis de Grimmond said. "He's also a Corvallan naval reservist, rank of Commander. Few civilian ships in all Montival are faster, in fact, save for some rich men's racing yachts, and they are not seaworthy."

Ignatius nodded. "Feldman is noted for going into peril," he said. "He's fought pirates abroad more than once. His ship is designed for that sort of work, high risk and high reward."

Shrewd, shrewd choice, my golden girl, she thought. *Feldman's family have obligations to House Artos . . . and originally the obligation was for protection against House Arminger, back in Father's time. He'd be more likely to dare my anger for your sake than anyone else you could have picked—certainly more than anyone who had to be simply outright bribed into it. And Corvallis . . . they've never much liked any Associate. They only joined the High Kingdom because there really wasn't any alternative when all their neighbors did unless they wanted their trade choked off. Fighting the Prophet's War with the rest of us helped, but factions there are still unhappy about it.*

"What do we have that could catch her?" Mathilda said.

"Nothing apart from one frigate in Astoria, the *Stormrider,* refitting after taking her latest anti-pirate patrol out of Victoria," Maugis said, touching a file-folder without looking at its contents. "The Royal Montivallan Navy base there is overburdened with more serious work and they sent her south on contract to a civilian yard."

"*Stormrider* . . . twelve hundred tons, complement of two hundred and fifteen, thirty marines, twenty-eight eighteen-pounder catapults and two twenty-four-pounder track-mounted chasers fore and aft, Captain Russ commanding," Mathilda said absently.

"Yes, Your Majesty; they're ten short of complement, losses in dead and seriously injured from a cutting-out expedition that was ambushed ashore."

Mathilda nodded, the anger she would usually feel at that distant and muffled. She would never have been surprised, though. It wasn't enough to look at maps. To truly grasp how big the northern sea-land country was you had to see with your own eyes the endless chains of islands from county-sized to bare rocks, and the fjord-riven coasts that ran up into Alaska—which she had. Big and steep, densely forested with enormous trees that came right down to the stony beaches and up to the glaciers, cut by rivers that made overland travel a nightmare, icy seas fog-bound and lashed by huge storms much of the year and full of reefs and rocks. With icebergs as common as driftwood.

That daunting inhuman scale was among the reasons the High Kingdom had never been able to do more than keep the Haida menace from getting completely out of hand. In theory the Crown of Montival claimed everything from Baja up to the Bering Strait; in practice only about a quarter of that vast stretch was remotely under law. Much of it wasn't even regularly visited, much less ruled.

Maugis went on: "Assuming the *Tarshish Queen* intends to make a stop in San Francisco Bay . . ."

"They will, my lord," Edain said. "The news from home . . . from my home in Dun Fairfax . . . is that my son and his friends planned a long overland journey. And they were not present in Newport when the *Tarshish Queen* weighed anchor. My guess would be that they're after heading for the Bay; for the Dúnedain holding there, Stath Ingolf. Wherever they intend to go in the end, they'll stop there."

Mathilda's mind clicked through a mixture of reports, maps, her own travels, the links of friendship and vassalage and kinship, and ran them all through the focusing mechanism of a lifetime's political experience. Rudi's twin half-sisters Mary and Ritva and their men had founded that Stath of the Rangers, in what had been rechristened Ithilien County in accordance with the Dúnedain . . .

Obsessions, she thought. *Or founding myth, if I was feeling charitable, which I am very much not just now.*

Just a little while ago the news had come that one Korean ship had been cast ashore north of the Bay, and the Dúnedain had had a clash with its survivors—acting together with a Haida skaga, a shaman of those piratical tribesfolk, and the cannibal Eaters who haunted the ruins of the lost cities. Mary's eldest son Malfind had died in that skirmish and her daughter Morfind had been wounded, as had Ritva's son Faramir Kovalevsky.

Mathilda felt a slight twinge of guilt that she hadn't paid more attention to Mary's loss. Grief made you selfish. In practical terms, though—

"She's going to meet the Mackenzies she's suborned to this lunacy there," Mathilda said flatly. "And probably pick up a few younger Dúnedain too. And . . . how did they coordinate this? Without getting into the message files or alerting anyone? Órlaith has been at Montinore Manor almost since she got back, when she wasn't here. So has Lady Heuradys. And there's nothing definite in the logs of the Castle Ath heliograph station. Very little but routine traffic."

"There I can speak," Edain said. "Susan Mika—Susan Clever Raccoon. I met her in the McClintock dùthchas, nobbut a few months ago, when she bore your messages to the little Princess."

"Little!" Órlaith's mother snorted.

Her daughter had inherited Rudi's looks, and was only an inch below six feet, built like a long-limbed blond leopardess; she could have posed for the warrior-woman on the cover of one of the pre-Change tales of chivalry and adventure her grandmother had liked, though the so-called armor on those usually looked as if they'd been designed for the eyes of thirteen-year-old boys rather than for combat.

Edain probably remembered helping her onto her first pony and tumbling about with her puppy; men were . . . rather soppy that way.

Mathilda searched her memory again. Then she stopped and snapped her fingers. A young Lakota named Susan Mika had enlisted in the Crown Courier Corps less than two years ago. Rick Three Bears was her uncle, and a friend of Rudi and Mathilda's from the Quest a generation ago, as well as important in the government of the Lakota *tunwan* that formed the Kingdom's eastern frontier. He'd sent a note explaining she'd gotten into bad trouble at home and asking them to find her a job. She'd done well in the Couriers, in fact . . .

Ignatius slapped his palm on the table, his face showing the pleasure of solving a mental puzzle: "Yes, she was the Rider I sent south with the dispatches from you for Princess Órlaith."

"Aye," Edain nodded. "And she met us at Diarmuid Tennart McClintock's steading."

Mathilda winced again. Órlaith was of the Old Faith, her father's religion, and like most maidens of that belief in the clans she'd lost her virginity at a Beltane festival in her teens, about three years after her first menses. To one Diarmuid Tennart McClintock . . . Mathilda's Catholic side had been angered; she'd been a virgin on her wedding night, not without considerable effort and inner struggle. And her political antennae had quivered too—lover to the next High Queen was a political position whether the parties wanted it to be or not.

"Diarmuid's handfasted to another now," Edain put in. "Just as we showed up out of the wilderness on our way north. But forbye they're still friends. She's probably called on him for aid, and some blades who'll follow him. Say another dozen, to match those my sons Karl and Mathun managed to persuade into it, they'll not want a great host."

To the others, which meant mainly Maugis: "Diarmuid's a *feartaic* down there, something of a minor chief, what they call a tacksman, like his father and grandfather before him."

The Mackenzies and McClintocks had always had fairly close relations, but a north-realm noble whose business was mostly within the Protectorate wouldn't know as much about the more southerly of the great pagan Clans. Mackenzies didn't have tacksmen, but then they hadn't been founded by someone as utterly obsessed with his somewhat deranged vision of the Highland past as the first McClintock. Juniper Mackenzie and her followers had just been improvising in a world gone mad.

"This Rider . . . she had speech with the Princess, more than once," Edain went on. "And our Golden Princess has all her father's golden charm. Charm that could bring the birds from the trees, Matti."

"I know that, Edain," she said shortly.

He shook his head. "Not the way someone who didn't nurse her or wipe her wee arse does. A mother is a different thing, blessed be."

He touched the back of his right hand to his forehead, a gesture of the Clan's version of the Old Faith to a hearthmistress—half reverence to the Goddess who was Mother-of-all and half ironic reminder to the High Queen. She was uneasily aware that the pagan part of Montival saw her as the Mother's surrogate for the High Kingdom, as they'd seen Rudi walking in the power of the Lord who was Her consort. It was politically convenient . . . but religiously it made her itch. Catholics . . . well, many Catholics . . . had stopped interpreting the Lord and Lady as demons and deceivers and moved on to *just misunderstood aspects of the Truth*; she wished the Old Faith would stop plastering the *interpretatio paganensis* on *her* theology.

But as the good Father told me long ago, debating doctrine with a witch is like trying to carve fog with a sword.

Ignatius stroked his close-cropped beard. "An ideal way to communicate in confidence. Nobody questions a rider of the Crown Courier Corps. She's been carrying regular dispatches down to Castle Rutherford and Stath Ingolf since. A few more in the pouch, or simply verbal messages . . ."

"There was the Yurok shaman we met at Diarmuid's steading," Edain said thoughtfully. "She said that there was something that Reiko, their Empress, must recover. Something to the south."

Ignatius nodded. "It definitely looks like a rendezvous inside the Golden Gate. Whatever mission our mysterious Japanese friends are on, it's south of there."

"Has this Grand Steward Koyama Akira said anything about *that*?" Mathilda asked. "We still haven't any real idea of what they're trying to *do*."

"Not a word. He is angered, but singularly close-mouthed with outsiders and foreigners. As I would be in his position," Ignatius said. "A formidably disciplined man, impeccably courteous and utterly unyielding. I think his command of English is better than he would have us think, which helps him be . . . skillfully unhelpful. We are still trying to find a Japanese-speaking interpreter who knows enough to be useful; there may be one in Boise, and there's a family of landholding knights in the Skagit baronies who may have kept it up as family tradition, but either will take time to arrive. And I would guess at a certain satisfaction on Lord Koyama's part that we are as . . . thunderstruck as he, and for similar reasons."

"I'd be thinking *gobsmacked* is the word you're looking for, Ignatius," Edain observed dryly.

Maugis nodded. "*Stormrider* might overtake her—she has more hull speed than the *Tarshish Queen* when she's clean, but she was due to have her coppering renewed in the next year."

"I doubt Moishe Feldman would shoot at a ship of the High Kingdom's fleet," Ignatius said thoughtfully. "Even if the Princess told him to, which she would not."

"She wouldn't tell him to," Mathilda said flatly.

She was quite sure of that, at least.

"But he would certainly run away from one if she tells him to do *that*, and we can't start flinging round shot or napalm shells at my daughter and my son! Bolts from a naval catapult are no respecters of persons."

"No indeed," Ignatius said. Thoughtfully: "Nor at the Empress of Japan, for that matter. We have enough enemies across the Pacific, it appears, without adding another!"

Mathilda gave a single sharp if unwilling nod to acknowledge the point. "My lord de Grimmond, put . . . sixty or seventy men on her, from the Protector's Guard. Select a commander immune to Órlaith's charm! Instructions are to secure the person of the Crown Princess and Prince John, but without using lethal force against anyone aboard that ship. Including the Japanese."

"Your Majesty, I'm not in the naval chain of command."

"Well, I'm not going to tell Tiph to do it, under the circumstances! Ignatius, do up the necessary documentation to regularize things. The High Queen *is* in the chain—holding the upper end. And jerking it hard right now."

Maugis stirred again; he knew he was being ordered to tell his men to make bricks without straw. She held up her hand. The impulse to protect his troops from impractical political demands was perfectly natural—essential—but sometimes you had to override things like that. Fighting was always at most a means, never an end, though those born to the sword tended to forget it sometimes. The purpose of having armed force was to use it to get people to do what you wanted, or resist their attempts to do that to you. Anything in the way of actual fighting was a regrettable by-product, like dirty water from a dye-works.

"I'm aware that it's an impossible thing to task them with, but it has to be done that way," she said firmly.

"Your Majesty," Maugis said, tucking his head in acknowledgment. His face grew grimmer. "My son Aleaume—let his person answer for his actions as it pleases you."

"My lord, Sir Aleaume's oath was to the dynasty, not me personally, and he did not violate any direct orders. And according to witnesses, he probably *did* swear personal fealty to my daughter . . . which is most irregular, but not strictly speaking illegal since she *is* the dynasty's heir, and once done carries an obligation of strict obedience as long as her orders are not direct treason. To be absolutely frank, if my daughter is running off hare-brained, I'm glad he's there to guard her person. He may have committed a serious error, he may have lost *my* favor—"

Implying that he was very unlikely to have lost Órlaith's, who would be High Queen in five years.

"—but I'm quite sure nobody will get to her except through him. Not as long as he can breathe and hold a sword."

Maugis swallowed and ducked his head again, radiating a mixture of anger at his eldest son . . . and beneath it, deep pride. Mathilda acknowledged both with a gesture.

"We'll suspend his post in the Guard and rusticate him out at St. Grimmond-on-the-Wold for a year or two with orders not to leave the boundaries of your estates while he contemplates the meaning of discipline and watches the grass grow and the sheep eat it. Then I'll find him some post on the frontiers for further reflection, somewhere uncomfortable and strenuous. The same for young Droyn, though his father my lord Count Chaka may add to it."

Maugis had been ready to hear the words *dungeon* or even *high treason*; his relief didn't show, but it was there.

And there are certainly enough people who don't like the Association watching me like a hawk from the outside for off-with-their-heads impulses now that Rudi's . . . gone. Now all Montival is ruled by an Associate.

At the Kingmaking she had seen her father in Purgatory. Heaven's mercy was infinite . . . but human beings, alas, were sparks of the Divine, not the thing itself.

And I'm the daughter and heir of the first Lord Protector, at that. Until Órlaith comes of age. Rudi, my love, you built well, but the realm is still new and young. Well, I have experience with young wild things, at that!

Maugis allowed himself a craggy smile. "Here is the first use Her Highness found for the writ from the Marshal."

Mathilda read the paper he slid across. It was a carbon copy of a standard typewritten logistics requisition on the armed forces of the Republic of Corvallis in the High Kingdom's name, for everything from spare bowstrings and underwear to tinned sardines and jam and pelletized alfalfa-fodder to boot-grease, to be delivered to a warehouse in Newport. Maugis had probably had to jar several clerks out of their comfortable routine to get it out of the continual flow of paperwork even a very modest army generated. Her brows rose. She'd been, effectively, Rudi's Chief of Staff during the Prophet's War, and she had logistics in her bones.

"At least Órlaith isn't being *incompetent* even if she's doing something deeply *stupid*," the High Queen said.

"Edain?" she went on.

"I can send a party of the High King's Archers after that pack of gossoons my sons took off into the wilderness."

"Cavalry would be useless, even light horse," Ignatius agreed, and Maugis nodded. "Too steep, too roadless, too forested. And little forage."

Edain made a gesture of acknowledgement. "Forbye warriors in good hard condition can leave foundered horses dead in their wake over a long run; I've done it. There's a question of law, there, I'm afraid, as well, Matti. It's not illegal for a dozen youngsters of the Clan to take their bows and blades and go on a bit of a trip to hunt and admire scenery and chase the pretty butterflies and listen to the wee birdies sing praise to the Lady of the Flowers, now is it?"

She snorted, but he was an old friend and had his full share of Mackenzie irreverence anyway.

"How many?" she said.

"The bigger the party the less ground you cover in a day, since you're bound by the slowest. Two-score, I'd say that will be the best balance."

There were about seven hundred bows in the High King's Archers at any one time; a little over half were Mackenzies. Any Montivallan could join if they met the tests . . . which started with a thirty-mile forced march in armor, before you got to the marksmanship part. The pay was quite reasonable, skilled-craftsman level, and there was the chance to strut about with the pride of an elite, but you earned all of it and more.

"I'll hand-pick them from those with the reconnaissance badge and take them out myself," Edain said.

Mathilda winced; Edain was rock-steady and a pillar of the Throne . . . and someone to whom she was Matti first, a lifelong friend to both her and Rudi. She had many loyal, able subordinates, but that was inexpressibly comforting.

"It's a lieutenant's command," she said.

He shrugged. "With another, Karl might do something . . . rash. Whereas meself meself . . . He's a man grown, but only just. Enough of the boy remains that he may not defy his father face-to-face, so. If only I can catch him to put my face *in* his face, as it were."

"Point," she said. "This is a political operation, not really a tactical one."

"Aye, Matti. And Diarmuid Tennart McClintock is a proud and hot-tempered young man, he might fight me personally in a challenge circle, but he'll not outright offer battle to the High King's Archers. Most especially if they outnumber him and are led by me, that being by way of precaution, you understand. So two-score is best all around, and it needs my aging carcass in person."

She raised a brow in question, and he grinned ruefully: "I'm not looking forward to it, mind, but though it'll hurt me more than it once would I won't slow them, not yet."

"Do it," she said. "Requisition what you need."

"No guarantees, Matti, not with my boys and their accomplices having so to say a long start," he warned. "We'll make up some by taking a hippomotive to the end of rail, and more by not going over to the Tennart's. Forbye they've been going hither and yon picking up people. With a Crown priority we can be at the railhead near Klamath six hours after we load. Good thing we pushed it that far last year."

She called up maps in her mind, and felt for the link to the land that had been there since the Kingmaking by Lost Lake. It gave her an intuitive feel for the possible, as if all Montival was a set of muscles she could sense the limits of.

Right now she was reluctant to use it.

I shrink from it, she conceded to herself.

And forced herself not to remember the scream that had echoed from the very earth and air and water as well as from her when Rudi fell. Her throat was still a little raw with it.

But I will do it. When I fought by your side on the Quest and in the war, Rudi, I bore wounds from edged steel. I went willingly under the shadow of Azrael's wings to bear our children in pain and love and blood. I will do this to keep them safe, my darling, and for what we built together.

"Don't try to follow them, except as far as you're heading for the same place," she said after a moment, her voice steady. "My guess is that they'll head for Stath Ingolf; it's close to the Bay and Órlaith has friends there."

"Ingolf the Wanderer himself among them, and her aunts Mary and Ritva, and Ian Kovalevsky," Edain warned. "They being the lords thereabouts."

Mathilda nodded. They'd been on the Quest together, fought together, shared hardship and danger and saved each other's lives. Together they'd been the first to hail Rudi—Artos—High King, far off in the eastern lands. Except for Ian, who'd fallen in with them on the way back west, in Drumheller, and he was a Quester by courtesy not least because he'd wed Ritva.

Edain was reminding her that they all thought of her as a friend first, and their monarch second and in a rather theoretical way. Off on their own in Westria with a message a month if that, they *were* the Kingdom, pretty much and for all practical local purposes. The High King and Queen traveled a good deal around Montival precisely to demonstrate that the monarchy actually existed; that was why Rudi had been down there. Plus . . .

"It's their children who are Órlaith's friend-friends, not Ingolf and the others," she said. "Go directly to Stath Ingolf . . . to the Eryn Muir, that's where they'll meet, there or somewhere close to it . . . and cut them off from the Bay. I'll give you an authorizing writ for Hîr Ingolf, putting him under your orders for the nonce. That's Crownland in a Crown province and they hold direct from the High Kingdom; I want him to have to think about disobeying a direct order, not just my theoretical opinions weeks after it's all a *fait accompli*."

Her head turned smoothly, rather like a catapult on its turntable. "My lord Maugis, please report after you've contacted Astoria about the *Stormrider* and checked on her readiness to sail immediately. They can send workmen along to complete repairs while under way, if necessary."

"Shall I accompany—"

"No, my lord, you may not take personal command. Do it by heliograph. If Edain's to be away, and I agree he must, I will need you here."

Plus the Navy belongs to all Montival, not the Protectorate, and your office is an Associate one. It's one thing to have some of the Protector's Guard along under naval command, but having you on board and in charge would be provocative.

She decided to sugarcoat it a little. With honesty, which was the best way:

"We're probably facing war . . . when we know more about what's going on. It's been twenty years since we called out the *ban* of the Association, much less the *arrière-ban*; you'll have more than enough to do. Chancellor Ignatius, please order a meeting of the Congress of Realms in . . . mmmmm, Dún na Síochána."

Ignatius nodded, thought for an instant, and began to write. "I will begin laying the political groundwork immediately. The quarters are incomplete and will be uncomfortable for the delegates, which may be for the best in encouraging them to be brief," he said.

Dún na Síochána was the new capital they'd been building for the High Kingdom; it meant Citadel of Peace, and it was on the site of the ruined pre-Change city known as Salem . . . which meant about the same thing, only in Hebrew rather than Gaelic.

"And draw up orders to Marshal d'Ath for the implementation of . . . Plan Baywatch, that was the one for pacifying the dead cities around the Bay. With the Eaters cooperating with a foreign enemy, they've moved themselves up the priority list. That will mean levies, we're going to need six or seven thousand troops for that, and their supplies. Infantry, mostly, and engineers. Mackenzies and Bearkillers and Corvallans, of course, but include a note that I want a field brigade of Boiseans as well, and at least a battalion from New Deseret. Yes," she went on to raised brows. "It's a long way but it'll help remind people we're all part of the High Kingdom. Instruct her to send the details to Fred . . . to President Thurston in Boise and to First Elder Mattheson in Logan. If she's going to stay High Marshal . . . she'll do the *work*, by God."

Maugis rose, tucked his helm under his arm and his gauntlets in it, clashed his right fist against his chest and bowed. Mathilda controlled herself until he'd gone; he was a devoted servant of the Crown and had been for two decades. The other two men were more than that, though they were that too; and they'd been on the Quest with her. Ignatius was her confessor and spiritual councilor as well.

"How could Órlaith and John do this to me!" she cried. "And . . . Rudi . . ."

Edain put an arm around her shoulders. "That's why, lass. They both need to be doing, don't you see? And that at once. Their grief will give them no rest, else. Vuissance and Faolán are still young enough to rest in your arms. Herself and Johnnie are too old for that, and too young to sit quiet on their own."

Ignatius nodded as he stamped his seal on the writ. "The young feel grief through their bodies, when they are freshly come to their full growth," he said. "It demands action. They think that they can outrun sorrow, or sweat it out like a poison. We know that it will always catch you, but it's not knowledge that can be transferred in words, even by a preacher with a tongue of fire. Which none of us here is. Only living long enough will do that."

Mathilda pulled a handkerchief out of her pocket, mopped her eyes and blew her nose.

"Edain . . . this is important. Something is happening down there. Something terrible. I can feel it in my bones, in my blood, in the air I breathe. It's . . . shadowed. As if I'm in a dream of darkness, with things moving I can't see. I haven't felt this way in a long time. Not since the war. Go save our children, old friend."

He nodded soberly. What they were doing was as much to *protect* her son and daughter as to bring them back for defying her.

I cannot lose them too! her spirit wailed.

Then her mind replied, the part that had been High Queen for a generation, and fought through the Prophet's War and the Quest before that:

The problem is that Ignatius is right. If you live long enough you learn things. And one thing I've learned is that you can *lose everything.*

Unconsciously her hand touched her stomach. *And this child . . . will never know her father. It's already cost my child that!*

CHAPTER EIGHT

DÙTHCHAS OF THE CLAN MCCLINTOCK
(FORMERLY SOUTHERN OREGON/NORTHERN CALIFORNIA)
HIGH KINGDOM OF MONTIVAL
(FORMERLY WESTERN NORTH AMERICA)
JULY 9TH, CHANGE YEAR 46/2044 AD

Edain Aylward Mackenzie blinked and coughed in the late-morning sunlight and batted a hand at the flies crowding around his face.

"Now we know why there was so much of a howling and growling in the distance among the beast-kind last night," he said.

He'd thought it might just be natural here, some quarrel over a predator's kill; these southern fringes of the McClintock dùthchas weren't like the Cascade forests he knew best. Though he'd been through them more than once, it being the only way to get down into the southernmost province if you didn't take ship. It was just as steep, but drier, much of it dense woodland but more open in some spots on the south-facing slopes. They were well into what the old world had called California and the High Queen's mother had renamed Westria after some tales she was fond of, and the forests even smelled different—spicier and harsher somehow, with less of the green mossy scent. Though right now . . .

"If we'd camped any closer we'd have winded it sure. Well, well, well!"

"Or if we'd been downwind. 'Tis the tale of the three wells, that it is," his second-in-command agreed.

Her name was Báirseach. She'd been just old enough to go to the Prophet's War in the Mackenzie levy as an Eoghan, an apprentice-helper, and had joined the Archers in time to catch the final nasty toil of hunting down the last guerrilla bands in the Bitterroot country away east. She stripped off a handful of needles from the branch of a young pine, crushing them and holding the results under her nose against the powerful musky-sweet rankness of the stink from the bodies.

Even standing carefully upwind it was strong enough to feel like rancid oil spread on the inside of your mouth and nose, and the buzzing of the flies was loud enough to seem like a great malignant cat purring at something vile. Several of the younger Archers were looking very pale, or green. There was nothing like a corpse lying unburied and unburnt for a while to remind even heedless youth that you were of the same very mortal flesh as any other animal.

"They're just somewhat over-ripe," she said. "A week?"

"Something like," Edain said. "Hot days, but this high up nights are cool, even in summer and this far south. Yet we're gaining on them, and that steadily."

"Now, I'd be thinking these dead spalpeens were bandits," Báirseach said, her red brows rising in a pale boney weathered face as she looked again and tried to reconstruct the scene.

"Aye, by their gear. Varied, and not much of it, and not well kept up," Edain agreed.

His second's blue eyes went around the site of the little battle . . . or possibly *brisk little massacre* would be a better term. Down to the little tarn where water pooled and then chuckled over smooth brown stones, then around the slope that led up from it under the tall sugar pines that turned the sunlight into a shifting dappled carpet. The coyotes and other scavengers had run or slunk or flown off when the High King's Archers had followed their noses here, and by the marks a tiger and a grizzly bear had taken turns running each out of the location some time ago when the meal was fresher. Few predators turned such down when one came along. Some of the flesh had been reduced to dried tatters, others slumped into liquid, the maggots had hatched some time ago, and the tufts of hair looked the more grotesque for it.

She went a little closer, picked up an arrowhead with a stub of broken shaft, examined it and then flipped it to him as she retreated. Edain caught it carefully by the wooden bit—all things considered, he didn't want to slice himself open to what was caked on it—and turned the metal triangle to catch a ray of sunlight.

"Broadhead, red-cedar shaft," she said helpfully. "One of ours. Clan make, hand-forged, not from a hydraulic trip-hammer in a Royal armory or a factory."

"Dun Fairfax smith-mark in Ogham, right enough, it's my idiot sons and their friends, who are half-wits whose vanity aspires to the lofty status of idiots, so," he agreed; she was Sutterdown-born, from the closest thing the Clan had to a city. "Went through a body and broke off on a rock, most like. Easier to let it lie, when they were in a hurry. And a bit spooked at what they'd done. Training will take you through your first fight . . ."

". . . But seeing the results is a wee shock, to be sure. I don't remember the two days after the battle, back in the wartime."

When someone of roughly their age said *the* battle, there was only one they could mean. He nodded, having been there and in the thick of things. She went on:

"And I was just scurryin' about with bundles of arrows and helping the wounded back during the fight, when I wasn't crying or puking me guts out or both at the same time. So they might well have skimped on things like the policing up of the field."

Mackenzies kept a number of spare arrowheads in a pouch on the war-quivers they took into the field, along with uncut flight-feathers from geese, and anyone could trim out and fletch a shaft at need. The razor-edged shapes like the one he held were cut and hammered out of a stainless-steel coffee spoon, with the stub of the handle wound around a mandrel, then heated and hammer-forged to make a tube that would fit the tip of a shaft. The spoons were one of the staples of the salvage trade though they were worth only pennies each, being so durable and to be had anywhere the ancients had dwelt—they were still used as spoons, for that matter.

This one had a tiny sigil tapped into the socket with a metalworker's punch, a straight line with two branches to the left and another with three to the right—"d" and "f" in the script of the old Gael. Mackenzie smiths made and stored the like by the thousands, working whenever there wasn't anything more pressing to do. They went to the Chief's Portion, or were bartered to hunters for meat and leather, horn and bone.

"But how . . . by Nuada of the Silver Hand, how did our youngsters get them to stand in a bunch like that, and them so agreeable about being shot at?" she said. "Look, there's some hit running away—out in a fan, you see? As if they'd been taken under an arrowstorm sudden-like from the very ground they stood on, somehow."

"And then fled in a panic; the which is more likely to get you killed than standing your ground," Edain observed.

"Aye. Most often if you run, you find you've run towards the Shadow Queen's scythe without knowing it. But those last"—she pointed with her bowstave—"were shot running upslope, which is *towards* the only cover about the place, and away from which they'd have been dashing if they'd been ambushed. Then it looks as a few were cut down with the sword close to the brush. It's impossible. Unless our youngsters had the *féth fíada* of *Aengus Óg* to render them invisible, the which I doubt, even if that McClintock with them *is* named Diarmuid."

Edain had been grim enough. Now he grinned, despite the gruesomeness of the scene. He'd seen far worse, in one place or another. If you took up the spear of your own wish you made your life's blood a free-will offering to the Dark Mother. By preference he'd die at home in the bed he'd been born in, with grandchildren about him ready to keen him to the pyre and then knock the bung out of the barrel at the wake. But he didn't expect it, and hadn't for a long time. Kings weren't the only people who knew they were walking towards the scythe.

"Earth must be fed," he murmured, then more briskly: "Take a look at the angles the shafts went in. Not the ones scattered up the hill. The most of them, right under the trees, where they were caught unawares and in a clump."

"The bodies've been dragged about and broken up too much by the beast-kind to . . . wait, look at that one! He must have been on his hands and knees, that shaft went in his neck and near-enough came out where his arsehole used to be . . ."

Edain's smile turned to a chuckle. He'd been leaning on his longbow, and he now shifted it to point upwards.

"How they got them to stand together so at the first, ignoring all else like youths watching the maidens dance skyclad about a Beltane pole, I do not know and cannot guess," he said, chuckling. "But if you were to climb those trees, and them so straight and thick and fine though less so than our Douglas firs, and look carefully . . ."

"Aililiú," she blurted, then shook her head admiringly. "Hunting blinds in the trees!"

"There's one among them with a pleasingly and usefully wicked habit of mind."

"Karl's work, or forbye Mathun's, but Karl would be my guess. He's a clever young bastard, when he's not thinking with his fists or his balls, that he is."

"When he's not being young, you mean," she said, then added: "Young and male, that is. Why's he not in the Archers, then? From the look of things we could use him."

"He's not overfond of being under my eye *all* the time," Edain said. "I don't altogether blame him for it, for all that he's still not fit to be let out without a keeper. As this whole matter shows."

"Oh, aye, plenty of the High King's Archers enlist to get *away* from home. By the Daga's dick, I did! Having your da as your commander too, that would be . . . a bit of another matter, so to say."

Edain chuckled. "For this I'm *almost* inclined to forgive him for making me miss going home for the harvest, forbye it's been too long since I tossed a sheaf."

The words were harsh enough, but he could feel the pride leaking out in the tone. Edain raised his voice:

"Scouts out, and the rest of us follow in skirmish column. Pursuit pace, wolf-trot—move!"

There were a few groans; he felt like groaning himself, after day upon day of relentless work. Not long after coming this way traveling northward, though that hadn't been as brutal. He was forty-two years old come this Samhain and a bit, and the oldest of the band he was chasing was twenty-six. He had a decade or more on most of his own command too. It told. Sweat soaked the padding of his brigandine, his thighs ached, and there were raw chafe-marks in places he'd thought callused beyond that long years ago. But he wasn't going to let them see it.

Them or my sons, he thought, as they fell into the wolf-lope again.

The seed doesn't fall far from the tree, though, does it now? However you managed it, Karl-me-lad, I'm something impressed. How old Sam would smile . . . Perhaps I'll kick your arse one time less if you tell me how! We'll catch you at White Mountain, or close thereafter, I think. There will come a day when you're better at this than your da, but not yet. Not quite yet.

The Dun Fairfax band and their McClintock allies came out of the shaggy wilderness, the trees and rampant feral grapevines and the odd patch of straw-colored savannah that stretched north of the salt marshes where it wasn't scrub forest over ruins. Karl Aylward Mackenzie had expected something of civilization soon, since there had been the odd lump of horse-dung and someone had been making a start on the road for the last few miles. Hauling away the rusted remains of automobiles and trucks, cutting back the larger bushes that had sprouted in the cracked asphalt and filling in potholes and digging away dirt where blocked culverts had flooded in the winter rains. And the scent on the breeze from the west was subtly different—tilled ground smelled a bit hotter and dustier.

Dogs barked and raced about as they came into the cleared stretch, a biggish square field in the faded but glittery brown-blond of wheat stubble. Shoots of green burr-medic clover pushed up between the ankle-high stalks the cutting bar of the horse-drawn reaper left. The clearing was edged with young dark-green cypress trees like man-high pencils. He blinked and shaded his eyes with a hand.

"Follow at heel, Fenris, Ulf, Macmaccon, Buagh, Dwyer, Uaid," he said sharply.

The greathounds were too disciplined and too tired to do more than pad along with their tongues out, which was fortunate for the nondescript farm mongrels doing the challenge. Mackenzies bred them for hunting game like boar and tiger, or for war, and the great rangy beasts averaged about the weight of a smallish man, with fangs to match and jaws that could crack a bull elk's thighbone.

A half-score of landworkers were at their tasks in the field, from a man with gray in his beard down to children as young as six or so scaring away birds and bringing dippers of water to their elders. The folk were carting the last of their wheat. It was earlier than that would be done in the Mackenzie lands, since summer came sooner and much hotter here. Otherwise much the same: pitching the stooked sheaves into a cart pulled by two big platter-hoofed horses and packing them on the high teetering precarious-looking golden heap. Gear lay piled under the shade of a big oak, under the guard of a woman nursing a babe.

Karl flung up a fist to halt his column, put a foot down to the left of his bicycle and took a swig from his water-bottle of salvaged aluminum encased in modern boiled leather. He was a young man not long past twenty, a year older than his brother Mathun and of a similar long-limbed build he'd gotten from his mother, along with hair much the same color as the reaped grain, and blue eyes. Their square cleft-chinned knobby faces were much like their father's, and the broad bowman's shoulders they shared, though both were still lanky with youth.

He corked the canteen, waved and called:

"Fair harvest, friends! Corn Mother and Harvest Lord be with you!"

They were far enough away they probably couldn't catch the words, but close enough the tone and gesture should travel. And he'd used the general terms rather than a specific deity's name, which was a witch's way of being nondenominational. From their dress—loose shirts left in the natural pale gray of linsey-woolsey, pants tighter and dyed blue with the odd copper rivet, laced boots and round floppy straw hats—they were probably Corvallan countryfolk by origin. The weapons they'd grabbed for when they saw two-score of armed strangers, crossbows and the odd eight-foot half-pike, argued likewise.

He was glad of it. Corvallis folk had a reputation for keeping themselves to themselves; minding their own business and not sticking their noses in yours, they called it, or cold standoffishness as others might put the matter. That didn't mean they wouldn't pry now and gossip later, but they'd be slower and less insistent about it, and easier to shake off without giving real offense.

They relaxed as they saw the kilts of the Mackenzies and McClintocks, waved back at him, called greetings blurred with distance, and got back to work. That wasn't surprising either; even in a place like this with reliably dry summers you never really felt secure until the sheaves were carted and in a nice well-thatched stack in the yard. If nothing else, birds were always too glad to take a share, whether it had fallen out of the ear to make fair gleaning or not. And then you itched to get it threshed and the grain in the sacks lest a careless spark send a year's work and the flour for a winter's loaves up in a whoosh.

After the threshing you worried about rats in the granary . . .

He'd missed the harvest back home because of this venture, and it felt a little unnatural. He could still remember his pride the first summer he was allowed to drive the reaper and take his turn binding sheaves and stooking. And watching his da carrying the Queen Sheaf for the High Priestess to weave into a woman's shape so She could preside over the harvest-home feast. And the dancing afterwards. It was a fine time to be a young man in Dun Fairfax, even if everyone was a little tired. Babes conceived in harvest-time were thought lucky.

Diarmuid Tennart McClintock's folk came up from behind while the dozen Mackenzies were halted—it was their turn for rear guard—and did likewise. Karl carefully did not grin at the set look some of them had as they slowed and stood down; at least they weren't falling over anymore, even the ones with four-foot *claidheamh mòr* greatswords in hide slings over their backs. Some of them were openly kneading their buttocks under the baggy wrapped-and-pinned Great Kilts they wore.

It wasn't that they weren't hardy, though Mackenzies often gently mocked their pretensions in that direction. But McClintocks were woodsrunners, hill-and-hollow dwellers from the uplands south of the Willamette who lived thinly scattered and seldom saw even a two-wheeled cart; their dùthchas was mostly rugged territory where nature had been unkind to the old world's works, roads among them, so it was pack-ponies and shank's mare for them when they traveled. The Clan Mackenzie claimed plenty of mountain country—up to the crests of the High Cascades in the east—but they had a nicely large chunk of the Willamette Valley too, fat flat fertile land, and that was where most of them dwelt. They weren't crowded even yet, but roads were good and bicycles common.

"Aught?" he asked Diarmuid.

The McClintock *feartaic* shook his head, but unconsciously looked over his shoulder. He was shorter than Karl and about five years older, a slim-waisted, broad-shouldered brown-haired man with the thin golden torc of the handfasted around his neck, a basket-hilted claymore by his side and a round nail-studded shield slung over a back clad in a light mail shirt. He'd sprouted a respectable close-clipped beard on the journey to go with his mustache, while Karl and his younger brother still scraped off all their whiskers . . . though as much for the fact that their scattering of fair down still looked embarrassingly sparse as for the fact that it was the custom for young single men among Mackenzies. It made the swirling blue patterns of his tattoos look a little odder to Karl's eyes as they peeped out from under the hair.

Diarmuid had been Princess Órlaith's lover, something of which Karl was frankly and wistfully envious. Presumably that was ended, but not a close friendship, not when he was ready to risk his life and leave a newly-handfasted bride at home as well to manage the Tennart steading with his mother, and her expecting their first babe.

Karl wouldn't have wanted to face *that* on his homecoming. There were places where a man could just tell a woman to shut up and expect her to at least pretend in public to do it, but those most emphatically did not include the dúthchas of the Mackenzies or their McClintock cousins either.

Thank the Mother-of-All, Karl thought. *And she didn't outright tell him not to go . . . still, she was not joyous at the thought, no she was not altogether . . .*

Though he supposed it would make a man reckless of death; he'd seen the young hearthmistress in question when they stopped at Diarmuid's garth and she'd been silent on the matter in public but tight-lipped.

"Nae, no' a thing I could see, wi' the blessin' of Cernunnos," the tacksman said.

The McClintock accent was rougher than that of Karl's folk, harsh with rolled r's and throaty swallowing sounds. Karl grinned, though he imitated the other man as he made the sign of the Horns to show respect to the Lord of the Beasts, as was fitting. Both Clans were mainly of the same branch of the Old Faith, though with differences of emphasis.

"He's the Lord of the Hunt and of the hunted both. Which face of Him do we call on?" Karl said.

Diarmuid smiled back and offered a silver flask from his sporran. Karl took a sip; the other man had refilled it with grape brandy at White Mountain. It wasn't as good as the smooth sweet pear spirit from his own steading he'd had in it originally, but it was welcome. Neither of them was formally sole leader of this branch of the expedition, and the rivalry between McClintocks and Mackenzies was as old as the Change . . . though *usually* mild enough, a matter of teasing, rarely more serious than an occasional good-natured brawl. It was still best to be carefully friendly; and the *feartaic* was a man to respect anyway.

"That's a matter for debate, but I hae nae doot at all of yer da's opinion o' the matter," Diarmuid observed pawkily.

"Oh, I think we're a bit ahead, to be sure. Yet true, Da's not the sort to give up."

"Were truer words ever spoken?" Diarmuid said. "My ain father knew him in the old wars, ye ken. *Think three times before ye cross that 'un, Diarmuid* he said tae me once; and this from a man who liked the hunting of bears, which was the death of him in the end. Well, I've done the thing now, but no' lightly, I'll hae ye know."

Karl nodded, torn a bit between pride and what he grudgingly admitted to himself was resentment. As a lad he'd glowed every time someone sang the tale of the Quest, or badgered his father into telling a bit after a mug or three before the fire some long evening in the Black Months.

There in the story was *his* da; the High King's trusted right-hand man and blood brother, who'd gone to Nantucket and back, won the sword-maid of Norrheim, dared peril and black evil and saved his Chief's life at the great battle of the Horse Heaven Hills. Yes, and he'd strutted and enjoyed the other children's envy, when Da wasn't around to tweak his ear for getting a swelled head, and tell him not to believe everything that came out of a bard's mouth.

When you came to manhood yourself, though . . . it could make you feel as if you'd be a boy all your life, having *that* looming over you. Diarmuid seemed to have an easier time with his father's memory, though that might just be that he was older or that his father had already passed the Gate or had simply been a well-respected and prominent man rather than a hero of legend and tale.

Well, I'm on my own journey now, and no mistake! If we can just get clear of Da, that is.

They were making good speed. Not as fast as the knock-down rail-riding frame they'd picked up at White Mountain and used down the great baking stretch of the Sacramento valley, pumping away at the pedals with the hot wind in their teeth like a horse galloping but for far longer. The dogs had loved it, lolling at ease with their noses in the breeze and their tongues flapping like pink banners of wet silk; keeping up with bicycles on their own four feet since they left the rails was hard for them.

Still, good time.

He assumed the High Queen would send Edain Aylward Mackenzie after them; that might be a bit of vanity, but he didn't think so. Even if his father had come into White Mountain right on their heels—the High King's Archers could *move*—they wouldn't be here just yet. Since that had been the only set of railcar frames to hand at the outpost, his band would have at least a day or two on them by now.

The thought made him snicker a little.

"Still seeing Da's face in your mind, when he finds the trick we played on him?" Mathun said, slapping him on the back. "And that last little detail you thought up—lovely! You've a right to laugh at your own wit."

"That I do, brother of mine. That I do."

"The wonder and joy of it, the more so as it's a thing so seldom seen."

Diarmuid joined in the laughter as the brothers cuffed playfully at each other. Inwardly Karl was a little worried, and glad to be past that stage along the rails, not least for the effort of knocking down the frames and carting them around the breaks in the ancient working. The scorching western side of the great central valley of the Province had been uninhabited after they passed White Mountain. By repute there were only a few tiny bands of skulkers in the hills that bordered it, and it had felt safe enough, but he didn't like it.

I'm tired, maybe that's what's making me see things out of the corner of my eye, he thought.

He'd expected danger and weariness on this venture for the Princess, and found them, but not so much the loss of sleep.

This is much better than the great valley, the Sacramento, he thought; there were rolling hills not far away, and low mountains to the west blue with forest. *Still hot, to be sure, but better.*

Gwri Beauregard Mackenzie came up, a dark-skinned woman of a few years more than his own age with her hair in thin braids tipped by silver balls; she was his second on this venture. Her home was Dun Tàirneanach, over towards the Willamette and well south of Dun Fairfax, and he'd known her for years, since a memorable Beltane feast, in fact. She was clever and a good archer and hunter, serious-minded and steady . . . and more to the point, her mother Meadhbh was a Priestess of the Triple Cords and a *fiosaiche*—seeress—of note. She'd done notable work with that talent during the Prophet's War.

Gwri was neither High Priestess nor seeress, not yet, but she had some abilities along those lines. The Princess had left it to him to pick who came along, from those willing and able to keep their lips from flapping in the breeze. On a venture as uncanny as this, with the breath of the Otherworld on your neck, he wanted someone with a bit of those skills.

And so, I do not like it when she frowns that way and looks about her as if seeking for something not to be seen in the light of common day. Good never comes of it . . . though it's best to know the threat before it strikes, or at least that there is one. Still, why could the foresight not predict a rain of beer, or roast pigs trotting by with knives and forks in their backs?

"I've an ill feeling," she said, confirming his stomach's verdict.

One of the landworkers—the middle-aged farmer, built like a knotted stump but with a slight limp to his stride—came over to the fence at the edge of the field, leaning eight feet of half-pike against it. The full sixteen-foot length was unwieldy for anything but serried ranks in a pitched battle, so throughout Montival they were made in two halves joined by a metal sleeve; that was easy to take down and left you with a top half that made a useful general-purpose spear and warstaff.

That he came by was no surprise, given that the cart was safely heading off. It was normal to be suspicious of outsiders, and just as normal to come and chat once you knew they weren't hostile. News was always welcome, and would be more so here in this out-of-the-way place, and doubly so with the shock of the High King's death nearby so recently making folk anxious.

What wasn't expected was what he said: "Diarmuid Tennart McClintock, and Karl Aylward Mackenzie?"

Karl and Diarmuid glanced at each other, startled; Karl felt his mind stutter, and wished he had a reason to pause and gather his wits. Luck or the *aes dana* provided one. A little berry-brown girl with hair that was a mass of black curls hardly confined by a red ribbon had followed the farmer. She hid behind the man, gripping his leg and peeking repeatedly out from behind him at the worn strangers with their odd clothes and great shaggy dogs, sometimes clutching at the little golden crucifix that hung about her neck on a silver chain. The beasts gave their slack-mouthed dangling-tongue toothy *look-it's-a-puppy!* grins at her and thumped the ground with their tails.

Not for the first time he reflected that dogs were better than men, on the average and in some respects.

Mathun crouched, grinning himself, and winked at her as he took a little figure of a running horse out of his sporran. It was well done, lively in the elongated and stylized fashion Mackenzies preferred; he liked to whittle with his *sgian dubh* when he had a little time. The farmer halted in surprise, then paused for a moment.

"Here," the younger Aylward brother said. "Do you like horses, little lass? I've a sister about your age and near as pretty, and she's mad for them."

A wordless nod, and he went on: "This, 'tis Epona, the Lady of the Horses, a Goddess great and powerful. Forbye she'll send you one of your own to ride in your dreams if you put it beneath your pillow, so."

The little girl's eyes went wide; the farmer laughed and urged her forward with a hand on her head and she snatched the toy, murmured *thankyouverymuchsir* and ran full-tilt back towards the oak with bare feet flashing and shift flying in the wind, waving the carving overhead and calling shrilly to her playmates.

"George Finney," the man said in the blunt Corvallan way, and shook hands with their leaders. "I'm yeoman here, holding this land in free tenure as a Crown grant."

When Karl and Diarmuid confirmed his guess he forbore to note aloud that Karl was an odd first name for a Mackenzie, or to ask about the famous-and-rare midname. He *had* been warned, after all, and evidently hadn't asked questions then either. There were times when Corvallan customs were agreeable enough.

"We sent for your friends when we spotted you, figured it had to be the party they'd warned us about," the man said instead. "They've been here since yesterday, camped out in my olives, and they told me you'd be by."

"Ah," Karl said, trying to look relaxed. "That would be Susan Mika."

The man nodded. "The Sioux girl, the Courier, right. Odd to see a Lakota again after all these years . . . strange folk, wild men if you like, but by God they can fight!"

Diarmuid nodded in turn and offered his flask, which the landsman took with a nod of thanks, and a gasp of appreciation after he sipped.

"So me ain father said of them more than once; fair deadly in open country. You'd have been at the Horse Heaven Hills, then?" he said.

It was a safe enough bet for someone the farmer's age with several visible scars, and there had been a contingent there from the folk of the Seven Council Fires as well.

The man surprised them a little by shaking his head. "I came in with a later draft, but then I carried a pike all the way from Walla Walla to

Corwin—my regiment was one of the ones that fought their way in from the edge to the center and up the steps of the Temple. Met my Pía there, she was a healer with one of the outfits from the Free Cities and everyone's field hospitals were taking whoever got brought in. There at the end they were as busy and as jumbled up as we were at the point of the spear."

"I've heard the street fighting was . . . hard," Diarmuid said.

"It gave a whole new meaning to *cluster-fuck*, those goddamned tunnels, the maniacs kept popping up behind us. . . . Pía sewed up seven cuts and a stab on me and got me a transfusion, I had blood squelching in my boots by then. Couldn't seem to settle after the war, so a bunch of us came down here. . . ."

His eyes went distant. Karl cut in: "Friends, you said? There being more than Susan?"

"Yeah, the Sioux Courier, and two young Rangers from their station at Eryn Muir, but they left day before yesterday. The Courier should be here soon—I sent José over to the homestead, where she's staying."

He smiled. "Filling my kids' heads with stories and doctoring people's horses, she has a good touch with both."

Karl nodded, smiled back, and winced inwardly; the more so when Diarmuid cocked a pawky eye at him. The dwellers *had* sent off a messenger, and he hadn't seen it.

"We'll wait here, then, and many thanks," he said, and the man nodded, shouldered his half-pike and walked off after his grain-cart and family.

Everyone was glad of a bit of a rest, not to mention meeting someone who could give them some idea of what was going on here. They didn't have long to wait; a rider came down the roadway at a canter, leading two remounts.

By then he had his own scout out, Boudicca Lopez Mackenzie of his own Dun Fairfax, who he'd picked for her skills as a skulker—the kind who said shooting game with a bow was a crude makeshift, because she could stalk deer and then cut their throats before they really noticed one of the human-kind was standing at arm's length. He thought a bit of that was vaunting, but grudgingly admitted she was the best of the Dun of their generation at brushwork, though he thought himself a close second.

She came out from under the war-cloak that turned her to an anonymous lump of vegetation and dirt and waved her arms in the *all clear* signal of Battle Sign.

The rider came on a bit, drew rein and hailed him. Susan Mika was riding a nondescript tough-looking little cob, and with a few individual touches—beadwork on the shoulders, fringes down the seams—to her tight leathers and more on her bowcase and the sheath of her shete. She'd been the go-between who'd brought Órlaith's word to him in Dun Fairfax, using her place in the Crown Courier Corps . . . or just serving the Crown, though the High Queen might dispute the point if it were argued to her.

She was his age, give or take, but much shorter—the Couriers all were, to sit light in the saddle—and a slim wiry bundle of steel-wire sinews, with a high-cheeked, proud-nosed face of a tint like old bronze and with a complex set of black braids on her head. Even for her horse-lord people she rode easily, and with a young man's automatic likerish appraisal he thought she'd probably be a wildcat in the blankets if you could get her interested.

"Merry meet, and merry part, and merry meet again," he replied, which was the Mackenzie formal greeting.

Right now she was all business, though she gave him a smile. "*Taŋyáŋ yahípi*, friends," she said, raising one hand palm-out. "Welcome. Good to see you at last."

"The Princess isn't here yet?" Karl asked.

"Not yet," she said. "We're expecting the ship anytime, but it's not as if you can tell that sort of thing to the day. And Faramir and Morfind had to take a message north to Mist Hills. Too suspicious if they balked at a regular order, but they should be back soon; from what they say it's only a long day's ride if you have good remounts and push it."

Karl nodded, though a Courier's definition of *only a long day's ride if you push it* meant *twenty-four hours of torture* by most other folks.

He knew Dúnedain customs well enough. They guarded the High King's peace when there was no war, and were scouts and raiders when there was, and by preference they lived in woods and waste places. The

Rangers thought it better than tilling the earth, and it certainly had its excitements and air of mystery, but it meant living a bit like full-time warriors under the discipline of command all your life, albeit it was also a family business.

"We're not to press on to China Camp the now?"

"What people don't see, they don't have to take official notice of," Susan amplified. "That's what Faramir and Morfind said."

"Ah," Karl said, and Diarmuid grunted.

Both of them meant the same thing; what the rulers of Stath Ingolf—which was to say the Dúnedain pair's parents—didn't officially see they wouldn't have to report to the High Queen. They might know, what with their own children involved; they might suspect; or they might just be very busy elsewhere. Nobody could tell for sure, which was pretty much the point.

"We'll get you a bit farther west, camp you out, and then rush for Círbann Rómenadrim when the ship comes in. Nobody actually lives there full-time, there's just the wharf and some boats and some sheds for storing stuff when a ship comes in, but folks go back and forth from there to the Eryn Muir all the time."

"Aye, that's fair ca'canny," Diarmuid said. "Good sensible caution," he added, when he saw how the others were baffled by the dialect term.

"And we've set up a campground here on the Finney farm—there's firewood, a spring and pool of good water, and supplies," she said.

Then she smiled. "Fresh-risen bread, vegetables. And a case of the red wine they make at *Tham en-Araf*. And a pig ready to over the fire, plus Faramir kicked in some of his mother's chipotle BBQ sauce—it ain't buffalo hump steak at the fall hunt, but I won't kick."

"Tham en-Araf?" Diarmuid said.

"Wolf Hall," she added. "Where Morfind's parents live—Lady Mary and Lord Ingolf—over the other side of the valley. The Prancing Pony in Eryn Muir brews damn good beer, too, now that some of the settlers here are growing hops, and Faramir brought some crocks."

Karl could feel ears perking up among his followers and Diarmuid smacked his lips; they were hungry, weary, and *thirsty* in more ways than one. That nasty little skirmish with the bandits had blooded the band without too much loss, no dead and only a few badly wounded who'd had to be left in the clinic at White Mountain. It had still left them all a bit shaken by the speed and brutality of the fighting, and they could all use a bit of a rest and a revel. His own ears pricked as well, but he turned an eye on Gwri. She was still frowning, and she shrugged reluctantly.

Maybe it's Da at our heels. I'm too old for him to grab by the ear and wallop on the backside the now . . . but my guts are shriveling at the thought of him, that they are.

White Mountain town was named for the towering peak just visible to the northwards, a volcanic cone whose top was still snowclad in July, tinged red now as the sun sank westwards; the ancient world had called it Shasta.

The commander of the High King's Archers found that cool pale sight a bit of a taunt by the Powers, given the way the hot dry air was sucking at the sweat it brought pouring from your skin down here in the lowland, leaving a rime of salt behind to itch in sensitive places. There was a green smell in the air from the irrigated fields that started twice long bowshot ahead and a densely forested strip along the river to their left, but white salt-tasting dust coated his face and hands, and it was hotter than he could remember the Willamette ever being. For a moment homesickness was bitter.

Not hotter than deserts across the mountains in summertime, though, he thought sturdily. *And Balor of the Single Eye knows I've seen enough of* that *country, on the Quest and in the war time and afterwards. Easier to take heat when it's dry like this, too. Now the sunrise lands in summer, Iowa and the rest, that was hard to take. You felt as if mushrooms would sprout from your crotch and armpits at any moment.*

"Nearly there, sir," the mounted scout who'd met them said; his comrade had galloped on towards White Mountain to alert their officers.

Edain grunted in reply as he jogged along the road between pale fields of faded golden grass and patches of eucalyptus and Valley oak with his unstrung bow pumping in his left hand.

The outpost itself was not far south of the ruins of Redding, a settlement of the ancients at the northward end of the great central valley of

Westria Province. The city had emptied in the year after the Change—it was just remote enough that the agony had probably been more prolonged than in the megalopolis farther south. What was left after the fires had largely been swept away in the floods since, especially the monstrous crests that poured like tidal waves of water and rock and rubble down the valley of the Sacramento as the great dams in the mountains lost their battle with earthquakes and corrosion in the spillways and cresting waters in wet springs.

The rammed earth fort was new, and the earth mound it stood on, and the little town at its foot, all laid out since the Montivallans came. It was well back from the tree-covered floodplain, safer since the natural rhythm of retreat and advance had resumed, though there was a floating dock out into the water of the broad river with several craft tied up that ranged from canoes to sailing barges.

The two squat towers of the modest fort rising into sight as they jogged bore the Stars and Stripes as well as the Crowned Mountain and Sword of Montival, both of course flying at half-mast just now. When the High Kingdom reached its hand out to this part of the new province the particular finger was in the form of a battalion of troops from the United States of Boise—what some stubborn traditionalists in that inland member-realm of Montival insisted was the United States of *America*.

Edain admired the Boiseans wholeheartedly as warriors—he'd seen them fight on both sides in the Prophet's War, which had been a civil strife for them—and they certainly worked like well-organized beavers, or bullocks, at whatever they turned their hands to. Their ruler for the first generation after the Change, Lawrence Thurston, had been a commander in the old American army, a Ranger in a different sense from the modern use of the term. Edain had met him once shortly before his death: a man very hard, and very able, and very much concerned with order and system. It had struck deep into the souls of his folk, under him and his son Fred.

People generally didn't mention his elder son Martin, the parricide, usurper and traitor who'd become the Prophet's puppet in Boise for a time.

Fred I like, what with the Quest and hence living in each other's sporrans for a year the way we did, and fighting the war in company with him; you know a man well after that. His folk in general, though . . .

The Boiseans assigned here had thrown up the fort almost overnight, then sent for their families or made their own while they built much else; they called such settlements *coloniae.* It had been less than a decade, but now there was a ring of modest but comfortable-looking farmsteads stretching out in a checkerboard, rambling low-slung whitewashed dwellings with red-tile roofs set in colorful little gardens and each with its wind-pump spinning. The square fields of yellow reaped stubble or green-and-gold tasseling corn were interspersed by roads and irrigation ditches, surrounded by pasture where horses and cattle and sheep grazed. There were ancient but newly pruned silvery-gray olive groves cleared of the thickets of spindly saplings that had grown up in the long years of neglect, and young green vineyards and orchards of peach and fig and more.

All amid a pleasant bustle of carts and children and the clatter and hum of folk about the close of their working day. Woodsmoke scented the air, a little different from what he was used to because much of it was eucalyptus burning, and the good smells of cooking. The oddest part was that there were few adults over thirty. Or children past their early years, though full plenty of those.

A column of troops perhaps two-score strong came trotting out of the fort to greet the newcomers, to the thutter of a drum and a complex bugle-call from the hoarse tubae on the gatehouse wall. An officer marched at their head, a red crest cross-wise on his helm and a vine-stock swaggerstick in his hand. The soldiers following behind him wore a plainer version of his armor of polished hoops and bands over chest and shoulders and belly, with big curved oval shields marked with the eagle-and-thunderbolts, short leaf-shaped stabbing-swords worn high on the right hip, and heavy six-foot javelins with iron shanks.

Their legs moved in perfect unison like a centipede as they jogged along at the quickstep, chanting:

"Yanks to the charge! cried Thurston.
The foe begins to yield!
So strike—"

—and each hobnailed right boot struck the road.

"For hearth and nation!
So strike—"

—another stamp.

"For the Eagle Shield!
Let no man stop for plunder,
But slay, and slay, and slay;
The Gods who helped our fathers
Fight by our sides today!"

—and they stopped with a final uniform crash of hobnails against the rock pavement.

They came to attention, rapped their long iron-shod javelins against their shields, then turned and made ranks on either side of the roadway, shield held against the left shoulder and spear to the side, the butt braced against the right foot, tanned faces like shapes carved from oiled wood and every point in precise alignment.

It was discipline for discipline's own sake, formal as a dance, but with an undertone of grim relentless intent. He'd seen them, or more likely with this lot their fathers, maneuver just like that during real fights with arrows thudding into their shields and globes of hard steel and liquid fire arching across the sky from catapult batteries. While the wounded screamed like the Woman of the Mounds on a rooftree . . . And it worked, chewing through the murderous bewildering complexities of battle like a power-saw in a mill through tough wood.

He tapped his bow to his brow, thus returning the punctilious salute of the officer of the detachment; the Boisean form was the right fist to the chest, then thrust out at eye-height. Enlisted men in full gear did it with their spears to the shield, then the spear held out.

It was all rather impressive, given how far they were from home—or how close they were to the arse-end of nowhere-in-particular—and what they'd had to work with.

But for all their virtues they mostly have a serious pickle up the back way, that they do, besides being just wrongheaded about a good deal and stubborn withal, he thought. *They're an easier folk to respect than to like, and that's the truth of the matter.*

"Commandant von Sydow will be anxious to see you, Bow-Captain Aylward," the young officer said. "Your command is welcome in our mess hall and the Commandant extends an invitation to dinner for you and—"

"It's in a bit of a hurry I am," Edain said.

Though the thought of a decent meal and a bath and a full night's sleep in a good bed did arouse longing. The plain fact of the matter was . . .

That I am after getting a wee bit old for this shite, he thought. *Or* have gotten, *so.*

He went on to the Boisean: "A party of Mackenzies and McClintocks? Coming through here also in a hurry, just now? My son Karl would be one of their leaders, and the tacksman Diarmuid Tennart McClintock the other."

"Why, yes, they left yesterday morning," the officer said with enthusiastic helpfulness; he had a faint blond fuzz on his upper lip, probably meant for a mustache.

Either that or a wee little caterpillar has crawled there and died and he didn't notice. Sweet Blodeuwedd's blossoms, they all look so young these days, like puppies, Edain thought.

Then, with a hunter's thrill at a successful chase: *Ah, good, we're still gaining on Karl!*

"Did they get bicycles here?" he asked.

One of the duties this outpost owed the High Kingdom in return for help and the land-grant was acting as a relay post on the overland route down to the Bay. It kept horses beyond its own needs for the messenger service as well as for official travelers, and stocks of bicycles salvaged, repaired and fitted with modern solid wheels. Elsewhere a stath of the

Dúnedain might serve the same purpose, or a daughter-house of the Order of the Sword of St. Benedict with its surrounding hamlets, or a Mormon village, or a feudal grant to an Associate noble, or some other group willing to tame a strategic part of the wilderness.

"Well, not just bicycles . . . what they took south was our new rail pedalcars," the lieutenant said helpfully. "Our engineers made them up after your party and the Crown Princess passed through earlier on their way north after the terrible news about the High King. So that bicycles can work on the rails, you see, the way you did in the Quest."

"The line down the west side of the valley hasn't been repaired, has it?"

He would most certainly have heard of a major project like that, one with military implications. Especially since this province was Crownland.

"Oh, no, sir. It's dry country, mostly, which helps, but still it's broken in a dozen places at least, flash floods and subsidence. Trampling by herds of mustangs, quite likely!"

For a moment the young man looked offended by the sheer messiness of nature; he was a Boisean, right enough. And probably by the way nature had reclaimed most of California-that-was. There was wilderness in Boise's territories, but a lot of it had been wilderness before the Change. Uniquely in Montival, there were probably nearly as many people in what had been central and southwestern Idaho as there had been fifty years ago. They didn't use the land there nearly as intensively, since it wasn't producing food for distant cities anymore, but it was all at least theoretically occupied.

Compared to the new Crownland of Westria, or even parts of the Willamette and Columbia Valleys, it was densely populated.

"It'll be a long time before it's worth the effort to repair that railroad," the young Boisean went on. "Generations. But your story about the Quest gave the engineers in our machine-shop an idea about how we could use the intact sections anyway, for some things. Light knock-down frames to hold the bicycles, so the whole thing can be taken apart and carried around breaks . . ."

Edain flushed and snatched the Scots bonnet off his head and clenched it in one knobby fist. They *had* done that on their way back from Nantucket. The idea had come to Rudi in Norrheim, and it had gotten them through the empty lands far faster than they could have otherwise despite all the damage a generation of rain and fire and landslip had made to the rails of the ancients; he doubted it could be done again, not back there at least.

Most people were familiar with the story, Karl and Mathun more than most. They'd have seen the chance.

"Well, we need your takedown railcars too," he barked. "And that at once."

The lieutenant's face fell. "Oh, I'm very sorry, sir—the first group of your party took them all. We're making more, but it's not the first call on the machine-shops . . . we don't have the right salvage metals on hand right now, we used up all our stock of aluminum pipe. . . ."

Something about the way the Boisean had said *first group of your party* struck Edain as ominous, somehow. Now he was fumbling in a pouch on his belt.

"As a matter of fact, sir, your sons said you'd be paying for the equipment he commandeered, since it isn't part of the fort's usual obligations. Here's the receipt he . . . Karl . . . signed. It was a bit irregular, but since it was them—"

The Boisean settler froze in shock as Edain threw his bonnet on the ground and stamped on it

"Go mbeadh cosa gloine fút agus go mbrise an ghloine!" he shouted. "With the toe of me boot to your arse, Karl, and the flat of me hand to Mathun's ear!"

Báirseach laughed until tears tracked dark and slightly muddy paths down through the dust on her face, leaning on her bow lest she collapse. A moment later Edain burst into laughter himself, picked his bonnet up again and dusted it off by slapping it against his kilted thigh. The Boisean was looking shocked and trying unsuccessfully to hide it. Mackenzies had a reputation for being open and carefree, but this was obviously beyond what he'd expected.

They wouldn't be getting to Stath Ingolf before Karl and Mathun, no matter how hard they pedaled. Now all depended on when the *Tarshish*

Queen made the Bay, which depended on the weather; or on how fast the frigate *Stormrider* came in pursuit, which depended on the Navy . . . and the weather. As for his own chase, Karl had beaten him fair and square, whether his sons were stuck waiting for the Princess while he caught up or were sails below the horizon when he arrived.

Or they beat me trick for trick. And such a trick!

"Well, we'll be taking up Commandant von Sydow's invitation, lieutenant. That we will, and a dinner will be welcome, though no more welcome than a bath first. And in the morning we'll be off at dawn, on plain bicycles."

It's never a joy to be outdone, he thought. *But when a man's outdone by his own child, there's a pride to it nonetheless.*

For a moment he missed Rudi Mackenzie with a keenness that bordered on physical pain.

How the Chief would have laughed!

CHAPTER NINE

GOLDEN GATE/GLORANNON
CROWN PROVINCE OF WESTRIA
(FORMERLY CALIFORNIA)
HIGH KINGDOM OF MONTIVAL
(FORMERLY WESTERN NORTH AMERICA)
JULY/FUMIZUKI/CERWETH 14TH
CHANGE YEAR 46/FIFTH AGE 46/SHŌHEI 1/2044 AD

The orange-red towers climbed out of the curling tendrils of sun-brightened mist, like sculptured pillars in the temples of some high God, and the long graceful swoop of the cables between them linking headland to headland, all still hints glimpsed as the mist thinned.

"The fog was very heavy when my father . . . when we came in; and it was still nearly dark," Reiko said softly; she must be feeling the pain of loss as well, but her face was quietly serene. "We saw the bridge only as a shadow and we were . . . preoccupied. This is indeed very fine! And the way it changes from moment to moment, each revealing a little more."

The wind was still from the northwest, and the *Tarshish Queen* stood in under plain sail—her gaff-rigged mainsails alone, sacrificing speed for quick reaction. There was a perceptible roll to the motion now, as they cut diagonally across the waves. Not far away to the north the huge rusted shape of an ancient ship slanted bow-upwards, water breaking white around it and spouting in foam through the gaps that time and Ocean had eaten. With the tide on the ebb you could see how thick the crust of barnacle and weed was on the remainder, life swarming about it in fish and seal and birds.

"That wreck's on the north bar, Your Highness," Feldman said from beside the wheel.

Then he jerked his head a little southward, without moving his eyes.

"There's another bar like it not far that way; sometimes bits are above the surface. The whole thing's like a horseshoe with the arch pointing westward, and a hole in the center kept clear by the tidal scour. They're both dangerous, not just shallow water but sudden waves that can come from nowhere and swamp you or pile you into something that'll rip your hull open bow to stern. Starting with *parts* of wrecks. The ones you can see aren't so bad, but there are a lot just beneath the surface, like rusty gutting knives. They shift around, too. Mainly after storms but sometimes for no reason anyone can tell."

Captain Ishikawa Goru was looking deeply unhappy at leaving his Empress' safety to someone else, no matter how competent. He was also keeping very quiet. Feldman knew this harbor. Ishikawa had only sailed through here once, on a one-way journey in a burning ship, and he'd observed enough to develop a healthy respect for the Montivallan skipper's seamanship and that of his crew. Órlaith caught the slight byplay as Reiko gave her naval officer a very tiny approving nod. Ishikawa was youngish for a senior command and a bit wild and brash by the standards of the Nihonjin party. Which meant he was only moderately buttoned-down by those of the more rule-bound parts of Montival.

"And your captain was either skillful, lucky or both to make it in safely on his first try without a modern chart or an experienced pilot, Your Majesty," Feldman added to Reiko.

"Ryūjin . . . sea-*kami* . . . help," Ishikawa said, with a shrug.

Ah, Feldman is clever; not least in using truth for praise. From what I've seen Japanese enjoy praise as much as anyone; when it's well-earned and from someone who knows what they're talking about, at least. But they're very modest about it. Or at least this small bunch of them do and are; I don't suppose they're altogether typical.

The ones here were all of the upper classes, as were the samurai of the

Guard waiting belowdecks with her men-at-arms, and in the direct service of the Chrysanthemum Throne. The only commoners in their party were Ishikawa's eight surviving sailors, with whom she'd had little contact except to note that they were much more carefree and less reserved with their local equivalents than their almost maniacally disciplined and studiously reserved overlords. At least when those overlords weren't watching; they didn't say a word if they were.

I don't know all that much about Japan, even as it was before the Change, apart from what happens when I think in their language.

Sometimes that conveyed information simply because of the assumptions and penumbras inherent in the words. What the Sword did wasn't like learning a second language; it was like acquiring the command you would have had if you'd grown up speaking it.

And doubtless they've changed a great deal since the Change, just as we have. Possibly changed just as much, *too. I know Reiko fairly well, I think—brief acquaintance but intense, these last few months.*

Like his sovereign the Nihonjin captain had known English—theoretically, in the written form—before his party landed here. Unlike her he hadn't become fully fluent yet. The sounds of English were difficult for speakers of Nihongo, and vice-versa, and nobody who actually spoke the language as their birth-tongue had survived the Change there to teach anyone else, so it was rather impressive that they'd done as well as they had.

Reiko still had a charming soft accent. Ishikawa's was just thick.

Though he had become at least understandable, unlike the Imperial Guard commander; perhaps it was because he was younger. The grizzled soldier was in his mid-forties, and Órlaith suspected . . .

Knew, she thought.

. . . that behind a stony calm Egawa fiercely resented needing foreign help in recovering one of his people's great treasures. Doubtless that tied in to memories of Japan's defeat by the ancient Americans in the great war of the last century; his Empress had let drop that his grandfather had died in that struggle, a hero who perished deliberately diving his flying machine into one of the invaders' warships. Apparently that man's son had grown up hero-worshipping the memory of the father he'd barely known, and *his* son had kept up the tradition.

Reiko didn't think that way. She was alarmingly intelligent, fanatically determined about anything she considered important or a matter of *giri*, of duty, and ruthlessly pragmatic to boot, focused on what she could do to bend the future to her will. That made her capable of grinding out astonishing results by sheer willpower.

Ishikawa indicated the course the *Red Dragon* had followed.

"Your Haida pilate . . . pirate and *bakachon* ship close behind—"

Órlaith winced slightly without showing it as the Sword-gained command of the language cataracted through her. Sometimes that was like having her mind split in two, and she had to pause and consciously unpack things.

Baka meant *idiot*, and *chon* was a contemptuous diminutive of what the folk of Korea had called their own land, *Chosŏn*; the other term the Nihonjin employed for their foes was *jinnikukaburi*, a new coinage that meant *human flesh cockroach*. To her Sword-trained ear it carried a freight of dread and loathing and sheer murderous hatred like a boiling cauldron in the minds of the users, a flame that could only be quenched in blood. If the chance for wholesale revenge ever came, she didn't think her new allies would be inclined to mercy.

Granted that from what she'd been able to learn Korea was currently ruled by a mad cult of diabolist cannibals who'd taken it over just after the Change and who were even worse than the Church Universal and Triumphant that her parents had fought. And they had been raiding and tormenting Nippon's survivors for more than forty years in an utterly grisly fashion.

Yet it is still a bit of a . . . rude . . . way to look at an entire realm and folk, even if one of them killed my father. I doubt the most of them chose to live so. Still, the folk of Chosŏn haven't injured my whole people as they have the Japanese, or threatened our very existence. And didn't Da say himself that you should keep in mind that fighting against Evil mostly means killing farmers that Evil has levied from the plow at spear-point?

Ishikawa continued, and her thought was a flicker beneath her attention to his words:

"*Bakachon* shooting firebolts and shells, gaining on us as we shipped water through very many leak and around plugs in holes below waterline, our stern catapults dismounted, sails ripped, fires starting already in rigging, many men killed trying to carry hoses aloft. Only *chance* of death from underwater wrecks, very sure death if we don't go through, no doubt on best odds. I think then enemy lose one ship on approach—four when we pass through, three land after us very close. But your reports say one wrecked to north later, perhaps turn back with bad hull damage."

"How many initially?" Feldman said, then repeated it more slowly: "How many enemy ships in pursuit of you at the beginning, back in Asia?"

"Twelve," the Japanese sailor said. "We sink five—burn with firebolt or napalm shell, dismast with round shot so they swamp and blake up in storm, one we turn on when it get ahead of others, that one we board short time and Imperial Guard samurai jump down hatch."

"Jump, Captain?" Sir Aleaume de Grimmond said.

The commander of her men-at-arms was red-haired, handsome except for his jug ears and rather melancholy by inclination.

Egawa Noboru spoke softly in his own language, and Reiko translated for the others:

"They cried *Tennō Heika Banzai!* And jumped with incendiaries in their arms. So that the fire would be sheltered from the rain and sleet and take hold quickly, and so they could fight off the *bakachon* damage-control parties until it was too late, while our ship broke away."

The Montivallans blinked, then bowed their heads for an instant to honor the memory of warriors so brave and so true to their oaths; the Catholics among them crossed themselves.

"Duty, heavier than mountains," Órlaith said, in Nihongo.

"Death, lighter than a feather," Reiko said, completing the proverb.

Egawa nodded crisply, but looked a little surprised that she'd known it. Órlaith crooked one blond brow a very little as she caught his eye for an instant. Ishikawa went on:

"Many *bakachon* . . . disappear along way. Much bad gales, much ice-berg, many long-range actions in bad visibirity. Hard to tell what to them all happen."

Brrrr! Órlaith thought. *And all Reiko* said *was that it was* difficult and troublesome*!*

Then everything else was lost as the fog dwindled again and sank towards the sea and streamed away in tatters, and the long curves spanning the open water became fully visible, their deep orange glowing against blue and white and green. Reiko gave a little involuntary gasp beside her, and Egawa grunted, a small guttural sound. Órlaith stopped herself from whistling with a slight effort of will; it seemed insufficiently reverent, and she drew the Invoking pentagram instead.

Sir Aleaume and Droyn Jones de Molalla crossed themselves; so did her brother John and Luanne. Even John's valet-bodyguard Evrouin did it, where he stood inconspicuously behind the Prince's shoulder. All of them were accustomed to seeing the huge structures of the ancients occasionally; enough so that they usually mentally edited them out of the landscape as irrelevant to modern life, unless you were looking for raw materials or needed a lookout post.

This was different.

It took a few moments for the sheer scale of the twin towers to north and south to fully sink in, soaring most of a thousand feet into the sky. But these were as cleanly delicate as spears, without the stark brutality of so many ancient structures. She could see Reiko's hand trace the curve of her sword, a lovely and deadly masterpiece crafted seven centuries ago by the legendary Masamune, as her eyes followed the long swoop of the suspension cables between, and the way they nestled into the hills that anchored them at either end.

"Ahhh," she said, her voice almost a crooning sigh. "Your ancestors built very well. And your father was right that those who conceived it deserved honor."

Órlaith nodded. "I've seen his face carved into a mountain in the eastern stretches of the realm with some of his kin, and Da said it was fitting for him to have that everlasting glory, for he had many great works to his credit. In peace as much as in war, helping his folk in times of dearth and drought. But this is the most beautiful of them."

The Japanese present made little bows in the direction of the bridge. Everyone except the sailors at work tilted their heads up as they passed beneath; Órlaith felt tiny for an instant, as if she'd walked out the front gate and found that she'd been living in a child's dollhouse and the furnishings of giants stood around her.

"And this time, they gave something godlike to the Gods, enhancing what They gave us," Heuradys agreed, with a sigh and a murmur and a look over her shoulder as they passed. "Apollon must have inspired them, He who loves beauty and due proportion in all things, in humans and their realms and the work of their hands. Hard to believe anything so big could be so beautiful. Like Mt. Hood or Ranier, or those waterfalls on the cliffs of the Columbia gorge."

Ashore in the wreck of San Francisco most of the great towers of the ancient world still stood, though some were twisted shapes of girder and some slumped against each other, tilted from the force of earthquakes and gnawing rust.

The bats and nesting birds must love them, Órlaith thought. Their lower levels were green-shaggy with vines, the upper dull rusted metal and sandblasted glass, with only a few shards glinting here and there in one great triangular mass. Birds soared about their nesting-sites like a shimmer in the sun, and you wouldn't think from looking in the bright light of day that the ruins were the haunt of terror. A thin thread of smoke from farther down the peninsula was the sole sign of the bands who prowled them.

Feldman nodded. "I've been here half a dozen times, and it's always impressive. The channel in the middle is usually pretty safe, the tidal scour keeps it thirty feet deep or better. Though the Bay is full of wrecks too, and not all of them are visible. Enjoy the sights—and now this is going to take concentration, I haven't been here for a couple of years and things shift. Mr. Radavindraban, leadsmen to the bows, if you please."

The ruins of San Francisco spread out on the hilly peninsula behind them as they turned north—

It's astern, Órlaith reminded herself with an inner chuckle. *At sea, behind is astern.*

—astern, edged with a thick fringe of intensely green salt marsh through which an occasional stub of stone or concrete or steel poked. Every possible spot, the islands the maps called Alcatraz and Angel Island and Yerba Buena and the decks of sunken ships, and little bits of higher land among the longshore marshes, was alive with fur-seals and harbor-seals, sea-lions and shorebirds. Sleek shapes slid into the water when the ship passed too close, and a score of brown wide-eyed heads lifted from a raft of sea-otters to stare curiously at the unusual sight of human-kind passing by.

Sir Aleaume passed her a pair of binoculars and she used them to scan about after a word of thanks to the knight; she wasn't a sailor and couldn't interpret the signs well enough to be useful looking for wrecks lurking beneath the blue. The others were doing likewise, equally interested in this southernmost outpost of civilization and symbol of the old world's fall. There were ruins everywhere—there would be for centuries, some would last for millennia like those statues in the Black Hills—but the ones where most of them lived had been worked by the survivors and showed it. Here the landscape of cataclysm was mostly as time and nature had left it.

The huge fringe of wooden houses around the adamantine towers had burned away long ago, mostly in the unimaginable violence of the firestorms that had run all around the Bay in the summer of the first Change Year. And up into the foothills where the ancients had let masses of fuel accumulate in the woods by suppressing the fire cycle. Sand-dunes laced with salt grass and dune weeds covered much of the northern tip of the peninsula that she could see, and elsewhere tawny grassland rolled amid ruin.

Farther south the hills were blue-green with renascent forest. More forest covered the East Bay across from them with the stubs of larger buildings or snags of wall rising like green-covered markers. Where reservoirs had burst the hills were gashed by long tongues of silt and gravel and rubble overgrown with shrub and vine, stretching out into the water.

There was a deep silence, save for the creak of wood and cordage, the lapping of water, the thrum of wind; by now, after most of a week at sea, those were pure background. The occasional sharp command echoed the louder, and the slap of feet on the deck as the crew on duty raced to obey, tweaking the sails or moving the wheels in precise increments.

They passed another bridge—one very long, but mostly tangled wreckage in the water save for the single middle span. There the towers leaned drunkenly apart, trailing girders like writhing windblown branches frozen in motion. Time and sea air had obviously eaten deep, and everyone looked up a bit apprehensively. Eventually the rest *would* topple; it was just a question of when.

"Soundings, Mr. Radavindraban," Feldman said as the schooner passed through on its journey northward.

The leadsmen began whirling their cords with the teardrop-shaped lead weights and casting them out before the schooner's bows, the ropes dropping down into the water while the sailors drew them in until they stood vertically as the ship passed over them.

"By the mark . . . eight! Eight fathoms even!"

"Thus, thus; very well, thus," Feldman said. "Steady as she goes."

"By the mark . . . five! Five fathoms even!"

"Port your helm, two points to port."

"By the mark . . . five! Full fathom five!"

"Port your helm, three points to port. Steady, steady as she goes. Very well, thus."

"By the mark . . . four! Full fathom four!"

She had grown to adulthood in a world where the sky was usually thick with wings, more so every year, but even to one of her generation the noise of the flocks here was stunning. Seagulls in snowy drifts, duck and Canuck Geese, herons and snowy egrets and uncounted others, and the osprey and bald eagles and hawks that preyed on them and the fish. A big pod of dolphins slipped by not far away, the school of white sturgeon they were chasing thrashing the surface into foam as a dozen of the sea-mammals leapt and dove, the lighter stripes on their sides flashing. The fishing must be fabulous here. . . .

Hmmmm, she thought, as she saw a patch where the water was reddish and nothing grew, and another of a strange metallic green.

Then again, perhaps I'd be a little reluctant to eat any fish that lived here year-round. Perhaps my grandchildren can.

"By the mark—four! Full fathom four!"

She completed her circuit and looked northwards again. Mountains ran like a ridge against the sea to the west, then fell away eastward in hills that were a mixture of forest and scrub and yellow-brown grassland, down towards the lowlands.

"Are you looking for something in particular?" Heuradys said, quietly.

Órlaith touched her lower lip meditatively with her right thumb. "No . . . but . . ."

Then: "I heard Da talking to Grandmother Juniper once about how the Sword gave him *feelings* at times. She called it his *spider-sense* for some reason."

Heuradys' brows went up. "What did she mean by that? I didn't think spiders had particularly sensitive senses except through their webs . . . though . . ." She frowned. "Wasn't there a legendary hero who had a Spider totem? But your father's was Raven. Of course, if *she* said there was something to it . . ."

Juniper Mackenzie was not only the founder of the Clan Mackenzie and its Chief until she retired in favor of her daughter Maude; she was Goddess-on-Earth and among the reasons the Old Faith was prominent in Montival. You didn't treat her word lightly on such matters. Or any others, if you were wise.

"Da didn't understand it either, and she wouldn't tell me—said it would spoil the jest," Órlaith said. "Sure, and she can be as mischievous as a girl of six, not a great-grandmother of six-and-seventy years. But she was serious enough about the thing itself, to be sure."

She laid her open left palm on the moon-crystal pommel of the Sword. It was the gesture her father had used, and now she could feel why.

"Da spoke sometimes . . . Mother less often, but once or twice . . . of how after the Kingmaking they felt as if they *were* the land of Montival, and not just as a manner of speaking. Da said he could *feel* it, almost like his own body in a way."

"Can you?" Reiko said.

She was listening with closest attention, as she always did when the Sword came up; being on a quest for a fabled blade of her own made that natural. She made a gesture with her *tessen*—a steel war-fan—and Egawa moved aside, as if casually stepping to the rail. The others did as well, granting the leaders as much privacy as was possible on board ship. Not that any of them would much *want* to hear these particular matters spoken of. The folk of Montival revered the Sword of the Lady and understood it according to their various faiths, but there was fear in that awe as well. It wasn't something that any sane mortal felt *easy* with.

"Mmmmm . . . a bit?" Órlaith said. "For a moment when I took it from the flames of the pyre. It's . . . muffled, somehow. I think perhaps nobody can bear its fullness all the time, and also because I *haven't* gone to Lost Lake yet; there's a rite there that only the Royal kin know of, a binding. Yet there's an *itch* as it were. Something not quite right. But I can't tell *what*. And to be sure, something will be wrong somewhere always, in a land as wide and varied as ours!"

She looked around at the disheveled loveliness of the ruined Bay. "This—there's a wrongness to it. The weight of steel and stone upon the land, it still . . . It feels out of balance. Like an ill note in a song, or one of those dreams where one leg is longer than the other."

"And the rightness?" her liege knight asked.

"There *should* be a city of human-kind here. With the harbor and the fine land and timber and the rivers running into it from the valleys all about, and a clime so mild and fine and the place itself with a beauty that sings to the soul, how not? Buildings and farms and workshops, yes, towers and walls and gardens and sails upon the water and a coming and going of ships. We have our rightful place in the great dance too."

"Like the beautiful bridge," Reiko said softly. "It is our nature to build, so the *kami* made us. We may do it well, or badly, but we will do it. We cannot do otherwise."

Órlaith nodded vigorous agreement. "But to take it all and cover it with the makings of our hands, no, that is an offense to the Powers and the *aes dana*."

Aes dana was how a Montivallan of the Old Faith—and some Christians, for that matter—would usually name the spirits of place, the mostly-unseen beings not as men were but lesser than the great Gods. Heathen might say *wight* or *alfar* or *aelfen*. *Kami* meant very much the same thing. Though strict Catholics usually referred to the patron Saints they believed watched over particular places or occupations, in her opinion it all came down to very much the same thing in the end.

She went on:

"The land will forgive as it heals. That's not altogether what I'm worried by, though. It's something more specific . . . but vague to the point of driving me mad, so."

Heuradys grinned. "I think I remember the High King saying that he didn't get *actionable intelligence* from it very often."

Órlaith nodded. "The Lady Herself isn't that much concerned with the ordinary affairs of our kind, the intrigues of power and the contentions of tribes and rulers and such. That's . . . you might say it's like the scurrying of ants, or those macaques they have about here leaping and chattering in a tree; important to the ants and the apes, but otherwise, not so much of a much. The Sword is . . . it's Her gift, but it's more *particular*. Tied to this land, and the human folk and the other Kindreds that dwell here; and it's linked to my family's bloodline. What Da said it gave was a sense of what could be," she agreed.

"He was not more definite?" Reiko said, and sighed.

"No. Forbye, he would say that it *couldn't* be described in human words spoken in the light of common day. Sometimes it prompted him, in peace often when it was a matter of the way we of human kind dealt with the other Kindreds and the land; or he would know the likely outcome of actions more clearly because of it. During the Prophet's War it was a matter of not needing maps, never being lost or forgetting the needful, knowing what the land could and should do; and who its folk were, and how best to bring them together to the Kingdom's need. A strengthening of what were already his strengths. And a knowledge of a new wrongness, when it arose. The Prophet, he was like a tooth being drilled, Da said; though he and the other magi of the CUT could cast shadow over what they did, and where."

Quietly she added: "And . . . remember what Diarmuid's mother said, when we guested at his steading on the way north?"

Heuradys tossed her head slightly in agreement. Gormall Tennart McClintock was a priestess of the triple cords, High Priestess on her family's land and lady of its *nemed*, its sacred wood. The knight quoted her words softly:

"The Earth's very self wept and keened him, when his blood lay upon it. It weeps yet, and rages, that the sacred King was slain untimely by the weapons of foreign men."

"Aye. I can *feel* that, more now that I'm near where it happened again. That will echo down the years, forward and back. Yet I'm not sure if that is all. I wish I could—"

A line of smoke suddenly rose from the hills behind the shore ahead. One long puff, then a pause, then another—what you got when you burned green boughs on a fire first made intensely hot, and then used a wet blanket to interrupt the smoke.

Órlaith watched the signal with satisfaction. One long . . . one long . . . three short, repeated and one very long to end.

That's it, by the Powers.

"You can put in, Captain," she said. "That's my Courier's code for *all present and accounted for at this location.*"

"Someone could have got it out of her, I suppose," Heuradys said.

At Órlaith's exasperated look: "I know, Orrey, but I'm your household knight. It's my *duty* to be paranoid about anything that could threaten you. You said yourself something was bothering you."

"Even if someone overran the whole of Stath Ingolf and took her prisoner, all she'd have to do is lie," Órlaith pointed out. "We arranged the code verbally, nothing written down, and it's a one-off."

"Good practice, my liege," Sir Aleaume said respectfully; he hadn't been a member of the . . .

Conspiracy, Órlaith thought. *Other people have to be honest around me, why shouldn't I follow suit? At least with myself!*

. . . conspiracy when Susan Mika, one of the Crown Courier Corps, joined it; her name meant Clever Raccoon in the tongue of the Lakota folk. Beside him, Droyn Jones de Molalla blinked, obviously making a mental note; he was a younger man, about John's age, tall and rangy and with the dark skin and curled hair of House Jones, the Counts of Molalla. Egawa grunted and nodded, understanding well enough. Then he said in Japanese:

"At home, perhaps not. The *jinnikukaburi* can twist men's minds, sometimes. But in ordinary terms, yes."

"Right, Your Highness," Feldman said, and relaxed a little as they turned and sailed close-hauled to the north with the wind broad on the starboard bow.

A channel was marked with buoys here, where the Dúnedain of Stath Ingolf maintained a landing at what had once been China Camp State Park. A quick check of the Castle Todenangst reference libraries via the heliograph net back at Montinore Manor on Barony Ath had shown that China Camp had been called that because Han fishermen had dwelt there for a while. The Dúnedain, more particularly her aunts Mary and Ritva, had renamed it Círbann Rómenadrim, which meant *Haven of the Easterners* in the secret language of that folk.

"Dúnedain?" Reiko asked, when she said that aloud. "So sorry, is that English?"

Her brother John pointed northwest, to the peninsula that closed that end of the bay. He was looking quite dashing in a prince-ish way with the golden spurs on the heels of his sabatons, his broad shoulders emphasized by a dark blue cloak of merino wool with a gold-embroidered hem, blowing in the sea breeze over his polished armor . . . and he was wearing a complete suit of white armor, burnished steel, kept bright by Evrouin's dogged care. The helmet resting at his feet with his shield had a crest of ostrich feathers dyed gold and purple.

And sure, when he's in full sunlight you can't look at him without getting spots before the eyes, which might actually be an advantage in a fight.

Órlaith suspected it was all carefully calculated, down to the way the wind tousled his seal-brown hair, which he also wore a bit longer than the usual Associate knight's bowl-cut. And the fact that the tooled leather of his sword-sheath contained, if you looked closely, something in musical notation.

So did the markings on the lute-case slung over his valet's back, and he'd *named* the instrument within. Azalaïs, after a famous female troubadour of ancient times, which she had to admit was a nice touch. Evrouin carefully kept it within reach for troubadourish moments of inspiration . . . except when they'd tied him up in a warehouse back in Newport, until he promised not to try to escape or report them to the High Queen.

And she had to admit John's manners had been perfect with Reiko, if also unaffectedly natural and friendly . . .

Except that in the way of nature John can no more not try to charm a female than he can not breathe, she thought a little sourly. *I love my brother, but sometimes I want to show it by clouting him upside the head, so I do, I do.*

He was using that charming smile as he spoke: "Dúnedain is what they call themselves, which means *Folk of the West*; or Rangers, in English."

"*Aa, so desu ka,*" Reiko said.

Which meant more or less *I see,* and they'd all picked up at least that much Nihongo since it was a common conversational placeholder, rather like *really*? or *is that so*? in English.

"A good place," Reiko said. "We have lookouts like that around all our settlements, there is nowhere far from mountains."

"By the mark . . . three! Full fathom three!" the leadsman cried as their lines came fully vertical.

"Mr. Radavindraban, do you make our mooring?" Feldman said, with his telescope trained to the left.

Port, Órlaith reminded herself.

From a cluster of low buildings on the shore there ahead a long pier ran out, much of it made of thick wooden posts that looked like old telephone poles and probably were. Two lines of them had been driven into the mud and secured by a lattice of more of the same, supporting a plank deck. A few single-masted fishing boats rode anchored to floats near it, but the portion farthest out that made the whole arrangement into a T about a hundred and fifty feet by fifty was a floating wharf, and vacant save for a pile of wooden barrels. Two figures stood on it, waving as they approached.

"Aye aye, Captain."

"Bring us in, then."

"Aye aye!"

"And we'll take sail on the mains now," Captain Feldman said. "Yarely, yarely."

The first mate nodded and brought his speaking-trumpet up again. The nauticalese included *let go the aloft halyards* and *outhaul the clew*. What it amounted to was letting the upper yards at the top of the sails down, and rows of sailors tying off the loose canvas at the bottom with the cords sewn into the surface of the sail. The ship came more upright, and then turned in towards the dock and leaned the *other* way.

Then a lookout cried: "Sail! *Sail ho! Three sail to sternward on the port . . . Christ, Haida! Orcas! Jesus Christ,* four *sail! Another one to the west, ship-rigged and a big'un!*"

Órlaith's head whipped around; the shapes were clear now, but still tiny-distant; three sets of sails to the south, two of them very hard to see because they were a neutral blue-green color . . . which meant pirates for certain, and probably Haida ones. The islanders of the far north weren't the only sea-thieves around, just the best organized and most effective, and their big low-slung sleek-hulled schooners didn't miss a trick. She couldn't see the fourth.

Captain Feldman was already training his telescope in that direction, then turning more directly south.

"The one coming in from the southwest is an RMN frigate, by the Lord of Hosts!" he said. "They must have run the Gate not long behind us . . . *Stormrider*, from the cut of her gaff. I thought she was in drydock in Victoria!"

Mother! Órlaith thought. *I should have known she'd act without hesitating!*

He turned the instrument. "The other three were hiding behind a wreck, that flat-topped one, a *tanker* they called them. Must have had a lookout up atop the hulk's funnel, that's taller than a masthead. Two of them are Haida—orcas right enough, big ones, three-masters, three to four hundred tons I'd guess. And that third one, I don't recognize her lines at all. The sails have slats and the bow is squared off above the cutwater. It's bigger than the *Tarshish Queen*, smaller than the frigate."

"*Bakachon!*" Ishikawa burst out. He used his own telescope: "The squadron flagship!"

Feldman looked at her. "I can evade the frigate, or the Haida and the Korean, but evading one means running into the other, Your Highness. I won't fight the Navy and I can't fight three ships the size of those with no maneuver room. If they can lay alongside or rake us from astern and bow-on we're all dead. I know a spot where I may be able to get out through the ruined bridge *if* they all start pitching in to the frigate, which they probably will, but I've got to start right now. Your decision—do we turn back?"

Órlaith took a deep breath, making her thoughts stop jabbering and dancing by an effort of will; from an expected meeting with friends to battle in the blink of an eye.

"Can you put us ashore?" she said. "There."

She pointed to the T-wharf; the figures there were close enough to be individuals now, and *they'd* noticed the other ships too now. One of them took off running, leapt to the back of a horse and heeled it into a flat-out gallop. Otherwise the long timber rectangle was empty except for the stack of big wooden barrels, hogsheads of some type.

"If we're ashore, the Navy has no reason to stop you. Nor a legal right, really."

"We can get you ashore if we use the longboats, and if we do it right now," Feldman said. "But I can't pick you up again. Not here. Getting out of the Bay is going to be damn tricky at best and Captain Russ of the *Stormrider* might arrest me now and argue about legal rights in an Admiralty court later."

"Then meet us at Albion Cove," she said. "If you can. If not . . . we walk, and fare you well. I have no complaints about how you kept up your end of the bargain."

He nodded and then bowed briefly and formally; there was a quiet approval in it as well as agreement.

"Your Highness."

"Right, everyone—let's go! Sir Aleaume! Load everyone, and fast, just grab the bugout bags. Shields up and eyes open, this may be a hostile landing. Those ships could have put landing parties ashore."

And what in the name of Anwyn's Hounds has been happening? she wondered, as the rush began to strip the covers off the longboats and swing out the davits; Reiko nodded to her guard-commander and Egawa barked his own orders.

The enemy . . . but the frigate? Mother must have been busy!

CHAPTER TEN

GOLDEN GATE/GLORANNON
(FORMERLY SAN FRANCISCO BAY)
CROWN PROVINCE OF WESTRIA
(FORMERLY CALIFORNIA)
HIGH KINGDOM OF MONTIVAL
(FORMERLY WESTERN NORTH AMERICA)
JULY/FUMIZUKI/CERWETH 14TH
CHANGE YEAR 46/FIFTH AGE 46/SHŌHEI 1/2044 AD

Captain Richard Russ, Royal Montivallan Navy, loved his trade and his ship *Stormrider*, and never more than on days like this—bright and sunny, just enough wind to blow spindrift from the waves, and a bit of tricky sailing in hand. The RMN's frigates were based on what the pre-Change world had called a *medium clipper* plan, and that meant speed and grace and handiness from the sharp bow to the elegant cruiser stern. As lieutenant, lieutenant-commander and captain he'd been through a great many storms, other perils, and chased pirates aboard her with only brief spells of duty ashore or on other vessels.

At home he was known as a solid quiet sort, a good Churchman devoted to his wife and three children and given to puttering around the rose-bushes in his garden, fighting nothing but the slugs among the cabbages and cucumbers and regularly attending the Astoria Chamber Music Society soirees where he played bass viol and his wife the violin.

At sea it was another matter, for another man.

Stormrider was Astoria-built; that was his native city, where he'd been born thirty-eight years ago and spent his first fifteen years as the second son of a middling-prosperous member of the Guild of St. Luke, patron of physicians. One who also owned a modest chunk of shares in a plant that preserved fish—their potted salmon and lobster were used at Court and by the Dukes of Odell, which had been a matter of immense pride to his late father, and still was to his mother, elder brother and three of his four sisters; the fourth was a nun-physician in the Sisters of Compassion and to give her credit genuinely didn't care about anything but God and her profession. He'd been headed for the Church himself, except that then the High King returned from the Quest and he'd eagerly shipped on a river-galley on the Columbia instead. Nobody had objected, in the wave of patriotic enthusiasm that had swept Montival just then, and on the whole nowadays he doubted he'd ever really had a vocation.

When they were off-duty, his Corvallan executive officer had been known to refer to him as *Purveyor to the Nobility and Gentry* because of the cursed potted fish. He laughed at that, mostly because it wouldn't do to get a reputation as a tight-arse; he'd learned that early, when his nick-name as a midshipman had been *Spotted Dick*.

The irony was that he didn't even particularly *like* the aristocracy. Astoria had been part of the Protectorate since early in the Foundation Wars, but it was also a prosperous chartered town of craftsmen and tradesmen and far-ranging merchants, self-governing under its Council of Guilds and Lord Mayor. It also wasn't an accident that he'd taken service in an arm that worked directly for the High Kingdom as a whole and operated strictly on merit.

Right now the XO was giving a sigh of relief. "*That* was tricky, Captain," she said, looking astern at the remains of the ruined bridge dropping out of sight to the south.

Russ nodded curtly. Running the Golden Gate had been relatively straightforward, but this one, the old Richmond bridge, had given him hives, even though they'd picked up a pilot in Astoria who'd been here recently. Virtually shanghaied him in the mad scramble to depart, in fact.

"We might wait for them here, where we can block the passage through the Richmond bridge," he said. "It's a chokepoint—cuts off San Pablo Bay completely."

She shook her head. "Captain, if anyone does know another way through Feldman's the man, and the *Tarshish Queen* draws a lot less water than we do, and since we can't actually shoot at them . . ."

Without that threat it was appallingly difficult to catch or stop an agile ship. You'd have to get close enough to launch a boarding grapnel; and it wasn't hard to pry one of those loose if it wasn't being covered by canister rounds or showers of crossbow bolts. It was like trying to catch a greased pig on a frozen river.

"I know Feldman a little—" she went on.

Like Moishe Feldman, Lieutenant-Commander Annette Chong came from a prominent Corvallan family, one with merchant-prince aspirations; there weren't so many of the magnates in the city-state that they didn't all have personal acquaintance, especially ones with shipping interests rather than banking or spinning-mills or foundries. Corvallis and his hometown were both basically mercantile oligarchies with some democracy stirred into the pot for flavor. Astoria was just more open about it, and possibly a bit less ambitious.

"—and sir, if you give him the least little wiggle room, all that you'll see is his topsails disappearing over the horizon. He's . . . clever."

Reluctantly he nodded. "You're right. Playing dodgem over the shallows . . . not a good idea. They'd be far too likely to get past us. Or decoy us onto something that would *really* give the shipyard work. And for that matter the Princess and Prince John might just go ashore."

His XO's hard amber-skinned face and slanted blue eyes were carefully impassive, even elaborately so. He hoped his own countenance was just as blank; there was obviously high court politics involving the Royal family here, which meant it was a good idea to carry out their orders without too much speculation if they could. The High Queen would presumably be grateful if everything went well, but the heirs would *not*. He hadn't heard that either the Crown Princess or Prince John were particularly vindictive, but remembering someone as the man who'd effectively arrested you . . . and considering that *she* would be running the whole of Montival and *he* the Protectorate later . . .

He ordered the leadsmen to the bows. Once you got beyond the old bridge passage was easier, but he'd still be much more relaxed when they reached the buoy-marked channel that led to the landing at the—absurdly named, in his private opinion—Círbann Rómenadrim.

Everyone rational knew that the Rangers' Historian had been a good Catholic and meant his tales of Middle-earth as a biblical allegory, after all. Even the Catholics among the Rangers treated it literally, though, and it didn't do to offend them.

Russ looked up at the rig stripped to fighting sail, and down the long sweep of the warship, noting the boarding and splinter nets taut and ready, the damage control parties standing by with their pumps and tanks, axes and crowbars and come-alongs, the pivoting launchers and their crews ready with boarding grapnels and coils of steel cable. The deck of the *Stormrider* was two hundred and twenty feet long not counting the bowsprit, flush from the break of the quarterdeck to the bow except for the hatchway coamings, and the broadside catapults were below on a full gundeck, fourteen to a side—the mark of a frigate, as opposed to the warsloops, which made up most of the RMN and carried their weapons topside. That gave the detachment of the Protector's Guard room to stand in armored ranks, like metallic black insects. Besides their usual gear they were carrying nets and poles, rather awkwardly, since those were tools more suited to a city Watch than the Protectorate's elite fighting unit.

He raised his voice slightly. "Sir Boleslav? If you would, please."

The thickset gray-eyed knight clanked up the quarterdeck ladder with his silent tow-haired squire Andrei at his heels carrying his helmet and shield; the senior nobleman's round head was shaven save for a plaited black scalplock over his right ear, which was a fashion in County Chehalis, something from the ancient homeland of House Stavarov. The effect was rather like a decorated bowling ball above the scoop-shaped bevor that covered his neck and chin up to the level of his lower lip; the Guard had chosen protection over sea-safety, which was within the nobleman's area of authority. What wasn't . . .

The soldier saluted first, fist-to-chest, and Russ returned it with the Navy's hand-to-brow. Their ranks were roughly equivalent, but his came from the High Kingdom, not the Protectorate, which gave him seniority; with the High Queen also Lady Protector the distinction was a little theoretical for now, but it was there. The orders from Her Majesty had specifically confirmed that, and to his credit Boleslav hadn't pushed at it . . .

Much, the naval officer thought.

"We will pursue, Captain?" the Guard officer said.

"We'll pursue by waiting, Sir Boleslav," Russ replied; technically the knight was a Captain of the Guard, but on a ship only one officer bore that title.

He indicated the mountains to port and the long low coastline and brown water ahead and to starboard, with the hills standing out farther north.

"That's the northern part of San Pablo bay. It's broad but most of it's shallow, and we have three times the tonnage and twice the depth to keel of Feldman's ship. Now that we're inside the Gate and the Richmond bridge he can't get past us. I don't want to get into a dodging contest with a ship I can't shoot at and that can go where I can't and can point a lot closer to the wind. We'll approach gradually, pin him, and then send a boarding party in the longboats. That's where your men come in. But we'll have to be very careful."

"This merchant is more nimble than a Royal warship?"

Russ controlled himself and pointed to the sails. "This is a *ship-rigged* vessel, Sir Knight. Mostly square sails. I'm *faster* than the merchantman with the wind astern or on the beam, but the *Tarshish Queen* is a *schooner.* Mostly fore-and-aft sails. Which are made to beat into the wind."

Boleslav frowned. "Her Highness and Prince John could go ashore," he said. "I am most straightly charged by the Queen's Majesty to secure their persons at any hazard."

"You can go ashore too if you have to, Sir Knight; that's why we have longboats on the davits," Russ said.

And did not add: *This ship isn't a destrier, and not just because it doesn't eat hay and shit. And why do you Associates all talk like old books?*

They just did. Considering who their grandparents had been, or who their grandparents had imitated and married, it wasn't even very surprising. Instead he went on aloud:

"And the commander of the High King's Archers should be here by now, or very shortly, to block things on the land."

Edain Aylward Mackenzie; if the High Queen told him to move quickly, he would move *quickly*. Possibly leaving Captain-of-Archers shaped holes in trees and mountains and any unfortunate human beings who got in the way.

Though with forty-odd men, that's a lot of land to block. Forty thousand *might make a go of it.*

"It is a large stretch of empty country," Sir Boleslav said, and scratched the shining dome of his head, possibly because it was a little sunburned. "Hard to find another small group."

All right, he's not actually stupid.

He grudgingly admitted that the Associate gentry were almost always brave, and seldom outright dim mentally; their faults tended to be the headlong arrogance and insularity born of growing up in a rural world where they were all the biggest bullfrogs in some small manorial pond surrounded by forelock-tugging deference, plus a tendency to see all life's problems as susceptible to solution via whacks with a war-hammer. But Boleslav's main qualification had seemed to be a stolid readiness to carry out his orders no matter what.

The knight surprised the captain by smiling slightly.

"So, we wait. Like waiting for a boar to come out of the thicket, eh?"

"Sail ho to starboard!"

The lookout's hail was punctuated by the shrilling of a whistle, something used only in emergencies. Russ snatched up a speaking-trumpet and shouted at the maintop:

"Where away? What ships?"

"Three sail, starboard, Captain! Orcas! Orcas! Three sail, two orcas, one some other sort of foreigner. Big ship, three-master, brigantine rig, sort of! They're coming out from behind a wreck near the Richmond shore!"

A ripple went through the frigate's crew at the lookout's hail, more a matter of tensing than movement; they'd all heard that cry of *Orca* before, though usually much farther north. Petty officers and bosun's mates cursed and shouted:

"Eyes on your work, damn your liver and lights! The officers will take care of the thinking!"

The sailor and the soldier looked at each other as the lookout repeated the hail, adding details with a slight rise to her voice. A lieutenant slung a long telescope over his back by its carrying strap, leapt and went up the shrouds like a squirrel with its tail on fire.

Russ put his own glass to his eye, and caught the flotilla coming out from behind the rusting canted bulk of one of the ancient world's absurdly large ships. The orcas were unpleasantly familiar, long low schooners with killer-whale figureheads and sea-colored sails. The other ship was basically a medium-sized three-master, but with details that precisely coincided with the reports on the ships who'd brought the men who killed the High King. A Korean warship, then; and apparently Montival was at war with Korea whether they wanted to be or not. It only took one to make a fight.

His lips curled back from his teeth a little. Avenging the High King was something that he would enjoy *much* more than getting involved in some sort of internal squabble in House Artos.

It probably wasn't worth the trouble now to try and raise a man-carrying observation kite . . .

"Haida; and a Korean," Russ said, and added gently: "I think that your men can stow those catchpoles and nets, Sir Knight."

Boleslav grunted, then smiled thinly. "Yes. This is a day for swords now, I think."

A shrug of armored shoulders. "Better so. I would rather fight to keep the heirs alive than chase them with a net like a butterfly to be pinned to a board."

At the naval commander's double-take: "I collect."

Doesn't pay to make assumptions.

Captain Russ ran the map through his mind, automatically adding wind direction and depths and known navigation hazards. He had to keep the heirs safe . . . but he didn't want to let them by him, either, if he could do that without endangering them.

The first priority is to keep those ships from getting past me.

"Chess is *my* hobby," he said. "And now if you would, I need the quarterdeck, Sir Boleslav. I hope it won't come to close acquaintance with our visitors, but if it does I'll be glad to have your men-at-arms."

The lookout called again: "The *Tarshish Queen*'s dropped anchor off the Círbann Rómenadrim wharf! Boats making for the shore!"

Russ hesitated for an instant, then shook his head and went on with what he'd just planned: his priorities had changed, and he didn't know and couldn't possibly find out exactly who was in those boats, they were too far away even to a lookout at the masthead. The Admiralty was in Astoria, the Marshal was in Portland, the High Queen was in Todenangst, and a small fleet of enemies was heading in the direction of the Crown Princess and the Prince, whether they were still on the merchantman or heading for the shore.

And I am here, *with a radically changed situation the high command won't know about for weeks.*

It was called "exercising initiative" if you did the right thing or got lucky or both, and "being a sacrificial goat" if you didn't. You couldn't just take refuge in following orders, either, not in the Royal Montivallan Navy you couldn't. This sort of thing was why they made you Captain, and why his teachers had told him *moral* courage was the first qualification for command.

"Helm! Come about, sou' sou'east. Number One, we'll rig the starboard catapults for bolt, if you please; firebolt. Load thermite. We'll start the dance with a warm salute from a distance."

CHAPTER ELEVEN

CÍRBANN RÓMENADRIM
(FORMERLY CHINA CAMP)
CROWN PROVINCE OF WESTRIA
(FORMERLY CALIFORNIA)
HIGH KINGDOM OF MONTIVAL
(FORMERLY WESTERN NORTH AMERICA)
JULY/FUMIZUKI/CERWETH 14TH
CHANGE YEAR 46/FIFTH AGE 46/SHŌHEI 1/2044 AD

Órlaith knelt against the stempost with her hand tight on the gunwale. The sailors were pulling hard in all the longboats, half-rising from their benches with a grunting chant and hauling until the strong ash shafts of the oars bent, anxious to get the heavy cargo of passengers ashore and get back to their floating home. With pirates close they'd feel as naked out here away from their ship as a turtle without its shell. Water purled back from the bow, and she could feel the dip and bite and surge, almost as alive as a horse. The *Tarshish Queen* carried more boats than most ships did because its master voyaged so often in places where regular docks and wharfs didn't exist. He'd taken on an extra set for *this* venture, just in case, and it thankfully meant that they didn't need multiple trips right now. Órlaith liked the way he prepared carefully.

You prepared as best you could. And then, as her mother had put it once when she was talking about the campaigns and perils of her youth, you rolled the iron dice.

Now to get ashore, pick up Karl and Diarmuid and their parties, and Morfind and Faramir and Susan Mika, hotfoot it over to Albion Cove—I'm fairly sure Baron Godric will help, that I am—and meet the Tarshish Queen *again. This is getting to be far too much like the joke about the sheep, the wolf and the cabbage! Then—*

Her head whipped back as one of the rowers found the breath to curse in amazement, and there was a huge rushing sound not quite like anything she'd heard before. The shore of the bay north of them, to the right, was a maze of small islands and stretches of renascent salt marsh and little wandering estuaries, intensely green with reeds and starred with great patches of golden jaumea and pinkish-blue gumplant. Trees were thick on the higher points, mostly willows.

The sound had been birds taking flight—thousands, tens of thousands, rising upward in twisting black skeins like veils of air and smoke, more and louder than she had ever heard.

Then she saw what they'd been fleeing and her cornflower-blue eyes went wide despite the sun-dazzle. Boats were coming out of the marshes. None of them were very large—most of them could be rightly called canoes—but there were . . .

"Morrigú!" Órlaith blurted, invoking the Shadow Queen in a voice that was half curse and half genuine prayer to the Goddess.

In Her aspect as the Battle Crow. *Badb Catha,* She who was terrible in majesty amid the shattering of spears.

"Holy Mary and St. Michael!" her brother John blurted from the rear of the longboat.

Forgetting to be suave and worldly for a moment, or grim and determined, and reverting to a very young man who'd trained to be a knight but never actually had anyone try to kill him.

"How many of the bastards *are* there?" he said.

Her mind gibbered slightly. *Scores of boats at least! Maybe more than a hundred!*

Then something in her mind said:

Ninety-eight visible just now. From one to a dozen Eaters in each. Over five hundred fighters, and there's more coming.

It was her own thought, but it had the same bronze-bell note as the

Sword gave her when she heard sincere belief. She could have counted the canoes and boats herself given time, but it was something to have a precisely accurate tally at her fingertips.

Heuradys spoke, but not to her. Quietly under her breath:

"Bright-Eyed One, Defender of the City, Lady of the Vanguard, lock shields with me today, I pray. And harken, O Alala, daughter of Polemos, to whom soldiers are given for their homeland's sake in the holy sacrifice of death. If this is the day the Spinners cut the thread of my life, I am ready to pay the ferryman."

And more boats were emerging as Órlaith watched, some showing as the Eaters cast off the nets of woven foliage that had hidden them. Canoes, and small pleasure craft of the ancient world—nothing more than twenty or thirty feet long, most smaller, all being paddled rather than rowed, though skillfully enough. She'd heard that the Eater tribes of the Bay used the like, fishing and hunting and fowling from craft they couldn't have made but could employ after a fashion—the aluminum and fiberglass hulls would last for a very long time. Perhaps if they'd been left to themselves long enough, another two or three or four generations, they'd have ceased to be Eaters at all, and become mere ordinary savages.

But they hadn't been left alone, and now they were taking the boats to war.

"Not feeling fey, I hope," she murmured to Heuradys.

From long practice they could understand each other with their voices pitched too low for others to follow.

"Oh, just touching all the bases, Orrey," she said.

"Well, this is indeed adventure, is it not?"

"No, then we'd be listening to someone like Johnnie here sing it," she said. "Now we're just doing it and it's a lot less enjoyable."

"I'm taking notes, don't worry," John said. "Evrouin has my pad, eh?"

The valet-bodyguard grunted sourly. He did have the lute-case over his back, but his hands held a glaive, the wicked blade and point of the polearm glinting and the hook at the rear sharpened like a razor on the inside of the curve.

Paddles flashed in the bright summer sun, throwing strings of jewel-like flashes into the air. The closest were long bowshot away, and she could hear the harsh rhythmic chanting of the paddlers as they whipped sprays of droplets aloft:

Ha-ba-da, *ha*-ba-da, endlessly repeated.

The chant spread like ripples in a pool, until the whole Eater host was grunting it in unison, and their paddles flashing in the same smooth unison as a well-practiced galley's crew . . . which was profoundly unnatural. You *couldn't* just duplicate the effects of long training. It took weeks of concerted effort to teach even willing and reasonably intelligent young recruits things like *pikes-up-files-left-face* without everything dissolving into a chaotic farce of collisions and tripping.

Moishe Feldman's ship had turned her prow south as soon as the boats were away, at anchor but with the sails loosely furled and ready to be hoisted in an instant when the boats were swung up again. She'd noted without understanding why that the sailors had rigged a second line to the anchor cable. Now faint commands came from the merchantman and deckhands hauled frantically on that stout cord that dipped out to meet the anchor's main line.

One of the oarsmen—they *had* to look behind—grunted in time with his efforts: "Skipper's got . . . a . . . spring . . . on . . . the . . . anchor . . . swing . . . her . . . 'round! Fast!"

The ship *was* swinging around, smooth and quick enough to make the hull heel over a little as it pushed against the still water of the anchorage. Suddenly it was hiding some of the onrushing small craft; another faint yell of orders, and then a massive *tung-CRACK* sound. It was tooth-gratingly familiar, heavy springs releasing and each set of twin throwing arms smacking into the hard-rubber stops at the end of their arc as a war-catapult cut loose.

She'd heard it hundreds of times or more in her life, at field-days when her parents watched troops drill, at feasts and festivals when they were used to throw bright colored lights into the night sky, or occasionally getting knocked out of a sound sleep when a castle garrison practiced, since her parents were most emphatically not given to disrupting training routines for their own convenience . . . but this was the first time she knew it was with deadly intent.

It was repeated eight times, one discharge treading on the heels of the last, and then the ship swung again, pivoting around the anchor cable even as it heeled and rocked back under the punch of recoil. The bow and stern-chasers pivoted on their trackways and cut loose as the ship moved.

A whistling sound went beneath the crashing noise of discharge; they were using beehive, canisters full of four-inch finned steel darts that flew free in a spreading cone just beyond the weapon's launching trough. Glimpses over the bulwarks showed the teams pumping at the rocking levers of the hydraulic cocking mechanisms. The Eater mass parted around the ship, streaming past . . .

Straight at us! she thought. *And none of them are running away!*

Turning around and paddling fast wouldn't actually *help*, but it was the natural reaction of undisciplined skulking savages suddenly caught in the open by modern weapons they couldn't understand or counter. If they were very fierce, trying to close with and board the *Tarshish Queen* and slaughter the crews of the catapults would be natural too. Instead the Eaters were doing the tactically perfect thing to accomplish the mission . . . if the mission was to kill *her*. And John and Reiko, of course.

They are *acting like automatons with no thought for their lives. Like breathing puppets. I don't think that happened even in the Prophet's War. Not on this scale, anyway.*

The end of the T-shaped wharf was directly ahead. The decking there was lower, floating on a thick raft of timbers so that it could adjust to the tides and linked to the pier running shoreward by a jointed section. It was much easier to get to from the water than the pier behind it, which stood about man-high above the surface for most of its length now that the tide was out.

Her cousins Morfind and Faramir were waiting on the dock, arrows on the strings of their powerful four-foot recurve bows of horn and wood and sinew; even then Morfind's fresh scar was a little shocking, the more so as her face was flushed with effort and excitement and brought out the purple of it. It must have gotten infected, but then, who knew what . . . no, she did know what would be on the blade of an Eater's axe. Both of them were in the mottled clothes Dúnedain wore as field gear, heavily coated with tan-colored dust and with the white Tree and Stars and Crown just visible on their jerkins if you looked carefully.

Let what's beneath your feet fight for you, her father had joked once, when he and some of his old friends were talking on a hunting trip and she'd been a silent presence hugging her knees at the edge of the light while the venison grilled. *It's so much easier that way than doing it all yourself, sure and it is.*

They could . . .

"Sir Aleaume, get your detachment out fast and form up at the base where the floating wharf joins the pier," she said crisply. "You from the *Queen*'s crew, you too, just leave the boats when we hit the wharf and everyone's out. You're not going to get back through that—"

She jerked her head at the mass of pursuing small craft and their chanting cannibal crews.

"—alive. You can rejoin your ship at Mist Hills with us, but stay back as much as you can."

Her mind was racing quickly; what could the sailors do? They were vastly more vulnerable to arrow-fire.

"Get ashore. Guard those horses," she added, pointing to the Dúnedain mounts, standing where the pier met the firm ground of the shore.

The bosun's mate in charge of the boats nodded; she thought he looked relieved that someone was taking charge of his group, because the choices ahead weren't the sort anyone sane *wanted* to be responsible for.

Because nobody *wants to be on that wharf when those canoes arrive. Which many of them are going to do, catapults or no. But every one Feldman kills is one we don't have to face . . . still, we can't just run, they'll catch us and swarm us under. We have to knock them back on their heels, give us time to find a point we can defend. How to do it, how to do it . . .*

Then she called to Reiko in the next boat, voicing her thoughts and adding:

"Your Nihonjin take the south side. We'll throw them back together and then retreat to the hills to make a stand on good ground—conform to our movement, there's no time for anything more complicated."

She got a nod and a brisk wave; the word was relayed to all four of the big launches. Reiko called:

"Captain Ishikawa and his sailors will keep the pier secure and retreat along it ahead of us!"

Órlaith waved assent. The Nihonjin seamen all carried *naginata*, polearms that gave them reach; if any of the savages waded through the mud to the pier they could strike downward.

Behind her the manyfold *tung-CRACK!* sounded again. The sound that followed was subtly different this time, a whistling moan, and she could hear something like hail on a tile roof combined with the sound a butcher's spring-driven bolt gun made when he stunned the beast before its throat was cut. Repeated many times. There was even a liquid *shurrussh*, as of water beaten into froth. This time they must be shooting canister, half-inch steel balls at point-blank range.

Mother-of-All, be merciful unto all Your children, she thought grimly. *We slay from need, not vainglory, to ward our lives and our friends, our homes and folk, obedient to our oaths and knowing that for us too the hour of the Hunter must come. As we are all Your children, so welcome all who fall here today to Your embrace, comrade and foeman. Greet them beyond the Western Gate, in the Land of Summer where no evil comes and all hurts are healed.*

Then the fresh redwood timbers of the wharf were approaching with shocking speed; there was a faint lemony scent to them, under the silt and fish and mud and tar—like any wooden structure in contact with the sea it had been painted with boat soap. Stronger than that was the harsh male sweat and leather and oiled metal of the men-at-arms around her.

As the boats approached the two Dúnedain drew and shot over the newcomers' heads, then shot again and again, a smooth steady knock-draw-loose almost worthy of a Mackenzie. They were shooting high, loosing with the points up at forty-five degrees, to drop the arrows down at maximum range.

She could hear the flat snap of the bowstrings and perhaps even the faint rushing whistle of the shafts. She could most definitely hear the shrieks of rage and pain where they struck.

Órlaith felt the skin between her shoulderblades crawl, underneath the armor and doublet. She knew exactly what that meant: if the enemy was in bowshot for the two Rangers, pretty soon they'd be shooting back. There would be a *little* time of grace, since the Eaters weren't as formidable with the bow, and they'd be in their canoes, but there were a lot of them. Her own bow and quiver were over her back, but the boat was too crowded and too unstable to make that worthwhile.

"Sir Aleaume, Droyn, we'll hold just in front of the pier," she said.

The knight had been taking a close look. He nodded and turned her general instruction into something more detailed:

"Men-at-arms and spearmen in walking castle formation. Droyn, crossbows firing rank-and-retreat on command at close range, we don't have many spare bolts."

He looked at her and she nodded confirmation before she went on:

"The Japanese will handle the other side. We'll back up to the pier, retreat down that to the shore and then make for that hill—"

She pointed to one not far from the shore, probably the one the smoke signal had come from; there was a low wooded strip just beyond the beach and sheds, then a fairly steep rise and higher rolling hills inland with scattered trees amid long golden-colored grass. She'd studied maps . . . but somehow she *knew* the lay of the land there now, the steepness of the slopes, the old laneway at the top of the ridge, the dense forest at the base of the ridge.

The knowledge had *fused* into an old-shoe familiarity like the woods around Dun Juniper or the streets of Portland. And the ground ahead *felt* welcoming, like a clap on the shoulder . . . from her father, at that. Possibly that was wishful thinking, but possibly not.

"—Then we'll make a stand as they come up the slope at us. We can't outrun them, they're not wearing anything but loincloths and bones through their noses, but they'll have no more coordination or discipline than a pack of feral dogs. I don't know why Eaters are after us—"

Though she suspected, particularly given the Dúnedain report of them cooperating with a Haida this spring. Doing certain things, living certain ways, made you more vulnerable to control by what her father had called the Malevolence and what Christians considered *their* God's great rebel Adversary. It opened a pathway . . . and then you walked down it and after a while there wasn't any way back and you didn't want to turn anyway. The Prophet's War had proved that, how it could steal on a person a little at a time.

Unfortunately it still seemed to be true, and she couldn't think of a better way to attract Its close attention than the existence of an Eater band. That attention would twist them to something even worse, and so on down a spiral that led to an oblivion with fangs at the bottom of the maelstrom. Best not to speak that aloud, though. It was uncanny enough to daunt even a brave man. The Royal kin stood for human kind with the Powers here in Montival; dealing with things of that sort was part of her job. Monarchs were High Priest or High Priestess as much as war-leaders and rulers.

"—But if we kill enough we may sicken the rest, and eventually the Dúnedain will come."

The two nobles nodded grimly, probably glad they were in their complete suits of plate—the men-at-arms had brought them on general principle, since they didn't take up significant room or weigh much on the scale of a cargo ship, though they hadn't planned on carrying them once they landed down south and set out overland into the interior desert. There hadn't been time to don hers in the scramble to leave the ship. Half-armor would have to do, and shields.

Things were starting to move very fast. Which was fortunate; there was no *time* to be afraid. Not so much afraid of death, as of dying with so much undone . . .

Out on the water the *Tarshish Queen* had slipped her cable and sheeted home her sails, with a final good-bye broadside of canister shot at the passing swarm of Eaters. The sails filled with a crack as a ripple of screams rose, but the thudding chant of the paddlers never ceased as they bobbed across the wake of the departing schooner.

A slightly larger boat held a man-sized drum, and as the canoes closed in on the wharf a savage with a finger-bone through his nose and his hair teased up into a thicket of bleached spikes began to beat it two-handed . . . with sticks that looked like and probably were human thighbones: boom-boom-*boom*-boom-boom-*boom* . . .

Órlaith didn't blame Feldman for making off in the least; for starters she'd just now told him to do exactly that. A moment more and the ship could have been swarmed by the Eaters and would certainly be pinned in this inlet by the approaching quartet, depriving her of any chance of a seaborne way to where she needed to go. And there was no time for the captain of the *Tarshish Queen* to ask her for fresh orders. In the ancient world there had been ways to talk over distances instantly, so that you could change plans on the fly. Modern times didn't work that way.

The floating wharf's decking was about a yard above the surface of the water. The whole construction was tarred, a massive raft held together by stainless-steel bolts and finished with a surface of three-by-four redwood planks, with tall piles driven deep in the harbor mud running through rings at each corner to keep it in the same place as it rose and fell with the water. Right now it was as low as it got, not quite touching the bottom of the bay but not far from it.

Two of the Protector's Guard reached out and caught the bumper of old cables along the edge with the hooks on the reverse of the blades of their glaives. They grunted with effort as they hauled on the shafts to hold the longboat tight against it. The Japanese poured ashore on the other end of the wharf, with Reiko calmly tying the chin-cords of her helmet as she stood among them. It made her face more of the bronze mask Órlaith had first seen, before the life behind started to peek out. Egawa was beside her, giving an occasional command in barking Japanese, and a young samurai behind her had the rayed rising sun of the *Hinomaru* banner standing up from a holder on the back of his cuirass.

Órlaith caught a bollard and stepped up with Heuradys at her heels unobtrusively ready to give her a shoulder in the backside. The sailors had leapt out with monkey agility; the armored warriors a bit more cautiously, not anxious to end their part in the battle early by drowning ingloriously in seven feet of muddy water. Even the massively buoyant structure swayed and dipped as nearly eighty humans swarmed over the edge in fighting gear, and several of her followers looked down at it dubiously as it moved under their feet.

The Japanese were a little less inhibited. Órlaith supposed it was because they came from a realm of islands where sea-travel and sea-fighting were part of everyday life. Montival was fringed by the ocean but most of her people would never see salt-water all their lives, much less voyage on it.

The warriors of Nihon instantly shook themselves into a well-organized mass, as colorful as a rank of exotic wasps with the lacquer of their suits, but as grimly businesslike as Boisean legionnaires in their own fashion. The long blades of the *su-yari* spears stood out as they were leveled; the men behind the rank of polearms had their seven-foot *bi-goyumi* bows in hand and the two swords tucked through their sashes and tied securely with the *sageo* cords. The Japanese sailors were farther back, their *naginata* ready. They didn't have the fine gear or ferocious stoicism of the Imperial Guard, but she thought they'd give a good account of themselves.

Hands seized Órlaith, and she almost drew and struck by blind reflex. Then she realized it was two of her men-at-arms, and that another pair were hauling the rest of her suit of plate out of a canvas sack someone had grabbed from her quarters during the scramble to get off the ship. The armor went on with a murmur of *Pardon, Your Highness*, and Heuradys got the same treatment a moment later, with less deference. The whole process was very quick with four pair of skilled hands working on the buckles, clasps and ties; everyone who fought in plate learned how to help other people on and off with it and she already had the cuirass on, which was the foundation. When they were finished she was covered from the bevor around her neck and chin to the articulated sabatons on her feet.

"Thank you, messires," she said shortly.

Fortunately they'd picked the foot-fighting set of faulds, the one that protected your backside too, rather than leaving it bare to help the leather on the seat of your breeches grip the saddle. The royal suit's relatively slight weight still surprised her, on the visceral level of memories graven in bone and muscle; the metal was a little thicker than its steel equivalent, but rustless, much stronger and much lighter.

Sir Aleaume blushed slightly when she shot him a glance but kept his eyes steady. He was her personal vassal now . . . but that didn't mean a noble wasn't supposed to exercise initiative, and she hadn't actually forbidden him to do it. She almost laughed aloud when she looked over at Reiko again, and saw the same process going on.

"Onegai itashimasu," Reiko said frigidly to her vassals as they began, though their actions were obviously unexpected.

That meant *thank you for this favor you're about to do,* more or less.

And a bitten-off: *"Domo,"* followed.

Which meant *very much* literally, and a brief curt *thanks* in terms of true equivalents.

The two men strapping the protective *suneate* to her legs both bent their foreheads to the dock for an instant after they finished, presumably in apology for touching the sacred and quasi-divine Imperial person, before she snapped brusquely that they should get back to their places.

Órlaith turned and looked seaward, sparing only one swift look at the departing schooner, a shape of strangely calm beauty as it heeled to the wind and its sails made a geometric off-white tracery against the dark blue of the water and bright blue of the nearly cloudless sky. The lunging bows of the canoes of the cannibal host were much closer and uglier, a clash with the warm comeliness of summer land and sea.

She gave a quick glance to either side. The Japanese and her own men-at-arms had formed up quickly; everyone looked concerned, and well they might, but nobody was panicking.

Not even me, and how I wish I could! she thought with some distant part of her mind. *This would be a lot easier if Da or Mother was here to tell me what to do!*

She'd been determined to strike out on her own, as her parents had done on the Quest. Now she was getting what she'd wanted . . . Someone was always listening when you made a wish, and some of those Someones had a pawky sense of humor.

John had his shield settled on his arm, with the Sword and Crown of House Artos on it crossed with the baton of cadency. He looked a little white about the mouth, enough to remind you that he was still short of twenty years, but steady enough.

Says the crone of twenty-one! she thought. *And to be sure,* he *isn't responsible for how this turns out!*

"The plumes on the helm work, Johnnie. You finally look taller than your big sister," she said lightly, and got a smile in return, and a lessening of the tension around his eyes.

Whatever she decided, folk would die because of it. It would almost be easier to die herself.

"Shields and visors!" Sir Aleaume snapped. "Blades! Protective formation!"

The men-at-arms knocked their visors down with the edges of their shields, a multiple metallic *shink-shink* sound, transformed from men to steel figures faceless save for the menacing black vacancy of the vision slits, like the fabled robots of ancient times. They drew their longswords with a slight hissing slither of steel on wood and leather greased with neatsfoot oil and held them in the ready position over the shoulder, hilt first. The front rank knelt, their kite shields braced against shoulder and the wharf's deck to make a wall, and then the second did likewise in a smooth ripple. Only the best few applicants were allowed into the Protector's Guard, and they practiced continually.

The points of glaives bristled forward as the footmen in their three-quarter-armor stepped up behind the knights and squires whose duty and honor it was to put their bodies in the front line against the foe, poised ready to chop and hook and thrust around and between them.

"Cousins!" Órlaith called to the two Dúnedain; they were literally that, the children of her father's half-sisters.

She pointed to the dozen large barrels on the south end of the wharf, which were full of *something* from the way they were making the structure dip in that direction even with the men-at-arms on the other end.

"Those tuns! What's in them?"

There wasn't much doubt, she could smell it and it was among the most familiar of scents around any sort of dock, but best to make sure. Faramir replied as he shot again.

"It's boat soap . . ."

Then with a double-take while his hand reached for his quiver, he blurted in amazement:

"When did you start speaking perfect Sindarin, my lady kinswoman?" he said in that language.

Just now! Órlaith realized, as the elegant liquid complexities settled into her mind.

She'd had no more than a few words before. Rangers all spoke what they called the Common Tongue as well, though they mostly used *Edhellen* among themselves.

She had the Sword . . . but it was a little eerie even so, and his eyes widened as she tapped her hand on the hilt. Then she dismissed it for now.

What mattered was the information and the idea it spawned, not how she'd gotten it. *Rock the enemy back on their heels while we break contact* suddenly became something much more concrete.

CHAPTER TWELVE

GOLDEN GATE/GLORANNON
(FORMERLY SAN FRANCISCO BAY)
CROWN PROVINCE OF WESTRIA
(FORMERLY CALIFORNIA)
HIGH KINGDOM OF MONTIVAL
(FORMERLY WESTERN NORTH AMERICA)
JULY/FUMIZUKI/CERWETH 14TH
CHANGE YEAR 46/FIFTH AGE 46/SHŌHEI 1/2044 AD

Moishe Feldman grinned tautly as the *Tarshish Queen* gathered way, sailing southward on a beam reach with the wind out of the west. Perhaps it was a fancy to feel that the ship was bounding forward like a horse given its head, but that long swooping grace was reality enough. The sheer joy of sailing was one reason he did what he did for a living.

He deliberately didn't look back at the longboats pulling for the wharf. For one thing, while he was perfectly willing to kill the Eaters—order it done, but it was the same thing in the eyes of the Lord . . .

And as Raba says in the "Tractate Sanhedrin," if a man should come up against you to slay you, forestall him by slaying him first, he thought automatically. *Which is a command, not a permission.*

. . . he didn't like to dwell on it more than he must. For another, looking back would make him wonder if they'd made a terrible mistake by putting the Princess and her brother ashore.

"Tide table and chart," he said quietly, and one of the quarterdeck gang ran to bring them.

He checked them, and looked at the chronometer repeater needle by the binnacle.

"Tide's making," he said quietly to the First Mate, and tapped a position on the chart.

"Not much yet, Captain, and we'll need more if you're going to try *that*," Radavindraban Madhava said. "I do wish we weren't missing those boat crews. I am so-certainly not liking heading into a fight shorthanded."

Radavindraban was an excellent navigator and First Mate in general, but Feldman thought he tended to be a little pessimistic. *He* thought Feldman was too inclined to expect things to work out, which was a new experience for the merchant.

"We'll manage, and by the time we've . . . arranged things . . . the tide will be up quite a bit. The boat crews may be safer where they are, too," he said, and leveled his telescope.

The images of the four ships sprang out at him as he scanned to the southward. The fallen Richmond bridge sealed off the Bay in that direction; *Stormrider* was pushing straight through towards him.

At a guess he plans to anchor off the wharf at Círbann Rómenadrim with cables fore and aft and springs on them, and make them come bows-on into his broadsides if they want to try getting past him. Conservative plan, but workable.

"If it weren't for the frigate we'd be facing a bit of a sticky wicket," the First Mate said.

He'd already spoken English . . . of a sort . . . before Moishe Feldman had hidden him from a howling mob in Jayapura and smuggled him out in a space hollowed out under a load of pink satinwood where the Raja's men hadn't thought to look. He still had a strong accent and used odd turns of phrase now and then. Feldman caught the meaning from the context.

It had taken a while to realize he was also an educated man with a talent for mathematics, a good grounding in navigation, and though not someone who went looking for trouble also a nasty customer in a fight. Quick-witted as well as intelligent, a good bargainer and honest in an unsentimental to-the-inch way, though his religion had a truly strange set of taboos, particularly about food. And he played a wicked game of chess.

In fact, he'd make a pretty fair Jew, the captain thought. *If it weren't for the multi-armed deities.*

As he watched, the three enemy ships parted to either side of the frigate, the two orcas going west and the Korean east . . . which confirmed his guess about their draught. That put the ship from Asia in the same deeper channel the *Stormrider* was using, which was more-or-less navigable all the way to the ruins of Sacramento, though the wrecks made it tricky.

"Steady as she goes, Mr. Radavindraban," Feldman said. "The first act of this comedy is going to play out before us."

"What are they trying to do, Cap'n?" he asked.

"From their courses, they're trying to get to Círbann Rómenadrim, where our . . . passengers . . . landed," Feldman said. "Either that, or bracket the frigate and sink or take her. Or both."

"And attack us too, yes, perhaps," the First Mate said.

"Oh, it's just the pirates and the foreigner who want to *attack* us. The frigate would probably settle for arresting us, if they manage to find the time."

Neither of them laughed, but he could see a pawky expression in the other man's dark eyes.

"As if they were expecting us," Radavindraban said thoughtfully. "Us, but not I think the frigate, no indeed."

Feldman nodded; he intended to promote the man soon, and that quick grasp of situations was one big reason why. "What they're doing is good tactics, if that frigate hadn't been there."

"But the frigate, it is here, Cap'n. Not good form to keep to a plan where circumstances have changed."

"The three of them outweigh and outshoot *us* quite comfortably," Feldman agreed.

I could take either of the orcas, maybe both. But not all three . . .

"But *Stormrider* changes the equation. Ah, here goes the Queen's Pawn," he observed aloud.

More sail broke out on the topmasts of the *Stormrider*; frigates were *fast.* For a ship-rigged vessel the frigate was extremely stiff, too, sagging very little to windward. That was the advantage of the deep keel.

The naval commander had run up *Heave to immediately and stand by to be boarded in the name of the High Kingdom* to his signal hoists, but that was pro-forma, to make the daily logbook entries look tidy.

And . . .

"There they go," he said.

They were too far away to hear the frigate's massive eighteen-pounder catapults cutting loose, the more so as they were on an enclosed fighting deck. It would be earsplitting *there*, with fourteen of them loosing within a second of each other. Weapons that size would rip *his* ship's frames loose from the scantlings after half a dozen broadsides even with hydraulic recoil systems, but they had their uses.

The broadsides she loosed were like elongated flickers reaching out towards the Korean. The nearly invisible passage told an experienced eye that she was shooting bolt, finned javelins about four feet long. The arcs were high, which meant they were aimed upward for maximum range. Bolt went a lot farther than round shot, though they did less damage when they got there.

Usually, he thought.

"I would be saying it is about a thousand meters . . . yards," Radavindraban said.

"Not extreme range, but close," Feldman agreed. "Another hundred, hundred and fifty, maybe."

Six bolts hit the water before the Korean's squared-off bows, beautifully placed for distance but a bit off on bearing. Through the telescope he could see the white bursts of froth where they struck, and then an eruption of spray and smoke.

"Firebolts," he said. "Thermite."

Bolt warheads from the massive naval weapons had three pounds of the mixture, and the steel shell turned to molten gobbets almost immediately on impact.

Not what you want slammed deep into your hull, he thought dryly.

Pirates usually wanted to take ships, not sink or burn, and rarely used firebolt or napalm shell. They kept some on hand though, for occasions when it was a matter of win or die . . . such as fighting a warship.

"Making good practice for a moving target at that range," Feldman said judiciously of the *Stormrider*'s catapult crews.

Four more of the bolts hit in the enemy ship's wake, doing no harm except to the taxpayers of Montival and any fish close enough to be quick-broiled. That left four. He saw three flashes of impact; one more must have landed short or gone over.

Very *good practice for that range.*

The Korean hadn't opened his portlids yet, the swinging hinged chunks of the deck bulwark that let the catapults fire and protected them when they didn't. Two more of the firebolts hit, ignited and then fell off into the water of the Bay. You could put a slab of steel plate on the outside of the portlid, if not over your whole hull.

The third hit lower. Fire and smoke spurted out instantly and the melted-through shaft of the bolt fell away, and a there was a scrimmage of motion difficult to make out at this distance even with a telescope. From the fact that the fire didn't spread it was apparently a damage-control team that knew its business, wielding axes and boring-tools to cut out the wound in their ship's fabric and packing it with dry sand to extinguish any sparks.

"Going to be interesting," he murmured; there hadn't been many pitched battles at sea since the Change, not around here.

It all looks so bloodless at a distance, he thought, remembering screams and stinks and the sound of splinters and edged metal whirring by. *A pawn doesn't shriek for its mother when a knight takes it.*

His First Mate sucked in his breath sharply as the orcas turned in towards the frigate, one each at bow and stern. With the wind out of the west—very slightly north of west—the Haida had the weather gauge. That meant that the *Stormrider* could avoid them only by turning downwind. The Korean to windward couldn't head right for the frigate, but he was turning to close as fast as he could.

It was very difficult for sailing ships with sea room to force an unwilling opponent to fight. But here there wasn't much room and all parties seemed eager to pitch in.

"Starboard your helm, five degrees right rudder," Feldman said, and the crew at the wheel repeated it back.

The *Tarshish Queen*'s bowsprit slid slightly to the right, westward, and she heeled a little more sharply; he looked up at the sails and shook his head, and the First Mate lowered his speaking-trumpet.

"We are going to go by?" Radavindraban said.

"We're going to give a very convincing imitation of an intention to do just that," Feldman said.

He watched the maneuvering ships calmly, glancing up occasionally at the pennants at the mastheads to check on the wind. At sea, things happened with majestic deliberation, until suddenly they happened very quickly indeed; it was easy to forget that you were dealing with massive objects weighing hundreds of tons but moving as fast as a trotting horse. The *Tarshish Queen* was quiet, only the odd murmur of voices and the creak and groan of the ship working and the thutter of sails as the angles changed and ropes were adjusted.

Feldman said more formally: "Mr. Mate, load the forward four port-side catapults with round shot. The sternward four with napalm shell. Make ready, if you please. The starboard catapults to load in opposite order."

Radavindraban turned and barked the orders. Feldman glanced up at the pennants again. The orcas were closer now, though it was probably his imagination that he could smell the lingering stink of fear and misery from them. Apparently they'd decided to close on the frigate and ignore him. Which was certainly a good thing with the boat crews gone, not to mention the Crown Princess and her men-at-arms and their Japanese equivalents. The *Tarshish Queen* wasn't in a condition to fight a boarding action with one pirate right now, much less two. With a little luck, he wouldn't have to.

He murmured under his breath:

"Praised be the Lord, my Rock, who trains my hands for battle and my fingers for war . . . Flash forth lightning and scatter them, Lord of the Universe: send Your arrows

and confound them, stretch out Your hand from the heights and deliver me from the stranger whose mouth speaks lies, whose right hand is the hand of deception!"

"The wharf is on fire, Cap'n," Radavindraban said quietly when the catapults were ready.

Feldman spared a quick glance over his shoulder. Not just on fire, but ablaze, like a stacked bonfire or a pagan funeral pyre. Damp timber baulks didn't go up that way unless you used something that helped it along quite a bit. The Eaters streaming by the *Tarshish Queen* to the attack had looked very focused, but not particularly technologically advanced, to put it mildly. It must have been the Princess somehow, she was a clever one in her odd way . . . and there was that entirely disturbing Sword . . .

His mind skipped through the things that might be available on a dock, and he smiled grimly as he turned back to his own task.

"I think that's a *good* sign, Mr. Mate."

The frigate looked bigger and bigger as you got closer, its masts towering to the sky. But a ship under sail was a thing in dynamic tension, huge forces barely contained. As he watched a bolt clipped the spar of the maincourse just where it crossed the mast, braced around as the ship ran with the wind abeam. Feldman winced in involuntary sympathy. The great length of wood—seventy-five feet of prime Sitka spruce thick as his waist in the center—was already bent like a longbow as it took the strain of the vast mainsail's draw. Now it flew asunder with a sudden snapping violence as it parted at the point of maximum bend. Splinters would be flying like arrows, and some of them would be as long as catapult bolts, too.

The *Stormrider* slewed and heeled as the tension came off her standing rigging. Lines broken and cut swung like curling whips in the hands of invisible demons. Hands ran upward on the ratlines to make emergency repairs, with catapult bolts whirring through the spaces aloft and cutting more line; the pirates and the Korean were probably using sickle-heads designed for that purpose . . . though they'd just as easily chop a human form in two along the way. The *Stormrider*'s headlong rush slowed, and she heeled slightly westward into the wind under the unbalanced stress on her remaining sails. A broadside of round shot lashed the water just short of the orcas as the malignantly bad timing of the injury to her sails threw off the frigate's aim. The orcas had taken Feldman's bait; they were used to merchantmen trying to run away from them and were ignoring him for now.

Normally I would *run myself*, Feldman thought. *It's not my job to fight pirates unless they can catch me and it* is *the Navy's.*

Occasionally . . . well, honest sailors hated and despised sea-rovers.

Both orcas turned and heeled with beautiful smoothness, cutting straight in towards the *Stormrider* and letting their sails out gullwing-fashion as they ran downwind, sacrificing their own firepower to close as quickly as possible while they hoped not to be battered to pieces or set aflame. Feldman put the spyglass to his eye to check their exact courses, and got an unpleasant view of the crews of their bow-chasers and broadsides pumping frantically.

I was right, he thought. *Heading for the frigate's bow and stern, they want to put in a broadside of case-shot and board right on its heels.*

The Korean was to leeward and couldn't do more than slant a bit more closely, but it should still be alongside in five minutes or less.

"Prepare to port your helm," he said to the crewmen at the wheel. "Mr. Mate, ready with the port broadside. Tell the crews they'll be switching after the first."

"Sir, Medical Officer Suarez reports that Lieutenant-Commander Dirkson won't be up anytime soon. She had to cut for the splinter in his stomach and he's under sedation."

Captain Russ suppressed an impulse to swear as the medical orderly saluted and gave his message. Dirkson had been in charge of the gundeck. The impact and rending crack overhead as the round shot struck the spar only made him snarl silently, though the sound was like his own legbone snapping, and he staggered slightly as the—now—badly mistimed broadside added to the unnatural movement of his ship. A volley of orders set the deck-crews hauling to adjust the set of the other sails to compensate, but nothing was going to change the fact that they'd lost a fifth of their sail surface and it had taken their edge in speed with it.

We're not going to make that anchorage in time to receive the enemy, he thought. *Not now. All right, let's see if we can encourage the enemy to make an unforced error.*

"Number Two," he snapped to his executive officer. "Go below and take command of the gundeck, keep up the fire on the Korean. Leave the orcas to me, just keep all catapult crews to starboard, and hammer the foreigner hard and fast until further orders or you hear the *receive boarders*. But have the starboard side loaded with beehive and case-shot, alternating. Be ready to switch the crews back and give one broadside at close range."

She left at the run. It was good to have subordinates who didn't need the t's crossed and the i's dotted. The loss of the spar was like a wound to one of his children. But unlike children naval vessels didn't exist for themselves, and *Stormrider* wasn't his yacht either. This was a warship, and it was here to win victories for Montival, even if it meant wrecking her and killing the crew.

There are times you have to be ready to destroy the thing you love, he thought grimly. *Not to mention yourself.*

"Steady, helm," he said.

"Aye aye, stea—" the petty officer at the wheel began.

There was a whistling, and then on its heels a soft massive sound, a *thuckk* with a crunch underneath it. A bolt had come arching down, a long-range shot from the Korean warship but still too fast to see except as a blurring flicker in the corner of the eye. It took the petty officer under the one armpit and slanted down and the chisel-shaped head exited in a shower of blood and scraps of meat and organ and bone just below the floating rib on her other side. The whole four-foot length of metal and hardwood wasn't perceptibly slowed either by the woman's body or by the light brigandine she'd been wearing—some of that came out as bits of metal and leather. The instantly-limp body pitched past him.

The bolt went by close enough that he could feel the wind of its passage, then sank two feet deep into the double deck planking and the oak carlins beneath. Russ was moving before he was fully conscious of the spattering gout of hot blood across his face. He spat to clear his mouth as he jumped to the bench and gripped the spokes of the forward wheel. The seaman on the rear wheel hadn't moved, but the cords of muscle on his bare arms stood out as he took a strain meant for at least two.

"Sir Boleslav!" Russ shouted.

The reliefs took the wheel. Captain Russ walked to the quarterdeck rail and called down to where a massive scrap of the mainsail had landed and covered most of the Protector's Guard men. He pitched his voice to carry; it was a skill you learned at sea with the constant burr of ships working and the wind in the rigging.

"Keep your men hidden, Sir Knight! Stay under the sail!"

Right now none of the enemy could see the *Stormrider*'s deck, since she rode so much higher than they did. That wouldn't last long, since the lookouts on their mastheads would have an angle of sight quite soon . . . but human beings were prone to seeing what they expected, and especially so in the heat of action.

"They'll grapple at the stern and bow!" he shouted, pointing forward and astern. "Be ready to move on my signal!"

The Chehalis nobleman gave him a fist-to-breast salute to show he'd heard; he barked his own orders, and eighty pairs of hands gripped the sail from beneath and spread it farther.

A glance to starboard showed the Korean ship still closing as fast as they could . . . despite a snapped spar of their own, on the gaffsail of their mizzen, and bulwarks beaten into splinters with several catapults lying dismounted. She was on fire in several places, but none of them had gotten out of hand yet and it looked as if their damage control parties were still operating. Blood was trickling out of her scuppers, and bodies were pitched overside to make room.

Plenty of guts and seamanship there, Russ thought. *But then, the same's true of the Haida.*

Stormrider had hammered them with round shot for several broadsides now, and their lighter structure wasn't taking it well. Five of *their* shot came aboard at that moment; two cracked off the bulwarks, two a little lower down into the hull at gun-deck level, and one took a seaman's head off cleanly as an axe as it blurred across the deck and out over the starboard side. The body fell, all the blood in it pouring out in seconds.

Their aim was excellent, but the more massive scantlings of the frigate would take it better. The range was closing, and a dozen of the eighteen-pound globes of cast steel smashed into the foreign warship, tearing gaps in the thin sheet-metal antifire sheathing, battering at timbers and sending lethal sprays of splinters pinwheeling across the deck.

"Mr. Smith!" he called.

A midshipman looked up from where he was overseeing a squad putting together boat pikes, fitting the rear shafts into the collars that turned the weapons into sixteen-foot poles that could be jabbed across the gap between two ships lashed together in a boarding action.

I am running short of lieutenants, he thought before continuing briskly, ignoring the young man's blink of horror at the way he looked before he realized it wasn't the Captain's blood.

"When the pirates attempt to board, their grapnels will be allowed to hold."

"Hold, sir?"

"Yes. Notify the other anti-boarding parties immediately, report to me when you've done it. And direct the grapnel launchers to be ready to put one each into them if they try to disengage, but only on command."

The midshipman was a youngster from somewhere far inland—the Navy tried to recruit from all over Montival, not just the parts near the coast—and looking desperately earnest under the scraggly blond nothing-much he fondly thought was the beginning of a cropped nautical beard. For a moment his face went slack with astonishment. Then he proved he was intelligent as well as disciplined and brave and glanced at the sail hiding the Protector's Guard contingent. He saluted and dashed away, hop-stepping over a body . . . or part of a body, at least.

Normally two large orcas would have some chance in a boarding action . . . but with the Guardsmen on board things were not normal.

"Not long," Russ muttered to himself, turning his eyes back to the orcas.

The reaver vessels were nearly bow-on to him now. The forward catapult of one cut loose—they were close enough now for it to sound quite loud even over the general din—and something flashed half-visibly through the air above. A cable and set of heavy wooden blocks fell into the netting over his head, and the gaffsail on the mizzen began to wobble. He could feel that through the soles of his feet and hear it as a rapid drumfire cracking sound; it dampened down as a rush of riggers went by overhead with their clasp-knives in their teeth, throwing themselves at the damage and tying down and splicing.

Driving in to board while the Korean distracted us would be a very good strategy if all I had was the sailing crew and the usual marine contingent.

He nodded, silent behind the blood-spattered mask of his face.

Of course, then I wouldn't have kept this course or given those orders.

He spared a single glance for the merchantman he'd chased all this way, and was mildly surprised to see him coming up quickly on the port bow, and not nearly as far away to the westward as he'd expected if they were trying to make the run through the ruins of the Richmond bridge while the warship occupied the pirates.

I wonder what he's *up to?*

"Port your helm, fifteen degrees left rudder," Moishe Feldman barked.

The wheels spun and the *Tarshish Queen*'s bowsprit pivoted from west of south to due south and then east of south. Now they were to windward of the frigate and both the Haida craft attacking it, and that meant they could close quickly if they chose. As they did the First Mate's voice boomed out through the speaking-trumpet to the deck crews, and they paid out the sails as the wind came more abaft the beam.

The merchant schooner's head began to plunge a little, and more spray came over the bow. Some of the spindrift reached the quarterdeck, and he blinked the spray out of his eyes. The two orcas swayed just enough to bring their broadsides to bear on the frigate and loosed, hammering scraps and splinters out of the bulwarks, then turned back and crashed alongside the Royal Montivallan Navy ship.

There was a deep *bunng* sound as their grapnel throwers released. The anchor-shaped grapnels flew up and were winched tight, and boarding ramps normally set into the deck rose and toppled forward, the spikes under their forefronts crashing down to nail the vessels together. Haida crowded forward onto the ramps, a hail of arrows from their archers arching over their heads to clear the way as they brandished spears and war-clubs and cutlass-like swords. A roaring chorus from hundreds of throats:

"Huk! Huk! Huk!"

It was the battle-cry they used when they drove home an attack regardless of cost, aiming to swarm the frigate under in the first rush. The joined ships were close to him now, the bow of the *Stormrider* barely a hundred yards away. He could hear the roar of voices—and then the deep shout of:

"Haro! Haro, Portland! Holy Mary for Portland!"

—as the black-armored forms of the Protector's Guard rose from behind the frigate's bulwarks at bow and stern, their shields blazoned with the Lidless Eye raised high and blades poised to strike. He estimated that there must be nearly a hundred of them, half men-at-arms and glaivesmen sheathed cap-a-pie in plate. The longswords and war-hammers smashed down, and the pirate boarding-parties bunched up, crowding into a solid mass on their foredecks and the ramps. Crossbowmen shot from the frigate's waist, taking the massed pirates in defilade, backed by crewmen and marines with long boarding-pikes.

"Aha, I didn't expect that," Feldman murmured to himself. "He was luring them in."

The portlids of the frigate's broadside suddenly snapped up in unison with a squeal and clack of mechanisms, revealing the throwing troughs of the catapults, the arms folded back to each side at maximum cock.

Tung-*Crack!*

Under that came a humming like malignant wasps; case-shot or beehive or both. The war-chant turned to screams as the hundreds of steel balls and darts slashed into them, though some beat the water between the two pirate vessels to froth or passed over the orcas' sterns.

It was time. Feldman raised the speaking-trumpet and called to the catapult crews who crouched along the deck—thinner than usual, but for one broadside where you didn't need the pumps three to a catapult would do.

"At the pirate's stern, fire as you bear! Wait for your shot!"

Each catapult-captain raised an arm for an instant in acknowledgment, not looking up from where they peered through the sights, left hand on the traversing wheel and the right on the elevation. The pirate's stern-chaser and the *Tarshish Queen*'s bow pivot catapult cut loose at almost the same instant as their bowsprit crossed the Haida's stern, and Feldman cursed to himself. *Someone* over there had been alert . . .

And may he grow like an onion, with his head in the ground! he thought.

Tung-CRACK.

The pirate round shot snapped out in a blur, and there was a loud painful-sounding crunch from the waterline just at the bow, a quiver through the mass of the ship. Radavindraban cursed in his own musical tongue and leapt down the companionway at the head of a damage-control party; that had probably opened the hull at the waterline, and would have to be plugged immediately, even if it meant throwing stores aside.

Feldman nodded grimly as he watched glass and wood fly from the orca's sternquarter windows; his own bow-chaser's shot going in. Then the broadside catapults cut loose, one after another at intervals of less than a second. The first four solid round shot all struck around the same spot—even at close range that meant his crews were *good*. Light flared from the throwing-troughs of the last four catapults on the port side as a crewmember stepped in with a lit towmatch on the end of a pole to light the fuel-soaked cord that wrapped the glass napalm shells.

Tung-WHACK, four times repeated, and a shudder through the deck. Below him along the deck the twin throwing arms of the catapults slammed forward into the stops, *here* and then *there* without any visible trace in between as the lanyards were pulled. The cable between whipped the carrier down the trough and the shells went on their deadly way.

There was always a bit of mental stress—something you felt in your gut and groin and the back of your throat—when you fired napalm shell. It wasn't entirely unknown for them to burst in the trough during firing . . . if you hesitated, and fear could make you do that.

Irrational, but there you are, it's people.

This time nobody hesitated, and the shells struck with malignant precision. The preceding four solid round shot had smashed open the stern windows of the pirate schooner and carried on into the interior.

And since orcas were flush-decked, beyond the captain's cabin and a few canvas-and-wood partitions was the open hold running forward to the forecastle, for stores and cargo—loot and shackled slaves, for an orca. Four napalm shells slammed through the tangle of broken canvas and tarred wood. The glass shattered, igniting the clinging liquid within, sending gobbets of burning napalm and burning wood and cloth forward into what amounted to a dry wooden box scattered with piles of *more* dry canvas and tarred rope and highly flammable naval stores.

Flame belched out of deck housings and portholes, and black smoke followed. Another gout of flame, and another, and then a bigger one, far bigger than the shells could account for and quicker than mere wood and cloth and rope could catch fire.

The careless mamzrim *must have left one of their own chests of fire-shell open.*

"Hard a'port! Port your helm, full port!" Feldman said sharply, suppressing an impulse to duck as someone on the stern of the ship he'd just destroyed managed one last arrow; it plunked quivering into the deck not far from him.

Then: "Let go the sails, on the run!"

The *Tarshish Queen*'s bow slewed eastward again, this time as fast as the rudder could push it, coming around in a half-circle as the ship did a majestic pinwheel. The sails came down with a rush and a whapping thump, the rigging giving a deep nerve-racking twang as it stopped the upper booms from falling into the folds of canvas.

Moments later the ship was traveling along its previous course, more slowly but stern-first; they'd be nearly vertical to the second pirate as they passed.

The catapult crews ran, leapt and dodged over to the opposite rail. Behind the wheel the heavier stern-chaser rumbled along the steel tracks laid set flush into the deck over the fantail.

"Fire as you bear!"

The stern-chaser let loose, an ear-hurting sound like steel planks slapped together right next to your ear, the crew cheering as the heavy ball cracked into the second orca's rudder. The four solid shot from the broadside hammered the stern transom, and then the napalm shells hit.

One burst in midair just after it left the trough, spraying the shattered wood of the pirate's stern with cupfuls of sticky acid-yellow fire. The other three broke up inside the stern cabin, which just meant that this orca would burn from its rear forward.

They were just close enough for Feldman to see the figure of the *Stormrider*'s captain by her helm, in the blue coat and trousers and the rather silly fore-and-aft cocked hat that the late Queen Mother had dragged out of some pre-Change book she liked and talked her daughter and son-in-law into making part of the RMN uniform when the service was first founded. It was too far for expressions without a telescope, but Moishe Feldman would bet on *flabbergasted surprise* this time.

The Newport skipper grinned in his beard as he whipped off his own practical billed hat and waved it genially, bowing as he did. The prow of his own ship came around, slowing again as it passed the eye of the wind and then still more. The schooner rocked in the low swell as it lay almost at right angles to the frigate with its bowsprit pointing due west and its bare masts making circles against the sky.

"Make sail, make sail!" Feldman roared. "Hands to winches, hands to heads'l sheets!"

The gaffs rose as the winches spun and whined, and the triangular staysails between the foremast and the bowsprit rose up the lines. They caught the wind and started to push the bow around faster; then the ship heeled as the mainsails cracked full and the hull began to gather way in a smooth, accelerating rush. The sluggish movement of the deck beneath his feet turned purposeful once more, and the wheel came live as the rudder had moving water to bite.

"Hands aloft to loose tops'ls! On the fore, on the main, lively, lively now, look alive!"

The rigging thrummed as parties ran up the ratlines to free and drop the square topsails, and others bent to the ropes on deck. In moments they were gaining speed on a southwesterly course that would take her past the old Richmond bridge by a spot he knew—just passable now that the tide had made a bit—and out into San Francisco Bay proper, ready to run the Golden Gate . . . which he could do much faster than the frigate, not to mention the time it would take them to send another maincourse spar up and rig it, heavy crew or no.

"Signals!" Feldman went on, alerting the crewman whose responsibility it was. Who had survived, fortunately.

"Ready, Cap'n," the ferret-faced sailor known as "Rat" McGuire said, throwing open the chest and poising to seize the coiled flags that conveyed coded messages.

"Run up: *Glad to help the Navy* and *The Princess and the Prince send their regards!*"

To himself, as the colorful pennants were made fast and went aloft to break out from the mizzen:

"And that little maneuver will open your eyes, I think, O exalted Naval captain."

Radavindraban was grinning as he glanced up at the flags while he climbed the short ladder to the poop deck.

"That will have him gnashing his teeth and coming after us . . . eventually, yes indeed," he chuckled. "Hotfoot and swearing, oh yes. We have the bow patched for now, Cap'n—slow leak, six planks cracked and a rib sprung—but we will certainly need to heave to and work on it for a few hours. Jacks to get the rib in alignment, then scarfing work and a sheet-metal patch. That will hold her until we get her back in the yard, or at a pinch beach her and come at it that way."

Feldman turned and raised his spyglass. The warship had managed to cut loose from the two burning pirates, and had enough way on her to put some distance between them. Though the damage-control officers were doubtless going frantic, he could see sailors on the yards wetting down the sails with spray hoses and hand-pumps. Pirates were jumping overboard from their flaming ships and swimming for it while the Protector's Guard crossbowmen methodically shot them down.

And usually I would—very slightly—pity the ones who made it to shore, Feldman thought. *But now . . . perhaps not so much.*

The other enemy vessel . . .

"If he's got the time to swear at us . . . yes. There, *Stormrider*'s on the Korean's stern and raking them now."

As he'd just demonstrated, the most devastating position for bombarding another ship was to lie astern of it with your flank making the bar of a T. That way you were shooting right down the length of her with your whole broadside. And the frigate's fourteen weapons threw heavy shot, and threw it very hard.

"A broadside every forty-five seconds, very good practice," he said with satisfaction.

As he spoke the Korean's mainmast lurched, twisted and fell across her forecastle trailing burning sails. Then the other two masts toppled, covering the whole length with flaming canvas.

"It is very good to see our taxes getting some uses," Radavindraban said.

"Ah, they're signaling *heave to immediately*," Feldman added. "That's immediately *repeat* immediately."

"Directed at us, I am supposing."

Feldman shrugged expressively. "Or at the seagulls and the seals." He turned to McGuire. "Signals, run up *Sorry cannot read your hoist* and *Princess bids you farewell*."

More soberly, the First Mate added: "We have two dead, Cap'n, and six wounded."

Feldman blew out a soundless whistle. "Better than it could have been, worse than it should," he said. "I'll go take a look. You have the deck, Mr. Mate."

"Aye aye, Cap'n."

The schooner had an excellent ship's surgeon, a cousin of Feldman's in fact, and Corvallis-trained at OSU's teaching hospital, but it was something he should do.

I wonder what the actual *Princess is doing?* he thought as he headed down the companionway. *As opposed to the ghost I just encouraged our naval friend to see here on board?*

Then: *The Lord knows, and I will find out in His good time.*

CHAPTER THIRTEEN

CÍRBANN RÓMENADRIM
(FORMERLY CHINA CAMP)
CROWN PROVINCE OF WESTRIA
(FORMERLY CALIFORNIA)
HIGH KINGDOM OF MONTIVAL
(FORMERLY WESTERN NORTH AMERICA)
JULY/FUMIZUKI/CERWETH 14TH
CHANGE YEAR 46/FIFTH AGE 46/SHŌHEI 1/2044 AD

"Reiko!" Órlaith called as her men-at-arms fell into their ranks on the wharf.

Reiko had her bow in her hand, and the broad helmet on her head, with the thick soft silk cords that held it tied around her chin in a knot that looked both complex, elegant and extremely practical.

"Those barrels are full of boat soap," Órlaith said.

Once again her Sword-granted knowledge of the language surprised her; the phrase that came to her lips was actually a bit more specific than the English term for that mixture of turpentine and boiled flaxseed-oil and tar.

"Roll ten along this front part of the wharf and break them open. Then leave the last two on their sides, in the center of the wharf. Knock out the heads facing us."

Reiko looked blank for a very brief moment, then began to smile; it was a remarkably carnivorous expression for a face usually suffused with a gentle melancholy; a nation of seafarers would know the stuff well.

Egawa's expression was harder to see because as well as his helmet with its new-moon-shaped crest he wore a *happuri* mask, a face-protecting armor that covered the forehead and cheeks, but his show of teeth was frankly shark-like. Reiko made a sharp horizontal gesture with the *tessen* in her right hand, speaking not a word. The Nihonjin set to their task at a run. Some of them were laughing outright; Órlaith thought she caught a couple of samurai giving her approving glances out of the corners of their immovable eyes.

The deck rumbled and swayed again beneath the barrels as two men rolled each. After that it was the work of seconds to rip the casks apart with wrenching and kicks and blows from the steel-shod butts of the *naginata*. The men skipped back to keep the dark thick pungent liquid from flowing over their feet; the enemy could see it . . . though the limit of their chemical knowledge was using mud to keep off flies.

But a few arrows with soot-blackened fletching were falling close now. She turned her head to check that the unarmored sailors had fallen back, and found that the Protector's Guard priest-physician had them assembling the knock-down stretchers that some of the men carried, obviously intending to use them as bearers to carry wounded. And there *would* be wounded.

Good thinking!

Running even a small fight would be impossibly complex unless your subordinates knew what to do, and did it. She turned her head to the two Dúnedain again.

"You have some fire-arrows, my kinsmen?" she asked; though the Sindarin term actually just meant *kinsfolk*.

Rangers usually did have firebolt shafts, along with an odd assortment of specialist gear. She glanced back and forth; the long side of the wharf was about long enough for seventy-five of the naked enemy to crowd into if they packed tight.

"Two incendiaries each," Morfind said, unconsciously touching the scar that marked the left side of her face.

"Good," she said. "You fire the last barrels on my word, and then the ends of the dock north and south. Then use your horses—"

Their mounts were tethered where the pier met the shore with a saddled remount each. All of them also had several bundles of spare arrows slung over the saddlebags at the rear.

"—to harry around the edges, lead some off if you can. You don't have to stay for a last stand, if that's what happens."

Faramir grinned. That made him look less melancholy and as young as his actual age, short of nineteen: his teeth and eyes and hair were bright against the dusty tan of his face.

"The smoke will bring the reinforcements faster," he said. "Both parties. And our folk from Eryn Muir, as well, and the ones from the northern Staths who've come in since the spring."

Órlaith made her voice *not* squeak with an effort; that did change matters.

"Reinforcements? Both parties?"

"On their way right now—long story. Susie took off to guide the clansfolk, they got in day before yesterday. And the Hraefnbeorg men are heading straight here as fast as their horses can carry them, six score of them, all Lord Godric could collect of his fyrd right away."

"Mist Hills men? You're *sure*?" Órlaith asked, with a single blink of astonishment.

Mist Hills was a little over a hundred miles away and tucked into a valley in the Coast Range, which along with luck and inspired leadership was why the little enclave had survived the Change. They must have started while the *Tarshish Queen* was still cruising down the coast. Why would they have mustered their fyrd and hotfooted it here?

Morfind answered her silent astonishment. "We were in Hraefnbeorg ourselves on orders on the seventh, couldn't get out of it. Then the Baron's younger brother . . . Deor the Widefaring, just back from traveling, well, everywhere . . . burst in and said we had to get going *right away* because the Princess and her brother were in danger. Started chanting like an epic and pretty soon he had them all roaring and grabbing for weapons."

Deor? The bard? Órlaith thought. *By Anwyn's hounds, what's going on . . .*

Faramir's face looked a little uneasy. "He's a runemaster as well as a bard . . . scop, they say. They, ummm, took him seriously."

Morfind shrugged. "We came back with them but pushed on this morning; I don't know Deor from Fëanor, not really, but . . . he looked as if he knew something. They should be here within, well, soon."

There was no time for explanations, but others needed to know the essentials. She spoke in English before she repeated it in Nihongo:

"We've got reinforcements on the way, my cousins tell me, arriving quite soon. We'll have to hold out until then."

If we can, she thought grimly.

Some of the sailors, the Montivallans and Nihonjin ones alike, showed relief. The professional warriors were more reserved, since veterans or not they were more conscious of the difference between reinforcements who were *on the way* and those that were or were not *here right now.* She could feel their determination shift—from a grim resolve to show no fear, die with honor and take as many of the enemy with them as they could to . . .

I think that now they're thinking: I'm going to fight like a mad bastard and come out of this a hero with a tale to tell, she thought.

She didn't intend to die right now either.

But then, people never do. Mother said once that the last expression you saw over the edge of your sword was usually a terrible surprise. That time she'd drunk more wine on Twelfth Night than she usually did, and she started crying afterwards and Da hugged her . . .

"Luanne," she said, and the young Bearkiller woman looked up from unlatching the cover from her quiver. "Take one of the Rangers' spare horses, we can use another mounted archer as flank guard. Now!"

Deep down she could feel the endless conversations she'd endured virtually from her cradle welling up and turning into decisions. There had been times when listening to the veterans rehashing had made her want to scream with boredom. But it had all sunk deep, soaking into her skin like scented oil under the fingers of a masseur. There was more to being High King or Queen than leading in war, much more, but it most certainly included that.

The sharp medicinal scent of the tar and turpentine distilled from pinewood mixed with the rich, almost meaty scent of the flax oil until it was overwhelming; hundreds of gallons flowed over the boards of the wharf about as quickly as cream skimmed from a milk bucket would have. The last of the five-foot-high barrels were pushed over with a *thud* that echoed through beam and plank and into the soles of her boots.

Egawa poised, pivoted, and kicked out twice. His heel punched into the boards that sealed the heads of the containers. They splintered and began to let out a steady stream of dark fluid, but it would take minutes to drain.

"*Kanpai!*" he shouted, bowing with ironic ceremony towards the approaching enemy and ignoring the occasional arrow.

Kanpai meant literally *dry cup*. *Bottoms up* was a close English equivalent.

Then: "We're going to make the sake nice and hot for you, *jinnikukaburi*! We're pouring it out like good hosts, so our guests should drink deep! We *insist*!"

The samurai didn't laugh aloud, or even move, but she could feel that they appreciated the bravura gesture; Sir Aleaume slapped his gauntlet against his steel-clad thigh and Droyn grinned when she translated, and it went down the Montivallan rank in a ripple of whispers.

Reiko nodded again to her Guard commander and put an arrow to her bow. The process always looked more than a little odd to Montivallan eyes; this was even longer than a Mackenzie longbow, and the grip wasn't in the middle but about a third of the way up from the bottom end. And a Nihonjin archer started with the bow held up over her head, drawing as it was brought down—precisely the opposite of the method she'd learned from her father and Edain. But as Edain *the* Archer had said to her when he first saw the outlanders shoot, at seventh and last it was what the *arrow* did that counted.

Reiko loosed, and the bamboo arrow shrilled as it rose into the sky and descended in a long arc. An Eater looked up at the last instant, probably a reflex at the slight hiss of cloven air. As the canoe went over the other Japanese archers gave a barking cheer and began to shoot. Reiko brought the bow down in a motion somehow calm and fluid as well as swift, and set the next shaft to the string without looking ahead, her movements as formal as a dance or a temple ritual.

Her dark narrow eyes met Órlaith's for an instant, and there was an inhuman detachment to them, like grass rippling in a slow breeze. As if the archery was a form of prayer, or meditation.

The Montivallan princess pulled her own longbow out of the loops beside the quiver, twitched a broadhead free and set it through the cutout in the riser of the weapon, a present from Edain's own workshop when he'd judged her able to use a ninety-pound draw without getting tired too quickly. Even the swatch of fur on the arrow-rest was from a wolf's tail, not the usual rabbit—Father Wolf was the totem animal of his sept.

She picked her target and bent to the task, exhaling slowly to still her mind and prepare her body for the sudden explosive effort—fast shooting was rather like snatching up a heavy weight over and over again. About a hundred yards now to the foremost paddlers thrashing the water as they strained, mouths gaping wide to suck in air and sweat sheening. She was only a fair–middling archer by Mackenzie standards; the sword-in-hand was her weapon of choice, and with that she was very good.

She drew past the angle of her jaw and released instantly without taking aim, letting the string roll off her fingers. Only beginners aimed; after that you just thought where you wanted the arrow to go and there it went. The surge of recoil, the flat snap of the string, and then the cloth-yard shaft was a long sweet arch through the air, and the wind was nicely steady . . .

The beat of the great drum stopped in mid-stroke as the broadhead punched into the back of the drummer just between the shoulderblades. He collapsed forward, scrabbled at the instrument and then rolled over the side of his boat.

A few seconds later another of the primitives took up the thighbones and began to beat the surface again—she thought she knew what the leather of the drumhead was, and didn't like it. The new beat was faster and lighter, an attack tempo. Still, the men behind her cheered as she shot and shot again. Arrows coming in the other direction were falling more thickly now; one thunked into the planks at her feet.

"Shield!" Heuradys d'Ath barked, pushing ahead of her and bringing her own up to protect her liege; she had Órlaith's slung over her back.

"Shield *now*, Orrey, by Athana! You're not going to stop that bunch with one quiver, not if you hit with every shaft you're not."

The Crown Princess blinked, pushed out of the diamond focus of concentration, handed the bow over and took the curved four-foot teardrop of plywood and wood, leather and sheet metal emblazoned with the sigil of House Artos, then ducked her head beneath the guige strap, adjusted its buckle to snug it tighter and ran her left forearm through the loops and took the grip in her hand.

"I'm going to helm you, too," her knight said. "You're sort of the *point* of all this, you know!"

She stepped up, unhooked the sallet helmet from her liege's belt and pressed it down on Órlaith's head, quickly snapping the chin-cup of padded varnished leather in place.

The visor was up, shading the princess' face like the bill of a cap, and the sun was high enough now that it wasn't directly in her eyes anyway, though the light on the water made the whole scene glitter. The familiar pressure of the sponge-and-felt pads gripped around the sides and top of her skull. The sallet muffled sound a bit—the sides came down to her jawline and a broad flared tail covered the neck—but that seemed less this time than what she remembered from innumerable previous times she'd worn a helm, as if the Lady's gift was magnifying what her ears took in.

The helm was graven with thin lines of gold inlay that mimicked the feathers of her totem spirit, the Golden Eagle. Sprays of that great raptor's feathers stood upright in holders on either side, as if to counterpart the black-and-white Harfang crest Heuradys wore, and the usual smooth curve of the visor was drawn down at the bottom into a beaklike point. Her father had done the same; you wanted your retainers to be able to see where you were at a glance.

"Sir Aleaume, let's discourage them and then start falling back," Órlaith said tightly.

About ten of the Eaters for every one of us, she thought.

The Sword let her make the calculation effortlessly. There was something to be said for ignorance, if the alternative was perfect knowledge of a sledgehammer swinging unstoppably for your head.

If they can swarm us in the open we're doomed. If we can get to that hill we're doomed a bit more slowly unless that help arrives and arrives in time . . . *Faolán and Vuissance are back in Todenangst with Mother, she can hold the reins until they're of age.*

An arrow banged off her shield without doing more than scoring the facing. Most were still falling short—drawing a bow in a canoe was even less practical than making love in one, and some of them were falling overboard when they tried to stand and draw properly.

The fourteen crossbowmen in the black harness of the Protector's Guard stood in their staggered double rank behind the wall of shields, their weapons at the port-arms. Droyn was in charge of them; nominally, since they had their own underofficer, but he knew the business.

They're Associates, they'll be happier with a nobleman standing there giving the orders and looking calm.

"Range ninety, sights down to battle setting. Fire and withdraw by ranks," he said.

The stocks came to the shoulder in a single smooth jerk, then the points swung upward a very little. Their position behind the kneeling shieldsmen left them covered to the midriff, exposing only the cuirass-clad chests and vambrace-clad forearms and heads in their light open-faced sallets.

"Take aim . . . *shoot!*"

Tung!

A brief massive unmusical chorus of vibrating steel. The short heavy bolts with their fins cut from salvaged credit cards were barely-visible blurs as they left the crossbows at three hundred and fifty feet per second, and you couldn't dodge in a boat.

She could see several canoes and boats pitch and roll over when they tried anyway. Unfortunately the rest kept coming as the crossbowmen pumped the cocking leavers, shot, pumped . . .

Sir Aleaume set the pace as the men-at-arms paced backward in an oil-smooth maneuver to the head of the pier. Órlaith and her brother and Heuradys fell in on the right flank, where the Montivallan line joined that of the Japanese. That put her next to Reiko; the Nihonjin woman spared her a single glance, nod, and slight smile; she returned all three. This was Órlaith's second battle, after the one with her father in the spring. From what Reiko had let drop she'd had considerably more experience in her people's ceaseless war. And it was their first fight together, of course.

Órlaith did a quick check that nobody had their feet in the spreading black pool of boat soap—some of it was dripping off the edge of the wharf where the enemy weighed it down, but that was all to the good, since it would float.

Crossbows and *higoyumi* snapped and spat, and the front turned into a semicircle that contracted in size as they backed onto the narrower pier. The chant of the Eaters changed: now it was a word.

"Meat! Meat! *Meat! Meeeeeeeeeeee!*"

A crashing bark broke out from the Montivallans that cut through the rising shrilling of the blood squeal, eerily muffled by the visors of the men-at-arms:

"Órlaith! Órlaith! *Órlaith and Montival!*"

Pride warred with an unexpected twist of pain; for all her life until this spring the High Kingdom's war-cry had been *Artos and Montival!*

"Auntie Tiph *told* me this would come in useful," Heuradys said.

She let her shield fall on its strap and raised a crossbow of her own, one more like an attenuated skeletal sketch of a crossbow, a pre-Change thing made of something called *carbon-fiber composite.*

It fired, a flatter sharper sound than the others, with a rattle beneath it from the pulleys. "Damn!" she said.

"You got him," Órlaith said.

"No, I was aiming for the one beside him, the thick-built one with the axe, he grabbed the man and yanked him in front. I think he's a chief, he's yelling orders from that boat and the others are listening . . . well, some of them."

"'Tis a crossbow, not a magic wand."

Órlaith looked to her right. Egawa raised his sword and shouted as the katana glittered in the sun:

"Tennō Heika banzai!"

That meant literally *to the Heavenly Sovereign Majesty, ten thousand years!* Or *Long Live the Emperor,* more colloquially. Nihongo was a remarkably compact language in some respects . . .

The Japanese ranks screamed out their response in a tearing guttural shriek:

"Banzai! Banzai! *Banzai!*"

"Adjust your fire!" Droyn said sharply. "Drop the bolts on the ones behind the leaders until they start their rush!"

The noise of onset was mounting, a blurring bestial snarl that spoke to something far below thought or custom or belief, as old as the ages when her ancestors had fought with stones chipped to fit the hand and the thigh-bones of zebra. Then the men-at-arms began to beat the flats of their long-swords or the shafts of their glaives against their shields, and the rhythmic booming was louder than the Eater's drum, echoing within her chest and gut. There was a hard menace to it, a *come and die!* more convincing than any words.

The foremost Eaters were packed crouching under the lip of the wharf now, dipping it towards them with their weight, clambering forward to the innermost boats to lie flat with the first arrivals or even just waiting in the water with only their hands showing gripping the edge and knives between their teeth. She could hear a black hot hatred in their chittering and squeals, and then the front rank boiled up over the long lip of the wharf's outer bar in a wave of contorted faces, snaggle teeth and fantastic ornaments—one had a huge mass of hair woven with diamonds and emeralds and sapphires from ancient jewelry stores, glittering like colored stars in a dome of hard mud.

Usually they don't—didn't—*fight straight-up like this. Something drives them. The Malevolence . . .*

"They're coming! Point-blank, point-blank!" Droyn shouted; his voice rose a little as he sensed the building charge.

And sure, he's very young too, younger than I.

A blast of arrows and bolts hammered into the Eaters as they leapt to the boards or heaved themselves out of the water, and the metallic copper-salt stink of blood suddenly overlay the sharp medicinal tang of the boat soap. But now they could plant their feet solidly to draw their bows of ancient ski-tips and modern wood, and dozens of shafts were coming at the Montivallans and Japanese. More and more of them crawled out, building into a mass of scars and stink and murderous intent.

Heuradys reached over and flicked Órlaith's visor down, and the princess raised her shield and crouched as the world shrank to a narrow band of light. Her head began automatically scanning side to side. One of the Nihonjin archers took a shaft through the eye and fell backward with boneless finality. Another arrow smacked into her helm, just above the left brow, and her head twisted to one side—transmitted through the metal and padding and straps, it felt like getting slapped upside the head by someone's palm. That had her looking at the Japanese for an instant.

She blinked as Egawa actually slapped another arrow out of the air with a sideways twist of his sword, sending it pinwheeling away. That was possible, but she'd always considered it more of a parlor trick than something you could really do in war, like the way her father could cut a buzzing fly in half with a flick of the wrist.

Blows landed on her shield like an irregular scattering of claps with a hammer as arrows struck, but nothing too bad yet. A few more banged and rang off her plate. They were only a dozen paces apart now, far too close for an exchange of arrows to go on for more than instants.

"Crossbows back!" Droyn snapped.

The more lightly armored Montivallan missile troops shot again and retreated; two were being helped along, one swearing at the shaft in his shin, the other with a tourniquet around one arm, rigid with agony until a comrade stuck a hypo of morphine into his thigh below the half-armor and pressed the plunger. Sailors dashed forward with stretchers, lifted them and a wounded Japanese onto the canvas and carried them back to the priest-doctor at the landward base of the pier. The shieldwall rose and rippled as they fell back by ranks with their shields up. Beneath taut readiness, a little irony ghosted through her mind: the Association forces had developed this tactic as a counter to the longbow arrow-storms of the Clan Mackenzie in the old wars . . .

The Japanese archers to her right slung their bows and drew their katanas in a swift hissing glitter, points skyward in the two-handed grip by the right side of the head. Perhaps it was the Sword, but she could hear the almost inaudible murmur as one young samurai's lips moved, repeating the same phrase over and over, the sword rock-steady in his armored gloves:

"Rin pyou tou sha kai chin retsu zai zen . . . Rin pyou tou sha kai chin retsu zai zen . . ."

That meant: *Heavenly ones who watch over warriors, stand before me!*

Reiko accepted her *naginata* and swept it forward into guard position and spoke as if to herself. Órlaith's mind stuttered slightly. The language was Nihongo, but not the living tongue; the words had the taste of the ancient to them, like copper green with patina:

"On the high heavenly plain
Primeval Kamurogi and Kamuromi live.
And in accord with them, my ancestor Izanagi,
In a grove of pine at Tsukushi . . .
Give us your favor, divine spirits,
Legions of heaven and earth,
Answer our plea!"

More and more of the Eaters piled onto the wharf, dancing and screeching with froth on their lips, encouraged by the fact that their foes were retreating. Ancient blades and hatchets were brandished, spike-studded clubs and crude spears made of whittled wood and ground-down knives. The mass began to pulse forward and back, a little farther forward each time as if an invisible barrier was being strained and was about to crack. And . . .

"Now!" Órlaith shouted, and the two Rangers stepped forward. *"Lacho Calad!"* Morfind shouted as she drew.

Half the Dúnedain war-cry: *Flame light!*

"Drego morn!" Faramir completed it, as the arrow left his string. *"Flee night!"*

The first two shafts struck neatly in the shattered heads of the half-empty barrels of boat soap mixture. The second pair landed in broken-open hogsheads at each end of the T-wharf. Volcanic white flame speared upward from each arrow's impact, with a core intolerably bright even in the sun and loud as a dragon's hiss. It left dots and bars fading across her sight, spattering and throwing gobbets of burning metal and wood and tar in all directions. The thermite in the heads made from salvaged beverage cans was as close to an explosive reaction as the Changed world allowed, burning hot enough to melt hard steel instantly and make it run like water.

This was a hot clear summer's day not long after noon, and the barrels had been in the sun since dawn. Spilled, the honey-thick liquor had had just enough time to develop a film of violently dangerous vapor and the heat smoked out more. A flicker of nearly invisible blue combustion ran across the layer on the planks faster than the eye could follow. Then fire caught with a bellow like the indrawn breath of a dragon.

She had expected something spectacular, but not quite this.

Nearly a hundred Eaters were standing packed together in pools and puddles, and it flared up around them just as they began their forward leap. Screams of rage and bloodlust turned to howls of pain and terror, but the instinctive gasps merely drew superheated air into their lungs and scorched them to char. In seconds the flames were roof-high, and Órlaith could feel it drying her eyeballs and making her blink even through the vision slit of the visor. A few managed to leap into the water, with their hair and loincloths and feet on fire, but the water close to the wharf was burning too. The war-shrieks of the rest died away for a moment of stunned silence, as the stink of burnt flesh filled the air along with bitter metallic black smoke. There weren't even many screams. The throbbing roar of the fire overrode what there were.

"Let's go!" Órlaith said, coughing and glad of the visor that hid her wince.

The Eaters were vile enough . . . but she'd been close enough to see their eyes as the world exploded in flame beneath them. It was necessary, but . . .

I wish I hadn't seen that.

CHAPTER FOURTEEN

CÍRBANN RÓMENADRIM
(FORMERLY CHINA CAMP)
CROWN PROVINCE OF WESTRIA
(FORMERLY CALIFORNIA)
HIGH KINGDOM OF MONTIVAL
(FORMERLY WESTERN NORTH AMERICA)
JULY/FUMIZUKI/CERWETH 14TH
CHANGE YEAR 46/FIFTH AGE 46/SHŌHEI 1/2044 AD

The Montivallans and the Japanese turned and jogged up the steep slope of the jointed, hinged section that linked the wharf to the pier and then along the pier itself, a surface just wide enough. The planking of the pier sounded different beneath their boots, more of a hollow drumming, though it was easily solid enough to bear their weight.

There was no point in getting winded trying to outrun the unburdened enemy. Armor was a massive deadly advantage . . . right up to the point where you fell down wheezing and feebly batting at whoever pushed a knife-point through the slit in your visor.

Canoes *were* spreading out on either side now, swinging around the pyre of the wharf that poured yellow flame and a towering shaft of black smoke into the sky with a hard stench of burning bone. It would be visible for miles already. The smell itself wasn't so very bad; she had attended enough funeral pyres since so many of the Old Faith followed that rite—though her father's had just been hot, no scent at all.

It was the knowledge that the bones had walked only moments before that made her swallow.

An Eater lunged up over the deck ahead, shrieking through filed teeth, then swung a rusty machete into the bare ankle of a sailor from the *Tarshish Queen*, dashing back towards them with an empty stretcher. The sailor yelled in shock and horror as much as pain as she topped over, then again twice as hands and blades greeted her below in a snarling flurry. Half the crossbowmen shot reflexively. Most of them missed, being on the move and startled. One bolt sank to the vanes in the Eater's forehead with a popping wet crunch, and he toppled back to jerk and sprattle in the soupy mud below.

Two of Ishikawa's crewmen rushed over and struck downward with their *naginata*, full-armed sweeping strokes driven by fury and fear, and the two-foot curved blades on the ends of the polearms sent sprays of blood-drops arcing into the air as they came up.

Órlaith was finding that fighting made you unpleasantly aware that on the inside you were mostly . . . various soft wet things. Very much like what came out of a pig at the fall butchering. And the pier was like running in an evil dream, with unclean death right beneath your boots.

Morrigú! she realized suddenly. *There are slits between the boards, wide enough for a knife or a spearhead!*

"Keep moving! No stopping!" Órlaith shouted, knocking her visor up again and forcing herself not to look down.

There weren't any arrows flying in just now, and the helm was like having your head in a metal bucket with a narrow strip cut in it. With the visor up it was like having your head in a metal bucket with a face-sized patch cut in it, which was better if not good. And there wasn't anything she could do about sharpened steel being shoved up into the soles of her boots—the metal of the sabatons didn't cover them, and stopping and trying to peer between the boards would just make you more vulnerable.

The mental effect was still like running over white-hot coals, and she could have sworn she could *feel* her feet sweating and her toes trying to curl.

Parties of Eaters were farther in, trying to wade through the mud closer to shore and then giving up and slithering forward on their bellies like a mass of human snakes; it was a good thing the tide was out and putting more soft ground between water deep enough to float a canoe and the high-water shoreline.

Luanne Salander had her borrowed horse well in hand, near where the doctor bent over the wounded. She also had two extra quivers from the Rangers' baggage slung on either side of the saddlebow; she trotted her mount out along that good firm sand just inside the high-tide mark, wheeled it right so that her left side faced the water, and began to shoot methodically with her four-foot cavalry recurve. The range was short, and the targets were naked Eaters trying to crouch under the pier and strike upward, or crawl through the mud. Neither could move very fast, and hiding behind the pilings supporting the pier wasn't much better . . .

Four broke out of the water and dashed at her, waving spears and knives, anonymous in their head-to-toe coating of thick slime. A shift of balance set the well-trained Dúnedain horse moving inland at a slow smooth canter, and she twisted in the saddle to shoot backward over its rump

"Hakkaa päälle!" she screamed as she loosed. *"Hakkaa päälle!"*

The formal war-cry came from Mike Havel, Órlaith's own father's father and the first Bear Lord. It meant *chop 'em down!*, more or less, or *get stuck in!*, the battle yell of his ancestors that his new-founded folk had taken as their own.

The Eaters were overtaking the horse in a flat-out sprint. It didn't occur to them that she was letting them do it until an arrow thumped into the breastbone of the first and the triangular head and eight inches of shaft stood out of his back. He took three dragging steps, staring down at the gray fletching, then collapsed forward less than ten yards from the rear hooves. Her next took the second in the back as he tried to flee, and the third. The fourth turned and couched his spear as if a boar were charging him.

Luanne's backsword came out, rising and falling as the dappled gray Arab horse bounded forward into a run with jackrabbit acceleration. She didn't bother with the shield slung at her crupper, keeping her bow in her left hand.

"Hakkaa päälle!"

Horse and rider hid the action for an instant; when the gallop slowed to a canter again the Eater was lying on the ground shaking and twitching with a massive cut to the head. Luanne wiped her sword on a cloth tucked through her belt before sheathing it and putting another arrow to her bow.

Faramir and Morfind joined her moments later; they'd sprinted down the pier and then vaulted into their saddles without breaking stride. The horses had stood still as statues save for a twitching of eyes and ears, despite the scents of fire and blood, until the Rangers' feet found the stirrups. Soon bodies bristling with shafts littered the tidal flat. It took training from childhood to make a really first-rate horse-archer; Órlaith knew she couldn't have done nearly as well herself, but all three of them were very good indeed. Of course, even if they'd shot their quivers empty and killed with every single arrow there would still be many hundreds of the Eaters, but the distraction gave the column on the pier time to get ashore and form up.

Behind Órlaith the wharf was still a pillar of fire, and she felt a profound sense of relief as her boots crunched on gravel rather than drumming on the planks. Fire was spreading to the pier's drier wood; the whole structure would burn down to the waterline. She could feel the savage heat on her face when she turned a glance that way. The little clutch of small wooden buildings that was Círbann Rómenadrim was ahead as they trotted inland, along a rutted dirt street. And it was—

"Deathtrap," Sir Aleaume said tightly.

She nodded; the furnace behind them demonstrated that, and sparks were settling on the dry shingles even now.

The Montivallan and Nihonjin warriors had settled into a uniform pounding jog—instinctively falling into step, a massive thudding sound beneath the rattle and clatter of their armor and gear as more than threescore feet hit the ground with every stride, with the sailors and their stretchers in the center of the formation. They went through the single scatter of buildings amid a strong smell of curing fish, then into the woods beyond with a sudden shock of shadow after the bright sun and cloudless sky. The ground right at the edge of the wood was densely grown with tangled, sticky coyote brush and bitter-scented wormwood and crimson-starred feral roses, and the fighters had to break ranks as they shoved and hacked their way through.

Órlaith's skin crawled under the sweat-sodden fabric of her arming doublet as the shade of the trees fell across her. She closed her eyes for an instant to make them adjust to the shadow faster. This would be the moment of maximum danger, as they moved into the insect-shrilling dimness of the belt of forest; the part of the Nihonjin force with long spears fell back, and the archers kept their *higoyumi* slung and forged ahead with their katanas glinting. Some drew the shorter *wakizashi* with their left hand. Branches and twigs crackled underfoot, spiny weed and brush scraped across their harness and poked for her face. She used her shield to push them aside, or break them with the edge. Dapples of light flicked at her eyes, and the crunching passage of so many feet buried any noise in the background.

A movement to her right, figures erupting out of the leaf-litter with soundless snarls, and suddenly everything slowed down. She started to draw the Sword, but Heuradys was already moving, a lunging thrust that glittered and flickered like metallic lightning in the beams and patches of light streaming through the trees. The narrow point of her longsword smacked through an eye and the thin bone beyond it and twisted free without even breaking stride.

"Alale alala!" the knight shrieked, and cut backhand behind her as they passed the clump of Eaters.

The brain-stabbed dead man leapt in a galvanic bound, precisely like a headless chicken, and her point laid open another's forearm so that he reared back in shock. The combination neatly tripped several more into the path of the Japanese.

The keen-edged curved swords moved in long looping drawing cuts, blurring-fast sweeps diagonally across the full width of a man with all the precisely-applied power of arms and shoulders and torso behind them, and the three savages seemed to explode into fans of blood and . . . parts. Reiko's *naginata* speared neatly though a throat, blurred sideways to lay open a thigh in a huge flap from hip to knee, whirled to dish in the side of a head with the butt-cap. An ancient sledgehammer smashed at her; she blocked with the shaft of the polearm held between her wide-spaced hands. The wood bent and cracked across as it stopped the twelve-pound lump of steel and left the wielder staggering; she promptly jammed the splintered ends into the Eater's throat, dropped them and drew her sword . . .

Another savage was standing with his hand cocked back, a javelin aimed at Reiko, the whetted head a spot of brightness in the gloom. Órlaith wheeled as she ran, tucked the shield into her shoulder and simply smashed into the half-seen shape of the Eater with a little crouch and leap just before impact: the technical term for it was *overrunning*.

He tried to wheel and face her at the last instant. The kitchen-knife head of the throwing-spear went over her shoulder, and the metal curve of her shield became the face of a two-hundred-odd-pound club moving as fast as her long legs could drive it. The shock jarred her as her body flexed but bones crumbled beneath the shield in a grunting wail of pain and blast of fetid air gasped out of a mouth full of rotting filed teeth. She chopped the lower rounded point of the kite down into the man's neck as she hurdled his fallen form.

From elsewhere in the woods and brush around her she could hear similar brief scrimmages, snarls and grunts, bang and boom of impacts on shields and armor, the wet thudding of edges in flesh, one high endless shriek that sank away into a bubbling moan and abruptly ceased.

A hatchet-head on a long shaft banged off the curve of her helmet as she landed and she staggered, but the blow had been oddly feeble. She turned her head and saw Reiko poised in a perfect follow-through, a spray of blood still following the curve of her Masamune sword. The Eater she'd struck was staring at the stump of an arm taken off a hand-span below the shoulder and shrieking mindlessly as the blood fountained; then he took one rubber-kneed step and collapsed.

Blue eyes met black, and both nodded gravely.

A last flurry. The sight of John laying a man's arm open from shoulder to elbow, and Evrouin using his glaive in a brutally economical stab-chop-smash rhythm, the steelshod butt nearly as deadly as the blade and hook, the stretcher-bearers they were protecting plodding on without looking up as they muscled their burden through the brush. Then the warriors were breaking through the inland edge of the forest and its fringe of brush, blinking in the bright sunlight, sucking in air that was pungent with crushed bayleaf and the spicy-dusty smell of the eucalyptus trees that were ubiquitous here in Westria. Nobody came out after them, not yet.

"Well, that was so not fun at all," Heuradys panted, and Órlaith nodded wordlessly.

Orange monkeyflower and purple-and-white ithuriel's spear starred the grass as they surged forward, going down beneath the boots.

"Slow down, close ranks, let the stretcher-bearers through first!" Sir Aleaume barked, and the men-at-arms and crossbowmen obeyed as discipline overcame instinct. "This isn't a foot-race, comrades. Crossbow squad first, skirmish order, spread out halfway to the crest and cover us, fall back to the crest after we get there!"

She'd been about to suggest that, and was glad she hadn't—thirty-odd men didn't need two immediate commanders distracting them by giving duplicate orders, and he had them well in hand. Instead she concentrated on climbing the steep slope herself, about a one-in-three and covered in knee-high golden-brown grass, the mass of slick dry stems a little slippery beneath the soles of her boots and hiding the occasional rock that threatened to trip her. If she did fall . . .

That would be suitably heroic, sure and it would, falling on my ass and going back down the hill like a toboggan in Yuletime!

Worse, it would make others put their lives in danger to save her.

The crossbowmen fanned out ahead, weapons at their shoulders as they climbed with quick agility. They halted fifty yards above up the slope, turning and facing the way behind, kneeling and covering the swordsmen and glaivesmen panting and toiling in their less heavily burdened wake and prodding down now and then with the butts of their polearms and the bottoms of their shields. The Japanese archers had stopped in about the same place, bows out and arrows on their strings, motionless as statues save for the slight movement of the *sashimono* banners some wore standing up from their backs. The silk rippled in the warm breeze, a slight rich fluttering sound.

Now and then Órlaith dug the lower point of *her* shield into the ground to help her climb; by the time she topped the edge of the steep slope and came out onto the more gently rolling crest only training was keeping her from panting like a bellows, and the clothing under her armor had that familiar sopping sweaty feel, as much greasy as wet.

There was a feeling of release and freedom on the top that made no sense but was true enough still. The hill was essentially a piece of plateau, eroded away on three sides, and the top was only gently curved before the steeper drop-off on the sides. On the north a narrow strip of flattish land connected it to the next hilltop, dipping slightly in the middle and only broad enough to take three at a time. The hill there was more broken, and more heavily wooded.

There was one tree on this hilltop, a big broad-spreading live oak casting an oblong of shade; the ground was hard and dry elsewhere, the grass knee-high where it hadn't yet been trampled, gold except for a few blue asters. Birds exploded out of the oak as the humans approached, iridescent green creatures with bright red heads and hooked beaks giving shrill *awk-awk* cries—the Dúnedain called them *bornaew*. Butterflies started up from the boots, drifts of orange Monarchs and paler Painted Ladies.

The leaders walked around the hillcrest from one sentry to the next to get a feel for the details of the position—what could be seen from where and how the folds and crannies gave potential cover. The slope was never less than thirty degrees except on the saddle to the next hill northward, and even steeper on most parts of the circuit. If the defenders stepped back from the edge, anyone coming at them would have to get to the crest of the hilltop before they could do more than loose blindly. Órlaith found herself nodding, as if her father or mother—or Edain or Lady d'Ath or Father Ignatius—were standing behind her making approving sounds as she picked the best ground on an exercise.

Reiko flicked her katana to one side as she walked, shedding a spray of blood-drops, and then wiped it with a fold of paper held between thumb and forefinger in the same motion as sheathing it; considering how sharp it was, she did that with considerable *savoir faire* and without looking down. You had to wonder what Masamune would have thought, if he could have known how far and how strangely his masterpiece would fare, in years and in miles.

"No water," Egawa said thoughtfully, looking around as they came back to the big live-oak.

Which showed a grasp of the basics, which surprised her not at all. They were all streaming with sweat, which except in very cold weather always went with fighting in armor, or running and climbing in it, and they'd been doing all of those. They ignored the thoroughly familiar sensation, but eventually you just couldn't ignore dehydration because you fell down raving and died. A human could do without food for days, if they absolutely had to; water, not so much.

"We won't be here that long," Sir Aleaume said.

Órlaith nodded and added: "You could be after saying our canteens should last us . . . one way or another."

Reiko translated that, and Egawa gave a grim smile and nod at what was both an observation and a warrior's joke. He aimed the point of his sword at the saddle joining this to the next hill northward and tried his slow, thickly accented English.

"*Jinnikukaburi* come that prace."

Aleaume nodded agreement, but Órlaith held up a hand and spoke in English and then Nihongo.

"That's the best ground tactically, but there are a lot of them and they're not organized enough to rotate fighters in and out of the front line. Most of them will try there where you said, General Egawa-san, but a lot of the rest will get impatient and come up the hillslope elsewhere. Just by accident, that may well be the best thing they could do."

The others nodded respectfully. Reiko said quietly: "This is proof that the thing we seek is something that will shake the earth when it is returned to my family's hands. The enemy . . . and the *bakachon* are but a finger on their hand, I believe now . . . would not put forth such effort otherwise."

Egawa gave a single sharp nod. "*Hai*, unquestionably true, Majesty; actions reveal priorities."

Órlaith translated, and out of the corner of her eye saw Aleaume and Droyn look at each other soberly. They had both come out of personal loyalty—and because she'd painted it as something out of a romaunt. Now the reality of what the term *Quest* meant was coming home to them, and that this was more than a war of human kind squabbling over territory and power.

And coming home to me, though I understood it with my mind. Now also with my gut, so to say!

"The reinforcements?" Reiko said briskly, in both languages. "Time is short."

They could hear the Eaters again now, a snarling brabble that rose occasionally into shrieks and gibbering squeals—battle cries inherited from those driven insane by horror, passing horror on down the generations.

"Sometime between one hour and three," Órlaith said.

"One hour would . . . could . . . be good now, Your Highness, but three would be a little late," Aleaume said dryly, and everyone chuckled.

"With your permission, Your Highness, we'll put the Guard men-at-arms and spearmen on the saddle, it's steep enough they'll have to come right into our faces with the crossbows on the flanks. If any crawl up the slope there they can kick them in the face. Our allies could hold the rest of the perimeter as they think best."

Egawa nodded crisply and spoke, with Reiko murmuring the translation: "We will form a reserve, here by the tree, to strike wherever the enemy try to scale the hill behind you. But we need constant observation on all three sides to prevent surprise. That will be difficult—single sentries could be overrun quickly and we cannot afford to lose men unless we must."

"We three can ride around the perimeter and spot enemy massing, or pick off lone wolves," Faramir said. "We'll have extra height, and we can retreat quickly and shoot as they come . . . you all right with that, Luanne?"

Luanne nodded quickly and looked away, absently checking the arrows in her quiver and then staring with mild surprise at the spray of drying blood across the back of her right hand. Faramir gave her a careful and respectful glance; they hadn't met, but after all she was the granddaughter of his mother's uncle, and she'd performed very well, up to the Bearkiller reputation. Órlaith supposed there was something inherently pleasing about seeing your kin live up to expectations.

"Steep for horses," he said, looking around. "Particularly at the edges."

"Well, it's the hill we've got," Luanne said.

"The others within reach all had much easier approaches," Órlaith said.

Luanne nodded. "So it'll have to do, steep or not. Shouldn't be a problem, really."

The Bearkiller was trying to make her voice cheerful, but she swallowed a little, and wiped the back of her hand across the spray of blood-drops on her face.

"I'll get used to this, I suppose," she added quietly, probably a thought she didn't altogether realize she was speaking aloud. "I think I understand Mom and Dad better now."

Except for the Japanese, I'm here with a force of untried youngsters, Órlaith thought. *We're doing well so far . . . and I couldn't have* gotten *this number of veterans to come along. So, they had their day. This is ours!*

The three riders spread out and the first sentries fell back to rejoin their comrades; with the extra height from horseback the mounted archers could cover the rim of the hill well enough to give warning of an attack without exposing themselves to be picked off, and further guard by keeping moving. Of course, if the Eaters came from all sides simultaneously . . .

Morfind called over her shoulder:

"I can see them moving in the trees down by the shore, about where we came through."

She unlimbered her binoculars. "Lots and lots of them, hundreds, it's their main body. And I can see groups moving out to either side, I think they're trying to surround the hill. More northward, they're getting ready to scale the hill there and come straight at us over the saddle."

"Some over here!" Faramir called from fifty yards to her right. "Moving west, inland, from tree to tree, by ones and twos and small groups. Coming in a steady trickle moving from cover to cover—about forty or fifty so far. Not trying to climb up to the next hill, the one south of us; the crest there's twice long bowshot."

So they could do little but make rude and antic gestures and slap their arses at us from there, Órlaith thought. *Unless they had a scorpion or a twelve-pounder field catapult about them, the which I doubt.*

"None here yet," Luanne called from her sector facing westwards, scanning methodically. "It's pretty open here—grass for twice bowshot and then only a few oaks, brush in the lowest parts. There are a few rocks . . . maybe concrete . . . big enough to give cover but not within two hundred feet. Rolling ground rising as far as I can see, then it falls away to the north."

Then: "Wait . . . I thought I saw something twinkling . . . gone now."

The Montivallans and their allies spread out into formation. The men-at-arms unfolded the hinged bars that ran down the inside of their shields and propped them up across the narrow saddle on the north side of the hill, making a staggered four-foot wall.

"One per file on overwatch," Aleaume said.

One man in five stood. A few went aside to relieve themselves; as her father had said to her once, great fear and a full bladder went ill together, and she made a note to find a spot herself before long. A few even managed to compose themselves as if to *sleep*, which surprised her a little and was either bravado or utter lack of nerves.

Underofficers checked canteens and quivers and reported the totals, and the half-dozen wounded were brought into the shade of the oak where the medics could work on them. The Japanese were relying on the Protector's Guard doctor, since they'd lost their last one when they landed in the spring.

She could hear Egawa telling his archers not to waste a single shaft. That was good advice, though it would be a pity to have your throat cut with unused arrows still in the quiver.

"Terric's dead," Droyn said quietly to Sir Aleaume; and, she thought, to her. "Took a spear right in the throat while we were in the woods. Hubreton got his crossbow and his bolts."

The two Associates both crossed themselves and invoked their Virgin to intervene for him.

"He was dark with curly hair," Órlaith said quietly. "From Molalla, originally. He joked about how he was going to get his fiancée a silk dress and his mother another milch cow and his father a new plow-team when he came back with booty."

Which had been funny, because if one thing was nearly certain about this faring it was an absence of loot.

"I'll see to that . . . assuming I can."

Both the noblemen looked at her for an instant, then nodded gravely. Her father had been famous for knowing the names and homes of nearly every warrior under his command, even when it was great armies in the war time. She didn't *think* she'd needed the Sword to do the same here.

"Blankwin got an arrow in the shin," Droyn went on. "He says he can stand in line and shoot, as long as he doesn't have to run very fast, and he doesn't want enough painkiller to turn him muzzy."

A tight smile: "And he says he doesn't intend to run away in any case."

"Let him try standing in the line," Aleaume said. "At worst he can shoot sitting down. The rest?"

"Fulk looks serious. Savaric will make it—"

Assuming we aren't all killed, Órlaith thought.

"—but he can't fight. Apart from that, superficial cuts and bruises."

Aleaume nodded and turned to her, taking his helm off for a moment to let more air into the neck-opening of his suit of plate.

"Your Highness, one dead, three seriously wounded in the crossbow squad. The men-at-arms and spearmen have only minor wounds so far."

No surprise there; a big part of what made plate-armored fighters so dangerous was the protection that let them take chances others could not. They had their vulnerable spots, but a naked man *was* a vulnerable spot from crown to toes. Men died because they'd been stabbed through something vital now and then, but the vast majority just bled out, and you could bleed from anywhere.

"And the Japanese are down three, two killed outright and one won't recover consciousness. As many more too seriously wounded to fight; one broken hand, a couple of leg wounds. Including one who actually had an Eater's tooth break off in his leg, that was nasty."

"Very good, Sir Aleaume. We'll let the enemy come to us. The longer they take, the better. Carry on."

Órlaith spoke to all the hurt men, which only took a few steps aside. Just a word of thanks and a nod to the Nihonjin, who weren't her subjects. They were showing an iron-faced stoicism, though none of them actually turned down the morphine. The Montivallans were cheerful or trying to seem so in a way that made her feel obscurely bad though she grinned back; except for Fulk, who was the blond youngster with a bad wound in his left arm, and *he* was unconscious.

They'd stopped the bleeding, disinfected and stitched the ugly stab-cut and got his cuirass off and elevated his feet on it. As she watched, the doctor finished inserting a needle and tube while his assistant attached the bottle of Ringer's Lactate they'd made up from powder and water.

Fulk still looked very pale under his weathered tan. Órlaith put a hand on his forehead, feeling clammy sweat, conscious of the rapid thready beat of his heart. The priest-medic looked at the Princess and spread his hands. They were covered in blood, and his assistant took the chance to seize them and begin wiping them off with a towel wetted in antiseptic. The fruity scent of medicinal alcohol mixed with the metallic, spoiled-seawater tang of the blood.

"Your Highness, I can't do a whole-blood transfusion now, which is what I'd like to, all our universal donors are in the shield line and we haven't got plasma either, just the lactate. I think he may be taking the morphine hard, some do. I'm afraid it's shock, and shock can kill in ways we don't understand. All I can do now is pray."

The clerical physician crossed himself and kissed his crucifix; he was dressed with rough practicality for the field, but had the white collar-tab of a Roman priest. The others had come for oaths of allegiance, or even for adventure. He had come because the care of these bodies and souls was the task entrusted to him by his God and His blue-mantled mother;

and he'd been almost inhumanly self-effacing on the journey, keeping to his canvas cubicle in the forepeak and praying when he wasn't working at his task or hearing confessions. She'd noticed he made John wait his turn without even discussing the matter.

Rudi Mackenzie had once remarked to her that genuine humility was the most formidable weapon the Church had in its arsenal.

"Padre," she said, and nodded respectfully to him as she knelt. "Praying can't hurt and may well help."

Silently she made the Invoking sign and called on the Lady in Her form as the Healer of Hurts:

Airmed, Goddess gentle and strong, from whose salt tears healing herbs arose, have pity and help this man: for he too is the Mother's child, however he calls on You.

Aloud to the unconscious man: "Don't you die on me, there, Associate," and bent to kiss his brow.

She wasn't sure if the Sword had anything to do with it, but a few seconds later he was breathing easier, and his color was a little better. The others *looked* at her as if she was responsible, though.

When everything was seen to she and Reiko sat; from the look of things they had another ten to twenty minutes before the Eaters finished massing their scattered gangs and came at them.

Heuradys offered her canteen. It was water—mostly, a little wine by the tang—and warm and stale and tasted like the sacred fountain of youth and joy that Arianrhod dispensed in Caer Rigor. They both took a ration bar wrapped in a dried cornhusk from a sack one of the crossbowmen was passing around, and Órlaith offered one to Reiko. It was a type used all over Montival with local variations; rolled oats and walnuts and hazelnuts and bits of dried fruit went into it, held together with a dollop of honey and baked into a rectangle. She hadn't felt hungry, but the first taste made her ravenous in a way she recognized from tourney and practice. Reiko bit into hers with a stoic expression and then looked down in surprise.

"This is quite good," she said. "Good enough for a treat . . . is there enough for all?"

Órlaith smiled. Most field rations would gag a rat—it had to last like iron just for starters, which usually meant *desiccated* and *very salty.*

"Enough for this morning, Reiko-chan, and one way or another we'll not be needing more," she said.

Reiko frowned slightly as she made that out, then gave a slight smile. If help didn't come soon they'd be too dead to eat, of course.

"This is standard issue throughout the realm, or something like it," Órlaith said. "Mind, it's supposed to be for times when every ounce counts. Regular rations aren't as . . . pleasant, so."

Anyone who'd eaten the twice-baked hardtack or regular smoked sausage or salt pork and badly-soaked dried beans and tooth-challenging cheese knew there was truth to that. It was tradition—established by her father—that when the High King or Queen led in the field, they ate what the common soldiers did. That shamed other leaders into following their example. . . .

Which Da said did wonders to keep the quartermasters on their toes!

"What do you use in your homeland?" Órlaith asked. "For warriors to carry with them, for the times they can't forage or have supplies sent up."

"*Onigiri,*" she said. "Cooked rice balls with salt, wrapped in bamboo leaves . . . with pickled plums, if they can be had, or dried mackerel flakes. And a flask of miso. And tea."

She sighed; tea was a rare luxury in Montival, grown on a few experimental farms or imported from Asia. When you had grown up drinking it several times every day, doing without was a real hardship.

"You can march and fight on that for a long time. And *ramen,* that is what we call pre-cooked noodles with dried soup powder."

"We call it ramen too," Heuradys said with a flash of a smile in the shadow of her raised visor. "Though you should see the faces Orrey makes if she has to eat it."

"You do not like ramen?" Reiko asked curiously.

Órlaith chuckled reminiscently. "Once when we were ten . . . well, I was eight and Herry was about ten . . . she and I decided to run away and go on a Quest of our own; to find the Solitary Fortress of Ice where the Super Man lives."

"Athana alone knows what we were supposed to do if we *did* find it or him. You were never very clear on that, Orrey."

"I was eight! It's supposed to be somewhere north of Drumheller, which is where we headed."

The two young women laughed; it was entirely genuine, though of course it did the warriors good to see the leaders carefree in their shared peril. The Nihonjin chuckled as well. Órlaith thought she heard something wistful in it. Reiko had loved her father, but as much in the way a devoted subject did a monarch as a child did a parent. She'd spoken of a mother gentle and kind and learned, an artist of verse and brush, and her father's close, shrewd advisor and helper—and who was also evidently half a decade older than her husband.

But Órlaith also had a strong impression of a life so dominated by duty that there was little room in it for fancy, or any but the most decorous play.

"*I* thought it was a bad idea from the beginning, once you went from talking to planning," Heuradys said. "We were further apart in age then, you know."

"True enough," she said to Heuradys.

To Reiko: "But even then, I thought to pack a big sack full of ramen packets to eat upon the way; we started before dawn and made about four hours' trot on our ponies. Da said at least the importance of logistics had gotten home—he was grinning, though he was angry too, since we'd made it almost far enough for people not to know who we were at a glance. And Mother was just angry—it was her idea to make me have the ramen and nothing else for dinner until the sack was all gone. I've never willingly eaten the stuff since."

"She watched me like a hawk, too," Heuradys grumbled, and explained to Reiko: "I was a page then—it's what you do before you become a squire and then a knight. Pages serve at table for their patrons as one of their duties, it's supposed to teach you humility. Mostly you take things from the kitchen staff and carry them to the high table. Humility for the page, colder food for the nobility."

Órlaith remembered the beginnings of stealthy movement with a pastry or a slice of brandy-glazed ham or lamb kebab while she sat glumly contemplating her fifteenth-plus bowl of Guard-issue field ration ramen and trying to decide whether it was worth going to bed hungry rather than put the horrible stuff in her mouth one more time. And her mother's steely brown eye and the slight clearing of the High Queen's throat to warn Heuradys off.

"She did not make you also eat the ramen, Heuradys-gozen?" Reiko asked.

"No, she said Órlaith was the Crown Princess and I was her page and she had to take my blame and punishment, too, because I'd followed and obeyed her; the liege is responsible for the vassal's acts when they're done in obedience. It made me feel awful."

She smiled reminiscently herself. "When I told my mother that . . . my mother Delia . . . she said that was the *point.* Orrey got her punishment, and I got mine, with the added knowledge that I was supposed to protect her against *herself*, at need, as well as enemies."

"And I knew you felt awful about it, and that made me feel bad," Órlaith said. "Which to be sure was also part of the point. My mother is . . . subtle."

Reiko nodded seriously. "That is good discipline, Orrey-chan," she said.

Órlaith raised a brow mentally. It had only been a month since she invited Reiko to use the familiar diminutive of her name, which was pronounced *Oorlai* anyway; Gaelic spelling being nearly as eccentric as English in relation to how words were actually pronounced. Tacking on *chan* meant more or less the same thing in Nihongo. It wasn't that Reiko wasn't friendly; in a shy way she was eagerly so. But "reserved" didn't *begin* to describe her.

"This is a way to make things real to a child," the Nihonjin woman said. "Physical correction is not enough, not when you are training character and mind as well."

"And in case it was all *too* subtle, also she tanned my backside for me until I howled right after they got us back," Órlaith added, and Reiko covered her mouth and laughed. "Mackenzies don't do that so much, but Associates are of another mind altogether on the matter."

Heuradys looked up at the clouds. "Auntie Tiph said I was getting too old for spanking when I got back home for Lammas, so she gave me some extra training sessions. She could really make you suffer with a practice sword . . . but at least I escaped the ramen, my liege."

Órlaith went on to Reiko: "So ramen's as common as dirt here. For soldiers, for travelers, for students, for anyone who needs something that that can be cooked as it is without much in the way of a kitchen."

"Ah so desu ka!" Reiko said. "I wondered why General Egawa was able to get it so easily for us. Even so, he thought ramen every day would make the troops soft unless he worked them harder," she added.

She sounded entirely serious. Rice-balls and pickled plums sounded like the equivalent of living on hardtack, dried beans and jerky, which could be done at need but wasn't pleasant. Though if you were hungry enough, you'd do so and give thanks.

They do love to live on willpower, our new friends, the Crown Princess thought. *On the other hand, willpower is the one resource they seem to have in abundance in Nihon nowadays, so to say. And if that's what you have, why not take pride in it? For it's a good thing to have in the toolbox as you might say, ready to come out when needed.*

John had been uncharacteristically silent while the women chatted. Now he carefully wiped *his* fingers, first on grass, and then wetted them with a few drops from his canteen and wiped them again on a cloth in the lute-case when he opened it. Then he tuned the instrument and strolled out in front of the ranks of men-at-arms, leaving his helm where he'd been sitting with his gauntlets in the bowl.

"Fellow Associates!" he called lightly, his fingers moving on the strings.

They looked up respectfully; he was a prince of House Artos, and a belted knight. And for that matter he *was* an Associate, with the jeweled dagger of that order on his belt, unlike his sister.

"I know how bored we all are waiting for the tournament to begin, without even jongleurs and dancing dogs to keep the folk in the gallery content while the bookies calculate the odds and the hawkers sell their popcorn and sausages in buns and small beer," he said, and got a laugh.

He struck a troubadour's pose: "Therefore I will improve the time! I give you . . . the 'Song of the Deeds of Sieur Roland'!"

Órlaith's brows rose as his fingers struck the strings of the lute, and Heuradys crooked one of hers. That was a bit of a daring choice; nobody had survived Roland's last stand at Roncesvalles.

On the other hand, it was well-known that on the stricken field of Hastings the Norman warlord William the Bastard—their maternal grandfather's idol, and according to wishful legend his ancestor—had listened while his knight-minstrel Taillefer sang the *Chanson de Roland*. Sang it on horseback as he rode towards the English ranks in challenge, throwing his sword into the air and catching it as he chanted the same verses that John did now:

"*Carles li reis, nostre emperere magnes*
Set anz tuz pleins ad estet en Espaigne:
Tresqu'en la mer cunquist la tere altaigne.
N'i ad castel ki devant lui remaigne . . ."

The ancient words rang out in a clangorous Old French where the Latin bones still showed plain, the song behind which the chivalry of the Duchy had charged and charged again and won the victory and a kingdom on that long bloody day. Órlaith leaned over and whispered to Reiko:

"Charles the King, our Emperor Sovereign,
Full seven years hath sojourned in Spain,
Conquered the land, and won the western main,
Now no fortress against him doth remain,
No city walls are left for him to gain . . ."

Reiko used a twist of dried grass and then a pinch of dust to be sure she'd gotten the last of the sticky honey off her fingers. After Órlaith's low-voiced account, she turned to her own followers and said—as if speaking casually to Egawa, but pitched to carry to them all:

"He sings of the deeds in war of their ancestors," she said. "From Europe. An ancient tale of a hero's last stand in a mountain pass, where he fell with honor by guarding the retreat of his *kōtei*."

She used the Nihongo word for foreign Emperors; *Tennō* was restricted to those of her line.

"It is part of a larger cycle of stories, like the *Heike Monogatari*, of the heroes who attended this ruler. An old story even as we would see it, from a time before the Genpei War."

Egawa's eyes lit a little: he was a devotee of the classic story of the struggle between the Taira and Minamoto clans for control of Japan, and had actually memorized thousands of lines, not just the most famous passages. Warriors spent a great part of their lives waiting or traveling or sailing from here to there, and even Egawa Noboru couldn't drill *all* the time, or leaf through heirloom manga.

Not even the priceless complete set of his beloved *Lone Wolf and Cub*, which was an inheritance from his father and his most treasured possession after his Mitsutada sword.

"A good gesture, Majesty," he said. "Though it still seems a little odd for a noble to sing in public. Given the difference in custom, they have some idea of how to lead, then, our hosts."

Reiko gave a very small snort—a sort of hmmmmm with a guttural edge—and used her fan to indicate their surroundings. Not the isolated hill in this alien but beautiful stretch of wilderness, with the pillar of smoke bending southeast and tinging the air with harshness. The great realm of Montival, the High Kingdom that stretched distances unimaginable to them, and had twelve times Nihon's people—four times that of even the much more numerous *bakachon*.

"Some idea of leadership, yes," she said dryly.

He didn't argue. Instead he leaned a little closer and spoke under his breath:

"This hill . . . the perimeter is too big to be held against any attack in force by the numbers we have, even if the enemy are naked savages," he said. "The best available, but not good."

Reiko made a gesture of agreement with her *tessen*. "There is none better within reach, I think." Egawa nodded. "And that saddle to the north, that is a very defensible chokepoint."

"Yes." With grim straight-faced humor: "Perhaps it is also like the stockyard and large abattoir we were shown."

She'd probably eaten more beef and pork in the last few months here than in any single year of her life in Japan; even commoners got a fair amount. Japan had nothing like that place on Barony Ath where cattle and pigs were driven by the hundreds at a time, because at home they simply did not slaughter large animals very often. When they did the business was handled by traveling butchers—that was a low-status occupation among their people, considered faintly unclean.

The system on the manor had been illuminating, and almost industrial. The whole process had been arranged as a climb in the darkness, leading to a spot with a moveable fence that clamped them immobile from both sides while a spring-loaded bolt gun smacked into their brain. Then a system that strung the carcass up to drain and be skinned and cut up as they moved by gravity along an overhead chain-belt past workers with knives and cleavers and saws and back down to ground level, where the end result went into wooden crates in a room kept just above freezing by ice and ingenious ventilation. It had even been thrifty, not usually a Montivallan virtue, with every part used down to the blood and hooves.

As long as the Eaters came straight in here they'd be almost as helpless. Both were impressively efficient arrangements for killing *en masse*.

"The Montivallan knights are good," Egawa admitted. "And that position gives them much advantage. For the rest . . . eventually the savages—"

In modern Nihonjin it seemed natural to apply *jinnikukaburi* to any of those who ate men; they used it for the little bands that haunted the ruins of the great cities on the main islands too.

His gauntleted hand moved around the three-quarters of the hilltop the Japanese would have to cover.

"—the *jinnikukaburi* will rush a part of the perimeter before we can get there, and we will have to retreat until we are back-to-back with the Montivallans. And unless these reinforcements the Princess spoke of arrive, there we will die one by one."

He snorted, an amused aside. "And yes, that will be before water becomes a problem, Majesty."

Reiko looked eastward. The pillar of smoke rose into the aching blue of the sky, and it would be visible for at least ten *ri* by now, a little more than twenty miles.

Órlaith and I have become close friends, she thought, smiling to herself as she thought the words in English and then repeated it mentally in her own tongue: *Shin'yuu.*

She hadn't had many friends, not in all her life; her position made it difficult. *It would be an irony if I make a friend only to die with her so soon after.*

"The Montivallan reinforcements will probably come," she said.

Then she shrugged ruefully. "Whether in time for us or not . . . perhaps there is a red cord around our little fingers, perhaps not, neh?"

CHAPTER FIFTEEN

Approaching Círbann Rómenadrim
(Formerly China Camp)
Crown Province of Westria
(Formerly California)
High Kingdom of Montival
(Formerly western North America)
July/Fumizuki/Cerweth 14th
Change Year 46/Fifth Age 46/Shōhei 1/2044 AD

Karl Aylward Mackenzie pumped at the pedals of the bicycle and gritted his teeth as brush flashed by on either side and the uneven surface of the ancient road hammered through the solid wheels. It wasn't the effort that bothered him, though it made him pant and sent sweat streaming all over his body and actually squelching in the padding under his brigandine. They'd all had a full day of rest and good eating at the Finney farm.

What bothered him was the fact that he was barreling down a southbound road towards an enemy as if it was a race at the Lughnasadh Games. If there were any onlookers, it wouldn't be roses or daisies they'd be throwing.

We were lucky with those bandits in the hills. But luck isn't a plan.

He'd been prepared for danger and hardship leading this venture; what was turning out to be worse was the feeling of always trying to do three things at once, each one of them needing all his attention. They couldn't even rely on the dogs to sense enemy presence, because the poor beasts were falling behind.

Sure, and didn't Da say that being led by the nose was for pigs at slaughter-time, not the human kind?

Their only scout was Susan Mika, up there on her wiry little quarter horse; at least *she* could ride with her reins knotted on its neck and an arrow to the string.

They should be getting very close now. He could see the Lakota begin to stiffen in the saddle, then duck and twist as something flashed by her—

"Off! Down!"

Karl shouted it as she drew, shot, and legged her horse up to a gallop in the same motion. A short scarred man with his hair worked into mud-covered spikes and naked except for a ragged loinclout fell out of the scrub a few yards from the road, writhing and screeching and pulling at a shaft sunk into the bone of his pelvis. A clutch of short javelins clattered down from his hands on the hard ground and rolled onto the faded white-gray of the asphalt.

As Karl spoke he jumped off the bicycle, let it fall and grabbed for the longbow in its loops beside his quiver. The others did the same in a crash of falling machinery.

Then he took a single instant to point and shout: *"Hounds! Mharú air! Kill!"*

The greathounds had been lagging and looking sore-footed despite the day's rest at Finney's farm. You wouldn't know it now. The big beasts bristled and launched themselves into the mass of brush and dry long grass to the east of the road like hairy bolts shot from field-catapults, mouths open, black lips curled back to show their fangs in saw-edge gapes and growling like a machine cutting rock.

Human screams followed almost instantly, and a thrashing and crackling among the brush. Another near-naked figure appeared, running up the sloping trunk of a small live oak with astonishing agility for a man who had a hundred and thirty pounds of war-dog hanging from one buttock by its fangs, and flailing wildly behind him with his bow to try and make it let go.

A moment later the dog ripped loose, fell a dozen feet into a crouch on the ground, whirled and eeled back into the brush, bleeding from a cut on the shoulder but not one whit daunted. The savage was a brave man; he raised his own odd-looking bow even though blood was pouring down his left leg in a dark glistening sheet.

Karl nocked, drew and shot in a motion as familiar as breathing, without even being conscious of making a decision. The range was short, only twenty-odd yards, and he was using a war-bow whose hundred and twenty-seven pounds of pull was designed to drive a bodkin through armor at three hundred paces. The path of the shaft hardly rose at all, and when it struck with a hard wet *thunk* sound it went completely through his target's body, breaking bone coming and going and arching off into the distance. There was a double splash of blood, a small blossom where the point struck and a longer trail behind, and the man fell out of the tree.

By then all the clansfolk were on the west side of the road, arrows half-drawn. A half-dozen of their foemen erupted into the open in flight from the dogs, and paid the price of panic as the Mackenzie longbows snapped. There was an excited belling from the greathounds; they were acting as if this was a hunt and they were driving dangerous game like boar towards the shooters.

Diarmuid's McClintocks were close behind. He took in the situation at a glance as he hopped off the bicycle—his Clan were feudists, ambush wasn't in the least strange to them, and there had been Eaters filtering up from the south less than a generation ago in their dùthchas. He screamed:

"McClintock abu!"

And ripped out his claymore in his right fist, snatched his dirk into his left so that it projected downward beneath the nail-studded targe-shield strapped to that forearm, and charged. His followers went after him, in no particular order but instinctively at double arm's length from each other, close enough to support and with enough space to work. An arrow whickered past Karl's face and another banged into his belly and bounced off, feeling like a hard punch through the leather of his brigandine and the small metal plates riveted between the two layers. One of his own followers was down with a shaft in the thigh, but then the McClintocks were at close quarters with the Eaters.

"Watch . . ." Karl wheezed, then forced himself to take a deep breath and shout loud enough for folk to hear through the flush of alarm. "Watch out for Diarmuid's folk! Close up!"

There was no point in spraying arrows blindly anyway, not with no clear target and a mere dozen archers—eleven now with the wounded man down. They advanced across the road in a few swift strides, and Karl felt as if he were trying to listen with his skin as well as the ears that heard grunts and cries and crackling brush and the brief tooth-grating clash of steel.

The McClintock tartan—mostly different shades of green and blue, with thin stripes of dark red—blended well with the vegetation, but they could see naked skin moving in there as the wild men turned to face Diarmuid's followers. He drew, shot—there was a wet cracking thump and a shriek—drew again . . .

Boudicca spoke to Gwri: "Back me."

The young seeress nodded and slung her bow, then caught the polearm Boudicca tossed to her. She poised it, brown full-lipped face intent as the huntress stepped closer still to the brush.

The cry of *McClintock abu!*—which meant *up the McClintocks!*—was sounding out now, then raw screams and an eerie up-and-down shrieking squeal that must be the enemy's battle call, like the call of man-sized rats.

Boudicca Lopez Mackenzie sank to a crouch with her black eyes as fixed and singular in their focus as a stalking cat, then to one knee, then drew and shot quick as a striking ferret with the bow slanted wide. There was a scream and thrashing from the brush as the arrow punched through below the fallen tree-trunk the savage was using as cover, and he collapsed over it and rolled forward halfway into view, thrashing with a shaft right through one kneecap and out the rear.

Two more Eaters leapt out, throwing themselves headlong forward. One had a short broad-bladed spear and small round shield; the other a hatchet in one hand and a long knife in the other. Boudicca nocked, drew and shot the man with the tomahawk at arm's length, so quickly that it seemed as if they were dancing to separate tunes with different tempos, and at so close a range that the feathers just had room to clear the arrow-rest before the point struck. It went into his throat, angling up between the arch of his jaw, and the broadhead erupted out his neck with half the clothyard shaft behind it.

The spearman was upon her then, and her right hand dropped from her quiver and darted towards the hilt of her shortsword. It would have been too late, betrayed by archer's reflex, save that Gwri thrust two-handed with the glaive from just behind her. The point struck the Eater's shield with a bang. The shrunk-on rawhide over the ancient trashcan lid turned the sharp steel spike, but the impact knocked him staggering back, and then she turned it and pulled with the hook on the other side to wrench him off-balance.

Karl exhaled and the string dropped off his fingers and the shaft whipped past Boudicca's shoulder and through the Eater spearman's body. The man spun away spraying blood from his nose and mouth and took three steps before he collapsed. Mathun shot beside him, face clenched in a rictus that nobody who'd known his lazy good-nature would have expected. The arrows were going out slowly, carefully aimed, none of the mad ripple that made an arrowstorm. The McClintocks were there, after all . . . but because they were there, the savages didn't have the leisure to shoot or throw javelins. The sound died down . . .

"We're aye comin'!" a voice called. "Hae a care, now, norrrthrons!"

"Heads up!" Karl called sharply.

With Mackenzies that wasn't a general alert. It meant *arrowheads up* and was an urgent warning against friendly fire—which his father had defined as friendliness of a most unfriendly sort.

The McClintocks came out onto the old roadway, looking variously exultant, shocked in the case of several with dripping wounds including a slash right across an eye, or grim: particularly the two who were carrying a limp body, a young man with old scars on the stump of one ear and the skull dished in above it and leaking slow blood around bone fragments sticking through the skin. Karl winced slightly at the sight, even more than the hand clapped across a bleeding eyesocket, and was glad of the light archer's sallet he wore. He'd been present as a child when the legendary Dun Juniper healer Judy Barstow Mackenzie said tartly to an injured hurly player that a man should bear in mind that a human head was like a china teapot full of jelly, and would react similarly if whacked.

"Aye, Dòmhnall na Cluaise is sped, may the Mother and the Horned One greet him beyond the Western Gate, and he feast with his kin before the forgettin' and the return," Diarmuid said heavily. "Forbye he was a good man, but he wuld drop his targe when he should hae been guardin' his left. The enemy is fled, those that live."

Karl looked around at a stifled keening sound. Ruan Chu Mackenzie was kneeling by the form of another of the little band from Dun Fairfax; his lover Feidlimid Benton Mackenzie, the young man's round fair face fixed in an expression of mild surprise. The arrow in his thigh had severed the big artery there clean across, the one that ran up into your groin and was as thick as your index finger. The great pool of blood around him showed the result, where his body had pumped out pints of it in seconds. Even on a healer's operating table with transfusions at hand that would most likely have been fatal.

Karl felt something run through him halfway between a grunt and a wince. He'd known Feidlimid all his life, since they were both running around underfoot like pups and in and out of each other's houses, as was the Clan's way with children. They'd been part of a clutch that usually sat on the same bench in Moon School, and they'd been made Initiates in the same year. He'd known some would likely die on this faring, but it was so *real* now.

Ruan's narrow dark face was set as he closed Feidlimid's eyes and bent to kiss him gently and straighten his limbs, though tears ran down his cheeks. Then he touched his fingers to the blood and marked his forehead with a single savage gesture before rising with the dead man's quiver in his hand. It held the full forty-eight shafts less the one on the fallen man's bowstring; he'd gone down before he could shoot even once.

"I told him we should stay at home until the levy was called out to avenge the High King, but he would have it so," he said quietly, his face hard.

Karl put a hand on his shoulder for an instant; he knew Ruan had been the more reluctant of the two to come on this faring. But he and Feidlimid had sworn the Oath of Iolas, which was a battle vow as well as one of the heart, and he'd followed despite his misgivings.

"We are all are born fey, my friend," Karl said; he made the Invoking sign and murmured a brief prayer to the Wise One and the Keeper-of-Laws for all who'd fallen. "Are you ready?"

"Aye," Ruan said shortly. "Let's be about it."

"Patch any of our folk or Diarmuid's who need it, then. Aye, and the hounds too, for that they fought with us."

Ruan's mother and father were healers in Dun Fairfax, and like most he'd picked up a good deal of his trade from his parents, and studied in Dun Juniper as well—the Clan's hearth-Dun was only a short walk from their home, which made it easier.

And I spoke to Feidlimid of this rather than another who'd have done as well because with him came Ruan, and we needed his skills. Well, so be it; I'll answer to the Guardians for it.

"Be about it!" Karl said to the others. "Fill your quivers and sling the extras from the bicycles."

Susan Mika rode up while Ruan was snipping off the linen thread he'd used on a slash; she had her bow cased and her shete in her hand, the broad-tipped slashing sword common east of the Rockies. There was blood dripping from the forward third of the edge, and she swung down casually in the saddle to pull up a swatch of dry grass to wipe it before she sheathed it, leaning far over with one heel hooked around the horn of her saddle for an instant. He'd seen plenty of expert horsemen even if he wasn't one himself, and the casual ease of that movement still made him blink a little.

The last pair of McClintocks came out of the brush as the snick of the shete sliding home sounded.

"They're a' sent on, *feartaic*," one shaggy redhead said to Diarmuid, her grin distorting the blue design of feather-tattoos that covered her face and neck.

She gave him his title of sub-chief with a duck of her head, and tossed her red-dripping spear a little to indicate how they'd been ushered to the Summerlands.

"Wha' tracks, Seònaidh?" he asked.

She cleaned the spearhead by plunging it into the earth several times before going on:

"Nae sign o' ain *truaillidh* more, by She Who Brings Fear."

Karl winced a little, and forced himself not to make a protective sign. A Mackenzie wouldn't have named Scathatch—the Devouring Shadow Beneath, the Dark Mother in Her most terrible form—so casually. Lady Juniper, the first Chief, had invoked Her in a battle early in the Clan's history, and the fearsome result was still a tale told in whispers. Still, even a stark southern hillwoman wouldn't swear by Her unless they were . . .

Extremely and with no doubt sure, he thought.

Susan nodded, looking east and south. "I didn't find any of the crazy bastards either," she said, looking a little grayer than her normal ruddy light brown.

The eastern rasp was stronger in her voice than usual, too. From what Karl had heard there hadn't been any Eaters out where she came from, even right after the Change. Cattle had outnumbered people there even in the ancient times, and there had been millions of acres of wheat in the ground when the machines stopped. Times had been very hard and many died, according to the tales not least in the wars that saw the refounding of her nation as a mighty power out on the plains, but it hadn't been anything approaching what had happened where great cities were near.

"'Cept the ones who couldn't keep up," she said, and touched her hilt. "Wouldn't take those scalps even if I had time," she added, answering a question he hadn't asked.

Karl thought for a moment. "Our wounded should be safe enough here. They're not straggling about so much as I would have expected from bare-arsed wild men."

"Aye," Diarmuid said. "You, Ìomhair a' Bhogha Mhaide, you stay with the hurt."

Harshly, when Ìomhair clenched his hand on his bow and began to object: "Yer limpin', mon! Ye cannae keep up wi' us in a run! Ye'll do aye more good here and the danger may be more. And ye, Ùisdean."

The McClintock he named looked up, hand hovering over the swatch of bandage covering one eye. The other was a blue-centered slit with the pain.

"Can ye fight, mon?" Diarmuid asked.

"Aye," the wounded man answered. "I can, that."

Then with an attempt at a smile: "Wuldna' claim tae be at my best, ye ken, *feartaic*."

Karl was somewhat impressed; that eye must hurt like the fangs of Anwyn's hounds, especially with the disinfectant Ruan had poured on it.

"You'll stay too, then."

Karl cast a glance back over his shoulder. This didn't seem nearly so much like a prank anymore, but he was more determined to see it through for all that. And . . .

"We lost a day waiting at the farm, that we did. My da will be through here sometime soon with the Archers, hotfoot on our trail."

He turned to Susan. "How far to the Princess?"

"Two miles."

"Let's go then. You lead, but don't get so far ahead we can't act together at need. We'll push it the now."

That didn't mean a sprint, but at a quick jog with no rest periods they could cover the distance in twenty minutes. He cast a longing eye at the bicycles as she reined around, but riding would be impossibly dangerous now. They wouldn't do the Princess any good getting killed before they arrived at the real fight.

"Ar aghaidh linn!" he barked. "Let's go!"

"About half an hour," Edain Aylward Mackenzie said.

The Bow-Captain of the High King's Archers looked at the state of the bodies lying beside the road and how many flies had drowned in the pool of blood under young Feidlimid.

His lips tightened at that; he'd known the neighbor-lad from his own

Dun Fairfax all his life. Not the brightest candle in the sconce, perhaps, and given to wild fancies and seeing the Fair Folk dancing down at the edge of the pasture on festival nights after the keg was tapped often enough. But good-natured and willing and lively, strong as a bear, a pretty fair archer and promising smith, and a friend to his own sons. It was not the first time he'd seen a likely youngster lying stark with all the promise run out with their life's blood, not by many a weary league in time and distance. And had to bear the thought of the family keening them without even the chance to lay their child out and carry the body to the pyre . . .

But I'm thinking it's the first time for Karl, and guessing that he likes war less now than he did when he was wild to be grown. Welcome you are to the club, boyo! We fought through the war time to give you peace for your childhood, but that ends now.

The living wounded, four of them, had been moved into the shade and given good first-aid; there was nothing more he or the High King's Archers could do for them. From the silent glare the tow-haired McClintock with the swollen knee was giving him as he leaned on his bow there was no point in asking questions, but there wasn't much need either.

The brush on the east side of the southbound track was thick, but one graycoat coyote slunk off from ripping at a naked body that sprawled on the pavement with an arrow right through the knee and a gaping wound in the throat. More squabbled in the brush. Hopefully no silvertip grizzly or big cat would get interested; there were plenty of both in this country.

Earth must be fed, he thought. *It's as much a return to the Mother as the pyre.*

Báirseach nodded. "Your lads do seem to be running into bad folk along the way, and them such sweet peaceable babes, eh? Those ill-doers in the mountains, now this."

"Aye, I'd not have thought 'em the type to leave a trail of bodies," Edain snorted, but it was a good point.

Ah, Chief, would that you were here! For that I miss you for yourself, also you're missed for your sword-arm, and even more for your wits. The which the lass has too, but not so tempered by time's hammer and anvil.

"Not a fight this size until the one Eryn Muir reported, with the Eaters and the Haida and the Koreans working together," he said softly. "Now, there's more here than the little Princess taking a wee stroll with her new friends from Japan, as if it were that time she decided on a Quest of her own when she was eight," he said. "And meself was the one sent after her then, too, *and* dragged her kicking off her pony. Caught me a good whack on the nose, she did; she has a temper, that one."

"She did? You were?"

"A rare taking Matti was in, and the Chief not what you'd call over-pleased himself. But this is altogether more serious than the High Queen thought or thinks, that it is indeed and without doubt. Once is coincidence, twice happenstance . . ."

"The third is a foemen's plan or a message from the Powers," Báirseach said softly, and made the warding sign of the Horns with her left hand. "I never thought the High King's death could be mere happenstance."

"No, nor I. His fate was tied to the land's. It's troubled I am. We're here on orders, but the orders were decided on from information that's not complete."

"What would the High King have said, do you know?" she asked.

Edain snorted almost-laughter. "He'd have said use my best judgment, and take the consequences."

He thought for a moment, looked up at the pillar of smoke to the southward, revised his first opinion and then called to the glowering McClintock. Another of his Clan sat beside him with a *claidheamh mòr* naked across his knees, but looked understandably preoccupied with a nasty face wound that had probably taken his left eye.

Edain spoke to the standing bowman: "Cateran, there may be another fight ahead and we needed to pitch in. Where precisely were my lads headed?"

The man glowered again, still more fiercely, and Edain said impatiently:

"Would you rather I catch them, or enemies like these Eaters overfall them, then? *And* your tacksman and your clan-kin, to be sure."

The one-eyed man spoke unexpectedly: "Get yer head out o' yer arse and tell him, Ìomhair, he's right—a wonder of the Powers for a Mackenzie boy, but there ye hae' it. Forbye I'm hurtin' too bad to think and ye were always too much of a *burraidh* for that."

The man he named thought, then grinned—unpleasantly. Edain would have agreed with his kinsman's appraisal of him as a dolt and a bit of a wild boar besides, but at least he seemed willing to take advice from his own kin.

"Aye, summat tae tha', Ùisdean," he said in the rough growling accent of his native mountains, thick enough to cut with a *sgian dubh*, and turned to Edain:

"The *feartaic* and the Princess, they maun hae need o' ye, lowlander. Word came—the Lakota lass—that the Princess is in danger at . . . what do the westfolk call it . . . ah cannae get m'tongue aboot it . . ."

"Círbann Rómenadrim?" Edain said sharply.

"Aye, thass' it. Danger fra more o' these *truaillidh*, these filth." He nodded at one of the dead Eaters. "So the war band went gangin' awa' in a' haste, yer twa yellow-heads at the fore. Not that we waur ever in danger o' bein' caught by ye, eh?"

He seemed to be deriving some satisfaction from saying it; Edain flushed and carefully didn't give him a shout. Getting into a slanging match with a McClintock was like mud-wrestling with a pig.

Báirseach glanced at the rows of bicycles left where they lay. "Drop our ma-shins too?"

He shook his head, calling up maps and past visits and what Finney had said. Decision crystallized:

"No, dropping them was right for them, not us. The young gombeens will be putting up any ambush ahead of us."

"Like dogs flushing partridges from the stubble, you might be saying."

"Aye, save these birds have sharp teeth and a taste for human flesh. Back to it, Archers! The Princess and the Prince may be in danger!"

He could feel the reaction, like a dog's ears pricking up and its hackles rising; a good commander had to be able to sense things like that. They'd given their all on this chase, but arresting was not what the High King's Archers were for. *Guarding* the scions of House Artos, even at the cost of their own lives, was very much their craft, trade and mystery.

"We'll pedal as fast as we may."

There might be an ambush like this one his boys and their friends had broken from the inside, but he doubted it. His father had called that tactic of sending a party on ahead the Irish Mine Detector, for reasons he'd never made clear; Edain had asked Lady Juniper about it once and she'd just snorted and rolled her eyes and muttered *Sassenach!*

Right now it meant that he could push his force three times the speed of those on foot.

"Ar aghaidh linn!" he said, and stepped onto the pedal. "Let's go!"

"It's ironic," Deor *Wid-ferende* said.

He rose a little in the stirrups and looked out over the bright dry grassland that rolled away before them; just ahead was his brother Godric Godulfson and the raven banner of Hraefnbeorg. Behind came the rest of the thegns and huscarles and fyrdsmen, three-score and all mounted, with a few packhorses bringing up the rear.

Standing hurt too, sharp pain up into his groin. The weary horse rocked back up into a canter, and seemed as miserable as he was. He felt for the beast, since it could not know *why* it had to suffer save that the human in charge demanded it. Sweat ran down from under his byrnie of fine riveted mail from Hinduraj and stung still more in the raw places.

"Ironic? Is that a poet's kenning for *pain?*" Thora said, grinning through the mask of summer road-dust across her face. "Like *whale's bath* for *sea?*"

Sweat tracked runnels of mud through it; she pulled her canteen from her saddlebow, drank half the last few mouthfuls and leaned a little aside in the saddle to hand it over to him. She was sweating more, since she was in Bearkiller cataphract armor—only slightly lighter than a knight's. On the other hand, she was the warrior by trade, and the water tasted like bliss.

"Here I'm famous for my travels, and this saddle is sawing me in half from the crotch up as if I were some city merchant used to a padded chair at a countinghouse desk beneath my backside, and smooth rails beneath the wheels for a tramcar ride home."

Thora snorted and shifted herself and reached under the faulds of her armor to pluck at the seat of her leather breeches.

"More *ironic* for me, oath-brother," she said. "I was raised to be a horse-soldier and after just a miserable little ride of five days I feel as if I want nothing more in all the world than a week in bed . . . alone, and face-down, with nothing but air on my arse. Or maybe air and goose-grease with comfrey and chickweed. Too many years on ships, both of us."

And perhaps part of it was that neither of them would see their thirtieth summer again. The years gnawed at a man, never ceasing, as the Malice Serpent did at the roots of the World Tree.

I can still do everything I could ten years ago, he thought. *It just hurts a good deal more, and for longer. Thora's right, time to settle. After this faring, of course!*

He handed her the other half of his last dried apricots, and they munched them down. Something sweet just before a fight was usually a good idea, and it helped him to settle his belly. He'd never taken Thora's fierce joy in battle. And while she didn't enjoy killing men she'd never met and who'd done her no harm, it didn't much bother her either if wyrd would have it so, hers and theirs alike. He himself sometimes saw the faces of men he'd killed in the early hours when dawn was still gray.

Hooves beat with a drumroll on the hard ground, adding the scent of crushed herbs to the powerful smells of horse-sweat and man-sweat, metal and leather. They were well past the belt the thick impenetrable scrub and forest that hid the remains of Petaluma, and they'd cut cross-country rather than following the old roadway to save time. It was open here and kept so by natural fires and grazing game, rolling hills covered in long summer-golden grass with oak and bay and bluegum in the swales and scattered elsewhere.

The golden hills of Westria, he thought, as the wind waved the grass like the locks of a hero in a song.

When he'd gone north as a lad he'd read those pre-Change tales that the Queen Mother had liked, and from which she'd taken the new name for this province. They'd moved him too, and they'd been eerily prescient—perhaps somewhere, in some other cycle of Earth, they were fact and he was the dream. The High King had spoken to him of such things, late one winter night when they sat over wine in Dun Juniper and the coals burned low and shadows moved quietly on the eerie carvings of the Witch Queen's hall and Artos' own strong jewel-cut features. Of how this was not the first world that had declined towards its wyrd, nor would it be the last.

He shivered a little as he came back to the hot sunlight of common day. They'd seen little except a few Tengwar runes on stones, deer and antelope sensibly fleeing, and once a grizzly had reared defiant a few score yards away, bellowing raw challenge before lumbering sensibly into a thicket of overgrown ruins to wait while they passed.

Beasts are wiser than men, sometimes.

A silence lay over the countryside but birds were gathering above, dark wings circling, ravens and crows and even the giant grace of a condor, unknown when he was a boy and still quite rare this far north. They'd had enough time since the Change to learn that when men gathered to fight a feast was likely spread for them.

Ahead and leftward a tall pillar of smoke was bending away to the east, faded and tattered but still plain; now and then they could catch a glimpse of blue, the surface of the Bay. That smoke was Círbann Rómenadrim itself, the wharf or the buildings aflame, or both. His mouth tightened, and as it did two horsemen came towards them, riding up out of a fold in the land and swinging wide around a patch of forest to their left. They were Alfwin Jacksson and his younger brother Sexræd. Alfwin had a name as a great hunter and stalker, which helped with such work.

Alfwin and I were close as brothers when I was young, he thought. *Not many would make time for all my fancies then; life was hard in Hraefnbeorg in those days.*

It was odd to come home and see the wild youngster now a solid householder with young children of his own. They were friends still, and the brown-haired man with a coarse cloth jerkin over his byrnie of scale armor—for concealment's sake—smiled tautly at him before he pulled up and raised a hand in salute to Godric:

"They're there, lord. The Princess and the Atheling stand yet, but the wild men are very many and they can't hold for long. Ten for their one, five when we've joined them. It's just as Deor said."

Even weary as they were there was awe in the glances the others gave him. He didn't feel entirely easy about it himself. Woden sent the mead of poetry to men like a flame in the heart; but He was also master of runecraft and the high magic, of oracles seen in dreams. The one and the other were closely linked, but he'd seldom had a seeing so clear and urgent. He could still feel it like a hand at his back, a whisper in his ear.

Godric thought for a moment, then signaled a halt and swung down. All the others did as well, some staggering as they gathered around. He shifted his round raven-blazoned shield from over his back to his left arm, pushed back his gilded boar-crested helmet for a moment, and looked from face to dust-caked, sweating face.

"Hraefnbeorg men," he said, pitching it to carry but not shouting. "Often have we boasted when the drinking horns passed in our hall at feast and symbel that of all men on Midgard we of the Saxon kind are the truest to our oaths."

There were nods and mutters of agreement. *Boast*, or *gylþ* to use the old word, had a special meaning among heathen folk like his. It placed your word in the well of fate, a solemn thing and one of dreadful potency and power. It bound not you alone, but also your kin, in a web of fate and luck and dooms. Kingdoms and great kindreds had fallen in fire and blood because of such, and the tales of them lived yet.

"Now is the day we make good our claim. We could not stand with Artos King in his last fight, he who held my oath and through me yours; wyrd wove it so. When he poured out his blood on our land—"

A thump of his spearbutt to remind them that it was this very soil he meant.

"—for us no man of Hraefnbeorg stood with him, though I had laid head and hands on his knees and given him my word. Now that blood calls out for vengeance from beneath our feet, and the heirs of his blood battle against harsh odds. Shall we stand by them?"

A short barking cheer ran through the threescore warriors, and Deor brandished his spear with the rest. It felt oddly comforting to march with his home-folk for once, as well as his blood-sister, to be one part of a single thing grown from the earth that had fed him.

Father, do you see me now? Are you content?

"Victory is in the All-Father's hand, He who sent my brother the seeing that brought us here. If our foes are many and fierce, then courage must be more and heart harder! Look to either side."

Startled, the warriors did so.

"Huscarles, landsmen, yeomen, you fight beside your neighbors, your kin, your sworn brothers, and I your lord will be at your head. We fight for our oaths, our families, and our land that feeds our children and holds the bones of our fathers and mothers."

He thumped the steel-shod butt of his eight-foot spear on the ground; the keen edges of the long head glittered in the afternoon sun.

"The spirits of those who bore us watch us now, to see our honor or our shame. All men die, all things also. The fame of your deeds alone lives as long as the world stands!"

They cheered again, and the lord of Hraefnbeorg grinned and drew his brother beside him, thumping him on the shoulder with rough affection:

"And we have a famous scop bred on our own lands to see our deeds and sing of them."

This time they cried *Deor* hail, and he felt himself flushing as he waved. That had not happened often, in an eventful life. Applause for his work, yes, but not this.

"We leave the horses here—"

This time there was a cry of joy with an ironic note, and laughs from the youngsters amongst them as a few rubbed their buttocks. The older men, the solid bearded householders and heads of families, were more grave. They had lived long enough to know down in the bone how quickly and easily a man could die.

"—and we march to fall upon the wild men, cut our way through, and make shield-wall with the athelings and their war band. Form the swine-array! The battle cries are *Hraefnbeorg* and *Woden*!"

A bellow arose, and a thunder of shafts on shields. The raven banner went up to flutter in the warm westerly wind behind the lord, carried by Deor's younger nephew Wulfric on a long spear; the lad's freckled teen-age face was pale and set with his determination to bear the glory of the post. Two with shield and sword stood to either side of him, and two huscarles with four-foot, broad-bladed battle-axes in their hands.

The rest of the fyrd fell in behind Godric and the banner in a blunt wedge—the swine-array of battle, Woden's gift to brave men, where the strength of each was the strength of all. Deor and Thora had a place of honor in the front rank only a little behind Godric's sword-hand, next to his son and heir Leofric. As honor usually did, it also meant greater peril. The mass behind them added weight, but they were at the point of the spear. Others would step forward to take their place if they fell dead or wounded.

"Follow me! *Hraefnbeorg!*" Godric called.

"Hraefnbeorg!" sixty voices bellowed in reply to his brother, a raw challenge to the world as they stepped off together.

Boots thudded, mail and scales and gear chinked and clattered, and in the rear of the formation two men raised long ox-horn trumpets to their lips and blew, the sound echoing in bone and skull and speeding out over hill and swale. The grip of Deor's round shield was tight beneath his gloved hand as he raised it to just below the nose-guard of his helm. They toiled up the long low slope to the southward, swinging a little west to avoid the patch of scattered trees and brush, and as they did the weariness fell away from him, and the weight of the byrnie and helm and shield.

Over the crest, and a wind was blowing through him, hot and holy, like the birthing of a song but stronger. The tread of the boots was like gray surf pounding the cliffs in a storm out of the Western sea, feeling the rock shake beneath his feet under the ocean's blows and glimpsing the *sae-aelfen* in the spray.

The ground ran upward now, rolling, through the black clot of the Eater host and towards the narrow place where the kite-shields stood embattled. And the silvery warrior with the feathers of the Golden Eagle on her helm stood, the Sword forged by Weyland-smith beyond the world bright and terrible in her hand, just as *Láwerce* had shown him while his body lay in the hollow oak.

Save that now the savages were aware of him and his folk.

They were still three long bowshots away, but somehow he knew how chiefs among the Eaters of Men were grabbing at their followers, shaking them and kicking backsides and slapping faces to make them turn around even in the grip of bestial passion. A spray of them headed towards the swine-array, then more, then gathering clots.

Behind and above them was the Darkness he had sensed; and threads of it running down towards a man among the savages. *He* was no savage, though: dark and grim but holding a baton carved with orcas and ravens, a mind subtle and strong with hard-won knowledge and bitter angers and long years of hatred. The dark power wove through the forms of Raven and Orca to the man in patterns of ruin and compulsion—it was as if it was a net woven through flesh and mind, holding helpless aspects of Powers themselves inconceivably mighty, twisting Their forms to its purposes and through them Their worshipper. For a moment he glimpsed carved longhouses beside gray seas, and mountains clothed in forests of majesty.

That knowledge flowed through him, past the blade-edge focus that his very self was becoming more purely with every stride. He strode through knee-high golden grass, but it was as if every pace also took him beyond this world of common day. The vast forces he had seen from afar were *here* now, so present and so real that their essence made the world translucent as thin-sliced horn or smoked glass. The sun-bright Lady who *was* the Sun; the terrible Crone with Her scythe and swarming crow-flock . . . and another, behind Deor himself. With him, through him, glimpses, black wings, a horse that was not a horse, a hall whose tables faded into shadow and whose carven pillars towered into the sky, a bridge that shone and glittered, slow steps echoing as he walked down to a well were *something* waited. Thoughts vast and shadowy and bright, more complex in their endless twine and turn than his soul could grasp save as uncomprehending awe, and a single blue eye. A grief and strength and sadness greater than worlds.

The first of the enemy were near; he could see two loping towards him. A female with a long knife and a mask made of human facial bones with their teeth replaced by a dog's, and a male with soot-blackened features swinging a jagged lump of metal on a thong attached to a wooden handle. Deor felt his right hand cock backward.

The heavy spear he bore was a thrusting weapon, but it flew like a bird arcing up into the sky. Then it descended, in an arc so pure that his soul ached with it, and an Eater collapsed backward as the steel punched through his breast and his flail-weapon flying free to strike one of his comrades. Deor's sword flared in his hand.

"Woden!" he screamed.

His body was light as thistle blowing on the wind, yet vast as mountains, swift as larks swooping beneath the eaves of home on a summer's eave.

"Woden! *Woden!*"

CHAPTER SIXTEEN

CÍRBANN RÓMENADRIM
(FORMERLY CHINA CAMP)
CROWN PROVINCE OF WESTRIA
(FORMERLY CALIFORNIA)
HIGH KINGDOM OF MONTIVAL
(FORMERLY WESTERN NORTH AMERICA)
JULY/FUMIZUKI/CERWETH 14TH
CHANGE YEAR 46/FIFTH AGE 46/SHŌHEI 1/2044 AD

"*They're stirring again!*" a voice shouted, interrupting the sound of whetstones filing notches out of well-used blades.

Órlaith slung the nearly empty canteen back to her waist and accepted the helmet from Heuradys. Her liege knight made sure that it was well seated and the chin-cup firm before she put her own steel gauntlets back on, grimacing a little at the way their leather interiors were sticky with cold blood now. They were both spattered with the stuff, running red in streaks or turning jelly-like and clinging across armor and the upper part of their faces where it sprayed through the vision-slits of their visors. There was no time to do anything but smear it aside to clear your eyes, and spit as it trickled down to your lips diluted with sweat. In some ways it was like working in an abattoir.

"You OK, Orrey?" Heuradys said.

"Better than I expected," Órlaith replied, with was true enough. "And the reinforcements are coming."

Heuradys nodded soberly. Órlaith tossed her head a little; the helm seemed to squeeze at her skull worse each time, but the relief of having it off for a moment was worth it. Then she took up her shield and set her hand to the hilt, taking a long deep breath as she did. Drawing the Sword of the Lady . . . when you did it in anger and hot blood and intent to kill, it was like no other thing on Earth. Her father had never gloried in war, but she was beginning to understand why his name had been one of terror to the kingdom's enemies. One that haunted the shattered sleep of the few who had faced him and survived.

Ahead of her the stretch of level ground northward was littered with the dead. Carpeted, in some places, lying sprawled across each other. There was an astonishing amount of blood, when scores bled to death. There was a ridge of bodies where the first charge had met the shields of the men-at-arms. The marks glaives and swords made on bodies were terrible gaping things, but she could see the difference where she'd fought herself. A little of that was that the enemy rushed towards her in particular, shouldering each other to get at her, but more of it was the Sword. Every wound it dealt was like the worst from a common weapon, like what a newly-sharpened blade striking with force and great skill and optimum angle made.

The thick layer of dead extended six long paces back now, to mark where the knights had retreated to keep their feet clear and as the trickle of hurt were dragged back and the line thinned. The ground had been hard and dry with summer beneath the grass. Now it was actually muddy in places, and damp over several dozen square yards.

Like spilling buckets on the ground. Bucket after bucket . . .

Flies were buzzing in hordes—she batted away one that seemed intent on getting inside her helmet—and swarming so thickly on the bodies that some of them seemed to move again. Flies and maggots were part of the wheel of things as well and had their rightful place, but that didn't mean she had to like them. The smell was heavy too, copper and iron and salt like seawater but not quite, with a faint tang of meat going off beneath it in the warm summer air, and the stink of bodies sliced open, like an outhouse badly kept. Overhead the birds circled, everything from condors and kites to ravens and crows. Their cries sounded peevish now and then, as if they were impatient.

At the alarm call half a dozen of her crossbowmen came running back with bundles of bloody bolts in multiple quivers slung around their necks, ammunition salvaged from their targets, and handed them out to their comrades. A few of the Protector's Guard men still had their swords or daggers in their hands as well, having taken a risk to put the Eater wounded out of their pain. Rumor had said the wild men ate their own dead; they now had visual proof of the fact, and that they weren't too fussy about exactly *how* dead. It was a relief not to hear whimpering or see broken shapes trying to crawl away.

And we will have to do the same mercy-stroke for our own hurt, if we can, at the last, she thought grimly. *I can feel that the others are coming, I can hear it on the air, feel it through the ground . . . but I don't know* precisely *when. And* arra, *time is very short indeed!*

The cannibals weren't necessarily stupid, and they knew the effective range of a standard crossbow to an inch. A little more than three hundred yards away they were grouped in clots and clumps, some down on the ground resting, some doing their chaotic war-dances even now. As she watched more and more took that up, the shrieks and shrill squeals and drumbeat rending the air. She sensed something behind them, something ordered and severe as they were wild, something full of a cold wisdom—

"Here they come," Heuradys said.

Órlaith looked over her shoulder. The Japanese were resting too, grouped around the now more numerous wounded. More than half of those were Japanese themselves; rushing parties of Eaters back from the edges of the hill had proved more dangerous than holding the narrow saddle. One of the samurai had gone tumbling down the hillside when he missed his stroke with the long spear in his desperate haste, and the screams had lasted for some time.

Egawa was down on one knee, a hand on the hilt of his sheathed sword and leaning on it slightly as he panted. Reiko was beside him, kneeling and sitting back on the heels of feet overlapping at the toes. She met Órlaith's eyes and smiled, inclining her head very slightly, and Órlaith returned the gesture.

How to spend an afternoon with your friends, she thought. *For those times when hunting or hawking or singing and dancing just won't do . . .*

Her head came back around as the Eaters began to move forward; they sent fewer arrows now, since they didn't have any reserve beyond what they'd carried, and few had many to start with. She knocked down her visor, bared her teeth behind the metal and . . .

. . . laid her hand on the hilt that felt like silver and staghorn and . . .

Drew.

A *shock* ran through the world, immaterial but entirely real, a flexing like a beaten drum. The Sword of the Lady *glittered,* looking more like diamond than polished steel in the hot sunlight, a shine like a silent roaring in her ears. The weight in her hand felt as if it was a bit less than two pounds, light for a hand-and-a-half longsword . . . though it had been heavier for her father. Within her—

The heat, the weariness and the fear were still there, the ache of bruises and the sting of sweat in a pressure-cut on one cheek. So was the taste of blood from where the inside of her mouth had been driven back against the teeth within. That had happened when two of them hit her in flying leaps and knocked her backward; Heuradys and John had hacked them apart while they scrambled to stab her and she thrashed beneath the weight. But none of them *mattered* anymore. A wind blew through her, like the beating of a million raven wings, bearing her up and making her weightless.

She *was* the land, and hers was its wrath at the blood spilled upon it, full of a keening sorrow and fury at the pain of its defenders, a hot pride at their courage and steadfastness in the face of certain death. Her father was there somehow, part of something infinitely greater but still exactly himself.

"Morrigú!" she shrieked. *"Morrigú!"*

The line of the knights stiffened and braced, with a deep shout of *Haro!* that was a snarling croak as much as a battle-cry. The Eaters came on beneath a shower of black-fletched arrows, then a rattle of javelins, and the crossbows replied—slowly and deliberately, each shot carefully aimed, to make the dwindling ammunition stretch. The loping mass was closer now, and the knights crouched a little behind their shields so that they were covered by the battered facings from nose to foot. The swords came up overhead, held hilt-forward.

A savage was heading towards her at a dead run, threads of spittle hanging from his open gap-toothed mouth, nostrils splayed open by what had to be deliberate cutting, and an ancient baseball bat spinning in his hand, with a knife hammered through the thick end. She stepped forward with the rest at the last instant, tucking her shield into her shoulder and keeping her head a little lowered.

Thump.

The Eater rammed into her shield and the bat came down, glancing off the curve of her helm and then into the shoulder-piece of her armor. The impact was wrenchingly hard, and she let her knees flex and then drove them forward again to tumble him backward. The Sword lashed down in an overarm cut, and there was a tug at her hand as it slammed into his shoulder and chopped through muscle and bone, from the angle of the neck down through the joint. The limb and a chunk of shoulder fell free, leaving a cut that took a fractional second to begin bleeding—so sharp that the veins and arteries were shocked into clamping down for an instant.

Even in the focus of battle something in her mind blinked astonishment. *Like an obsidian razor. And nothing harms it or dulls it. Nothing.*

On her left John took a step back, grunting, as a club made from a cut-down sledgehammer smashed into his shield. He stabbed over the edge, a little clumsily because the blow had thrown him off-balance, then cursed frantically and tugged as the point lodged in the bone of the Eater's face and wouldn't come clear. The man's body followed, jerking the point from side to side as he thrashed and dropped his weapon and clutched at the shield in reflex. Spearpoints turned towards him to take advantage. Evrouin had his glaive stuck in a man's rib cage; his dark eyes went wide as he prepared to throw his body in the way.

Órlaith stepped in and struck with her own shield, knocking the wounded Eater off her brother's point; in the same instant she cut upwards with the Sword to block a machete. Only the retraining she'd made herself go through let her parry with the edge like that.

Ting!

Her eyes went wide behind the visor, as the top half of the ancient garden tool pinwheeled upwards. There had been a hard tug on her wrist this time too, but little more than she'd have felt at lopping through a wet straw mat on a practice field with an ordinary weapon. Heuradys stepped in and blocked a spear aimed at her liege, took a thrust to the shoulder from another that screeched off her armor and cut the man's leg out from under him—being merely a very good sword skillfully wielded it went halfway through the knee-joint and had to be tugged out and he flew backward when she punched a polyene-covered knee upwards into his descending face.

For long moments the three of them were fighting in unison like a dance or three bodies with one will, a continuous block-strike-block seasoned with blows from armored elbows and knees. The whole line took a lurching step back; the knights were like steel towers, but the brabbling weight of the savages threatened to overwhelm them, every instant one misstep from utter disaster for them all if the line broke. Out of the corner of her eye Órlaith saw one of the crossbowmen sling his weapon, draw his sword and take the little round buckler slung on the scabbard in his left fist, preparing to step in when the men-at-arms were forced back from the narrow stretch they could still cover nearly shield-to-shield.

Órlaith knew she was fighting well, but she was at ten-tenths of capacity, and everyone in the shield-line was performing to their limit. Each enemy who came within reach of the Sword's edge died, but it was impossible to keep stopping men forever if they had no fear of death at all . . .

Knowledge crystallized. The Eaters were being *flung* at her, as much a weapon in someone's hand as enemies in their own right. They too were part of Montival, a part that was like an illness, a grating wrongness . . . but she could feel how their savagery was used and twisted.

"Cover me!" she shouted through the snarl of voices and bang and clatter and rasp and the loud hiss of her own panting in the closed helm.

She took a step back as John and Heuradys stepped in, her brother's sword looping in a figure-eight and her liege knight moving in an astonishing blur of speed.

A moment's thought, and she knocked her visor up, reversed the

Sword of the Lady, holding it up with the pommel to the sky. The sun caught in the antler-cradled crystal like white fire.

"Free!" she shouted, and went to one knee as she thrust it downward.

Into the soil of the kingdom it had been forged in the World beyond the World to embody, into the land and air that linked every living thing.

Shock rippled through her, and her skin roughed as if she had been plunged into cold water. There was a sense of *severing*, as if invisible cords had been cut and recoiled like giant whips, and the assault hung in the balance. A new note entered the Eaters' shrieks and chitterings and squeals, an almost pitiful tone of bewildered doubt. Somewhere a man knelt screaming, with blood flowing from eyes and nose and ears and lips.

And beyond the enemy, a sound from the northward: horns, ox-horn war trumpets sounding a long resonant *hurrr-hurrr-hurrr.*

"Hraefnbeorg!" Deor shouted again as swine-array trampled over the bodies of the first band of Eaters to shatter on their shieldwall, like a pot thrown at the side of a house.

They toiled uphill under the banner of the ravens; the grade was slight, but now he could feel it again in his thighs. Arrows were whipping towards the Mist Hills fyrd, not many yet nor very hard driven, but each one was potentially a death and when you heard the *whhhpt* sound past your ear something inside you knew it. There was a grunt and cry of pain from behind him, and a man stumbled out of the array. The ranks moved to close up, and the battle-boar went its many-legged way forward.

Deor's shield went up a little. It was one taken from those hung in his brother's hall—good swords might be passed down from sire to son, but a good shield was lucky to survive one afternoon of strong warriors and heavy blows. This was the type their father had made from the pattern of the ancient Angles and Saxons: three feet across, a convex form like a huge dish with a single handgrip in the center behind the steel boss, the raven painted across its surface in black on red below a coat of varnish. He crouched a little as he jogged and held it up and forward. An instant later an arrow hit it at an angle and snapped, the hard twist of impact a surprise as it always was.

"I've seen a lot better shooting than that," Thora said contemptuously beside him, doing likewise with hers—made by craftsmen in New Singapore out of lacquered bamboo and elephant hide, and held by a forearm loop and grip Bearkiller-fashion. "I've *done* a lot better than that."

He opened his mouth to pant out a reply, and—

Shock.

Something seemed to run through earth and sky, blood and bone, up from the hard soil beneath his feet. For an instant that lasted perhaps half a heartbeat he was *aware* of himself as he had rarely been before; seeing his life as a complex web of choice and circumstance, each step turning his feet to a new pattern that in turn became his fate. And he knew the things that had bound him, constrained him, *limited* him with a stark clarity. The moment passed, but left him feeling a little different within—light, clean, and somehow more purely himself. He felt *free*.

"Something happened," he panted.

"No *shit*!" Thora said.

The clumps and clots of Eaters who'd been rushing toward the fyrd slowed and wavered. Deor saw one man among them with a double-bitted axe stop and shake his head again and again, clasping his hands to his head, the gesture clear even across a hundred yards of distance. Then he stopped and looked at the force approaching, looked back over his shoulder. He ran out in front of his fellows, bellowing; between distance and the thick clotted dialect Deor couldn't understand a word, but he could feel the rage and fear in it. Muscle ran thick over the man's arms and shoulders, in contrast to the knotted sinewy scrawniness of most of his fellows.

"Upuzzi yuh fukk'mup!" he screamed.

Pointing the weapon at the shieldwall he loped forward; after a moment more and more followed him, until it was a mass several times the fyrd's numbers. The savage chief was not without wit, either; he was aiming a little to one side of the boar's head . . . right at Deor, in fact, and looping in so that the westering sun was behind him. It wasn't the handicap it would have been later in the day, but it didn't help, or hurt the savages to have the sun at their backs. Six paces to his left Godric Godulfson snarled a grin in his gray-shot beard and held his sword aloft, then chopped it down and to the right as he turned in that direction. His sons followed with the banner and the whole blunt wedge swung to follow, the adjustment as automatic as the spacing of a yard to either side everyone kept, fruit of many days practice in the fyrd-muster in the slack seasons of the farming year.

"Woden loves brave men!" Godric roared. "Charge! *Woden!*"

"*Woden!*" the whole small host bellowed, as the horns sounded again and again.

The Hraefnbeorg fyrd broke into a bellowing charge behind their lord, not a dash but a hard swift pounding lope, every left boot coming down in unison to a massive chant:

"*Wo*-den! *Wo*-den! *Wo*-den!"

The loose mass of the Eaters came closer and closer. Deor could see mouths gaping and eyes going wide and glancing from side to side among them, and the crowd—it would be too much to call it a formation—rippled like tall wheat in a breeze as the wedge of red-and-black shields came closer, the boar-crested helm of Godric at the head and the serried ranks of spearheads and raised swords and axes behind him. There was no crash of impact or transmitted shock; instead the savages rippled back like the rings of water when a stone dropped into a pond. Here and there an Eater dashed forward to thrust or strike; then two or three of the Hraefnbeorg men could hit at the same time from as many angles. Already at an advantage with their shields and helms and metal byrnies, their order and impetus carried them through the enemy in a single headlong rush.

The last gave way before them; not running so much as recoiling. Deor sucked in a breath despite his panting as he saw how few the line of tall shields ahead were. Princess Órlaith snapped up the visor of her helm and called out.

Órlaith looked to either side as she rose. The solid mass of the Hraefnbeorg men was plainly visible now. The Eaters weren't pressing in with the same mindless fury, but they weren't running away either—or at least most of them weren't, and they were still very many despite the trickle running westward for the woods and the Bay. A glance over her shoulder showed the Japanese retreating from the hill's southern edge towards the tree, holding their formation but moving back to keep the mass of Eaters who'd finally surged up onto the hilltop from lapping around their flanks.

"Sir Aleaume—" she said, then realized he wasn't on his feet. "Droyn!" she called instead. "Take over here! They'll rally in a moment. Collect bolts, get ready!"

The squire nodded curtly, blood spattered red against his brown face. The knights straightened as the Eaters recoiled from the advancing Hraefnbeorg formation, then swung back like an opening door. The Mist Hills levy came through it, their banner flaunting proudly and the Saxon broadswords and heavy spearheads running red. A few of the faces showed wounds, a few limped, but the thick carpet of dead beneath their boots was the main hindrance. Their leader grinned at her, a middle-aged man with a graying beard and a helm with a rampant gilded boar on its crest, swinging his sword up in salute.

"Many thanks, my lord," she said, crisp despite the desert dryness of her mouth. "Now follow me!"

There was an odd feeling in her hand where she held the Sword of the Lady. It was unmarked; blood seemed to flow off it, as if a million tiny invisible jets of cleansing water . . . or light . . . were scouring it ever clean. And now there was a *tightness* to it, a feeling of vast forces holding each other in check, or nearly. As if she had cloven some substance thick and yielding and gelid, that would close in behind the stroke rather than trying to openly oppose a greater power. The chittering squeals and weird shrieking of the Eaters had died away. Now it began again, rising to an ululating chorus. John and Heuradys flanked her, and the Saxons parted to give them a place. The world narrowed again as she knocked her visor back into place; it took a little more effort, since the right hinge had been bent a bit when it shed a thrust that *almost* went into the eyeslit.

The Nihonjin had held when their leaders saw that help was coming. Now the Saxon wedge formation swept in around their left into the Eater mass, and Órlaith raised the Sword as she ran at their head. The savage in front of her threw himself back in a near-summersault as it came near, dropping the hatchets he held in either hand; there was an odd expression in his eyes and slack face, as if something *lifted* from his mind as the Sword approached.

He trembled for a moment and then bolted to the rear and leapt down the hillside, tumbling and rolling in his eagerness and coming back to his feet running. Another was pushed towards her by the press at his back, and she struck grimly—a figure-eight, slicing through the shaft of his spear and then back to take a neat disk off the side of his skull.

Others pushed in as he fell; she kept her shield up and struck with economical thrusts and short, controlled chops, even then on some level horrified by the results. Heuradys and John were slowing, slightly but noticeably, and she felt a twinge of eeriness at how she wasn't. Part of that was the lighter weight, even more the lack of friction—nothing caught or held the blade's infinite smoothness when it struck. Part of it was something sensed, as if she knew that there would be a price later.

I'm sending the weariness down the road, she thought. *I'll pay the price for it then. If the Mist Hills levy hadn't come we'd all have been dead in fifteen minutes more, so we would and certain sure, but they aren't enough to do more than delay things!*

Still, she had to do what she could.

"My lord!" she called to Godric. "You have three-score?"

Godric whipped his shield's leading edge forward to punch an Eater in the face, with the flat laid along his arm, using it like a twenty-pound set of brass knuckles. The savage fell, and the huscarle beside the baron brought his four-foot axe down on another with a shout. The broad blade of the weapon chopped three-quarters of the way through the Eater's neck, leaving it lolling on a scrap of muscle and skin and white sinew. The Saxon chief jerked his head aside to dodge the flow of blood, and it went down the front of his mail byrnie instead of—possibly fatally—into his face to blind him.

"Yes, sixty-two with my brother Deor and his oath-sister," he said, side-stepping closer until he was shield-to-shield with her brother John and close enough to talk.

You could do that while fighting, if you had to. It usually wasn't a good idea but needs must.

"Send a score or so back to the men-at-arms, they're nearly worn out."

Godric wasted no time; she felt an inner relief that he wasn't the sort of man who needed a long explanation when there was no space for it.

"Leofric," he barked to the young man on his left; there was a strong family look to him, though the hair of his beard was much lighter. "Take Beorn and Paega and Hengest and their households and bolster the north-realm men behind us. Go!"

Leofric stepped back and turned without a word and moved through the formation grabbing men by the shoulder. Meanwhile the Hraefnbeorg force spread out, turning from a wedge to a wall three deep bristling with point and edge. The Eaters broke back from it like surf on rock and drew off again, glaring and mouthing and gathering their scattered gangs. Órlaith looked to the Japanese; their faces were iron, but the strain was showing.

"Reinforcements!" Reiko called, raising her sword in salute; the tone was almost lighthearted. "Most welcome! More soon, I hope!"

Godric looked at the Crown Princess, and she nodded as she spoke.

"Another two-score, or a bit more. Mackenzies and McClintocks. I'm told they should be here any moment. And hopefully the Dúnedain will show up, what with the smoke. Though they may send scouts first to see what's happening."

He grunted and looked about. The Associate men-at-arms were leaning on their shields and panting, as his son led eighteen of the Mist Hills fighters to shore up their line at the narrow place that joined this hill to the one northwards. That more than doubled their numbers, and at least it let the more lightly armed crossbowmen who'd been filling the gaps to step back to the flanks . . . those of them left on their feet. The rest of the Montivallan position was a semicircle facing southward, and most of that was the newcomers. The Eaters eddied in chaos beyond them, and more were pouring up over the lip of the hill. Órlaith answered his unspoken question as Reiko and Egawa trotted over; the *Heika* murmured a translation for her commander as Órlaith went on:

"Our ship hit them with darts and case-shot while they were on the water, and *we've* been killing since we came ashore, and they must have lost every third blade they started with, counting the hundred or so that burned when we fired the wharf under them."

"That was you, Highness? Ah, clever! They've been fighting you on your terms, and they've neither the gear nor the training nor the order for it," the man said. "Thunor with me, I've never dreamed of so many bodies on a single field!"

Órlaith had; she'd grown up on tales of the Prophet's War where this would have been a moderate-sized skirmish, with armies numbering tens of thousands and whole cities and castles and provinces changing hands more than once. But Mist Hills had been out of touch with the wider world until well after that. The real point was . . .

"We've hurt them very badly, but they're *not running*," she said grimly.

Godric grunted thoughtfully, and Egawa did too.

Small bands with strong bonds might literally fight to the death, or defenders who were surrounded by enemies asking no quarter and giving none.

As we are now, Órlaith thought.

But no larger force pressed on an assault until everyone fell. Except that the Eaters looked to be doing just that; they attacked, fell back a little, then rallied and came on again instead of backing off. As if something were overriding their sense of self-preservation; not only for their individual lives, but for the little groups that were losing all their hunters and warriors and dooming the rest to starvation and death.

Deor spoke, his thin tanned face haunted. "Princess, this is more than a battle of human kind. I can *feel* the bale and ill-will of the Power driving them on. Through a *drymann*."

She didn't know the word; it was from the Mist Hills tongue of lore, related to the one other Heathen folk used, but distinct from it.

Then she *did* understand it. *Sorcerer,* it meant. How easy it became to rely on the Sword . . .

And he knows what he's talking about, she thought. *Or he wouldn't be here with his kin. His vision saved our lives. House Artos owes this man a great deal. Unfortunately the immediate reward will be more peril of his life.*

"A *kangshinmu?*" Reiko said sharply, and Egawa grunted again when Órlaith nodded, since that was at least close to the real meaning.

Kangshinmu was the term the Japanese used for the type of magus who led their enemies from across the Sea of Japan, though the word was in the enemy's tongue, *Chosŏnŏ*, rather than Nihongo. Then Egawa's eyes went to the Sword of the Lady, and he nodded thoughtfully.

She followed his thought. "Yes, this is proof against such, if I can bring it to him. I thought I'd severed his hold," she said. "But it closed up again. Whoever it is . . ."

Faramir and Morfind had come up, leading their foam-slathered horses; Luanne was close behind, with a folding bucket they'd mostly filled from the last in their canteens. That was good practice, horses couldn't force themselves to keep going on willpower the way human kind could, for it took discipline of the soul.

"The skaga," Morfind said grimly, and her cousin nodded. "The Haida shaman, the skaga. Like when Malfind was killed."

"The skaga used the Eaters when we fought them this spring," Faramir licked his lips, and his cousin nodded vigorously, absently touching her scar. "Drove them, somehow. And . . . we shot at him, point-blank, and nothing hit. He just twisted and let arrows by, or batted them out of the air with that wand."

Deor glanced at them and nodded gravely. "And he is still here. Him at least."

Órlaith's gaze locked on the scop. "Can you tell where he is? He's hidden from me. Cloaked."

Deor closed his eyes, then turned and pointed, southwestward. Not directly towards the dispersing smoke of the pyre of the dock, but—

She couldn't feel where the skaga was herself. If anything there was an absence in that direction, a sense of muffling and binding and blinding. Oh, the enemy was strong, strong! But she could feel the land itself, and how it lay.

Steep, but doable going down, she thought. *With luck.*

"I can feel him," Deor said. "I'm a scop, not a *drymann* myself, but I have some runecraft. And the All-Father is my friend and protector, as the Crow Goddess, the Threefold Queen, is yours, Princess. And as the—"

He looked at Reiko, and bowed deeply in respect. "As the . . . the Power I see behind you protects you, great and sovereign lady."

"Power? Behind me?" she said, focusing on him. "What do you see, seer?"

He licked his lips. "A woman . . . a Goddess . . . who flames like the Sun itself, as if the sleeves of her robe were the Sun's fire arching through Heaven while she dances," he said. "She holds a mirror and wears a necklace of fiery jewels, and carries a sword that she holds over your head. I do not know Her name, but it seems to me She is some great Power of the Other World, ancient and strong. Her face . . . I cannot look at it for long before awe overcomes me even with the eyes of the spirit. But it has a look of yours, lady, as if you were close kin."

Stark astonishment broke through Reiko's control for a moment, and Egawa's eyes went very wide as he turned his head to glance at her.

"Amaterasu-ōmikami," he murmured, and bowed low for an instant.

"She is here to protect Her people, however far we journey from the Land of the Gods," Reiko said with soft awe. "Ancestress, I will be worthy of You."

Decision firmed in Órlaith's mind. Then her lips quirked; it was more a case of there being nothing else she could do except die to no great purpose. That made *deciding* surprisingly easy, even if it was something you very much didn't want to do.

"Droyn!" she said.

The squire took a few steps to join them, keeping an eye cocked on the milling mass of Eaters beyond the field of death.

"You heard?"

When he nodded, she went on: "If we kill this shaman now, the rest will run. But we can't charge him wholesale; it would take too long, he'd just retreat and keep the savages in front of him like a shield, and we have to guard the wounded."

Everyone within reach started to draw breath, getting ready to volunteer, and she raised the Sword—there was no better way to snap attention back to herself.

"No time for volunteers or objections," she said.

And sheathed it with a click that sounded exactly like metal on metal; some things about it were ordinary . . . which was itself profoundly odd.

"Will you come, Reiko?" she said.

"Yes," the Empress said simply.

Then a sharp gesture with her fan to Egawa. "You heard, General. A small force may do this, a large may not. You may come, and none other of our men."

"Heika," he said unwillingly.

"Heuradys and John, you're with me."

"And I, Highness," Evrouin said. Bluntly: "I'm not here because you locked me in a room, your Highness, or because I was afraid to face the High Queen. I'm here because protecting *him* is the job I swore to do. So . . . with all respect . . . get out of my way and let me do it."

Órlaith nodded: "Deor—"

"And I," Thora said, and Órlaith nodded curtly.

"Malfind, Faramir, Luanne, we'll need you because you're mounted, you're going to open the way and maybe cut off his retreat. *No* objections!" she added as others opened their mouths again. "There's no time. We'll go there"—she pointed just to the southwest of the saddle the knights held—"when the next attack comes in. The rest of you, hold hard here."

That next attack wouldn't be long; the noise from the Eaters was rising again. A murmur went among the fighters, and canteens were passed. She accepted one and sipped rapidly, feeling the water dissolving into her tissues. Everything depended on them now. They all ate one of the sweet ration bars as well, and a damp cloth let her get the clotted blood from around her eyes. One of her samurai handed Reiko another *naginata*, plainer than her original weapon whose shaft had been hacked through. It looked just as deadly as she spun it overhead and Egawa gave his final brief instructions to his command.

"I leave this position in your hands, Lord Godric," Órlaith said to the Hraefnbeorg leader. "And I take your brother to stand beside me. Fell fighters and grim, those of the Saxon blood, and none are more true to their oath."

She said it first in their old tongue, then in modern English, and felt the pride bristle through their ranks. Her blood-spattered armor was getting respectful looks as well. She went on:

"You have saved my life already; now I rely on you to guard my back while I do the work the Powers have given my House."

That use of their own terms was leaning on the Sword again, but she saw the point of the Lady's gift: no monarch could learn every bit of language and rite current in every corner of the High Kingdom and among Montival's vastly varied peoples on their own. The Sword gave every community a ruler they could trust and speak to as one of their own, so that none felt they were under a foreigner's power.

And it will go on, even if I fall too. John can take it up, or if we both die here Mother can come for it and keep it for Faolán and Vuissance and the sib yet unborn she carries.

One thing she was very sure of was that no hostile hand could grasp the Sword of the Lady and live.

Órlaith took a deep breath. The two Dúnedain and Luanne Salander moved ahead, making a trio with Faramir at the apex. Thora Garwood caught Luanne's eye for an instant as she passed and made the Bearkiller salute, fingers to brow, and the younger woman returned it. Heuradys finished checking her liege's armor and gave one strap a last tug to check its soundness.

"These are really good suits," she said absently. Seriously: "Athana put her shield over you, Orrey."

"And the Morrigú ward you, Herry," Órlaith said, checking hers in turn.

The other pairs did likewise; Evrouin tried to demur when John went over his crossbowman-style half-armor, and was briskly told to shut up and get ready. Órlaith looked at Deor:

"You hang back behind a little," she said. And before he could protest: "You can tell where the skaga is. If you're killed or crippled before we get to him, what's the point? Call out directions."

She looked around. *Well, good company to die in, if I must,* she thought. *And Da to talk with if I do.*

"You guard him too, Johnnie," she said to her brother.

He grinned under the slightly battered visor of the ostrich-plumed helm.

"We poets should stick together," he said, and held out a hand to Deor. "You wouldn't remember me, I was a spotty brat when you were last at Court."

Deor smiled back as they shook hand-to-wrist; he wasn't a conventionally handsome man, but the expression was charming.

"On the contrary, your Highness, you were a very promising . . . spotty brat."

They shared a chuckle, and Thora joined. "You on my shield side as always, eh?" she said. "We'll just slip the Prince in between. A handsome man on either arm—what more could a shield-maid wish?"

Egawa silently gave his sovereign the bow to one knee with fist against the ground that his folk reserved for their commanders in the field and drew his katana with a swift hiss and flicker as he rose. Órlaith decided she would keep the Sword sheathed until the last instant before the charge. She didn't know how well the enemy magus could sense its presence or movements, but there was no sense in taking chances.

Ahead of them the three riders slapped each other on the shoulder before they set shafts to string. The two Rangers bowed slightly towards the west, and Luanne kissed her crucifix, crossed herself and murmured:

"Sancte Michael Archangele,
defende nos in proelio;
contra nequitiam
Et insidias diaboli esto praesidium!"

Órlaith thought that quite grimly appropriate. On the whole she was perfectly satisfied with having come down on the pagan side of her family's two religions, for a whole set of reasons that just started with political convenience. But you had to admit that Christianity's dark anti-deity made a good fit for the situation they found themselves in.

"Keep the line I showed you until I order otherwise. Bull straight on through," she called to the riders.

The noise from the Eaters to north and south was building again, the hammering of feet on the ground and the rising squeal and squall of their voices. More and more poured over the edge of the hill southwards, and the Hraefnbeorg fyrd planted feet and raised their shields. There was a ripple and growl as their heavy battle spears were leveled. Her father had said that dash wasn't their strong point, but they had guts in plenty and were stubborn to the point of madness, and as usual he looked to be right.

John ostentatiously cocked his ear at the shrill brabble of the enemy.

"A fair top tenor chorus, but no bass section at all," he said, and Deor gave a snort of laughter as he whisked his sword through a figure-eight to loosen his wrist.

The savages were surging forward and back as they screeched, a little more forward each time—it was a familiar pattern by now. Soon—

The wave snapped into a screaming charge, bare feet pounding over the bodies of their scattered dead.

"Now!" Órlaith shouted, and drew the Sword.

CHAPTER SEVENTEEN

CÍRBANN RÓMENADRIM
(FORMERLY CHINA CAMP)
CROWN PROVINCE OF WESTRIA
(FORMERLY CALIFORNIA)
HIGH KINGDOM OF MONTIVAL
(FORMERLY WESTERN NORTH AMERICA)
JULY/FUMIZUKI/CERWETH 14TH
CHANGE YEAR 46/FIFTH AGE 46/SHŌHEI 1/2044 AD

Órlaith's voice came from behind him: "Keep the line I showed you until I order otherwise. Bull straight on through."

Faramir Kovalevsky, Ranger of Stath Ingolf, raised his hand without looking around, and settled his light helm as the three riders moved forward and his attention narrowed to a focus like a spearpoint.

He checked that everything was ready one last time; it was as much for the soothing feel of long habit as anything. The cut on his face just stung where the Protector's Guard medic had put antiseptic and three stitches into it, but the arm was starting to hurt like Udûn beneath the dent in the light vambrace. On the other hand, it hadn't crimped the muscle enough to really matter. You could ignore pain, at least for a while, and what mattered here was performance.

"Been good to meet you, cousin," he said to Luanne. "Pity it was so brief."

"Yeah, and even more of a pity about the mad screaming cannibals crashing the nice carefree Gunpowder Day BBQ family reunion," she said, and flashed him a grin. "I hope we have more time later. I've heard a lot about Eryn Muir and I always wanted to visit it."

"I hope the company will be better in the Halls of Mandos, if that's where we're going today," he said.

He didn't add: *Though before we get to our afterlives I* would *like to have gotten laid just one more time.*

Many of his best friends were women, but generally there were a few things you just couldn't say around them. They struck the female ear differently.

"I'll settle for Purgatory," she said dryly. "Though I have it on good authority some pretty skanky people end up there; Órlaith's maternal granddaddy, for instance. *I* would have figured him for the Seventh Level of Hell, but I'm not God . . . which is probably a good thing."

Morfind was quiet; lately only Susan Mika had been able to draw her out of her shell, and that when the three of them were together. They all exchanged a slap on the shoulder and he and his cousin put their hands to their hearts and bowed westward towards Valinor and That which was beyond it. Luanne murmured a Latin prayer, and they all twitched a shaft free and set it through the arrow-rests in the risers of their bows.

His mouth felt dry, but he didn't want to shake the last drops out of his canteen; the horses had needed it more anyway. Instead he worked his mouth and spat.

"I'm scared too," Luanne said gently. "It's easier to handle than I thought it would be, though."

Morfind snorted. "Let's get *going*," she muttered.

Faramir looked over to his left, a brief flicker of his eyes. The Eaters would be trying another rush across the saddle any instant from the look of it, but with the Hraefnbeorg men to help the men-at-arms should be able to throw it back.

Once, maybe twice or three times, he thought. *If they keep coming on the way they have, not more than that.*

An equally quick glance over his shoulder showed the Japanese and the rest of the fyrd in a semicircle. There seemed to be no end to the savages coming over the edge of the hill now that they couldn't hold the whole perimeter anymore. The air was heavy with their stink, and the smell of blood, and the smoke from the fire at the wharf.

Órlaith knocked down her visor and set her hand to the Sword.

Like Anduril, he thought, feeling a thrill even then. *Flame of the West indeed!*

If this was a last stand, at least it had all the classic elements. He could imagine dying, but somehow it included listening to the song of the deed as well, and standing among the crowd when the Stath gathered to hear their *Book of Valiance,* the record that told how a Ranger fell. And girls being impressed, definitely that was in there somehow.

On the other hand, nobody will know or care how the enemy *dies.*

Faramir was eager for revenge, even after an hour and more of savage fighting so far this day. The Eaters and their new allies threatened this land that was his home; the same alliance of evil had killed his cousin Malfind and wounded Morfind and nearly killed *him* and they'd killed his lord and kinsman the High King. Besides which he just objected to the Eaters' existence on general principles, and doubly so to the new enemy from across the Western sea. That force was behind their attack, the *galor,* the sorcerer-lords and the dark Power they served, what the very ancient Folk of the West had called Morgoth.

It all gave him a new appreciation for *the Histories.*

"Now!" Órlaith called, and drew the Sword.

Something like a hot clean wind went through him. He couldn't imagine a Montivallan unmoved when the Sword of the Lady was drawn on a field of war. They moved towards the edge of the hill. It was going to be a tricky bit of riding; a steep slope, brush and rocks, and enemies to face. But the Arab horses the Rangers rode were no block-of-muscle knights' destriers, being compact but immensely strong for their modest size, quick, intelligent and sure-footed as cats, and his Suldal was better than average even for that breed. He'd ridden lands like these all his life, and been lifted to the saddle before his parents as soon as he could walk.

At least the sun's not in our eyes, he thought.

He took a deep breath, called on Tulkas the Strong—the Valar he felt the closest bond with—

He was a little worried about Morfind, though.

"Dago!" she muttered to herself. "Kill! *Dago in yrch!"*

Luanne was quiet but ready; she was a bit older than he, though still short of twenty years. Faramir knew it was her first real fight, and he was full of admiration for how she was facing it.

"At least there's another Bearkiller here now," she murmured, and stood a little in the stirrups. "I can't see anyone between here and that wood we're heading for."

"Good," Faramir replied. "Let's get right to the jump-off point. I don't want to be exposed longer than I have to."

They all signaled their horses forward—there was nothing deliberate about it at their level, you just thought where you wanted your mount to go and it did . . . provided it was as well-schooled as a Ranger's, or a Bearkiller A-lister's. For these, reins were merely a training aid in colt-hood. Faramir clucked reassuringly to his as the horse tossed its head and snorted. It was in the nature of the beasts to be cautious of their legs; Suldal was brave, but he was also intelligent for a horse and knew perfectly well that they were approaching a slope far steeper than it would try on its own. He liked his horse and had raised it from a colt, but at seventh and last a Ranger's horse was a weapon, as were the Rangers themselves, guarding the honor and homes and hearths of the kingdom.

Another deep breath and they broke into a slow canter. Then over the edge—it felt a little like a game young Dúnedain here played, over at Wolf Hall where his uncle Hîr Ingolf dwelt, swinging back and forth on a rope over the hillside reservoir and then letting go to fall with a tremendous splash. Horses and riders both threw their balance back a little—the mounts were going down the slope half in a controlled fall and half by squatting back on their haunches in the very worst spots. He let his thighs do the work of steadying him and concentrated on looking ahead—and to either side, everywhere there might be an enemy.

There.

The slope ahead stayed steep until it leveled out into a brush-grown swale that gave into open forest. A group of Eaters was there, resting on their haunches and waiting to swarm up to the assault on the men-at-arms. They caught on when the horse-archers were halfway down the hundred yards of slope and the others were running full-tilt at their heels close behind. He drew the cord past his ear—the real trick was to do that without giving your horse misleading signals, which would kill them both right now—and loosed. Just a target, just a target, a boiled-leather outline stuck up on a spring-loaded stick.

Don't watch the arrow, it's going to go where it's going to go, snatch out another, draw, shoot.

Time enough for three, the last into a man just left of him in the act of throwing a hatchet, and it whirled through the air to catch him a hard thump on the shoulder. Slap the bow back into the harp-shaped scabbard, hook the shield up in the same motion, right hand across and the sword is *out* and *up* and *slash* backhand down to the right, all done to the stopwatch a thousand times.

Only this time he wasn't aiming at a pumpkin or a gourd or even the pig's or sheep's head from the butcher's shop that advanced students used.

A hard jarring thump up through his wrist and arm and shoulder, and another spike of pain from the deep bruise. The snarling face fell away backward with the poised spear tumbling away. Brush clawed at his face, reaching for his eyes with iron-hard claws, and he ducked down along the horse's neck. His sword held out beside it towards the next terrified and terrifying face.

"Lacho Calad!"

"Drego Morn!"

"Hakkaa päälle!"

Órlaith went down the hill in a controlled fall-and-skid with her backside nearly touching the grass as her feet moved crook-kneed, and once on her back for a few heart-stopping seconds—without slowing in the least. A frantic dig with her heel at a mostly-buried rock and Heuradys' shield levered against the backplate of her armor and her own momentum got her back on her feet and back into the sort of run where you couldn't slow down unless you wanted to tumble arse-over-teakettle.

At least I don't have to worry about the edge of my own Sword, some distant part of her mind thought mordantly.

Usually there was a real risk to running in the rough with something sharp and pointy in your hand, but the Sword of the Lady wouldn't cut her, or anyone of the blood of House Artos. Reiko was running beside her, the *naginata* spinning above her head as if it were a stabilizing gyroscope, a wordless focusing scream ululating as she charged. Egawa was nearly as agile on his sovereign's other side: his war-cry was *banzai!* but Órlaith supposed it would be rather strange for the Nihonjin ruler to shout what would effectively be *long live me!*

The horses rammed through the Eaters' wavering rank and into the dappled gloom beyond and the fighters on foot crashed into the scattered mass right on their heels. One horse was rearing in front of her—not mere reflex, but striking out with both hooves at once, and a body flew backward. Reiko cut a man's feet out from under him—literally—with a double-handed sweep that let the full length of the *naginata* swing out to give the cut immense leverage. Órlaith lunged with the flat parallel to the ground and the Sword slotted in between an Eater woman's ribs even as a blade made from half a pair of garden shears grated along the lames of Órlaith's breastplate. The savage's experience-born instincts had betrayed her; against someone who wasn't wearing armor that would have been a deadly blow.

"Alale alala!" Heuradys shouted, the cry the worshippers of the Olympians took to war.

She ducked under the swing of an axe, broke the man's bare foot with the point of her shield, punched him under the jaw with the upper curve and cut into the wrist of another trying for the weaker armor at the crotch by stooping low and stabbing upward; the savage lurched off clutching her half-severed limb.

"To the right, to the right, he's moving!" Deor called from behind Órlaith, and she swerved in that direction.

There was a clash of metal and thumping back there, and John's breathy shout: *"Haro!"* Evrouin's voice snarled curses in English and vile Spanish.

In the medicinal-smelling dimness under the eucalyptus the Sword of the Lady burned like a crystal flame. Bands of Eaters were skulking closer.

"He's trying to get back to the water," Órlaith called, her voice like a silver trumpet as she leveled the blade. "Hold him! Don't let them slow us down!"

The three riders put their horses forward as the rest of the party followed, ducking and weaving in the saddle with reckless abandon through the brush and wood with their swords bright in their hands.

They moved forward in a rough wedge through the brush with Órlaith at the point, all of them stabbing and cutting and smashing with shields at the figures that rose up ahead or darted in; after a moment Thora and John turned and guarded the rear, taking the insanely dangerous role of walking backward, with Deor in the center of their formation adding his shield wherever needed. She could hear the scop chanting as he fought, not loud but using the hard alliterative rhythm to pace his efforts:

"Swa stemnetton, stiðhicgende
hysas æt hilde, hogodon georne
hwa þær mid orde ærost mihte
on fægean men feorh gewinnan—"

Using the Sword as a brush-clearing tool felt very strange, but a four-inch trunk of scrub oak toppled sideways when she hacked at it, leaving a slanted disk of pale wood smooth as a cabinetmaker's plane could have produced. She hurdled the stump and dodged the branches whipping at her as the trunk fell and pinned several Eaters to the ground, putting her shield up as she thrust through with a gasping grunt of effort and another slash that scattered twigs and branches in a spray.

The Eaters were more and more reluctant to approach the glittering deadliness in her hand, shaking their heads and whining and breaking to either side as she approached. Their numbers were still growing, though. It was like breasting an ever-growing tide.

He's calling them back against us. We have to do this now *or we die.*

"Now!"

She plunged through, slashing the Sword left and right, feeling muscle and bone part under the edge. Through the screen of Eaters, and all three of the mounted fighters were around a single figure, striking at him in a flicker of steel glinting through the sun-shot dimness.

He was no scrawny-wiry Eater stunted by disease and malnutrition and naked save for a breechclout. Instead he was about six feet, and well-built in a lean muscular way, like a well-fed man active all his life. He wore a blackened steel helm shaped like the upper half of a raven's head with the bill as a visor, and a spray of feathers across the crown. The countenance beneath the bill was square, the sparse beard the same dark-brown color as the twisted queue of hair that fell past his shoulder, and the face was somewhere between ruddy and olive in color.

First-Folk and incomer mixed, she thought.

Like herself or Diarmuid, but with more of the first and less of the latter.

His clothes were well-tanned breeches and boots of sealskin, a wool shirt dyed green with nettle and a leather tunic sewn with small iron rings like miniature bracelets linked together by pivots; the sword-scabbard at his side was splints of whalebone bound with sinew. Around his throat was a necklace of bear and beaver teeth. His left hand held a short carved staff shaped like an oddly elongated double-ended paddle with puffin beaks strung to it; the main shape was two orcas eating a seal, the bodies of the great sea-predators in turn carved with ravens and eagles. Something similar was painted on the leather surface of a small round hand-drum hanging at his side over the scabbard of his sword.

The three young warriors were spinning their mounts with immense skill, leaning over in the saddle to slash at their foeman . . . and he was calmly twisting and ducking, as if he started each dodging movement *before* the blow was started and he was doing a slow stately dance through the thicket of swift edged metal. Both the practical-looking cutlass-sword in his right hand and the wand in the other moved. There was an occasional *ting* of steel on steel, a *tock* as the wand slapped against the flats of the blades.

Luanne crowded her horse in close and leaned over to thrust with the backsword. The enemy—the skaga—turned his body out of the way. Then he stepped forward and thrust his sword a foot deep into the horse's breast. There was a scream, like a human hurt but enormously louder, and the beast reared and toppled backward. Eaters rushed in, chittering, and the two Dúnedain turned their horses into their flood. The mounts danced in place, lashing out with hooves and teeth as the riders slashed frantically.

The skaga came out of his fighting crouch as Órlaith drew near. Until now his expression had been merely serious and abstracted. Something flickered in it as he looked at her. She'd hear how the magi of the CUT had been like something hollowed out from the inside. This was different. There was a man there, a human being. But also something . . . else.

"*Kíl 'láa,*" he said.

Which meant *hello*, she suddenly knew. And he knew she knew. From the reports—scouts, spies and escaped slaves, mostly—she knew the modern Haida spoke English among themselves for the most part. Their upper class of warrior captains and clan chiefs and shamans kept the ancestral language alive, and used it as a badge of rank and for ceremony. Roughly the way Associates did Old French, though more often.

And for lore and magic, she thought, *they use it for that too.*

"This plan may be bungled into wreck by fools," the shaman said, in that clicking tongue full of stops and breathings. "But there will be another. You will not ruin my folk again. We are strong now, with powerful allies . . . in this world and the Other Place."

"We'd be a deal less set on ruinin' you if you'd stop raiding our villages and killing and robbing and carrying off our folk for slaves," she pointed out as she came forward.

Her mouth and tongue and throat felt strange, as the new knowledge used them in ways they'd never been stretched before. This was a speech even less like that which she'd been born to than Nihongo was.

Unexpectedly, fury blazed at her. "I have seen—from the lives before! I have seen the *Xaayda*—"

Which was what his folk called themselves, and outsiders had pronounced as *Haida*; like many such names it simply meant *The People.*

"—lying dead by their thousands, untended, none to put them in their box and mount them on the sacred poles. Their skins rotting and brains cooked with fever, their villages deserted, the few alive left selling their sacred things for whiskey to kill their grief! We will never let you gather the strength to break us again!"

She felt his utter sincerity. He had certainly seen what he claimed; and it might well be from his previous lives. The High King had seen visions of the chain of ancestry through the very Sword she carried, down through uncounted generations.

That didn't mean the way this man had let those visions shape his life was wise. Her father had used the Sword to show even bitter enemies their ultimate kinship. For that matter, the chronicles told that the skaga's folk had been raiders and reavers long before the incomers from the Old World sailed to these lands to shatter and to build. They'd carved memorials of stark magnificent beauty to their dead chiefs . . . and thrown the bodies of dead slaves, of which they'd had a multitude then too, into the sea for the fish. If it hadn't been in the middle of a battle and deadly peril, Órlaith would have sighed, or perhaps groaned.

She knew that she herself descended from half a dozen tribes who had well-founded grudges against each other, or outright killing feuds; not to mention that her grandfathers had fought each other for a decade and then personally met before their assembled armies in a personal combat neither had survived. The blood of all mingled in her veins and helped make her what she was.

And I none the worse for it. For I am the land, and through me the braided past and its future yet to be, as Montival is meant to be.

She'd also learned that there was simply no point in talking to a mind so focused inward and pastward. And as her parents said, at the point where talking was futile you had to start hitting if you didn't want to get hit yourself.

"Herry, help John and the others keep them off. I'll handle this—"

"And I," Reiko said. "Egawa-san, guard our backs."

With gentle smoothness, Órlaith raised the Sword of the Lady. From the corner of her eye she saw Reiko bring her blade *Kotegiri* up into the two-handed ready posture. When she moved forward, there was a sense of *pressure*, behind her and before. As if it took a very long time to take each step at normal speed. The world outside her and the shaman slowed to a background thrum and burr; Reiko beside her as well, though not so much. Her face was set in the shadow of the glade, but her red-lacquered armor seemed to shine with extra luster, as if a beam of sunlight were following it like a cupping, shielding hand.

The carved wood of the shaman's wand moved and the sense of pressure increased. Gasping, she raised the sword and it faded back.

"You cannot stand against what is locked in this," she said.

"*Please* don't tell me that the dark fire will not avail me now," the skaga said sardonically; in English for that moment.

"Some of my relatives are Dúnedain, but I'm not," she grated, and struck.

It was a hard twisting backhand slash; that at least seemed to be proceeding in normal time, and sparks flared where he parried. The blade in his hand sprang back notched, and he lurched and then twisted hard to avoid Reiko's overarm cut. Órlaith could see how he did that now. She was *connected* to that other place to which he stepped aside. Reiko was not, not quite; the fire that flickered about her bent the boundaries of it with astonishing raw strength, but lacked the sharpness of focus the Sword gave her ally.

He gestured again with the thing of power in his left hand, and cold poured over Órlaith; the cold of northern seas. Something moved beneath that non-sea, something black and sleek and powerful, deadliness in its icy intelligence and the mouthful of teeth shaped to rend and tear. Thoughts vast beyond human ken gripped and twisted at the fabric of things as fins and flukes bent the sea.

"Morrigú!" she called, and raised the blade her father had brought from the Otherworld.

White light seemed to blind her for an instant, and great black wings enfolded her and bore her up in a way that was more real than the world of waking day where she stood with her boots on the leaf-mold. The hostile *presence* faded—twisting away, as if it were swimming through oceans of space and time trailing blood amid stars like grains of sand. She had not killed It—she didn't think anything could. But she had hurt It. Or the Sword had, through her.

The shaman staggered and gasped. "That thing is not for humans to use! What can wound the *Sgaana xaaydagaay,* who give me power over the *buxwbukw,* Those Who Eat Men? Do you know what it is you grasp? Better you had pushed your hand into a fire or a bear's mouth!"

"'Tis *unfair* that I keep a magic sword about the place?" she panted.

Steadying herself was an effort that felt like hoisting a boulder overhead. There was still a taut smile on her lips as she mocked:

"This from the man who just tried to feed me to a salt-water bogle, and would that by chance be a magic *wand* you're after doing it with? Grimy arse, said the kettle to the pot!"

She lunged, and there was another grating of steel on not-steel, sparks and a ragged cut in his sword and an impalpable blow from the carved wood that was far heavier; this time like a flint-hard beak that would have split her very mind if it had struck her fairly. Crows and ravens tumbled in not-space and not-time, slashing at each other with beaks and claws.

For a long moment the Sword was held in the X made by wand and blade, and then he was twisting against that holding force as Reiko struck down at his legs with her katana. Slowly to his eyes, or to Órlaith's now, but with a furious purity of intent that was beautiful even then. The not-place they inhabited *twisted* as the skaga began a motion that would have leapt over the Nihonjin blade and thrown himself back from the Sword of the Lady—

Tung!

The crossbow bolt was still fast, though not the blurring flash it should have been. She could see the carbon-fiber shaft turn and the four-bladed point glitter along its razor-honed edges, but at the same time there was the faintest hint of something else. White wings, gray eyes sharp as diamond, a crested helm and monster-painted shield and a bitter spear.

The northern shaman could deal with two deadly threats, but not three. Movement seemed to *snap* back to the world of common day, and he was staggering, dropping wand and blade, grabbing at the black shaft that transfixed his face from his cheek to where the point rammed out of the back of his neck in a shower of blood. Then he dropped, twitched, tried to speak, and went still.

Órlaith felt herself start to buckle at the knees and fall, reached out and grabbed blindly and found herself leaning against Reiko's armored form; even on the verge of collapse they were careful of the blades they carried. Another body staggered into them; it was Heuradys, half giving support and half taking it. The pre-Change crossbow clattered against them as it swung on its sling.

"Saw you had him pinned . . . took a chance," the knight of Ath wheezed, her hands shaking. "Athana strengthened me, but it was like aiming in a hurricane. Wish I could get that feeling out of my *head*."

"He was strong indeed, by all the Gods of my people," Órlaith agreed, controlling her breathing.

The Sword flicked out and cracked the orca-graven wand in half. Something jolted up her hand and arm as it did, and squeezed at her chest beneath her armor; only the other two held her upright.

"Good to have a magic sword on your side!" Heuradys said, and the Nihonjin nodded with a slight breathy chuckle as she said:

"Very good."

"Good to have friends," Órlaith said. Her hand thumped feebly at Reiko's shoulder. "Good to have true friends!"

The three young women hung for a moment with their helmeted heads together, trying to embrace with arms gone feeble, then started to straighten and smile at each other. There was noise enough around them—screams and weapons clashing—to remind them that things were far from settled, and much more worldly dangers could kill you just as finally.

Then the dead man's eyes opened. They were black as tar, a blackness that shone and somehow *drew*, soft with an infinite malice.

"Hāidēs Ruler of Many!" Heuradys yelped.

She sprang back convulsively, as someone might from a spider on their pillow, as the hands and feet began to scrabble clumsily at the earth. Reiko's blade went up and her lips set; she was obviously planning to deal with the revenant in the traditional way—by taking its head. The Crown Princess recalled that she'd mentioned seeing similar things in her homeland when the enemy attacked, and her own parents had told her of the like in the Prophet's War. Things that had once been men killing until they were hacked apart and burned; things whose very blood and spittle bore a spirit-taint.

Órlaith looked into the eyes, into a whirling circle of dissolution that was eternally motionless, a nothing that thought it was everything, a futility that believed it was perfection. Where there were no lies because there was no truth, only an endless chewing of stale memory into smaller and smaller bits beneath the gaze of the Solipsist.

"No," she said. "I will not leave even a bitter enemy so. Find freedom, man of the People. Find *truth*."

She stepped forward and thrust. For an instant bewildered pain and hatred ran through her in a shuddering wave. Then it was as if a door opened—not for her, though she was enough *of* it to see and stand on the threshold for a moment.

The skaga took his hand from the dorsal fin of the great creature that bore him on a journey, one she sensed had been far longer for him than her. He made a gesture of thanks as it turned and dove into water like froth-tipped icy jade; his eyes caught hers for seconds, and he nodded, then turned to those who waited for him.

Mist hung in tendrils from the great Sitka spruces and red cedars and Douglas fir about the cove. Long canoes hewn from just such trunks were drawn up on the shingle, their forepeaks carved with images of that Power which had borne him here, and beyond them countless red-draped racks of drying salmon scented the air. Huge longhouses of mossy plank were scattered about, their beams fantastically carved and smoke lifting from holes in their high-peaked roofs. Even more elaborate were the great sculpted and colored poles of clan-crests that rose before each one, and innumerable others that stood about; a new one was making on a frame that held it until it could be erected. Each told a story . . .

No, a thousand thousand stories, she thought.

At first glance she thought the figures who danced towards the shaman were monsters. Then she saw that they were humans in mask and costume, and that the work was beautiful, though wholly strange to her—faces elongated and crested and fringed, some of them as large as the bearer entire, stylized yet vividly true to what they depicted. *Presences* floated invisibly above them; Orca, yes, and Raven and Beaver and Wolf and Bear. Welcome flowed out, and a sense of homecoming, but not for her.

The sight faded, and the body before them was limp in the ordinary messiness of human death.

"Bunch up," Órlaith said. "No sense trying to move—we'll make a stand here."

The savage chief she'd seen before, the squat one with the cut-marks on his nose and the double-bitted axe, was half a hundred yards away, peering out from beyond a tree, then turning and gesturing to followers she could barely see at all. There was blood on his body from half a dozen minor wounds, but blood on his axe too. She recognized grim purpose in the way he rallied a band, pointing towards them and screaming at the savages. *That* one knew he could yet carry the day and avenge his folk if he killed her.

"That's the Sword, by Brigid the Bright!" Gwiri Beauregard Mackenzie said.

She was nearly gray under her natural brown, and not just from the sounds ahead—crack and thud and hard unmusical clangor, shouts and screams of uttermost agony. It was still blurred with distance, but unmistakable. Like an open fanged maw waiting to greet them.

"I can feel it!" the young priestess went on. "Can't you? The Powers are in contention here, and the world's self screams at the weight of it. Aye, it tears the cloth the world is woven from back to the threads that made it!"

"Where?" Karl shouted.

"There! There!"

She pointed frantically. Diarmuid and Karl looked at each other; *there* was a stretch of scattered woods just south of them, at the base of the hill where the wink of steel showed the fighting. He could see figures moving there, but the line of brush and tall grass at the edge of the trees blocked close sight. It was double bowshot anyway, six hundred paces.

"Anwyn take it—" Karl began.

Then there was a shout of alarm from Boudicca at their rear, and faint with distance a well-known roaring:

"Hold there, ye little iijits!"

The voice was all too familiar, from their earliest days. Karl looked at his brother this time. As one, he and Mathun bounded forward, and the whole band followed. They ran through the line of scrub with woodsman's skill and scarcely a moment's check; once they were under the canopy of the trees the brush was lighter.

"There!" Gwri shouted—screamed, rather, the whites showing all around her eyes.

There were times Karl was profoundly grateful he had no trace of the Sight, and could simply give the Powers their due without the Otherworld creeping in at the corners of his eyes. This was one of them, because there *was* a sense of something wrong. The hair crept at the back of his neck under the rear pad and strap of his helm, and he did not want to even imagine what it must be for Gwri.

Suddenly an Eater was running at him . . . and the skinny savage looked near as frightened as Karl felt, under the soot that coated his face save for a band across the eyes. There was nothing wrong with his reflexes, though: he whipped up the knife in his hand. The Mackenzie smacked the bow in his hand down on the man's wrist, and the tough yew cracked bone. The Eater wailed and stumbled; Karl seized his neck and threw him face-forward into the trunk of a tall bluegum three feet away with a hysterical strength that astonished even a young man proud of his muscle. There was a crunching sound, but he was bounding past before the body hit the earth.

"Forward!" he shouted.

They dashed into a more open stretch, sun slanting in from the westward, failing at last even this long summer's day. Incongruously pretty butterflies burst upwards as Karl skidded to a halt. He recognized the Princess as the figure in the middle distance—how not, in that silvery suit of plate with the Golden Eagle feathers of her sept framing the helm? She and her friend Heuradys and someone in foreign armor were standing over a body, holding each other as if for support. Others were behind her: he thought he recognized Prince John, from the rather flashy polished harness, now sadly battered, and a shorter man who was his follower whirling a glaive over his head and spraying red from both ends of it.

The ill sight was the band of Eaters a little to the westward. There were gathering for a charge, with a leader leaping and screaming and whirling a long double-bitted axe around his head, pointing and calling his gang forward. He looked notably strong, much thicker-set than most of his scrawny scavenger band.

A hundred paces, he thought. *Not point-blank, but not far either.*

There were other savages closer, and turning to look at them, but that was the threat to Órlaith. He yelled to Diarmuid:

"Keep them off us while we shoot, man!" and put an arrow to his bow even as he knew that eleven bows weren't enough, not even eleven Mackenzie longbows. There must be near five-score grouping ready to rush, and the shooting was bad—trees and patches of cover, and they were close enough to get to handstrokes in a few seconds at a run.

Then behind him that same familiar rough voice: "Arra, ye gombeens—"

Then an instant's silence as his father took in the situation with the swiftness of a lifetime as a warrior, and much louder with a hard edge of command:

"Ah, *shite*! Deploy to me right, double-line harrow, *deploy*. Action front, target yon loathly grugach and his band. And you young bastards, with us the now, together with us, so!"

He didn't need to turn his head to know that the High King's Archers were falling in to his right, westward. He heard the infinitely familiar chant next, like a cold cloth to the face, steadying and taking the glaze of horror off things:

"We are the point—"

Then Órlaith's head whipped around as she heard voices from the north, equally distant from her little band and the gathering Eater mob:

"We are the point—
We are the edge—
We are the wolves that Hecate fed!"

The arrows came right on the heels of the chant, a hard blurring ripple through the brushwood. A man beside the savage chief pitched backward with a gray-fletched clothyard shaft through his throat and smashed through his neckbone too. Another plowed through his own upper arm and more into the band around him. They dodged, scattering as the next volley snapped in, and the next. The kilted archers in their green jacks were running forward, coming in from the north and halting every ten paces in a pattern she remembered seeing from earliest childhood, moving easily through the trees and brush. The voice that directed them was familiar too, and not Karl's or Diarmuid's:

"Wholly together—draw—loose! Forward—halt—wholly together—draw—loose!"

Karl and Mathun, she thought. *But there are too many for just them. That's two or three-score longbows. Is that their da, by Lugh of the Long Hand?*

A rider on a quarter horse was with them, shooting too, and raising a shout:

"Hokahe!"

That was the Lakota war-cry, and it meant *up and at 'em,* pretty much.

And a tearing scream:

"McClintock abu!"

Swordsmen with claymores and *claidheamh mòr* and gruesome Lochaber axes loped forward in a unison more like a wolfpack than a regiment. The wounded chief with the axe hesitated as the band bore down on him, then screamed frustration for an instant before his face calmed:

"Ufukkinrun!" he barked, and turned and dove into the brush. The rest followed him.

"They're running!" Deor yelled. "They're all running!"

His oath-sister beat one back with her shield, but he'd simply been rammed into it by the press behind him; his bad luck as he fell flat and she stamped accurately with a bootheel. More and more came dodging through the woods. The band who'd been about to overrun Órlaith and her friends before the archers struck had been in some sort of order as they retreated. Order as Eaters understood such things, but what she saw now was blind panic.

Perhaps literally so. "Pan has their souls! *Panikon deima!*" Heuradys shouted exultantly.

Above on the hill horns were sounding; the deep sonorous burring snarl of the Hraefnbeorg fyrd, and others that were higher, lighter, several notes together in a haunting chorus, and voices like hawks at war.

Now it was a flood and crackle and crazed screeching as hundreds of the Eaters went by, wholly taken by the terror at their heels, ignoring even the arrows that scourged them from the newly-arrived Mackenzies as they threw their weapons aside and ran heedless. They parted about Órlaith's little band where they stood shield to shield, like water around a rock in a swift stream. Behind them came the reason; mounted fighters, score after score of them on white and dappled-gray horses, in spired helms and round shields graven with the silver Tree and Stars and Crown, wearing the light breast-and-back of jointed plates, mail sleeves and armguards the Dúnedain bore when they rode to open war.

"Lacho Calad! Drego morn!"

Most of them passed by, shooting and slashing with their long-hilted curved swords. Órlaith would have expected Faramir and Morfind to follow, but instead they were kneeling by the fallen horse. She sighed heavily and sheathed the Sword, walking over to them.

Luck doesn't go on forever, she thought.

It had run out altogether for Luanne Salander of Larsdalen and the Bearkiller Outfit. From the look of it the horse had landed heavily on her legs and pelvis and rolled over her before it died; her lower limbs pointed in directions that made Órlaith wince just to contemplate. There was a fair amount of blood, and more was leaking out of the corners of her mouth. The two Rangers each held a hand, and they were gripped with a white-knuckled clench despite the two empty morphine syringes lying beside her. Sometimes that could only help with the pain, not stop it. You didn't have to cut loose the sodden clothing to know a wounding that could only end in death, over hours of soul-crushing agony until you died like a beast. Anyone would know, who'd seen battlefields, or even been around horses and knew what happened when a thousand pounds of bone and muscle crushed a human body against the unyielding ground.

Deor's friend Thora Garwood stepped forward and drew her dagger.

"I am a Bearkiller, of this woman's folk, and a Sister of the A-List as is she. It is my duty by the oaths of the Brotherhood we both swore to do her the final service."

She touched the small blue burn-mark between her brows as she spoke with a somber formality.

"Are any here of this warrior's blood-kin?"

"We are," Faramir said. "Our mothers are aunts to Luanne's mother. And we are her friends and comrades-in-arms."

"I am her kinswoman," Órlaith said; they'd both always acknowledged the link, at least. "And her friend and comrade-in-arms and her sworn lord by right of blood and oath."

"And I," John said, with a slight catch in his voice. "And I am of her faith. I will have masses said for the peace of her soul, I swear it."

It was obvious by the Thor's Hammer at her neck that Thora wasn't Christian. Luanne's eyes tracked to him and she nodded as he knelt beside her and held up his crucifix. She couldn't really speak, but her lips moved a little as he said the words:

"O my God, I am heartily sorry for having offended you. I detest my own sins and faults because I dread the loss of Heaven and the pains of Hell, but, most of all, because they offend You, my God, Who are all Good and deserving of all of my love. I firmly resolve, with the help of Your grace, to sin no more and to avoid the near occasions of sin, Amen."

He touched the silver figure of the Man of Sorrows to her lips and added:

"Sáncta María, Máter Déi, óra pro nóbis peccatóribus, nunc et in hóra mórtis nóstrae. Ámen."

Thora looked around and met their eyes. They all nodded agreement to it; it was something that was necessary, and they were all profoundly glad there was someone else who could be trusted to do it. She knelt swiftly as John rose and held the weapon before Luanne's eyes. The younger woman nodded sharply, consenting, and freed one of her hands to grip Thora's convulsively for an instant. A small sound echoed in her throat, choked off hastily. Thora put her left hand over Luanne's eyes and turned her head, placed the point behind the ear and did what was needful with a single hard skilled motion. There was a heavy twitch, and merciful stillness.

Then she closed the eyes, stood, threw the knife to sink point-first in a tree and quiver like a giant bee before she stalked off into the woods to stand with her back to them, hands clutching her elbows across her body. Deor went to her side and stood silently, not speaking or touching her but shielding them both with his presence.

Kilted figures approached. Diarmuid Tennart McClintock was the first, with his caterans behind him waving their blades and caterwauling a screeching triumph. He signaled them to silence as he saw what lay before the feet of the living.

His eyes met hers. "Merry meet, Oorlai," he said gravely. A glance at Reiko. "Majesty. Och, we were later than I could hae liked, though."

She nodded back to him. "And merry part, to you and yours, Diarmuid my friend. Not *too* late, which is the thing of importance, eh? War not being calligraphy, and so rarely perfect."

She lifted her eyes a little at the two tall yellow-haired young men trotting up in Mackenzie kilts.

"And merry meet again, Karl, Mathun, and all of you. My thanks, and a hundred thousand thanks more. The fight was looking ill and grim before your arrows arrived, and never was I gladder to see shaft fly. That I'll swear to, by all the Gods of our people."

Behind them was an unmistakable figure. Edain Aylward Mackenzie, Bow-Captain of the High King's Archers. In green brigandine and tartan kilt, longbow held in the crook of his left arm, square-built and square-faced, with a new gray-shot short beard that must be the result of weeks when shaving was a luxury he couldn't spare the time for. His eyes were hard and level as he strode up, and his mouth like a steel trap. Behind him was a lanky red-haired woman in Archer gear, and she was smiling thinly as she reached into her sporran and pulled out an envelope impressive with ribbons and red wax seals, if looking a bit battered as well.

That was a Royal writ if Órlaith had ever seen one, and she had. Once she'd read it, or it had been read aloud in her presence . . . then things got very sticky.

I do not have will for this, not now, she knew. There was a hollowness inside her, and a weariness beyond words. *But it must be done, none the less, and done now. I will not let you delay me, old Uncle Wolf. I know what's necessary, and it seems you do not.*

Hooves clattered; Edain and his officer glanced around and relaxed. A party of the Dúnedain rode up, with the black-and-silver banner of the Stars and Crowned Tree amongst them fluttering from a slender lance.

Órlaith recognized the two leaders instantly when they pushed back the cheek-pieces of their helms and removed them; tall blond women in their forties, eerily similar save for Mary Vogeler's eyepatch and scar. The other was her twin sister Ritva Kovalevsky. Faramir and Morfind stood and started to bristle as their mothers—and commanders—drew rein, trying their hardest to be adults instead of just on the cusp of it.

Mary held up her hand without looking at them, but the palm was in their direction and signaling *silence.*

"Bow-Captain Edain," she said, looking past Órlaith—carefully *not* looking at her at all, in fact, or acknowledging her presence. "Good to see you again, my old friend."

She held his eyes, and glancing back and forth between them Órlaith could see him hesitate and then decide something. Not so long ago the Crown Princess could remember a little resentment at the way her parents and their old comrades from the War and the Quest and the years before could communicate in a sort of code of glances and spare gestures and elliptical phrases. Now she was glad of it. Nobody but one of those blood-bound friends could divert the force of nature who commanded the Archers.

"Aye, Mary, Ritva," he said a little cautiously. "It's been too long, sisters of my heart. Though I'm here on the High Queen's orders."

Ritva smiled; she'd always been the merrier of the two. "And we seem to meet on battlefields a lot, Edain."

"Happen that'll come to pass, if you seek out low and base company," he said dryly.

Morfind was scowling, which made the scar on her cheek knot; Faramir's pale brows went up. His eyes darted between his mother and his aunt, and then he leaned over and whispered urgently in his cousin's ear. Susan Mika slid out of the saddle like an otter dropping into the water and went to stand with them, her face proud and grave.

"It's important that we meet with Hîr Ingolf and Hîr Kovalevsky to discuss this skirmish," Mary said, naming the husbands who with them made up the ruling quadrumvirate of Stath Ingolf. *"Due to circumstances of which the High Queen has no current information* and which would *certainly affect her decisions."*

When he opened his mouth she added, before he could speak:

"Over at *Tham en-Araf*. Where they were planning to return directly once the pursuit they are leading *right now* is completed and for which your help, Bow-Captain, and that of your Archers is *badly needed*. All four of us *really* want you to come and confer, Edain."

Tham en-Araf was Wolf Hall in English, in the Valley of the Moon on the western slopes of the Mayacamas Mountains to the east between here and Napa—though the Dúnedain called them the *Ered Luin* these days, which name was by report gradually prevailing due to absolute stubbornness. Wolf Hall had been rebuilt on the foundation-ruins of a mansion that had burned before the Change; the name was ancient too, though modern-sounding to a Montivallan ear. The Vogelers dwelt there when their duties didn't call them into the field, as the Kovalevskies did at Eryn Muir, and a settlement of Rangers had grown up around it in the last generation. Living scattered as was their fashion, but cultivating vineyards and groves there as well as their more usual occupations.

And it was two days' travel away, if you didn't push yourself and risk breaking your horses' wind, at the other side of Stath Ingolf's territory.

"As there is *absolutely no reason* to stay here," Mary went on.

Ritva took it up: "We won't be back to Eryn Muir for at least *three days*."

"By then things will be *cleaned up* here," Mary finished.

Órlaith mentally translated that: we didn't see you, we're going away, be gone by the time we get back and we'll deal with the High Queen and everything can be tied up long enough in messages that take weeks to go back and forth. Edain looked rebellious for a moment—he *did* represent the Crown, after all.

On the other hand, so do I in a manner of speaking, Órlaith thought. *So do I.*

She rested the Sword's point in the dirt at her feet, and her crossed palms on the crystal pommel. That was a statement. She carefully said no word aloud, and looked away, though it was hard not to throw herself into the arms of her father's blood-brother and closest friend and her uncle-by-choice, even if it meant a wallop on the backside.

Many believed that the weapon from beyond the world could not be used in a way that the Ones who protected Montival forbade, and her bearing it here was a powerful argument that They approved of what she'd done. On the other hand, Their thoughts and reasons were not those of human kind.

"Aye, Mary, Ritva," Edain said after a moment, sighing. His mouth relaxed a little. "Does my heart good to hear you finishing each other's sentences like that. Fair takes me back, that it does indeed."

"You'll come?" Ritva asked; her face was calm, but Órlaith thought there was a pleading in her eyes.

"Aye. Aye, that might be best. For surely the Powers are at work here, not mere maneater savages and pirates, nor mere foemen of any sort. We learned back in the time of the Quest that it was best to listen when They spoke, hard though it might be."

Órlaith translated that as well: he'd do his bit to convince the High Queen that her position made it necessary to let her children do this, hard though *that* might be . . . and that he'd let his sons do likewise.

He turned and barked at the High King's Archers. "Well, you heard the lady. We've more fighting to do this day, and then we're off to Wolf Hall to consult with the leaders of the Dúnedain hereabouts."

His second-in-command's wary blue eyes narrowed and he gave her a slight crisp shake of the head. She rolled them upward and then closed them in what seemed a mute appeal, put the hand that held the writ to her brow, then nodded and tucked it back into her sporran. *She* wasn't protected from the High Queen's anger by childhood friendship, nor was she one of the Questers who'd crossed a continent with Rudi Mackenzie and Mathilda Arminger and shared the dangers and the glory. Several of the rank-and-file were openly gaping; she stepped close to them and hissed something inaudible, and they stiffened into a parade rest. Edain went on, his eyes following a bird swooping from tree to tree.

"Though if there was something to see here . . . if my halfwit balls-for-brains elder sons were here for instance . . . I would be inclined to clout them across the ear for their insolence, so. Leaving the receipt for me to pay indeed!"

Edain Aylward Mackenzie could still move very quickly when he wanted to. A hard *thock* sound rang twice, and his two tall sons were rubbing the sides of their heads and looking like sheepish six-year-olds caught absconding with apple tarts cooling on a windowsill rather than tried fighting-men. He was grinning as he shouldered his bow and led his command away.

"I might be inclined to do some clouting myself, but of course there's nobody here," Mary Vogeler said, still looking up into the branches. "Possibly there was someone, but we missed them. Completely."

"Nobody at all," her sister agreed gravely as she turned her horse.

Then she leaned over and tweaked an ear sharply as she passed; her son yelped in surprise and twitched.

The impulse to smile left Órlaith quickly. "Bring Luanne," she said, looking up the hill. "We have things to do."

"Farewell, knight of the Association and the High Kingdom," she said, bending to kiss Sir Aleaume de Grimmond's forehead. "May your Mother of God fold you in her blue mantle, and the gates of Heaven open for your valiant soul."

The dead of their band were laid side by side now; the Japanese fallen were at a little distance among their own. Both numbered a half-dozen each. Aleaume's face was very pale, and looked younger than it had in life, settling into an inhuman peace as the early-evening breeze moved a lock of his russet hair on his brow. The death-wound had been under the armpit where the armor was thin mail even in a full suit of plate, and across into the upper lungs. But gentle hands had withdrawn the weapon, wiped his face clean of the blood his mouth had sprayed in the last convulsion, and laid him on his back with his sword naked on his breast and his gauntleted hands crossed on the hilt. His legs were crossed at the ankles as well—so would his effigy be on the tomb in the church of his family's home manor at Grimmond-on-the-Wold on Barony Tucannon. It would portray him as he was now, in full armor, and that posture marked a nobleman who'd fallen in battle, as civil garb and heels resting on a lion or hunting-hound spoke of peaceful death at home. The holy oil of Catholic last rites glistened on his eyelids.

Droyn looked up at her. He wasn't weeping, because in the northrealm that was accounted disgraceful in public for men of full years, but his eyes shone wet and there was a catch in his voice as he spoke:

"My Lady . . . he had become like an elder brother to me. I couldn't reach—it was too far—"

She put a hand to his shoulder. "He was your brother in arms, and none are closer," she said gently. "Only fate and the will of the Powers decided who should fall. You will carry his shield and his sword to his family, and tell them of how he died. But for now we have work to do."

Her voice rang louder as she stepped back and drew the Sword. *That* caught the attention even of the doctors and their helpers for an instant; several of the Ranger healers were at work, and they had horse-litters waiting for wounded who'd been stabilized enough to be moved.

"On your knees, squire Droyn de Molalla of House Jones," she said, and Droyn fell to both with a clank of armor, looking a little startled.

The tone she used was solemn; this was a legal act, and required witnesses.

"This man is of full years, though young, of good birth, and skillful and courteous in those arts and graces which are becoming to gentlefolk. He has served House Artos as page and esquire-at-arms, and this day has proven valiant and fearless in battle, facing death without flinching in obedience to his oaths. For his valiance and loyalty I am therefore minded to dub him knight; which is my right as his liege-lady, as scion of House

Artos, and as one who herself wears the golden spurs and belt of knighthood. Do any here dispute my right, or know of an impediment in this man? If so speak now, or hold your peace thereafter, for you may be called to court under oath as witnesses of this ceremony."

Nobody did, though the silence was broken by stifled groans from the hurt. Droyn's eyes grew wider as it came home to him that she was using the Sword of the Lady for this; it was a rare honor, and one that would be spoken of all his life and by his descendants after him for as long as the chronicles were read.

"I dub thee knight," she said, and the flat of the blade rang on his armored shoulder as she struck; the sound was more like a great crystal bell than the usual clank of metal.

"I dub thee knight," she repeated as she flipped it to strike the other side, and then sheathed it.

"Receive the collée," she said, as she pulled off her right gauntlet.

That was a slap on both cheeks, delivered forehand and backhand, and she gave it in the full old style her mother's parents had brought back, a hard smacking buffet both ways that rocked his head on his neck. This was a rite for warriors, one that belonged in places where the iron smell of blood hung heavy. Droyn was solemn as he drew his own sword and presented it across his palms, but almost exalted now rather than on the edge of tears. Órlaith held it up and kissed the cross the hilt made before returning it.

"Take this sword, Sir Droyn de Molalla, knight of the High Kingdom of Montival. Draw it to uphold the Crown, Holy Church, your own honor and your oaths to your liege, and to protect the weak as chivalry demands," she said, in the form used for Christians.

"I will, my lady and my liege. Before God and the Virgin and St. Michael, I swear."

"Then rise a knight! And I will be the first to welcome you to the worshipful company of that most honorable estate."

She put her hands on his shoulders and exchanged the ritual kiss on both cheeks; she might be his liege and heir to the Throne, but at moments like these all knights were equals, a kinship that knew no other rank and crossed all boundaries of faith and homeland. John and Heuradys stepped forward to do likewise, since they bore the golden spurs too. Evrouin and the other Associates bowed low.

"And now we've got to . . ." she began, sheathing the Sword.

Then she fell to her own knees, and toppled onto her side and then her back. Blackness flowed in like warm honey, and she smiled at the anxious faces of her friends above her; Reiko put a hand to her forehead to check for sudden fever.

A barking in the background and the curse of someone snatching for a collar and reconsidering at a snap, and a greathound was anxiously nuzzling her and looking for a hurt to lick better with sorrow and joy struggling on its gruesome barrel-sized face.

Órlaith reached for the Sword, fumbled its sheathed length onto her chest and wrapped her arms around it. She *would* have smiled at the way Macmaccon's eyes held the same expression of worry as her friends of human kind, but suddenly that was too much effort.

"Just . . . need . . . sleep . . ." she said; and did.

CHAPTER EIGHTEEN

Eryn Muir
(Formerly Muir Woods National Monument)
Crown Province of Westria
(Formerly California)
High Kingdom of Montival
(Formerly western North America)
July/Fumizuki/Cerweth 15th
Change Year 46/Fifth Age 46/Shōhei 1/2044 AD

Órlaith leaned on the balustrade before her and looked out across Eryn Muir, her hands on the flat polished claro walnut surface of the railing, feeling its dark smoothness. The redwoods towered all around them here, rising straight as candles two hundred feet and more, seeming to reach the sky even though this flet and its guesthouse was itself ten times the height of a tall man in the air. Your eyes had trouble adjusting and it could make you dizzy when you realized that yes, they were trees and yes, they really were so huge. The lordly forest stretched for miles along the little creek that you could just hear burbling over brown stones far beneath, and up the sides of the low hills to east and west, until the sight faded and blurred into an umber shadow where beams of light slanting in from the westward were like golden spears edged with an explosion of green.

Reiko was standing beside her, and suddenly chuckled softly. The Crown Princess turned her head and raised a brow, absently reaching down and ruffling the ears of Macmaccon as he raised his muzzle from her feet. The Nihonjin woman touched the hilt of the katana thrust through her sash as she spoke:

"A thought I had yesterday, as our ship sailed under the great bridge and into the Bay," she said. "Of what my father's sword *Kotegiri* . . . my sword now . . . had seen since Masamune forged it so long ago, how it had witness . . . witness*ed* so much of the history of my people. The words that came to me were: *Tranquility like rice bowing before the sickle, and deeds like skies full of storm.*"

She was wearing an *Hōmongi*, a semi-formal walking-out woman's kimono, ultimately a gift from Lady Delia's collection at Montinore, though one of her samurai had brought the garment in his emergency pack and had been scolded for it.

And sure, discipline must be maintained. On the other hand, it's a bit of a charming gesture. At times these Nihonjin seem businesslike beyond the bounds of humanity, but things like that remind you that they're not so altogether and always.

The fabric was a shimmering pale blue silk; an elongated pattern of autumn foliage in brown and white and orange wrapped around the lower hem and then the back of the right sleeve and shoulder, and the front of the left. Órlaith had done the complex hair-knots she sported herself, under Reiko's direction and with Heuradys' advice and assistance.

"If steel could talk, so to say?" Órlaith replied. "Being more mobile than walls, despite those having ears. And the pattern holds here as well."

The Dúnedain had built their settlement at levels from fifty feet to little lookouts at thrice that. Most of the individual flets scattered between weren't large, like this one just enough to hold a fair-sized cottage with a railed walkway-verandah all around. The circular platforms were supported from below by a ring of graceful curved beams that flared up like giant bowstaves from a support collar around the trunk, the tops rising above the floor planks to make the balusters of a four-foot parapet railing, their ends carved into the heads of birds where they bent outward.

Reiko nodded. "*Hai*. The battle, the *kangshinmu*, and now"—she made a pointing gesture with her fan—"this. Once more, terror and then peace. And though these happenings are part of the history of Montival, it will also be part of ours, as much as Nagashino or Dan-no-ura."

A few flets held structures of several stories, or the platforms merged to form larger areas from trunk to trunk where the master trees grew in close-spaced arcs, legacy of offspring sprouting from the stumps and roots of ancestors fallen a thousand years ago and more. Flexible footbridges suspended from swooping arcs of cable linked the flets, woven of lath and cord and light planks; they and the balconies were all fringed with planters of wood or wicker, mostly growing vines with colorful blossoms, trails of greenery and flowers falling into space, or arching over pergolas or trailing from pots. The whole looked as if it had grown, and then been pruned by the hands of human kind.

Reiko made a small appreciative sound, and Órlaith nodded.

"They know how to use wood here, sure and don't they?" she said.

The basic construction material was redwood also, culled from trees fallen in storms or taken in carefully-judged thinning operations from younger growth where the kingly trees had recolonized their former range over the generations since the Change. The timber was highly and rightly prized, a lovely golden-red-brown color brought out by varnish and polishing, strong and light and easily worked. With only a little care it was nearly impervious to decay and insects, too. There was other wood in plenty, skillfully chosen for its look and character and use, and here and there designs were picked out in colored glass or metal.

"It is not as we would do it—there is more, ummmm, *intervention* with the material," Reiko said. "But in its own way, for its own place and its makers, very good. The forest itself provides the *fukinsei*, the irregularity of nature. So do the homes, adapting to the places and shapes of the trees. Yet in them there is also design, intentionality, an order that springs from thought, each contrasting with the other. So grand, yet so small when one sees it against the forest: that gives *seijaku*, tranquility. And it *is* made of wood, of materials that grew and must ultimately decay and pass as we do, as even these giant trees must: transience, a beauty that fades, *wabi-sabi*."

Most of the wooden surfaces were lightly carved, with running sinuous designs based on leaf and tendril. Sometimes on larger walls there were scenes from life or what the Rangers called their *Histories*—not far away someone had been working on a panel of low-relief and inlay work that depicted a dragon stooping on a town built over piles in the midst of a lake, with a great mountain looming beyond. The chips had been neatly swept up and used as mulch in a nearby planter, and the tools hung in a net bag from a peg as the artist had just stepped away—which they probably had, when the call to arms came.

Órlaith inhaled deeply of the cool damp air. Eryn Muir wasn't actually within sight of the sea; Amon Tam and a set of lower hills shielded this valley to the west. But you could feel the Mother Ocean in the air keenly even in high summer once evening began, scented with the pungent-spicy smell of the trees and the deep vegetable decay of the woodland floor far beneath the platform of this flet. It was never hot here, and she was glad of the green Montrose jacket of fine green wool she wore beneath her plaid; someone had found one to lend her that almost fit. Her House badge and a spray of Golden Eagle feathers rested above her brow on the Scots bonnet, and she and Heuradys had renewed each other's Dutch Braid—or the Ranger fashion, depending on how you looked at it—left to fall loose now and not clubbed.

It didn't rain here in warm months, though the fall and winter were wet, but the sort of fog whose last tatters drifted through the great trees now was a daily thing and kept growth thriving. That included the vivid moss on shingle roofs, and the dense green turf on others, starred with flowers, many like white-and-pink mountain yarrow that had medicinal uses or the dwarf lavender grown for their scent.

"I think the Dúnedain would say that to build well you must use Aulë the Maker's gifts of skill and thought and planning, but remember that Yavanna his Lady grieved for the trees which His children used in their crafts, and that they have a beauty of their own which we cannot match. Which may be another way of saying the same thing."

Reiko nodded. "This place is itself a *shimenawa* about the body of the forest," she said.

That meant the sacred rope of rice straw draped with white plaits that marked a place—often a tree—as the abode of *kami*. The two friends were dropping into and out of English and Nihongo sentence by sentence and sometimes phrase by phrase. That was easy for Órlaith, and it helped Reiko perfect her originally purely theoretical command of Montival's common English tongue . . . which was something she'd made truly astonishing progress with in the scant few months since her arrival, grinding out results by sheer intelligent persistence.

I've known many who are strong-willed, Órlaith thought admiringly. *But few more . . . more focused than Reiko-chan! She makes me feel a little sloppy and careless, sometimes.*

The Nihonjin gestured to the view before them with her fan and returned to contemplating the sight as the lanterns came on among the trees, like twinkling stars of different colors but scattered at different levels among the giant redwoods. One of the things Órlaith liked about her was that she was fully comfortable with silence. In fact, she could talk quite eloquently with it.

The sun was falling westward, beyond the low mountains and the sea beyond. This wasn't Órlaith's first visit, but it was the first as anything like an adult, and the settlement had grown much and matured in the years since. She'd slept all the while the horse-litter had brought her here from the battlefield and through that night and morning, woken up half-conscious long enough for the baths and to wash down some bread and fruit, then slept until well into the afternoon.

The Sword could mobilize every reserve within her, but it was the wielder who eventually had to pay the price. The duel with the skaga had drained everything that the fighting had left. She'd been busy since she woke, partly to reassure the rest that she'd taken no lasting damage, and this was her first chance just to *look*. Every Stath in the far-flung Dúnedain network considered itself unique. Often they went out of their way to be so. But they'd all willingly sent help, skilled workers and materials and supplies, once they saw the plans for this, despite the expense of distance.

Now she felt alert and relaxed, though still faintly tired; and ravenously hungry with a gnawing in the gut, which could be a pleasant sensation when you knew you could eat soon and well. Grief for Luanne and the other fallen was there, but like the pain of her minor cuts and fairly extensive bruises could be put aside for now. There was no shame in feeling the joy of life more fiercely after coming so close to losing it. The shadow of the Hunter's wings would fall on her too one day, and she suspected she would not outlive the tally of her father's forty-six years, if that many, nor would she die in her bed surrounded by consort and children and kinfolk.

We of House Artos are not a long-lived breed, it seems. Da knew it long before he met his fate, but he was the happiest man I knew—with his mate, with his children, in his work.

Even the ugly memory of edged metal slamming past before her face, close enough to feel the wind on her skin, was faded for now; even the memory of the skaga's eyes, when the Thing he had thought to control and use took him at last. Dreamless sleep and time added a little distance. She watched the slanting beams of light shift and fade, the lanterns seeming brighter as the sun sank beneath the mountains westward, and then spoke quietly.

"My father said more than once that you should live each day as if it was your last, and as if you would live forever . . . always both at the same time."

"Hai, honto desu," Reiko replied. "Unquestionably true. Simple . . . but very hard."

A quirk of a slim eyebrow. "As you told me your grandmother put it, if the path of wisdom was easy, any fool could follow it."

The sough of wind in the branches above was the undertone of the trees' millennial existence, and a barely perceptible sway moved the fabric of the flet beneath them. The sound was like the slow breathing of some great dreaming beast, and the movement the flexing of its ribs.

"That is music, neh?" Reiko said, turning her head and closing her eyes to listen.

Órlaith looked up and let the sound echo through her mind, watching as the crescent moon gleamed through a gap in the boughs, like faded silver against purple-black.

"And they've been making that sound here every day for ten thousand years—the ancients' books say this forest is that old. It's stood here since the Ice withdrew, since before the first tribes of human kind found these shores, when only the beast-kindreds and the wild Powers walked here."

The redwoods dominated the life of the place, but they were far from the only giants; some of the Douglas fir were nearly as tall. The floor was dense with fern and flower wherever a little sunlight penetrated, and the upper reaches and the canopy held scores of other plants that made their life on those living monuments, down to the algae that grew on moss. Game was mostly invisible from this height but thick on the ground, not least because the Rangers carefully spread their hunting and gathering in time and space to avoid stressing any one spot.

Birds fairly swarmed. Just here a flock of rufous-colored chickadees chattered and swirled about a set of thick planks bored with the holes they preferred for nesting, swooping after insects in acrobatic drifts, but they had competition from emerald-green flycatchers, and hummingbirds flitted among the flowering morning-glory vines that lined this balcony or over the flowering roofs.

Reiko smiled. "So your voice and mine and these others are woven into something very ancient at this sunset."

The stillness of evening didn't quite swallow the sounds humanity made, but encompassed them, like a warm bubble of hearthlight seen across hillsides in a lonely place. Folk were busy on the walkways and bridges and around the flets, the permanent dwellers and their children, and lately incomers from elsewhere in Stath Ingolf and warriors from other Staths of the Rangers come south since the spring on the news of the High King's death and the presence of new enemies here. They had provided many of the fighters who'd ridden to the relief of the encircled force at Círbann Rómenadrim, and given the blow its crushing weight.

And today, there were the guests; of the Crown Princess' followers, of Reiko's party, and from Deor's folk.

Diarmuid and Karl and Mathun were frankly gaping as they came off one of the connecting walkways and stood a few paces away; Órlaith smiled a little at the homely forthright sound of their voices, lowland lilt and mountaineer burr. They seemed to have become fast friends and comrades on their journey here, which she was glad to see. For its own sake, and because putting Mackenzies and McClintocks together like that was a little risky, like asking dogs and cats to cooperate on a hunt. Sometimes she thought they were divided by their similarities.

"Sure, and while I'm fair certain the hospitality will be of the best, not to mention the food and drink, I'm just a wee bit fearful that we'll wake up tomorrow naked on a green mound with long white beards and a hundred years will have passed," Karl said. "You feel that just a wee bit at Dun Juniper sometimes—more in the *nemed* there, the sacred wood—and more at Mithrilwood, but not so strong as here, so."

Diarmuid grinned. She still liked that smile of his and the way it made the swirling blue tattoos on his handsome face shift, apart from fond memories of the Beltane Bower. It didn't produce the old tingle and flutter that seeing it had brought once, the desire to touch and be touched, which was convenient but . . .

Sad, she decided. *Da and Mother loved each other from their days as children; you could warm your hands at it like a fire on a winter's night. And you could see that the years just added new layers to it, each in its appointed time, and would have into their deep age. Well, Clíodhna's three sweet-songed birds will whisper a name in my ear one fine day, and in the meantime I have work to do. And supper to eat!*

"Weel, at the least we didna get here by chasin' a white stag heedless over hill and dale and leaving oor fellows behind, eh?" Diarmuid said.

The three young men laughed, and the McClintock tacksman hitched at his plaid and shook his head.

"How'ere often a white deer leads 'em astray in the tales, still the puir fools do it, though if they ever heard a ballad in their ain lives they must ken nae guid will come o' it. It never does."

"Worse luck than refusing an ugly, smelly old beggar-woman a tumble or a lift across a ford running high with spring, that it is," Karl agreed. "White deer are not sent to guide you to a pot of gold, so."

"Did I see hide or hair of sich unchancy creature, I'd say to mesel', *Diarmuid lad, past time tae gang aboot fur home, where the parritch is bubblin' on the hob and yer wumman waitin' with a mug o' beer.* And then I'd run like buggery, screamin' as does a wee bairn afeerd. Nor stop until I was tae hame wi' cold iron hangin' above my door."

There was more laughter at that; she thought some of it was bravado over genuine unease.

Mathun nodded and crossed his muscled bare arms and put on mock-solemnity: "Nor did any say *enter of your own free will* when we arrived, the which always made me want to say *No, no, don't do it, ye iijit! Don't take sip nor sup they offer!* When our Da came to that part with a tale, and we around his knees with our eyes like saucers."

More lanterns were being lit as dusk stole through the heights, on posts or swayed out to hang from ropes overhead. The alcohol flames and mantles were bright as stars through the tinted glass and metal fret-work or globes of colored paper. Some of the Rangers were in their mot-tled working garb, with shaggy hooded cloaks and flexible strapped elf-boots, but others had donned the long full-sleeved embroidered robes of linen or fine wool that both sexes among this folk wore for festival and formal ceremony. Garlands of flowers were woven in hair mostly grown past their shoulders, now loose or elaborately braided.

Faramir and Morfind were in that style, since they had quarters here and their own clothes to hand. His robe was black with goldwork around the hems and in two bands down the front, hers a very dark blue worked with silver. Roses glowed against her black hair, and blue hyacinths in his yellow curls.

Susan Mika was walking between them as they strolled in from a flet around a trunk a hundred yards distant, also with flowers in her raven braids—and two eagle feathers over one ear—but wearing a deerskin tunic tanned butter-soft and bleached to a snowy whiteness, edged with fringes and a blue-and-red yoke of beadwork and elk teeth over the shoul-ders. Her leggings likewise fringed, and her strap-up moccasins deco-rated with colored porcupine quills. She looked small but not in the least childlike between the two tall Rangers; they were all three hand-in-hand, chatting, smiling at each other a good deal and snatching the odd light kiss.

Even Morfind was cheerful, who'd been scowling or blank-faced most of the time Órlaith had known her; though she granted that had been mostly in a desperate life-and-death battle and after a bad wounding and a sore loss. And as you'd expect with a young man in his position Faramir looked like a cat who'd fallen into the cream-vat and was licking its whiskers with an expression of dazed self-satisfaction.

Órlaith raised a mental brow in mild surprise, then shrugged and smiled fondly. Happiness was rare enough that she wouldn't grudge any to her friends, though she did feel mildly envious . . . and very slightly curious about some details. She couldn't recall offhand what taboos Dúnedain had about first cousins; that varied widely from folk to folk, from forbidding such matings to encouraging them.

Her brother John was standing not far away on this guest-quarters flet and talking with Deor and his comrade Thora, but Órlaith didn't think it had the same significance, though the two poet-singers—one aspiring and one of established reputation—were deep in animated conversation that was probably utterly technical. Evrouin was a tactful four paces away, with the lute-case over his back.

It's amazing how boring it is to talk *about music that's a pleasure to* hear, she thought.

The Bearkiller A-lister listened tolerantly with her thumbs in her sword-belt and sniffed at the odd waft of cooking odors that mingled with the clean, cool damp smell of forest.

The two men were peacock-bright beside her plain brown garb; Bearkillers tended to be ostentatiously unostentatious, while John . . . or more likely his valet Evrouin . . . had managed to dig up an Associate noble's garb of tight hose and curl-toed shoes, loose-sleeved shirt and thigh-length jerkin and dag-sleeved houppelande coat and chaperon hat, and it all *almost* fit well. That had probably soothed his foppish soul, and prevented too much longing for the baggage chest aboard the *Tarshish Queen*, which Órlaith privately considered to be the equivalent of the tattered stuffed bear he'd dragged around when he was six. Deor wore the embroidered tunic, pinned cloak and cross-gartered narrow hose of his folk, with rune-graven gold bands on his upper arms.

The three of them looked up as musical notes sounded through the colored dimness, silvery tubular bells and icy bamboo flutes and some sort of plucked instrument strung with metal. Nearly everyone else in sight did too, and there was a general forward movement, checked by looks at her and Reiko. Only her samurai remained still, waiting and passionlessly alert.

"The summons to dinner," Órlaith said at Reiko's questioning look. "And sure, there's many an official banquet I've looked forward to far less. Let's go! Fighting is hungry work, I find. Macmac! Stay, guard!"

Macmaccon stirred and whined as her foot withdrew from beneath his jowls; he hadn't been willingly out of contact since the battle, and they told her he'd insisted on lying at her feet while she slept, baring teeth and glaring through slitted eyes and growling like millstones at anyone who approached unless accompanied by someone he knew and trusted. That was a little inconvenient . . . but she wasn't going to turn away such fiercely unconditional love.

There were a number of ways to get from the ground to the interlinked flets, but only the hollow redwood with the stairs inside was navigable for dogs and not all of them could learn to use it; most of the community's canine dwellers were ground-based, like their horses. And unlike the numerous cats, one of which was peering over the edge of the roof at him with that peculiar indignation its breed reserved for intrusions by strangers in their accustomed space. The Rangers had made an exception for Macmac, though. For her, and because he bore a stitched cut on one shoulder as a mark of honorable battle against the Eaters.

"Hungry work, yes," Reiko said, sounding pleased with the phrase.

She gave Macmac a slightly dubious look as he laid his head on his broad paws obediently and sighed like a melancholy hairy bellows; her folk used their Akita breed for hunting and guarding, but less often than Órlaith's father's Clan and were less likely to dwell close with them as well. They had less to spare for beasts that ate the same foods as men, and things had been harder still in the terrible times just after the Change.

There had been years when many of Reiko's people were fully hungry enough to eat dog-flesh, something many Montivallans considered almost if not quite as disgusting as cannibalism.

"And fighting of the sort we did even more so," Reiko added, falling in beside the Crown Princess in a rustle of silk, seeming to glide effortlessly, and making a small gesture that brought her retainers in her wake. "It will be pleasant to eat. Though I had heard that the leaders here will not be present?"

"None of the senior ones, they've all gone walkabout, as it were," Órlaith agreed. "Found urgent business elsewhere and put the telescope to the blind eye."

Reiko blinked at that, and then chuckled as Órlaith explained the story about the legendary English sailor and hero-rogue named Nelson. He'd been a contemporary of the even more famous Lucky Jack whose name voyagers swore by, and featured in the cycle of stories that told his life.

She went on: "Their presence wouldn't be politic, seeing that I'm here without Mother's permission . . . though I've received no formal order forbidding it, to be sure. Doubtless that frigate bore such, and Edain's second had a writ with a menacing look about it; but the one sailed away after the *Tarshish Queen* . . . limped after, rather . . . and the other is in Wolf Hall, and they'll solemnly discuss it there while we abscond, skipping over the hills like spring lambs and singing a merry song. 'Tis easier to ask forgiveness than permission."

Reiko smiled, and opened her fan to cover her mouth in a gesture that suggested ironic discretion among her folk.

"Your mother is . . . stern," she said, not altogether disapprovingly.

Stern seemed a good word to describe contemporary Nippon, from what the visitors had let drop; not least what they'd let drop unintentionally, in the assumptions their words and actions revealed. Hiding the who of things was possible, but hiding what you were was near-impossible, even if you tried, which they didn't.

"She loves her children like a tigress her cubs," Órlaith said more soberly. "But it's harder for her to show it free of worry and . . . and a desire to control, to protect us, than it was for my father, who was always more at home with his own heart. Especially when we're grown, as John and I are the now. I think it may be that her own father died when she was ten, and her mother . . . well, there was love there too, but it was like a running chess match between them as well. And of course when you're born to rank, your parents' authority changes but doesn't decrease when you're of age."

Reiko nodded thoughtfully. "Difficult, for a family to be raised at court. I have much to thank my parents for, that they made my life and that of my sisters as . . . as normal as it could be. Perhaps your mother will reconsider her stance when she receives detailed reports?"

Órlaith made a weighing gesture. "What happened here was a powerful argument for our view of things. Yet it's truly said that you're ever a babe to the one who bears you, and also that the head is the heart's servant by nature."

Behind them Egawa rose from his kneeling position; he'd been gravely considering a hummingbird that had flown in a slow curious circle around his head. Apparently the little creatures didn't exist in Japan, and the Nihonjin found them endlessly fascinating. The two samurai who were never far from Reiko fell in behind their commander, spears in their hands. Órlaith's guards for the day were a pair of Rangers in back-and-breast and spired helm, carrying shields and deadly-looking long-hilted curved swords on their shoulders. That spared her battle-weary men-at-arms and the equally exhausted Mackenzie and McClintock clansfolk from a duty that would keep them out of the feast, but she hadn't bothered to even suggest that the Imperial Guard samurai do likewise.

Heuradys leaned against the balustrade just far enough away to give the two of royal blood a little privacy, while close enough for someone with her reflexes to draw and strike at a threat; she'd managed to find an Associate outfit like John's, probably from the same source, and though it was a bit large—made for a man, and not a small one—she carried it off with unconscious style, somehow managing to make her entirely practical longsword and dagger look like jewelry rather than killing tools. When Órlaith and Reiko moved she glided in front of them with a slight bow in passing, tucking a rose she'd been toying with over one ear beneath the liripipe of the chaperon hat.

The suspended foot-bridge had a bit of a sway and flex to it, which Órlaith found exhilarating, as she did the steep drop to either side beyond the woven guardrail. That was a matter of how the Powers had made your inner nature; she'd always enjoyed heights and climbing, and ever since she had terrified her parents and nannies running around the towers of castles and scaling the branches of apple-trees as a child, and Heuradys was much the same. They both liked gliders, for that matter, though John excelled them both in that skill. She noticed that Susan Mika seemed quite content to keep her friends on either hand and not look down, despite a proven courage as scrappy and indomitable as a wolverine's. The Rangers had been raised hereabouts and were casually at home.

More and more joined the procession as they traveled and other bridges linked to this, the path growing broader, and two Rangers went ahead carrying paper lanterns on long bamboo poles. As they passed home-flets families rose from their own tables on the verandahs and bowed gravely with right hand to heart; Órlaith nodded in return, though Nihonjin etiquette required Reiko to glide forward with her eyes trained ahead in a style that made her seem to float. The pleasant burble and trill of Sindarin conversation was musical in the background, and there was distant song and the sound of instruments. Rangers considered skill at both as necessary to life as Mackenzies did, in their rather different way.

The walkway was covered at intervals by arches of woven-willow trellis grown with mats of climbing roses whose blooms had pink leaves and pale centers, their musky scent strong and a scattering of petals lying on the flexing planks where they turned the passageway into a tunnel. It led to what was by far the largest flet; or rather a collection of flets merging their circular forms together, where a clutch of the largest redwoods grew close enough. The carved support-beams below curved into each other like interlacing fingers, and the looping edge of the platform enclosed thousands of square feet, punctuated by the trunks that made rough-surfaced reddish-brown pillars eight feet thick at the least.

Most of the surface was occupied by the hall where the Dúnedain of Eryn Muir met for feasts and assembly, song and dance, and where the single warriors without near kin here messed regularly; it was a building with a set of steep and wildly irregular shingled roofs whose rafter-ends were carved into the heads of Golden Eagles. On the balcony around it and in courtyards within were gardens of pathways and benches, edged with wooden planters bearing pruned bushes, blue-blossomed Manzanita, flowers like bright-yellow gumplant and arrangements of colored rocks kept wet and shiny by the frequent mists.

The carved screens that made the outer walls in summertime were mostly folded aside now. The pillars supporting the roof were single forty-foot trunks of richly-grained bigleaf maple, carved into the shapes of the Valar, as Rangers called the Powers who governed and pervaded the world. The rendering in the hard golden wood was lifelike, but done in a slightly eerie elongated style.

Each had two figures facing away from each other, a Lady and her Lord: Órlaith recognized King Manwë and Varda Starkindler, Aulë the Maker and Yavanna the Giver of Fruits, Oromë the Huntsman and Vána of the Flowers, Mandos the Judge and Vairë Fateweaver, Lórien Dream-giver and gentle Estë the Healer, Tulkas the Strong and Nessa the Dancer. Stark solitary Ulmo of the Waters was to the westward, and Nienna the Merciful at the east.

Around the centermost and largest of the tree-trunks was a circle of screens carved in abstract patterns showing no human face. That was for Eru, the Source Beyond, the ultimate Power behind time and space, Who was also named Ilúvatar the One Unknowable.

Órlaith halted and made the Old Faith's reverence along with the clansfolk, clapping her palms softly together twice and then bowing with the hands pressed together, thumbs touching her chin and fingers on her brow. The Japanese followed suit with a surprisingly similar gesture, the Christians (all Catholic as far as she knew) crossed themselves, and Deor and Godric and the Mist Hills folk bowed—to Manwë, she noticed, who of the Valar was most like their All-Father.

The vast airy hall within was lit by lanterns hanging from the intricate spiderweb of rafters high above, with pools of light fading into dimness. The tables were set out around the fires that flickered red in bowl-shaped hearths, topped by fire-hoods and chimneys of light aluminum hammered into decorative patterns picked out in gaily-colored enamel. The light of the flames seemed to grow greater as the sun dipped farther behind the western hills and the deep gloom of the forest darkened.

The oldest Ranger present was the physician Ioreth, whom Órlaith had met briefly at Círbann Rómenadrim.

Though I was barely conscious, Órlaith thought as she inclined her head and the Dúnedain made a knee and kissed her extended hand.

"*Le Suilon, Ernible,*" the healer said in formal greeting as she rose; the word implied reverence. "Be welcome, Princess."

The next most senior was a man in his thirties named Bragolon Darby, with his left arm bandaged and hanging in a sling, standing with her. He was lean and weathered, with a scar over his left eyebrow, and the upper joint of his right middle finger was missing.

"*Mae l'ovannen, Ernible,*" he said, which meant much the same thing.

"*Êl síla erin lû e-govaned vîn,*" she replied: *a star shines on the hour of our meeting.*

Órlaith hadn't met him before, but she knew him by name and the sketch in the files she'd looked through before setting out from the north. Below the four founders he was commander of this part of Stath Ingolf, and his formal title was Captain of Eryn Muir. They were apparently a handfasted pair, standing to greet the guests with grave courtesy. Each group of guests was given a bow and a few words, and a young *obtar*-apprentice led them to their table.

The courtesy showed again as they bowed to Reiko in the Nihon style, at forty-five degrees with the head bent, though they didn't attempt the language:

"Be welcome to our hall, Majesty," Ioreth said.

Baron Godric was an old friend here and had been since the Dúnedain first came to found Stath Ingolf, but Deor was as new to the place as John, and they had a similar look of makers storing up images for later use as they took it all in.

The tables were covered in cloth of unbleached linen, and places were already set, among skillfully woven cedar-withe baskets of long loaves of fresh wheat bread with poppy-seed in their brown crusts, earthenware butter-crocks, bowls of olive oil and olives, others of apricots and figs and oranges, platters of cheeses and elegant glass pitchers of wine and cool spring water with sections of lemon floating in it. Órlaith took her seat and refrained from boorishly tearing off a hunk of bread by an effort of will. It was fresh enough to have the intoxicating smell of the bakery, and was probably still slightly warm.

"Folk of the West," Bragolon said, raising his voice a little when all had been greeted and the summoning music died away.

He spoke in English with the soft Dúnedain accent—probably using what they called the Common Tongue out of courtesy to the outsiders present. The term had a double meaning; that it was the commonest language in Montival, and that it was . . . well . . . rather *common*.

"Tonight we are honored by the presence of allies and neighbors like Baron Godric Godulfson, but also by great lords; the heir to our own High Kingdom of Montival, bearing with her the Sword of the Lady, and Her Imperial Majesty of Dai-Nippon, Montival's ally in this war that is upon us against the Dark Power. They and the warriors who accompany them have ventured upon a Quest to far lands, in the most desolate and perilous of wilderness. They seek a lost and storied treasure, a thing of power for long ages, an heirloom of the Yamato House. One whose loss or finding may shape the fate of Middle-earth for an Age to come, for good or ill."

There was a hush made of indrawn breath and watching eyes. *This speaks to their very souls,* Órlaith thought. Ioreth whispered to him and he added:

"Though in another sense they're not here at all; our own Lords Ingolf and Ian, and the Ladies of the Rangers of Stath Ingolf, can't see them. Perhaps they're wearing a Ring!"

The tension dissolved in laughter. Young adults made up the most of the audience, what the Rangers called *ohtar* or squire-apprentices, and those just old enough to be ranked as *roquen*, knight-warriors.

Mostly they looked cheerful, even those with bandaged hurts; they'd just won a victory that would be famous in the sort of epic tales the Dúnedain loved, taken revenge on an enemy they loathed for past injuries down their kin, and they were part of events that would be more famous still. The cost hadn't been too great either, and these were a warrior folk. Not exactly fierce lovers of battle like some, but they prided themselves on their willingness to pay the price of guarding the peace of others.

"So we will not question them—"

A declarative statement, but nobody could doubt it was an order as he glared for a moment.

"—nor seek to make them speak more than they wish, for secrets are part of such affairs. We've fought and shed our blood by their sides; two of our own will join them when they depart."

Heads turned to look at Faramir and his cousin Morfind, with curiosity and envy mixed. Her face set, and his fair skin had a fiery blush despite its tan, of which he seemed miserably conscious. Órlaith sympathized; they were nearly three years younger than she, and she could remember vividly the period when *everything* seemed hideously embarrassing.

"As our ancestors fought the Dark Lord while the Ringbearer sought Mount Doom, we will fight this war that they may fulfill their Quest. And this night we'll give them a feast to send them on their way that they may remember with joy in hard and bitter places!"

Or remember with bitter sadness as we stare at some piece of weevil-seething hard-tack or moldy jerky or suck on a rock forbye there's no water, Órlaith thought, and inclined her head graciously.

This time there was a cheer, and then a scraping of benches as the Dúnedain all stood and faced westward with their hands over their hearts and heads bowed.

Ioreth spoke the blessing for all them. Dúnedain only uttered it aloud on great occasions, though she could see many moving their lips to the words, and a whisper like a faint soughing breeze accompanied it:

"To Númenor that was, and beyond to Elvenhome that is, and to That which is beyond Elvenhome and will ever be."

The rest stood as well and remained respectfully silent until it was finished, as was fitting when you were a guest in another's house and on their heart-land. Nobody here was such a fool or boor as to offend against a host's sacred things. The Catholic minority among the Rangers murmured their own grace and crossed themselves as they sat; to them the Valar were angelic beings and Eru Ilúvatar another, more ancient name for the creator-God the Bible spoke of. She noticed with amusement how Sir Droyn at the high table and the rest of her Associates at their separate seating relaxed a little as they did likewise, reassured that everything about them wasn't altogether pagan and of the Otherworld. There weren't many Rangers in the Association lands, where the Church dominated so thoroughly.

Poor dears, how their eyes would go wide at Dun Juniper! Órlaith thought affectionately. *Especially at the Beltane festival, with the pole and the bowers and the Green Man prancing through waggling his whapping-stick and all the lasses trying to touch it for luck!*

She signed her plate—a very handsome blue and white chinaware with a motto in Tengwar around the rim—with the Invoking pentagram of the Old Faith and murmured:

"Harvest Lord who dies for the ripened grain—
Corn Mother who births the fertile field—
Blessed be those who share this bounty;
And blessed the mortals who toiled with You,
Their hands helping Earth to bring forth life."

Then she set aside a crumb and a drop for the house-hob, whatever the Rangers might call the one of the *aes dana* who warded this place; the Mackenzies and McClintocks scattered about did the same. Others of her party made their various small rituals. Thora and Deor and his folk hammer-signed the air before them, thanked the wights and invoked *Earth who gives to all;* Heuradys dipped a crust of bread in her winecup and then the dish of oil and spoke, clearly but softly, as she threw the morsel into the flames of the hearth and watched it flare up:

"Home-loving Hestia who is the flame of the hearth, you whom I have always honored first and last, accept this offering of bread and wine and oil, and bless all who join us in this meal."

The Nihonjin made a gesture with palms together and then spoke a soft-voiced *Itadakimasu* towards their hosts.

There might be some faith or place that *didn't* have a thanks-offering at meals, but she wasn't aware of any. It was one of the minor graces that made life homelike wherever you went, and gave it form and meaning.

More of the meal appeared . . . literally, since the kitchens were on another smaller level of flet below this one, and sections of the floor sank down and rose again with wheeled trolleys loaded with covered dishes, which were in turn pushed around by adolescent helpers. She'd heard that Hîr Ingolf and Hîr Ian had designed and helped build the system with its smooth-acting counterweights; they were both amateur engineers of note. The Rangers expected their leaders to share the common work, and honored a maker's skill highly.

The Nihonjin smiled and bowed thanks to their hosts again when those trays turned out to include bowls of steaming rice. Which for them was the equivalent of leaping in the air with glad cries while snapping their fingers and clicking their heels.

Sure, and if there was tea, maybe they would *do that!* Órlaith thought.

"Please, where does this come from?" Ishikawa Goru said as he accepted his eagerly.

In a fundamental way to Nihonjin rice *was* food, and everything else a garnish; it was their equivalent of bread, though they'd settle for noodles instead. The fact that rice was an expensive luxury in the central parts of Montival had been a trial to them. The fact that they'd borne it with cheerful willing stoicism didn't mean they weren't happy for the familiar taste.

Faramir answered the sailor; Morfind and Susan beside him were whispering and feeding each other morsels on their forks and Morfind was actually giggling, at which Órlaith boggled for a moment.

"If you go east up the *Côf* . . . the Bay . . . and then up the river that flows into it, the Mallenduin . . ."

He noticed bafflement among the north-realm visitors, and clarified:

"—What the ancients called the Sacramento, there are huge marshes, many days travel across and low islands among them . . . it's a maze that shifts with every winter flood. The ancients grew a lot of rice there, and it grows wild in patches still, though thin and scattered. We gather it there. Most summers we of Stath Ingolf send expeditions by boat up the Mallenduin, to gather and fish for sturgeon and hunt—there are uncountable thousands of hippo and water buffalo there. Even tigers have problems with grown water buffalo, and they leave the hippos alone, so they breed fast and we're the only predator."

In the course of the translations and explanations it turned out that the Nihonjin knew what water buffalo were, more or less, but had only the haziest idea of a hippopotamus from pre-Change books. Órlaith had never seen a living one herself; north of here Montival was too cold for escapees of that breed from zoos and parks to survive in the wild, though things were very different as you went south. The delta of the Sacramento—

Pardon me, of the Mallenduin, she thought; it meant *Goldriver.*

—had proved to be ideal for the big river-pigs, and hordes of them had bred up and joined the water buffalo and the crocodiles and tigers and the native tule elk and muskrat and beaver and capybara and wild boar and much else. Hordes of other animals from the grasslands of the great Central Valley migrated to the marsh edges during the dry hot summers too.

Eyes widened a little at his description of going after the irascible amphibian giants from boats with heavy crossbows and harpoons, and even more when a Ranger showed off a carved sword-hilt wrought from a single one of their huge teeth, nearly a foot long. It *did* sound exciting. She'd been far too young for something that dangerous when she was in Westria before, and anyway the Dúnedain of Stath Ingolf had been fewer then, and still feeling their way into their new home.

"Even salted for wintertime or travel the meat's not bad in a stew, the teeth are prized, the fat makes good soap and lubricant, and the hides are very valuable for shields and saddles and the like. The northern merchants always want more for machine belting. The buffalo hides too, it's nearly as thick and tough . . . they're more or less like lean beef to the taste, their horn makes good bows and springs and cups, you can render their hooves for glue, things like that," Faramir said.

"*Hinu, hinu!*" Susan said, which was an exclamation of interest. "That sure sounds like a fun hunt!"

Morfind looked up as she poured the three of them more of the red wine.

"We make camps on the islands in the marshes to smoke the fish and jerk and salt down meat and salt-cure the raw hides so they'll keep for tanning later, and we gather some of the rice while we do it," she said. "It's beautiful country, especially at sunrise and sunset, though the bugs can be bad. Not just a sea of reeds . . . and even the reeds make paper and mats. Wild fruit and herbs and greens are more than anywhere else I've ever seen, and it's nearly empty of humans, but . . . haunted. Good training for working in wetland, and for handling boats. You'll have to come with us sometime, Suzie. It's hard work, but sort of like a festival too."

The Lakota brightened, then made a moue. "I wish I could invite you guys to the *makol* for the buffalo hunt, but . . . probably not."

John started questioning the Ranger pair on hippo-hunting, which led on to crocodiles in the same marshes, whose old bulls could be fifteen feet or more and push a ton in weight, and the peculiarities of looks and behavior among the tigers and wild boar, sitatunga antelope and curious birds who lived amidst the islands and reed-beds.

Órlaith concentrated on eating for a little while, starting with a soup of abalone, mushrooms and scallions and bamboo shoots seasoned with sorrel that the Japanese seemed to appreciate as well while the conversation turned on hunting dogs and bows and spears and the habits of every sort of game.

She liked hunting, and nearly everyone did it, except some townsmen, Christian clerics and the odd strict Buddhist. Cernunnos and Lady Flidais permitted it to those of the Old Faith; it was part of the nature of human kind, just as it was for wolves, provided it was done with care and respect for Their power and the lands and beasts under Their protection . . . which was one of the things the Crown ensured everyone did, often through the Rangers. It was useful work too, yielding leather and meat, bone and fat, and also necessary in most places to protect farms and livestock or people or often all three.

It was in the nature of tigers and lions to see her kind and their livestock as food, for wolves to eat sheep and coyotes and foxes to chase lambs and raid henhouses, and for grazers from rabbits on up to feast on garden and field if they could.

John was considerably *more* fond of hunting than she, though. So was Heuradys, for that matter. Associate nobles tended to be a bit obsessed on the subject.

Karl and Mathun and Diarmuid were soon joining in enthusiastically from the other side of the table and everyone's favorite *then the boar broke through the thicket* story came out, along with the *really impressive* buck that got away. Even Egawa tried to join in, to the limits of his shaky English and with Ishikawa doing his best to translate.

Under her usual slightly lofty politesse Reiko seemed frankly bored with the subject, and they exchanged a look of mutual sympathy.

"I thought your home was too crowded for much game?" Órlaith asked quietly.

Reiko nodded. "Sado-ga-shima and the other refuges, yes; only small things and birds for hawking. I like hawking because it is . . . quiet."

Órlaith nodded; they'd done a little falconry together during Reiko's stay in the north, both for its own sake and as a disguise for private scheming. The Nihonjin form of the sport had some interesting minor differences.

"They say the hunt is the shadow of war," Órlaith observed.

"*Hai*, and I am not fond of war!" Reiko said, and laughed behind her fan. "Not fond enough to welcome its shadow as a pastime. But the main islands, they are more like—"

She made a gesture encompassing the resurgent wilderness that covered much of Montival.

"And General Egawa's work has taken him there all his life. To the new settlements, and on salvage missions. The settlers must make war indeed, or the animals would eat all their crops and their plowing beasts. And the food is valuable."

"I'm a little surprised that so many survived to breed," Órlaith said; from what the books said, Japan had been fantastically crowded, even more than old California.

"I think because so much of my country is mountain forest," Reiko said. "More than eight parts in ten of the whole. Very many people in those days, but also much remote mountain where animals could hide . . . and the dying was mostly very swift *because* the cities were so very large. Few managed to escape them; enough to destroy the countryside in the plains and foothills and along the roads, but not to scour every woodland bare. Then there was so much land growing back in scrub that animals had very much to eat."

Her tone was clinical. Órlaith recognized it, and remembered her elders going still when she or one of her contemporaries used it among themselves; as the cataclysm grew farther away in time and fewer and fewer of those who'd lived through it as adults survived, so the children of the Changelings regarded it more and more as history. Tragic, yes, but not *immediate* in the way that haunted their grandparents or great-grandparents.

"And also . . . I think many of the people who worked in—"

Her much-improved English failed her for *zoos* and *wildlife parks*; Órlaith supplied the words. They were fairly recondite even in her dialect of the tongue, since both concepts had more or less vanished in the modern world. The closest thing to them were the vast areas of Crown Forest, the noble hunting preserves in the Association lands, and areas reserved for religious or secular reasons or both in many other places—in the Clan's dúthchas they were under the protection of Cernunnos and Lady Flidais, though the Mackenzies were perfectly aware of the ecological reasons as well.

In most places humans dwelt if you wanted to see wild animals you simply walked a little way from your house. In many, the animals came to *you*, which was one reason few went far from their front doors without a spear or bow. Though like other apex predators, humans were the main risk to their own kind.

"—worked in zoos and wildlife parks were very dedicate . . . dedicat*ed*. Those who knew that they would die, they may have spent themselves, their lives, to help their charges escape."

Órlaith nodded soberly. That had happened on this continent too, though in most cases they'd simply released the beasts before trying to save themselves; it had helped that there were so very many places where animals were kept here—game ranches in Texas alone had seeded species which spread all across the southern tier of the continent. From what she'd seen of Reiko's people, they were more likely to make any task the center of their lives and give it complete and utter devotion to the exclusion of all else.

Ishikawa was politely floundering as he tried to translate for Egawa; his English was much better than the general's, but not nearly as good as Reiko's, and his vocabulary was centered on matters nautical and on engineering and war. Órlaith took pity on him and helped a little before withdrawing. Evidently there were tiger, leopards, bear of several kinds, boar and a fair selection of grazing beasts including feral livestock all over the main islands of Japan. From what he said, probably more life and more varied life than those lands had seen in thousands of years.

The more time for me to enjoy the food, Órlaith thought when her self-imposed task was finished. *I'm hungrier than I can remember being ever in my life . . . eat nice and slow now, girl! Learning to live with the Sword is complex. Da was always a trencherman who could put John Hordle to shame, though he was as trim as a tiger all his life, not a spare ounce on him. Mother struggles with that. Was this part of it, that the Sword draws on your body?*

The Ranger's feast was good, and varied; the four founders of the new, or renewed, Dúnedain had had different likings, and they'd thrown in things from *the Histories,* not to mention what recruits had brought with them since. Aunt Eilir, Juniper Mackenzie's eldest daughter, had a Mackenzie's tastes, as you'd expect. The salad of wild miner's lettuce, onions, tomatoes, chickweed and purslane with hard sharp cheese crumbled in and dressed with garlic-infused oil and wine vinegar could have been from her hands.

Her husband *Little* John Hordle was given to what a deeply rural Englishman would like, one who was also six foot seven and three hundred pounds of boisterous enthusiasm, as much for a feast as for a fight . . . or for growling about playing bears on the floor with a clutch of giggling children. She took a slice of a cold pork pie shaped like a squat barrel and simply seasoned with sage, salt and pepper and remembered him fondly; from the strong taste and texture she thought the meat was boar-loin.

Aunt Astrid had died—heroically, of course—not long before Órlaith was born; she ate some of the fresh steamed asparagus with lemon butter and almonds in her memory. Her spouse Lord Alleyne had been English and a countryman too, an old friend of John Hordle, and he'd lived long enough for Órlaith to meet him and guest with him and the Hordles at Mithrilwood. But he'd been a Loring, of a family that had produced far-traveled governors and commanders in the days when his kind ranged and ruled the world around, sampling its good things as they went with lordly insouciance. The lamb tagine with green olives was his sort of dish; so was the chicken marinated in yoghurt, spiced with hot red chilies and turmeric and baked in an intensely hot clay oven.

Someone had been polite in the kitchen, too: besides the soup and rice there were seafood and vegetables dipped in batter and deep-fried in tempura style, pickled vegetables, and skewers of grilled salt-dressed chicken and other things. None of it was exactly Japanese food—she noticed several abortive reaches for containers of shōyu, fermented soy sauce, that just weren't there. Any of it might have been seen in most of Montival, but it was to their taste and convenient for their chopstick-based style of eating.

The flaky honey-sweetened pastries full of spiced apple, raisins and walnuts and the custard-and-berry tarts and sliced peaches in cream were just good.

And if it's one thing you can be sure of getting in Westria, it's wine worth drinking, she thought, and poured another glass for Reiko, who did the same for her; Nihonjin etiquette encouraged that sort of mutual small courtesy.

Montival had many fine vineyards in the Willamette and Yakima and up the Columbia and as far inland as Boise, mostly pinot noir and pinot gris, Gewürztraminer and Sémillon and the like, but the ones here were contributing some varieties that just didn't do well in the north, and it was more a matter of reconditioning and pruning them than slow starts from scratch.

A happy hum of conversation and the clink of cutlery filled the hall; a harpist was playing to flute accompaniment, and doing it rather well. Reiko sipped at her wine again; she'd learned to like the grape despite being reared on beer and sake, and this was a very nice Zinfandel from over at Wolf Hall with notes of anise and pepper.

"Quite good," she said. "And it goes well with these *enoki maki.*"

Which was Nihongo for skewers of mushrooms wrapped in pork and grilled.

"Chancellor Ignatius thinks that excise taxes on wineries here will be important eventually, since the province is Crownland and the taxes go directly to the High King's fisc. And Westria can grow things the rest of Montival can't, so there's a natural basis for exchange."

"Rice?" Reiko asked with interest.

You couldn't grow up a monarch's heir and *not* be interested in crops and taxes, not if you were going to do the job right. Tilled land and field-workers were the foundations on which all else rested, and politics was essentially about who got how much of what they produced.

"Rice eventually, definitely cotton, possibly sugar, and a lot of warm-country fruits like these oranges and lemons," Órlaith said.

She smiled a little sadly: "I found his lectures on fiscal policy a bit dull sometimes, but now . . ."

She gestured with her head to the hilt of the Sword hung over the back of her chair.

". . . now it looks sort of restful."

Reiko nodded silently; Órlaith flushed a little as she remembered that Nihon had been at war virtually since the Change. Montival had been lucky by comparison, even with the Prophet's War and the Haida reavers and all the internal scuffles in the old days, like the one which had killed her grandfathers.

"It was not the most fascinating part of Grand Steward Koyama's time as my tutor either," Reiko admitted with a slight shrug, lifting one of the grilled mushrooms to her mouth in her chopsticks and eating it with delicate finesse. "But as the saying goes, a *koku* of rice is a *koku* of rice."

The term that came to Órlaith's mind when she said *koku* was *ten square feet*, or a measure of weight which meant a little less than a pound a day for a year; after a moment something prompted her to think *six or seven bushels*. It also had an overtone of *a year's ration*.

As the meal wound down two of the Nihonjin rose and bowed to the older Dúnedain present, politely saying:

"Gochisō-sama deshita," as the others nodded and smiled, and Reiko gestured with her fan.

Those words meant *it was a feast*, which was literally true besides being good manners. The Nihonjin were a pleasure to be around that way . . . unless they decided you were an enemy, in which case you were in very bad trouble. From what she'd seen and sensed and from the old tales they were capable of a chilling ruthlessness, for all their subtle courtesy.

Deor and John had been deep in conversation again. Her brother grinned and shook his head, then leaned back and peeled an orange as the *ohtar* made another round, setting out bowls of nuts and dried fruits and the sweet nut-studded wafers that they called *lembas* and similar nibblements, and pots of various hot and cold herbal tisaines. She noticed that plenty of the Folk of the West seemed content to stay with the wine on a festive occasion like this, though most of them were pacing themselves and using appropriate foods to cushion the impact. There was precedent in *the Histories* for reveling. The guards of King Thranduil, for example.

Though I wouldn't care to walk about this place tipsy, considering how far it is to the ground.

"Oh, no, my friend," John said to the scop as he separated the segments of the orange and popped one into his mouth.

They were much more common here than farther north, where they were still special treats for Yule and the like. Few of the big citrus orchards had survived to greet the pioneer Montivallan settlers. Unlike the deep-rooted olive and vine they needed human help during the dry summers, and this was the northern edge of their range in any case. But individual trees close enough to water had lived and been brought back into production here and there.

"Not for my *sister*," John went on to Deor. "I don't sing praise-songs for my own family. You can do *chantaire* style just as well as I; better right now, and you know it."

"Your Highness, I must bow to your command," Deor said; then he turned and winked at Órlaith.

When he rose and walked over to the musicians he had the almost-too-steady walk of a man who wasn't drunk by any manner of means, but was definitely a trifle elevated. Thora shifted over beside John and gave him a friendly prod with an elbow.

"You're smart as well as good-looking, eh? He needs a nudge, sometimes, even after all these years. And I'm not qualified to do it when it comes to music."

John grinned. "I must be a Prince metaphorically as well as literally," he said, and grinned wider when she winced at the pun and mimed a clout, one that landed but not hard enough to sting.

Órlaith felt mildly envious. She had had the impulse to actually give him the proverbial whack on the back of the head more than once.

Deor bowed to the Dúnedain around the harp and soon they were talking animatedly; one pulled a sheaf of musical notation out of a case at her feet and opened it. The Mist Hills man looked it over and nodded and tapped a page; the Rangers glanced at each other, smiled, and launched into a tune's opening bars.

Wait a minute! Órlaith thought; then it died down before she could be sure.

Most of the hall had glanced over when the sound died. Now Deor raised his hands and smiled. It transformed him. She'd seen him fight, and he'd done it with courage and skill. She'd seen him starkly confronting things of the Otherworld, with knowledgeable determination. But this, making music before an audience, was the thing for which he was *made*.

"Friends," he said, falling into an alliterative half-chanting style. "Comrades of the battlefield, shield-brothers and shield-sisters. Yesterday I fought with you, and our Princess and Prince John, against the savages and the ill-wreaking *drymann* who drove them on. If we walk among the living today, it is because she wielded well against the sorcerer the Sword the Gods forged, forged for the line of her blood! Many and mighty were the deeds her noble sire did when his fist held the brand wrought by Weyland-smith, but not unworthy are those his heir has done, young though she is."

Heuradys snorted very faintly; Órlaith quirked a brow at her. That wasn't entirely fair, Reiko and she had been nearly as important there at the last, but art and politics were closely intertwined. Sometimes both required . . . simplifying . . . things for the sake of a smooth story-line.

"Someday I will make a praise-song for her, worthy of that field and all the heroes who locked shields there amid the splintering of spears! But for tonight, I will use the words of another; the troubadour-knight Odard Liu de Gervais, who fell on the shores of the far eastern sea, defending our High King and Queen on the quest of the Lady's Sword. I have seen his grave, where the folk of Kalksthorpe make offering even to our own day to honor his courage; but what he sang lives yet."

Now Órlaith sat bolt-upright, unable to reply when Reiko looked a question. That song she knew, and she'd never thought it would be used for *her*. It had been composed for her mother when she was younger than Órlaith was now and Lord Odard had loved her hopelessly and served her and his friend Rudi Mackenzie to the death . . .

He bowed again, waited for the accompaniment to swell, and began—using the smooth melodic modern north-realm style with easy fluency, his strong baritone filling the space effortlessly. She'd never heard a better rendition, as familiar as it was, and even with the high standards of Court for comparison, and he'd made a few changes on the fly that fit the scansion perfectly:

"The one who'll rule over our fair land of Montival
Shall reign just and wisely, and give each a fair ear
For no truer lady treads on this good earth
So let the hall ring for the Light of the North!
Let the hall ring for the Princess of Montival
Let the hall ring for the Light of the North!

Lady by grace and Princess by birth
So let the hall ring for the Light of the North!

She carries the Sword for the honor of Montival
Before her in battle our foes flee in fear
With her inspiration our heroes charge forth
So let the hall ring for the Light of the North!

Let the hall ring for the princess of Montival
Let the hall ring for the Light of the North!"

He bowed as cheers rang through the hall; it *would* have rung, if the walls weren't open, and it was certainly loud. In one or two cases there were even young Rangers standing on the tables to hail her, which wasn't their usual style at all. When it died down she rose in turn, and her mouth quirked. The Sword had *helped* her again; he was perfectly sincere and meant what he sang. Which left her few alternatives . . .

"Deor Godulfson, called the Wide-Faring, it's no gold ring I'm having to bestow this day," she said. "But I will not forget this gift, and the greater one of your own making when I hear it. The High One said truly that our deeds alone live forever, but it is words that *make* them live."

Deor came forward and went gracefully to one knee. "Ring-giver, I will ask a greater boon than gold of you. Let me and my oath-sister take a place in your band on this Quest and be of your sworn companions! Our swords and our lives are yours to command."

A smile. "And two poets are better than one, they say."

She opened her lips slightly and then closed them.

That's not a bad idea, at all, at all, she thought. *We've suffered casualties. They're both tried fighters—Thora is really impressive and Deor is better than average—and they've more experience with travel in different lands than anyone I know. Even Uncle Ingolf. And Deor's a runemaster; I owe him for more than his song, that I do. He got the Mist Hills men moving and that saved us. They're a bit older than the rest of us, but not exactly middle-aged yet either, so they should keep up well enough.*

"If what you ask of me is certain hardship and likely death, Deor Wide-Faring, I cannot deny you. Welcome to our company!"

Thora stood for an instant. "And there should be someone from the Outfit on this faring, to stand by the blood of the Bear Lord that you bear, Princess," she said bluntly. "And to avenge my sister of the A-List, Luanne Salander. I drink to her; may she feast with the High One!"

The hall rang with cheers again, and John rose to thump the singer's back as he returned to his place. Dúnedain singers joined the harpists and flautists and someone who was performing on what looked like an upright xylophone and sounded like crystal birds giving voice, and the Ranger's music resumed. It was extremely pleasant on the ear, but all the lyrics were in Sindarin.

"These people, the . . . Dúnedain? I think you also call them . . . scouts?" Reiko said after she'd shrewdly followed Heuradys' murmured explanation of what had just happened.

"Rangers," Órlaith said, reaching back for a moment to lay a finger on the pommel of the Sword. "The Scouts are another group, and far off eastward, in the Mountains of Yellow Stone, and a curious one. I've visited there. The Dúnedain are more widespread, and have their own tongue—"

She winced slightly and put a hand to her head, though there was no real pain.

"Problem?" said Heuradys sharply.

"*Pedin edhellen* . . . I mean, I just got the Quenya too. That's *two* languages the Dúnedain have, Reiko-chan. Sindarin they speak coequal with English in the life of common day. Quenya they use for lore, so fewer of them know it well. Powers, but it's pretty, though!"

For a moment the new vocabulary tumbled through her mind like a cascade of images; a green shore where silver waves beat on glittering sands, a tall white tower with walls like lace carved from crystal, a mountain whose top shone like a star, a forest of trees as majestic as redwoods, but with smooth gray bark and leaves of silver and green amid golden flowers.

Reiko's regular and almost-delicate face was frowning slightly, as if she searched her own memory:

"Aren't those words from stories?" she said suddenly.

"Ah . . ." Órlaith began.

Reiko's face cleared as she smiled with delight. "Yes, I remember Dúnedain from them too, I didn't recognize it when it was spoken aloud. But I loved those stories! I could read them, you know, even if I was not pronouncing correctly then in . . . ah, in my head. My tutors used them for teaching me English as a child because they were my favorite after the *Heike Monogatari*. I liked that one very much because it has Tomoe Gozen, Lady Tomoe; Éowyn was much like her . . ."

John had torn himself from rapt contemplation as a song came to an end to catch the tag-end of the conversation; he made a seated bow and recited, "The sound of the Gion Shōja bells echoes the impermanence of all things; the color of the sāla flowers reveals the truth that the prosperous must decline. The proud do not endure, they are like a dream on a spring night; the mighty fall at last, they are as dust before the wind . . ."

He dropped the bardic tone and said with a smile, "Alas, I cannot recite it to the sound of the biwa in your beautiful language, Majesty."

They'd agreed to use first names among themselves, but more formality was necessary for him than for his heir-to-the-Throne and not at all incidentally female sister, at least when he was speaking in front of Reiko's compatriots. Who were ceremonious even compared to Associate nobles, and fiercely jealous of their *Tennō Heika*'s dignity.

"But even in translation it's a fine tale," he said, with obvious sincerity; Órlaith could feel it.

"Gionshōja no kane no koe, Shogyōmujō no hibiki ari . . ." Egawa Noboru said, the same opening lines in Nihongo.

Apart from a few labored words on hunting, it was virtually the first conversation he'd ventured during the banquet, though he'd eaten heartily if courteously.

Órlaith looked at the squat, brutal-looking commander of the Imperial Guard with a slight surprise. Though she supposed it was less unlikely than his liking for the haiku of Bashō, which she'd decided she loved herself now that she could understand them in the original. She also thought he glanced at John with a bit less of the pawky skepticism he'd hidden under impeccable manners before.

And John's managed to pay Reiko a compliment that impresses Egawa too, who usually looks at him like a bear protecting her cub, or Macmac protecting me. *I would most truly like to clout you from time to time, brother of mine. Charm is all very well, but you take it to excess.*

Reiko inclined her head with a pleased look. "But . . . the Tale of the Heike is *real* . . . well, it's a tale about the Genpei War, between the Taira and the Minamoto clans, long ago, and the Genpei War certainly happened, if not everything in the tale. Ancestors of mine were very much involved! These other stories, of the War of the Ring . . . you mean . . . they are true?"

"Ah . . . opinions differ," Órlaith said.

The Montivallan nobles all looked at each other for an instant. Sir Droyn snorted very slightly while holding his wineglass up to a candle-flame, making his opinion plain without being tactless. Órlaith cleared her throat.

"The Dúnedain certainly think so."

She gave a glance over at Faramir and Morfind; they and the Lakota Courier were fast in a head-to-head conversation again. All three of them *were* short of twenty, after all.

Says the crone of twenty-one years, she thought, and lowered her voice as she went on:

"They can get sort of . . . I'd be saying shirty about those who mock it. *Okori-yasui,* I think your folk would say. And as far as they're concerned, they are the Folk of the West from the tales, reconstituted, you might say."

Her more or less great-aunt Astrid, Mike Havel's sister-in-law and Luanne's grandfather's younger sister, had founded . . .

Or refounded, in her telling.

. . . the Dúnedain Rangers together with her *anamchara* Eilir, grandmother Juniper's eldest daughter and therefore Órlaith's own aunt, by blood and without qualification. They'd been about of an age, fourteen or so at the time of the Change, and had become *anamchara*—oath-sisters and close comrades. Astrid had modeled her group on those tales, which had been her strongest interest before the Change, along with horses and archery. Which had, oddly, been mere hobbies and mere amusements then. The traumatic aftermath of the old world's fall had turned Astrid's fascination into an obsession; she'd taken to claiming to be herself a descendant of the heroes they spoke of, the royal line of Númenor.

That had been back when things were more fluid and little groups had come together around this or that leader, succeeding or failing according to luck and ability . . . even around a pair of teenage girls, one of them lost in waking dreams that suddenly fit the new world rising from the ashes of the old. Even outright lunacy hadn't been a handicap, as long as it looked as if it would work in a world itself gone mad; hence the rise of the Church Universal and Triumphant and the long wars against the Prophet with whose echoes she'd grown up, as well as much else for good or ill.

Aunt Eilir and her man John Hordle were still very much alive. Sir Alleyne, Astrid's consort, had just died last year up in Mithrilwood, the Ranger headquarters in what had once been Silver Falls State Park. He'd been a man she liked, kindly and very able, but . . .

When Aunt Astrid died, he became the keeper of her dream. And a trifle . . . single-minded about it, so.

"What is your opinion of the matter, Orrey-chan?" Reiko asked, her bright tilted eyes still sparkling with interest.

Órlaith winced slightly. Egawa's eyes gave a very slight twitch every time Reiko or she used the –chan suffix, which could mean several things but in this context was an expression of close friendship, particularly among women. She liked and admired Reiko too, and they had things in common besides the deaths of their fathers on the same day and at the hands of the same enemy. Or even being the daughters of rulers and heirs to thrones. But it was harder to be politically and diplomatically . . . vague . . . about her own opinion with a real friend.

Like its elder sibling love, friendship was a set of obligations willingly assumed, truth and trust among them, not just a pleasure or a feeling. At least it was if you were to be a friend worth having.

And I suspect Reiko simply hasn't had any friends before. Not as an adult, at least. Loving relatives and devoted retainers yes, friends no. And it's not natural for human kind to live without friendship; by the blessing of the Youth I'm rich in that. She's a bit like a hungry person finally finding a laden table and she needs all that formidable self-mastery not to gobble.

The stories the Rangers called *the Histories* and treated as sacred books were set in the lands across the Atlantic, purportedly in a very distant past, even more distant than Arthur or Charlemagne or the Black Prince.

As stories she'd always loved them too, but . . .

"I am genuinely in doubt about the matter, Reiko-chan," she said. "And so was my father. Though he said the Dúnedain could have taken far worse models for their lives."

It wasn't the only case where people were uncertain as to whether pre-Change records were fiction or not, or part-fiction and part-truth. It was simple fact that things had been possible then that weren't now and vice-versa. If that had happened once, why not before? Nobody but a few old-fashioned diehards gave much credit to the ancients' cosmology of uniform, eternal natural laws anymore.

And it was also simple fact that the ancients had been in the habit of writing down fiction in the same forms they used for fact, which made it hard to judge, and also true that tales grew garbled over time. While studying at the university in Corvallis she'd seen six or seven different opinions in the works of pre-Change scholars on how much of Homer's Iliad and Odyssey were history and how much fancy, all sounding equally confident as they contradicted each other. Heuradys believed Homer pretty much the way the Dúnedain did their *Histories*, of course.

Then there were the tales of King Conan, a favorite of streetcorner story-tellers throughout Montival and for all she knew beyond. There was a detailed history of the Hyborian Age written in the form of an essay, albeit one that had a very odd obsession with the color of people's hair, and the maps were not dissimilar to those in *the Histories*, but . . .

Faramir looked up. He didn't seem angry, but his offhand confidence was all the stronger for it.

"Well, of course *the Histories* are true, not necessarily every single word, but mostly," he said. "Granted that a lot of the ancients didn't *accept* them as anything but tales, how could the Historian have known so much . . . like the languages . . . if the Valar weren't inspiring him? It would be Lórien Dreamgiver, of course."

"He may not have known himself how true they were," Morfind added. "Visions can be like that, so he bent them a little to the contours of his own mind and age."

And it became harder to tell what had been fact from what had been mere tale-spinning with every passing year. Her father had told her in confidence that as a young man he'd always thought *the Histories* merely wonderful stories, and Astrid utterly barking mad, though functionally and usefully so. Until he returned from the Quest to Nantucket with the Sword of the Lady and found he could speak the Elvish tongue. Including grammar not contained in *the Histories* at all, and thousands of words nobody had known, some of them for *concepts* that nobody had known.

For colors that the human eye could not see, for instance, she thought. *I can see what* Light of the Two Trees *means the now, the same way I do when I think* red.

Dúnedain scribes and bards had followed him around at times for the rest of his life taking notes; he'd endured them for kinship's sake, and because the Rangers were so useful to the High Kingdom, and of course because Astrid had given her life on a mission of great importance that had been crucial to the outcome of the Prophet's War. He'd said more than once, and in public, that the least of what she'd done meant that ten thousand souls still walked the ridge of the world who would have lain stark on the battlefields otherwise.

He'd also said privately to his eldest daughter a few years ago that when you found you could say *Eat shit and die, arsehole!* or *I want a shredded pork sandwich on a bun, with a pickle on the side* in a language, it made the theory that it all had been made up from whole cloth by a long-dead Englishman less convincing. Even if the Englishman had *thought* he was making it up.

"You've a point there, Morfind," she admitted.

"Well, if *the Histories* aren't true, then they should have been," John said diplomatically. "Some damned fine song lyrics in them, too."

"By now two generations of the Rangers have grown up speaking Sindarin as their cradle-tongue along with English, so you could say it's a language as real as any other," Órlaith said . . . also diplomatically.

Naturally the Rangers believed in *the Histories* as strongly as Christians believed in their Bible. In some cases they believed in *the Histories and* the Bible. The human mind was a wonderful thing, as Grandmother Juniper was fond of saying.

Heuradys seemed to be following her thoughts, as so often in their long comradeship.

"There's nothing in *the Histories* that's outright impossible, any more than in the Tale of Troy or the Tale of Arthur," she said thoughtfully, turning the stem of her wineglass between her fingers. "I mean, yes, there's the magic ring . . . rings . . . but we've got a magic *sword* right here and we're looking for another."

"One that I have seen in visions," Reiko said, nodding. "As did my . . . as did Saisei Tennō before me."

"And there's the Dark Lord with evil powers, but by Hāidēs and Persephone, Orrey, your own father killed a Dark Lord with evil powers . . . and used his magic sword to do it. And *you* and the Majesty just killed an evil magician *working* for the darkest of Powers, didn't you?"

Órlaith shuddered and made the warding sign of the Horns. Reiko nodded emphatically; again her side of the Pacific had its own analogues and they'd followed her here. Tales from the Prophet's War told of such, too, ones she'd heard from first-hand witnesses she trusted. John crossed his arms thoughtfully and said:

"Not to mention your crossbow bolt, Herry. And the people in *the Histories* seem to live pretty much the way actual people do, you know, farming, fighting with swords and bows—it's a lot more realistic than most of the stuff written before the Change. More like real life and real history. There are even big ruins and lost cities all over the place—those faces of their rulers the ancient Americans carved into the Black Hills that Suzie's relatives showed us when we visited the Lakota lands, Orrey. They're pretty much like the Argonath in *the Histories* with the statues of Isildur and Anárion."

"A point, brother of mine," Órlaith agreed.

"And the face of Tašúŋke Witkó," Susan Clever Raccoon said, and added: "That means *Crazy Horse*, one of our greatest war-chiefs. He's carved there too. Not far from the Four Big Wašíču Guys."

"Right, Suzie; I remember thinking it was a pity they didn't complete the whole statue," John said. "He'd have looked very imposing on his horse, judging from the model."

"Yeah, but have you seen the way they were going to have him pointing?"

She grinned and put out her arm with her index finger foremost. "That's sorta rude to our way of thinking, you know? Like this." She clenched a fist and extended the middle one.

John raised his hands in acknowledgment. "God knows *we* couldn't finish it, anyway, not without an army of ten thousand working for fifty years."

Karl Aylward Mackenzie returned to her brother's original point. "Aye, but you're right, Highness, *the Histories* of the Rangers don't have the things that make you scratch your head and wonder what they'd been drinking and how to get some. Whether they're fact or no, there's nothing where you go *oh, that makes just no sense* the now."

"Nae rockets tae the moon or dinosaurs on islands or clockwurrk men fra the future come to kill their enemy's grandparents," Diarmuid agreed. "Forbye, a fine stormy tale they are."

John took up the thread: "So it could be as true as, oh, R . . . the Majesty's *Heike Monogatari*. Basically true, just . . . spiced up troubadour-ishly for added interest. You know, more dramatic tension, taking out the boring bits, simplifying the narrative, have the villain get off the coach and kick a dog on his way indoors, that sort of thing."

"Like *Beowulf*, or *The Battle of Maldon*," Deor added, and then glanced at Thora. "Or the *Völsunga saga*."

"Or Lady Fiorbhinn's *Song of Bear and Raven*," she said.

Susan Mika nodded, and her face took on the considering look of someone remembering a verse they'd memorized.

"That one gets sung a lot up on the makol in wintertime when there's not much to do," she said.

Órlaith felt her mind shudder inwardly a bit. The Black Months could be hard enough in places like the Willamette. She'd loved her times among the Lakota, but those had been in summer, the great buffalo hunt and the festivals where they gathered many thousands strong for trade and council, celebration and dance.

Susan went on: "I always liked this part, it's got my Uncle Rick in it, which is cool. It's in Book Three . . ."

"The Return Stanzas," Deor agreed. He hummed wordlessly, supplying the slow undertone as she half-chanted in her light high voice:

"Rick, Lakota incantan
Lord of the tunwan wide
Rode to meet King Artos
At great Des Moines to bide
"No walls defend my kinsmen,
No river, lake or tree.
For long we ride in plains so wide
Their ends no man can see."
So spoke wise Rick the war-man,
Victor of many a spoil,
For he had seen with plains-eyes keen
The fruit of Cutters' toil.
And as he stood in Iowa
There eighty thousand strong

Mustered close a vast grim host
To cleanse the red-robes' wrong.
"Such a mighty force as this
We could not face alone.
With rails to tread, our elders said,
Soon all our land they'd own.
I shall not lead my tribesmen
For yields of dust and bone.
A pledge to make that will not break
I must secure and hone."
He pondered long and deeply
For all his people's sake,
And in the end he faced his friend
His homage then to make
In view of all the bossmen,
Full-binding as a cord,
His oath to pledge about the edge
of the Lady's holy Sword.
In your High Kingdom, Raven,
Our honor shall abide.
For you have been 'gainst foul Corwin
And with you we shall side;
Then you shall be our bulwark,
And we your eastern guard.
So sky and sea and earth and thee
witness for time unmarred!"

Everyone raised their glasses in a toast, and Heuradys added:

"And who could say the Valar aren't real? I know Athana is, I can feel her hand every time I make an offering, and they're actually pretty much like the Olympians, or the Powers the Mackenzies and McClintocks reverence. Or the Aesir, come to that."

Karl Aylward Mackenzie finished his fourth apple pastry.

"'Tis plain sense you're speaking, Lady," he said, dipping his fingers in the bowl of warm scented water and wiping them on a napkin. "Why, even the figures of them here look like those in Dun Juniper or the god-posts outside Sutterdown. A little, at least. I didn't get much through this thick head of mine in Moon School, but that the Powers wear many faces, that I did get well into my chine. And though they say the Otherworld was more distant before the Change, at least for the years just before it, still it wasn't entirely absent. Otherwise this sword of Her Majesty of Nihon wouldn't have the name it did, eh? For *that* story happened long, long before our grandparents' day."

Órlaith nodded respectfully. *None of the Aylwards are stupid, even if they're not scholarly hairsplitters like some.*

John rolled his Catholic eyes and sighed at that, and Heuradys stuck out her Old Faith tongue at him, before ostentatiously turning back to Órlaith:

"Your father met deities around every hill, back on the Quest."

"Twice, once in a dream and once through a seer who was in a trance."

"Or angels," John said stubbornly.

"You use your titles, Johnnie, and I'll use mine. But it wasn't around every hill, Herry. And . . . *the Histories* have dragons and orcs," Órlaith pointed out dubiously. "And Ents. You don't see things like them around. Which is a pity, I'd have liked to meet Ents."

"I have seen . . . the *kami* are very real," Reiko said. "And the Grass-Cutting Sword. So why not the great eight-headed serpent whose tail contained it?"

"Passenger pigeons," Heuradys added suddenly. "I mean, all the chronicles say they were extinct, but they've come back, right? Starting with Nantucket, where the Change began?"

Morfind nodded. "And *the Histories* themselves say the orcs and trolls faded and dwindled in the Fourth Age, the Age of Men. But . . . now, who knows? We did meet a *golor,* an evil magician; met him twice and killed him, though sooner would have been better."

She touched the scar on her face. "And the Eaters are enough like *yrch* for everyday use. If Morgoth of old twisted elves into orcs back in the deeps of time, before the rising of the Sun and Moon, why not the same with humans now? And the Elves set out for the Uttermost West to usher in the Age of Men. So maybe here in the Fifth Age, we'll get them all back again eventually."

"Powers, I hope not the orcs and trolls, Eaters are bad enough!" Órlaith said, but she nodded too; Morfind had a point.

"Well, fauns and centaurs, then," Heuradys grinned.

The Dúnedain themselves occasionally spent winter evenings squabbling over what Age this was in their reckoning; the consensus was that it was the Fifth, with the Change marking the beginning of it as the destruction of the One Ring had started the Fourth. Some of their Catholics held out for this being the Sixth, with the ministry of Christ marking the Fifth. The odd eccentric said seventh or eighth, on the theory that they were getting shorter.

Órlaith wished Luanne was here; for herself, but just now also for the sardonic look she'd have given. Her grandfather Eric Steelfist Larsson, Mike Havel's brother-in-law, had always held to the *barking mad* interpretation of his younger sister Astrid, and had been known to refer to her during her life as Princess Leg-o-Lamb.

Which according to campfire stories drove her into fits. A great lady and a warrior for the legends, but by all the tales she was . . . difficult.

"Well, the Dúnedain in this age are real enough," Órlaith said. "There are thousands of them, all over Montival."

"Except where the barons get a hair up their . . . noses about it, in the Association territories," Heuradys added. "Pity. They're useful. If my lady mother or my lord my father had estates further north or on the coast, I think they would have endowed a *stath*. The way those idiots kicked up a fuss in the House of Peers when the Counts of Tillamook invited them in was a disgrace."

Órlaith nodded. *Useful to the realm, and the Crown, and to Lord Chancellor Ignatius' lasting pleasure, inexpensive to the Exchequer, except in grants of land which nobody else is using or wants to use anyway.*

"It's not as if they asked for manors, or even land that would be valuable under the plow," Heuradys added, echoing her thought.

Rangers didn't farm much beyond truck gardens, though they had many excellent artisans, and the places they settled had good hunting but mostly little land suited to the plow. Their main trade was danger: escorting caravans, patrolling against or hunting down bandits, scouting into the perilous wastelands of the dead cities to protect salvagers, slipping through forests to find pirate bases.

Their place in the Great Charter also made them available to communities that needed outsiders to keep the peace or deal with malefactors because their own methods had broken down, though the Rangers were rather picky about that and had given some self-satisfied lords unpleasant surprises when they sided with their underlings. In war they scouted and raided and operated behind enemy lines. Her father had been fond of saying they did more to keep the High King's Peace than several armies thrown together.

People who wanted a nice secure life, a normal one where you rarely went more than a few hours' walk from the fields you tilled, tended to drift out of the Rangers. Those of the opposite temperament drifted in, often by marriage.

John looked up at the stars. "Getting late, if we're to be off early," he said. "And hearth or no, it's a bit chilly, too, with the walls open like this."

Then he grinned, that reckless expression Órlaith knew. "I'll give them something to wrap it up. Something appropriate for a Quest, by St. Jude!"

He moved down from the dais and spoke to the musicians. They'd gone back to gentle background work, and listened keenly. Then they took up a slow rhythmic tune, like the pace of a swaying march. Silence fell as attention turned to him, and he began.

She recognized the words; they were from a book of poetry that Captain Feldman had lent him, but the tune was new, and his:

"We who with songs beguile your pilgrimage
And swear that Beauty lives though lilies die,
We Poets of the proud old lineage
Who sing to find your hearts, we know not why—"

"Ah!" Reiko murmured.

Órlaith nodded and closed her eyes for a moment, letting the images flow through a mind lit by wine and war and things beyond the world of common day:

"What shall we tell you? Tales, marvelous tales
Of ships and stars and isles where good men rest,
Where nevermore the rose of sunset pales,
And winds and shadows fall towards the West:
And there the world's first huge white-bearded kings
In dim glades sleeping, murmur in their sleep,
And closer round their breasts the ivy clings,
Cutting its pathway slow and red and deep."

The hall had fallen entirely silent, and she saw tears on some faces when she opened her eyes.

"And how beguile you? Death has no repose
Warmer and deeper than the Orient sand
Which hides the beauty and bright faith of those
Who make the Golden Journey to Samarkand.
And now they wait and whiten peaceably,
Those conquerors, those poets, those so fair:
They know time comes, not only you and I,
But the whole world shall whiten, here or there;"

A voice murmured *mujō*; that meant transience, or the melancholy of things that were impermanent—life, in particular.

"When those long caravans that cross the plain
With dauntless feet and sound of silver bells
Put forth no more for glory or for gain,
Take no more solace from the palm-girt wells.
When the great markets by the sea shut fast

All that calm Sunday that goes on and on:
When even lovers find their peace at last,
And Earth is but a star, that once had shone."

A long moment when only harp and flute sounded, and then her brother's voice soared again, triumphant:

"Yet sweet to ride forth at evening from the wells
When shadows pass gigantic on the sand,
And softly though the silence beat the bells
Along the Golden Road to Samarkand.

We travel not for trafficking alone:
By hotter winds our fiery hearts are fanned:
For lust of knowing what should not be known
We make the Golden Journey to Samarkand!"

CHAPTER NINETEEN

ERYN MUIR
(FORMERLY MUIR WOODS NATIONAL MONUMENT)
CROWN PROVINCE OF WESTRIA
(FORMERLY CALIFORNIA)
HIGH KINGDOM OF MONTIVAL
(FORMERLY WESTERN NORTH AMERICA)
JULY/FUMIZUKI/CERWETH 15TH
CHANGE YEAR 46/FIFTH AGE 46/SHŌHEI 1/2044 AD

One of the ironies of this strange place is meeting little bits of things that are familiar amid so much that is alien, Reiko thought as she yawned and slipped beneath the covers on her futon.

Eryn Muir was crowded right now, and she and Órlaith and Heuradys were sharing a room as they had on the ship.

Though with Lu-anne then too. Such a great pity that she fell . . .

It had been an odd experience to simply be one of a group of young women on a journey rather than the axis on which everything turned. Odd and rather refreshing. The Bearkiller had been perfectly respectful, in a foreign way, yet also . . .

How do they say here? Good company, *yes, and* fun. *She died very well. And she was young, but the young are no more immortal than the old. Duty is heavier than mountains.*

It was easier to prepare herself for sleep because it turned out that the Dúnedain used very much the same type of bedding that her people did, the combination of *shikibuton*—flexible stuffed mattress—a *kakebuton* comforter, and a pillow stuffed with chaff, though they called it all a futon-set. It felt luxuriously warm as soon as her body-heat had been caught for a little while, and the linen covering was as crisp and smooth as the cotton she was more used to.

Two of them were in Western-style bed frames hinged to the walls of this wedge-shaped room, one for her and the opposite for the Crown Princess, and one was set out on the floor for Órlaith's inseparable liege knight. But they could all be rolled up for storage in the daytime in the way she was used to. Except for the patterns embroidered on the comforter and some differences in the texture of the fabric it might have come from home; it was exquisitely clean, and smelled very faintly of lavender, which must be included in the padding.

There was a little stove built into the wall, but they hadn't bothered with a fire though it was chilly and damp outside. The quilt with its linen cover was quite warm enough; in fact the contrast of cool air outside and warmth within was perfect for rest. Though it would have been perfect if they could have used it to brew some *sencha*—she missed the way tea helped you center yourself.

The Rangers seemed to save their lavishness for public things and public occasions, and live rather plainly themselves; they reminded her of an order of warrior monks, save that they had families. From what she'd heard they *did* have warrior monks here, orders both Christian and Buddhist; there hadn't been time to enquire more. That was an institution that had been tentatively revived in the homeland, on a small scale and only in the last few years.

The walls even had racks for swords and stands for armor, bows and quivers, both in use now; this was a barracks, more or less. Her gear had been meticulously cleaned and repaired . . . and then General Egawa had gone over it carefully, testing the new lacing cords . . . and then she'd done the same herself. Someone had even found her replacement arrows of the right length, though they were crafted from the fine cedarwood favored here rather than bamboo.

The inner wall—the wedge shape of the room was squared off where the point would have been—also had a shelf bearing a few books in a strange script, and a lantern turned down to its lowest, so that it was a very dim blue spot in the dense darkness. More light came through the windows to either side of the door, though it was slight and very diffuse.

From the ceiling over her bunk hung a banner; she smiled drowsily at it as it stirred a little, pale in the darkness. She'd made it herself.

Waiting for Órlaith to awaken had been hard. None of them had been sure what the deep sleep had meant. Nobody had dared to wake her when ordinary noise or the jolting of a horse-litter or having her armor removed didn't.

There was nothing to do until she woke, after seeing to their wounded and arranging proper cremation for their dead, and the possibility that Órlaith *wouldn't* wake at all simply did not bear contemplation. To pass the time when she wasn't sleeping herself Reiko had asked for cloth and ink and a brush and centered herself by making a banner in the ancient *hata-jirushi* style, a rectangle meant to be hung from a crossbar with the long side vertical. The device she'd chosen was five overlapping bamboo leaves point-down in a fan and three gentian flowers above, complex enough to be a bit of a challenge. The symbol was also ancient, the *mon* of the Minamoto clan, and mustering the calm needed to make the strokes smooth and sure had helped.

She stilled her mind as she grew warm and comfortable and drowsy beneath the comforter; the wine she'd drunk made her more so, and the fact that you did not recover from exhaustion of the sort she'd known in the battle with one night's sleep, even a long one.

And remembering how she'd learned the brush had been soothing while she knelt poised with sleeve held back, ready to make a stroke. Recalling long afternoons with her mother and her sisters, with the shoji slid back to show the courtyard garden and give them light, and Mother's smile when she achieved the poised relaxation needed for a perfect trace. And the memory of her little sister Yōko's tongue peeping out of the corner of her mouth as she concentrated fiercely on the first elementary practice moves . . .

Then she *was* asleep. She could tell by the fact that the light was no brighter, but everything was perfectly visible as if by day, down to the way a ruffle of golden hair curled on Órlaith's brow and how Heuradys' hand rested lightly on the hilt of her sheathed dagger.

Reiko was standing, and in her armor again; she turned and tucked her swords through the *uwa-obi* around her waist and took the banner down, rolling it up and tying the ends before looping it over a shoulder like a bandolier. Somehow she managed to do that without looking at the bed, for she was obscurely unwilling to see her own head upon the pillow.

Or even worse, not *to see it,* she thought, in a way that seemed curiously detached from action.

Órlaith's great dog twitched and whined in its sleep by the door—it was a little disconcerting to have a dog in your bedchamber, but she had to admit that the huge beast was as formidable a guard as any, and utterly dependable. She paused for an instant and let it resume its slumber. Something told her that unlike a human being *it* would not be bound by the fact that she was asleep and dreaming, and might take exception.

I have had these dreams before, she knew and thought. *The desert and the castle in it, the creature with eight heads and the Grass-Cutting Sword. And I have seen* Kusanagi *in the hands of Takero Yamato . . . and for an instant, he saw* me. *Or my . . . our . . . Ancestress through me. What now?*

The door opened silently beneath her hand. That was more terrible than the dream itself, that her hand could feel the carved wood of the knob against her skin. The guards outside were alert, but neither the samurai nor the Dúnedain *roquen* stirred as she passed, though one did blink and frown and glance about. There was a lamp high above; experienced warriors wouldn't have one close, for that would simply kill their night-vision without extending the range of sight.

Everything was still perfectly clear to her.

Is this how a cat sees? she thought. *Is this how it feels to them, to move invisible through a night-world in which we are blind?*

A dove stood on the railing outside, cocking its head and staring at her. Beyond was blankness, thick fog hiding everything beyond arm's reach and the canopy of the trees and a moonless sky; to her it was as if the world vanished into infinite caves of mist and smoke.

There was a muffled silence, even the creak and rustle of the trees subdued in the windless stillness, and a low dripping sound as the saturated air condensed and fell, tiny drops touching the skin of her face like a mere memory of rain. The dove bobbed its head, and she realized it was a *hato,* a type familiar at home but one she'd never seen on these shores.

Her breath caught as she remembered Who had doves for messengers, and then a warrior stepped from the mist onto the balustrade and down to the walkway. Reiko's left thumb started to push on the guard of *Kotegiri* and her right hand move to the hilt. Then she froze, her lips slightly open in astonishment.

The figure was Japanese—but not of the Japan she knew. Nobody had worn that *o-yoroi* style of armor, like colorful laced-together curtains of silk and steel hung from the shoulders and breastplate, for a very long time; she had never seen it except in books of history and old prints. Beside it, her own *Môgami Dô,* inspired by those worn late in the Sengoku, the Age of Battles that preceded the long peace of the Tokugawas, was a thing of yesterday. He—

No, she, Reiko recognized. *That is a woman samurai, an* onna-bugeisha. *That gear makes it a little harder to see.*

Such were rare but not unknown in her people's history; several had been very famous.

—*She* had a *naginata* in her hand, a bow and quiver over her back, and a narrow-bladed sharp-curved *tachi* slung by two *ahsi* hangers edge-down from her belt in the ancient manner. Her long hair fell past her shoulders, confined by a *tenkan* with a triangular fretwork ornament over the brows and two red tassels at the sides. The weapons and gear were rich, fine steel and elegant lacquer, and there was the figure of a small silver tiger at the end of the *tsuka* hilt of the sword gripping with claws and teeth, but it all had the look of well-kept equipment that had seen long hard use.

The stranger went to her knees with a supple catlike grace and bowed her head to the floor; but to the dove first, and only then turning to make obeisance to Reiko. For a moment the long black fall of her hair swirled about her face.

Reiko's eyes went to the bird, but it bobbed again and took wing, circling above the stranger's head and then vanishing into the mist.

Perhaps to Hachiman!

She made the small gesture to the warrior that meant *you may rise.* Like many minor things of custom that was extremely ancient, and she was obeyed at once. The other was startlingly *real* when they stood face-to-face, with the *onna-bugeisha*'s eyes politely lowered and her head a few inches lower than Reiko's. Perhaps thirty years, perhaps forty, a striking face with the weathered look that came of a life lived mostly out-of-doors. There was a small white slanting scar along her left cheekbone just below the eye, the mark of an unsuccessful *yokomen uchi* strike where only the very tip of an enemy's sword had split the skin. Probably that had been the last mistake the wielder ever made. Her hands on the polearm looked narrow and strong and rather battered by time and training and battle. Beads of moisture starred the armor and the other woman's long hair, just as Reiko felt them settling on herself.

Perhaps even eerier was the scent. It was clean but strong, the smell of a body that exercised hard and washed often, but long before her people borrowed the use of soap from the Westerners. And wearing armor whose backing and cords no amount of care could entirely free of the faint tang of blood and sweat. That was the way warriors smelled when they set out on campaign—one of her earliest memories was of her father in his armor lifting her for a moment as he left the palace with the horses of the Imperial Guard stamping in the background. He had had that scent as she threw chubby infant arms around his neck, before he handed her back to the nurse and her mother gently chided her as she wiped away the tears.

Do ghosts have a scent? Reiko thought, with some part of her consciousness that observed from a distance. *Am I a ghost here, or is she?*

The stranger's face had a well-ordered calm; beneath that, Reiko thought, a deep sorrow; and stronger than anything a hard purpose. It was a face she had seen before on those entrusted with a task that must be done even though the doer hated it. She touched her own lips as if to say *please do not speak* and then turned and leapt back to the balustrade. Then she extended a hand to Reiko.

It was firm and hard, callused and dry beneath hers; entirely a physical thing.

A flash of alarm went through her as they stepped off over a gulf of space. Existence whirled, and a cold wind blew. The air grew clear as they descended in a turning, swooping movement like a dream of being a bird—

That is the southern point of Honshū! she thought in amazement; the view was like one from the fabled aircraft of old, far higher than a tethered balloon. *Kanmon-kaikyō, the Straits of Shimonoseki. But where is the bridge? Where are the ruins? This is the land as if it were stripped of the work of human hands.*

There had been cities on both sides before the Change, huge factory works all up the coast of the island along the Inland Sea, and it had been joined to Kyushu by a double-towered bridge over two thousand shaku long, still standing though canted by earthquakes. And an unmistakable black tower to the north itself nearly five hundred shaku tall, topped with a glass globe.

And the passage is wider, the shores steeper. As if there had been less silting.

They stooped lower. She had dreamed before of the Brave of Yamato, in the fight where the Grass-Cutting Sword had acquired its name. That was a time so ancient that her vision of it had had the very taste of the immemorial, a time before history and chronicles, the time of legends. Like the smell of green bronze, but completely present, completely concrete.

The feeling here of a barrier between what she saw and what she *was* grew lesser, as if the distance she covered was smaller than it had been. The view added to it, familiar and distorted at the same time. If anything it made the blow to heart and mind harder this time. She had stepped into history as well as legend.

With a chill Reiko saw the tall forest to north and south, and the little villages of thatched wooden houses and their fields that were all that marked the narrowest spot of the sinuous passage. But there were human beings in plenty to be seen as they descended, and ships. Hundreds of them, but *tiny*, even by the standards of the modern age, much less the era of wonders just before the Change.

They spiraled through a low-lying cloud, and she grabbed reflexively at the banner slung across her chest as it started to come free of its knot. The fine white fabric blew across her vision, and when it streamed behind her as she held it spread with both hands they were much closer to the surface, descending now as if down a steep stair with *something* beneath her feet. The air was cool with spring, and full of the salt smell of the sea. And a tinge of smoke; several of the ships were aflame.

She could see the vessels more clearly now. Small wooden things with square platforms at the bows, and most of them had only one mast, now taken down and bound the length of the vessels. Crude hut-like wooden structures rose at their sterns, and long oars drove them. Closer to the shore were a few larger ships, still modest and with a Chinese look to their lines in her eyes.

And all were here to make war. Arrows flew in clouds between them; some wallowed in pools of dispersing red, their rowers and warriors bristling with the blizzards of shafts that had swept them. As she watched one ship whose oars beat the water to froth crashed into another, and warriors swarmed across in a storm of shouts and flashing steel. Reiko could hear their voices, the crash of metal, the screams of the wounded, see bodies by the hundreds bobbing in the water amid arrows and oars and broken spear-shafts. The sun was well past noon, and the battle hung in the balance. It had been a long and bloody day, and both sides seemed grimly intent on a fight to the finish.

Her heart hammered; she knew exactly where and when she was, now, and that she was watching the deeds which had broken the old order of things in Japan and ushered in a new. It was the twenty-fourth day of the third month of Genryaku 2, the day that the last dying echo of the Heian age had ended, and the rule of the first of the Barbarian-Subduing Generalissimos had begun. The day that the curtain-walls of the *bakufu* had first enclosed her people.

I know this battle!

One fleet flew a white banner, the other a red. Most of the fighters wore versions of the archaic armor the *onna-bugeisha* bore, though usually less of it and simpler; many of the rowers had nothing but a *fundoshi* around their loins and a headband as they heaved at the looms of their oars. Bizarrely, a great pod of dolphins swam through the carnage, until it dived and disappeared beneath the red-bannered fleet. Eyes were turned up to them now, more and more as shouts and pointing spread the news and men tore themselves away from matters of life and death. . . .

No. Their eyes go to the banner. *I do not think they can see me or . . . who I suspect this is, who held my hand. Not clearly at least. The sun would dazzle them too much at this angle.*

The white flag blazoned with the bamboo leaves and gentian flowers billowed again. More hands were raised to point; combat died down as they approached one of the square-bowed ships a little larger than the others. Those about it bore the white banner, but apparently its own had fallen. A few bows aimed hesitantly upward by a warrior's reflex to strike at anything unfamiliar, but other hands knocked them down. More and more fighters doffed their helmets and dropped to their knees, making obeisance. Shouts rose; some mere incoherent noise, some words.

The language was Nihongo, not utterly strange like that of Yamato Takeru's day, but so different from the speech she had been raised with that only parts of it could be grasped amid distance and excitement.

Hundreds showed raw terror, but that did not include the two at the stern; there was wonder on their faces, but no fear. One was in armor as colorful and elaborate as the warrior-woman; a young man, of her own years or a little more. In his right hand was a *gunbai ichiwa*, a commander's solid signal-fan. His helmet was off, and his topknot held his hair clear of his face; this was before the age of the *chonmage* and the shaved pate.

Like everyone she could see he was of her folk. She had rarely seen a man so beautiful, in a wholly masculine way, and never one so utterly alive even in stillness; there was a charm and a force crackling in those features, keen intelligence, and a tensile grace in the smooth ease of his stance and movements.

I would trust this man with any task, she thought. *But I would never take him lightly. And any enemy who did him an injury should also kill him instantly, for he would never forget it, any more than he would a favor done him. This is a man to be loved, or slain.*

The one beside him in a posture of protection was an ogre by comparison. For a moment she thought—this was a dream—that he was an *oni* in truth, an *oni* with an iron club. Six and a half shaku tall and broader in proportion, with shoulders like a plow-ox and bare legs beneath his armor knotted with muscle. His face was ugly in a way that might be pleasant when he wasn't in a battle and primed to kill, knotted and scarred with injuries and with a bristle of sparse beard that matched his cropped hair. The white wimple-like headdress of a *sōhei* fighting monk was pushed back on his shoulders, to reveal a black cap. A *naginata* which must have been heavy even for those monstrous hands rested on his shoulder, and altogether he looked like an amiable but very dangerous bear in human . . . or part-human . . . form.

The two women alighted on the roof of the cabin. Reiko flung her arms up, and the banner spiraled into the air and caught on a rope at the stern of the ship. The wind strengthened and it streamed behind the ship, the *kamon* of the Minamoto showing clear. A sudden roaring cheer went up from everyone on the ship, and from many others nearby.

A banner has been granted by Heaven itself, and it flies from their flagship. What clearer sign or greater omen could the kami *grant?*

For an instant Reiko's gaze met that of the bareheaded commander's, and he saw her. His eyes widened. Then he started violently; it was obvious that she had vanished from his sight like mist in a dream, and now he doubted if she had been there at all. The bearlike warrior leaned close and growled at him and he blinked and shook his head. Then the handsome features returned to their set of hard determination.

He shouted to the crew and the samurai who crowded the vessel, pointing to the flag and they roared again, an endless surf of noise; she could see the exultation there, the sudden conviction that the *kami* favored and fought for them. And how it built their battle-fury, like a wind of fire rippling from man to man and ship to ship.

Then the war-fan chopped around to point at one of the red-flagged ships, and the oarsmen fell into a chanting rhythm as archers put arrows to their strings and raised their bows to draw.

The woman beside her spoke for the first time, but seemingly to herself:

"You are more fortunate than my own lord, Yoshitsune-sama; you eclipsed him as bright daylight does a pale lantern that gutters and dies. More fortunate . . . for a little while, a very little while."

"I cannot watch this," Reiko said, her eyes bright with tears.

Because I know what follows the terrible victory. The treachery, the betrayal by closest kin and lord, the years of flight and despair, the lonely death in the cold north, the last retainer dying upright.

"You can, Heavenly Sovereign Majesty. Because you must. Too much flows from this day to all our days to come. Subdue your soul. It is your *giri*, and your karma, daughter of the Empire, daughter of the Sun."

The battle continued, but now there was a driving force to it.

Like a heavy weight shifting, shifting, until it topples down a mountainside.

The man she had seen snapped orders, conferred with his captains by signal and by coming alongside, drove his men forward, himself led boarding charges that swept enemy craft like tsunamis of steel and blood. When he fought with his own hands his *tachi* moved with deadly skill as he slid through the complex obstacles of battle like wind through bamboo, and his monk-companion hewed men down like saplings before a forester's axe.

At last his ship approached another, a larger vessel with slatted sails, and led more to it. He gestured to his massed archers with the fan. The *yumi* spat and arrows hissed until the ship with its red banners and reddened decks seemed to float in a red sea.

Oars drooped unmoving from its sides, the hands on their wooden shafts limp in death. The general's ship ghosted towards it, while men stood in tense silence with arrows half-drawn.

"Take the ladies alive and unharmed!" the commander snapped. "The young Majesty as well, and secure the sacred things! Quickly, men, quickly!"

Figures moved amid the bodies still or groaning and thrashing, coming from below the decks that bristled with embedded arrows. They must have awaited the outcome of the battle there, in darkness. Not samurai, but women in elaborate and colorful Court robes, their long hair fluttering a little in the breeze and their faces set with a proud sadness and only here and there a silent tear. The commander's expression changed as he saw the three bundled objects they carried, and the child one led by the hand, and heard the low murmur of:

"Namu Amida Butsu!"

That prayer meant: *I venerate merciful Amida, Buddha of Infinite Light and Life,* and it was often uttered just before a life's expected end, to ensure entry to the Western Paradise.

"Quickly, you fools!" he shouted.

The giant monk bellowed and leapt to the ship of death. Others followed him, or missed their jump and drowned in their armor.

"Namu Amida Butsu!"

As his callused feet thundered on the deck the women turned as one, stepped up to and over the rail of their own ship on the opposite side and into the ocean.

All but one, who fell to the deck with a cry of despair as the monk's *naginata* slammed through the edge of her robe to pin it to the wood and tripped her helplessly. The bundle she carried skittered off across the red-running planks, and without breaking stride a samurai flung himself through the air and landed on it, gripping at the deck with fingers and toes as if he would burrow into the wood to hold it safe. Two more *bushi* collided in mid-air as they tried to do the same and fell stunned.

Another warrior rushed to the side of the ship and stabbed with his long spear. The second of the bundles bobbed on the surface as a gashed hand released it, and half a dozen of the near-naked oarsmen dove after it, swimming with the ease of fishermen born.

But of the Court women there was no trace; they had sunk without the slightest effort to swim or struggle, their robes and the water they had deliberately inhaled dragging them down. The general bowed his head and the fan hung limp by his side.

Reiko stood, stunned and awed by the self-discipline of the women's gesture and the iron pride behind it.

They made nothing of defeat and less of death.

A motion from her guide, and she took her hand again. They stepped off the rail, in eerie counterpart to the six ladies an instant before. She expected to feel the cold shock of seawater, and in a sense she did as it moved against her skin. But there was no smothering, no darkness; vision became a thing of ripples and shimmering blurred shapes, as if she were seeing with something else besides her eyes.

So clear! As if I saw with sound!

Perhaps that was less than fortunate, for all around her were a gradually descending army of the dead. The fallen warriors and those who had leapt to their deaths rather than concede defeat drifted downward in a host of corpses fading to the edge of her not-sight.

She and her guide flew through the water as they had the air, turning in an arching spiral. A woman sank away from them, the richly robed child in her arms, their faces calm but their eyes staring as if at an impossible horizon. For an instant Reiko saw something else herself; a city of broad avenues beneath the sea, castle and temple and mansions, a chime of slow unearthly music beneath a sky of purple cloud.

Then all her attention went to the long cord-wrapped bundle falling away from the two bodies, turning with dreamlike slowness. The wrappings hid it, but she could *feel* the supernal power locked within, majesty like thunderheads piling on a horizon shot with lightning, like the winds of typhoons uprooting sea and land. A blaze of brilliance that called to her very soul.

"No!" she said, and stretched out her hand towards it.

It was beyond her reach, falling and trailing thin strings of bubbles, falling toward the abyss. But something shot past, as if her reaching hand had thrown it as a thunderbolt. A dolphin, slipping through the waters with an arrow's grace. The animal's short beak closed on it and it curved into a pirouette, a gesture at once playful and somehow reverent, the black upper body and white making a curve through the blue sea. She met its eye and felt a joy that was all the more painful by contrast with the bodies sinking about them. It hovered before her, and seemed to nod.

Death came towards them both—a great death pale gray and white-bellied, swimming with an almost mechanical stiffness. The dolphin's eye was full of life and mind, alien as it was to her. The shark's was fixed and glaucuous, simply a machine to guide another machine to the food it desired in a sort of passionless hunger for everything that was. With nothing within save a drive to replicate itself until all the world was *shark*.

Kotegiri flashed into her hands. Darkness flowed towards her with the great hōjirozame shark, she struck with ferocious concentration into the midst of it. The edge that had cut the steel wrist-guard as men fought through the streets of burning Kyoto slashed home. Vision returned, and the torpedo shape flopped limp and half-severed, drifting towards the depths trailing a dark banner of blood that roiled out through the waters like clouds.

The water about her flexed; her hand clamped on her guide's as something came up between them. It was another dolphin, a big one ten shaku long. Her hand and the guide's closed on the long curved dorsal fin, and they were surging upward. Their heads broke the water, and she gasped in air she hadn't realized she needed until that very moment.

What she saw was not the strait and the gruesome wreckage of battle. Instead there were mountains ahead, black against the setting sun. A river, pouring down to the sea, and a long wooden bridge, and both dolphins moving towards it.

I know this place, she thought again. *This is Ise. The bridge to the Inner Shrine.*

She had seen it before, several years ago, not long after she was declared the heir when hope for her brother was abandoned. The bridge had been burnt ruined stubs, and more ruins had stretched all about. Then it had been an armed Imperial Navy ship, with her grim-faced father showing her what little was left of the holiest fane in all Nihon. She had blurted out an oath to restore it someday, and his unsmiling face had nevertheless held a hard approval.

Now the bridge arched across the flood, obviously recently renewed. Otherwise all she could see was a figure kneeling on a simple platform on piles at the water's edge. The structure gave the watcher and a few standing attendants a place near the bank backed by trees and looking out over the river, though there was a hint of larger structures higher and inland. Birds swooped through the trees along the river, and reeds bent in the mild breeze of a summer evening.

She and her guide glided upright as the dolphin stopped, and the one before it made a spectacular leap. The wrapped bundle landed with a clatter on the boards; the figure there started up in surprise and shock. It was a woman of middle years in an elaborate, archaic kimono of crimson and green and white, with an enclosing headdress of gold and white cord and green *aoi* leaves. Her gentle unworldly face reminded Reiko strongly of one of her mother's elder sisters who'd spent most of her life in dreams.

She is Saiō, Reiko knew.

It had once been custom that a daughter of the Imperial House spend some time as High Priestess here, at the nation's most ancient and sacred shrine.

She is of my line. She will know what it is that she sees, even in its ceremonial wrappings. Perhaps especially so.

The priestess stared incredulously at what lay before her, then raised her wide eyes to the departing fins of the dolphins. Then she fell to her knees and extended a trembling hand towards the bundle, drew it back, sat with tears running down her face.

Reiko walked towards her, knelt and sat back across from her, an unseen presence. Once more she reflected that this must be how a ghost lived . . . though she was the living soul among the presence of the long dead.

Or do life and death have any fixed meaning here? Perhaps for me now all time and all lives exist at once? she thought. *I walk through the ages of our being, the happenings that forged our legends and our souls, and at each I touch, and am touched.*

This shrine had been dedicated to her Ancestress in a time long past even if this was the year she believed it to be. Wordlessly she appealed, and held out her hands, her palms framing the High Priestess' face.

She knows what this is, Reiko thought. *Now she must know what is to be done. She may not see me, but she will feel.*

Shock went through her, as she was *filled* in an entirely non-physical sense, filled with purpose. Then heat, and light. She *was* light. But not mere flame; within that fire was inconceivable structure, complexities beyond even the beginnings of comprehension.

The *Saiō* reached forward again with a sigh of exhaled breath and took up the bundled treasure. Her head bent over it, and tears rolled down her face; tears of joy, of wonder, of fear and humility. Her attendants rushed forward in a rustle of silks as she rose and led her away, one on either side.

Silence fell like an exhaled sigh as they vanished up the path towards the Shrine. Her guide sank down opposite her and they sat for a while in silence amid the deepening shadows, where the loudest sounds were birdsong and the *plop* of a fish leaping. Dragonflies glittered in the last rays of the sun, making their dance of victory.

At last she spoke: "Why am I here? What purpose is achieved by it?"

"What did you do, Majesty?" the guide replied.

"I bestowed a banner; I rescued a treasure," she said. "The Grass-Cutting Sword. But why was it necessary that *I* be the one who did these things?"

"Even the Great Kami accomplish their ends through others. Even fate proceeds through the deeds of mortals."

The weathered face of the warrior-woman smiled very slightly at her dissatisfaction and spoke slowly in her archaic Nihongo.

"What era-name did you choose, Majesty?"

"*Shōhei,*" she said. "Victorious Peace."

"Then *that* is the object of your pilgrimage," she said.

"Does this voyaging in dreams across space and time bring me closer to that?" Reiko said sharply. "To victory and peace for our people?"

"Majesty, it brings you closer to that which you must find, but equally that which you must *become*. All life is a pilgrimage. It is not the destination, but the journey itself that shapes the pilgrim's soul, step by single step."

"And is that why you were appointed as my guide in this, Lady Tomoe?"

The other almost smiled. "You recognized me, Majesty?"

"At once. As you know. I heard your tale long ago, as a small girl, and it struck deeply into my heart."

"As They who sent me know. When you heard the tale, it was preparation for the journey you have made this night, and the greater journey of which it is a part. In my life I walked the Way of the Warrior, and then the Way of the Buddha, to find and to lose myself, that I might be *fit* to guide you. This is a step on your path. Rightly seen, all voyages arrive at the same harbor."

Darkness fell; not simply the dying of the light, but a deeper night, warm and welcoming. As it fell, she heard the other's voice speak once more, soft with yearning:

"And by offering guidance, the guide guides herself."

"*Obayou*, Reiko-chan!"

Reiko woke with a start, for a moment unaware of herself. Was this her room at home in the Palace, with the attendant breathing softly in her sleep at the door? Was she on the ship, and her father sitting on the quarterdeck contemplating the shapes of the waves?

No. I am in Eryn Muir, across the eastern sea. My journeying begins again.

"You're getting up late, sleepy-head," Órlaith said to her with a smile; she was in her traveling clothes, with the sheathed Sword wrapped by its belt in one hand. "We thought you must need it."

Light leaked around the shutters of the windows; light, and fresh crisp damp air full of the wild spicy scent of the redwood forest, and an intoxicating aroma of things grilling and baking. Reiko slipped out of the coverlet and reached for her robe; it was time to wash, to dress and eat and be upon their way, though her muscles were still stiff and sore from the brutal exertion of battle.

Work is the best medicine for that, she thought, putting the tumbled images of savagery out of her mind.

"Where's that banner you made?" Órlaith said casually as she sat to pull on her boots. "Sure and it was an interesting thing, and I wanted to see it again. There wasn't much time after I woke up yesterday with the day half gone already."

Reiko froze as she reached for her comb. Slowly she turned and looked up, face unmoving. The wall above her bunk was bare save for the carving down the lines where the broad redwood planks joined.

After a long moment she picked up the comb and began to run it through her hair.

"I made a gift of it," she said softly. "To one who needed it more than I."

Órlaith looked at her for a moment, nodded, and finished pulling on her boots. One of the things Reiko liked about her friend was that she never pushed when it was obvious that Reiko didn't wish to speak. Everyone had been polite to her, but the Nihonjin woman thought that was probably a rather unusual attribute here.

"Would you please send Egawa in? I need to speak with him for a moment before we leave," she said.

"Certainly."

She seated herself on the bed—it was low, about the height of a general's folding camp stool—and drew her fan, composing herself when she found her pulse quickening and mouth dry. Breath in, breath out . . . Not so much the prospect of telling what she must, but at reliving it in her mind.

"Majesty," Egawa said, going to one knee and giving her the abbreviated field bow. "All is in readiness."

"Sit, General," she said.

One who knew him as well as she did could see his mild surprise as he sank back on his heels and bowed. As he did, he saw the vacant space above the bed.

"You have conferred great honor with your gift, Majesty," he said.

In their own terms he was right; calligraphy from a member of the Imperial family did convey honor. Especially from the *Tennō Heika*'s own hand. Japan was less ceremonious than it had been in former times, if only because her people were so few, but that remained true.

She took a deep breath, watching how the bright beams through the windows lit the bare little room and cast craggy shadows across Egawa's face.

"A man dreamed of being a butterfly," she said. "He woke . . . but perhaps then he was a butterfly that dreamed it was a man."

The general's eyes narrowed; it was a well-known parable and paradox. "Another vision, Majesty?" he said.

She gestured assent, keeping her gaze straight in front of her. "In a dream, I bestowed a banner. In a dream, a dolphin bore the Grass-Cutting

Sword to Ise at my command, lest it be lost. In a dream, an *onna-bugeisha* was compelled by duty to aid me and through me to aid the man who slew her lord . . . who was his kinsman."

Egawa was no fool, and quite knowledgeable. His eyes went back to the bare wall where the banner had been, and his lips moved in a name. She nodded, once, very slightly.

"I have told you this, General, and I shall tell Captain Ishikawa, because I may not return alive."

She made a gesture with her fan before he could speak. "My sisters will continue the line if I do not return. You may not; Captain Ishikawa may not. One of us must. With *Kusanagi-no-Tsurugi*, and with what I have seen."

After he had left, she gathered herself, conscious of an incongruous longing for a cup of hot tea.

"And are we a dream our grandparents dreamed? Or *their* dream of their ancestors come again?"

"No." She tucked her fan back into her sash. "The past makes us, but we are entirely ourselves."

CHAPTER TWENTY

ALBION COVE, BARONY OF MIST HILLS
(FORMERLY MENDOCINO COUNTY)
CROWN PROVINCE OF WESTRIA
(FORMERLY CALIFORNIA)
HIGH KINGDOM OF MONTIVAL
(FORMERLY WESTERN NORTH AMERICA)
JULY/MÆDMŌNAÞ 20TH
CHANGE YEAR 46/2044 AD

Deor Godulfson stood and watched his brother ride for home, his huscarles at his back. The lord of Mist Hills turned and waved once more in the saddle, and then there was only the twinkle of the dawn-light on the spearheads as the horses wound up the track eastward into the densely forested hills and disappeared amid green trees and gray-white patches of fog speared by sunlight. There was much to do for Godric Godulfson at home, with war begun, and he hadn't lingered past breakfast and farewells. From what they'd heard the first troops from the north would be arriving within a month.

As they turned to look out over the ocean the light of the rising sun just clearing the Coast Range peaks behind them glinted off it, like hammered silver sequins sprinkled over blue-green waves of the cove and the Pacific beyond. Little waves hissed up the sand, and small spindly-legged birds skittered over it amid the litter of wrack and kelp-strands. There was no driftwood; the thrifty folk of the hamlet gathered it all for their fires. He felt a sense of welcoming and farewell, the woven life of the land and people and the wights that watched over rock and hearth.

Hraefnbeorg and all the farms around it would be a bustle of preparations and mustering and going-over of gear and rolling-out of supplies and twice-baking of biscuit; it was a good thing the harvest was over and the grain stacked. Deor had privately taken his elder brother aside and warned that this was the first move in a very long game, and to pace himself and their folk's efforts to the long haul. After the last two weeks, and most particularly since he'd roused the Hraefnbeorg men to a peril he alone had seen, he found his brother took his warnings with complete seriousness.

Which is a little strange in itself. I'm a man grown at last, it seems, and one whose word is a thing of weight.

"Good of him to offer us land," he said.

Thora snorted. "Thanks to us, he got a chance to save the heir to the High Kingdom. He *did* save her, and right under her eye and her brother's, too. Oh, and he saved her brother, did I mention that? The heir to the Association, which happens to be the biggest single chunk of the High Kingdom?"

"Undying fame," Deor agreed. "He earned that. Lady Fiorbhinn's *Song of Bear and Raven* will live forever . . . but I think the *Chrysanthemum and the Rose* may rival it. That's the title I picked."

"Undying fame my rosy pink undying *arse*," Thora said with that Bearkiller bluntness she'd never lost. "Mind, your brother is a brave man and a man of honor and acted like it, even when it meant locking shields and walking towards a line of spears. But he wouldn't be human now if he didn't realize that the Princess and the Prince are honorable too . . . which means after this is all over, they'll think of gifts and rewards."

"My brother wouldn't ask for a return for doing his sworn duty," Deor protested. "I know he took the death of the High King hard."

Though . . .

Thora put his thought into words: "He won't have to *ask*. They understand good lordship, that pair. They'll just see to it anyway."

Deor shrugged and smiled, adjusting the harp-case slung over his back. That *was* part of good lordship, the quality that made followers eager to serve and stay loyal when it meant going to a hard place. It wasn't so much that vassals were greedy for reward, as that they wanted to serve those who acknowledged their worth. Sometimes that meant praise, or standing by a subordinate in a lawsuit or quarrel, or something as simple as remembering a birthday; sometimes it meant gold, rank and land, publicly bestowed to confer honor as well.

"True enough. Still, it was generous of him to make the offer. It's a lot easier to give land out than to get it back and as the saying goes, the Gods aren't making any more of it."

"Maybe we should take him up on it, when we get back," Thora said. "I'd like to settle among heathen folk, and that stretch he showed us is *good* land, the only wealth that's really real. The brush needs thinning and the vines have to be cut back to the stumps and regrafted and the orchards likewise, but work never bothered me. Good pasture, at least, and Morfind says she can get me the services of stallions from her parents' stud over at Wolf Hall; they know horses, those two. We could start small with ordinary grade mares, hire a few helpers on shares . . ."

"A quiet life?" he teased. "For Thora Swiftsword, famed in song?"

"Famed in *your* songs, maybe," she said, and gave him an affectionate punch on the shoulder.

Then she shrugged, a little defensively. "Mist Hills isn't as much out of the way as it was that day we first met. We could visit the north every year; in the summer, say. It's only a few days on a good ship to Newport, and they have a rail connection. And we could travel to the new settlements down on the Bay . . . pardon me, the *Côf* . . . or over in Napa . . . more often. They're growing."

"There's good music to be had here now, that's true," he said. "Besides mine, that is."

He exchanged a glance with her and smiled as they looked out over the bay. They'd met here—on that beach less than a long bowshot to the west, where the boats from the fishing hamlet had put out to take the crew of the battered *Ark* ashore, just sixteen years ago come this October. And where the *Tarshish Queen*—her successor as the pride of Feldman &

Son's fleet—was tied up at the new pier today, looking considerably more trim. Of course, the *Ark* had just survived several thousand miles of a stern-chase with Suluk corsairs who'd been after her all the way from Hawaii, shooting bolts and round shot as they went.

"Full circle," he said, all that was needed.

Until that hour he hadn't been sure that anything but cannibal savages and raiders nearly as cruel survived *anywhere* on the earth outside the little land of his birth. And she and her shipmates hadn't known there were anything but murderous wild-men *here,* for that matter.

"The storm was getting worse, and it was cold," Thora said, her voice a little wistful for that first and freshest venture of an adventurous lifetime. "Damn wet, too."

Neither of them thought the brisk wind off the ocean this summer's day anything but pleasant, though he'd thrown a corner of his cloak over his shoulder, and his dark curls tumbled a little in it. The coast of what had been Mendocino was never actually *hot,* and right at the water's edge it made you glad of a jacket and wool wrap many days even in July. No matter how the sun shone and the blue-green waves sparkled, that water out there was *cold* with the northern current. Rich in life, but not for humans to frolic in. That had been one of the pleasures of the tropic lands for them both, tumbling in the waves like seals.

Then she chuckled, probably thinking along the same lines: "I've never been so bloody glad to set foot on land and eat fish stew, after seriously wondering whether I was going to be drinking Lord Aegir's salt ale and having dinner in Valhöll or Fólkvangr. Which I hope to do . . . someday . . . a day not very soon."

Captain Moishe Feldman caught the last of that as he strode up briskly. "Old friends, I was very sure my father would find some way out of it, even before we saw Deor's signal fire and thanked Him who spared Jonah. Or at least I was telling myself that I did, and doing so very hard."

They both shook the captain's hand, and the three clapped each other on the shoulder as well. They and the Corvallan skipper *were* old friends, even if they hadn't seen each other often enough to be close ones, and they were all much of an age. Deor thought that Feldman also felt a little wistful envy that he would never speak of, for a man who could travel simply for the sake of seeing new things, without the burdens of family and dependents.

The merchant captain looked around.

"And hasn't *this* changed, and for the better?" Feldman said. "I'd hardly recognize it, if I hadn't seen it since that day."

"Save for the bones of Earth, yes," Deor said, not without pride at what his folk had wrought.

The piers of the old-world bridge at their backs across the mouth of the Albion River still reared in a high tangle of rusty steel, though he thought bits and pieces had been cut clear for salvage since then, re-forged for knives and nails and spades and whatever else was needed. There had only been a few lonely fisher-families here sixteen years ago, in the little hamlet on the patch of flats just inland of the bridge. They'd dwelt in cobbled-together shacks that saw outsiders from the rest of Mist Hills perhaps ten times a year, and nothing to the seaward at all. All of it teetering one minor disaster away from collapse, one boat lost to a storm or a bad hearth-fire getting loose.

Now there were a dozen households; those who plowed the sea, and a smithy of their own and a little boatyard. The houses were comfortable modern ones, fieldstone foundations below and squared logs above, steep turf roofs with chimneys of salvage brick trailing white plumes. The whole was defensible, at least against a casual raid; stout shutters and fences meant the houses could be held in a pinch, hinged slits meant they could support each other against attackers, and there were bows and spears and swords, simple helms and sealskin jacks with metal scales racked inside every door.

There were also long sheds where fish drying over slow smoky fires added a rich salty-smoky pungency to the salt freshness of the air, and gardens in raised beds fertilized with offal and ash and seaweed, and barns for a few milch-cows and horses who added the usual tang. Big sailcloth tents on spars had sheltered most of their party last night, but the travelers who'd slept in them had taken them down as a courtesy.

Folk were busy about the work of boats and gardens; even the ten-years-wonder of a visit from the Princess, their own lord, a merchant ship and exotic foreigners all in a few days space didn't mean idleness for long. Work didn't wait; it never did. The place was prosperous now in the terms Deor had grown up with, meaning that with a great deal of hard skillful labor and a modicum of luck common folk could have full bellies for their families every day, dry warm beds and enough clothes for their backs that there was one set to wear and one to wash and one carefully kept packed away for festivals, weddings, funerals and holy days.

"I've seen . . . we've all seen . . . much worse," Feldman said, echoing his thought. "Most of the human race lives in places like this, after all. If they're lucky."

He made a waggling gesture with one hand. "Allowing for local details."

Chickens and ducks pecked for bugs and slugs amid the rows of mulched beans and tomatoes, lettuce and cabbage and chard. Figures in shapeless stained sea-garb and oilskin hats were calling back and forth as they walked towards their drawn-up boats, carrying long oars over their shoulders and sacks with bread and cheese and cold meat and flasks of beer for their lunches out on the water. By evening they'd be back, with sardines and jack mackerel and Chinook and albacore, and baskets full of spot prawns. As far as seafood went, much of the time they could eat like kings here . . . though even in the usually calm summer season he noticed the long considering looks they gave sea and sky.

A white-bearded elder who was probably the last here who remembered the world before the Change sat on an upturned barrel and worked on the part of a big net draped across his lap with a coil of hemp cord, a boat-shaped little net shuttle of oak polished smooth as silk by use, gnarled fingers and infinite patience. Toddlers played around his feet with his equally creaky dog helping to keep watch, and a cat stalked by with regal arrogance. Deor could hear the thump of looms and the wet sloshing rhythm of a churn working from the settlement and someone singing to pace their work:

"Churn churn churn
This is churning day!
Til the golden butter comes
My dasher will not stay.
Pat pat pat,
Make it smooth and round,
Now the golden butter's done
Won't you take a pound—"

An irregular clanging came from the smith's forge and then a brief howl from a grindstone, some tool being made or refurbished; he knew how crucial that was, not having to let tasks hang fire while you sent repairs elsewhere.

A girl not far from womanhood but still barefoot and dressed in a child's simple calf-length shift herded a clutch of honking geese past them with a wide-eyed glance, then used her switch to keep her charges moving. She blushed and scampered faster when Deor gave her a grin and a deep Court bow, her brown hair fluttering at her shoulders beneath her kerchief and her *seax* thumping against her thigh. There was a willow-wood flute thrust through her cloth belt, and a wicker basket over her back for the wild onion and sorrel and sea rocket and field mustard she'd pick during the day.

"That bow from you is something she'll boast of the rest of her days," Thora laughed. "After that duet last night."

"When I'm given hospitality, I sing," he said, leaving unspoken that he did it with the same skill whether the hospitality was in a palace or a fisher's cot. "And she's actually not bad on that flute, she must have a good ear."

"So does he," she said with a sly grin.

She nodded to the spot not far away where Prince John waited and spoke with his sister and Reiko, with his left hand on his sword-hilt and the lute-case across his back and his crimson cloak blowing in the wind.

"A likely lad. And not too young for *me*," she said.

Deor nodded, then raised his brows when she added: "Good breeding stock there."

Feldman coughed delicately and looked up at the sky. "Well, I'd better be getting aboard. I'll see your gear's stowed; close quarters, I'm afraid, with the horses."

"Not the first time I've slept in stable-straw, Moishe," Thora said. "And it's not for long. I did it all winter once, and it was a cold land."

Feldman shook his head. "I told them that there are horses to be had in Topanga," he said. "They all looked at me as if I'd suggested something very nasty. What do their precious nags have that the ones we could buy there don't? Besides the ability to take up space and foul the bilges? A horse is a horse."

Deor wasn't sure he was entirely serious. He had yet to meet a Feldman who couldn't put on bland convincingness at will when they were saying something outrageous. As a guest in Moishe's home he'd seen the whole family down to the twelve-year-olds do it as a game around the dinner table with the prize going to the last one who started to twitch helplessly.

Thora laughed and shook her head; she'd bound on a folded kerchief to control her wiry dark-red curls, and a broad-brimmed leather hat hung down her back by its cord.

"A horse is a horse . . . said the *sailor*! Packhorses, maybe, but these are steeds for our scouts and mounted archers. You need a teammate and a comrade for that, not a servant. Would any woman do, if it was troublesome to pack your wife along?"

"No," Feldman said, grinning back. "Though some sailors think so. But then, I never felt inclined to marry a horse."

When they'd laughed and he'd left Deor glanced at the royal party and went on:

"John *is* a likely lad, Thora. Handsome, quick and steady with the sword, keen-eyed, no fool—a bit full of himself, but he's young—and an even better poet and singer than he is a warrior."

"Talented, you'd say?"

"Yes, but that's not the point. Talent is cheap, it's application that makes a scop, or any other maker. He *works* at it, he doesn't just make a toy of it. If he wasn't born to be a ruler, he could be first-class."

"Well, then, there you are. Nice to know we still have the same tastes in men!"

"But he's a Prince of the House of Artos, oath-sister. The High King's son."

She grinned and raised a brow. "I wasn't planning on asking him to pledge me handfasting," she said.

"One poet about the place is more than enough?"

"Odhinn and Freya, yes! And I doubt the PPA wants a pagan warrior-woman fourteen years older than their next Lord Protector in their fine palaces. Can you imagine the Catholic clergy and the ladies in their spired headdresses fainting left and right, or leaping screaming and headlong from the windows of the castle solars? They'd be less horror-struck if he took up with *you*, brother, far less. I don't want to fight *that* many duels!"

He joined in her chuckle at the thought, but shook his head.

"A tumble's one thing—all you'll get from me on that score is envy—but a Prince's get are royal," he said bluntly. "If begetting's really what you had in mind, and not just fun."

"Would it matter? We're a long way from the Association lands."

"Not nearly as far as it was in the old days," he said, throwing her own point back at her. "Also Westria is part of the High Kingdom—and not just in theory anymore. In another twenty years . . . and this may be the heart of the realm, in the end."

"He's heir to the Association, not the High Kingdom."

"Not heir, no . . . as long as his elder sister lives."

Thora winced and drew the Hammer. "Victory and long life to her!"

"Victory and long life *I* say too, but neither of us is a Norn, and you've seen what a cautious guarded life she lives!"

"She's a fighter born, that's true," Thora admitted with ungrudging admiration. "And a leader. She has the *baraka*, the shine, the magic that pulls you after her. She went down that hillside in full plate as if she were running towards a feast, not a fight, and we all followed like wedding guests. Agile as a cat, trained to a hair, and quick, quick . . . though her friend the knight is just as good at that part of it."

"It's not written in the Well of Wyrd . . . as far as we know . . . that she'll have heirs of her body, either," Deor pointed out. "Some don't, no matter how healthy they are and no matter how hard they try, and nobody can tell why. If she doesn't, *his* line inherits the Throne of Montival and the Sword."

Thora shrugged and he plowed on: "And he's also the descendant of the Mackenzie chieftains, the Lord Protector and the Spider . . . and your own folk's first Bear Lord. Do you want to start pulling threads in a web that tangled?"

"Not much of a problem in Mist Hills, if we avoided politics . . . and neither of us ever wanted to play the game of thrones!"

"*We* don't. A child of yours . . . and his . . . might, when she was a child no more and developed an itchy foot and a roving eye and felt cramped in the fields she'd known all her life. Oh, *that* could never happen, not with a child of *yours*."

She winced a little at the sarcasm, and he went on: "Or a Court faction might come looking for someone with the right blood to be used as a front for their ambitions."

"That doesn't look likely."

"Not now, but children are hostages to fortune and fate," he said.

"That's true whoever their parents are."

"But more true of some. We're speaking of a child blood-linked to one of the mightiest realms on earth; one likely to be mightier still in the future. That you or I wouldn't cross a barnyard to pick a crown falling out of a manger and rolling past our feet doesn't mean others think the same—you know they don't."

She raised the hand that had been resting on the basket hilt of her backsword.

"I hadn't decided on it; just thinking," she said. "And it's not as if we had the leisure for it now anyway."

He nodded and put a hand on her shoulder. "It's your decision to make, oath-sister; and I'll back any you do make, my life long. But think three times."

"And three times more, and one more for seventh and last," she said, completing the old Heathen saying, and looked about with a sigh as she squeezed his hand with hers. "It's *not* the end of the world here anymore, is it?"

"No. And the sea isn't the world's end here either . . . not anymore."

The ancient road running inland had been repaired and shored up until—unless the weather was very bad—you could drive an oxcart all the way to Hraefnbeorg, rather than the packhorses scrambling around gaps and through streams of his younger days. The sea-harvest went that way and Earth's grain and fruit and meat the other, and things like barrels of Gowan's applejack and his own family's pinot grigio to wait aging in a cellar for the odd coasting merchantman who put in on a speculation. There was even a little open-sided temple now on the bluff above, where the folk met to make sacrifice and feast on the greater festivals, rather than just the altars in each house. Within stood images of Woden and Thunor, Frīg and Sib and some of the others; the carving and coloring were raw and crude, but powerful.

"More gulls than I remember," he mused.

"More food for them, when the fishers here clean their catch. You can tell how rich a harbor is, by the gulls."

He nodded. They'd both seen that the world around. There were plenty of the white-and-gray scavengers stalking along the beach with that air of bad-natured beady-eyed suspicion or going by overhead in raucous flocks.

"It'll be like Portsmouth or Darwin next," Thora said dryly.

Deor smiled a little sadly himself. The boy who still lived within him *was* astonished at the growth. The man who'd walked the streets of Portland and Corvallis, Darwin and Zanzibar and Sambalpur saw how it was almost lost in the wooded hills about, eucalyptus and patches of scrub and grass rearing higher inland amid oak and fir and young redwood. A harbor seal not far away gave them a mournful look from its huge liquid eyes and then undulated into the water, unafraid. More of them were sleeking through the shallows; the dwellers of Albion Cove took seal elsewhere in season, but spared them and the otters who frolicked in the kelp forests hereabouts. As an offering to Nerthus in Her aspect as Lady of the Sea, and to the *sae-aelfen* and the wights.

"It's time," he said with a sigh, feeling Thora's sympathy; he was leaving home again, and earlier than he'd intended.

A chattering bunch of youngsters in kilts went past, the Mackenzies that Órlaith had called to her aid, and they followed them towards the pier. Deor smiled at the sight; he remembered his time in the dúthchas fondly, though Clansfolk on the cusp of adulthood always looked a little younger than their years to him. For all their bows and swords they might have been on their way to a Beltane festival with flowers in their hair and frolic on their minds. He'd done that himself, and enjoyed it.

But then, Lady Juniper seems like a girl sometimes, and she was only a little younger than I am now at the Change, he thought. *They're a more carefree folk than mine, though brave and hardy enough at need for anyone.*

One of the Mackenzies looked graver than the rest, though no older; a handsome dark slightly-built young man with the sickle and flowering branch of Goddess Airmed, the Lady as Healer, embroidered on his haversack. That was a craft sign among the Clan as well as simply being the sigil for one of their Gods. Their eyes met for a second, and Deor inclined his head politely.

"Let's be about it, then," he said to Thora. "Didn't think we'd be back aboard a ship so soon, eh?"

She slapped his back. "You left home on a Feldman ship going north with me and Moishe," she said. "Now it's another, going south. Who knows what we'll find, eh?"

"How is the ship, Captain?" Egawa Noboru asked.

He absently ran his hand over the freshly-shaven pate of his head, back towards the topknot, and blinked out at the sea where the last stars were fading in the west as the dawn cast long shadows before them. There was a twinge, but the wound he had taken to keep the knife from his *Tennō* was paining him less and less. It had been functional for some time, which was the crucial thing. Battle scars were a mark of honor, but that one more than most.

I failed in my most basic duty that day, when Saisei Tennō *died; though it was at his express order that I stayed by his daughter's side and not his. This wound shows that*

I also succeeded. This pain bears witness. And she is his true and worthy heir. When Prince Yoshihito's ship was lost many despaired; but I never did. Not for a moment.

With a stark inner grin he reflected on how much faster the hand would have healed when he was the Majesty's age. Now it would probably give him a little trouble for the rest of his life, when the hand was cold or he was very tired. The various aches of battle, minor wounds, and fast travel by horse were more painful than they would have been back then too, of course. It did not matter; his body would serve his will, and his will would serve the Heavenly Sovereign Majesty and the Land of the Gods as long as necessary.

"The vessel is fully serviceable, Egawa-sama," Ishikawa Goru said.

He preferred *Lord Egawa* to *General*, coming from the naval service as he did. Both were equally respectful, though Egawa sometimes thought that interservice rivalry in a military as small as the modern Empire's was more trouble than the gain in esprit was worth.

"The pumps appear to be active," Egawa said.

He indicated the *Tarshish Queen* with a slight jerk of his chin, where it was moored to the little jetty; twin pulsing jets of water arched out into the calm surface of the small bay on the seaward side.

"They are pumping out the drinking water, Lord General, and replacing it with fresh; there is a hose and piping from a spring on that hill running out to the dock. Very good spring water from the bare rock, and it takes little time or labor, so one might as well replace old with new."

Egawa grunted, hiding his approval. It was the sort of meticulous precaution that appealed to him; so was the attention to detail on Ishikawa's part that had made him check things like the quality of the local water supply even though they'd arrived fairly late yesterday.

"Good to be back within sight of the sea!" Ishikawa went on, taking a deep breath.

Egawa nodded; he'd spent more time away from the smell of saltwater since arriving on these shores than he had in the whole of his life before, and the iodine tang and the familiar smell of drying fish from the racks around the little fishing village were reassuringly homelike. Though every detail was different, from the construction of the houses to the names they gave their local *kami* to the boney horse-like faces of the people, if you stepped back and let your eyes slide out of focus a little it was not so very different from a fishing village at home.

He longed for Japan, but this place made him less conscious of it than he had been in the eerie settlement in the air among the giant trees. Though his youngest child, his daughter Emiko, would have been entranced; she loved stories of the spirits, and was never happier than when she was allowed to help in offering flowers and water to the mirror on the family's *kamidana* altar with her parents on either hand to guide her small chubby hands.

The *Tarshish Queen* looked to be in good order as it floated at anchor here in what the *gaijin* of Montival called Albion Cove, in the lee of a little island a hundred yards from the shore. But though Egawa was familiar enough with ships and their ways—you couldn't be a soldier in Japan nowadays without spending a good deal of time at sea—he wasn't the expert that Captain Ishikawa Goru was. The Imperial Navy officer was young, just thirty, but the former Majesty had picked well when he chose him. Also he'd gone over the *Tarshish Queen* from keel to maintop in Newport, making a most meticulous inspection before they sailed.

"Battle damage?" Egawa said.

He could see patches in the antiflame sheathing and newish-looking bits of wood here and there, and he'd caught glimpses of the naval action in the Bay during their hilltop battle ashore with all the ships battering at one another. Including, happily, the ultimate sight of the *bakachon* vessel disintegrating into burning splinters under a hail of heavy round shot and flame-shells.

Ishikawa's handsome young face smiled slightly as he bowed. He was probably thinking of the same sweet sight.

"Some damage, yes, Egawa-sama," he said cheerfully and pointed to her bows.

"But mostly minor, only one serious strike. They took a nasty hit at the starboard bow towards the waterline; they tell me it was from the stern-chaser of one of the pirates. That stove some planking and cracked a rib, but it has been repaired well. Very well, for temporary work done at sea. It would hold even in a bad storm, I think, much less for the short voyage we face, though of course shipyard repairs will be necessary eventually, scarfing in a new timber. And I think replacing one hanging knee. A sound ship. I look forward to commanding her sister, though I miss the *Red Dragon*—she and I knew each other's ways. Well, she died valiantly, and what more can one hope for, neh?"

Egawa grunted thoughtfully. A ship built to the same drawings as this one had been just down the ways and ready to fit out as they left Newport. It was about the same size as their lost *Red Dragon*, about ten parts in a hundred larger, and under differences of detail about as well-armed. The Montivallan princess had negotiated with the merchant house who owned both and secured her for the *Tennō*; she ought to be fully equipped when they needed her, and with Ishikawa's sailors and the Guard samurai to help under their direction they could return to Japan . . . if their casualties weren't too high before then and they didn't have to fight seriously at sea.

All depends on circumstances. Still, I would prefer a larger crew even if we must ship foreigners. And an escort would be welcome. What we bear is precious, even apart from the treasure we seek. I was right when I thought that the seeds of greatness were in the heir; now they have begun to flower.

A little grudgingly he admitted: "That ship will be a generous gift, if we live to receive it. Even allowing for how large this *gaijin* kingdom is."

The Imperial Navy struggled to keep up the number of its keels, between the constant grind of operations and shortages of everything starting with labor. War used things up and wore them out; that was its nature. The new ship would prevent a hole opening up that would be difficult to plug.

"*Hai, honto desu*, Egawa-sama," Ishikawa said. "Very true, Lord Egawa."

Then he sighed a little. "Though greedy as it seems, I would rather have that frigate! Magnificent! Like a great tiger gone to sea. A perfect ship . . . if only she were flying the *Hinomaru*."

"So would I, if we had the men to sail her, Captain," Egawa agreed.

This time his tone was one of suppressed envy, at the thought of a fleet of such craft bearing the red-rayed sun on white. Japan didn't have specialist warships yet; the IJN was made up of armed transports able to carry cargo, or troops into an assault, or to fight at sea. The biggest were closely equivalent to this trading vessel. Which was equipped to trade through pirate-infested seas, and in lands where the inhabitants killed and robbed by preference and traded when they were looking down the business end of a catapult and the point of a boarding pike.

The *bakachon* had nothing better; not as good, in fact, though more numerous. Numbers were Japan's great problem; the enemy outnumbered them three or four to one, and past a certain point quantity had a quality all its own.

If the jinnikukaburi *were not always fighting the Mongols in Manchuria as well as us, things would be . . . very difficult,* he thought.

He didn't want to say *hopeless* even in the privacy of his own mind.

We need peace! Several generations of it, at least. More people, more rice land, more of everything. *Then we would be on a sound footing. In numbers is survival. As it is, our* Tennō *has put it very well: the existence of our people balances on the edge of a blade—a blade we here hold in our hands. An honor, yes, but a terrifying one.*

He looked north. "That *jinnikukaburi* ship they told us of came ashore not far from here," he said thoughtfully.

"Yes, lord General. I rose early and borrowed a horse and guide. Definitely one of theirs; it grounded and broke its back. The enemy thoroughly stripped it before they left overland, though. The scale of this country is daunting—you would discover outsiders only by accident or if they were very careless."

"How many enemy ships does that leave?" Egawa asked.

"There were a dozen in the flotilla that pursued us from the homeland," Ishikawa said.

They shared a glance. It had been highly suspicious that such a strong squadron—twelve ships was a substantial portion of the enemy's navy—would have been waiting to intercept them as they made the passage up the west coast of Honshū. They'd had to run all the way north of Hokkaido before they could turn east across the Pacific, up to the latitudes of ice and fog and endless storm in the cold Kamchatka seas and then down the Aleutian chain. Though Ishikawa had insisted that was the best tactical choice anyway, given that their ship was better-found than the enemy vessels.

The sailor went on:

"So sorry, Lord Egawa, but it is impossible to say precisely. Counting the one that burned in the great bay south of here while we fought, we know that seven are definitely sunk. I am morally certain that at least two more foundered in the storms. Perhaps all of them—but . . ."

"But it would not do to be over-optimistic," Egawa agreed. Then, slowly: "The Heavenly Sovereign Majesty informed you of her . . . her vision?"

He didn't know precisely what to call it. From what the Majesty had said, it had been more than seeing, if not quite participating. Perhaps *haunting* would be closest, though the thought of the living haunting the dead was . . . disturbing.

"Hai," Ishikawa said; he was usually cheerful and rather brash, but now he looked somber enough. "Dan-no-ura!"

"Hai," Egawa said; there was a breadth of meaning in the simple word.

The last great battle of the Genpei War, a struggle whose name and outcome had echoed down the history of Nippon ever since. He could well remember how his father had told him and his brothers the story, in the long nights when winter storms threw chill rain and sleet against the walls of their house and they sat with little covered braziers beneath their robes.

Ishikawa hesitated, then blurted: "The Majesty seems . . . different, Lord Egawa. Since we departed southward from Newport."

He fixed the younger man with a beady stare. "Different? How?"

Ishikawa ducked his head, drew in a breath and licked his lips before he continued: "The Majesty was always firm and decisive. But now . . . now it seems more . . . effortless, neh? As if the burden is less. She is . . . one feels as if one has caught fire in her presence. As if . . . as if one could do more, accomplish more—one's own will tempered and wits made keener."

Egawa's face relaxed, or at least as much as it ever did. "Unquestionably true. The Heavenly Sovereign One is still very young for such responsibilities, which would bow the strongest shoulders. I was among those who saw to her education and I always saw the potential . . . but now we see the flowering of it."

"Yes, unquestionably. Let those who thought a woman could not truly rule in her own right only look at the Majesty!"

Egawa grunted again; he preferred to think of her as an exception, made possible by the divine blood which flowed in her veins. To be *Tennō* was a thing utterly singular in any case. Ishikawa went on:

"How her example heartened all on the voyage here—who would dare complain when hunger and cold and thirst and danger were as nothing to her? Her conduct with the Montivallans has won us great advantage, and she was truly magnificent in the battle."

A shadow passed over his face. "And . . . the visions both she and the former Majesty have had. I cannot believe that she is otherwise than the very voice and hand of the Great Kami, stretched out to counsel and protect Their people."

"Extraordinary, neh?" Egawa said, with dry understatement.

Ishikawa brightened, taking his words more at face value than he had intended. "We live in extraordinary times, lord! A terrible, terrible loss that *Saisei Tennō* fell, of course; we will all mourn the Majesty for the rest of our lives. Yet when—"

His voice stumbled ever-so-slightly as he forced himself not to say *if*.

"—we return . . . with a strong alliance, and the great treasure we sought . . . and now that we know how completely true the former Majesty's visions of its importance to our country were . . . well, our names will live as do those of the heroes of Dan-no-ura itself!"

"Hopefully, not the way the names of the Taira live," Egawa said dryly, deflating the younger man's enthusiasm a little.

To himself: *Though that may be optimism in itself. If we fail, there will be nobody to read epics in Japanese. Still, better that I must work at restraining a noble stallion than prodding a reluctant ox.*

Ishikawa laughed. Perhaps dutifully; a superior's jest was always funny, and Egawa's humor was rare enough anyway.

"I would very much like to see a squadron of those frigates crushing the enemy fleet," he said. "Then we could land and sweep the whole realm of the *akuma* sorcerer kings with the sword and cleansing fire. Avenge our dead and rid us of those filth forever."

Egawa nodded, his left hand clenching unconsciously on the scabbard of his sword and the thumb pressing ever so slightly on the guard as images of a sky ablaze from horizon to horizon lit his mind for an instant. His lips curled slightly back from his teeth.

"We would need troops as well as naval help for that, even if the enemy are engaged elsewhere at the same time."

He forced himself to think dispassionately; it was hard, hard. Then he went on more slowly:

"Though I would be satisfied to see Korea made harmless to us," he said. "I would not want to have to conquer it. And to rule it . . . still less."

"*Hai,* lord Egawa." Ishikawa ventured a small joke of his own. "It is full of *chon* cannibals, after all."

Egawa shrugged with a clatter of armor. "Even if we beat them in the field and pursued a *Three All* policy to its conclusion—

Which meant a policy of *burn* all, *kill* all, *destroy* all; it was an old saying.

"—then we would have to garrison the empty land or the Han or the Mongols would take it without even a native population to give them problems, and be on our doorstep. Which would be a great improvement over what we have at present, but still a problem in the long term. And there are rumors of a Russki kingdom in the Amur valley; we know far too little of that."

"We might settle the land ourselves," Ishikawa said, though there was doubt in his voice.

"No. Too many angry ghosts; more, if we laid it waste. Conquests on the mainland have never gone well for us, not in the long run—despite the fact that we tried even before Heian. The islands south of Japan, I think that is where we may look for gains after the *bakachon* have been thrown down. We are not a people suited to continents. Islands are our karma. Islands, and the sea."

"Yes, this is wisdom, lord Egawa," Ishikawa said respectfully, bowing. "Turning their backs on the sea is the great mistake the Tokugawa made, when all the Asian oceans could have been ours, Taiwan, Hainan, Luzon. You may know I myself was second-in-command of the survey mission to Taiwan several years ago? Virtually empty in the western plain, and much good rice land. Less of the farmland is ruined by ancient buildings and roads and other works than is the case with Honshū or the other Home Islands except for Hokkaido where the climate is so cold. It would be a valuable addition if we managed to take and settle it before the *Shina* return."

"Just so, and it is an old possession of ours from before the great war of the last century, rightly part of Dai-Nippon. Well, enough daydreaming of the fruits of victory before we have cut our foes down. Let us be about the work of the day, Captain. The prize is before us, and the enemy will not be idle."

The captain bowed again. They walked towards the pier and the Imperial Guard and the sailors fell in behind them. Obviously dreams of glory were still in the forefront of Ishikawa's mind, though; perhaps he saw himself as a viceroy, ruling *han* fiefs of his own from a castle-town, perhaps as an admiral of fleets sweeping southward. Egawa was inclined to be tolerant there. That was appropriate for a young warrior. His older sons were the same, under the stern self-discipline he had passed down from his own father, eager for accomplishment and distinction in the *Tennō Heika*'s service.

Only someone who knew the Imperial Guard commander well would have known that he was smiling.

At the thought of two broad-shouldered young men named Takayoshi and Kogorō, and a stripling of promise called Ryōma. Of an infant resting in a daughter-in-law's arms. And at the memory of a formidable tart-tongued middle-aged woman named Haruko, smiling herself, as she showed a little girl how to loft an eagle-shaped kite on a windy hillside.

With the last cherry blossoms blowing down the slope and settling like pink jewels in the blackness of their mingled hair.

CHAPTER TWENTY-ONE

PARTICIPATORY DEMOCRACY OF TOPANGA
(FORMERLY TOPANGA CANYON)
CROWN PROVINCE OF WESTRIA
(FORMERLY CALIFORNIA)
HIGH KINGDOM OF MONTIVAL
(FORMERLY WESTERN NORTH AMERICA)
JULY/FUMIZUKI/CERWETH 24TH
CHANGE YEAR 46/SHŌHEI 1/2044 AD

"This is my first visit here too, Reiko-chan," Órlaith said. "We're just now making even the Bay area really part of the Realm, and it's a process far from finished."

"As we found, Órlaith-chan. Some of the people we met objected to the process of integration." Reiko said dryly, her face calm. "Strenuously objected. Forcefully, even."

Then both of them chuckled, and Órlaith went on:

"*Hai, honto desu ne!* Here we of House Artos haven't even really started."

The Santa Monica Mountains stood blue and beautiful to their north as they approached; the coastline of Westria turned east-west here for a stretch, before resuming its southward slant. There were ruins in sight as well, but mostly small and much worn by time and often covered by the rampant plantings that had once surrounded them. In a new place you saw the old world's leavings more, with less of the filter that mentally removed or diminished them on your own home ground. There was very little low land; a bluff stood inland from the beach, and beyond that the ground rose steeply into tumbled vastness.

Less comely was the long form of a rusted hulk, a monster ship of the ancient world that had come ashore long ago, probably not long after the Change itself, just a little westward of where the old Topanga Canyon Boulevard intersected the Coast Road.

How long ago that was showed in the bulk of sand on its northwestern side as well as the gaping rust-holes and the massive white streaks of guano from nesting seabirds. Together they made a new spit extending hundreds of yards out into the ocean in a curve of white where the longshore drift and winter storms had piled it. Cargo containers that had once turned the ship into a hill of goods had been pushed off to make an interlocking tangle in the sandspit and catch still more of the drift in a way that absorbed the blows of winter storms.

"Those are interesting hills inland," Reiko said, shading her eyes with her *tessen*. "More . . . wholly unfamiliar to me than those in the north, or even where we fought the battle. We have left the lands of . . . of green mountains with tall trees behind, neh? I must readjust my expectations. That a landscape does not deliver what my eyes expect does not make it hideous, simply . . . different."

It's a smart girl you are, Reiko-chan, Órlaith thought affectionately, and raised her binoculars. *I have to trot to keep up with you betimes.*

A few slender trails of smoke rose from the narrow strip of ruins and flat ground along the shore, and a few more inland—perhaps hearths or forges, perhaps small wildfires in this dry summer season. Winter was the wettest time all along the coast of Montival, but summer drought became more and more pronounced as you went south and by the time you got hereabouts it was near-absolute.

Closer and you could see how narrow canyon-valleys ate their way backward into the low bulk of the mountains, and the olive-gray-green of the tough twisted chaparral which covered much of them. Taller trees—slim spearpoint cypress, blue-tinted eucalyptus, stone and umbrella pine, smallish oaks—stood out where something caught a little more water and soil. Here and there were rows of silvery-green olives snaking across the slopes, or a patch of vineyard or small grove of figs.

"Reminds me of pictures of Greece," Heuradys said thoughtfully. "Mom Two . . . Lady d'Ath . . . got a lot of them, after she decided to follow Athana, and I always liked them. Maybe that was one reason why She ended up as my patron too. The Gods know what Greece looks like now, of course."

"God and the Chancellor," Órlaith said. "He gets the Badia reports."

Badia was an old monastery in the hills of Umbria where the Catholic Church was now headquartered; that was what the word meant, in fact. The Vatican was tumbled ruins in the larger ruins of Rome.

"Ah, but that's political stuff, Orrey. It's interesting to know that Rhodes threw out the Venetians and joined the Hellenic League, but that doesn't say how it *looks*. Which I'd like to know, being sort of an honorary Hellene."

"You are?" Reiko asked, raising her brows.

"Well, since I worship the Olympians and they come from that part of the world. Though they're Christians there now as far as I know. Still, I was rooting for the League."

John grinned at Feldman. "Were you for the Venetians, Captain?" he said. "Corvallis being our foremost mercantile city-state."

He snorted. "Some of the history department are, but no, Your Highness, I wasn't. Renaissance Italy was an interesting period but not what you'd call a Golden Age for Jews."

Reiko sighed. "We know so little of the outside world in Japan!"

"Well, we'll change that after the war . . . granted, that will take quite some time, I'd say. The more I learn, the bigger the job looks, so to say. But then Montival and Dai-Nippon will hold the North Pacific as allies, each powerful in its sphere. There's no reason Japan shouldn't become a great naval and trading nation again, in touch with all the world."

The Japanese all nodded, polite small gestures with a fierce eager agreement within that Órlaith could see . . . or perhaps that the Sword of the Lady conveyed.

Near the shore a tall flagpost bore a banner with some sort of botanical theme; Órlaith turned her field glasses and made out a fan-shaped spray of five saw-edged leaves, pointed ovals in dark green on a yellow field edged with black. A familiar bright blink about its base must be spearheads.

"That banner is a little like the house *kamon* of the Minamoto," Reiko said. "Though without the three flowers above, and I do not think those are bamboo leaves. Odd."

Feldman ordered sail struck and they ghosted in on the mizzen gaff and forestaysail alone; the wind was from the north, carrying the drier dustier land-smell, and the deck heeled like a shallow roof as the *Tarshish Queen* sailed reach across it. The morning was almost painfully bright, the sun beating down from a cloudless sky, and little whitecaps topped the waves as they cut across them with a corkscrew motion that had a few of the landsmen hanging over the leeward rail giving their breakfast back. Spray burst backward along the deck like jewels.

"It's my third trip here, Majesty, Your Highness," Feldman said. "It's not a major port, to put it mildly. Barely even a minor one, though the approach is straightforward. If it weren't for the way that wreck protects a bit of the shore in its lee you couldn't put in here at all, you'd have to anchor in an open roadway and barge things back and forth and pray for good weather . . . well, harder than sailors always do."

"I wonder what was in it?" Órlaith asked, looking at the huge wreck; the idea of something like that floating seemed absurd, though she knew it had.

If it was clothes or tools, it would be a treasure-house.

Feldman grinned sourly. "I asked, your Highness. Television sets, radios, some things called CD players, and electronic clocks. From Korea, oddly enough."

Reiko frowned slightly; she was in traveling garb today, the pleated divided skirt or very loose trousers that her folk called *hakama*, belted on over a short *hakama-shita* kimono, both of a medium grayish blue; garb worn by men in modern Japan, or by women when they did something more than ordinarily active, but upper-class women's riding dress in the Association lands.

The which gave us both a quiet joke when her samurai discovered they all looked like cross-dressers imitating noblewomen out for a ride. Mind, for those who like to wear the other sex's clothes, the PPA is paradise, the garb being so different for men and women.

She'd never seen the point, herself; she just wore what she liked or what was convenient or bowed to local custom out of courtesy or political calculation. Heuradys did the same, only with an elevated finger to custom. But the Goddess made individuals each in their own way.

In the Mackenzie dúthchas, they're out of luck—a kilt is a kilt! And men and women even wear their hair much the same way. Ah, well, Montival is a broad land, and varied. There's always someplace to suit any taste.

Reiko's swords were thrust through her sash; she wore socks that divided to make a separate pocket for the big toe, and stout sandals with soles cut from tires, a marker of high status in Nippon as it was here. Pre-Change rubber that had not grown brittle and cracked grew scarcer every year. A curious straw hat like the gently curved top of a mushroom sheltered her face, secured with broad soft silk cords tied about the chin in a complex knot.

Órlaith was in civil garb as well, kilt and sock-hose and ankle-boots, loose saffron-dyed *lèine* shirt gathered with drawstrings at the wrists, plaid pinned at the shoulder with a knotwork broach of silver and turquoise, and Scots bonnet with a spray of Golden Eagle feathers in the badge of House Artos.

John was peacocking in his polished suit of chrome-steel plate and plumed helm, and Heuradys and Droyn and the men-at-arms were in full harness as well with their shields across their backs; Egawa and his samurai were in full fig too, down to the banners in holders on their backs. Egawa looked just as unhappy as Droyn about their lieges' choice not to don armor, though Heuradys had simply sighed and given her a speaking look.

Órlaith was fairly sure the reasoning was sound, though; they wanted to look impressive *without* looking like a storming party coming ashore ready to sack and burn. That was also why she'd made sure that the portlids of the *Tarshish Queen*'s broadside would stay closed, and the bow and stern-chasers would remain pointed fore-and-aft. Though both sets would be loaded and cocked.

Without false modesty she knew she *was* fairly striking . . . and she bore the Sword of the Lady.

These lands were part of Montival . . . in theory. The theory was much more tenuously connected to reality here than it was farther north. Civil garb would also probably be much more comfortable, though that mattered little if she was making a mistake, of course; arrows and sword-cuts were very uncomfortable indeed. Still, though the sea-breeze was no more than pleasantly summery, the feel of the sun on her hands and face hinted that it would get very warm indeed once they were far enough inland to block it. This was a long way south of the Willamette.

The armor would have to be cached soon anyway. It would be an elaborate form of suicide where they were headed, inland into some of the hottest, driest desert on earth.

"Only here three times?" Órlaith asked the merchant captain. "What do they have to trade?"

Feldman's eyes narrowed, as if he was opening and leafing through a filing cabinet in his mind, sorting and cataloguing.

"Not much, and that's the problem. Some good white sea-salt," he said without hesitation, and pointed with his telescope. "They send most of it inland, though. It *might* justify someone on a regular run if they had, say, a few hundred tons per year available consistently, but they don't."

There was a stretch of drying pans along the shore just westward of the wrecked ship, and the skeletal metal shapes of wind-driven pumps. It looked like a smallish facility and rather haphazardly laid out.

Though probably a basically efficient one, Órlaith thought. *For that the sun's brighter here and it doesn't rain as much.*

"Apart from that, little bits of this and that . . . olives, olive oil, oranges, lemons, dried figs, some fruits like pomegranates that ship well," he said. "A little merino wool and angora goat-hair. Maryjane and tobacco—both of good quality, according to appraisers I trust; I don't smoke myself."

Órlaith made a slight moue. Tobacco was simply filthy, in her opinion, and not many people in Montival used it, which made it expensive and hard to come by. Some did, though, especially in the port cities. She'd tried maryjane, which had a certain following in Corvallis among students and the mildly raffish elsewhere, and just didn't like the way it made her feel slow and stupid.

"Good-quality raw opium, and there's always a market for that," he went on.

Everyone nodded. That was the base for morphine, the main painkiller available in the advanced parts of the modern world, save for ether.

"There's wine and brandy, but . . ."

He made a grimace; it must be truly dreadful.

"And salvage goods; watchmaker's tools, convertible machine tools, bicycles, mimeograph machines, manual typewriters, sewing machines, rubber still in the original packaging, optics; occasionally something startling in the way of artwork or gold and silver. But not much of anything at any one time. You'd be surprised how fast a ship can swallow profits if it has to sit at anchor waiting. We leave it to the smaller coasting outfits, and even they don't touch here very often. I did Crown charters for the relief effort four years back, though. My father sent me, he was already ill then. It just barely paid expenses, and that's not counting the capital cost of tying the ships up when they could have been doing something more profitable, but—"

He shrugged expressively and raised his hands. "We picked up what we could for the return trip, even salvage brick and marble and roofing tile, just to avoid going back in ballast, and I ended up letting it sit in a vacant lot until I built my new house. We've *still* got some on our hands, even with the way Newport is growing and donating part of it to the Newport Town Hall and the synagogue. The trip was basically a mitzvah, your Highness."

Mitzvah meant a good deed that pleased God, more or less. Órlaith snapped her fingers as the memory came clear.

"Ah, they had a drought and a bad fire here, and my parents scraped up some relief aid by shamin' folk into it, I remember hearing of that, though I was out east in the Valley of the Sun just then. At Chenrezi monastery, for the new Abbot's elevation. Food, cloth, medicines and tools. The good monks and the folk they lead wanted to contribute, but it was too far for provisions so they sent money, of which they are usually short."

Karl Aylward Mackenzie was standing not far away, leaning on a longbow tucked into a greased-linen bag and looking eagerly towards the shore as the breeze ruffled his flaxen hair on his brow. His long queue swung down his brigandine as he turned his head to speak.

"Aye, Highness. I remember, that I do. Herself went about saying we should remember that the Mother loved all Her children, so do dig deep, lads and lasses, and please Her while you earn threefold return. Lady Maude didn't exactly make it *geasa* as Chief and Goddess-on-Earth, but then again, she didn't exactly not, either, you might say."

Sir Droyn nodded. "Bishop Anastasius preached a sermon on it in Molalla," he said, and crossed himself: "I remember it well, because it was at my last Mass at home before I went to court as a squire. He took the lesson from Corinthians: *And though I have the gift of prophecy, and understand all mysteries, and all knowledge; and though I have all faith, so that I could move mountains, and have not charity, I am nothing."*

Karl tossed his head in agreement. "Dun Fairfax sent some wheat and barley and bolts of linen from our joint store; to be honest, 'twas the oldest of what we had, though still sound. I helped with the wagons to get it to Sutterdown."

Órlaith nodded, and thought of the question that would tell them the most of their landfall. "What do they buy, Captain? What is it that they need and desire?"

"Pretty well everything, but they can't afford much. Tools and instructional books lately, I've heard. Must have decided that if they want modern goods they'll have to make as much as they can themselves. Which is sensible. The coast south of here is an utter wreck or complete desert for a long, long way, and this area just has too much land covered in concrete to amount to much. Pity, because you can see that if it wasn't covered up some of it would have been very good land indeed."

Reiko had been looking very still, which with her was a sign she was remembering and organizing her thoughts.

"This Los An-ge-les was a very large city, neh?" she said. "Half the size of Tokyo. Yet some survived, and remained civilized? How?"

Chancellor Ignatius had assembled at least skeletal files on every part of Montival, even the parts that didn't know they were in the kingdom yet, using everything from explorer's diaries to merchants to agents in place to tapping into his Church's parallel network. Órlaith had read them all as part of her education, and gone over the updated ones dealing with the far south of Westria again once she and Reiko determined where they were heading and began to assemble their party.

The reports on this part of the world had made grim reading, even more so than most. And since she bore the Sword she found that facts and figures were more *real* to her, as if the part of her mind that dealt with them had been given a goose in a sensitive spot, or developed an extra muscle that enabled her to translate them into flesh and blood.

"Water," she said, and swept her arm from northeast to due south. "Fourteen millions there, and there was another great city about a hundred miles south, millions more, and millions more than that just barely south of there in the realm that was called Mexico. It's not exactly a desert, not this side of the inner mountains, but then again it's not very wet either, and the Change came just at the start of the dry season here. All but a little of the water the cities used came in aqueducts from hundreds of miles away, and most of the rest from deep pumped wells. And the day of the Change, it stopped flowing. Or within a day or two at most."

She'd been speaking Nihongo, since Reiko and her compatriots were the ones least familiar with the story. Reiko winced, and Egawa grunted thoughtfully while she repeated it in English for the rest.

"You can do without food ten or even fourteen days before your body fails, if you must, Lady," he said then; he'd been easier with her since the fight at Círbann Rómenadrim. "Months, with only a little food now and then; I did that myself once, on a long mission behind enemy lines. But water . . ."

They all nodded when Órlaith translated that too. Water was an entirely different thing; and the symptoms of the lack showed up within a few days at most, less if you were working hard. First raging thirst and a swollen tongue making breathing hard, then savage headaches and cramps and weakness, then raving delirium and hallucinations, then unconsciousness and death; and you weakened fast enough that moving to *find* the water became impossible fairly soon.

"So most perished . . . very quickly. The ones moving about were the first to go," she went on. "What little water there was in pools and such quickly became filthy—the clouds of flies hid the sun, the reports say. So many died so quickly that places on the fringe that *did* have water could survive, if they also were able to defend themselves for a little while, or even just hide."

"A little like the Willamette," Karl said, surprising her; she hadn't though he was interested in history. "Save that there it was plague in the camps around Salem that was, the folk the first Lord Protector drove out of Portland."

Órlaith nodded; sometimes the worse was the better. "Topanga was one such refuge, it's a narrow canyon with year-round springs and streams most years, not too many folk even then, and easily blocked off."

Everyone was somber and silent for a little while. Most of the time you could think of the time before the Change as something far distant. Seen between the covers of a book, like the German Wars of the last century or the terrible plagues that had swept the Western Hemisphere when outsiders first came, or the Iron Limper's huge pyramids of heads before that, to be dealt with on the surface of your mind, the part that analyzed and used numbers to make a model of the world.

But now and then it came home to you that an entire world of humankind had perished in bewildered agony within living memory, hitting you in the guts and the blood. Few of those who'd lived through that time spoke of it much; the ones who babbled obsessively of horrors or hid bread in corners and wept inconsolably when it went moldy mostly hadn't lived this long, though from what the oldsters said there had been many such in the early years, driven mad or nearly. Not all the damage had been physical.

And the ones who did live through *the terrible time didn't really* live it, *not the way most did,* Órlaith suddenly realized. *For the tales are all of how the tale-tellers survived, but the* true *story of the first Change Years is one of death, not survival.* Our *parents' parents were like someone who falls off a sheer cliff a hundred feet high only to hit pine-boughs covered in snow and lives to walk away. Does that not once, but over and over again, all the way down the mountainside to the flats below. So their stories are true . . . but so exceptional they're misleading, as that lucky plunger would be to the next thousand people who went off the same cliffs, so. It couldn't be otherwise, for the dead died with their stories untold and unknown, vanishing like mist in the sun.*

She shivered a little and rested her palm on the hilt of the Sword, closing her eyes and opening her mind.

There was a *singing* when she did that, a vast crystalline humming, a sense of lofty unused chambers in her mind, clean and swept and ready for habitation. It made her feel her father's presence too, somehow: nothing definite, more like a scent or a taste, but unquestionably there. That temptation was one reason she didn't do it too often. And when she pushed at it as she did now there was a sense of where she was in Montival.

Less knowledge of the sort a map or book might give than a *feeling* when she asked for it. Oddly, as she moved away from the lands she knew it was stronger, less overlaid with her personal experiences. Here along the coast it was like the scent of sage and fennel, and a feeling of . . . infancy, of people and land not yet fitting together but taking tentative steps. Like a child seeing a dance and moving through a few of the steps.

The dead city inland and southward was a wound, deep and painful but dry and cauterized, an itching keloid scar that only epochs of time could remove. Yet even there sun shone, water fell and trickled, life gnawed, roots burrowed and bit, the very air bound materials a molecule at a time. Like the plates of Earth grinding deep beneath in a world of heat and stress; mills grinding slow, but exceeding fine.

The mountains and desert beyond were more as they should be. Lizards basked, insects scuttled, animals and plants and birds native and not grazed and hunted and bred and sought their own dynamic in a universe of alkali and drought where day was a sword and night was a shield. All like a huge balance swinging, wildly at first as a monstrous pressure was removed, and then more and more gently. Human kind was part of that spare clean hugeness, as wholly as coyote and sidewinder, and with all of it the spirits of place were woven through the world of tangible things and utterly at one with it, matter and otherworld part of a greater pattern that rose up into complexities that even the Sword could only suggest.

Except there, she thought, shuddering. *Except there!*

When she opened her eyes, Heuradys had moved unobtrusively to shield her in a way that give her as much privacy as was possible on the quarterdeck. Reiko leaned close.

"The *shintai*?" she murmured; that meant dwelling-place-of-a-spirit, which was as good a description of the Sword of the Lady as any Órlaith had heard. "It spoke?"

"Yes," Órlaith said equally softly. "You remember what the Yurok shaman said? At Diarmuid's steading?"

"A good thing in its own place can become bad in the wrong place?" Reiko said; one of the things they had in common was a good memory.

"Oh, yes, very bad indeed. Wild and strong and . . . lost. Trying to shape things as it knows they *should* be, lost in memories, as if it had dug a hole and jumped in and pulled it after itself. And waiting for us, Reiko-chan. Waiting."

Then she shook her head and spoke something closer to the truth she had felt:

"No. Waiting for *you*, *Tennō Heika* of Dai-Nippon. Waiting for *you*."

"That's a coaster out of Astoria, I think," Feldman said thoughtfully, as he belted on his cutlass and settled his round peaked cap prior to going ashore. "Ah, yes, the *St. Sebastian the Martyr.* One of Andre Langlois' ships; they're in the coasting trade. They must have pushed their round this far south, maybe on a speculation. An honest firm but not what you'd call adventurous."

The leadsman in the bows called out sharply: "By the mark, three! Full fathom three!"

A pause as he hauled up his weight and examined it where beeswax lifted a sample from the bottom.

"Bottom is clear sand and shell!"

"Strike all sail," Feldman went on in his captain's voice, brisk and crisp. "Mr. Mate, stand by to drop anchor, bow and stern. This is good holding ground."

"Aye aye, Cap'n," the officer replied.

The little harbor had only two real seagoing vessels, besides quite a few fishing boats from single-man rowboats to fair-sized smacks; they were tied up to a rickety-looking wharf built along the inside of the wrecked giant. And looked comically small there, like a child's toys floating in a bath. Boats piled high with fresh vegetables and produce were putting out even as she watched, and the bosun and a pair of crew with boarding pikes moved to keep them at a distance until they were given permission.

The ship the merchant had pointed out first was a two-masted schooner about half the *Tarshish Queen*'s size. Feldman tapped his telescope towards another, somewhat larger and a three-master like their own ship.

"That one I don't know, your Highness, but from her lines . . . see the raised fo'c's'le? She's southern, one of the Hispano realms. Brigantine rig, about our displacement but a shorter hull and a broader beam. Two catapults a side and a stern-chaser."

Órlaith focused her binoculars on the name written in letters of weathered, flaking gold paint around the stern of the three-master.

"Virgen de las Esmeraldas," she read in *español*; there was a blue-mantled figure drawn below it with a child in her arms. "Virgin of Esmeraldas, in English."

"Right. The king there has been encouraging trade lately, mostly by burning out the pirate nests in the Galapagos and not stealing *too* much himself," Feldman confirmed. "Palm oil and soap, abaca hemp rope and canvas, cocoa, coffee, raw rubber, cotton cloth and prints, that sort of thing; they're mostly interested in metals, and in luxury goods they can't produce like wine and brandy, and in a few things like chronometers. And they build pretty fair ships. Hmmm. From her looks, she took damage, storm or battle. Probably stopped here for water and to refit before heading farther north."

Órlaith touched the hilt of the Sword again. "Aye, Esmeraldas. Their ruler . . . *Rei Hernán I* . . . has exchanged letters and envoys with us of late, if not ambassadors."

Reiko sighed softly and spoke in her own language: "The world is so wide."

The last of the sails came down; the ship coasted forward another hundred yards in water gone pond-quiet in the lee of the wreck-sandspit. At a sharp command the anchors went down with a rumble and splash, at the head first and then the stern as it swung around. The schooner came to a halt with her side facing the beach after a single sway and bob as the cables went taut. The peaceful-looking bulwark was well within catapult distance of the beach and the straggle of houses and sheds that made a not-quite-town up above the high-tide mark amid the larger crumbled, brush-grown ruins of the ancient world.

None of those was *very* large, and the newer houses had all been built from their materials. The largest had stucco walls, the smaller were frankly cinderblock or walled with rammed-together rubble bound with clay or simple adobe. She thought the faded red tiles that were the commonest roofing were probably salvage too, but many of the dwellings had colorful flowers about them or growing up the walls in blossoming vine as well as truck-gardens and pens for goats. Several small windmills spoke of tube wells.

"I'll signal when it's time for the main party to come ashore," Feldman said. "Incidentally, there are trebuchets covering most of the harbor—high-angle weapons on turntables. They're over behind that earth berm planted in scrub—but that's just a reasonable precaution by the Topangans."

"And sending Karl ashore with you is a reasonable precaution for us," Órlaith said; the captain hadn't wanted it. "Also he's a friendly sort and folk like him, which might help."

"And I'll take some men-at-arms ashore when Captain Feldman reports things ready, and then signal for you once we've secured a perimeter, Your Highness," Sir Droyn said with implacable politeness.

"Perhaps it would be best if I also followed with some of the Imperial guard before you landed, Majesty," Egawa said, almost treading on the end of the knight's sentence. "For the sake of symmetry."

The young Montivallan knight and the grizzled samurai looked at each other in momentary surprise; Droyn wouldn't have followed the Japanese, but it was obvious they were saying the same thing for the same reason. The two young women glanced at each other with a shared smile; behind them Heuradys d'Ath looked at Droyn and nodded soberly.

"The biter bit! You can only override your guardians every so often," Órlaith said in resignation.

Feldman was politely impassive as he called: "Mr. Radavindraban! You have the deck!" and turned to the boats on the davits, stepping in with casual agility.

On shore they had been stirring and pointing as the newcomer dropped anchor. Órlaith looked at the higher ground inland and nodded to herself as she caught the winking of light off something polished—at a guess, it would be a telescope or pair of field glasses. Doubtless messengers were scurrying and Morse code was being flashed by mirrors. She hoped it wouldn't take too long to locate what passed for authorities here, and waited quietly with a hunter's patience while the two big longboats were crewed and lowered, pushed off from the side of the boat and rowed up to the sand.

The warriors jumped free and deployed in a smooth disciplined movement that left them drawn up in ranks while the sailors made fast . . . though not pulling the boats up far enough that they couldn't embark again quickly. They were double-ended whaleboats and could switch directions instantly, for precisely this sort of situation.

The onlookers ashore had surged back at the show of martial force, then hesitated when everyone stopped. One of Karl's archers walked forward with a white rag on the end of her unstrung bow, waving it back and forth and shouting encouragingly. The watchers were obviously just the inhabitants, none armed beyond the casual blade at belt or odd spear you'd expect anywhere strangers might arrive, but one—a youth, she thought—went inland with flying heels, and it wasn't very long before a larger body came down to the water.

Not in any precise order, but moving close together, and one carried a long metal pole with the same botanical flag.

"I don't think they're of a very decisive type, here," Órlaith sighed, as conversation began; not just between the newcomers and the locals but among the locals themselves, accompanied by frequent gestures.

The bosun had let the bumboats approach after Feldman's first mate looked them over with a pawky eye for possible treachery. Heuradys went to the side, flipped a coin down and came back with a stalk of six-inch yellow fruits that Órlaith recognized after a second as bananas. An instant later she realized that that was their name in Nihongo too . . . with an added hard-to-define feeling that the word wasn't much used there in modern times. She'd eaten them only three times in all her years herself, but she remembered how to peel the brown-spotted yellow covering back. Reiko watched and copied her, and then her eyes went a little wider at the taste.

"That is most excellent!" she said after a moment. "So smooth and sweet, like apples and plums together! I suppose it is too cold in Nihon to grow these. I have seen their pictures in books."

"Just barely warm enough here in a sheltered spot, *Heika*, and they must water them a great deal," First Mate Radavindraban said with a bow. "They don't ship well, alas."

He sighed, then smiled brilliantly when Heuradys handed him one. "My thanks, lady! Very common where I was born, yes indeed."

Órlaith tossed the skin into a basket; she thought they'd probably appeal to the horses. An occasional neigh came from below, now that they'd scented land and were making it very plain they wanted out of this cramped uncanny place where the ground moved. Heuradys had waited until her liege's hands were free before having one herself, and she did it dexterously left-handed.

Ashore, the talking was going on. Órlaith sighed, and looked over her shoulder. The green-blue waters of the Mother Ocean were empty except for a few little fishing craft with single lugsails. Nothing else . . . for example, no sign of the tall masts of RMN *Stormrider* beating down hell-bent to enforce the will of the High Queen.

Not yet, she thought, and then aloud: "Not decisive at all."

"You want me to get ashore and goose them?" Heuradys asked, her voice carefully neutral.

Reiko raised a brow. "I think I have finally mastered English," she said. "That is a 'don't tell me to do that' question that is not a question, is it not, Heuradys-gozen?"

"Oh, I wouldn't dream of telling my liege that," Heuradys said, then felt at her nose as if it had grown.

Reiko didn't see the reference to the classic children's story, though she chuckled when the knight explained it. Órlaith sighed again; Herry had never been shy about telling her when she was screwing up, though she was more tactful about it in public than she had been when they were little girls together.

"No, I've told my people what to do. They're out there getting things ready for us. We'll let them go and do it."

The crew lofted and racked their oars and leapt out of the longboat as soon as the keel grated on sand, pushing it a little farther while they stood knee-deep. Not as far as they might, though: he'd warned them to keep it ready to float quickly, just in case.

Moishe Feldman waited until the probably-unnecessary and possibly-unwelcome archers deployed and then stepped ashore, up to the gunwale and then off the prow and down on sand that was only damp rather than washed by the low combers that hissed across behind him, as suited a captain's dignity. He smiled to himself as he did; there was always a little bit of a thrill to that, a hint of new things and a wider world as his boots hit the shore.

The tide was on its way out, and there was the usual litter of wrack—strands of seaweed, bits and pieces of shellfish, here and there some drift-wood, with the odd pair of gulls quarreling over a titbit. Small fishing boats were drawn up higher, often chained to posts driven deep, and mostly pre-Change hulls of aluminum and fiberglass; this area was seriously short of timber for anything more modern. Nets dried on stakes, some with plastic-jug floats still attached, and several score people were about their business. There was a strong smell of fish—fish drying, fish smoking, fish and offal just plain decaying amid a pile of empty shells that buzzed with flies. Skinny-looking mongrels danced and barked, baring their teeth at the Mackenzie greathounds until various owners arrived and dragged them away by their collars and ruffs. The unclaimed ones decided discretion was the better part of valor when someone shied a pebble that thumped into a narrow rump.

"By *God* I'm glad I sail out of Newport!" someone in the boat's crew muttered; Feldman didn't rebuke them.

Mainly because nobody local was close enough to hear, but also because he thoroughly agreed. Newport was Corvallis' window on the Pacific, with a rail link to the city-state's territories in the Willamette, a thriving and growing little city in its own right, a place of traders, deep-sea fishers, seafarers, shipyards and all their ancillary crafts. A place that regularly saw craft from all over the Pacific basin and as far away as Europe and Africa. *This* sleepy little sandspit . . .

Though I've seen far, far worse.

The old coast road, roughly patched here and there, ran along the base of the bluffs inland; a new-made branch in plain rutted sandy dirt with some gravel thrown on top ran to the wharf in the lee of the ancient wreck, and a pair of oxcarts were moving along it in opposite directions but similarly piled high with barrels, bundles and crates, two-wheeled things made from the axle of an ancient car with a wooden superstructure and larger wooden wheels on the old hubs. Each pair of oxen trudged stolidly with the driver walking beside, leaning into the yokes.

He was the business of the party who marched towards him with armed youths at their backs after one of the pagan archers went forward and waved a handkerchief on the end of her bow.

"Top of the mornin' to ye, yer honors!" she called cheerfully. "And would you be coming to parlay, the now? A hundred thousand welcomes!"

Moishe had backing too—the two Dúnedain, Susan Mika, the Mackenzie contingent and six sailors with cutlass and crossbow. All trying their best to look tough—which they were and which they appeared—and friendly and unmenacing at the same time. Unlike many places where he'd leapt from the longboat to the shore he was fairly sure nobody here intended violence, which as a man of peace and trade he thoroughly approved.

That didn't make it absolutely certain there wouldn't be any, of course; there had been places where peace and trade required thumping. And from the number of spears, something had the locals more nervous than ever. He could see a few patched minor injuries, too. There had been fighting here, and recently.

"Jared!" he called, as the Topangan party came closer.

We're in luck, he thought. *Some of the Brains are here already.*

For some reason lost in the years of chaos right after the Change the Topangans called the members of their five-member sort-of-governing council the *Brains*. They elected a new one when a predecessor died, grew feeble or just didn't want to do the work anymore; it was rewarded solely in prestige and a little extra neighborly help. He'd never been able to tell if the title was official, or even if "official" meant anything at all here. The ones Feldman had met *were* quite intelligent, if a bit parochial. They also deliberated slowly in his experience, and everything important had to be put to a general meeting of adults for a vote as well, often several times.

Then people decided if they wanted to pay any attention to the result. Topanga made Corvallis look as tight-arsed and over-regulated as Boise. It was all rather like dealing with a Mackenzie Dun's *Óenach*, only more quarrelsome and with less religion folded in, and far more people entitled to attend and speak . . . and speak . . . and speak . . . at length . . . than any single Clan village.

"Good to see you again!" he said.

He waited until they were close enough to speak normally. Shouting always sounded angry, the more so when comparative strangers were involved. It wouldn't do to just assume they remembered him, either. They probably did, but you never knew. His smile was perfectly genuine; he liked most of the people he met, apart from the stubbornly stupid, the vicious and the dishonest. He'd known merchants who were sourly convinced that the bulk of humanity fell into those categories, and he'd always wondered why they had picked a line of work where you had to spend so much time dealing with human beings who weren't neighbors or relations.

"Moishe Feldman here, of Feldman and Sons, captain aboard the

Tarshish Queen; I was here with that grain shipment four years back, and you were kind enough to invite me to stay at your house."

Jared Tillman led the Topangan greeting party; he was a man in his sixties, quite tall but a bit stooped now, with a shaggy mop of white hair and a closer-cropped beard of the same, though he had most of his teeth. He peered at Feldman, pulled a pair of glasses with incongruous upswept pink plastic frames studded with costume gems out of a pocket and looked through them, then relaxed slightly. The glasses seemed to help, though they'd do nothing for the cataract growing in his left eye.

"Hey there, Moishe," he said, shaking hands with a grip still strong. "Good to see you again too."

His son Connor was behind him, shorter but with the same lean build and long face, about forty and still clean-shaven. Moishe thought the youngster behind *him* was Jared's oldest grandson, in his teens now and looking much more sullen than the happy-go-lucky boy on the edge of puberty the merchant remembered from four years ago. There was a strong family resemblance.

He was also rather dramatically dressed, in leather pants fastened with copper studs, strapped moccasin-like boots, and a chest bare except for a flamboyant cloak made from the hide of a full-grown male cougar with the head at his shoulder, all fasted with a jeweled golden brooch that must be salvage work and garnished with a ferocious-looking necklace of fangs and claws. Variations seemed to be fashionable among his peers. Besides that he had a bow, quiver, shortsword and dagger. His leanly muscular chest and shoulders were tanned brown, and there were lighter summer streaks in his shaggy dark-brown hair.

"And Kwame," Feldman added. "Good to see you again too. Hope things are going well."

Kwame Curtis was a bit older than Jared's sixty-odd, stocky and missing several fingers on his left hand and clean-shaven and very erect in bearing, wearing an antique Fritz helmet of the old Americans and a back-and-breast cut and hammered from salvage metal. Feldman hadn't gotten to know him as well, but he was fairly sure two of the youngsters were his children, from the cast of their features.

They were also about the same wheat-toast-brown shade of skin as Sir Droyn, while Kwame was considerably darker. The Corvallan merchant knew that the color of one's skin had sometimes been considered important before the Change. Important in the way people nowadays thought of your tribe or clan or realm, what religion you followed, what your home city was or which lord held your oath. It seemed odd, but then much about the pre-Change world was deeply strange, even for one like him who was well-read in the ancient histories. And human beings were tribal by nature; if they couldn't pick sides about one thing, they'd do it about another, down to which end of the boiled egg they opened at breakfast. Jews had millennia of experience with the phenomenon, from both sides.

The two older Topangans looked at each other. "Hey there, Moishe," Jared said again. "Long time."

His son Connor added: "Those goods you brought in after the fire did help."

The youngster behind Connor spoke up: "Kept a lot of us from starving to death, you mean, don't you, Dad?"

"This would be a really good time to shut the hell up, Conan," Connor said tightly.

"Fine, OK, we weren't hungry and we fed all that wheat to our pigs and goats," the young man said, and stalked away.

Jared and Connor exchanged a glance. Feldman could interpret it quite precisely. Connor was saying *Was I really that much of an asshole at his age?* And Jared was replying: *Every bit as bad, and I'm enjoying the hell out of this.* It was a dialogue as old as fathers, sons and grandfathers.

Kwame was looking at the Mackenzie archers and the trio right behind him.

"You're not exactly hauling wheat and dried beans this time, are you, Captain Feldman? Because those look like soldiers to me—soldiers who're trying to look relaxed because someone told them to."

At that point Karl Aylward Mackenzie waved and shouted cheerfully: "And the top of the mornin' to you, your honor!"

Feldman shook his head. "No, not wheat, but it's an official—"

Quasi-official, sort of, kinda.

"—charter from the Crown this time too. What I've mostly got is passengers, including some very high-ranking ones, and naturally they have an escort. They need to use Topanga Canyon to get inland, then through the Valley likewise. Is that a problem?"

"High-ranking?" Jared asked sharply, and his son fairly bristled. "Look, I know you guys up north claim we're part of the, umm, High Kingdom—"

Feldman held up his hands. "On oath, they're not here to collect taxes or make you sign the Great Charter if you don't want to," he said. "Honestly, the Crown Princess—"

"A Princess?" Jared asked. "Christ, and I thought Disney was dead."

That reference went over the merchant skipper's head, but he'd been born only a decade after the Change, and he'd grown up hearing things he didn't understand from those who were adults before the old world fell. It made for a gap between generations greater than anything since, and, he suspected, greater than any before back to Noah and the Flood. In this specific instance he winced slightly and spoke earnestly:

"The heir to Montival, Jared; Crown Princess Órlaith Arminger Mackenzie, of the House of Artos. And her brother, Prince John Arminger Mackenzie. Anyway, they have other things on their mind and you're just topography they have to cross."

"Running around without her father . . . No, the ship from Astoria said he was dead? They hadn't heard the details when they left."

"Murdered by foreigners . . . agents of the ruler of Korea . . . it's a long story."

"So she's High Queen or whatever?"

"No, not until she's twenty-six. Until then her mother's High Queen Regnant . . . ruling monarch. But . . . ah . . . she's got these Mackenzies along, and McClintocks, and some Associates . . . ah, knights and men-at-arms, and they all take monarchy pretty seriously. A word to the wise: you should too while they're here. It's the wave of the future, and right now a wave is landing on your beach with . . ."

He combed his memory for a local metaphor.

". . . some royal surfboards riding it."

He turned his head; Morfind and Faramir were in Ranger working garb selected for the dry lands, mottled muted light brown, rock-gray and olive green with the Stars, Tree and Crown on their mail-lined leather jerkins, and long hooded cloaks hanging from their shoulders. Susan Mika was in brown Crown Courier leathers with some Lakota additions in the way of beadwork and fringes; fortunately she didn't have scalps down the seams of her leggings, which he thought might have added to the stress factor.

All three were wearing swords and had quivers, bowcases and shields slung over their backs. It was time for a little unity-in-diversity pep-talk.

"Montival's a big place, there's room in it for anyone," Feldman said. "I'm from Corvallis . . . well, Newport . . . as you know, and we're a representative democracy. These two are of the Dúnedain Rangers from Stath Ingolf—"

"Mae govannen," they said gravely, bowing with their hands on their hearts, then continued in English: "A star shines on the hour of our meeting."

The two older men and Jared's son did a double-take.

"And Rider Susan Clever Raccoon. Of the Crown Courier Corps, and the Lakota *tunwan*, the people of the Seven Council Fires."

"And the Oglála *oyáte* too if you want to be picky," she said cheerfully, then grinned, held up her right hand palm-out and said: *"Haŋ.* That means hi, basically."

"And we've got an actual monarch along. A Japanese one," Feldman said. "Sorry if this is a bit of a shock, but there it is."

"Japanese? People survived there? Who is it, the Emperor in person?"

He watched Feldman's face. "Wait a minute, you're saying it *is* the . . . you're not fucking with us, are you, Moishe?"

"I'm afraid not, Jared, Kwame. Empress, actually. And her samurai. And they take it very, *very* seriously; they're serious people, and you very much don't want them pissed off at you for her sake. Fortunately they don't expect foreigners to touch their foreheads to the ground, but a bow would be tactful."

"Knights and samurai . . . samurai and knights . . . Princes, Princesses . . . Empresses . . . guys in kilts with bad movie brogues . . . fucking *elves*; I've lived too long," Jared muttered to himself, touching a hand to the side of his head for a moment. "And I'm not even high."

"Ah . . . I'm very sorry, good sir," Faramir said politely, inclining his golden-curled head. "We're *not* elves. I apologize if there was a misunderstanding."

Jared looked relieved, until the young Ranger went on: "We're Númenóreans; descendants of the Folk of the West exiled here to Middle-earth. Friends of the elves."

"If there were any around," his cousin Morfind put in. "Not yet, though. They're welcome anytime as far as we're concerned but we're not holding our breaths."

Kwame looked as if he wanted to clap his hand to his head too, or tear out clumps of hair, but was too disciplined. The youngsters behind them started to chatter excitedly and point out to the *Tarshish Queen*, until he turned and barked into the rising brabble:

"Quiet! Or go back to your mommies!"

The noise subsided, though not the bright-eyed curiosity. Feldman patted the air soothingly with both hands.

"Look, Jared, Kwame, as I said, all they want is to go through Topanga to the Valley, then through the Valley inland, and maybe pick up some supplies and packhorses, for which they'll pay handsomely. I'll be staying here until they get back, and I'm willing to buy a cargo which will give you credit on First National."

Even if it's more unsaleable tiles and bricks and bathroom fixtures worth maybe three percent over scrap value. It's a mitzvah to make peace and anyway the charter terms cover it.

The two Brains looked at each other; Connor leaned forward and whispered urgently to his father. Then the senior man turned back to Feldman.

"Ah . . . normally there wouldn't be a problem, Moishe. If you vouch for their behavior, we know your word's good. But . . . right now there may really be a problem."

Feldman sighed. "Let me hear it."

CHAPTER TWENTY-TWO

PARTICIPATORY DEMOCRACY OF TOPANGA
(FORMERLY TOPANGA CANYON)
CROWN PROVINCE OF WESTRIA
(FORMERLY CALIFORNIA)
HIGH KINGDOM OF MONTIVAL
(FORMERLY WESTERN NORTH AMERICA)
JULY/FUMIZUKI/CERWETH 24TH
CHANGE YEAR 46/SHŌHEI 1/2044 AD

Karl Aylward Mackenzie stood easily with his strung bow in his arms and his right boot up on a block of crumbling concrete at the edge of what had been a road along the coast, not a quarter bowshot from the beach, while Captain Feldman conferred with the local headmen. Or possibly the equivalent of their First Armsman, or some combination of the two. From the looks of things, they weren't altogether happy with what he was saying.

Behind him the *Tarshish Queen*'s sailors rested in the longboats that had brought them ashore, ready to leap out and push off and leap back in at a moment's notice; he grinned a little to himself at the fact that the McClintocks were all still on the ship, doubtless because of their reputation for being rudely hot-tempered. The Princess had said they should be friendly, and friendly they'd look, down to keeping their bonnets on and their helmets slung at their belts. Neither he nor any of the other of the young Mackenzies were going to have a problem getting going quickly if things went into the pot just because they weren't standing as if they had a pike rammed up the arse.

The armsman was looking at them now and then, calm but narrow-eyed and attentive. He was the one with the fingers gone, and was armored in a rather crudely made back-and-breast and had a helmet of the type oldsters called a *Fritz* for some reason.

A warrior, that, and a good one in his day, though too old for much in the way of handstrokes now. A commander, then.

His hard intelligent features revealed little, unlike his companion who was looking baffled and vaguely indignant at the same time. Behind the whitebeard was another man, shorter but equally lean and long-faced, obviously his son and looking pretty old too—forty or so, Karl thought, though the way most people's faces turned to leather under this southern sun might be giving him a few more years. Behind both of them was a set of younger men . . .

Well, nearly all men, he thought, catching a lass's eye for a moment and winking before she turned her nose up haughtily and looked away.

The younger sort were obviously there to back up their leaders if needs must, having bows or spears in their hands, shortswords at their waists, and many carrying round shields over their backs as well, though he didn't see any armor to speak of besides arm-guards that might be fashion as much as protection. Some had belt-quivers with little darts as well, which puzzled him until he recognized the tubes like long flutes as blowguns, which was interesting.

Sure, and wasn't Lady Heuradys' second mother said to use such now and then? Of course, she was an assassin then . . .

One of the young men started over in his direction. The middle-aged man behind the whitebeard said something which seemed to roll off the younger man's back . . . and yes, there was a family resemblance there too; grandfather, father and son, then.

He was grinning as he approached, and Karl made a quiet gesture to his clansfolk: *be easy,* so that there would be no pack-bristle. Just to be sure, he gave a sharp *heel* to the dogs as well—they'd been quiet but cocking a hairy eye at the local mutts, a couple of whom had drifted back and were making little barking rushes now and then as if to say *we'll run you off our territory whenever we like, you just see if we don't,* despite the fact that the biggest of the skinny sharp-muzzled mongrels was about half the weight of Fenris or Ulf or the Princess' dog Macmac.

The greathounds' massive heads turned towards the human stranger as well, but his word restrained them. Macmac looked back over his shoulder to the ship, just to check that Órlaith had nothing to say on the matter. Dogs and men weren't all that different in their inclinations, though human kind were supposed to be better at mastering them.

Yet if this lad isn't a young ram exchanging a head-butt with his sire and proclaiming how he's a grown man the now with each swaggering step, I've had never seen one . . . Or been *one, come to it, and that recently.*

The stranger was a little younger than Karl, or Mathun for that matter; younger perhaps than Faramir or Morfind, who with their Sioux friend were up with the leaders. Too young to raise more than a thin wisp of brown beard on his tanned face, and a trifle shorter than either though broad-shouldered and leanly strong. His torso was bare save for an archer's bracer of rather crudely tooled leather on his left forearm, a handsome cougar-skin cloak pinned at one shoulder, a necklace made from its teeth and claws, and the hide quiver slung over his back. His bow was a single stave of lemonwood, strung to be ready for action but with no arrow nocked.

Karl cast an expert's eye on the weapon and decided it was made honestly and with some skill, but with no particular subtlety and more of a hunting tool than a war-bow by the standards he'd been reared in. The grip was simply rawhide thongs wound around the middle, for instance. Save for the size it was the sort of thing you gave a ten-year-old for practice.

"Conan Tillman," the local youth said, extending his hand. "Hey there. Welcome to Topanga. That's my dad and granddad over there; he's Connor Tillman and granddad is Jared, who's a Brain."

Though from that flick of his eyes he'd rather be talking to Boudicca or Gwri or Gwenhfar or pretty Rowan, Karl thought with amusement as he took the offered hand.

Which was natural enough, and he completely agreed they were easier on the eye; from the way he'd silently counted them he must be surprised the lasses were so many. Well, customs differed.

And young Conan is after telling us he's not son of no one in particular.

"Merry met, Conan Tillman of Topanga, and merry part and merry meet again. You'd be named for the ancient king, then?"

"Ummm, the guy in the stories? Nah, my granddad's dad was called Conan. Maybe *he* was called for him."

"A name of might, still. Karl Aylward Mackenzie I am, of the Clan Mackenzie and Dun Fairfax; the totem of my Sept is the Wolf," Karl said, and shook; there was only a little testing squeeze. "This long lout here with his mouth hanging open and the flies buzzin' in and out, he's me little brother Mathun; also a Wolf, but a bit of a mad pup."

Mathun aimed a slow fist at him, and Karl grinned and rolled his head out of the way before he named the others, and saw the local's lips moving at the unfamiliar sounds. By now Karl had heard any number of ways of treating English; the clipped staccato of the Association lands, the rasping nasal twang and slurred vowels of the easterners from over the mountains, which came in many different sub-varieties, the growling clotted burr of the McClintocks, and the smooth fluting of the Rangers. He'd been making an effort to tone down the Clan's musical up-and-down lilt and peculiarities of sentence structure for the stranger's sake, which he suddenly realized he'd heard his father doing now and then too with *cowan*, outsiders.

Conan's accent reminded him of the neutral Corvallis dialect more than anything else.

Moishe Feldman's, say.

But even flatter, more old-fashioned, and with an odd habit of a rising tone at the end of every sentence, as if they were questions even when they weren't.

"You guys are from Montival?" Conan said, trying and failing for a casual confidence. "You've got a *Princess* with you?"

"To be sure, though it's more a matter of her having *us* along," Karl said; which tactfully left out the fact that Topanga was also part of the

High Kingdom. "Not to mention her brother, Prince John. We're Mackenzies in service to Crown Princess Órlaith of House Artos, the Lord and Lady bless her, and I'm Bow-Captain of this band."

Conan's hazel eyes went a little round. "There's *really* a Princess?" he said. "Like in the old stories?"

He peered out at the schooner anchored a hundred and fifty yards offshore, as if he expected gauzy wings and pointed ears, or at least a flowing train. Karl made charitable allowances for backwardness when he went on:

"The very same," he said. "Warrior princess, mind."

"Ah . . . no diss meant, but how old is she?"

"Twenty-one summers and a very small bit," Karl said.

"Must be nice," Conan muttered, casting a glance back over his shoulder.

"She's a braw leader and a bonny fighter, and not so stodgy as her elders. Or mine," Karl said. "Me own da was not overjoyed when I set off on this faring, I can tell you that."

"Would've pulled us back by the ear, that he would, if he'd had his way. But we had ours instead, the which is more enjoyable by a mile and two yards, so!" Mathun said.

Karl pulled a silver flask out of his sporran, one graven with an elongated face surrounded by curling hair, and took a nip.

"*Sláinte mhaith!* Your good health!"

He held it out; Conan accepted it and sipped.

"Nice! What is it?" he said, examining the engraving on it for a moment before handing it back.

"Brandy from pears, to be sure; I got it at Eryn Muir, the Dúnedain garth. That's the one where they live in their flets . . . houses set high in the great redwood trees, linked together with bridges."

Conan's eyes went wider. "Uh, there really are people like out of those Tolkien guy's stories? They live in *trees*? Man, that is, like, *so cool*. I wish I could see that!"

"Indeed there are, and some of them do, and it was worth a journey of hard weeks to see the same. Your kin have their steading hereabouts?"

That required a moment or two for the meaning of *steading* to get across, since the local dialect used *place* or *home* for that concept, and apparently Topangans said *family* or *bunch* rather than *kin* as well.

"Nah, our place is about halfway up the Canyon . . . that's north of here a few miles. Granddad came down 'cause the ship from Esmeraldas pulled in and the Brains wanted to talk with them about something, and he brought Dad and me along because *hablamos español* and he doesn't much—my mom speaks it. We're not the only ones of course, but we're family and we were there. The Esmeraldans've got a pretty thick weird accent in their *español*, but I can talk with 'em, turns out they're straight enough."

A scowl. "Though Dad handled the real dickering stuff."

After a little chat—Conan Tillman was almost pathetically eager to hear about the outside world—

The which I would be too in his place. This place is yokeldom's very homeland.

—Karl asked: "Did you kill that big cat whose pelt and sharp bitey clawy things you're wearing yourself?"

Hunting was usually a good way to break the ice.

"Yeah!" Conan said. "He was taking sheep and stuff over on Old Topanga, right out of pens next to houses, and everyone was scared it would be kids next. So I went after him. Lost a good dog when we treed him, God-dammit, but I caught him clean. Behind the left shoulder. At about thirty yards, not a long shot but the angle was tricky and there was brush in the way. He came right down and sort of staggered in a circle for a second and flopped, and I managed to get to him before the dogs tore the hide too much."

"Ah, that's needful work, by leave of Cernunnos and Lady Flidais. Warrior's work, to ward your folk."

"You've got cougars up north?"

"That we do, and their sad ways with sheep are much the same. Also tigers, and we saw lions farther north in Westria, roaring betimes and shaking their manes."

"Westria?"

"Ah, that's the new name for what the ancients called California."

Conan shook his head at the irrelevancy and went back to hunting: "Tigers . . . are they as big as they say?"

"Big enough. The biggest . . . oh, say eleven, twelve feet with another three for the tail. Around the weight of a small pony, or three big men. Mind, most run say two-thirds that, when they're grown."

"Whoa!" Conan said. "You've hunted them?"

"That I have. Though not alone, that would be foolish. Do you get the lions here yet?"

The Topangan shook his head. "Nah, not yet—I've heard they've been spotted up in Simi Valley, that's northwest of here, and we're getting more of those weird antelope things that bounce like rubber balls every year, and I hear the ones with the funny horns that don't need to drink are all over the desert country out east. You never saw that stuff around here when my dad was a kid."

"Cougar are fierce enough; cunning beasts too, by the Horned One. And was that nice lemonwood popper of yours what you took him with?"

"Yup. Here, have a look."

Karl took it and drew it; as he'd thought it was a simple self-bow about seventy pounds weight, just on the low edge of being useful for war, though perfectly adequate even for big game. You generally got within a hundred yards for hunting, and the beast kindreds weren't known for donning plate, or even mail, and rushing at you waving swords with fell intent. He'd seen a sixty-pound bow put a broadhead right through a big bull elk at close range, breaking ribs going in and coming out.

"Not bad," he said as he eased off—you didn't release the string unless there was a shaft on it. "Make it yourself?"

"Yup. Well, Dad cut the wood a couple of years ago and roughed the blanks then left it in the attic to dry, but I finished and tillered it. Say, that's a different way of drawing you've got. Can I try on yours?"

Karl had drawn Clan-fashion; drawing *inside the bow* it was called, starting with the bow down and your feet planted wide and your body leaning forward, then coming back into a slight squat with your arse stuck a bit out, which safeguarded your spine. In between you drew with a twisting heave of your whole body, putting your shoulders and back and belly into it as well as your arms, rather as if you were trying to push two doorposts apart.

He silently handed over the six-foot-six length of yellow mountain yew and black-walnut riser and polished antler tips. A serious Mackenzie bow was usually the user's height plus half a foot. Conan handled it with careful respect, examining it closely from one end to the other.

"Hey, I like the way the grip's shaped to the hand. And this shelf right through is for the arrow, right? What's the wood for the limbs?"

"Yew, mountain-grown; heartwood on the belly, sapwood on the back. Separate riser of black walnut root, with the limbs pegged and glued in, the which means you can use shorter lengths of yew, and you can replace them too," Karl agreed.

"Cool. It would be sorta long for the brush you get around here, though."

His own bow was about chin-high on him.

"I think it's heavier than mine, but let me give it a try—"

The Topangan drew the way a lot of *cowan* did, dead upright with his feet at right angles and his whole left side pointed at the imaginary target. After a moment his right arm began to shake with the string a little over halfway to his ear and the muscle bunched hard under his skin.

Karl's weapon would have overbowed him even if he was a Mackenzie, but he was probably strong enough to have drawn it—just—if he'd known how, despite Karl having thirty pounds of solid muscle on him. You had to be strong, yes, but no amount of putting brute to the bow could make up for lack of skill.

"Christ!" the Topangan said respectfully. "What's the *draw* on this monster?"

"A hundred weight a score and seven . . . a hundred and twenty-seven pounds. With a clothyard shaft at full draw."

He'd noticed that Conan drew to the ear, also common outside the dúthchas. Mackenzies drew past the angle of the jaw, an extra couple of inches. Karl added:

"We say you should take a tenth of an archer's naked weight, count that times seven or seven and a bit, and you've got the right draw for their war-bow when they're full-grown. Less for huntin', of course."

He grinned at the Topangan and slapped his brigandine-covered chest. "Seeing as the deer don't wear steel, d'ye see. Or even tigers."

"*Christ!*" Conan said. "You can really hold that for a real draw? And more than once a day?"

"Oh, I manage. And we think twelve shots within a count of sixty reasonable. Perhaps we'll shoot at rounders some day, or hunt while we're here if there's time."

Conan clapped him on the shoulder. "Dude, totally!" He waved over the watching youngsters. "This is my friend Billy—"

"Let me get this straight, then," Órlaith said.

One of the houses in the not-quite-town on the shore was evidently a combination of the informal headman's—headwoman's, rather—family home, workshop, warehouse, fish-drying shed, stable and a tavern or inn or eating-house for sailors and inland Topangans who came down to deal with them or swap for the coast's cured fish and salt.

It had a pleasant courtyard enclosed by rubble walls overgrown by bougainvillea in a mound of crimson blossom, rather badly set flagstones, and tables oddly constructed of slabs of what looked like polished granite fitted together, held up by more of the same rectangular shapes turned upright. She thought she'd seen countertops like this in ruins; the poles that held up the woven-straw umbrellas over them were aluminum, and so were the frames of the chairs, whose seats and backs were modern rawhide. The headwoman, who was leathery and fiftyish and had hook-and-line scars on her fingers, had set out rough brown bread and olive oil and brine-cured olives and toasted chickpeas and carafes of a truly vile red wine, flat and harsh and very strong. She'd welcomed the silver coins of Montival, but a gift of a dozen cans of tinned pork-loaf and a crate of ship's biscuit from the stores they'd brought had lit her eyes even more when they said they'd be staying for a bit.

Fortunately there was water to cut the wine with, because Órlaith felt she had to drink some for form's sake. None of the local leaders seemed to think there was anything wrong with it, which told a story.

Less bound by diplomacy, Reiko had taken a single sip, winced, and put the glass down. Heuradys had simply sampled the scent of hers and poured it back, and John's smile had become rather mechanical as he made himself drink one glass of half-and-half. Oddly to northern eyes there were also jugs of orange juice, an exotic luxury for wealthy merchants and nobles in Corvallis or Portland, and Órlaith switched to that once her courtesy glass of diluted desecrated grape-juice was down.

"You've a long-standing quarrel with the folk over the mountains in the valley northward, the . . . Chatsworth Lancers?" Órlaith went on.

Kwame nodded. He'd exchanged a single look with Egawa, and given another long appraising one at Droyn and the men-at-arms in plate and crossbowmen in half-armor, another at the samurai, and a half-incredulous one at Diarmuid and his tattooed McClintocks. Droyn was here with his visored sallet and gauntlets resting on the table, but the rest of the party was setting up camp in a vacant lot. Save for the mounted part of her followers, the Dúnedain cousins and Susan Mika and Thora Garwood, who were exercising their horses up and down the beach. From the sounds outside the folk of the two Clans were following her orders and making friends with the younger locals.

"Yeah, ah, your Highness. There were horse-ranches there at the northern end of the Valley at the Change."

His blunt finger moved to show the locations he meant. There were two maps on the table, one of Topanga Canyon and its immediate neighbors, the other of what had been Los Angeles and environs. Both were pyrographed with hot needles onto soft-tanned bleached hide, probably from yearling does, work done with patient sure-handed skill; she wasn't surprised that Curtis understood that good maps were a weapon and a deadly one at that. The lay of the land was obviously taken from maps of the ancient world, which was standard practice, but the names and political boundaries were modern.

"Up here the Valley wasn't quite built up completely in 'ninety-eight—hobby farms for rich people who liked to keep horses, mostly."

Órlaith nodded, ruffling Macmac's head where it rested in her lap. She loved horses herself, but the thought of them as a *hobby* was very strange. They were the way you traveled fast, or the way you avoided doing work with just your own muscle when you couldn't apply wind or water power. Still, *hobbies* like that had been important in a number of places, preserving breeds that were crucially important today. One such had given the sires of most of the draught breeds that hauled rail-cars and heavy loads all over the High Kingdom.

"And they had their own wells and water tanks and stored food and fodder. Some of 'em got together and forted up in those big houses and barricaded themselves and their nags, some pulled up into the hills until most of the people were gone. The Great Dieoff—"

She could hear the capitals.

"—only took a couple of weeks."

He and Jared looked very grim for a moment; Connor sighed slightly, as at an oft-told tale.

"Then they used their horses to take over what was left of the Valley, with this family named Delgado running the show. We had a showdown with Bruce Delgado, the first one, about seventeen years ago—"

Órlaith nodded admiringly at the explanation of how they'd foiled an invasion of their steep and rocky home; so did Egawa, as his sovereign translated quietly.

"Now that was somewhat clever," Órlaith said. "But unless they're too stupid to walk and fart at once you'll not get them to advance heedlessly up a narrow road below a cliff full of waiting boulders again," she observed. "With heavy horse all bunched together to catch the rocks with their teeth, at that!"

Curtis shrugged. "Delgado was clever, but he was an amateur. It's a good thing he died, though; he could learn from his mistakes."

"Sure, and that's the problem with relying on clever tricks and cunning ploys against an enemy who outweighs you. It's easier for them to get smarter than for you to get bigger."

Jared frowned and then nodded. Kwame gave her a long look. "That's . . . ah, no offense, but that's rather strategic thinking for . . . ummm . . ."

Órlaith grinned amiably. "For someone so young, Captain Curtis? Ah, that's my parents and teachers you're hearing. For that my father and mother commanded great armies in a long hard war when they were not much older than I am now, and I not yet weaned, and I was reared among . . . reared *by*, really . . . its veterans. No disrespect to those who've fought for their homes here, but we've had more wars and bigger ones in the north since the Change, alas, and learned accordingly."

She noticed something, a tattoo on his left forearm; an anchor crossing a globe, topped with an eagle. Her brows went up:

"You were in the . . . Marine Corps, it was called, Captain?"

"Yes," he said. "The Marines were—"

Órlaith smiled. "I *did* study history. And my father's father was a Marine. Mike Havel, you may have heard of him; hence I recognize their sigil. And he was a warrior in a thousand accordin' to *the Histories* and to those who knew him, with his own hands and as a commander both. And a fine ruler of the Bearkillers who they revere to this day, and his son is Bear Lord the now, Mike Havel Jr. A credit to your Corps."

"He was a Marine?" Curtis said. "I have heard a little about him, but not that he was a Gyrene . . . that's another word for Marine."

"He was . . . Force Recon, I think they were called. Scout-sniper. He fought in the Iraq War far across the eastern sea in the desert lands; 1991, in the Christian calendar."

"Damn," Kwame Curtis said, looking at her searchingly. "So did I. We may even have crossed paths. I take it you didn't get the interesting accent from him?"

"No," Órlaith chuckled. "That was from my maternal grandmother, Lady Juniper Mackenzie, first Chief of the Clan Mackenzie. *Her* mother was Erin-born, Lady Juniper is still very much alive. My other grandmother Sandra Arminger died only eight years ago, but Mike Havel passed the Western Gate when my father was ten. And there were . . . family complications, so to speak, so I didn't know either of my grandfathers personally."

In fact they'd killed each other in a single combat neither had survived. This Curtis struck her as shrewd beyond doubt and probably intelligent as well, so he probably knew that perfectly well. It was certainly famous enough that any number of sailors would have told the tale here, probably at one of these very tables. There was no need for her to get explicit about it.

"To business, though. You were speaking of the leaders of Chatsworth? The House of Delgado?"

Kwame cleared his throat. "So after Bruce Delgado was killed, his younger brother Mark more or less took over the Chatsworth Lancers, after some fighting. Bruce kept him in the background while he was alive; suspicious of the vicious little rat, I think, and with good reasons. Bruce was about eight years older."

"Mark's wife is the brains of that team," Jared observed.

Kwame nodded. "He's not stupid, but yeah, Winnie's a weasel in human form, it's not just a nickname."

Droyn smiled. "There's precedent—Robert Guiscard, the Norman warrior who became Duke of Sicily by craft and arms. Robert the Weasel, in the modern tongue. Famous for his, ah, cunning."

"That pair are cunning enough. But it took him years to get back all the parts of the Valley that had broken away from Chatsworth; by then there were more people than right after the Change and things had settled down. He only really finished it this spring. Since then he's been pushing at us like his brother did. Ummm . . . the problem is that someone, just lately, has been supplying him with equipment. Stuff we've never seen before. He used it to mop up the last holdouts, ones who had forts."

Órlaith's brows went up. "Equipment? Of what type, precisely?"

"Wheeled catapults pulled by a four-horse team, like a God-damned Civil War field gun and just about as effective. They've got at least a couple of different types, or they can be altered real easy to shoot different types of ammunition."

"'Tis the latter, if they're anything like ours. Do you have any close observations?"

"Connor Tillman here led a scouting party and saw it in action in the fighting when Mark's bullyboys squashed the last groups fighting him in the western Valley. Who, frankly, we were helping on the quiet, which royally pissed him off when it didn't work out as well as we'd hoped."

Jared stirred. "Worth trying," he said. "It delayed things, at least."

"Yeah, and it convinced him Southern California isn't big enough for both of us," Kwame replied, evidently an old argument.

"You're sure this gear is not of their own making?" Órlaith asked slowly. A tiny alarm was ringing at the back of her mind.

"They're just about up to making horseshoes and lance-heads and repairing a plow. We've got better smiths and *we* couldn't have done it," Jared said, and Kwame nodded.

His son Connor nodded too, and went to the entryway to the courtyard. "Hey, Conan! Get your mind off that girl and your ass in here!"

"My son was with me, mmm, Highness," he said to Órlaith. "He's damned good at sneaking around without being seen."

The young man came in just in time to catch that, frowning fit to make a storm, and did an almost comical double-take to hear himself praised. His father scowled at him in turn.

"He's good for something, at least, besides playing up to his name."

Somewhat to Órlaith's surprise, Conan Tillman made a clumsy but reasonably correct knee to her and bowed his head. She rose and extended her hand for the kiss of homage, and he not only did it but drew his shortsword—not noticing the slight shift from Heuradys d'Ath as she stood behind her liege and the fingers of her right hand flexed—and offered the weapon hilt-first over his left forearm in proper form. He must have been taking some quick lessons from her people outside. She touched the hilt and the steel and said:

"Arise, and know that your homage is accepted, Conan Tillman of Topanga. Let this sword be bound to the High Queen's peace, and drawn only in its defense, and hers."

Connor seemed to be flushed with irritation, and *his* father amused and alarmed at the same time, and Conan at least a bit exalted. Kwame had watched Heuradys instead, narrowly considering her stance and movements. He nodded to himself as if confirming a thought; probably that when Conan had put his hand to his hilt he'd been three-quarters of a second from falling backward with a narrow longsword-profiled hole six inches deep through one eye and into his brain.

Which was completely true.

"Conan helped with these," Connor said, notably *not* entitling her. "He's the one who got closest."

He pulled a rolled sheet of paper from a haversack he'd been wearing that had held the maps; it was tough modern rag-pulp paper, and he weighed down the corners with cups and bottles. The Montivallan commanders leaned forward. It showed a field catapult, one with a shield and split trail and two spoked wheels. The drawing was fairly detailed, and someone had done a color-wash afterwards to add more realism; there were four views, frontal, to either side, and from above. The outline of a man with a long spear or short pike was drawn beside it for an easy reference on size.

"That's not one of ours," Feldman said, and the Montivallan nobles all nodded agreement. "I know all the designs manufactured in the High Kingdom, as far east as Boise and New Deseret. From those cranks, it has a geared mechanical cocking mechanism, not hydraulics, and a straight spring recoil absorber. How accurate is this, Connor? Conan?"

"I was behind some brush about fifteen feet away for a couple of hours while the crew pulled maintenance on it," the youth with the ancient king's name said. "I saw them take parts off and put them back on. There was a guy in odd armor giving them directions, like, showing them how."

"Odd?" Órlaith said.

"Yeah. Little plates linked together with chain mail, and a big curved sword—sort of heavy towards the tip—and a helmet with flaps on the sides and a spike on top and a leather guard with metal studs down his neck. He had a bow across his back, sorta like the ones some of you folks carry—like the Dúnedain ones, only skinnier."

Recurve, Órlaith thought. *And that armor . . . the clash where Da died . . .*

Reiko made a sharp gesture with her fan, and Egawa and Ishikawa grunted expressively.

"Bakachon," she said.

Then she gestured to the plan. "That is very similar to ours, because they copied our designs. A shipboard weapon, but intended to be easily dismounted and put on a field carriage."

Órlaith closed her eyes for an instant. The little warning was growing shrill and loud now.

"Baka-chon?" Jared said questioningly.

Kwame had given the Japanese a swift, not overly friendly look.

"I think the . . . ah, the Majesty . . . means Koreans. I was stationed there and on Okinawa for a little while before I got shipped out to Iraq in 'ninety-one."

His right hand touched the missing fingers, and his eyes looked back over a stretch of decades before he went on:

"*Bakachon* would mean something like, ah . . . *dumb gook*."

Órlaith smiled grimly. She'd decided not to bring up the matter of contentions among the Powers just yet, or the sorcerer-kings who ruled the Korean peninsula in modern times. Even in terms of the politics of human-kind, things were plain enough, and Topanga seemed to be a bit old-fashioned that way.

"Since they killed my father the High King only a few months ago, Captain Curtis, I'm not going to rage at a smidgen of disrespect, so. For their rulers, at least, and what they've made of the place; no doubt the common folk are no worse than others with the same teaching would be. The same dynasty misruled part of Korea before the Change, I understand."

Jared blinked. "Wait a minute, *Kim Jong-il* survived the Change?"

"That was his name, yes," Reiko said. "His grandson rules them now, as sorcerer and priest of the dark powers and God-King, claiming a right to command all mankind."

Kwame's face twisted. "Luck of the devil!"

Reiko made a gesture with her fan and spoke dryly. "That is more true than you can possibly understand, Captain Tillman. Though we would say *akuma* rather than demon."

The younger Topangans were looking bewildered; Órlaith brought the discussion back to the present.

"And now it would seem they're helping your enemies."

The Topangans nodded; that certainly trumped any lingering habits from before the Change. Órlaith considered for a moment. Then:

"Could you give me a brief summary of Chatsworth's numbers and gear and yours, Mr. Tillman, Captain Curtis?"

They did, and Órlaith felt a slight inward wince. The ratio was not good. On the other hand, the Topangans had maintained themselves this long, which argued for basic strengths in their position as well as craft of the type the dark-faced commander had explained.

And best of all, they're telling me the truth. Perhaps not all of it, but they haven't lied . . . and I've finally come far enough that they don't know or don't credit the Sword's powers in that regard. Like the sailor in the story who walked inland with an oar over his shoulder until someone asked why he was carrying that strange-looking winnowing fan.

"We need to consult briefly, if you would excuse us, gentlemen."

When they'd left she looked around the table; Droyn, Feldman, Heuradys and Diarmuid of her folk, and Reiko with Egawa and Ishikawa.

"We've two choices. Involve ourselves in this, or take ship again and try from . . . Long Beach, wasn't it, Captain Feldman?"

"Yes," he said. "That's up to you, your Highness, but central LA is . . . very dangerous. Worse than San Francisco, if anything. Quite considerable salvage expeditions have just disappeared there, presumably overrun and eaten."

Órlaith sighed. "Including a few sent by my Nonni Sandra, to salvage artworks. Now in putting this expedition together, my concern was to keep it light and nimble. And here we are, where a battalion's worth of heavy foot, a few score men-at-arms and some artillery would be most welcome!"

Feldman spread his hands. "I could dismount some of my catapults, Your Highness. The problem is that if another ship shows up while they're gone . . . well . . ."

Órlaith nodded. "And our legal position is questionable. Fighting Eaters in self-defense is one thing, but attacking a civilized state within the boundaries of Montival . . . questionable, even though they haven't signed the Charter. For neither have the Topangans."

"The ones in our way are in league with enemies of the realm and technically in breach of the High Kingdom's peace," Heuradys pointed out, and Diarmuid and Droyn nodded vigorously. "You've reached your age of majority if not Crown age Orrey, so you have the rights of the High, Middle and Low Justice in provinces that are Crownland and not in obedience to the Throne. Westria *is* Crownland and obviously nobody here in this part of it is in vassalage. Technically these Chatsworth people are rebels if they don't submit at summons for making unlawful war, and you could take their heads."

"There is that, though we've never pushed it. Still, it would be easier if . . ." She snapped her fingers. "Ah, I have an idea there!"

Reiko frowned and spoke: "If we go south, these . . . Chatsworth Lancers might attack us anyway; there is nothing between them and that place, is there? They are in league with the enemy—and perhaps under their control. Also the *kangshinmu* of the enemy seem to have influence over the minds of other *jinnikukaburi* . . . Eaters."

"That they do," Órlaith said.

"So with time to gather them, they could bring overwhelming numbers against us before we crossed the ruined city. There would be many opportunities for ambush or night attack."

"Also, Majesty, your Highness, this means that at least one more *bakachon* ship is here. Many pr . . . places to hide south of here, neh?" Ishikawa Goru put in.

Feldman nodded. "Any number, Captain Ishikawa. Not much water available I imagine, but if they have local help that wouldn't be an impossible problem. Which means they could show up where we're anchored at any moment."

Reiko moved her fan decisively. "Better to fight here," she said.

"Agreed," Órlaith said. "Though I'm uneasy about turning this into a straight-up battle, that I am."

Reiko nodded, her eyes narrowing. "Better to split the . . . Chatsworth Lancers . . . from the *bakachon*, if possible, neh?"

"It'll require the talents of all us, in various capacities, and a few days delay at least, but needs must. First—"

CHAPTER TWENTY-THREE

PARTICIPATORY DEMOCRACY OF TOPANGA
(FORMERLY TOPANGA CANYON)
CROWN PROVINCE OF WESTRIA
(FORMERLY CALIFORNIA)
HIGH KINGDOM OF MONTIVAL
(FORMERLY WESTERN NORTH AMERICA)
JULY/FUMIZUKI 25TH
CHANGE YEAR 46/SHŌHEI 1/2044 AD

Sir Droyn Jones de Molalla squinted a little because the afternoon sun was bright and hot ahead as he looked up at either side of Topanga Canyon Boulevard.

Steep mostly, and then some of it's very steep, he thought. Easy to defend, but hard to till! In most places this would be a hunting preserve or just another stretch of nothing-in-particular with a few goatherds and maybe one manor and a few farms.

He was in half-armor right now, his back-and-breast and vambraces and the faulds protecting his groin and upper thighs, with the visor removed from his sallet. And he had half a dozen of the crossbowmen with him, as well as the locals' war-captain and several of his men. Droyn had been glad to get astride a horse again, even this sorry little borrowed nag, and see something new, even if it was steep and rocky and scrubby and dry. Sweat was running down under his breastplate and arming doublet, a familiar experience, but the sun was fierce enough that he was glad he wasn't a redhead like his mother.

"So, you're from the Portland part of Montival?" Kwame said, as the land rose to the crest northward.

Droyn thought he should have entitled his guest Sir Droyn, or my lord, but he was an outlander . . . and a man of rank, in the rude backward fashion of this place. One had to make allowances for isolation; and he was old enough to have been adult and set in his ways before the Change, which meant more allowances still. Men that old were rare now, and women of those years only a little more numerous.

"Yes, Captain, I'm from the Portland Protective Association's territories," Droyn said. "Part of the High Kingdom of Montival, and far from the least part."

He didn't know how much Curtis knew about the north, and it would be tactless to assume he knew less than he did. Her Highness had stressed how important it was to be diplomatic right now. He went on:

"From County Molalla, southeast of Portland and on the border with the Queen of Angels Commonwealth."

"That's what the de Molalla part of your name means?" Kwame said.

Droyn made a modest gesture with his free hand. "Yes, House Jones holds the county as vassals in capite of the Lords Protector of the PPA. And through them of the High Kingdom. But I'm my lord my father Count Chaka's third son, and so can expect only a modest inheritance. In my own right I'm just a knight in the Royal Household and the Crown Princess' personal vassal."

"Don't be too humble, son," Kwame said.

Droyn nodded. "Yes, my confessor says that false humility is an insidious form of pride. I am proud of my House, of course, for these arms have ever been at the forefront."

He tapped the shield slung over his back which bore the Lion-and-Assegai of House Jones, quartered with the royal Sword and Crowned Mountain of House Artos.

"That's our family crest. Chaka is the name of a—"

Kwame nodded; there was sweat on his dark craggy face too, but he was ignoring heat and effort with commendable toughness in a man of his years.

"I've heard of Chaka Zulu."

Droyn nodded back, relieved. "My grandfather's line were lords and princes in Africa, until they were cruelly enslaved after ill-luck in war and ground down by oppression."

"Oppressed by who?" Kwame asked.

Droyn hesitated and looked down. "By . . . Protestants," he said reluctantly, then glanced up with a flush of anger when the older man burst into laughter.

"Captain Curtis! These are weighty matters!"

Kwame held up an apologetic hand.

"Sorry. You're not even completely wr . . . ah, there's an element of tru . . . ah, you're even somewhat right about that. First Church of Honkey, Metho-bapt-etyrian. How exactly did, ah, House Jones turn things around?"

Droyn controlled his temper and went on: "After the Change my grandfather was a freelance man-at-arms with a fighting tail of his own, who threw his support to the first Lord Protector, performing great feats of arms in the Foundation Wars and becoming one of his right-hand men, so winning first knighthood, then lands and title and restoring the high and noble estate to which God has called our line."

"I can relate to that," Kwame said, smiling rather oddly.

Droyn felt very slightly guilty. That was the polite, official story, the one that got written down and taught in the chronicles at Castle Molalla and sung by the troubadours at feasts and tournaments. He didn't doubt the broad outlines, but though nobody was going to tell him otherwise to his face, from hints and deductions about his grandfather Droyn suspected the family had fallen a long way by the time the ancient world perished, and that the old rogue had actually been some sort of petty bandit chief with a group of ruffians at his heels. And a rough one at that until Grandmother civilized him.

Many noble houses skipped over the period just before the Change with a few vague generalities. Still, back in the Protector's War Droyn's grandfather had died sword in hand at the head of his men as a gentleman of the Association should, and noble blood would out even if circumstances eclipsed a line for a while. Droyn's Grandmother Phillipa had run the County for a long time and raised his father; there had been many widows-regnant then.

Kwame coughed into one hand, and Droyn controlled any offensive sympathy or offer to slow down. Old age came to those who didn't die young, and you could see that the Topangan had led a life of honorable accomplishment in war.

"Ah, Droyn isn't exactly a Zulu name," he observed.

"No, it's Old French," Droyn said cheerfully, moving on to safer ground. Any Associate nobleman could recite family trees until the cows came home. Most would, too, at the first opportunity. "My grandmother Countess Phillipa was of the Society before the Change—"

"The Society for Creative Anachronism?"

"Ah, their fame has reached far Topanga?"

Kwame coughed again, knuckled his brow as if in pain, and nodded. "You might say so. LA had most varieties of geek life. We heard that they were important up north after the Change."

Droyn frowned; he didn't know that term *geek life*, and perhaps the Topangan soldier misunderstood. Two generations of isolation might well have distorted memories without the sort of meticulous chronicles the Association kept, and of course there was his age to consider.

"The Society were a band of noble knights and their households, very learned in the arts and courtesie of gentlefolk and strong in arms. Hence they were ready to rescue and guide the commons when the world fell into ruin, and restore civilization as it had been under the great kings of old . . . Chaka, Charlemagne, William the Conqueror, Richard the Lion-heart, Arthur of Britain. Well, I grant that others managed too after a fashion, but . . ."

Captain Curtis made a small groaning sound, but shook his head when Droyn raised a brow; doubtless it was some small pain of age—he had to be at least threescore and ten—or from one of his many creditable wounds. The man looked like he'd been carved out of tough old vine-root and then hacked at until the axe got dull, but that was elderly in modern terms, past the age the Bible set as the span of man. That didn't necessarily mean he was unusually favored of God, but it might. He decided to make the basics clear:

"And my lady my mother's kin were also of the Society; she is a daughter of the Dukes of Odell. Many Society families are of high birth and noble blood, mostly from the ancient aristocracy of Europe."

"They are?"

"Oh, not all of them, but many. The knightly families and the nobility, of course, not the ordinary retainers—stout fellows those, though, and some have risen to rank and estate by worthy deeds. Our Society nobility is of the best blood of France and the Norman kingdoms; hence their traditional names. Though some are of Iberian descent, of the line of the fearless hidalgos who won Spain back for Christendom and then brought Holy Church to the Americas by their dauntless feats of arms."

He crossed himself. "Thus overthrowing demon-worship and saving many souls from the pangs of hellfire; or at least long eons in Purgatory. And many of them wed noble ladies of the Incan and Aztec realms. So you can see how the Associate nobility and gentry unite the glories of the past with the bright promise of our own age in Montival."

Kwame covered his face for a moment. "Yeah, I can see how that all hangs together."

"So it's fitting that as House Jones unites the bloodlines of princely Africa and noble Europe, we should take our names from both traditions. My eldest brother is Viscount Mpande."

"Very sensible . . . You work directly for the Princess, though?"

"Crown Princess, she's the heir to the High King's Throne under the Great Charter," Droyn corrected politely. "Yes, I'm her vassal-at-arms. Liege knight."

Kwame frowned slightly. "I thought that, ummm, Lady d'Ath was her liege knight?"

"Oh, yes. Her first—they're childhood friends. I'm the second. Sir Aleaume de Grimmond was another when we started this Quest, but he fell in the north."

Droyn sighed sadly and crossed himself again. "We were like brothers; but he bore himself very valiantly against the wild men. So a knight must expect to fall."

"So, what's she like to work for?" Kwame asked, focusing keenly. "The Crown Princess."

Droyn frowned, wondering how much it would be polite and politic to say. "Well, she bears the Sword of the Lady—the Lady being the Virgin Mother of God, of course, whatever the pagans say—and thus she's the chosen of God, monarch by Divine Right, so it's a privilege to follow her."

Kwame nodded tightly.

"And she's dauntlessly brave, a fine knight like her father before her even if they are clansfolk . . . and like her mother in her youth . . . and she is very, very smart, Captain Curtis. Also—"

He made a spread-fingered gesture; how to convey the truth to someone cut off from the modern world for so long?

"She does bear the Sword, which gives her many powers. To thwart evil magicians and break their fell enchantments, for example."

Kwame nodded. "I'm absolutely sure it'll see off any evil magicians we run into, and demolish any of their, ummm, fell enchantments," he said, his voice oddly neutral, though the sentiment was perfectly orthodox. "OK, we're getting close to the Wall."

Droyn put up his fist to halt the column and dismounted in the fashion of a knight on active service, swinging his right leg over the horse's neck and sliding down with his back to its body. That left you always ready to face a foe. One of the crossbowmen came forward to hold the reins, and Droyn nodded to him before he walked slowly and thoughtfully forward. The cracked, faded asphalt of the two-lane road was pointed more or less northwest here; there was a high rocky bluff to the left and the ground dropped off to the right very steeply indeed, and for several hundred feet.

He went over to the verge; the Topangans had smoothed the slope below, covered it with a revetment of smooth dry-fitted rocks to keep it from eroding, melted asphalt and let it run down over the surface, and built a breastwork along the edge. None of the work was very neat or tidy, but all of it would get the job done. Just climbing up and down that slope on foot would be very slow and might require ropes and pitons. Doing it in armor and carrying a weapon would be even slower and make you more likely to fall.

With defenders dropping rocks on you and shooting, impossible. A night attack? No, not if there were any defenders at all.

And there was no position within range where archers or crossbowmen could rake the defenses here. Even for scorpions or catapults rigged for bolt it was at extreme range or just beyond.

In the other direction they'd built a wall about twenty feet high across all but one lane of the road, and then back into the bluff, continuing up to parts that were very steep and rocky, with a fighting platform on the inside behind crenellations and staircases backward to allow forces to rush up—and to deny all cover against missile weapons for anyone who took the wall and came down it. The trebuchets were a bit farther back, but they were pre-registered and could drop their high-trajectory loads more or less where they wanted, which would be the road on the other side of the wall.

"Yes, I wouldn't want to have to storm this."

From the maps the road went in this direction for another half-mile, then bent back in a series of steep hairpin curves down into the valley to the north.

The air was hot and still in the lee of the wall, full of the sounds of insects and jays screeching, dark-eyed juncos chipping and tweeting, and dry spicy scents as well as horse and man sweating. Nobody was going through the open gate right now, though from the dung oxen and horses went this way fairly often, and from the tracks in it bicycles did occasionally too. It was logs in a metal framework and covered with more sheet metal, from the looks what the ancients had called telephone poles, which made handy construction timbers. More lay ready to be rushed across to brace against the inside of the gate when it was swung closed, but however strong a gate it was always the weakest part of a wall.

"Well, this is our primary fortification," Kwame said. "We've been strengthening it over the past decade or so too."

Droyn had been giving it careful consideration while they spoke. "It's extremely well-placed," he said. "Couldn't be better, given the terrain."

Which was true, and avoided being too blunt about its shoddy makeshift construction and very modest size. The older man pointed back and to their right.

"We have an observation post there too, called the Top of Topanga. With good warning, this position is very strong."

"You certainly can't get at it from over there"—Droyn indicated the steep drop—"and I presume there's no good path over those heights to our left?"

"Not for quite some distance." Kwame's brows went up. "You're an expert in fortifications?" he said. "You seem a bit young for that. No offense."

Droyn shrugged in a clatter of plates; he was young, young to be a knight at all, though not implausibly so. Though of course he'd had a noble's education and all Associates were born to the sword.

"Oh, no, not an expert, just the basics. I can lay out a fortified marching camp or the like. I did grow up in castles . . . my family's, and Todenangst and I've seen most of the strong places in Montival at one time or another, traveling with the Court, and studied their plans."

"What do you use as construction materials for those?" Kwame asked.

"Steel-reinforced concrete, and for the biggest structures salvaged cargo containers filled with various things and concrete and faced with more."

Kwame looked very thoughtful. "How do you move heavy freight like that around?"

"Horse-drawn railways and careful organization and enough manpower, where there's no navigable water. And patience. It gets done if you keep working at it."

He left out the dreadful labor camps the first Lord Protector had employed in the early years where uncounted thousands had died under the whip. Nobody, or nobody you wanted to know, was proud of that part of the Association's history, and most would prefer that it gradually faded into oblivion—though people in the rest of Montival were less charitable. He went on:

"Pyramids and cathedrals and . . . what's it called . . . the Great Wall of Cathay, that could be seen from space? They were all built without powered machines, and we have hydraulic cranes and the like, and better materials to use."

"Pyramids. Yeah. Sometimes I'm sort of glad we're out the way here. Or were until now. What sort of dimensions on the forts?"

"Some of the highest castle walls—Todenangst's inner keep—are eighty feet high and twenty or thirty thick and machicolated all along the top, with gate and wall towers and reversed approaches," Droyn said proudly.

And remembered the awe he'd felt as he rode towards that man-made mountain for the first time, heading to Court for page duty.

Kwame blinked again. "Good God, how do you take something like that without explosives?"

"You don't," Droyn said bluntly. "Smaller castles can be stormed, albeit at a high price, but the major works are essentially impregnable to assault or artillery if they're garrisoned and have the standard year's worth of rations. You can starve them out, but . . ."

"You'd really better not be in a hurry," Kwame said dryly.

"Exactly. Or you can take them by treachery, of course."

"How many of the damned things are there?"

"Several hundred, but only thirty or so of the major ones."

Kwame frowned. "I heard you had big wars up there. With those things all over the place, it sounds like everything would be gummed up and stalemated."

"Well, in the Foundation Wars and the Protector's War . . . some call it the War of the Eye . . . the Association had the castles and others usually came to grief when they tried to attack us. That was long before I was born, of course—before my father was, for that matter."

He left out the fact that the early Association had used improvised castles to nail down conquered lands in the initial drive, and then built more and better ones to hold them, not least against rebellious peasants pushed into the manorial system. Everyone was part of Montival now and the Portland Protective Association only about a quarter of the total, but if Norman Arminger had had his way there wouldn't be anything else but Association fiefs in the western half of this continent. He supposed that would have been good because Holy Church spread with the Association . . . but it would make things a bit dull.

"In the Prophet's War when my father was a young man, for the most part Montival had the castles and walled cities and the Church Universal and Triumphant didn't, their core being mostly eastern plainsmen, horse-archers, and it hurt them very badly in just the way you thought. Castle Campscapell in the Palouse changed hands twice, and we took Boise by escalade, but those were all after someone opened the gates from within. I've heard the late High King say it would have cost him ten thousand men to storm Boise if it could have been done at all. Major castles are even worse than cities because the circuit of their walls is so much smaller relative to the size of the garrison within, and an attacker can't get an overwhelming advantage of numbers at any one point."

"Ah."

The Topangan looked at the wall, which was obviously made of anything that came to hand mortared together with cement. He sighed.

"We could use one of those walls here now. On the other hand, then we'd have had to have all the stuff in our backgrounds that made you people develop them. All right . . . Sir Knight . . . how would you take this? And the Canyon?

"Well, I wouldn't try to use mounted knights," Droyn said, and got a dry chuckle from the older man.

This reminds me of the way they used to drill us with hypotheticals, he thought, remembering his time as page and—until very recently—squire.

"Artillery, basically, for this wall, and it's low enough for wheeled siege towers or even just scaling ladders, it really should have a ditch in front and a drawbridge. Secure the flanks with light infantry, crossbowmen . . . or McClintocks, if I had them . . . bring up engines, batter it down, drench it with napalm shell, then massed crossbowmen shooting—or Mackenzie longbows, if I had them—and heavy foot charging under their cover, dismounted knights and men-at-arms and spearmen. It would cost, but you could do it."

"Same thing down the road?"

Droyn nodded. "Being very careful to secure the heights above the road each time and bringing up the catapults. It would cost, of course."

He thought of something one of his instructors had told him. "If you outweigh your enemy, you don't have to be brilliant to win. You just have to be . . . not stupid. It is the weaker side that requires inspired leadership."

He smiled. "Your stroke with the avalanche, for example, Captain Curtis."

"Yeah, but Mark Delgado isn't stupid and I'm right out of inspired. I hope someone has some on them, and that someone isn't him. How many battles have you fought in, kid, ah, Sir Knight?"

"Mmmm, two, Captain, both this year and both small; one charge of knights, and a defensive engagement holding a hilltop on foot. But I was well-taught."

"Apparently. And now the Chatsworth God-damned Lancers seem to have the artillery. And we don't. The trebuchets have limited range and they're not mobile. We've tried to hire machines from passing ships, but the fact of the matter is we've found out we couldn't raise the cash to hire a kid in a canoe with a slingshot in his back pocket. We're just plain poor."

"Well," said Droyn, "we're seeing if we can do something about that. The Crown Princess has some very persuasive friends."

Moishe Feldman took a sip of cocoa slightly spiked with rum—quite good rum—and smiled at his host here in the captain's cabin of the *Virgen de las Esmeraldas*.

"Most excellent cocoa and even more excellent rum, Captain de Mendoza," he said, quite truthfully.

Antonio de Mendoza y Pacheco was a slim man of about Feldman's mid-thirties and similar medium height, with smooth dark-brown skin and well-tended curly black hair and a neatly trimmed mustache and pointed chin-beard framing bluntly handsome features. There was a crucifix around his neck, hanging on the breast of a loose shirt of snowy white cotton embroidered along the hems and neck. Snug breeches were tucked into half-boots . . . of which the right had a dagger-hilt showing. His long fawn-colored coat, a narrow-bladed sword with a complex swept guard and the baldric to which it was fastened were hung on the wall near the door, with a floppy-brimmed hat sporting a plume of some colorful feathers. Feldman's plain blue jacket, round peaked nautical cap and his cutlass hung there as well.

"Both are from my esteemed father-in-law's estates," Mendoza said.

The smell of cocoa and tobacco mingled not unpleasantly with wax and the sea-breeze through the open sterncastle windows . . . though there was a slight and less agreeable whift from the bilges. Silence stretched, with the Esmeraldan waiting with patiently attentive courtesy; which proved he was no fool.

The captain's cabin of the *Virgen de las Esmeraldas* was a bit larger than Feldman's on the *Tarshish Queen*, and the ceiling—the quarterdeck was above—was a bit higher as well. The curved wall of windows at the stern lit it brightly, but not too brightly with the sun overhead, and there was a pleasant moving dapple of reflected light on the ceiling above. This ship had roughly the same displacement as his, but it was broader-beamed. That made it slower, but there were advantages.

"He is as fortunate in the produce of his lands as he is in his son-in-law," Feldman said.

The décor was darkly rich, carved chanul and teak in shades of reddish brown and chocolate buffed and waxed to bring out the grain. One corner held an elaborate little shrine with the Virgin and a prie-dieu.

The silver pot and service were ornately wrought with Classical figures, and there were a pair of well-done oil portraits on the walls; one of a smiling, plumply pretty woman in a long white dress seated with three children standing to either side of her, and one of a stone-faced man in an elaborate uniform holding a scepter in one hand and a sword in the other, with a thicket of medals on his chest and a jewel-encrusted golden crown on his head—His Majesty Hernán the First.

Whose father Antonio had been a successful warlord who'd marched down from Quito in the chaos, famine and desperate mass migrations of post-Change Ecuador and made himself President for Life of a chunk of the northwestern coast covering several score thousand square miles. His son had decided to change the title to something more modern now that monarchy was fashionable. Feldman supposed it was all to the good; it would make usurpation and civil wars a little less likely, at least, if Hernán's dynasty generated some legitimacy by lasting a generation or two. Long enough that nobody living remembered anyone else on top.

Captain Mendoza should pump the bilges out more, Feldman thought automatically. *Apart from that, a well-found ship. Overmanned, though. Even if wages are lower in Esmeraldas than Newport, extra crew still eat and take up space. And a bit lightly armed for long voyages far foreign; maybe he's trying to make up for fewer catapults with more cutlasses.*

"More, Señor Capitan?" the Esmeraldan skipper said, smiling as put his cigarillo in the ashtray's holder and lifted the pot.

"*Muchas gracias,* Don Antonio," Feldman said.

They were speaking Spanish; Feldman's grasp of that language was much better than the other man's English, which was functional at best. He'd apparently had a nanny who had been an American tourist's child when the Change stuck them in Ecuador, and without that he wouldn't have been comprehensible at all.

"You are too kind; and *Don* is far too formal. Señor is more than sufficient for a mere merchant like myself," he said . . . or purred, with a wide white smile. "Though I hope to have a hacienda of my own eventually, you understand, and be enrolled among the new hidalgos of the realm. Truly my homeland has entered a golden age under our good and most noble and able King, one in which prosperity is general and anything is possible to a man of ability and character, with the help of God and His mother."

The southerner faced the shrine and crossed himself, and then made a little bow to the portrait of his monarch.

That and the fact that you can't mention His Majesty without a half paragraph of flattery tells us something about the Golden Age, Feldman thought dryly.

"And your Spanish is also most excellent, which is a relief among these isolated peasants," his host went on.

The sailor squatting by the door was also smoking, but something much harsher; he had a machete and hooked knife at his belt, and his face and bare muscular dark torso were heavily scarred above the ragged canvas pantaloons that were his only garment. A straw hat hung on his back by the cord around his neck, and there was a printed kerchief wrapped around his shaven head and tied at the back.

His snake-steady eyes never left the Corvallan as his captain went on genially:

"Believe me, it is a relief to have a conversation with a civilized man, a man of culture, one of the *gente de razón*. These Topangans, they are honest enough peasants, but . . ."

He shrugged his shoulders eloquently. "Peasants nonetheless. Believe that I mean no reflection on Montival; there are many just as backward in the hinterlands of my own country."

"I gather you do not expect to sell your cargo here," Feldman said, after a further brace of mutual compliments.

Which I suspect cover a damned judío *somewhere in the background,* he thought, and shrugged himself—mentally. If he'd been prickly about that, being a merchant was the wrong line of work; he'd have gone to Degania Dalet and taken up farming. *And I've met far less courteous ways of putting it.*

Mendoza laughed gently as he shook his head. "You choose to joke, Señor Captain Feldman. I would never have put in here if our casks had not been contaminated during the storm and I had not heard it was a reasonable watering stop. They could not buy one hundredth part of my cargo with all the wealth of their little tribe."

"Don Antonio," Feldman said—and found no further objections to the title. "—I profoundly sympathize, as one who has experienced the irritating delays . . . and the attendant loss . . . of trade by sea."

The cargo was in fact a rich one; a hundred and fifty tons of processed cocoa and cocoa butter ready to be transformed into drinks and confections, along with hibiscus-vanilla-scented palm oil soap (and dried hibiscus petals in sacks), bricks of high-quality indigo, a good deal of fine cotton cloth and planks of exotic woods that were naturals for the furniture and cabinetry markets—mascarey, tangare, Fernán Sánchez, jigua, higuerón, ceibo, sande, virola and guayacán. That sort of thing was in high demand these days, and overall there was an almost sensuous pleasure to reciting the names and contemplating the value . . . and beauty and usefulness . . . of what the Esmeraldan had below his hatches.

Mendoza raised his eyes to the ceiling. "And would you believe they tried to hire me to engage in one of their petty local quarrels? That is why I intend to sail with the morning tide, having replaced my water and taken on some fresh provisions."

Feldman sighed in sympathy, sipped, and put his cup down. "You were intending to dock in . . ."

Mendoza's eyes were blandly unreadable. "Portland, I had thought. I have not made this run before, it is so new, but I have spoken with those who have. A good market, and a very fine selection of goods for the return. And there is an acting Esmeraldan consul, himself a merchant of Portland who acts for those of my kingdom who trade there—there is a similar arrangement back in our capital."

"Yes, Portland is an excellent market . . . but no better than Newport," Feldman said. "Which has rail connections with the Willamette and the Columbia Valley, and is considerably closer. The Columbia mouth is tricky, even with a pilot . . . and the Astoria pilots charge highly, to discourage foreign traders from going upriver themselves. The Guild Merchant of Astoria prefers to see those cargos sold in their own city . . . for obvious reasons."

"Obvious indeed," Mendoza said and waited, showing that he knew something of bargaining.

"I admit there is a certain rivalry between my city and Astoria . . . but I assume you have heard of the First National Bank of Corvallis?"

"Indeed. Their letters of credit and other paper are accepted in Esmeraldas at very modest discounts these last few years."

"And at full face value in Newport . . . *and* Corvallis . . . *and* Astoria and Portland; in fact, everywhere in the civilized portions of Montival and as far away as Hawaii and Darwin. Now, I am currently under a government charter—"

True enough . . . for government work, Feldman thought, as he went on.

"—but my firm often deals in cargos of the sort you are shipping. It strikes me that our meeting is a gift of fortune; and as men of business, it is our duty to our trade and our families to seize opportunities, is it not?"

"Indeed," Mendoza said calmly. "And to distinguish between the true opportunities and unjustified risks."

Feldman didn't let the rhetorical trick throw him off stride.

"If *I* were to purchase your cargo, you would be able to save considerable time and expense by simply docking in Newport and unloading to my warehouses, rather than spending at least weeks, possibly months vending it in bits and pieces . . . with wages and charges mounting up . . . demurrage costs, warehouse rental fees . . . awkward dealings with bureaucrats unsympathetic to a foreign captain . . . cabals of merchants who all know one another combining to bargain down an outsider . . . all the problems of a strange port without contacts."

"Yes, that would be so . . . given a fair price, of course. But then I have to fill my hold for the return voyage or lose half the profit; I am not going to sail home with nothing but ballast and banker's drafts."

Feldman nodded. "And I am also in a position to provide a fair percentage of your return cargo. In bulk, immediately, saving you more valuable time."

"You are?" Mendoza said. "I am primarily interested in metal and metal goods. Esmeraldas prospers under our wise and benevolent King Hernán—"

Another of those little bows to the portrait.

"—Demand for tools is high, and we are not so well-provided with ruins to mine as you are here in *el norte*. And His Majesty is concerned to increase our capacity to build naval catapults. We do not care to be dependent on foreign sources for things so essential to national defense."

"Just so," Feldman said, adding to himself: *and so essential to keeping His Majesty's fundament on his Throne.* "Corvallis is closer to Eugene . . . a source of salvage goods . . . than Portland is to Seattle, and Corvallis is a major market, a distribution center, *and* a center of manufactures. I could arrange several hundred tons of copper and PVC pipe, for example; steel springs; machine tools and hydraulic cocking mechanisms from Donaldson Foundry and Machine, who I deal with myself; and wines and brandies of very good quality, comparable to the ones you get from the south—judge us not by the swill here—and goods exotic in your home, such as apple-brandy."

"This would take . . ."

"Impossible to be certain; perhaps a couple of weeks. With a letter of introduction and funds immediately ready for you to draw on from my firm's line at First National, you ought to be able to conclude the rest of your cargo quickly. The sellers will want you back, you see, on other voyages."

Mendoza's brows went up. "You are in a position to move this much by yourself, Señor Capitan? The cargo is of course not all mine, though this ship is. I represent a consortium of both merchants and landowners. And—just between ourselves—several officials close to His Majesty, themselves wealthy and powerful men."

"Oh, not quite by myself; Feldman and Sons is a considerable firm, but not so considerable as that. I doubt if any single merchant house in Corvallis is, or anywhere else in Montival."

"Nor could any single family in Esmeraldas. You would put together a consortium, then?" Mendoza asked politely; he knew Feldman was wealthy, but could have no idea what his relations with his peers were.

"I have contacts with other houses in Corvallis—Chong and Company, Antonelli Merchant Ventures, several others—which would enable me, or rather my brother Abraham who handles our branch in Corvallis City itself, to place the whole of it much more promptly than one, who . . . forgive me . . . however able, does not have the contacts we do."

"You can tie up so much capital on a chance encounter?" Mendoza said, both impressed and a little skeptical.

"Not in cash . . . but First National will be willing to accept the cargo itself as collateral for a short-term loan of working capital while it is on our hands; they know us, you see. In that way we can pay you immediately and in full without risking liquidity problems."

Whereas you would have to put up much more in cash, went unspoken.

"Which means, if the price is agreeable of course, I would be willing to take the entire load and have my brothers make our own terms with the others. At my own risk, and of course risk means profit; with a modest discount for purchasing it in bulk."

"Ah." Mendoza's expression grew cautious.

He might or might not have heard of Feldman and Sons, but he *had* seen the *Tarshish Queen*, which was worth more than his ship by itself and probably as much as the ship and its cargo, or nearly. He'd been particularly impressed by its armament; his own catapults were serviceable, but fewer and older. The ship and its condition argued for a well-financed, well-run firm. And one with good political connections as well; governments did not allow what amounted to private warships to those they did not trust.

On its face Feldman had just made him a very good offer, making his forced stop here a stroke of fortune rather than a costly *mis*fortune. Connections and trust were the framework of business, and he was being given an entry into the Corvallan world that would make him a profit now on this voyage and possibly much more later if he ventured north again.

It wouldn't be free, of course, but it would be less than he'd expected to lose as the inherent disadvantage of being a foreigner who didn't know the local ins and outs.

"And this *agreeable* price and *modest* discount?" he said skeptically.

Feldman named figures; Mendoza laughed with a theatrical scorn worthy of a demented raccoon, and they settled down to a dicker. The Esmeraldan turned out to have a very fair idea of market conditions in central Montival . . . as of about eighteen months ago. Information traveled slowly, and knowledge was power. When they had finally finished to their own satisfaction, Mendoza poured the rum neat into small glasses rather than in tiny dollops into the cocoa, and added slices of cut lime.

"I think we are now both sure that we have swindled each other down to the shoes on each other's feet," he said happily. "A fair bargain, then."

"The best sort," Feldman said sincerely as they shook.

Then: "And now, Don Antonio, I am willing to concede a quarter of a percentage point on the net, if you are interested in another little venture . . . for which there would be a cash reimbursement, drawn on

First National, equivalent to the cost of your delay here with a little for your own trouble. Understand, if you wish to simply take the deal we have made, I will raise no objection."

He reached into the attaché case on the table and drew out several crackling parchments. "These, you will see, are sight drafts on First National. Good as gold anywhere in Montival . . . well, anywhere they can read . . . and as you mentioned readily negotiable in your own kingdom."

"They are indeed."

Mendoza touched the commercial paper, keeping a poker face but unable to prevent his fingers from lingering a little. Feldman had judged his man well; the Esmeraldan skipper was more than intelligent enough to realize that a side-venture paid in cash did *not* have to be shared with the backers who'd financed nine-tenths of his cargo. It wouldn't be all that much compared to the total profit of the voyage . . . but it would be quite a considerable share of *his* personal profit when the voyage was put to bed, and with a good deal on the cargo nobody would be looking too closely.

"This *other venture?*"

"It has to do with the difficulties the locals mentioned to you. They could not pay you for your risk. My principals can . . . and without risk, there's no profit, eh? If either of us were men frightened of risk, we would stay home and be content with squeezing out a miserable pittance from safe trades, no?"

Mendoza sat silent for a while, sipping at his rum; once his eyes went up to the ceiling, usually a sign a man was doing mathematics in his head. Then he looked at the sight drafts again. Once Feldman had signed them they *were* cash, exchangeable for bullion or local currency over a large chunk of the Pacific basin. His home city's banking system wasn't as sophisticated as that of Corvallis, but it was well up to that concept. And much easier to carry . . . or to hide . . . than gold.

"Purely for the sake of my curiosity," Mendoza began, "what precisely would be involved?"

The Theatricum Botanicum had been a combination of open-air theater and garden before the Change; since then it had been used by the Topangans to hold the general meetings by which their loose government functioned, or didn't. Mostly it seemed to concern itself with defending the Canyon in their perennial struggle with the folk of Chatsworth, with a sideline in preventing internal disputes from becoming violent, as much by directing the force of public opinion as anything more formal. In a small close-knit community this sort of arrangement could work quite well.

The amphitheater was a natural one improved by the hand of man, a two-thirds circle of steeply sloped wooden benches leading down to a stage. Pepper trees and olives with narrow gray-green leaves grew around it, overshadowing the borders and giving a fair amount of shade, helped by the fact that the sun was heading towards the Santa Monica Mountains. If they'd had good lighting, or even mediocre, she'd have tried to get the meeting called for after dark, but local technology didn't run to incandescent mantles or limelight.

As it was Órlaith kept an eye cocked at the sun, and listened to the chatter and burble of the crowd as it gathered. Her own seat was in the front row center, easily accessible to the short staircase leading to the stage. The air smelled spicy and dusty and hot, and as the seats filled of wool and sweat and the maryjane cigarettes and pipes of which the locals seemed extremely fond.

The Topangans were alerted to sessions by messenger or semaphore signals, and apparently any adult could attend, speak and vote. Órlaith found it fairly familiar. The same system of sitting around talking and then voting by show of hands or dropping wooden counters in a bucket was how Mackenzies ran things at the level of each Dun, though they also had the *Óenach Mòr*, the Great Assembly of delegates, to steer the Clan as a whole under the guidance of the Chief, *the* Mackenzie, Herself Herself.

The four hundred or so gathered—with another hundred waiting nearby and seeing to horses, carts, bicycles and children—were probably a fair chunk of Topanga's adults and they crowded the place. They didn't take a census here either, but she estimated the population of the canyon at no more than two thousand and probably less. That meant the system had the merit that if the assembly decided to fight, it would be the voters themselves and their immediate families who'd be walking towards edged metal in the hands of angry strangers.

She was a little surprised there *were* that many Topangans; she hadn't seen a patch of grain on the steep and rocky way up to this halfway point much larger than what the old world would have called a front lawn, and there wasn't enough grass here to support big herds either. A good deal of the rough land was covered in Himalayan blackberry, which at least produced edible fruit, stands of tall strong-scented fennel, which could be eaten . . . and many waist-high thickets of Teraccina splurge and Russian knotweed, which were actively poisonous. She'd also seen hemlock and climbing mats of waxy-leaved and highly toxic Cape Ivy.

The Topangans fished, and they planted olives anywhere they'd grow, which was many places since once they were established olives would usually yield *something* even in places you wouldn't think would support a cactus. They planted slightly less hardy trees and bushes like pistachios and figs and grapevines and peaches wherever there was a patch of soil and a possibility of steering some runoff to it. They carved out gardens, often terracing them, and built up the soil with their own wastes and animal dung and ashes and clippings. They raised chickens and turkeys that could live mostly on the insects and wild seeds, and ate the rabbits and deer that tried to eat their vegetables and any birds they could catch and any edible wild plants they could find or encourage. And they pastured sheep and goats wherever they could, and a few horses and cattle and the odd pig.

They were a laid-back folk; in fact they gloried in how laid-back they were, probably to make an inescapable austerity seem like a choice. But they worked hard and got . . . just barely enough, and that only most of the time.

When we bring the High Kingdom's peace hereabouts, I think a good many of them will just leave, she thought. *Finding better land nearby, or working their way north on ships and such. Having this many people in so hard a stretch of country is an accident of history. The ones who feel the strongest link to the place and its ways will stay and have an easier time of it.*

Some of her own party were here; in civil dress, not armored and not overly armed . . . though swords were in evidence. A lot of the locals carried shortswords or big knives as a matter of course, though they stacked things like bows and spears, helms and shields outside. Reiko and her two commanders and a pair of samurai stood out in their colorful kimonos and *hakama*.

When there were enough present the senior Brain—Jared Tillman, currently—looked at his watch, nodded, and stood.

"All right, let's get going," he said.

The crowd all stood, and a song began—irregularly at first, and then louder as more joined in, ending with a rousing chorus:

My Canyon, 'tis of thee
Sweet land of the hippie
Of thee I sing!

She recognized the tune; people in the United States of Boise still used it, though with different words. She even knew what hippies had been, vaguely; Grandmother Juniper and her Singing Moon coven had apparently been called that sometimes before the Change, though the word had dropped out of use afterwards in most places.

Her grandmother had laughed about that and said: *Well, we won, didn't we?*

When people had seated themselves again, he went on:

"Well, let's get this show on the road."

Which seemed to be a ritual phrase, as much as anything was here. The Brains were considerably older than the crowd on average—she thought the youngest was in her forties—but wore the same plain shapeless clothes and sandals and moccasins, or in one case bare feet; a few of the spectators were wearing nothing beyond a loincloth and a headband, perfectly comfortable in this climate. The Brains sat on pre-Change folding chairs, with seats of worn nylon, and a couple of them clutched papers.

Jared stood and peered at the crowd, apparently not needing his pink eyeglasses. "You all know the Lancers are getting ready to take another slap at us."

Someone shouted: "You were the one who wanted to mess with things out in the Valley, Jared!"

"Shut up, Lou," Kwame Curtis said. "I was against that too, but we've got to deal with Mark Delgado now—and he's got better weapons. It's water under the bridge now, you can't say *sorry about that, let's pretend it didn't happen*. We've as well as numbers on us this time."

Jared nodded: "And Mark's a meaner son of a bitch than his brother Bruce ever was, and his crowd got rougher while they put the Valley back under Chatsworth. If they break through, I don't think they'll leave anyone except the ones they want for chain gangs and whorehouses. He doesn't just want to beat us, he doesn't just want to boss us, he wants us *gone*. And most of his important guys want revenge for the Battle of the Avalanche; half his Lancers lost their fathers there, or brothers or uncles or whatever."

There was a building murmur of dismay.

"We've stopped them at the Glenview Wall before," someone shouted, and got a chorus of growls and cheers.

Kwame waited it out and then said flatly: "We can't hold the wall against what they're going to throw at us. Without outside help, we're . . . fucked. Just . . . fucked."

Órlaith could feel his sincerity; most others here seemed to be accepting it too. Eyes swiveled towards her, but she remained quiet until the Brains called for a vote on letting her address them. It was nearly unanimous; she heard someone say:

"Can't hurt to listen."

She walked up the staircase and turned, thanking the instructors who'd drilled her in public speaking; she was a little nervous, but she'd spent a fair amount of time on stages. She knew the kilt and lèine, plumed bonnet and plaid she wore were exotic to their eyes, but she hoped not threatening the way a suit of armor would be. And there was a reason for her to wear the Sword.

"Friends," she said. "I am Crown Princess Órlaith Arminger Mackenzie, eldest child and heir to High King Artos of Montival and High Queen Mathilda. Four years ago, my parents sent aid to you when you faced hunger and many of your homes were burned. House Artos counts it their duty to help all the folk of Montival."

That got another murmur, a thoughtful one. The High King *had* sent shiploads of food, along with cloth and medicines and tools, and his representatives had simply handed it over, wished them well and departed. Few really appreciated being the recipients of charity, but human beings *were* capable of gratitude, especially if there was grace in the giving. That went doubly for promised help when they were feeling desperate.

"Now I and my followers . . . and our allies from Japan . . . are here and ready to help you once more; this time with sword and counsel, if you will have aid of us."

To be sure, we didn't come here to help you, and by "counsel" we mean "do what we say." In fact I was only vaguely aware of your existence before I took up the Sword. We're on a mission of our own and here against my mother's will. Still, it's all close enough to true for government work . . . when you are *the government, or part of it. And it's partly* because *of me that they're in this fix.*

There was more talking among the attendees. One shouted:

"Hey, Kwame! Can these people do us any good? I mean, yeah, they've got, like, nifty stuff. Really cool shit. Everyone groks that. But there aren't very many of them."

The War Brain stood. "We're a hell of a lot better off with them than without them," he said. "With 'em we've got a chance. As far as I can see, without them we're . . . fucked. And I've been doing this shit since before the Change, remember."

Órlaith waited for silence and went on. "But Montival is a kingdom of laws, governed by the Great Charter. I cannot simply make war as pleases me, even though I am convinced your cause is the better, and there is no time to consult the High Queen."

Who *would* almost certainly help the Topangans if asked, but who would also haul Órlaith and John back north by one ear each. Nor could any help arrive in time to do much good, from the way things looked.

"Under the Great Charter, I *can* act to keep the High Queen's peace by defending a signatory realm from attack with whatever force I have with me. If the Participatory Democracy of Topanga signs the Charter, I can act. If not, not."

The noise was deafening this time. She raised a hand, until it gradually died.

"The High Kingship is not simply a matter of politics, though, of making laws and leading in war," she said. "My father did not take up the Crown because he desired it, for he did not; he carried it as a burden that he bore for others, and in the end it killed him far too young. Nor did he do it simply because it was necessary to put down war and disorder, that ordinary folk might live as they pleased and each reap what they sowed with none to put them in fear, precious and good though that is."

She laid her hand on the hilt of the Sword of the Lady, and took a deep breath.

"The Powers—however you see and name Them—set my father's steps on the path that led to the Crown of Montival, and hard was that testing, that took him from the Mother Ocean to the Sunrise Lands and back. As a symbol and embodied power, they gave him this: the Sword of the Lady, forged for the hands of House Artos in the world beyond the world. Together he and my mother mingled their blood on the point of it and drove it into the living rock of Montival on the sacred shores of Lost Lake, and so bound themselves and the line of their descent to the land for all time past and time to come. I draw it now, not in threat, but to show you that I speak truth."

She drew the Sword into a breathless hush; there were gasps even then, as the more sensitive felt the world shudder. For a moment it was only glinting steel to the eye. Then she raised it high, so that it caught the rays of the sinking sun.

It *caught* that light, drank it, and gave it back. Brighter and brighter, like a shape of white-glowing diamond. A light that should have seared her eyes but did not, though others threw up their hands against it; a light that drew you in, to depths beyond depths.

With that light went a . . . not quite a sound. A humming note, a crystal chime that rang to the confines of her mind in a torrent of image and sensation.

It was her mother lifting her high while she kicked and gurgled before the windows of a castle solar, and John's chubby toddler hand in hers and her father turning and winking at her during a solemn procession. It was a crisp apple plucked from a roadside tree exploding in her mouth with savor, and it was the face of a friend by a campfire's yellow light laughing and passing the leather bota of rough red wine while the venison grilled, and it was the taste of a first kiss in the cool scented dimness of a Beltane bower. The redwoods of Eryn Muir in the warm evening light; snow blowing in trails of white feathers off the peak of Mt. Hood; a desert shining in stillness beneath furnace heat; the feel of a golden sheaf on the end of her pitchfork as she lifted it to the cart in the Mackenzie dúthchas.

It was . . . *home.*

And it would be different for each who beheld the Sword, *as* each one of them knew home to be, down in their heartstrings.

"For the lord and the land and the folk are one; so you are my folk of blood and bone, a common past and a common fate; your land is my dear homeland also; and I am yours."

She lowered the blade and sheathed it. There were no voices now, though she heard the raw sobs of those moved to tears by sudden overwhelming emotion.

"You are a free folk, people of Topanga. Make the decision that seems best to you."

The silence grew as she strode down the stairway and out of the amphitheater.

CHAPTER TWENTY-FOUR

PARTICIPATORY DEMOCRACY OF TOPANGA
(FORMERLY TOPANGA CANYON)
CROWN PROVINCE OF WESTRIA
(FORMERLY CALIFORNIA)
HIGH KINGDOM OF MONTIVAL
(FORMERLY WESTERN NORTH AMERICA)
JULY/FUMIZUKI 26TH
CHANGE YEAR 46/SHŌHEI 1/2044 AD

Reiko dreamed, and knew again that what she dreamed was real.

In that dream she walked amid the smell of burning, the dry unclean scent of things not *meant* to burn, with an undertone of scorched and rotting flesh rising to a cloudy sky.

People of her own folk wandered the streets of a great city, seeming to be almost as much ghosts as she. They were aimless for all their urgency. Their language was only a little strange to her, but their speech was disconnected, and mainly about food. Many were hollow-eyed, hangdog men in the worn remains of yellow-brown uniforms and peaked caps. Others wore shabby Western clothes, or mixtures of those and *wakufu*, Nihonjin clothing, with here and there a kimono—almost always on a woman. Ash drifted on the air. More of the space between the grid of streets was vacant than not, showing only the stubs and scorched rubble of buildings, or marks where the wreckage had been shoveled and pushed back out of the way.

The wreck of a castle stood out among the ruin of buildings modern as the first half of the last century had reckoned such things, with a thin bitter haze of smoke drifting in threads from part of it where the keep had risen, the sort of subterranean fire that could smolder on for months after a structure fell. Most of the people were on foot, and all of them looked thin, thin with the pinched faces that came of years of ever-worsening hunger. Now and then a bicycle or a rickshaw pushed through; her eyes widened as she saw a motor vehicle *actually moving*, though it did not look much like the many wrecks she had seen, being black and higher-set and boxy.

Once a woman with a bandaged face suddenly threw herself off the road and into the remains of a building, screaming a child's name as she knelt and scrabbled in the burned dirt. After a few moments several others moved to pull her back with rough kindness. She fought against them with hands marked by savage festering burns days old, twisting, sobbing:

"Please! I know she is here, I hear her calling *mama! mama!* to me. Please let me go to her, she is so small, she is frightened of the fires and noise!"

Folk looked at Reiko, but without seeing; brushed past her, touching in a way that was terrible in its lack of connection. The gap of time was less than it had been for Yamato Takeru's age of legend, or the days of the first Kamakura shogun, but something else separated them, something that resisted her presence. Something that tried to make it never have been, a fantasy that drifted away like mist.

The Change, she thought.

The thought itself rang like a bronze bell struck with a log hammer. Rang with truth.

I can feel it. It approaches, only a few generations away now, and all of time and space and possibility is compressed before it. Like a monstrous wave rippling down from eternity through the very substance of things, a standing wave across the years of mankind. Existence grows thick *with it, thick and slow and heavy and . . . fixed in place by its weight. Until the tension breaks in a flash of light and pain, and the great wild magic at the heart of things is loosed upon the world once more.*

At last she came to an open space of gardens and trees and pavilions. The buildings within were wooden and in the ancient style, low with roofs whose ends swept up. Several of them had burned as well, and the others showed scorch-marks where utter effort by desperate men had saved them; some of the trees had the yellowing leaves that meant they had been killed by the blazes.

As she entered the gates a little motor vehicle sped by on its way out; it was like a small box on four wheels, painted olive green with a white star on its sides and hood. A *gaijin* in an American military uniform sat at the wheel, round-faced and ginger-haired and grinning, with a rifle of some sort in a scabbard beside him. The small rear seat was crowded with cloth-wrapped bundles and a dozen swords—*nihontō* of several different styles thrown carelessly together like sticks of firewood despite their classic lines.

Her feet moved through the landscape of death.

I know this time, she thought.

With sorrow and bitter pride:

Just one century ago. Our armies broken; garrison after island garrison dying where they stood in storms of fire and blood, or left bypassed to starve; our fleets crushed wreckage upon the sea-bottom from here to Guadalcanal and beyond. The cities are ashes and the people starve. Shōwa Tennō *my grandmother's grandfather has surrendered to save the nation from absolute destruction. Egawa Noboru's father lies in his mother's womb, and* his *father is dead after he crashed his flying machine into a battleship, trying to hold back the invaders off the shores of Okinawa.*

And I know this place; *it is the Atsuta Shrine, where my father sought the Grass-Cutting Sword . . . and found it gone, long gone.*

She walked up to the entrance of a building where a sliding door lay battered aside; it was only then she noticed that she was in a kimono, and wearing wooden sandals that she stepped out of in lifelong reflex before she placed her feet on the raised floor. Within and down a corridor, she followed the sound of weeping.

In a spare small room a man dressed in a bedraggled white robe and purple *hakama* knelt, the tears running down through blood on his face—blood still liquid, dripping from a wound dealt by a heavy blow. He was old, and the lines of age and those of grief mingled to make a countenance like the *Ishio-jo* mask of a Noh drama.

"Curse him, curse the foreigner, curse all his thieving generations!" he mumbled over and over again.

A shortsword lay bare near him on the tatami, an antique *wakizashi*. As he struggled for self-control he reached out to it with one hand, while the other began to pull at his *suikan* robe and the kimono beneath.

This time when she opened herself the light that filled her was warm as the memory of her mother's arms, the terrible majesty muted by a compassion fully as infinite. Reiko knelt and touched his hand before she sank down opposite him. The old man jerked convulsively and looked around. He saw nothing, but he *felt*.

He gathered himself, breath slowing, tears dropping more slowly and then ceasing. When he was calm, his hand went towards the blade again.

No, Reiko said/thought.

Her breath was in her throat and her lips moved, but no sound came from them. The thought itself darted between mind and mind. She was herself . . . and something greater, something beyond humanity.

The man jerked again, but when he spoke it was to himself, as if taking both sides of an argument.

"No? Yes! I must make apology. I have failed in my duty to the *Tennō*, to the nation, to all my ancestors who were priests here for fifty generations, to the Great Kami themselves. The Treasure that She gave us is lost!"

Yet at Dan-no-ura it was cast into the sea, Reiko thought to him, remembering that very moment. *And it was returned by no human hand, to the hands of the one who brought it here.* Amaterasu-ōmikami *guards Her own, though the will of the* kami *may be accomplished in ways and times mortals cannot understand. Have faith!*

"The *gaijin* thief will take it over the sea to his own country!"

Yes, he will; it is the nature of warriors to plunder the defeated. And for three generations of men it will be lost to us, though all will believe it still kept here—even the very Emperors who receive the semblance of it at their ascensions. Yet what is lost can be found.

"Three generations?" he whispered.

In that third generation, warriors of our people will sail the eastern sea to reclaim it. With their swords in their hands and unbroken steel in their souls, and the cry of Tennō Heika banzai *upon their lips. This I promise you.*

Something relaxed in his face. His eyes still lingered on the pure curve of the ancient weapon, marred only by the very faint blood-etching of use.

"But it will not be restored in my lifetime. I am an old man, my sons are dead in battle. Why should I remain here to eat shame?"

It is your giri, *and your fate. Our people are adrift, cut off from all that they believed, doubting everything because what they were told by faithless men of power was false. They have suffered for putting their trust in lies. Shall* you *now use your death to tell them a truth that would be a whip of fire on their bleeding souls, the last cut that severs them from what they are?*

"What can I do, one helpless old priest?"

The men of war have failed in their duty; let them *make apology with their lives to the Emperor, and to his people who they have delivered to disaster.*

"And I?"

Now be the priest you are pledged to be! Our people need the idea *of the Grass-Cutting Sword more than the thing itself . . . for now. And that* now *is your inescapable duty. You must bear that which cannot be born, for their sake, as the* Tennō *has accepted the unbearable shame of defeat that our generations may live. Follow him! Let the suffering you cannot show and the truth you cannot speak be your atonement.*

The man bowed his head. When he raised it again doubt and wonder were in his eyes. Now he knew . . . or suspected . . .

"I am not alone, am I?" he whispered. "I am not speaking to the figments of my mind."

No. You are never alone, man of the Shrine, not while you serve Me and I protect the Land of the Gods. As you failed to guard the Treasure, now you must guard this secret. Treasure it, and pass it on as you would the other.

Slowly he bowed forward on his widespread hands, until his forehead nearly touched the mat.

"I hear and obey, Great Lady, Immortal One Shining in Heaven," he said.

She began to rise, to feel herself fading back to the waking world and the present. Then suddenly she *knew* there was one last thing she must tell.

And another thing is promised you. Your curse . . . know that made here, in this time and place and for this sin . . . that curse will strike home more surely than any weapon made by human hands. Like a tiger stalking through a maze of years and darkness, it will bring his line to its end in utter ruin. You will be avenged, kannushi *of Atsuta. Most terribly avenged.*

CHAPTER TWENTY-FIVE

Participatory Democracy of Topanga
(Formerly Topanga Canyon)
Crown Province of Westria
(Formerly California)
High Kingdom of Montival
(Formerly western North America)
July/Fumizuki 27th
Change Year 46/Shōhei 1/2044 AD

Connor Tillman grunted resentfully as he pedaled westward down the broken roadway behind his son and the stranger in the kilt, sweat running down his face and knees braced as cracks and holes hammered at him.

"Are there Eaters in this Malibu place, then?" Karl asked.

"Dude, it's like, nobody really knows, not really," Conan replied. "People disappear there, that's for sure. If you're dumb enough to go there without some company. Or stay too long, or all go to sleep at the same time. Other times everything's fine, but, like, it's fine when there are a bunch of you and you keep your eyes open and you go in and get what you want and get out, you grok it?"

"We'd say *ken*, but yes," Karl said with a smile. "So the answer is most likely yes, but on the other hand, perhaps not."

So they talk funny. Big shit, Connor thought.

Now and then the surface went soft but difficult where sand had drifted across it. He was in good shape; he was also many years older than his son, and most of the strangers didn't look a hell of a lot older than Conan. Lately everyone that age tended to look younger and younger to him, too.

I'm turning into my dad. And that doesn't even seem as bad as it would have once. Bummer, man.

Once they were a few miles west of the junction of Topanga Canyon Boulevard and the Coastal Highway they all had to weave around the rusted hulks of cars and trucks as well, though some of them had been worked over for salvage; leaf and coil springs in particular were highly prized.

There had been a lot of traffic on this stretch of the coastal highway between LA and Malibu at six fifteen in the evening of that March day forty-six years ago. You could see skeletons in some of the cars where they'd crashed into one another, grinning out through the dusty grimy windscreens, a few with scraps of skin and hair still dangling.

More bones lay thick in the brush and scrub by the road, though those had been scattered by coyotes and feral dogs and carrion birds long ago, and cleaned up to white by the ants and such and by decades of bleaching sunlight. A lot of shopping carts and dollies and such lay there too, used by the refugees to try and haul supplies.

The skulls lasted longest, and there were a few of those in sight every couple of feet. Sometimes a gold tooth gleamed. The bones didn't particularly disturb him. The Canyon's dead had been decently buried even when things had been worst from the older folks' accounts, if necessary in communal graves. But bones were there anywhere you went on a salvage expedition, which he'd done since before he was as old as Conan was now. It had freaked him out the first couple of times, yes, but that was a long time ago and everything actually looked less gruesome these days.

What bothered him now was the Montivallan bicycles.

Damn, why didn't we think of this? he thought . . . as he pedaled.

There were plenty of bicycles in Topanga; from what his dad said, it had been the sort of place where a lot of people used bicycles even back before the Change when cars worked. Every household had at least a couple now, and there were enough spare parts to maintain them.

But most of the machines spent most of their time in storage sheds or under tarps, more so every year, because the supply of tires had run out long ago. They got used again when a new set showed up found still in its packaging in a ruined store or garage, and that was among the most prized of salvage goods.

The young archer from the north swung a fist up and they all stopped for a moment, swigging from their canteens and letting the cool sea breeze dry their sweat. That let the horse-drawn wagon catch up to them too. The four mounted scouts fanned out ahead of them, sitting their horses with arrows on the strings of their short recurve bows and scanning the ruins to the south and hills to the north with methodical care. None of the Montivallans seemed to think it was anything special that three of them were women; in Topanga women usually only fought if the fight came to them, though there were exceptions.

Connor's father had muttered *Well, Women's Lib still lives, by God!* But not too loudly.

The Montivallans had functioning bicycles because they'd just accepted that they couldn't make pneumatic tires, and substituted *solid* rubber ones instead. They gave a rougher ride and you had to be careful not to get Melvined by the saddle dropping away and then smacking you unexpectedly in the balls, but they worked. They'd had a bunch of bikes so equipped on their ship, and Connor, Conan and half a dozen other Topangans were using them now along with the northerners. That cut the twenty-mile trip to Malibu from a long day's hike there and another back down to something manageable.

With enough daylight once you got there to accomplish something; a day and a half all up, rather than three or four, and less time meant less risk. The slowest element was the wagon and its four-horse team, and the riders on horseback.

Dammit, we could have done these tires ourselves, it's not like making watches! We could have, like, cut strips out of truck tires or something! Why didn't the old guys do this years ago? It wouldn't have been perfect, but it would work. Fuck it, we will *do that now!*

All the times he'd busted his ass when he could have pedaled, or just *coasted* most of the way from the Tillman place to the ocean . . . and it was a lot easier to push burdens on a bike than carry them on your back too. And bikes didn't eat precious food when they weren't working, the way horses and mules and donkeys did.

Why didn't we think of it? Hell, maybe it's because there are a lot more of them to have *ideas.*

That sort of thing had happened a lot since the northerners showed up a few days ago. His dad had actually cried when one of them told him that they were making new wind-up record players and that it would be—theoretically—possible to replace the treasured salvaged one that had finally given up the ghost a couple of years ago. It had been hideously embarrassing in a way he'd thought he'd put behind him when he married Luisa, though at least the old man had waited until the strangers weren't there before he opened the taps.

Plus Connor would have to listen to more scratchy Steely Dan and weird electric guitar sounds if one of those new machines ever made it down here; he'd thought he'd gotten past that, at least. Though apparently the things were made to order and ferociously expensive, ten times the price of a good horse.

The sea hissed against the beach to his left, or against the rubble edge of the roadway where the beach petered out. Or was hidden by ruins where there was a little more in the way of beachfront property, always an endless blue presence and a sound of gulls. The hills rose to his right—the Santa Monicas were barer here than they were around the Canyon. A rabbit scurried across the road, and he reached reflexively for his blowgun, but they weren't here to hunt for the pot.

And Conan's frisking around them like a puppy, damn it. That bothers me too.

"Forward," Karl said, and motioned.

The guys in kilts—there were two bunches, the ones he was with today who wore tailored kilts and were called Mackenzies, and the others with baggy wrapped kilts who called themselves McClintocks and had wild tats—seemed to have a whole language of broad gestures. They called it Battle Sign, and it was a lot like the ASL deaf people had used before the Change, but simpler and designed to be readable from a distance. They used it when they didn't want to make noise, and a lot of the time they used it even when they spoke too, to keep in the habit so they could just stop talking if they had to.

They all leaned into their pedals and got going again. Now and then landslips had covered the roadway or the ocean bitten chunks out of it, and they had to dismount and manhandle the wagon around and then shove or carry their bicycles. They were rarely out of sight of the water; once he looked north and saw a herd of springbok bouncing like a mass of manic tennis balls across a hillside and away over the crest in horrified surprise at the sight of human beings.

When they reached the boundaries of what had been Malibu proper the hills inland gentled down and swung away from the coast, silent under a bright noon sky. Many of the town's buildings had burned at one time or another, and spiny, weedy growth reached across or sprouted from their cracked foundation-pads, some of it still waxy green despite the summer dryness. Piles of tumbleweeds rested where wind had trapped them against something solid, though he thought there weren't quite as many of them as there had been when he was a kid.

Other structures still stood, the breeze whistling in broken window and sagging door; one had simply disappeared under a mound of purple and crimson bougainvillea where a freak of ground channeled water to its roots. Birds flitted in and out, and in the middle distance a coyote trotted across the road on its own business.

"We'll go on foot from here," Bow-Captain Karl said as they stopped at the edge of what had been a small, rich town. "Helms on the now."

The northerners all took off the odd cowflop-like things they called bonnets and put on their helmets, open-faced bowls with flared neck-guards that would give fair protection without restricting sight or hearing. Plus more shade than the bonnets would; you could tell they came from a place with a lot of rain and cloud.

Karl went on: "Bring the bicycles in the wagon, we'll need to load that when we get there. Thora, you and the riders are rear guard. Boudicca, Gwri, point."

The Mackenzies seemed an easygoing lot, not much given to martial stiffness, but Connor both admired the way they obeyed instantly and spread out, and resented it. He was tempted to argue for the sake of the thing. What did being a Topangan mean, if not telling people who tried to give you orders where to head in? But he decided not to; not least because it would be like stepping backward in time, with the young longbowman playing the part of his father and his own son looking on.

Also it would be stupid to pick a fight with someone doing the *right* things. Connor hadn't lived nearly forty years in the world the Change made by being that sort of stupid.

Karl looked around as they walked forward, eyes narrow. "There's more land that could be farmed here," he said slowly. "More room between where the houses stood."

Connor nodded silently at the enquiring look the archer gave him. The way his father told it, Malibu had been full of rich people who liked big lots and parkland, sort of like Chatsworth but not so fortunate. By the time the refugees from LA got this far, they'd been *really* hungry, and there was enough running water around here to keep them from dying quick.

"Why haven't you Topanga folk settled any of it?" the Mackenzie asked curiously. "Plowland being something you're fair short of, it seems to me."

"Some people tried," Conan said. "A couple of them lasted . . . what was it, Dad?"

"Two months," Connor said. "Back around the time I married your mother, just after the Battle of the Avalanche. But they may have been missing longer. Some of their friends came out here and checked on them and they were just . . . gone. Like they'd walked out the door and never come back."

He looked at Karl. "There's even better land a bit farther up the coast around Oxnard and Ventura, really good open land not built up, and lots of it. We haven't tried that, either."

"We should," Conan said, with a sudden blaze of enthusiasm. "We could all just pick up and move and not have to scratch at rocks anymore. Let the Chatsworth pukes spend their lives breaking up parking lots."

His father ignored him and went on: "Because it's the sort of flat open country the Chatsworth Lancers would really love if they could get at it. If a lot of us left, enough to keep one another safe, they'd be able to swarm through the Canyon and run a lance right up the ass of whoever had moved. And if it was just a few . . . well, I told you what happened to the Roghayeh family."

Conan glowered at him and then spoke, ostentatiously to the Mackenzie:

"The way the old folks tell it, a day or two after the Change, a like, huge *horde* of people came up the Coast Road from LA. Mostly on bikes, but a lot on foot too, some dying every step of the way but there were so many they just kept coming, day after day for a week or so and then a trickle for another week. We pulled back north into the Canyon and blocked the road and stood 'em off, but they ate everything bare and drank the creeks dry all the way to Santa Barbara."

"Farther," Connor said grimly. "A few got most of the way to the Bay. Lots got to Paso Robles, at least."

Silently: *I used to get bored when the old guys talked about stuff like that, maybe because it was them talking. For Conan, it's just interesting history that happened a long time ago. And your granddad's favorite stories aren't as boring as your dad's when you're his age.*

One night just after the last war with the Chatsworth bunch . . .

Christ, was that nearly two decades now?

. . . Connor and his father had gotten truly wasted with wine and weed; they'd both been in that one, after all. Jared had helped hold the Wall, and Connor had saved Topanga village from a sneak side attack when he ambushed a Valley probe trying to infiltrate along the old hiking trails, and he got back far enough ahead of them to give the alarm. The older and younger Tillman had started getting on a little better afterwards; his father had taken him more seriously.

When things got late that night Jared had talked about what he'd seen when Kwame sent him and a few others to scout up this road, a year after the Change. They'd needed to know . . . and after that, they'd known. Not all of them had come back, and for years afterwards the Brains had leaned hard to keep people from going outside the Canyon at all.

Most of the time he didn't pay much attention to the old man's stories and feels, especially that oh-we-had-it-rough-in-the-Change stuff, but . . . the tone hadn't been hectoring that time, or superior, just flat and . . . factual, spoken while he stared at the wall. His father had bad dreams for a few weeks after that, because he'd brought the memories back. Connor didn't, words were never quite like the real thing, but it wasn't something he liked to think about much.

"And some of 'em . . . their kids and grandkids . . . are still hanging around, I bet," Conan said. "So when we come this way to salvage, it's a bunch together and we don't stay after dark."

Karl nodded and whistled. Four of the monster dogs jumped out of the wagon and sat at his feet, staring up at him intently with their ears cocked . . . and their heads were easily over his belt-buckle while they did it, despite his being a six-footer or better. They probably weighed nearly as much as he did, too.

I wouldn't want those things staring at me, Connor thought. *Jesus, those fangs are as big as my little finger. If those are hunting dogs, what the hell do they hunt? Elephants?*

Part of the answer was obvious: they hunted people who gave their owners grief. He'd seen pictures of dogs that big, Great Danes and Mastiffs, but he'd never been sure if they were exaggerations. Now he knew they weren't. The thought of how much these things must *eat* every day made him wince. And that made him feel . . . poor. Which was a novel experience; nobody in Topanga had much more than anyone else. He couldn't even pretend these kilties were a-fucking-ristocrats like some of the northerners; from the way they talked it was obvious that they were just farmers and blacksmiths and hunters and whatnot back home, much like his people. They even seemed to run things in a basically similar way, talking and voting.

They certainly seem to get a lot more out of it, for sure.

The Mackenzie consulted his map, an old Rand McNally, looked around and snapped his fingers and pointed as he said sharply:

"Scout!"

The dogs split up and went ahead down the ruined street; they moved in swift bursts, stopping dead and sniffing with their black wet noses every ten or twenty yards, their ears cocked.

Karl made another sign, and two women followed, the ones named Boudicca and Gwri, Connor thought. Boudicca moved like a cat, and like a cat seemed to sense things with her whole skin. Her bow was slung and she held a gruesome-looking weapon in her hands, shaped like a heavy butcher knife with a hook on the reverse mounted on a six-foot pole. Gwri had an arrow on the string and slightly drawn as she followed, black eyes never still.

The rest of them came behind at a distance, arrows ready too. Connor slipped a dart made from a tenpenny nail stabilized by a plastic bead into the tube of his blowgun and brought it up. Some preferred a tuft of feather to steady the dart, but he'd learned on this type as a kid . . . and they weren't going to run out of either nails or plastic beads anytime in the next ten generations or so.

The dogs stopped, looking around and sniffing and then crouching slightly with their muzzles pointed at one building, a two-story structure with an arcade below and a second-story balcony running along its length. Most of a red-tile roof was still intact above.

Boudicca threw up a hand and everyone else halted too—the Topangans after a few extra steps, when they realized the northerners had frozen in place. She tapped two fingers towards her eyes, then used them to indicate the building on the seaward side of the street. The ground-floor windows and doors had been glass and the fragments of them lay amid drifted dust and sand and shreds of tumbleweed; gaping dark holes of empty windows loomed behind the balcony above them, with a length of cord swinging in one. That might be the wind . . .

The woman with the polearm—glaive, it was called—knelt under the balcony, then looked backward at Karl.

He made a sign. She nodded, crouched back on the balls of her feet, poised, then leapt suddenly and thrust the glaive upward with her hands low towards the base, quick as a snake's strike. It plunged up through what must be a hole in the floor above, crunching aside tattered board. Where there had been silence, there was suddenly a shriek of agony as she bared her teeth and wrenched it back.

A man leapt up howling, and was transfixed by three Mackenzie arrows in the time it would have taken to count that high, twisting and jinking under the massive impacts that smashed the broadheads through bone, then falling back out of sight. Another dashed out of the ground floor, a long knife in either hand, face a mass of hair and bulging eyes and brown broken teeth.

Connor had the blowgun's carved mahogany mouthpiece to his lips; he aimed and shot with a deep *huff!* of exhaled breath that turned into a hissing *psfth* in the tube. The nail split the man's Adam's apple from ten yards away, the yellow bead dancing against his skin as he collapsed in convulsions and sprayed blood from nose and mouth.

Boudicca brought the steel cap on the butt of her glaive down on his temple with a swift flick and a crunching sound you knew would come back to you later, then nodded a single brief gesture of thanks to Connor.

He found that warmed him, which was a little odd from a girl only a bit older than his daughter Maria, but there you were.

Two more figures started upright on the balcony itself, turning to sprint back indoors; one had a spear and one a pre-Change fiberglass bow and a clutch of arrows thrust through a rag belt, and he was trying to put a shaft to the string as he ran. Out in the street, Gwri drew and shot before the one with the bow could take more than a couple of steps. The arrow hit his back with a hard wet sound, like a sweaty hand slapping a shoulder, and he pitched forward.

In the same instant Boudicca had dropped the glaive, drawn her shortsword and snatched her little steel buckler in her other hand and sprinted unhesitatingly into the derelict building with two of the other Mackenzies and a brace of the hounds at her heels. There was a gurgling shriek from inside, and snarls like great sheets of ripping canvas, then thumps like bodies falling down a stair, then silence.

"*Sin é!*" she called out from inside. "That's it! Got two!"

A third figure came out on the balcony, then dropped to the floor and did a scrambling crawl so that the balustrade gave some cover; Gwri's next arrow went up in a blurred streak and slammed into the aged wood of one newel post, into it and halfway through in an explosion of bone-white splinters on a line that would have bisected him if the post hadn't gotten in the way.

The hidden figure turned into a scrawny, near-naked man as he sprang up and ran full-tilt down the rest of the balcony, dodging right and left as he ran, with four near-misses close enough to feel giving extra speed and some thin shrieks to his flight. Then he leapt down to the street, vaulting from the balcony to the roof of a rusting van, down to the pavement like a ball bouncing, then hurling himself up to catch the gutter of a roof that had slumped to within ten feet of the ground when the building gave way and half-collapsed. He went up the gapped tile surface in a rush as agile as the feral monkeys that infested the Santa Monicas.

That mad dash put him better than two hundred yards away, but the dogs were almost at his heels, soaring in huge leaps of their own. One missed its jump to the ruined roof and dropped back to the pavement with a yelp; the other two made it, but their paws made them scrabble and lurch on the tile. Which was probably why he kept running straight away and didn't dive head-first through one of the holes in the roof. Connor wouldn't have wanted to go into a confined space with those beasts on his heels either.

Conan's father saw from the corner of his eye that his son was drawing, though it was a long shot. Karl was leaning forward with the head of his nocked arrow pointing down. There was a brief twisting pull as he brought it up and drew in the odd northern way, then the hard snap of the bowstrings and a *whippt* of cloven air. On the crest of the roofline the running figure lurched up on tiptoe and seemed to flex like a whip as he was struck and flung forward. It was too far to hear the wet smack of steel in flesh, but Conan's arrow went through the same spot barely a second later.

"Anwyn take it, lost the arrow," Karl said mildly as he came erect again.

Crap. These people really are as good with their bows as they like to think they are.

I didn't think anyone could shoot so quick and be accurate with a draw like that monster. A hundred and twenty-seven pounds, Christ!

Karl grinned at Connor's son: "Not a bad shaft there, boyo."

Conan shrugged, flushing under his dark tan. "I missed."

"No, you didn't—I knocked him out of the way. 'Twould have hit him, so, had I not shot. He'll not be bothering us more, though, either way. Likely they were laying up and keeping an eye on us, planning to strike in the dark. Assuming they really were Eaters, the which is also very likely."

"Aye, likely on both counts," Boudicca said from just behind the Topangan. "There was a nest of them up there, and not a pretty sight, by the Dagda's dick."

There was a necklace on the red-dripping point of her leaf-shaped shortsword, held up for Karl and incidentally Connor and Conan and their fellow Topangans to examine. The thong was ancient plastic, probably fishing line, but the finger-bones and teeth were much more recent, and so were the dried ears. He supposed the bones could have been gathered from the roadside skeletons, but he didn't think so and the ears certainly weren't. He contemplated them with distaste as the Mackenzie flicked them to the ground, cleaned her sword with a swatch of weeds and sheathed it.

Conan gulped: "Well, I guess that settles the question of whether there are Eaters in Malibu."

Connor had also suppressed a slight start when she showed up; the Mackenzies all moved lightly, but he thought he could do about as well himself. He'd been a hunter all his life, and a scout in war. But *she* was like a ghost even by those standards. The dogs padded back as well, licking their chops and waving their tails with an air of self-satisfaction; half the northern archers were standing with their backs to the action, their eyes moving, and the mounted four were farther out still.

"If we didn't get them all," Connor pointed out. "And if they don't move away now."

He looked around at the ruined town. If there was a little tribe of Eaters in residence—resident at some parts of the year, at least—they might well have dozens of routes for moving unseen, holes knocked in walls and tracks through the tangles of saplings and brush that choked the spots between buildings. They would most certainly know every thicket and crevice and bush of the ruins better than an occasional visitor.

His skin crawled at the thought of being here after sundown, and having them swarm out at arm's length . . .

The two Mackenzies who'd followed Boudicca into the building appeared briefly on the balcony, looked around, performed the mildly gruesome chore of retrieving arrows, waved, and turned back. When they'd rejoined their companions, there was a brief joint prayer. They seemed to do that sort of thing a lot. This one asked someone called *The Mother* to witness that they'd killed the Eaters because it was necessary and not for kicks, which it sure as shit had been.

There had been Wiccans in Topanga and still were a coven or two—hippie territory, after all—but they and the Mackenzies had found as many points of difference as agreement after half a century of separation. That had seemed to bother the locals more than the visitors, who simply expected to meet strangeness among strangers. Connor considered himself a lazy Buddhist, like a lot of his compatriots, but some people needed more red meat on that side of things.

He was just getting used to the notion that the Canyon was not only small, poor and isolated, but conservative and backward as well. Other places seemed to have changed more since the Change, while Topangans preserved more of the old way of seeing things. Or at least his generation had, for all that they'd grown up exasperated with their elders for dwelling in the past.

"I misdoubt the rest will try us tonight if there are any more," Karl said. "Not after this. It can't be a large band and we probably killed every third fighter they had, aye, or better. Forbye they must hunt game and gather for the most of their food by now, so they're at our throats by habit and because we're on their runs, not because they must."

Connor looked around again. "I'd just as soon not chance it. There's no telling where they'll pop up—there might even be intact sewers so they could travel underground."

Karl nodded. "Right you are, and that's a good thought. We'll pull out a little east on the road back and camp in that stretch of open ground after we get what we came for, keeping careful watch, so. I'd rather not be within bowshot of any buildings hereabouts after sundown."

He looked at the map again. "And the target will be one street over, I'm thinking, the sporting-goods store?"

The Mackenzies chuckled at the name, with the sort of laughter that a mildly dirty joke got, which was a bit bewildering. Conan laughed too when one of them explained it to him. Evidently *sporting* had a slightly different meaning up north these days.

"Yeah," Connor said, ignoring the byplay. "We cleaned it out six years ago and the stuff you want was still there. Never saw any use for it."

"But now we do!" Conan crowed; he was getting his color back, after the brief spasm of deadly violence. "Flying! This is gonna be, like, *so cool*!"

From fifteen hundred feet the Top of Topanga gave you an unsurpassed view northward into the Valley, all the way across to the Santa Susanas lying blue on the northern horizon and the San Gabriels eastward; two hundred and sixty square miles of ruin all laid out below you, and with a lot of detail if you used a powerful telescope. It was one of the reasons Chatsworth had never been able to rush the Wall by surprise.

"Why didn't we think of this?" Jared Tillman said. "Once the Chatsworth Lancers came up with the damned catapults."

"Were loaned the catapults by Kim Jong-Il's grandson, apparently . . . and ain't *that* a kick in the head . . . but you've got a point."

Jared and Kwame sat waiting patiently in the shade of a stone pine. The tracks up here weren't passable for wheeled vehicles anymore, what with washouts and landslips and plain decay; thickets of bamboo-like Giant Cane had to be slashed out of the way to widen the narrow footpath, and it would take a while for the packhorses and people plain lugging things to get here and this part of the plan to get moving, and they were spectators now anyway. They couldn't have done it earlier, it was too likely to be noticed.

Jared took another long draw on his pipe, the sweet musky odor of the weed trailing back west with the prevailing wind from the north.

"And apparently Kim Jong-Il's grandson is sort of a cheapjack Sauron knockoff these days," he said. "With his lackeys puttin' on the orc."

"Well, that's the version we're getting," Kwame said judiciously. "I'm sure not feeling much love for them from the northerners, *or* the Japanese."

"If he's arming Mark the Merciless and Winnie the Weasel, I'll go with the Dark Lord thing."

There was a persistent updraft here, warm and dry this time of year, and the sun-warmed stone at his back was easy on his old bones.

"Damned if I know why we *didn't* come up with this," Kwame said thoughtfully. "Yes, it's a desperation ploy and it would be much more so for us to try alone, but we *could* have done it with some practice if we'd thought of it. Done most of it, at least. We're not exactly combat virgins ourselves."

Jared grunted; he wasn't, and had the scars to prove it. But Kwame had been a professional in the Marines, and led Topanga's fighters at need for more than forty years in the intervals between raising olives and goats. Yet . . .

"I think Connor was right. There just aren't very many of us and most of us are busy squeezing out a living most of every day and trying to relax when we're not doing that or sleeping. The amount of wondering time we've got is limited," Jared said. "He's right about the youngsters thinking the sun shines out of the Northerners' orifices, too, though I'm not as worried about that as he is."

Kwame shrugged. "Not worried about outsiders corrupting our pure Topangan culture and leading our youth astray, you mean? Christ, Connor has grown up, hasn't he? And you and I have gotten past the age when you think you're going to save the day by being serious every minute."

They shared a chuckle, and Jared jerked his thumb northward, indicating not the Valley or the corpse of California beyond but the inhabited lands after that.

"There are millions of them up there, Kwame, and they've got a lot bigger leisure class who can sit and think, and hire people to make stuff."

Kwame began to laugh outright, and Jared glanced at him with a flash of irritation that would have been sharper except for the pipe he was smoking.

"You were, what, twenty when the Change hit?" the War Brain said.

"Yeah, twenty and a bit. You were thirty, right? Doesn't seem so important now."

Kwame nodded. "Not between us, no. But maybe it's a bit more ironic for me seeing jaws drop at the awesomeness of a huge, huge population of *nearly five whole millions* in a country covering a third of this continent, say a tight teeming crowded cheek-by-jowl average of two-point-something people per square mile, with seventy-five thousand in their biggest city? Greater LA had what, twelve million? SoCal maybe sixteen all up?"

Jared laughed himself; it was funny when you looked at it that way. Laughing was better than letting your memories bleed and then sobbing and getting sad-drunk, anyway. A bit of casual conversation with Moishe Feldman came back to him and he went on:

"What's really ironic is that they say *Des Moines, Iowa* is the giant sophisticated metropolis of North America, the place people in *Montival* talk about with awe, the biggest city between Panama and the Arctic. A hundred and fifty thousand square-headed blond hicks eating bacon and cornbread in the center of flyover country and they're where the action's at. Whoa, man! I guess we Angelenos are the hicks now."

Kwame grinned unsympathetically. "No, our grandkids are the hicks. With cougar-tooth necklaces. We seem to have rejoined civilization as Inbred Cousin Jeb from Toothless Holler, like it or not. We're the real Beverly Hillbillies."

The reference went past Jared, until he searched his memories for old reruns seen when he was a kid and laughed. Then his voice grew wistful:

"Did you know you can just go in to a restaurant in Portland or Corvallis or Boise and order a burger or a pizza?" he said, and sighed; so did Kwame. "I heard one of the . . . guys with the crossbows . . . grousing to his buddy about how much he missed that. That and cold beer."

"And you didn't strangle the bastard?" Kwame exclaimed.

"Not when he was in armor and I had four decades on him, but God I felt like it. Burgers! Cold beer! Dude, no shit, tell me! I've been missing it a hell of a lot more than you have, and for forty-six years."

Spit ran into his mouth at the thought . . . and memory . . . of a cheeseburger smoking off the grill with a side of fries and onion rings, despite a reasonably adequate dinner not long past. In modern Topanga you ate what you had, if you had it, which was mostly mush and vegetables and olives and a little cheese or fish or maybe rabbit if you were lucky. If you went to someone else's home, you ate what *they* had . . . which was mostly pretty much the same.

For a wedding or a funeral, in a good year, someone might slaughter a goat and roast it to be washed down with lousy wine accompanied by actual *bread*. The Valley had a couple of restaurants; the Canyon didn't. The closest thing was the sort-of-bar Maureen's family ran down at the beach which catered to sailors when a ship was in, and she just served booze and snacks and would cook what you brought her. He was used to it all by now, but he hadn't grown up that way.

"I, for one, welcome our new Oregonian overlords," Jared intoned, and blew a smoke ring.

Then he had to explain it for Kwame, whose parents hadn't been into movie adaptations of H.G. Wells—that one had come out just before he was born—and who hadn't watched *The Simpsons* either. He returned his gaze to the view behind him. The shadows were lengthening to the west, and . . .

"You know something?" Jared said. "It just occurs to me that this view really *has* changed since the Change. Crept up on me but this makes me think back. Changed even in the last ten, fifteen years."

"Well, yes," Kwame said. "I should think so."

He'd always had a more precise diction than Jared, though he could also cuss better than anyone else in Topanga, which might be the Marine Corps talking.

The finicky part must be Annapolis, Jared thought.

As far as he knew Kwame was LA born and bred and his father had been a high-powered lawyer with political connections in the California

Democratic Party. He'd just happened to be visiting Topanga on leave that St. Patrick's Day of 1998. Down from the family home in Calabasas for dinner at the Inn of the Seventh Ray with one Anne McGillicuddy, and he'd still had the ring in his pocket when the flash of light and pain hit. Since they were both still alive and still married forty-six years later, with two sons, two daughters and a round dozen grandkids, at least something positive had come of the evening the world ended.

Jared found one son and four-and-counting grandkids enough effort . . . though being a granddad had most of the fun of parenting and far less work. Maybe that had been different before the Change, but he didn't think so.

"Remember the fires in 'eighteen?" Kwame went on. "God, the smoke was almost as bad as the Change Year. Must have been another couple of dozen people died of black lung coughs that time, even with everyone tying wet cloths over their mouths."

Jared nodded, trying to see the view as someone who'd come to it new would.

There were some tall buildings, whose earthquake-canted, fire-scorched, rusted hulks were still visible down in the huge oval basin, but most of the San Fernando had been wall-to-wall suburbs and low-rise commercial buildings, nearly all built in the classic balloon frame style of two-by-fours and plywood under the stucco or siding. Fall brought the hot dry Santa Ana devil-winds and sparks from something or other. The Valley hadn't gotten the sort of week-long firestorm towering into the stratosphere that had consumed central LA a couple of years after the Change, hot enough to burn asphalt and steel itself, but by now nearly everything that *could* burn in a normal flame *had* burned one year or another. Unless someone was actively protecting it, and sometimes even if they were.

The swimming pools had turned into traps for runoff, gradually filled with rubbish and silt, became little seasonal marshes and then grew up in thickets of locust and oaks, false banana and bamboo, citrus and morning glories and impenetrable tangles of roses. The ditches and storm drains had blocked one by one, and once the water couldn't run away the pavements and foundations had concentrated the winter rains on former lawns and gardens, doubling the effective total on the areas that weren't covered, and *they'd* grown up in hardy trees or bushes, whose roots were breaking up the pavements one slow inch at a time.

People had gradually turned the concrete-lined LA river into a series of ponds that shrank and swelled with the seasons and dried out totally only in bad years; mainly by dumping stuff in and packing dirt layered with plastic around it as checkdams to catch the winter floods that poured down the streets, supplemented by the natural tendency of junk to wash downstream. And the water-table had risen steadily again, now that it wasn't pumped dry by deep wells; more springs and seeps and natural swamps had reappeared every year . . . except in the occasional drought.

From here, going on a couple of thousand feet up and miles away, most of the San Fernando Valley looked more like a sort of scrubby patchy savannah interspersed with dusty bare zones of cracked, tilted concrete foundation pads, instead of a ruined city. Though the gridwork of roads still divided it and brick chimneys and the snags of cinderblock walls poked up here and there, sometimes through block-sized jungles of artichoke thistle taller than a man. The most orderly-looking parts were where those lawns and parks and laboriously-cleared parking lots and such had been turned into groves and fields and pastures, miserable enough compared to what the San Fernando had been before the city grew over it, but lavish by Topanga's standards. There were patches of that activity scattered around most of the Valley where small groups had managed to ride out the Dieoff, though the north and northwest had the most. He supposed that given enough time it would all look that way, centuries of hand-labor sweat undoing two generations of mechanized frenzy.

"All our visitors had was old maps and pictures."

"Yeah," Jared said. He sighed. "I hope we did the right thing, signing up with Montival."

"After that . . . fucking amazing thing with the Sword . . . there wasn't much opposition."

They sat silent for a moment. Jared shook his head. He didn't *think* alien Montivallan mind control rays were penetrating the tinfoil beanie he wasn't wearing . . . but something very strange had happened. Also he now believed what the newcomers had frankly stated about the bearer of the Sword being able to detect falsehood.

It probably makes you immune to genital warts, too. I thought the Change had opened my mind but maybe it was just putting the key in the lock.

Kwame voiced his thought or something like it: "I'd be willing to believe it glows blue when goblins are near if they told me so. Flets in Muir Woods, pardon me, Eryn Muir. But you know the really scary thing?"

At Jared's enquiring look he went on: "One of them told me it could stop evil magicians, and undo their *fell enchantments*."

Jared chuckled. "Why's that scary . . . Oh. Oh, *shit*!"

Because it means there may very well really be *evil magicians running around. Casting fell enchantments on those who* don't *have the Sacred Snickersnee of Contagious Goodness handy and someone with the right DNA to use it. Oh, I do not like that at all. Serious bummer. Maybe Kim Jong-Il's grandson really* is *a cheap Sauron knockoff with the Identity Bracelet of Power. One McGuffin to Rule Them All . . .*

Jared cleared his throat, and by unspoken mutual consent they moved on to more mundane things.

"That Great Charter's not bad when you read it, like we have to pay a share of taxes we impose on ourselves . . . but Topanga doesn't have taxes so our share is zero."

"We actually get more power than a State did in the old days," Kwame said. "People are free to leave anywhere they're living—I like that, and the prohibition on slavery and debt-peonage is sorta reassuring—"

"Christ, yes. I've been worrying about *that* coming back for years. Nice to see someone taking real precautions so that it doesn't sneak up on us."

Kwame nodded. "Tell me. Remember the fight we had to go through to stop people putting the POWs to work in the salt pans after the last war? But we get to decide who can settle permanently here, which I also like. Not that people crowding in to take our goat cheese and rope sandals are going to be a big problem, but still."

"But how many countries in the old days had great constitutions on paper that were just so much hot air?"

"Point," Kwame said. "Even us, sometimes. But I've got two counterpoints."

At his enquiring look the old Marine went on, holding all the digits on his left hand, the index finger and thumb:

"Mark Delgado. Winnie the Weasel. Their merry band of thugs."

"Point, dude. Like, *three* points."

"Two's as many fingers as I've got on that hand," Kwame said, blank-faced until he winked.

They both looked at the Montivallans already here. Heuradys d'Ath and Droyn Jones de Molalla were facing off with Prince John watching.

"Let's warm up," d'Ath said.

All three were in what they apparently considered plain practical clothes in their part of Montival. That consisted of pants, boots, long sleeveless vest-like things they called jerkins made of soft leather lined with light mail secured by patterns of tarnished copper rivets, and loose-sleeved shirts closed at the wrists by studded leather bracers. All in shades of olive green and brown and gray respectively, with small heraldic shields embroidered over their hearts.

They also all had a look that bothered him with a teasing half-familiarity until he thought way back. It wasn't just that they'd all have been medium-tall or better even before the Change, which was unusual in Topanga now . . .

Well-fed jocks, he thought suddenly. *Gym rats.*

LA in the last decade of the twentieth century had been full of people who put a lot of time in at the gym or marathons or rock-climbing or whatever. The idea of deliberately lifting heavy weights or running to nowhere because you had too much food was sort of bitter irony now.

They're not skinny people who have to work hard all the time on just enough food. But no, not gym rats either, not quite. They don't do it for the way they look.

He snapped his fingers. "Pro athletes," he said. "That's what they look like."

"Right," Kwame nodded; when you'd been around someone long enough you didn't need to talk as much. "Gymnastics or pentathlon, maybe."

"Or martial arts, yeah."

Droyn took a golden ring off his finger and flipped it high up into the air with his thumb, like spinning a coin. D'Ath drew her longsword and struck, and the ring settled neatly over the sharp point and came to rest a few inches down, where the blade widened enough to stop it.

"Those aren't big chopper-style swords like the Lancers use," he observed.

Kwame nodded. "Cut-and-thrust bastard longswords, European fifteenth-century style, the great-granddaddies of the rapier. My classes in military history strike again. These people use plate armor, I've seen their suits—miles better than anything Chatsworth has, even better than the real medieval stuff too because the steel's higher grade. You can't cut that with an ordinary sword, you have to be able to stab through the weak points . . . and there aren't many weak points."

Heuradys laughed and flicked the ring up again with a snap of the wrist, and Droyn did the same trick, dodging to the right to get under it like a big brown lynx leaping for a bird. The point of *his* sword ticked the rim of the ring; it circled for a moment and then settled down, and they repeated the process, moving like a game of tennis.

Jared thought of some of the other northern weapons he'd seen. "Yeah, that's why a lot of their stuff looks like giant can-openers on sticks. That's what they are."

After a moment Prince John made a motion to the short Hispanic-looking man who seemed to be some sort of bodyguard-cum-personal-assistant, and whose jeweled dagger was a mark of status in the Association territories, a sign that you belonged to the warrior caste. The man opened a handsome-looking leather case and handed him a lute, a beautiful piece of work in some rich dark reddish-brown wood, the surface of the neck inlaid with mother-of-pearl.

"If knights will dance, they should have music," John said while he tuned it.

He began to strum a tinkling tune. The movements of the game turned to a leaping galliard, without slowing at all.

"Jesus," Jared said quietly, trying to imagine how long you'd need to learn *that* trick. "You're not going to pick that up in the intervals between milking the goats. Useful, though."

"You said it. They can put those points *just* where they want them." Kwame smiled grimly. "You know why Delgado's Lancers . . . the actual Lancers, not the militia . . . are better than anything we have, man for man?"

"They're on the top of the heap down there; better gear, more time to practice. But these people make them look like cheap imitations."

"That's because they *are* cheap imitations. Without even knowing it. These people, their granddaddies may have been King Arthur weeaboos who got to live the LARP after the Change, but *they* aren't. That isn't costume they're wearing, those are just their clothes, if you know what I mean. They may not be much like any knights that ever lived before the Change, but whatever they are, it's the real thing now."

The Japanese contingent arrived. Instead of their colorful kimonos and *hakama*, or even more colorful armor of lacquered steel and silk cord, they were in tighter-fitting garb of dark matte cloth, stuff that would be nearly invisible after sundown and left them bleakly impersonal now. The jackets had hoods with face-masks that left only a strip over the eyes visible. They carried their two swords—the scabbards were black anyway—and some had those super-long bows and quivers. Others were fiddling with . . .

Shuriken, throwing stars, by God, Jared thought. *Yup, climbing ropes, climbing claws, grapnels, all the good stuff, they* said *getting down the steep parts wouldn't be a problem.*

"Instant awesome, just add ninja," he muttered . . . but softly. "What do you think of our new Japanese allies? I don't think I met more than a couple before the Change—Japanese-Americans don't count. Though they're probably why we eat sashimi. And I read a lot of manga, but these dudes strike me as seriously strange."

Equally sotto voce Kwame replied: "I was through Japan a couple of times in the Corps, mostly on leave. They *were* strange . . . you haven't lived until you've been nearly trampled by a horde of schoolgirls dressed as Chip 'n' Dale trying to beat the opening lines at Tokyo Disneyland . . . But they weren't particularly scary and they weren't much like outtakes from *Seven Samurai.*"

"But these guys *are* scary and they *are* like refugees from *chambara*-land."

"I think I know what happened."

"What?"

"Someone over there, maybe someones plural, who was very tough and very smart and very lucky and very, very *crazy* and obsessed realized the Change had knocked everything loose. He saw a chance to start partying like it was 1941 again, which he'd wanted to do for years, and took over whatever was left of the place."

Jared watched one of the dark-clad men draw his sword in a blur of speed, strike through a thumb-thick branch in the same motion, cut twice more in the time it took to breathe in once, and then wipe and sheathe the savagely sharp blade without looking down. The severed top of the sapling hit the ground just after the blade slid home. All of the black-clad figures went to their knees then, sitting motionless with their hands on their thighs.

"Probably convincing anyone dubious about the Ways of Our Forefathers to repent the same way Toshiro Mifune there just convinced that now headless and limbless scrub oak," Kwame added.

"Or maybe he wanted to party like it was *fifteen*-forty-one," Jared said.

"Or like 1998's idea of 1941's idea of 1541," Kwame said. "And everyone else got to live out his fantasy, and by now they think it's perfectly natural and was probably always that way."

"Whatever," Jared said; it was hard to get concerned about something so distant in time and space.

He looked at the scrub oak. The tough wood had been sliced so neatly that not even a single splinter marred the smooth slanted surface of the cuts.

The Brain took another pull on the pipe. "But I'm glad they're on our side."

CHAPTER TWENTY-SIX

PARTICIPATORY DEMOCRACY OF TOPANGA
(FORMERLY TOPANGA CANYON)
CROWN PROVINCE OF WESTRIA
(FORMERLY CALIFORNIA)
HIGH KINGDOM OF MONTIVAL
(FORMERLY WESTERN NORTH AMERICA)
JULY/FUMIZUKI 28TH
CHANGE YEAR 46/SHŌHEI 1/2044 AD

The smell of alien cooking drifting through the soft darkness of late twilight made Reiko's nostrils twitch behind the black fabric of her mask; some sort of stew of beans and meat and tomatoes with hot peppers. She brought the monocular night-glass to her eye, movements glacially slow and careful, and focused as she peered through the branches of the spicy-smelling sagebrush towards the target several hundred yards away.

Six catapults rested on the rough cracked surface of the ancient pavement, all under a tent-style roof of netting studded with pieces of vegetation strung between street-light posts dead since the Change; right now they were rigged to throw four-kilo round shot, though they could propel finned darts considerably farther. Unmistakably of *bakachon* manufacture though copied from a decades-old Nihonjin design, with that ugly squared-off look that came of cutting corners on production for the sake of speed. The two-wheeled, split-trail carriages were the type kept knocked down in the hold of a raider ship, ready to be assembled on the beach.

The Japanese had copied those.

Good. They have brought them together to guard them. And to guard them they have deployed . . .

Most of the figures around the campfires that bloomed through the twilight ahead looked like crudely armed militia. Which meant *gaijin* peasants, different from the ones in northern Montival only in that they were dressed more poorly, smelled as if they bathed less often, and looked less well-fed. Disturbingly hairy peasants, not least because many wore hair and beard in shaggy profusion. They were dressed in sandals or bare feet and rather unkempt pants and tunic-shirts of wool and linen and leather, and were mostly round-eyed and beaky-faced and a little paler than a Japanese with an equivalent amount of exposure to the sun, though some were much darker.

Those odd hair colors look natural on Órlaith and Heuradys by now, she thought.

The thought ran through some corner of her mind, as her training automatically noted numbers—around fifty militiamen in all—and weapons—mostly made by the peasants themselves, or salvage—and dispositions and state of alertness—which was low, but the pairs of sentries farther out made up for it.

But mostly it still appears like a costume, somehow, as if it were a badly-made coarse wig. This is probably simply unfamiliarity. If I had lived here for years instead of months, it would cease to be distractingly strange.

A dozen men sitting apart looked quite different, neatly barbered with clipped beards and shoulder-length hair combed out and sometimes caught back in silver ties, dressed in tight trousers and tooled boots with higher heels made for stirrups. Taller and more muscular, too; obviously better-fed for most of their lives, and though mostly young they had plenty of scars. They sat on folding chairs around their fire instead of squatting on their hams or resting on the ground, and ate from plates brought by deferential servants rather than dipping spoons into a common pot.

On stands nearby was armor that would cover chest and back, shoulders and thighs, arms and shins, and helms with wire mesh face-protectors. It all had the dimpled look of steel cold-worked by hammering over a wooden form, and the metal shapes were fastened to soft deerhide backing by copper or aluminum rivets. Tall lances—often with aluminum shafts—rested in portable wooden racks, but the men kept their long straight swords by their sides, matched by daggers at the other hip. A line of horses were tethered behind the tents, one for each; those would be the ready mounts. A soft nickering from a field another few hundred yards northward, and an earthy, grassy scent on the warm breeze showed where the main mass of horses were waiting.

Her lips curled back from her teeth a little at the sight of the half-dozen men who stood by the catapults themselves, in coats of small steel plates linked with mail, flared shoulder-pieces and spiked helmets, dao-style swords at their waists.

The enemy.

She had faced many enemies here in Montival, sword in hand. But this was *the* enemy, the ones who had killed her father and tormented her people since before her birth or his. The sun was setting, but the moon had risen. She crawled backward with a soft, smooth motion, one *sun* at a time. When she flowed over the low wall of tumbled, fire-cracked cinderblock overgrown with some prickly vine only a few crackles sounded, lost in the greater buzzing and chirping of insects in the night.

Egawa was waiting, and the two Topangans were back, the father Connor with his blowgun ready and the Conan son with the bow, the elder in dark clothing and the younger with his bare torso and face streaked with an effective camouflage of stripes made of soot and grease-paint. Connor put his head close to her ear.

"That's the main horse-herd back there, right where we thought. We can't get at it unless the guards pull out, but there are fifty head at least."

Reiko nodded. "Go. Be ready when you hear."

They moved off, noisier than her samurai trained in Silent Movement . . . but probably quiet enough.

Egawa quickly sketched the distribution of the guard posts for her—there were four, plus walking sentries closer in. She looked, nodded, and tapped each with her fan. Pairs of her men slithered off. They had hours to reach their targets, and they would use them to move inch by inch.

A samurai in black produced the signaling device the Protector's

Guard men had brought with them; a hemisphere of mirror, a tube lined with more mirrors, a stick of lime and burning compounds mounted in a screw-set holder before it, and a little piston bellows arrangement at the end of a rubber hose to make it burn bright. Reiko set up the tripod herself, her fingers sure and deft; though it was a Montivallan design, she had used similar ones often enough before.

The signal fire on Top of Topanga was clearly visible through the telescopic sight mounted in a bracket to the side. She looked through the sights, adjusted the screws until the crosshairs were centered on the white-painted stake planted beside the fire, then lit the light and shut the cover while Egawa pumped at the bellows. Within the container the lime would be burning with incandescent brightness, but no light escaped.

After a few moments a man walked before the mountaintop fire and then back again, the agreed-upon sign for *waiting on your signal.* The watcher with the telescope would be a little distance apart.

The crafting of the joints was very tight; when she put her thumb on the lever and pushed it the light was a complete surprise. Her approval was less a thought than an emotion, the respect she had been raised to feel for all those who paid meticulous attention to detail.

Clack, muffled and soft as the metal parts struck rubber buffers, and then *clack-clack,* barely enough to hear with her head next to it.

She paused, with her thumb still on the spring-loaded shutter control. This time two men walked before the fire—and back again, and then repeated it. They had seen her light.

Clack . . . clack-clack.

Egawa stopped pumping the bellows at her nod, and she turned the valve that closed the combustion chamber. The flame died—she could tell eventually because the heat radiating against the gloves she wore was less, lost in the warm summer night. She'd sent the *target is here* code and it had been received. The telescope up there was very powerful and showed much detail, but the camouflage had been well done, and only a ground survey could be sure.

It cools down more after dark here than it does at home, she thought, turning back to watch the target directly. *Perhaps because the air is so much drier.*

It grew cooler still, though still warm. Most of the Valley militiamen ahead lay down and wrapped themselves in thin blankets patched together out of scraps, or simply wadded their jackets under their heads as pillows. The elite retired to tents that servants had erected for them and laid themselves down on cots, most of them removing their boots. Though one of them always remained awake, no doubt to command. The *bakachon* detail guarding the catapults was replaced with another; every so often the picket posts in the scrub around the catapults were relieved. It was all military routine, dull and necessary and reasonably competently done.

Reiko looked at the stars and the moon. It would be quite some time and there was no point in burning energy she would need later. She laid her head down on her arm and almost instantly dozed off into a state halfway between real sleep and meditation.

And was elsewhere.

At first the experience was so alien that nothing would focus at all—save that centrifugal force made her body lurch back and then to one side, and that trees and rocks and darkness flashed by outside through windows of clear glass.

Like a glider!

She had traveled in military gliders, two-seaters, a few times. That let her mind grasp the experience enough to realize that she was in an automobile. Not for the first time, but this was no rusting, moldering relic, and it was *moving*. Even the air was strange, full of scents for which she had no names save that they were metallic and acrid. Strange lights glowed from the dashboard, and twin beams split the gloaming ahead.

Of themselves her hands shot to the front and side to brace herself; some part of her noticed that she was in a kimono of pale blue with designs in gray and silver, not the night-fighting gear her waking body wore. The impression of rushing speed was greater than flight, save perhaps for when the glider came down to land again. She blinked and her eyes adjusted, and she could make out that she was on a steep winding road in forested mountains, in a moving automobile. Somewhere in the north of Honshu, at a guess. And this was a car of the type that the Change had left stranded by the millions on the roads of Japan, and which her folk had been mining ever since, sleeker and more rounded than the boxy machines of the years of the Pacific War.

Slowly her head turned to see the driver. It was a woman—Japanese, she was sure, though in a Western dress—with her hands clenched tight on the wheel, a frown on her face. No more than a few years older than Reiko.

She is preoccupied. She is not paying attention to that which she does!

The machine was traveling far faster than a galloping horse, and through darkness and steep curves. What would happen if it ran off the road or struck a tree didn't bear thought. Reiko's teeth were bared as it took one of those curves, though the woman seemed to be handling it with some skill.

"Slow!" burst from her. "You must slow down!"

The woman started slightly, and the vehicle began to drift. With a gasp she worked the wheels and pedals and the automobile jerked to a stop by the side of the road. Hot metal pinged and clicked. Yet the pressure on Reiko felt greater, if anything. A crushing weight, shuddering with horror, like a great shape falling from forever over her head.

The Change! It is coming, and with it terrible death for all but one in a thousand of our people. This cannot be more than a few scant years before, no more than ten at most. The monstrous thing presses me like an insect beneath a mountain of glass.

Grimly she forced herself to *see.* The woman looked entirely ordinary; an intelligent face, pretty, forceful normally but a bit frightened now, breathing quickly. Her eyes hunted through the space Reiko occupied, where she saw and smelt and felt the touch of cushions and metal and felt her own presence. But there was something . . .

A nexus of lines of light? Reiko thought. *She shines with it.*

As if she was *permeated* by possibility. Suddenly Reiko understood.

"You . . . must . . . be . . . careful," she said distinctly, and the woman started violently. "You must!"

"Who is there?" the driver said. "Please, is someone there?"

The *Nihongo* she spoke was entirely clear, but of a form Reiko had heard only from a few elderly people; an educated Tokyo dweller's version of the old Standard Japanese. The woman's eyes grew very wide as she seemed to see *something*. If not Reiko absolutely, at least some sort of outline or presence. Despite that awe and fright her voice was nearly steady.

"Are you . . . a *kami*?" She shook her head. "Amazing! Are the old stories true, then?"

"A *kami*? I am . . . yes and no," Reiko said.

She felt sweat break out on her brow with the effort to resist the *weight*, the force that tried to exclude her from this moment, to make her *impossible*.

"But the *kami* are very real, Princess," she said. "And that is why you must be careful. Because of she who you bear."

The other's hand went down to lie on her stomach. "She? A daughter? And how do you know? I haven't even told Fumihito yet! Oh . . . either I am hallucinating, or . . . why?"

A tremulous smile. "Would a hallucination speak with that very odd dialect? Like someone from Sado acting in an old Kurosawa historical!"

"You were in danger," Reiko said. "It is . . . it is essential that you live. For she who you bear is of the seed of *Amaterasu-ōmikami*, and she will . . ."

Even under the stress of that moment, Reiko hesitated: how to tell truth without cruelty?

". . . she will be the instrument that saves our people in a time of . . . terrible crisis yet to come."

Reiko could feel herself start to fade, as if she was toppling backward, very slowly, over an infinite cliff.

"Don't go!" the other woman said, reaching out to her. "You can't just say that and leave—I have so many questions!"

"I cannot stay," Reiko said, with wrenching effort. "Listen, please! Just this. When all seems lost, do not despair. Trust Egawa Katashi, trust him with your child's life. This will seem as a dream, but remember that."

The woman nodded, already seeming a little more distant. Reiko forced out one more sentence before she was altogether gone:

"Farewell . . . great-grandmother."

She came instantly alert at a hand on her foot, then relaxed with the *tessen* halfway out of her sash.

Please, let that be the last of these visions!

She drew a deep breath and put it out of her mind. That was Egawa. He held his wrist near her face and held back the cover for an instant so that she could see the dim remnant illuminated hands on the watch-dial.

She rolled on one side behind the ruined wall so that she could look back to the south and used her monocular. The fire on the hilltop was still clearly visible. When she used the glass it sprang close. A figure passed in front of it—but this time it was a figure carrying something, something through which the fire passed in a diffuse red glow. She nodded and restarted the light, and a young samurai crept close to keep the pump operating. This time she locked the thumb-piece down—the light would be a beacon now.

Then she turned back towards the enemy, stretching as she did so without movement—pitting muscle against muscle on her bones to make them limber and quick.

That continuous light was the signal for launch. If nobody happened to see it first, and it wasn't that easy to spot. Egawa had started his stopwatch when she locked the light down, the ancient hands still very faintly glowing.

It had taken hours for the Japanese and the others to steal through the evening in this great wilderness of brush and ruined buildings. Sometimes they had evaded inhabited places more by the scent of smoke and sheep-pens and chicken-coops than by sight or sound. Several times they'd hidden from goatherds moving their stinking beasts about to graze on the thorny, spiny vegetation that sank its roots into the rubble. Now and then there was the incongruous scent of roses from feral plants that had survived the decades and the fires.

Nobody had been caught. And now the next wave would be coming.

She smiled the way a hawk might, if it could. Some of them were much more likely to run into local fighters than those who had infiltrated down the slopes. Others were much less so . . .

Thora Garwood clenched her thighs and leaned forward slightly, keeping the reins slightly slack as she moved through the Gate and down the winding switchbacks to the north.

The well-trained Dúnedain horse responded perfectly, walking forward into the darkness beneath a sky spectacularly frosted with the diamond band of the Milky Way and lit by a three-quarter waxing moon low on the horizon. The air had gone from hot to merely warm when the sun went down, here where the mountains blocked the sea-breeze; warm and spicy and dusty, with a hint of smoke somewhere. It didn't even smell strange, not after so many different lands.

Fortunately the Rangers used the same signals to school their horses, she supposed taken from the same rodeo-natural-riding-and-dressage mélange the Bearkillers had drawn from. Astrid Larsson had been the Bear Lord's sister-in-law originally, after all, and Morfind and Faramir were right behind her, his grandchildren. They'd been trained by the Luanne Hutton who'd married Eric Steelfist Larsson; she'd been the Outfit's original horsemistress.

The sun had painted the mountains ahead a salmon-pink when it went down; she'd rested under a pepper tree and watched it, before Deor helped her suit up. She was in her own battered and well-used armor, what the Outfit called cataphract harness; it was a bit lighter than knight's plate, with more mail, and a bit less complete, and they used a round shield a yard across rather than the big kite types. Fortunately, all that made her gear look a lot like what the Chatsworth Lancers were supposed to wear. More so because she'd had bits and pieces patched or replaced here and there around the world whenever they'd run into armorers . . . or just plain blacksmiths . . . who were up to the job.

Not *very much* like the Chatsworth version, of course; from the captured examples the real thing was much more elementary, and they didn't even try to make metal-to-metal joints, using leather where flexibility was essential. They also used a doubled-edged chopper style of sword that was, if the examples shown her were any indication, badly balanced and a bit too heavy for skilled swordplay—she'd just kept her backsword and belted on a sash whose knot and tag-ends covered the hilt.

Plus reportedly either none of them were women or they were few enough for their faces all to be known, so she'd left her helmet on despite the different profile. People saw what they expected to see, so in half-light and, more important, when they wouldn't *expect* anyone in armor on a horse to be anything but one of their own, it might well do. Or it wouldn't and the whole mission would be fucked but she'd be too dead to be embarrassed. She'd have laughed at that, except that it would be out of character.

"On the whole I'd rather be back in Hraefnbeorg, picking the site for the house," she said quietly.

Deor had a tunic over his mail shirt and rode a little behind her. Luckily Topangans and Valley men wore them baggy and shapeless.

"Now that you mention it, oath-sister, so would I," he said.

The Topangans had supplied her with a Chatsworth-style lance, about twelve feet long including the head, and made of aluminum pipe counterbalanced with lead in the butt. The metal was ridged, and had a grip of rawhide wound around it, and overall was about as practical as the ashwood shafts she'd grown up with though much harder to replace if damaged. She carried it easily, steadying it with her right hand and the butt braced against a ring welded to her stirrup-iron.

Been too long since I used a lance or spent much time in the saddle. Hope I don't have to do anything fancy, she thought. *Then again, picking tent-pegs out of the ground probably won't be on the program, it's not a Gunpowder Day festival at Larsdalen, after all.*

A sudden slight sadness came over her. *It would be nice to see the Bear Gate once more before the end, and my folks and the sibs and their kids.* She had three brothers, all handfasted, and ten nieces and nephews who hardly knew her except by reputation. Then she narrowed her consciousness down to a single point of focus.

The road dipped downward, weaving in switchbacks and then straightening out to the north; the foothills beyond the Gate were no-man's-land, used only for rough pasture and hunting. The land grew much smoother and a bit drier as the road became a straight highway. That was part of a grid in the low flat valley, and there were more ruins—many of them things you couldn't see from above, like concrete overgrown with vines. A pike pivoting between two poles marked the official border, and a low patched-up building with the letters ST TE ARM fastened to its façade stood nearby. Smoke came from a rusty sheet-metal chimney through the ancient flat asphalt roof, and light leaked out of the windows.

Three men came out as the sound of hooves approached; the first held a lantern in one hand and a spear in the other, and two had strung bows. None of them was wearing armor or looked very remarkable, and doubtless they had families or someone who would miss them. That was their wyrd; all human kind ever born lived until the moment they died, and not a minute longer. If you carried a spear you had no cause to complain if you died on one.

"Look, you hippie freaks know the road's closed at sundown for . . . Sir!"

The peevish note died as the man detected the lance and armor. "Sir, we're under orders to keep the road closed at night!"

"This is a secret mission," Deor snapped as she stared straight ahead—he didn't have quite the local accent, but at least the voice was male, and a scop could imitate anything on short acquaintance. "Raise the barrier, clear the way, and don't say a word to anyone."

The tone of authority overrode the fact that the words made no sense at all long enough for Thora and the riders behind her to come close enough. It also focused their attention on her, and not on the frankly foreign appearance of the others or any slight noises from the night around them . . . the sort men infiltrating to surround the building would make.

Squinting against the light of the lantern—it was an antique originally designed to burn kerosene—his eyes suddenly went wide and his hand clenched on the spear-shaft.

Perception and action flowed through her with no pause between one and the other. The lance tossed up, her hand slapped home on the balance-point in the reversed overarm grip, and as the blade came down to the right angle she stabbed with the vicious precision of a rattlesnake striking.

The honed steel rammed into the base of the man's throat, just above where the collarbones met, with a familiar feeling—soft and heavy, with crisp undertones as the steel parted the cartilage of the windpipe. The man had no time for more than the expression of surprise and alarm that had already begun before blood poured into his mouth and lungs from the clutch of big arteries that ran through that spot. The lantern landed with a clink of metal and a tinkling of shattered glass and the oil in the reservoir caught with a *huff* and pool of dancing blue flame.

She dropped the lance as he fell and her backsword hissed out, even as she threw a leg over the neck of her mount and slid to the ground with her shield up and her back to the beast.

Three horse-bows snapped right behind her, and the chunking smack of impact in meat and bone followed so quickly that it merged with the sound of the strings. Neither the Topangans nor their neighbors practiced mounted archery for some reason, but there was nothing wrong with Faramir or Morfind when it came to the art, and allowing for her size and the limits it put on her draw-weight, Susan Mika was about the best Thora had ever encountered, her own very considerable talent not excepted.

At about ten feet range, not even the pale fickle wash of starlight and moonlight and the guttering remains of the lantern and what leaked around the shutters made any difference. One of the bowmen actually managed to begin raising his weapon before a set of fletchings bloomed against the dull undyed linen of his tunic in a way that meant his breast-bone had been split and the point lodged in his spine. He went down thrashing, but only with his arms and only for a moment. The other fell instantly limp, a shaft in the left side of his chest and another—someone showing off—standing four inches deep in his right eyesocket.

Thora charged right after her feet hit the ground, and before the Valley militiaman shot in the spine stopped thrashing, with Deor beside her. They had ten yards to cover before they reached the door of the border post. They kept their shields up and ran straight, with Deor a pace behind and on her right hand, the way they had often before—they didn't go looking for fights but a fair number had come their way. Nobody shot at them, but arrows went by overhead from the road, and something grunted and then screamed once up on the flat roof, the sound dying down to a whimper.

According to the Topangan reports, tinder and dry pinewood was piled there in an iron basket. Evidently someone had tried to light it, which was bravely done even if it was reflex, and they'd met knife-sharp steel traveling at two hundred feet a second.

Two other men burst out of a side door and tried to run north. They took a few paces and then just silently fell over, face-planting on the cracked concrete. A lot of Topangans used blowguns; they didn't have anything like the range or armor-penetrating power of bows, but you could use them lying down behind a bush and they were even quieter than arrows, and accurate within their limits if you knew what to do with them. The fleeing men had each just had four or five tenpenny nails driven into various parts of their bodies, sent by the locals who'd swung wide behind the station while all attention was on the road.

By that time the door of the station was opening, inward. Whoever was inside was coming out—sensible enough, since there were two big windows and the place was indefensible even for the briefest moment, with no way to prevent people standing outside, breaking the windows and shooting arrows or bolts or even blowgun darts at him. This was a customs post, not a fort.

He had a shortsword in his hand, but his eyes were still dazzled by the light of the wall-mounted lanterns inside. And obviously had no idea of what was going on, save that it was something very bad.

Thora tucked her shoulder into her shield and hit him full-tilt. The impact made her grunt and put the taste of iron in her head, and a passing thump on the doorframe as they both went back through it made her glad she was wearing her helmet. You could get permanently punchdrunk in this business if you weren't careful. Or permanently dead even if you were.

She staggered into the room, skip-stepping to get back into stance, and he flew back until he hit a wooden table and knocked it skidding back across the faded uneven tiles, spilling a jug of something on the floor to splash dark liquid and wine-scent. The man snarled and crouched and managed to get back upright, and he'd kept hold of his blade. He didn't have a shield, though.

Thora kept hers up under her eyes and slanted, whirled the yard-long backsword up—you had to be cautious that you didn't hit the ceiling when you did that indoors, but there was enough room here—and brought it down in a diagonal backhand left-to-right slash as she advanced a stamping step and twisted her torso to put more weight into the cut.

The man couldn't dodge backward, and had to block or have his bones broken even if the buff-leather jerkin he was wearing held out the edge, which it wouldn't. Not having a shield, he used the two-foot blade in his right hand instead. The impact didn't quite tear it out of his hand, but there was a crash and skirl of metal as the edge of the heavier weapon slid down to the simple cross guard of the shortsword. Her Bearkiller weapon had a much more complex basket-guard hilt.

Which has a couple of uses besides protecting your fingers.

The swords strained against each other, while the Valley militiaman tried to gouge out her eye with the thumb of his free hand until she raised the shield to block him. He had a cropped bristle of black hair and was short and scrawny, but nearly as strong in the arms as her. Which meant nothing if . . .

She suddenly relaxed her sword-arm and let the combined blades snap down towards her shoulder. The edge of his sword struck the steel that joined her backplate and breastplate hard, which would give her a bruise even through the metal and padding. In the same instant she pivoted the blades around the point of contact and smashed the bronze bars of the basket hilt into the man's heavy blue-stubbled jaw in a high right jab.

That put her neck far closer to an enemy edge than she liked, but the militiaman was suddenly in no mood for cutting. His jawbone cracked in at least one place under the impact of the two-pound set of brass knuckles into which she'd converted her sword for an instant. He dropped his weapon and screamed, spraying bits of tooth as well as blood, and she gave him a knee where it would do the most good, throwing his spasming body away with a heave of her shield to give herself room for a finishing stab. The backsword's thirty-six inches of blade could be awkward in a room full of furniture and walls.

Movement out of the corner of her eye, and she spun into a stepping lunge more urgent than making sure of a disabled man who'd dropped his blade.

"Hold!" Deor barked, and struck her sword up with his in a sharp hard clangor that vibrated into her wrist.

The movement had been a woman a little younger than she in a shapeless dress darting out of a doorway, holding an infant in the crook of one arm and stretching a hand out to the militiaman with the other.

I didn't see anything but an outline and a target, she thought, taking a sharp breath. *Freya! I might have skewered the kid!*

The target's face was mostly hidden behind a fall of sun-faded yellow hair, but she didn't draw back under the menace of the bright metal. Instead she ducked under it and grabbed the writhing man, seeming to try to guard him and child both by putting her body between them and looming armored death and squeezing her eyes shut.

"Thanks!" Thora gasped to the scop.

She wasn't the sort who got the shakes or bad dreams after an ordinary fight. Warriors fought, killed and died; that was their wyrd, however grim. But there were memories you simply didn't want in your head. There was enough there in hers already without another, and just by accident at that.

Now she stuck her head through into the next room; it had been made by walling off part of a larger pre-Change one with adobe bricks, and the single window had strong iron bars across it to deter thieves. They were on the outside and for defense, but they'd work just as well to keep someone in. There was a tousled bed, a chest of drawers that must have been pre-Change, a cradle, and a lidded bucket that contained used diapers from the smell. A jug and basin and half a loaf of bread wrapped in a cloth rested on a plank shelf laid on pegs driven into the interior wall.

"Go there!" she barked to the woman, then repeated it after she swatted her with the flat of her unbloodied sword to attract her attention.

"Go there!"

The civilian's eyes flew open; Thora pointed with the blade.

"In there, and stay there!"

The young mother showed commendable presence of mind; she grabbed the wounded man by the back of his jerkin and dragged him into the room and pulled the door closed on her own. Thora swept the fallen shortsword over to it with her foot and drove it home point-first under the bottom of the door with three kicks of her bootheel, making a nice solid wedge that would take a long time to dislodge.

The child was bawling before the third blow sounded, a high shrill sound that went into the ears like needles.

Deor winced. She knew he liked children and could usually charm them effortlessly, but he liked them much better once they were old enough to walk and talk.

"Are you sure you want years of that?" he said.

"As opposed to the calm delights of what we're doing right now?" she grinned, sheathing her unbloodied sword as they went out again.

"All secure," she said.

She stepped over the staring-eyed body of the man who'd taken the lance-head in his throat, avoiding its pool of blood; someone led up her horse and she swung easily back into the saddle.

Faramir nodded back to her. "Nobody made it out. We went a couple of hundred yards down that road—Morfind and Suzie are still there, behind some walls."

Which meant that anyone who came trotting up the road was going to get an unpleasant surprise. Someone might have been stationed nearby and quietly left when they saw the station overrun, but that was a little more sophisticated than she thought any of these yokels could manage. Even if they did, the news could travel only as fast as a man could run, or at a pinch a horse. It wouldn't get where they were going much before they did.

A column of Topangans on bicycles was coming down the old Boulevard; at her wave they kept straight on, pedaling briskly. She and Deor and the Dúnedain legged their horses up into a loping canter—a little risky in the dark, but acceptable on a road with no wrecks on it.

Now they had to get past the lookouts along the line of the old Ventura Freeway, but earthquakes had savaged it, and she'd picked out a spot with local advice and a long look through a telescope. By then detection would be less crucial anyway. This plan didn't depend on everything going right . . . not entirely, at least.

And damned if I can see anything else that would have a chance of decisive results, she thought. *She's right about that. It's the* win big or plant your face into the dungheap *type of scheme sure enough, though. Either we all die or we bring it off and live . . . most of us, at least.*

Her head went up and she looked at the sugar-frosting sky. "What do the wights say?" she asked Deor.

He grimaced a little. "There's a babble. Too many hungry, angry ghosts here; too many evil deaths, too much pain too close in time. I'm glad we didn't go farther south, through the bones of the old city. The shadow of horrors will lie there for a long time."

Then he frowned, looking northward. "And there's another darkness there. As with the skaga back at the bay, but . . . thicker. Less of a good thing twisted, more of an . . . otherness."

"A shadow of evil?"

"Not . . . not in any sense we can know. As if the thing itself were nothing we have words for, but the shadow it casts *here* in the world of things is evil indeed."

Thora shivered and shrugged. "Well, let's get on with our part. It may be risky, but it needs doing."

Deor surprised her by nodding vigorously. "This isn't just a contention of kings. More is at stake."

"And this wasn't the riskiest part of the job by any manner of means," she said, looking up again.

"Didn't Mike Havel do something like this, back in the early days?" Deor asked.

"Yup. The Bear Lord's Flight," she said.

"Ah, yes, I know that song," he said.

"And there's a tactical analysis, too," she said, as she signaled her horse into motion. "That one says he was lucky, but crazy."

Both were taught in every A-Lister steading and Strategic Hamlet in the Outfit's territory. She supposed the descendants of the first Bear Lord living elsewhere were equally aware of it.

"Like granddaddy, like granddaughter, eh?"

CHAPTER TWENTY-SEVEN

PARTICIPATORY DEMOCRACY OF TOPANGA
(FORMERLY TOPANGA CANYON)
CROWN PROVINCE OF WESTRIA
(FORMERLY CALIFORNIA)
HIGH KINGDOM OF MONTIVAL
(FORMERLY WESTERN NORTH AMERICA)
JULY/FUMIZUKI 28TH
CHANGE YEAR 46/SHŌHEI 1/2044 AD

"People up north still do this for fun?" Jared Tillman said.

"It *is* fun," Órlaith said, with a reckless fighting grin that was . . . mostly . . . perfectly genuine.

Although we don't do it in the dark, aiming for a target we've never seen except through a telescope with murderous enemies at the other end. Not for fun, at least! Though . . . these are the people who killed Da. That *needs doing.*

"And there are military uses for them. Not many that gliders don't do better, granted, but occasionally for special-operations work. My grandfather Mike Havel used some to land an assault force on a castle by night, only a little while after the Change. One built by my other grandfather's troops."

"Castle, right," Kwame said; the word seemed to bother him.

"Motte-and-Bailey. More of a timber and sheet-metal prefab fort on an earth mound, actually, but the Association always called them castles. As an aspiration, I'm thinking."

Kwame looked at her and she spoke, thankful for the distraction. "My mother's father was . . . a man of dreams, in his way; and in those dreams he was lord of many castles. Which, by the time he died, he was in truth. Though he never got to build a real one in *that* spot. As a matter of fact, the Clan Mackenzie built a fort there a generation later, to hold against the Prophet's men—the old Highway 20 pass over the Cascades. That was before I was born, of course."

Heuradys was at the edge of the Top of Topanga's steep drop-off. She had a length of silk thread on a stick and was watching it as she held it out over the edge. There was plenty of light from the bonfire in the iron hearth, though you had to be careful not to blind yourself by looking directly at it.

"Still a consistent updraft," she said. "A bit slower, but not much."

Órlaith could see the light Reiko's beacon gave with the naked eye, now that she knew exactly where it was. She'd also lined it up with three much larger landmarks that were visible by moonlight, so she couldn't go far wrong even if she lost it, and she'd checked that the others had done the same.

"Check," she said.

She and Heuradys went over each other's machines one last time and hugged briefly but fiercely before they took up their hang gliders and let assistants strap them in. The harness that held you dangling beneath the framework that supported the wing was like a padded trough from chin to knees, fastened at the back. She reached around to make sure that the snap-clips were easily accessible; she'd need to get out of the cumbersome thing quickly. Then she bent down, grabbed the bar, and carefully lifted the whole ensemble. It wasn't all that heavy, and two locals were assisting by holding the tips of the blunt triangular wing.

Assembling and testing the hang gliders farther back in the canyon had been simple enough; unlike most things made post-Change, the fabrics and wires and frame of synthetics and light metal alloys just didn't decay much, not on the scale of decades, though you could build something workable if not as good out of laminated bamboo and piano-wire and silk.

There were six of them ready to take off; herself, her liege knight

Heuradys, John, his armsman-valet Evrouin who'd mastered the art when he did to keep up with him, Sir Droyn and one of the men-at-arms named Engherrand, who came from a family affluent enough to indulge in such a risky, fashionable sport. A few rich men elsewhere also used them, but odds were that anyone who'd had the resources and leisure to become familiar with the flying wings were north-realm gentry.

She gave it one more check herself. She was wearing a mail-lined jerkin and her helmet and arm-guards, and apart from that the usual tough clothing you wore in the field—and no kilt tonight, just good strong deerskin breeches and knee-pads. The others were in the same. Every ounce counted in flight. The Sword of the Lady was at her waist, but she'd secured the scabbard to her thigh with an extra length of buckskin thong just above that knee; it was a little awkward, but it would keep the length from flapping about and it would be only the work of an instant to tug the bow knot free. Her wing had a big white stripe of reflective paint from one tip of the triangular top surface to the other, too; they all did. That would give each following flier something to watch for ahead and below.

"Morrigú, Crow Goddess, You who are terrible in majesty amid the shattering of spears, be with me now," she said quietly, with her mind focused within. "I fight according to my oaths for my folk and Earth that feeds them as they toil with Her, for their hearths and hopes and children. Badb-Macha-Nemain, Lady of the Final Mysteries, know that if this is the day of my people's need, I go to You consenting, with open eyes."

The brief prayer helped. So did the feeling from the Sword, a building fury like ocean waves growling deep as they broke on fanged rocks, cold and powerful. The others formed up behind her, staggering themselves to right and left so that she had enough room for her takeoff run. She'd broken her left arm in two places once, falling out of a tree when she was nine. It had hurt for quite some time, though she remembered mostly being angry at the way the cast and the nurse kept her from doing the things she wanted to. Falling several hundred feet onto rock if something went wrong . . . well, at least it would probably be quick.

One deep breath, another . . . this was paradoxically so much easier when people were looking at you . . . how much of life was playing a role?

For me, a whacking great lot of it, from birth.

"And here I thought *go jump off a cliff* was a metaphor, so I did!" she said softly. "All those invitations I've received, and only now am I taking them up!"

"On three, Orrey, and I'll meet you there," Heuradys said, her voice crisp. "One . . .

John was murmuring to himself, with Droyn and the other Catholics: *"Sáncta María, Máter Déi, óra pro nóbis peccatóribus, nunc et in hóra mórtis nóstrae. Ámen."*

"Two . . .

"Three!"

She sprang forward—previously she'd paced it out, and found the run to be fifteen strides and a leap. Over the edge this time instead of stopping, and *push* back with her right foot against the parapet of the lookout's edge. Throwing herself forward, and the harness held her cradled in its trough, horizontal in the same plane as the wing.

There was a *whump* as the fabric struck the air, and a dip as she pulled the bar back to turn the nose down a little and gain airspeed . . .

The slopes along the front of the Santa Monicas made an invisible ladder in the sky as the Valley gave up the heat of the day. The hang glider still sank—one foot down for every seventeen or so forward—but the column of air that enfolded her was rising faster than that. The moon-washed ruins and scrub beneath her hardly approached at all for the first few miles. Even then, on her way to edged metal and anger, there was some of the joy of flying so; this was as close to a bird's dance with the spirits of Air as human beings could come.

Then the long straight glide, like tipping over the edge of a hill as they left the band of rising air. Just because it was straight didn't make it easy; Air was a living thing, and a playful inconstant Power. You steered by shifting your balance, forward and back and to either side. Like swimming . . . a bit like making love, too, though with a cool ghostly lover. It wasn't calm here, either. The air looked clear, but every patch of ground below sent its own gusts upward. Once she ran into a pocket that seemed to drop her a dozen feet in a heartbeat, as if she'd run into a vacuum. Her teeth clicked together hard, but then the wing bit again.

The dot of light was brighter and closer. Soon, soon . . .

Soon we'll all be down. If the others are still behind me!

It was something new to worry about, at least.

Connor Tillman was horrified when he realized one of the Mackenzies was making a noise, actually *talking*, with the God-damned Chatsworth pukes only a couple of dozen yards away through a night that would have been perfectly still if it weren't for the insects and some night-birds and a coyote howling in the middle distance. Talking when it was just about time for things to start. He didn't particularly like them, but he'd thought they knew better than *that*, and so did the other bunch in rather different kilts.

The Topangan crawled in the direction of the noise to shut the crazed northerner up . . . until hands seized him out of the darkness; he remained in control enough not to use his knife in the instant before his arms were pinned. At least three someones—strong someones—had grabbed him, including one pair of hands over his eyes and mouth.

The hand came off his eyes, though the other across his lips remained clamped hard.

"Wheesht!" a voice hissed in his ear.

Which obviously meant *quiet*; it was reinforced by the prick of a blade behind the ear, just a single touch and then withdrawn.

The paddock where the Lancers were holding their horses ready to deploy was a small park and several lawns and what had been a parking lot until the asphalt was broken up and carted away a generation ago. The mounts crowded it, restless and nickering and shifting now and then, the more so because in a display of insane machismo a lot of the Chatsworth types used entire stallions as their warhorses, what Connor thought of as trying to prove you were hung like a pony. The Topangans and one of the Mackenzies and a bunch of the . . .

McClintocks, that's what they're called.

. . . were outside the line of street where guards paced back and forth, sheltering behind snags of cinderblock wall. One of the kilted northerners was on his . . . no, her knees, it was the woman named Gwri, the dark one with her hair in small tight braids tipped with silver balls—sensibly muffled with a kerchief under her helmet for this work. Her face had a sinuous design in dark-green and brown and burnt ochre drawn on it now; Mackenzies didn't tattoo like their relatives, but they did paint their faces for war when they had time.

She was kneeling up behind a fragment of wall, with her arms out to either side and palms up, *swaying* slowly to left and right, with an arrangement of rocks and scratches in the dirt before her and objects at the points of a pentagram inside a circle—a feather, a bone, things he couldn't see clearly. And as she swayed she chanted or half-sang, very softly, words that trickled into your ears like warm honey, her eyes heavy-lidded. Like your mother singing to you in your cradle . . . and Connor's mother had died in childbirth; he'd been raised by his father and a bunch of neighbors, he didn't remember her at all.

Except that somehow now he *did*, with an overwhelming sense of homecoming, like staring into the hearth as it flickered low while it rained outside.

"Sleep of the Earth of the land of Faerie
Deep is the lore of Cnuic na Sidhe
Hail be to they of the Forest Gentry
Pale, dark spirits, help us see—"

Conan was on the other side of her. He was staring wide-eyed . . . and then his head turned very slowly. Connor rolled his eyes to follow his son's gaze. The Valley sentries were walking in pairs, weapons on their shoulders . . . and one pair was passing by right now, a spearman with a shield and an archer, both wearing simple metal pots and leather jackets with rows of overlapping stainless-steel washers sewn on with wire. They stopped, and one brought the spear down with a thump and a weary sigh, and rubbed a hand over his face. The other yawned enormously. Neither seemed conscious of anything but boredom, silent darkness and fatigue.

"Christ, what a waste of time!" the spearman with a blond queue tied back with a rag said in the middle of the yawn. "The freaks never come this far. And a whole day spent shoveling horseshit. I can do that at home. Well, shit from my ox and the milk-cow."

"This is bullshit too," the bowman said sourly . . . and yawned as well, enough to make his jaw click audibly. "We don't even get to keep the horseshit, I could use it for my new truck field. Easy to work but it keeps trying to turn back into sand if I don't feed it right. Tomatoes like it sandy but not *too* sandy, and there's fucking cutworm to think about. I'm wondering if trying tobacco on it next fall wouldn't be a good idea. Finicky stuff to grow but there's always a market for something that habit-forming."

"Yeah, but you can't eat tobacco, so in a bad year the price of everything else goes up more. And I'm worried about Jenny myself; that damn boar hog just isn't safe if I'm not there to check the pen, not when she has to look after little Bob too. Now that he's running around like a puppy and getting into everything. I should be *home*, dammit."

"Well, me too, but what're you going to do? Tell Mark Delgado *sorry Mr. Big Chatsworth Boss on your high horse, you can't have that war right now, I'm too busy*? We get something off the taxes, at least. Maybe the boss will finish off the freaks and we won't have to worry about shit like this anymore. That'll make salt a lot cheaper too; I hear he's going to build up the pans on the coast when we take 'em over. And we've got the new gear."

"That's something else is bothering me. I don't like those creepy foreigners who came with it. I swear they look at us the way I look at that damned pig. Christ, I'm tired, can't stop yawning. Why couldn't someone else draw middle watch three nights running?"

"You and the dice, Bob, you and the dice."

Gwri reached into a pouch at her waist and dropped something into the palm of her left hand in an odd spiral-circular movement, then took up a little of it between thumb and two fingers, raising them to her lips:

"White is the dust of the state of dreaming
Light is the mixture to make one still

Dark is the powder of Death's redeeming
Mark but that one pinch can kill—"

Then she blew sharply across them. A dark glitter seemed to hang before her fingertips for an instant.

"Sleep!
Harken in your dreams
Sleep and do not wake
Nothing's as it seems
Iron bonds will break—"

Conan's eyes were bulging even more. Connor's did too, when the first Valley sentry just sat down and leaned against a stump of concrete and let his head fall back. The hands holding Connor relaxed as he did, and he settled down on his belly to watch. He did *not* understand what was going on.

Bruce Delgado would have hung a sentry who decided he wanted a nap more than doing his job, hung him from a lamppost and left the body for the birds as a hint to anyone else who felt sleepy on picket duty at three in the morning. His brother Mark had men like that flogged to death with wire whips or dragged with a rope around their ankles and the other end fastened to the saddle horn of a galloping horse. The sentry's partner bent to touch his shoulder, yawning again. The singsong chant continued:

"Hearts will be set free
Wrongs will be made right
Sleep and dreams will be
Justice in the night
Dreams will be
Justice in the night—"

The song died away, and the second sentry lay down in the dust of the highway. Both of them were asleep; uneasy sleep, by the way they twitched, but deep and slack-mouthed. Connor felt sweat break out over his whole body, running clammy down his flanks. Two of the northerners—McClintocks with the tattoos and the baggy kilts—started forward with their long dirks drawn and the honed edges catching the moonlight in little icy glints. Silent hairy deadliness like wolves with steel for fangs.

"Nay! Don't kill them, Diarmuid," Gwri said quietly, and the two caterans halted and looked over their shoulders at their *feartaic*. "Ill-luck, to misuse a gift of the Mother so without strong need. There are Powers in contention here, and the ones who favor us wouldn't like it."

"Aye," the McClintock leader said softly; he had a torc of twisted gold around his neck, covered now with dark rags to keep it from glinting. "Seònaidh, ye've the lighter hand, ye tap them a lullaby. Tak care, 'tis *geasan* work here, nae sich sport as a feud in the hills."

A redhead with a blue design of feathers tattooed over her face and neck slid over the wall; she still had her dirk in her hand, but she struck with the ball pommel of the weapon rather than point or edge. And carefully, adjusting the angle of the heads to rap them behind the ear. That didn't mean they wouldn't hurt when they woke up . . . or even that they absolutely, certainly would wake up at all. Being knocked out was never a joke, though this was a lot less risky than getting hammered at random while they were resisting.

Then she dragged them both back into the shadow of the wall by the collars of their jackets. With a grin she used the dirk to snip two roses from the feral bush by the wall, then sheathed it and arranged the two militiamen on their backs with their hands crossed on their chests and the flowers tucked into their fingers. A silent snicker ran through the clansfolk. Connor supposed he'd have found it funny himself, if he hadn't been trying so hard to avoid a *bring me my brown pants* moment.

Diarmuid turned to Connor and spoke near his ear: "Gwri's a *banabhuidseach*, ye ken." At his incomprehension: "Witch. Spellweaver, like me ain mother. But I'd no thought she was powerful enough tae lay that on 'em. Few are, gae few. Most times a spell is a chancy thing, that might be doing aught and might be just wind and wishes. This is . . ."

Connor felt his eyes grow wider still. *I've got a lucky rabbit's foot,* he thought. *Don't think that's in the same league, no indeedy.*

"I'm not so strong, most times. I had . . . help," Gwri said bluntly. "My mother told me of such things from the wartime."

She nodded towards the road and the paddocks. "They may not be asleep there, the rest of them, but they'll not be spry. Sluggish, rather. And the ones who sleep on their own will sleep deep and dream hard."

Diarmuid pulled a watch out of his sporran and checked it. "Time. Let's be aboot it, then."

He smiled, a remarkably carnivorous expression in the darkness. "Ahhh, reiving horses by moonlight. Taks me back tae happy days, that it does!"

"Now!" Reiko said.

A samurai handed her the *higoyumi.* Another flicked a lighter and she touched the bulbous tip of the arrow to it; it lit brightly, and she squinted to keep it from entirely killing her night-vision as the naphtha-soaked fiber within flared up. She had memorized the direction and distance anyway, and so closed her eyes to let that knowledge flow out through hands and arms. Over her head, center the chi, draw as the bow came down, hold the gloved hand back . . .

The arrow arched away into blackness. So did a dozen more; she opened her eyes to see them tracing yellow arcs through the night, as pure as any she'd ever made on graph paper in her trigonometry studies. A growing brabble of alarm rose. And in half a dozen places in the brush around the enemy encampment, sentries started up. So did the Japanese warriors who'd crawled close, inch by patient inch over the hours of darkness.

They struck, but not silently—not after the blade or the metal batten of the nunchaku struck or the wire had settled round a throat.

"Tennō Heika banzai! Banzai!"

Light flared up from the direction of the artillery park; someone there had dumped the spare fuel onto the fire . . . which was exactly what she'd hoped would happen. That would blind those near it, and it would add to the beacon effect of the fire-arrows. Dark-clad figures came hurdling back over the wall ahead of them, grabbing for the longer weapons they'd discarded for their patient stalks. Her heart swelled with pride. This wasn't the ground they'd trained on, but her samurai were adapting very well . . .

The commander of the Imperial Guard leapt to the top of the wall ahead, standing with his feet braced.

"*Bakachon!*" he shouted. "Hear me!"

His sword was drawn, and held over his head. They would see the glitter there, at least. And if they saw the black night-fighting costume, so much the better. The enemy knew of the School of the Hidden Door, and they feared its adepts. Reiko spoke a fair amount of Korean, learned for military purposes, and she thought she detected that barking tongue in the confusion around the fire. An arrow flickered in their direction, a fluting whisper through the darkness.

There was nothing hidden about what Egawa shouted. They *wanted* the enemy to attack them . . . be entirely focused on them, in fact. Then they wanted them running back and forth between threats and unable to deal with any of them well; that was the plan, at least.

"I am General Egawa Noboru, Commander of the Imperial Guard of the Sovereign Majesty of Victorious Peace, victor in seven pitched battles, thirty-seven skirmishes and ship actions, and four duels! My father was Egawa Katashi, leader of the Seventy Loyal Men, who saved the dynasty and our nation! His father was Egawa Osamu, who dove his aircraft into a *Beijin* battleship! His father was Egawa Takeo, who lost his right arm leading his men in the storming of Mukden! For uncounted generations, the Egawa line has served their Emperors and Dai-Nippon! *Tennō Heika banzai!*"

Then in their own language just before he jumped down: "Come to us and die, filth!"

This time she could definitely hear shrieks of: "*Waegu! Waegu!*"

That was what the enemy called her people, and there was fear in the sound. Time to take advantage of that, to keep them off-balance. As in sword-work, where a series of blows ultimately left the opponent with no counter.

She drew another arrow from her quiver, raised the bow, lowered it and drew. This time she used a needle point, and the billowing flames illuminated the targets from her position even as they blinded those beside them. One of the men in Korean armor staggered, turned, grabbed at a catapult and slowly crumpled to the ground.

Loose.

It would probably take the enemy about five minutes to organize a counterattack.

Loose.

And about twice that long to kill her and every one of her party, if anything serious went wrong. Órlaith had promised that she'd find the Grass-Cutting Sword and send it back to Japan if Reiko fell, but while Reiko didn't doubt her she hadn't come here to let new-found friends do her duties for her. Not to mention friends just now in *even more* peril than she was.

Loose.

The fires rushed up towards her as she sent the hang glider down steeply. Distance was hard to estimate at night, even with fires billowing up—the last fire-arrows streaking in from the Japanese positions a little eastward, a bonfire blazing. She let the night flow into her . . .

Now.

She suddenly pushed on the bar with all her strength. The nose went up and the wing staggered in the air as its surface turned nearly horizontal to the direction she'd been moving, transformed from a wing to a giant brake. Motion ceased for a moment. . . .

And she began to fall, her hand going back to scrabble the first buckle of the harness loose. Her body swung down; light webbing struck the soles of her calf-boots an instant later, slowing the fall as her weight punched through. The broad surface of the wing struck the surface of the camouflage netting an instant later. That jerked her to a brief stop and made her teeth click together and she grunted as the harness squeezed at her chest. She hit the second catch, dropped three more inches to the ancient pavement and ripped the Sword of the Lady from its sheath while her left hand undid the thong that bound its sheath to her leg.

Shock.

Suddenly the flame-shot darkness around her was brighter; not with more light, but as if her eyes were making better, no, making fullest use of what was reaching them. The world became as much pale as dark, washed-out and flat, like a cloudy morning in the Dark Months rather than deep night. Strain and fear, even fear for her followers and friends, was suddenly as faint and ghostly as the light itself. Instead she felt light and strong, both angry and . . . lucid. Not quite as she'd felt in the fight by Círbann Rómenadrim—less of fury in it, more of thought.

Because that's what I need, she knew.

Everyone seemed to have dashed off from this exact location—precisely the point of the plan. A dead man lay on his side by a catapult with an arrow driven through his throat; she recognized it as one of Reiko's from the fletching. Another in the odd Korean armor trotted up, but apparently didn't see her immediately; instead he turned in the direction the fire-arrows had come and raised his own bow. It was a recurve, a composite of horn and wood and sinew, much narrower than the Montivallan equivalents and with rounded instead of flat limbs. But from the way it flexed as he drew, fully as powerful.

Not wanting to feel quite so much like an assassin, Órlaith spoke:

"Drop that bow, soldier."

The words were in his own language, and he did—but only because he was going for his sword in panic reflex as he spun on one heel towards her, his narrow dark eyes flaring wide in alarm. The sword was a *dao*-saber in the old Han style, not unlike the horseman's shete common over the Rockies, and with what looked like a cavalryman's reflex he whirled it up over his left shoulder for a backhand slash. Órlaith lunged instead with the right-foot-forward duellist's stroke, long arm and long blade and long lunge aiming at a point behind the man's back, wrist and arm braced for impact and long training making her keep the flat of the blade horizontal so that the edges wouldn't stick on a rib.

The point broke the mail links between the steel rectangles of the Korean's coat-of-plates with a distinct, almost musical *ching* sound. Not as easily as it would have cut so much string, but not as hard as it would have been if steel were meeting steel—nothing as sharp as the Sword could stay that sharp for more than an instant if slammed into hard metal. An edge that thin would break or curl . . . and the Sword's edge just faded into air like the thinnest fraction of an obsidian shard. But nothing on Earth could harm it, nothing at all.

There was an expression of terrible surprise on the Korean's face as he staggered backward, surprise and a dawning revulsion—as there might be on any man's with twenty inches of razor rammed through his lungs. But Órlaith had an uneasy sensation that the surprise had begun before that. The Korean warrior had looked normal enough, just one more hard-faced man of war. Yet something had changed as the Sword touched him, as if the veil of many years had been stripped away from his eyes and left the absolute truth of his own existence there instead.

That was what was supposed to happen when you made accounting to the Guardians of the Western Gate, before you entered the Summerlands. Her variety of the Old Faith had never made much of punishment in the Afterlife, except that singular self-inflicted one of knowing fully the cause and consequence of everything you'd been and done without possibility of untruth even to yourself.

Right now she was realizing that that might be just as serious as the Christians' hellfire.

She thought of what Reiko and the others had told her of what Korea was like under its sorcerer-kings, who ruled as living Gods. Or demon-lords exulting in a universe of pain and horror, the sort of place where family quarrels were settled by roasting and eating the loser's infants before their eyes and then lowering them into pits full of starving dogs or flesh-eating insects an inch at a time. It had all been sincere, but she'd assumed at least some part of it was the natural fruit of long enmity. Now she didn't anymore. Her father had told her more than once that you had to fight Evil, but what that mostly meant was killing Evil's conscripted farmers. This one, she suspected, had been rather more than that, however his life began.

The thought flashed through her and away even as the man toppled backward, blood that looked more black than red in the darkness spraying from mouth and nose. Some of it glittered like rubies for an instant where the spray passed before the firelight. She took another step and tossed the Sword upwards, caught it in the double-handed grip as it sliced through the netting with no more effort than it would have if she'd waved it through a cobweb, and brought it down in a straight overarm cut, putting her back and gut into it and clenching both hands and wrists at the last moment with a *huff!* of expelled breath.

The slash landed precisely on the spot where the coil-springs of the catapult were welded to a plate that resisted the cocking mechanism's pull on the right throwing arm. Hard impact jangled against her wrist, and there was a ringing *tung* as the thumb-thick rod parted and the springs sprang into extended bobbing uselessness. She struck twice more with flashing speed, cutting part of the anchor-point between the recoil mechanism and the main frame and then into the rods that joined the cocking system to the throwing arms. None of the damage could be repaired by snapping in a new part, and nobody was going to use this device again without a lengthy visit to a foundry and well-equipped machine-shop, of which the closest set she knew was in Corvallis and about eight hundred miles northward as the crow flew.

Just as the edge struck steel for the third time a caroling cry of: *"Alale alala!"* sounded from above and then a hollow hissing *shump* sound as a hang glider's wing struck the netting about halfway across the battery position. It had been perhaps twenty-five or thirty seconds since her own feet punched through and she dropped to the ground.

Thank Lord and Lady in all Their forms! Órlaith thought, with quick sincerity. Aloud:

"Here, Herry!"

Heuradys d'Ath landed in a cat-crouch as she shed the harness and spotted her, reslinging her longsword from where she'd had it over her shoulder to her belt as she rose—drawing a long blade from across your back was damned awkward, and worse still rather slow.

She also had her pre-Change crossbow cinched across her chest; it weighed nearly nothing, but that must have been awkward. She loosened it as she trotted springily up and snapped a blackened-aluminum bolt into the firing groove. Her teeth flashed white for an instant beneath the shadow of her helm.

"By Wingfoot Hermes, isn't this fun?" she dryly said and put it to her shoulder, standing slightly crouched and ready to snap-shoot. "Covered, Orrey."

"Now that you mention it, no, it isn't," Órlaith said dryly. "I'm going to work down this line."

But she was grinning as she turned away so that they were three paces apart and back to back. Walking backward to keep her covered wouldn't be easy, but if Heuradys d'Ath wasn't up to it, lead would float.

Another hiss and *whump*; someone else had landed. It was awkward having people arrive one at a time, but trying a mass landing at night in a confined space like this would be asking for disaster. As it was, each landing made the next easier, as the bright reflective paint on the upper surface of the wings guided the next flier in. Herry gave the shout to draw them; Órlaith was single-minded action now. The catapults were as alike as peas in a pod; she wouldn't be surprised if the parts were genuinely interchangeable, something usually worth the trouble only for the few genuinely mass-produced items . . . and military equipment. She walked steadily from one to the next, making the same three hard fast precise cuts and leaving ruined scrap behind.

Until the last.

A figure rose up before her then, in wild baggy costume of many colors, all muted to an infinitely drab taupe in the uncertain light; a tall three-pronged gold crown of filigree was on his head. He smiled at her like worms writhing in a pool of ink.

I . . . see . . . you.

The world froze.

CHAPTER TWENTY-EIGHT

PARTICIPATORY DEMOCRACY OF TOPANGA
(FORMERLY TOPANGA CANYON)
CROWN PROVINCE OF WESTRIA
(FORMERLY CALIFORNIA)
HIGH KINGDOM OF MONTIVAL
(FORMERLY WESTERN NORTH AMERICA)
JULY/FUMIZUKI 28TH
CHANGE YEAR 46/SHŌHEI 1/2044 AD

"Here they come," Boudicca hissed.

Karl started violently—he would have sworn by Cernunnos' horns and a lifetime's hunting by day and night that nobody was close except the others lying under their war-cloaks in the hot darkness, but she was kneeling just behind him.

Well, that was why you talked her into this, he thought; at least it made the sneeze he'd been suppressing go away. The local vegetation smelled like a dried bouquet from his mother's herb garden.

Ahead of him, two hundred yards southwards, was the enemy camp that held their artillery. Most of an old parking lot was covered by netting strung between the long-dead concrete lampstands, and beneath it were the neatly-spaced shapes of six war-catapults, field-pieces; the low red glow of the banked campfires flickered on the undersurface of the camouflage cloth, like the roof of a big low tent. The lumpy shapes of men snoring on the ground in bedrolls lay beyond it, with an occasional sentry pacing through, and a line of tents. Horses were drowsing along a tethering line behind them; he could smell the beasts, their wastes and their fodder and their own earthy-sweet scent.

Then he could hear the hooves drumming through the ground and into his belly, even if they couldn't be heard through the air yet. They were coming from the north, just as planned. The McClintocks and Topangans had overrun the horse-herd and its guards.

"Everyone up!" Karl snapped. "Right now our Nihonjin friends should—"

They'd insisted they would take out the sentry-posts. Karl had grumbled about it, but on reflection having two separate groups who didn't know each other well and couldn't speak more than a few words of each other's languages crawling through the night with knives between their teeth and minds primed to lash out and kill was a little risky. He wouldn't have wanted the Mackenzies and McClintocks both doing the task, for instance.

Suddenly fire-arrows were streaking through the night towards the enemy camp. There was a brabble of shouting and the glint of steel. The position of each enemy guard-post was known to him; he heard a grunt not far to the front and the wet smacking sound of a blade hitting flesh, then a series of Nihonjin war-shouts.

"That should get their attention good and proper, so," Boudicca chuckled. "That being the point."

Someone in the camp dumped split, tinder-dry pinewood into the watchfire and started blowing on a whistle; which lit the camp and woke everyone up, and also alerted anyone else who might be in the neighborhood and made the lit camp an island in a well of blackness to anyone close to the fire. The moon was still up, and the stars were as bright as anywhere Karl had seen them, even the dry eastern country around Bend, over the Cascades. He'd have smothered fires and put the lanterns *out* if he'd been in charge of a nighted camp that suddenly came under attack, and made no more noise than he absolutely had to. Not that he'd ever been in that position, but he'd listened to the tales of dozens of those who had since he was a little lad.

The local equivalent of knights came boiling out of their tents, some of them stumbling a little as they stamped into their boots, and dove into their armor with commendable speed. With considerably less wit they all swung into the saddle as soon as their grooms brought up the horses which had been standing ready on the picket line behind their tents and took their lances in hand. Just then a single rider came down the pathway from the north, the shod hooves of his horse striking sparks from the broken pavement. He nearly died on a dozen points, but he was yelling some password as he pulled up and pointed back the way he came. And now the neighing and squeals of angry, frightened horses and the drumming of scores of hooves came from that direction too. Mingled with it were a chorus of banshee shrieks; casting a glance in that direction Karl caught a glint of metal, and he could imagine the grinning tattooed faces. That was the sound of McClintocks doing what they loved best, stealing someone else's stock by moonlight.

Doing it very well the now, too, Karl thought. *Have to get the story of that—didn't expect them to get it moving so very quick. Were the enemy all asleep there?*

There were eleven in his party, now that Feidlimid was sped—and Gwri was with the McClintocks, a feeling she'd had. The remaining ten all came up to one knee. Now they stood and let the war-cloaks fall back from their shoulders and tossed back the loose hoods that had covered the helmeted heads. The material was much the same in concept as the camouflage netting over the catapults, though finer-grained: loose mottled fabric sewn with loops for bits of twig and leaf, and they'd carefully consulted the Topangans on what grew hereabouts. You could hide very effectively even in daylight and plain sight with them; at night you looked like a bush even quite close by. Their faces under the helms were covered in war-paint; Karl and Mathun used gray and dark amber, for the fur and eyes of their sept totem, Father Wolf.

The militiamen up ahead had been startled out of sleep and were running around and bumping into one another, waving spears and swords and a few of them loosing arrows blindly into the night—which might actually be dangerous, but just by way of accident. More flights of Japanese arrows came in on their position; *not* loosed at random. There were few things more terrifying than being shot at accurately with arrows at night—you couldn't tell where they were coming from, and Mackenzies had used that tactic themselves more than once, from the stories. There were other armored men there, in the gear that had been described to them as Korean. One of them whirled and slumped, trying to hold himself up on the frame of a catapult, and then falling.

"Waegu! Waegu!" they screamed; an officer or underofficer of some sort got them lined up and moving away towards the Japanese position.

Then a war-cry: *"Juche! Juche!"*

Not something I'd like to do, playing where's-the-spear in the dark with the Nihonjin. But not our concern. Now, those Chatsworth Lancers . . .

The way the Topangans put it was that the Lancers loved their warhorses more than their children . . . and they were *very* fond of their children. The Princess had explained her thinking a bit more. Each was a marker of rank and a huge investment and they belonged to each high-status warrior individually, not to their realm as a whole. The leader there—Karl could see the ostrich plumes on his helmet, nodding bright—screamed:

"Follow me!"

The command was reinforced by a youth with a trumpet, the brassy scream cutting through cries and confusion. The Lancers fell in, two ranks of six, and headed out . . . northward, towards the approaching dark mass of horses being driven against their will through a night full of obstacles that menaced their legs. The lances sloped forward, and the horses began to trot . . . towards their precious spare chargers and towards the Mackenzies they hadn't seen with their fire-blinded eyes up there ten feet tall in the saddle. Ten feet tall and silhouetted against the fire.

Beside him Mathun was muttering, probably without knowing it:

"The nock to the cord
The shaft to the ear
And a knight's breast-plate for a mark!"

That was an old ditty from the wars against the Association, fought and won before any of them were born. Won by the Clan's arrowstorms not least. All of them had a bodkin-pointed shaft shaped like a metal-worker's punch on the strings of their longbows, and three or four more clenched between a forefinger and the grips of their bows, a snap-shooter's trick. He waited until the approaching horsemen were figures with faces, not just outlines, the drumming of their hooves building as they legged their mounts up to a reckless canter.

And sure, against the Topangans what they're doing would probably work. Probably. Even in the dark. They're brave, that they are, but . . .

He waited until he saw their commander's figure straighten in shock as he realized what stood in their way, and what it was that glittered coldly from the points of the bodkins.

"Draw! Wholly together—loose!"

He drew with a grunt and shot, stripped another shaft from beneath his finger and drew, shot, drew, shot, drew, shot, drew, shot.

The others were only a little slower and the range was less than fifty paces and the vision as good as could be expected with the sun down. Half the first volley of ten struck men; one more hit a horse, and the beast's piteous, hideous scream split the night as it reared and dropped and rolled, legs kicking in the air.

Epona, Lady of the Horses, pardon human-kind that we bring Your children into our quarrels.

One of the hits stuck thrumming in a shield. Another skewered a shoulder and a lance dropped to the ground and its bearer lost all interest in anything but making his escape bent over the neck of his mount.

The Mackenzies were chanting as they shot; it helped you time the continuous hard effort, kept it smooth so that you tired less.

"We are the point—
We are the edge—
We are the wolves that Hecate fed!"

A Lancer pitched back over the high cantle of his saddle with a shaft through the eye; someone showing abroad, Mathun at a guess, or getting dead lucky. Karl's own first punched through a hammered-steel breastplate and dimpled the backplate that stopped it; the man he'd hit might live for hours, or a few minutes if he were luckier, but he crashed to the ground leaking blood around the arrow and from nose and mouth. Another whanged off a helmet, and the man reeled and threw up both hands in uncontrollable reflex at an impact like a metal-tipped club slamming into his head. The fifth slapped into a belly, sinking feathers-deep in the leather between two plates, which was pure bad luck . . . for him. The man hit began to shriek like a rabbit in a wire snare before he hit the ground. It cut off when he did, perhaps lucky this time, lucky enough to break his neck.

"We are the bow—
We are the shaft—
We are the darts that Hecate cast!"

By then all of them had drawn and loosed again and again and again in a ripple of practiced skill, shooting off the clutch of arrows they held against the riser of their bows. A few seconds later several riderless horses galloped past, and one dragging a limp shape with its boot caught in a twisted stirrup.

One remained; the youth with the trumpet, who was unarmored, with gangling hands just a little too big for his sleeves, about fourteen at most and pale-haired. He looked around him with eyes so wide that the whites showed in the dim light. His pupils had swollen wide too, enough that he could probably see the painted grinning faces, and the light on the many arrowheads pointing in his direction; it probably looked like dozens to him. He dropped the trumpet to dangle by its strap and fumbled at the hilt of his light boy's sword, his face milk-white in the moonlight.

"I wouldn't, if I were you, laddie," Karl said, in a not-unkindly tone; the boy had the right reflexes, at least.

The hand poised, uncertain, and he went on: "Off to your mother now, and leave the red work of Badb Catha to those of full years for it."

He stuck his face closer and jerked a thumb over his shoulder:

"Boo!"

The boy reflexively thumped his heels into his mount's sides and thundered off. Mathun chuckled.

"You've not made a friend there," Karl's younger brother said. "For that he'll hate that you should lightly him."

"'Tis the Crone and the Keeper-of-Laws I was thinking of," Karl said shortly. *"Sith co nem; nem co doman. Doman fo ním, nert hi cach."*

In the old tongue that meant: *Peace to Sky, Sky to Earth, Earth under Sky, strength in each;* or that each doing of human kind had its own laws and guardian Powers, war not least. It was ill-luck to kill an *eòghann*, an apprentice-helper, by design.

He looked about. *And that's it for Lancers fool enough to try and ride into the unknown in darkness,* he thought. *They could have given us hard trouble if they'd been less rash, come at us on foot say behind a wall of shields. Of course, they've never met Mackenzie longbows before.*

"Who's hale?" Karl said crisply as he reached over his shoulder for another arrow from his quiver. "Who's hurt?"

They all answered; mostly at once, but his ear could pick out their voices. Nobody seriously injured, serious here being unable to run and fight. An ambush was vastly to be preferred to a stand-up battle.

"Forward, the Princess needs us! On me, at the trot!"

They fanned out on either side as he loped forward, instinct guiding his feet through the night. The netting was mostly fallen, much of it was on fire, and he could hear the clash of blades ahead. And something bright, something more than steel, something that *called* to him, to them all. The Sword of the Lady had been drawn in anger, and the impalpable substance of Earth flexed and shook.

By the time they reached the catapults, the horses were thundering about them.

The world snapped back into motion and Órlaith staggered. A horse—where had it come from?—leapt over the last catapult, its white blaze and rolling eyes wild in the night. The beast landed badly, staggering into a three-quarter fall that saved itself only with a wild lashing of hooves.

That brought fourteen hundred pounds of terror-maddened charger crashing into the *kangshinmu*, breaking the stasis. Half a dozen arrows thumped into him at close range instants later, but even as he flexed beneath the impacts his eyes were *drawing* at her again, like a pit infinitely deep.

She thrust. The Sword seemed to leap forward almost regardless of her will, and a brightness shielded her for the instant that they were face-to-face. A shield to her, but she had never heard agony equal to the squeal from the sorcerer's lips as he seemed to burn from within in a pitiless white torrent when it transfixed him. She yanked the weapon from beyond the world free with frantic strength and swept the long blade around in a humming cut. The body crumpled as the head flew free, but it seemed oddly diminished, and there was little of the firehose spray of blood that such a wound usually produced. Órlaith stumbled three steps and went to her hands and knees, retching uncontrollably. The remains of bread and stew spilled and spattered, filling her mouth with sour vileness that still tasted better than the inside of her mind as she spat frantically.

"Orrey! What's *wrong*!"

Heuradys was on one knee to her right, and Reiko was to her left. She wiped one gauntlet against her lips, heedless of the rough hardness.

"He made me see the whole world of things through *his eyes*. Like being trapped in a maggot . . . *being* a maggot . . . in a giant corpse, eating and shitting and eating through it . . . the whole *universe* like that, forever, everything you ever touched or knew, all maggots and shit . . ."

She retched again, dry-heaving, and brought the crystal pommel of the Sword to her forehead.

"Oh, Brigit the Bright have mercy on Your child . . . Mother-of-All . . ."

Coolness spread through her mind; enough that she could gasp a deep breath, spit again, rinse her mouth with the canteen thrust into it, use the Sword to lever herself upright.

Droyn was limping over to the last intact catapult, a grim expression on his face and the thermite warhead he'd brought along in his hand.

"No. Leave the last, it'll make a demonstration tomorrow. Now let's get out of here."

Some of the frantic worry on Heuradys' face abated; she brought up a captured horse, from the scores milling around. Reiko squeezed her shoulder and stepped back. Not far away Diarmuid was flapping his plaid in the face of a dozen of them, turning them back as they tried to break loose. The Japanese were mounting, and some of her other followers. And bodies were being slung over some of the captured animals.

"Mount, everyone! Count your numbers and make sure nobody's left, dead or alive!" she shouted. "The rest are ready to cover our retreat. We've done what we came for!"

Deor *Wid-ferende* gasped. "They are coming!"

Thora pushed a body off the parapet of the watchtower with her boot and turned and sat as it thumped down onto the pavement below, her face shadowed under the brim of the helmet. The smells of blood and death lay heavy in the little fortlet atop the old freeway.

"They are?"

"Something . . . broke. As when the *drymann* died at the Bay. The Princess is coming."

A wry smile. "I'll have to get the story from eyewitnesses, this time."

A curse and a heavy tread, and Kwame Curtis came limping up. He hadn't done much fighting with his own hands, but a grown son and a grandson right by him *had*, and the old man had been effective at getting his folk into the fight, which was a stand-up one in a style they rarely used. He looked around in the flickering light of the single torch on a pole still burning.

"I hope this was worth it," he said grimly. "We took a lot of losses, considering how many people we have in all."

Deor bowed. "You will find the Princess delivers on her promises, Captain," he said.

Thora nodded without getting up, unscrewing the cap of her canteen; it was wine cut one-to-three with water, which did duty for sterilization and at least attenuated the local plonk. Her tissues soaked it up greedily, and she could almost feel it spreading out through her body. She handed it to Kwame, and he swigged.

"If they end your war and free your people from this threat, are the losses worth it?" she asked him, and got a steady nod. "Then consider it blood well spent, Captain. Every one of us must dree his wyrd, be it what it may, well or badly. I've seen lives spilled to much less purpose—some king's vanity, some lord's greed, a mob's panic or hate, grudges both sides can't leave alone like an itching scab."

Kwame sighed and sheathed his sword. "Point." He cocked an eye at both of them. "If the Lancers take their lesson. I'll admit the Valley must have lost eight for our one, at least."

Thora looked off northward. "If they try coming at us after this we'll break them," she said flatly. "Now we have catapults and they don't. And if we go the other way, they won't be able to stop us. Hopefully they'll see that."

Deor was looking in that direction; the fires and clamor were far enough away that they could seem tiny and very distant.

"As a performer—" he began, and Kwame snorted.

"I saw you in the storming party," he said.

"Well, I'm a singer of heroes," Deor said with a tired grin. "I have to go where they congregate, not so? But a scop is what I am at seventh and last, and *as* a performer, I can tell you that House Artos are no mean force when it comes to the . . . part of kingship that's also a performance. And that may matter as much tomorrow as weight of metal."

CHAPTER TWENTY-NINE

PARTICIPATORY DEMOCRACY OF TOPANGA
(FORMERLY TOPANGA CANYON)
CROWN PROVINCE OF WESTRIA
(FORMERLY CALIFORNIA)
HIGH KINGDOM OF MONTIVAL
(FORMERLY WESTERN NORTH AMERICA)
JULY/FUMIZUKI 29TH
CHANGE YEAR 46/SHŌHEI 1/2044 AD

"My ship, I think she feels naked without the catapults," the captain of the *Virgen de las Esmeraldas* muttered to himself. "Your Highness," he added quickly.

Órlaith grinned beneath the hand she was holding to her brow under the Scots bonnet with its plume of Golden Eagle feathers in the clasp. The shade of it was welcome on this bright hot morning, but for form's sake she was wearing a green Montrose jacket as well, with lace at cuffs and throat and a double row of silver buttons, and a knotwork broach of silver, gold and turquoise to hold her plaid at her shoulder.

Heuradys was in full plate, which would be much less comfortable in the sun that was baking up off the pale weathered asphalt of the roadway, and from the Ventura Freeway behind them . . . but which also made a statement. Nobody else here had anything like it; what the Chatsworth Lancers wore was a feeble third-best, and the militia were even worse-off.

"Esteemed sir, I doubt she feels nearly as naked as the people the catapults are keeping under their eyes," she said to the Esmeraldan captain.

She spoke in *español*, which she'd known fluently since she first bore the Sword, and found herself slipping into the rather pronounced dialect of that widespread tongue that was his native speech—*aguetatar* for *watch over*, for instance, and dropping the final *s* sound on a lot of words. It was very different from the choppy *norteño* version still spoken by some families and districts in Montival. He gave her a sharp glance when she slid into his own forms of speech; Feldman had told her there were no flies on Capitán Antonio de Mendoza y Pacheco, and she was inclined to agree.

He wasn't exactly naked, either, however his ship felt; besides a well-made back-and-breast of steel inlaid around the neck with gold tracery he wore a high-combed morion helmet, arm-guards, and an outfit of close-cut beige cotton twill beneath it all, as practical-looking as possible if you were going to wear steel armor in hot weather, which was the only type his homeland's climate had. His left hand rested on the complex hilt of a long narrow sword; that and a foot-long poignard hung at a belt of tooled leather worked with gold studs, and he had a small round shield of engraved steel slung over his shoulders.

Several of his ship's officers had plainer versions of the same gear, and sometimes half-pikes, apparently how gentlemen or people with aspirations in that direction in the Kingdom of Esmeraldas dressed for war. Their fifty or so crewmen were a good deal wilder-looking; most had helmets, some had one form or another of light torso-armor, and a few wore nothing but rag loincloths. All had machete-swords, knives . . . often quite a few knives . . . and either crossbows or sixteen-foot boarding pikes. Their lean muscular dark bodies shone with sweat from their jog up the Canyon, and their hard scarred faces looked ready for anything.

Feldman's crew from the *Tarshish Queen* were similarly armed, though they looked more uniform because all of them had the same brigandines of reinforced walrus hide, and they had a businesslike stolidity rather than the wolfish, raffish look of the southerners. Her men-at-arms and crossbowmen stood between them, and the Mackenzies with their long-bows in their arms; the McClintocks were wildest of all, with their tattoos and shaggy hair, and the Japanese were discreetly in the background for this internal Montivallan business. The Topangans were a rather shapeless mob, and a bit noisy, but obviously ready for action if they must, their metaphorical tails up with the other night's success.

And hopefully the other side's depressed in equal measure. There are few here with the discipline to take ups and downs in stride.

Best of all were the five catapults on improvised field mounts resting across the roadway in front of them, borrowed from the Esmeraldan ship. They were rather old-fashioned by Montivallan standards, but solidly made and well-maintained; nobody would enjoy getting in the way of round shot or bolts from them—that was certain.

"You will pardon me, Don Antonio," she said, and they parted with bows and more mutual expressions of esteem. "But again, many thanks."

"Friendly sort, and polite," she said to Heuradys as they walked away.

Her knight looked over her shoulder for a moment. "He'd like to be a lot more friendly, or I miss my guess," she said dryly. "Also considering where his eyes are directed right now."

"Mmmm," Órlaith said in agreement.

The man wasn't bad-looking at all, and she had an impression of a forceful but subtle personality, though her thoughts were on other things right now, of course.

"Can't blame him, really," she said with a chuckle. "Where would he be seeing two warrior maids as fair as us? Or see two more shapely arses? Enough to overwhelm any man, so it is; or any who likes women, at least."

"I think we terrified him nearly as much," Heuradys said slyly. "I get the impression the girls are more . . . demure where he comes from."

"Like the Association territories, only worse," Órlaith agreed.

"Oh, I don't know about that. You don't know what *terrifying* is until you've seen a council of Countesses settling things over tea before the House of Peers meets to go through the motions."

"I have, that."

"No, you haven't," Heuradys said with conviction. "You're the Princess, I'm just the other daughter of a baron and they talk in front of me in ways they wouldn't with you. Sometimes so I'll tell you."

They halted where Droyn sat his horse—much like a northern-bred courser, and spoils of the raid—bearing the banner of Montival on a lance. He was in full plate too, though he had his helm slung at his saddlebow and wore a chaperon hat instead, his face like carved oak and eyes unreadable behind his treasured heirloom Ray-Bans.

The Chatsworth array was drawn up around a thousand yards farther north, with their single solitary remaining working catapult standing in lonely state in their front rank. They had about a hundred and twenty heavy horse; and about ten times that of foot, mostly looking like militia and not too different from their Topangan equivalents, save that more of them bore actual pikes rather than just spears.

"I'm not very impressed with those pikemen," Órlaith said. "Even just standing there."

"Yup, not enough drill," Heuradys said.

Pikes were very effective for a range of specialized military tasks, but they had to be used in unison, in mass, and the troops carrying them had to be able to maneuver quickly over rough ground and change direction without getting their long weapons tangled. All of that required a lot of training; not as much as a man-at-arms or even a good archer, but a lot, much more than a crossbow required. You could tell immediately when you looked at a pike regiment from say Corvallis, or one of the Free Cities of the Yakima League, that they really knew what they were doing. Citizens there had to practice from their teens at muster-days and at an encampment of a few weeks in the slack seasons of each year. Most of them might not be able to do much else of a military nature *but* drill with pikes, but they could do that. These . . . were not so much.

A herald rode out from the . . . not-necessarily-enemy . . . ranks and halted about halfway between them. At her nod Sir Droyn advanced to meet him, giving no sign of how the knee he'd wrenched when he landed his hang glider was bothering him, which was precisely what she'd have expected. After a moment of talking, the northern knight shook his head and pointed to her and turned his horse.

And one reason I'm giving Droyn this duty is that we'll have to leave him behind when we cross the mountains, which will cut him to the heart. Best make a public show of trust and honor first.

"They wanted to meet midway?" Órlaith said when he returned, scowling.

"Just as you said they would, Your Highness," Droyn said. "The arrogance of this little backwoods chieftain! I made it plain they would be coming to you—diplomatically, as you instructed."

Órlaith smiled. "Make allowances, Sir Droyn. These people have never left their homes. As far as Mark Delgado is concerned he's a king, more or less, and the son and brother of kings."

Sir Droyn snorted. His father's County could have crushed everyone in this part of the world in a week or two, and not worked up much of a sweat doing it. That was precisely the point, of course; this part of the world *was* isolated, and didn't have any basis of comparison . . . until now.

After a little while there was a churning in the Chatsworth ranks, and two figures rode out with an escort of half-a-dozen lancers behind them. Droyn bristled a little. He'd probably have preferred they come barefoot and holding out their hands like supplicants. Or possibly barefoot, holding out their hands with symbolic nooses around their necks; the way a beaten foe had to her maternal grandfather, if they knew what was good for them.

"Easy, Sir Droyn, easy," she said, and chuckled. "That's what my father always said—let them up easy if you can after you've knocked them down. He also said that you should kill a man or make him a friend; there's not much use in falling between the stools."

Though if you could get a man to consistently *act* as if he was friendly, that would do; not least because if he did it long enough it became a habit. Something her mother had told her a long time ago about that came back; that most people found acting one way and thinking another painful, and eventually if they couldn't act the way they thought they'd start thinking the way they acted instead.

Some people aren't *that way, and they're dangerous,* she'd added. The *like* my *mother* had hung unspoken between them for an instant.

Nonni Sandra had still been alive then. As Lady Regent and probably more discreetly later as Queen Mother she'd always been polite and amiable, right until quiet untraceable ruin fell on someone like an anvil from a clear blue sky.

That one may smile, and smile, and be a villain, she thought. *And knowing my Nonni, she may well have been thinking that while she did it.*

Mark Delgado and his wife Winifred drew rein and dismounted; their horses were good-looking even by northern standards, and their Western-style saddles were tooled leather studded with silver. He was around fifty, give or take, and she a decade younger; both of moderate height, he stocky-muscular and she trim, and both dressed in pre-Change blue jeans, a treasured rarity these days even where salvaging was good. Only those packed in sealed plastic and away from light, heat and water stood much chance of being in good condition and even those didn't last long. There were mills in Corvallis and Boise that could make an acceptable substitute, and hand-loom workers tried elsewhere, but cotton of any sort was still very pricey.

Their heeled boots were new-made, and he wore a modern leather jacket over a checked shirt, with tasseled fringes down the seams and a black Stetson with silver conchos around the band. You could see where a sword-belt usually went around his waist, but he wasn't wearing it right now, which was smart. She had a broader-brimmed hat with turquoise as well as silver, and a long-sleeved, thigh-length blouse of embroidered cotton. His face was square, olive naturally and darkly tanned, and with bowl-cut hair of very dark brown; clean-shaven but with a hint of thick stubble, the sort of man who had to shave twice a day. His wife had long brown plaits caught with jeweled clasps, and a narrow pointed-nosed clever face and unreadable blue eyes.

Mark's eyes went over her gear and Heuradys' and Droyn's, then over the ranks of troops behind her, lingering on the catapults; then they snapped back to Heuradys when she moved slightly to put herself forward and to one side, and you could see him recalculating something on a more personal level. His wife's gaze settled on Órlaith's face instead, after a dart to Heuradys. You could see thought moving there, like goldfish beneath the surface of an ornamental pool, but her face was politely blank.

Órlaith held up a hand before they could start. "Welcome, Lord Mark, Lady Winifred of House Delgado."

She was entitling them the way she would Associates of rank, which was the closest equivalent she could think of. Both of them were very slightly taken aback, and then Mark Delgado puffed up a bit at the respectful terminology. Winifred simply noted it with a dip of her head, acknowledging that it meant the negotiations would be amicable . . . at least to start with.

"I am Crown Princess Órlaith Arminger Mackenzie, heir of House Artos and the High Kingdom of Montival. Just as a formality, it's customary in Montival to touch the hilt of the Sword of the Lady when greeting the Crown Princess or the High King or Queen."

Which was more or less true, in some circumstances, but she had an ulterior motive here. She pulled the sheathed sword out of the frog at her belt and held it out over her forearm. The Delgados looked at each other and then touched the crystal pommel.

Both started slightly as they did; Winifred's eyes went very wide for an instant as if memories were suddenly flashing through her mind. Both then looked intensely thoughtful for a moment, and glanced at each other. You could see them both becoming *more* concerned, as if their sense of what had happened over the last few months suddenly clashed with their memories of it.

Órlaith smiled grimly.

"You may have gotten more than you bargained for when you dealt with the Koreans," she said, and swallowed at the mercifully-fading memories of the *kangshinmu* as she put the Sword back in its sling on her arming belt. "That should clear things up a little."

Mark Delgado was going red and clenching his fists. "I kept thinking I was being too agreeable to the sons of—"

His wife touched him on the sleeve. "Deep waters, *mi corazón*," she said; people in Topanga and the Valley almost all spoke English, but they salted it heavily with Spanish loanwords and turns of phrase.

Órlaith nodded. "Let's go to the pavilion. We can talk out of the sun, at least. Sir Droyn, please see to Lord and Lady Delgado's escorts. And have the troops stand easy. It's a hot day, and it would be a pity did any keel over with sunstroke."

The pavilion was actually sailcloth from the *Tarshish Queen*, strung on ropes the sailors had rigged up to the supports of the old freeway overpass. Beneath it was shade, and olive gloom, and a smell of hot canvas and dust. That put them very close to the watchtower the Topangans, with her help, had stormed the other night, which was by way of a hint.

The furniture and rugs were another loan from the Esmeraldans, this time from Don Antonio's cabin; she was running up a bit of a debt there, but it was the sort she could pay comfortably. Moishe Feldman's new home in Newport was rich in a quiet, rather restrained fashion, but his cabin on the ship he used for his personal voyages was just plain and comfortable. The Esmeraldan's gear would impress the people she needed to overawe just now. And lying between them was the sheathed form of the Sword of the Lady.

Right now it could have been simply a very fine sword . . . save that it was never entirely that. The effect could be very subtle, but it was always there. Nor was the effect of a sword in itself without value. They were discussing politics and power, after all: and in a sense the sword was the power of which all others were shadows. The whole truth was more complex than that; but that was *a* truth.

The wine that Evrouin poured for them all was Feldman's too, from a selection he carried partly for cabin use and partly as samples for potential customers. The Valley's rulers sipped dutifully as a gesture of accepting hospitality, then checked slightly and glanced at their glasses.

"Is that salvage?" Winifred asked. "It's in unusually good condition if it is—that sort of thing has been getting harder and harder to find in a state worth drinking."

"No, my lady, it's from my family's estates, a vintage laid down when I was about twelve," Heuradys d'Ath said. "Montinore Manor, to be precise, on Barony Ath. Just a little west of Portland, in the Tualatin Valley. Feldman and Sons purchases from us in quantity for export to Hawaii, among other places."

It was a nice touch. The more intelligent of them here, a group among which the Delgado family were certainly numbered, must be uneasily conscious of how much they lived in and off the old world's skeleton. Montival was building anew, and a small thing like a well-made pinot noir and a well-printed label and an elegantly blown glass bottle were effective symbols to add to the weaponry. Mark's eyes flickered to his wife, and she nodded slightly.

"Well, to business," he said. "I've got to admit, ah, Princess . . ."

"The usual style in which the Crown Princess is entitled is *Your Highness*," Heuradys said gently. "My lord."

"Ummm, Your Highness, you hurt us a bit the other night. Still, the Valley's standing. You didn't crush us. You didn't even weaken us much. We've got reserves and your new Topangan friends don't."

"Ah, but *your* new allies?" Órlaith said.

"Gone, as you must know," Delgado said. "Except the dead ones."

He touched his hand to his forehead. "Something damned odd was going on there . . . but that doesn't alter the basic balance."

Órlaith inclined her head slightly; he believed what he'd just said, more or less, though he was putting a bold face on it.

"You're certainly not beaten to your knees," she said, in what was not quite agreement. "That's often the best time to make a deal, don't you think? While you still have bargaining stakes."

Winifred's face was entirely expressionless; she would be formidable at poker. Except that her pupils expanded a little, and Órlaith wasn't entirely sure she'd have caught that without the Sword. The woman certainly thought she had a point. Órlaith sipped from her glass and let Heuradys take up the tale, as she laid aside her helm, bevor and gauntlets.

"Lord Mark, let me summarize. Without those catapults the Koreans leant you . . . for purposes of their own, as should now be obvious . . ."

He gave a chuckle. "Like I ever thought otherwise. But there they were."

"And now they're *not*. And without them you have no prospect of taking the Canyon—which is now part of Montival and a signatory of the Great Charter."

Órlaith touched a finger to a copy of it lying at her elbow, the size of a slim book in a tooled-leather cover of deep brown stamped with gold lettering.

Heuradys went on: "Topanga is therefore under the Crown's protection. From now on, if you attack the Canyon, you attack Montival; we gave you a sample of what that means."

His face flushed slightly, and his hands clenched. *That's his tell,* Órlaith thought. *A choleric man, and a masterful one, who doesn't like being thwarted. Not the first I've met. . . .*

"What's more, with our assistance and the catapults *we* have, your opponents can go down Topanga Canyon Boulevard all the way north to the mountains and break anything you try to put in our way. Especially since you don't hold the Ventura Freeway anymore. You can't stop us if you don't bunch up, and if you bunch up the catapults will smash you."

The weapons were right at their backs this moment, emphasizing the point.

"If we're dumb enough to try to fight on your terms," Delgado said stoutly. "There are more ways of killing a cat than choking it to death with butter. You don't have enough troops to hold the Valley if we harass you and refuse the type of battle you want to fight. There's a lot of scrub and wreckage down here. Good luck and a happy time to you combing us out of it."

Órlaith smiled. "Very true. If the Valley were strongly united behind your House, breaking them would take far too much time and too many troops. However, my intelligence is that your hegemony over the Valley is recent in parts and none too popular anywhere. Spare me the formal denials."

The implication of that hung unspoken between them: if he couldn't hold his border, chunks of his lands would break away or join any invader who offered good terms. Possibly some of his own Chatsworth Lancers, if that invader menaced their homes, fields and herds and offered a settlement that guaranteed them. It took a very loyal populace indeed to watch their own homes burn and bleed for strategic purposes; that or an enemy thought to be wholly merciless anyway.

Delgado was a fighter, whatever else you might say about him. He snarled; you might almost say he growled. Órlaith held up a placating hand:

"Let's not let emotions get in the way, Lord Mark, Lady Winifred. These are matters of State and too important for feelings of injured pride, or arrogance. On either of our parts."

Winifred's eyes fixed on her for a moment, and she leaned in to whisper urgently in her husband's ear. Órlaith ostentatiously looked aside for a moment, until he cleared his throat and went on roughly:

"You think you can beat your way through the shell to get at the meat inside? Ah, Your Majesty . . . Highness."

"Lord Mark, I *know* I can; and you're no fool, so you at least strongly suspect it as well. As those catapults—just what one ordinary warship carries—should show you, the art of war as the Changed world allows it has advanced elsewhere in ways completely beyond your capacity to match here. Needs must when the devil drives, and we've been driven hard in ways you have not, and learned painful lessons."

"Plus there's the matter of scale," Heuradys pointed out, turning her wineglass between her fingers. "You're used to thinking of armies numbering hundreds. The High Queen disposes of dozens of ships and thousands of troops even just counting the Navy and the guard regiments we maintain in peacetime. We can mobilize tens of thousands fairly easily, and hundreds of thousands at a pinch. What we have here . . . what gave you that unpleasant sucker punch . . . is simply an escort, what the heir takes along on a trip."

He grunted; the escort was about a quarter as large as his whole elite force.

"You've been left to fight your own quarrels here because nobody cared. Now we do, thanks to your letting those Koreans meddle. We have a grudge against them, and grudges are like the flu, catching if you aren't careful. They've left you in the lurch, haven't they? And Korea is a very long way away. The Columbia Valley is much closer. A week's sailing . . . and a ship can carry a great deal."

A great deal of troops, weapons and supplies went unspoken.

"What are you proposing?" he growled, looking back at the Crown Princess.

Órlaith nodded; that cut to the heart of the matter. "Topanga has signed the Charter, which guarantees their borders. If you sign as well, that guarantees *yours*. You get very nearly complete internal autonomy—at this distance from the Willamette, even more than the usual. It also guarantees the peaceful succession of your heirs."

Unlike his deceased brother, Mark Delgado had four living children.

Órlaith smiled slightly. "I'll throw in the Simi Valley; you've as much claim there as anyone. And your southeastern frontier with the LA Basin is of course as of now undefined. That's potentially a rich salvage trade you've got there when it's developed, and you get to keep most of it."

"I need access to the sea!" Delgado growled. "We've needed it for years . . ."

"You'll have it," Órlaith soothed. "That comes under the free trade and free passage provisions . . ."

Then the dickering began. Fortunately it was morning, and she had that copy of the Great Charter at hand; it had been originally drawn up to be as soothing as possible to a dozen different varieties of bloody-minded localism, including some far stranger and stronger than this pair's little second-generation warlord's domain. John's man Evrouin came in with a light lunch about noon, and the bargaining continued.

Even more fortunately, apparently Winifred Delgado had been collecting information about the north for years, just on general principles, and had a reasonably accurate idea of how far above their weight the Chatsworth Lancers would be punching if they tried to fight, and she had filled in her spouse. Neither of them looked very happy a few hours later, but they'd just lost a war, and they'd still managed to get up with their table stakes untouched.

Also I think the Koreans frightened them. There are sharks in the pond at the bottom of what they thought was their home pasture and now they've seen the fins. Seen things happen in their own heads.

The main difference between them was that Winifred looked as if this was something she'd expected sooner or later, and just regretted not being able to grab off more before it did.

When they'd both placed their hands with hers in gingerly fashion on the Sword and sworn—honestly for the moment, but with hidden reservations that didn't surprise her at all—she nodded. Both broke out in a bit of a sweat as they withdrew their hands from the staghorn hilt.

"Now, you two remind me of my mother's parents, just a bit, and not in a good way. So I'm not going to give you a lecture on good lordship," she said. "For that I have an aversion to wasting my breath, and within very broad limits how you run your own lands is as much your own business inside the Kingdom as out of it. That's how Montival works."

The two hard wary faces across from her nodded almost simultaneously; they'd grasped that that was the practice as well as the theory, and it was the main reason they'd agreed.

That and the catapults, she thought, and went on:

"Instead I'll say a few words on the subject of wealth and power."

She pulled a Montivallan rose noble out of her pouch and spun it on the table; after an instant it fell over and she rested a fingertip on it, pushing it to the middle of the table. This was from the Crown mint in Portland, and bore a rose on one side and the Virgin on the obverse, with a clean milled edge and Latin motto. The simple fact of being able to coin to that standard made Winifred thoughtful, she could see.

"Wealth and power being the two faces of the same coin. What is power, Lord Mark?"

His hand dropped unconsciously to where his sword-hilt would have been. She shook her head.

"A sword means nothing without an arm to wield it; and the arm is attached to a body, which has a head, the which can think. You can control what you think . . . unless you run into nasty people of the sort I've just removed . . . but one sword isn't much in the usual run of things."

Mark Delgado grunted. "I know enough to keep my Lancers behind me," he said.

A stark grin showed he had his own subtlety, and he put in before she spoke. "That's a balancing act. You need to be tough, but not unpredictable. Fear and respect are sort of kissing cousins, but they're not exactly the same thing."

She nodded. "I thought you a hard man, and a clever one," she said. "So a ruler must be. Goodness is a nice dressing on the salad, but a good weak ruler is worse than a right bastard of a man who knows what he's doing and does it. Strength comes first, for without it you can't do anything, good or bad or indifferent."

Delgado gave her a thoughtful nod with genuine respect in it, and she looked at Winifred.

"And you, my lady, I think know that swords in loyal hands can do many things . . . but they cannot plow, or reap, or weave. Or *make* a sword, come to that. You're thinking that the Great Charter says any of your subjects who wish to can leave, but that it's a long way to anywhere else, travel isn't free and it is risky, it's more risky still with children and old folk, and people can't take their farms upon their backs. Or their milch cows or their anvils or much of anything else. And nobody is going to *give* them a house or blankets or a working farm or livestock or an established craft trade somewhere else."

Winifred nodded cautiously. "Yes, Your Highness. That had, ah, occurred to me. Sweat equity of that kind is sort of immobile. Territory's just . . . just dirt, on its own, without people. But people need dirt, and they accumulate stuff attached to the dirt."

Apparently the implications hadn't struck Mark Delgado quite the same way. He frowned uncertainly.

Heuradys chuckled dryly. "That's true. But as many Associate nobles—"

She touched the jeweled dagger at her belt, and the two local rulers nodded to show they understood what it meant.

"—found when we introduced that rule up north after the Protector's War, it's only true to a certain point, and that point depends on many things. A lord can do useful services for a peasant and provide things he needs or at least wants besides the land itself, things the peasant is usually willing to pay for, the more so as you throw in inertia; but peasants are *absolutely* essential to lords. And water tends to seek its own level, sooner or later."

Órlaith nodded. "There are many lords . . . and many free cities . . . and for that matter many clans and autonomous villages and tribes and whatnot . . . who'll welcome any pair of willing hands attached to a strong back, albeit that means starting at the bottom and staying there for a good long while. But there's excellent land going begging and not used for anything but rough grazing or hunting in many a place not two days travel from cities like Portland or Corvallis. Flat, fat well-watered land without pavement on it. And skills . . . a competent blacksmith or carpenter or leatherworker will never lack for work. If not in one place, then another."

Mark Delgado was looking a little alarmed. Winifred's eyes narrowed before she spoke.

"It *is* a long way to the north. Knowledge about that will spread slowly; it'll take longer still for it to become *real* to people."

Órlaith nodded again. "That will give you time. I suggest—for it's up to you—that you use it wisely, for your own children's sake. Get ahead of the curve, so to say. You have to make your folk *want* to dwell here, so you can benefit from their labor. For as to wealth and power . . . they are the source of it; the work of their hands, the craft of their minds seeking their own advantage, which is yours too; and their children. You've the makings of a rich lordship here, but it will take many years of hard work; and it's better to have a smaller share of much more rather than a bigger share of much less."

"Something to that," Mark said, neutrally.

"Now, those children of yours . . . the oldest are?"

"Jack's eleven," Mark Delgado said suspiciously. "Ellen's eight."

Órlaith smiled. "Just a suggestion," she said. "But in a year or two . . . depending on how things go . . . you might want to pay a visit to the north, and have them with you. You might want to foster them at court for a few years, even, when they're a bit older and after you've seen for yourself how such things are managed there. By way of education, and the making of contacts and friendships, you see? Entirely up to you, but you might want to think about it."

Mark Delgado frowned; his wife was obviously thinking very hard indeed.

"You actually want us to do well, don't you?" she said.

Órlaith shrugged. "Yes, and for exactly the same reasons I just advised you about, you see? If you prosper, the Crown prospers."

There was more to it than that—among other things, she wanted the common folk of this little not-quite-bandit kingdom to prosper too—but what she'd said was true enough. And she'd given them both enough to think about, and while they were thinking how to make Montival work for them and theirs, they wouldn't be thinking about how to make it *not* work and get advantage from that.

"We'd better reassure people," Winifred said.

The troops on both sides stood to again as the principals emerged from the pavilion and walked out into the middle of the highway, where everyone had a clear view. There was a rousing cheer from the Topangans as the Valley's remaining catapult was turned over—Don Antonio was getting it as part of his fee—and another from *both* sides as Mark and Winifred went to their knees to put their hands between Órlaith's and swear homage.

Sure, and most of the people here carrying spears are more than happy to take them home and put them back in the rack over the door, she thought. *It's a good day's work . . . ruler's work . . . and now, back to the real task.*

The celebration was modest; gold could not buy more than the land yielded. Fortunately the Valley used money enough that it was possible to send out an emergency call for provisions over a fairly wide area, and folk freed of the prospect of a long war were willing to sell more. One farmer with a lump the size of a pigeon's egg behind his ear had been virtually cackling as he brought in a very handsome boar-hog trussed in the back of a two-wheeled cart and had even volunteered to help slaughter and butcher it. There was plenty of the terrible local wine, which the locals themselves were thoroughly used to.

As the party wound down, Órlaith found herself in a corner of the pavilion—several had been rigged up on the same spot as the negotiations—with a plate of the roasted boar, along with bread and fried tomatoes and several other things. As usual, a fight left you ravenous for some time; she found that was more so now that she bore the Sword. Moishe Feldman sought her out, and they sat on a pair of the folding chairs; Heuradys moved to the fore to screen their privacy, standing casually close enough to hear but with her sphere of personal space keeping others at a little distance, nibbling on a fig herself.

There were times when Órlaith found court protocol at home more than a little stifling, but at least there it kept people from outright trying to grab her attention by pushing their faces into hers. Heuradys . . . and the hand she rested casually on her sword-hilt and those level, slightly ironic amber-colored eyes . . . did the same here. John and Deor were singing a part-song somewhere not far distant, a northern ditty from Portland, and the locals were wildly enthusiastic. The wine probably had something to do with that, but the music more.

Firelight and lamplight made a flickering mystery of the nook; local technology didn't run to the sort of brilliant light an incandescent mantle on a Coleman-style lantern could produce. They both rested their plates on a surface of cracked concrete, some sort of fallen pillar. His held fried chicken, and she'd heard him checking that it and the potatoes were fried in olive oil rather than lard. He was fairly liberal about the precepts of his faith, or at least flexible enough to make traveling among strangers practicable, but not *that* flexible.

"To life," the merchant said, raising his glass. "And to a war that didn't happen, Your Highness. Or mostly didn't. I don't like wars; they interfere with trade."

"Doing my job, Captain," she said, feeling a glow of pride at the thought.

It *was* her job; warriors chose to take up the sword, but there were plenty of ordinary folk still walking the ridge of the earth today because of what she'd done this last little while, their homes unburned and their crops unwasted and themselves not lying stark and sightless as the gore-crows pecked out their staring eyes. Her father would be proud. And whatever their differences, so would her mother.

"I don't like wars either," she said. "For one thing, the outcomes are never certain." She went on: "My thanks again for squaring Don Antonio, that was important—force is better used as a threat than for bloodletting, and a threat's the better for being unspoken; so his crew and catapults just . . . standing there . . . were very valuable. I couldn't have done it, I'm too foreign, and I'm a ruler not a trader, and I don't think he would have trusted someone of my age and sex."

"The more fool he, Your Majesty. Though to be fair, the Sword itself and its bearer are . . . disturbing to those not used to them."

She grinned and swallowed a forkful savory with crackling. "Perhaps, but my parents always said that you had to deal with folk as they were, not as you would have them. Forbye, I think you've information for me, and that more precious than rubies the now."

He nodded. "I've been making some enquiries while I scoured around for the supplies," he said. "It turns out there are still some Jews in the Valley, not all that many but more than a minyan. I attended services at their synagogue, and then some of them and I had a bit of a chat."

"Your being known as my agent the now didn't hurt?"

"Quite the contrary. House Artos has its supporters here; part of the conversation was them checking on what they'd heard with me to see how accurate it was. We didn't get a chance on the relief charters a few years ago, because relations between Topanga and the Delgado lands were too tense for more than a few hurried words."

"Your folk do get around!"

A chuckle. "Even the Change couldn't get rid of us all. Nothing ever does. Not quite."

The smile turned grim. "Some have compared us to cockroaches because of that . . . but I notice that those who said that are mostly extinct. And we are not."

"For I will bless them that bless you, and curse them that curse you, and through you all peoples will be blessed," Órlaith quoted. "In fact, my father said Jews were any realm's anti-canaries."

Feldman frowned a little then chuckled. "Ah, the old story of how they took canaries into mines to detect poison gas? And if we flock in, it shows the air is good?"

"More that the rulers are doing the right things, he said," Órlaith said, remembering her father's smile. "And securing useful subjects to the realm's benefit; merchants, scholars, craftsmen and artists and makers who sharpen wits and make folk in general less sleepy. Speaking of useful, what *did* your people here tell you that you wished to pass on?"

"For starters, that the Koreans have . . . disappeared. Heading south and west, any that survived; and absolutely nobody was sorry to see them go. Apparently they were on their best behavior while they were Mark Delgado's allies, but it's hard to completely conceal what you *are*."

Órlaith sucked in a breath. "South into the ruins of LA."

Feldman nodded. "That's where they'd have concealed their ship. Or ships. The old harbor there is an impossible tangle. It would take a fleet to search it. Or even to blockade it."

She sipped at her wine—they had *not* set out their own stock with the barrels of the local stuff everyone could tap.

"Not a surprise, but good it is to have confirmation anyway. There's more, I'd be assuming."

Feldman finished the drumstick of the chicken, wiped his fingers on the coarse linen napkin and nodded.

"This goes back to the Change, more or less," he said. "A group . . . mainly of my people . . . came through here from LA, just as things were getting very bad indeed. Needless to say, a crazy Jew led them."

"Such is often the case," Órlaith said dryly. "Often great things come of it, from my reading of the Histories, for good or ill. Better this time than . . . oh, Sabbatai Zevi, I hope!"

"Considerably, from what I heard. Jacob Lefkowitz was his name; he had been a soldier, and he was a rabbi . . . Conservative variety."

"A stickler for your Law?"

"More of a label for a . . . denomination. Which meant more back then. And he led them on a camel," Feldman said. "On a group of camels. Bicycles and pushcarts too, but plenty of camels. It seems he had a revelation . . . or said he did . . . that people would blame us for the Change."

He shrugged expressively and spread his hands. "Not totally unreasonable, though fortunately wrong this time. We got blamed for the Black Death, after all, not to mention droughts, hangnails, the common cold and the consequences of everyone else's unacknowledged blunders. As it turned out he needn't have worried about that, people were too busy dying for scapegoating. But at least it got his group moving fast and in a direction like the deep Mojave, which was so unlikely—settling in the Mojave to avoid dying of thirst—that it saved their lives. Apparently he was familiar with the area. A couple of hundred of them, all in all, via the camel farm he . . . liberated."

"There was a camel farm in Los Angeles?" Órlaith asked in surprise. "Some of my grandmother's people . . . liberated . . . horses and wagons and tools from an outdoor museum exhibit, but camels?"

"Evidently. Evidently there was at least one of anything you care to name in Los Angeles, before the Change; the people I talked to were mostly older, and they got very nostalgic about that. Camels are remarkable animals—very efficient, in the right climate, though it's a pity they're *tref*."

Órlaith shrugged. "Most Christians won't eat horsemeat, which is odd when you think about it."

Feldman nodded. "And they're still out there, or their descendants are."

"The people or the camels?" Órlaith asked with a chuckle.

"Both. There's some contact . . . clandestine, mostly. Somehow the Delgado family, Bruce and then Mark and Winifred, ummm, failed to inspire perfect trust, shall we say. And Jacob's people are . . . suspicious. To a fault."

"And wasn't it convenient that I drew a line on Lord Mark's map excluding the Mojave from his domains?" she said. "And he objecting not at all to being denied the rocks and salt and Joshua trees and Gila monsters."

"You may not run into the *bnei Yaakov*; it's a big desert. But just in case . . ." Feldman said.

He extended his fist and then opened it as he turned the hand. She took up the thing of metal and enamel he offered and held it up to the light.

"Ah. The Star of David."

He shook his head. "Mogen David. *Shield* of David. And another name for Him. And may He go with you, Your Highness, and be your shield too. The world is not so oversupplied with good rulers that we can spare any."

"A very pretty piece of statecraft, Majesty," Egawa said as she finished the explanation. "Fragile, I suppose. Still, when we arrived here our enemies had the stronger allies, they were standing in our path, and war threatened our passage. Now after a week's work and one small battle . . . granted, one with features I will enjoy telling my grandchildren . . . the land is reduced to obedience, and our way is open."

"For now; there will be counterstrokes. But as you say, well-done for an improvisation," Reiko replied.

They were sitting on a tarpaulin in an open field, an encampment where the party that would take them over the mountains waited; fires and voices were dying down, and the moon rose enormous and ruddy over the blue-black peaks. The light was stark on the bare slopes, bone-white, blood-red, midnight-blue; so different from the mountains of home, where the very word brought images of mist and pines and bracken. She raised her eyes to the bright alien stars.

"They are extremely different from us," Egawa said thoughtfully. "But there are fundamental similarities. This reminds me of some aspects of our history; very ancient ones."

She nodded. "Different from us. Different from one another, also; and that too is a difference. We have been one people with one tongue and customs and beliefs for a very, very long time."

"Unity is strength," Egawa said. "These divisions . . . it makes me doubt them, Majesty."

Reiko snapped her wrist and her fan opened; then she slowly closed it, one steel batten overlapping and locking with another until it was a rod of metal.

"Unity is *our* strength, General. Truly. Long ages have forged it; long ages tempered it, in blood and fire and slow strong growth. Their differences . . ."

She opened the fan again, until it was fully extended and each component separate, pointing in different directions yet joined at the base.

". . . may well be theirs."

The insects were loud in the night. She cocked her head a little to listen to their shrilling:

"Semi no koe . . ." she said: *Cicadas singing.*

"Keshiki wa miezu . . ." Egawa replied: *No sign.*

"Yagate shinu," she concluded: *Of dying soon.*

"We have faced men who opposed us, and we have cut them down," Egawa said. "We have faced evil *akuma*, and our guardian *kami* have protected us."

"Now we face more terrible enemies," she said.

"Deserts and hardship, Majesty?" Egawa said, smiling slightly.

"Those. And ourselves, General. And ourselves."

CHAPTER THIRTY

ERETZ BNEI YAAKOV
(MOJAVE DESERT)
CROWN PROVINCE OF WESTRIA
(FORMERLY CALIFORNIA)
HIGH KINGDOM OF MONTIVAL
(FORMERLY WESTERN NORTH AMERICA)
AUGUST 12TH/HAOCHIZUKI 12TH/AV 19TH
CHANGE YEAR 46/SHŌHEI 1/5084TH YEAR OF THE WORLD/2044 AD

"I've seen deserts before, but none like this," Órlaith muttered to herself.

She felt a little groggy despite sleeping through the day in the shelter of the tarpaulin, or perhaps because of it. It was hot; the sort of hot that meant you felt baked in the shade but if you stuck any part of yourself out into the sun it *grilled*; it made her regret that so much of her blood came from lands of mist and cloud and scant sun, because even though she tanned fairly well and had been keeping covered as much as she could her face and hands were sore and skin peeled. Her mouth felt gummy, not quite dry but getting there, and there was a thrum as of fever in her veins. She took a smooth rock out of her sporran and popped it into her mouth, working it around until the saliva began to flow a little.

The whole encampment was in the shade of a red-rock cliff striped horizontally with paler color. It ran northeast-southwest and turned into a narrow canyon, so it would provide some shade even at noon. There was a smell of warm rock and dust and aromatic, almost creosote-smelling vegetation. She carefully checked her boots before she pulled them back on—scorpions liked to curl up in the toes, for some reason, and made objections of stinging force if you jammed your toes into them while they took a nap.

The fact of the matter is I can feel the place coming alive, in a spare sort of way, she thought. *We're just doing what the birds and beasts and bugs do here; sleep in the day. Summer daylight here is the anvil of the sun indeed!*

Heuradys came in with their share of the rations, and Reiko and Egawa followed her, and John; Diarmuid too, and Karl and the Dúnedain. They all sat in a circle around the folded cloth and ate and drank with slow care, sipping the water at long intervals, and eating the crackerlike biscuits with nuts in them, olives and dried fruit. The olives were salty, but that was a necessity too—Órlaith could feel where a rime had been left on her skin where sweat dried during the day. In fact you were seldom conscious of sweating here; the atmosphere was so dry it sucked the moisture right out of your pores.

She rubbed a little of the oil into her face—it stung in her cracked lips—and her hands. They couldn't wash—that was often the case in the field, but more so here—yet the dry heat made the smells less offensive.

"Well, friends, according to the map, we have made exactly . . . no progress in the past five days."

She laid it out and tapped her finger down on it; they were at a place that had been called Emigrant Canyon in the old days.

"This is the castle that the Majesty and I have seen," she said, stabbing at a spot farther into the Valley of Death.

"It's plainly marked. There's a road of the ancients, and we can go along the foot of the mountains. We set out in the evening, and . . . somehow . . . in the morning we're a day's march from where we started, but no closer to where we were supposedly headed. If I take the lead, more often than not I look around and you're all gone, unless we blindfold you and rope you to my belt . . . the which is scarcely practical for long, and there was that time you all started dragging *me* in the opposite direction while swearing you weren't doing it! It's getting fair monotonous and we're running short of supplies and time. Now, does anyone deny that this is happening?"

Several faces clenched in frustration; there wasn't a single one here who wasn't strong-willed to the point of being bullheaded. She held up a hand.

"No complaints, mind, no anger. I'm not interested! I've enough complaints and anger of my very own, thank you all. Just . . . does anyone deny that this is *happening*? And that we cannot afford the time? We've been delayed again and again on our road here, and that may very well have been in the enemy's plan."

Silence grew as the first stars appeared overhead. At last Karl spoke. "No, that's what's been happening . . . and Princess, I've heard something much the same."

At her raised brows he went on, a little reluctantly, as if speaking of it was an effort:

"When your da and mother went to Lost Lake for the Kingmaking, *my* da guarded their back, standing rear guard as they walked down the last trail. Once he told me that he was needed not at all for that. For even the strongest will could not take a step after them; your path twisted aside if you tried, and your eyes were . . . shifted elsewhere. If your will wasn't of the strongest, you couldn't make yourself even *want* to try."

She frowned. "I think . . . my parents may have said something of the sort, but not in detail."

Karl nodded in turn, his boney young face unwontedly serious. "For that they wouldn't *feel* it, do you see, Princess? *They* can go there, for the Powers allow it. For other folk, not so; and it's been that way at Lost Lake since. Now and then my father . . . and I with him, once or twice . . . have hunted the woods near there, on the slopes of Mt. Hood, while the High King and Queen were at Timberline Lodge."

That was Crown demesne, and visits to Timberline were cherished marks of honor for guests, but the High King's Archers went where the Royal family did. Most of the millions of acres of woods around Hood had been some sort of preserve before the Change, though now they bordered on the territory of the Dukes of Odell to the east and the Counts of Molalla to the west.

Karl went on: "No paths lead there, though there were roads to it before the Change, aye, and after, until that day. Cross that territory as you will, you won't catch a glimpse of it now, even if maps say you should. It's . . . a place apart now, beyond the hills we know."

There were uneasy glances among some of those present; Diarmuid made the sign of the Horns.

Heuradys spoke, her voice cool, though she touched the owl amulet of Athana she wore. But that One was patroness of reason:

"That's the holiest spot in all Montival," she said. "And sacred to House Artos. Why should we have the same problem here?"

Órlaith laid the Sword across her knees, and her hand on the hilt. She was reluctant herself: these were sacred matters. But these folk had followed her into this peril, with more than a hint of the Otherworld to it, and she owed them an explanation.

"My father and mother bore the Sword to Lost Lake . . . to E-e-kwahl-a-mat-yam-lshkt, Lake at the Heart of Mountains," she said softly. "That was the goal of the Quest of the Sword of the Lady. Before that full many had walked there in the light of common day. When he and my mother mixed their blood upon the point and drove it into the rock of Montival they did more than pierce stone. They drove it through time itself, through all the days of their ancestors and their descendants; and theirs and mine is the mingled blood of all who have dwelt here, and it will run down through all their generations. It became the pivot about which this land turns. My father carried the Sword away, but . . . *it is still there.*"

At their puzzlement, she went on: "From that moment, it always *was* there. It always *will* be there. From the time the Ice withdrew and the first tribes of human kind wandered into this land, in the time of the Gods who were before the Gods, forward to a destiny unknowable, through all this cycle of Time and Space. And so that spot now dwells in all those times, and none; it has stepped *aside* from the world where we dwell. Only my blood can walk that path."

Silence rang as night fell. "More I cannot say," she whispered. "I will not know the fullness of it myself until I journey there for my own Queenmaking. We say that the lord and the land and the folk are one; it's a proverb. But it is *true*."

Reiko spoke at last. "Yes. Then what bars *you* from this spot we seek?"

Órlaith met her eyes. "What it holds, and should not," she said. "That which belongs to you and yours."

Reiko nodded, and addressed the others: "Such things . . . a thing which embodies the spirit and history of a land and a people . . . they are things which can be terrible. Not evil, not wicked in themselves, but . . . perilous, as any great force of nature. An earthquake is not evil; a tsunami is not evil; but they can destroy, especially if you are heedless of them. This is why such things are so often hidden away. *Kusanagi-no-Tsurugi* is one of three great treasures of *our* people. The jewel, the mirror, and the sword."

"Ah," Órlaith said. "But only one of three, where we have only the Sword."

Reiko nodded. "I think . . . what the Sword of the Lady is to your land, together they are to Nihon. But separate aspects. The jewel to sustain, to . . . to nourish, as a mother nourishes her child. The mirror for wisdom, for insight, as the mind and soul inform and guide the body, and look inward on themselves for self-knowledge."

Órlaith made a gesture of agreement. "So for you this Sword is more singly such a thing as a *blade* would symbolize?"

Reiko inclined her head, and moved her fan gracefully. "The Grass-Cutting Sword, that embodies *power*, the power of Fire and Air that is the soul of the Immortal One Shining in Heaven . . . who is my Ancestress. The warrior heart and power that a ruler must have, to protect, to guard, neh?"

"Justice carries a sword," John murmured. Reiko looked at him approvingly.

"And to punish the wrongdoer, yes. But separated from its proper place, from the proper hands, that power runs wild, seeking, not finding, twisting the very frame of things. Because it is apart from wisdom and peace."

Órlaith nodded. "And this land, to protect itself, has drawn a wall about the place. *That* I have sensed. An . . . absence."

Reiko hesitated, then went on: "To control it . . . that only I can do. I have seen . . . it has been granted to me to see the Grass-Cutting Sword through the history of my people, from the time of legends to that of our grandfathers. How it is entwined with the blood of my House, and both are mingled with the fate of Dai-Nippon. It was forged for the hand of the *Tennō*, the lord of the land, of the blood of the Sun Herself. Apart from that hand, it can wreak terrible things. So it was kept apart and secluded for many ages."

Órlaith looked around at her followers. "All of you, my dear comrades, came because I called you. Some died, and all of you have risked death and shed your blood for me. But at the seventh and last, this isn't something a war band can do. We're not here to make war, or to take with the hand of power. This is a pilgrimage, the righting of a wrong, the forging of a destiny that links us with the Powers. In the end, it's something that Reiko and I have to do—me to take her through the barriers this land has thrown up against a power that is not of its native soil, her to claim it by right of blood and her willingness to do what is needful at any cost and pay the price of it. And so here, for a while, we must leave you: because only we can make our lands whole again."

She touched the Sword again. "No, Johnnie," she said, to forestall him. "You're my brother of blood, but this could only come to you if I were to fail and fall. Fail and die. Until then the burden's mine. You will have your own tasks."

Indeed you will. For you too have dreamed; what those dreams mean, we do not yet know. But not of this.

Gently: "Herry, sister of my heart, you are my shield and my right hand and my most trusted advisor, but this once I have to go without you."

Heuradys nodded and looked aside, swallowing; John pounded a fist on his knee and bent his head. Egawa turned and began to bow.

Reiko caught his eye and made a single sharp sideways gesture with her fan. "No, General. From this you cannot guard me. It is for this that I was *born*."

They both rose and stood side-by-side. "Wait for us," Órlaith said. "And that is the hardest thing we could ask of you."

Three days later Reiko went down on one knee, bending her head. "Perhaps . . ." she managed to croak.

That did duty for perhaps we should have waited for sundown.

Órlaith touched the empty waterskin at her side. That filled in for an entire day without water and we wouldn't be able to move at all.

Reiko blinked again and again, until her eyes unblurred a little. That did nothing for the headache, which she could ignore at worst despite the way it pulsed through her every time the heartbeat sounded in her temples. And nothing for the weakness and feeling like a bad fever, which she could not. Her broad domed *sandogasa* straw hat at least gave her reasonable protection from the direct sun, as much as from the rain it was originally intended to shed. Órlaith wore a light beige-colored cloak with a loose hood, which did about as well.

Water, the Nihonjin thought, and then immediately wished she hadn't. The problem with losing your mind is that affects your self-discipline.

That almost made her giggle, but she controlled herself in time, afraid that if she did there would be no stopping.

Must not stop, she told herself. Keep—

Órlaith paused beside her, wheezing. The scabbard of the Sword clattered against the rocks beneath. With a dull clank . . . which meant they were on . . .

A touch beneath her elbow. That was not support, it was the idea of support, and she found herself able to stand. The rock beneath her feet was pale, very pale—somehow a white shade of black, and smooth except for a fissuring of cracks. Asphalt, after half a century of merciless sun.

Road, she thought, the thought as sluggish as her thickening blood. *Ancient road.*

The desert had been surprisingly densely scattered with them. Asphalt and dirt and gravel, lying still and often almost as if the ancients had simply walked away a little before. Sometimes with cars still resting on them, not as badly rusted as the ones she was used to. Sometimes the doors were open, sometimes shut; sometimes only bones near them, sometimes a grinning blackened mummy peering out through the glass, sometimes you walked a mile before the broken scattered skeletons lay by the wayside.

They crossed the road. Then gravel crunched beneath their feet. It was as if she was pushing wooden stumps down at the ground. Also as if she was pushing herself. Pushing through something resilient, endlessly patient, something that pushed at her mind to turn it about, as if soft impalpable hands nudged and nudged and nudged at her shoulder. The Sword at Órlaith's side was a white beacon, the prow of a ship parting the wave, the point of a spear. At times she hated it, because without it she could lie down and stop and that feeling of willful exclusion, of wrongness, would stop too.

The tension in her head mounted and mounted. She coughed, then retched dryly and put her hands to her temples. There was an almost irresistible urge to grab and pull, pull, pull until the skull popped.

A note of music, as if something had parted. A steel wire behind her eyes, somehow. Heat poured out of her, and sweat broke out all over her body. She crammed her cracked lips against the skin of her wrist, and the thick salty sweat burned them like a wave of fire, shocking her mind back into a glassy lucidity for a few instants. Something crackled beneath her feet, something tawny.

Grass, she thought. *Brush.*

A cliff loomed ahead, pale rock dripping as if it had melted—marble, flowing down the rock.

Órlaith made a choked sound beside her and toppled, toppled forward, crawled into the shade of the cottonwoods. Water glimmered and she plunged her head into it. Reiko coughed again and collapsed. Her outstretched hand fell into coolness, and she writhed forward like a snake. Hand to mouth, water touching her tongue.

Pull, she thought, and grabbed Órlaith's sword-belt with both hands. Pull!

The other woman slid backward over dried grass. Her face turned sideways, water running from her slack mouth and from her nostrils, and she coughed and sputtered. Reiko stretched her hand out again, licked the water off her palm with her swollen tongue, repeated it until her throat and stomach began to ache. Then she set herself to push Órlaith over on her back, an effort that left her shuddering and striving not to vomit up the water she had swallowed. After she lay panting for a while she fumbled at her belt until the cup atop her canteen was in her hand.

Slowly. Into the water, fill it. Pull it back. Don't spill!

Slide a hand under Órlaith's head. Tilt it up. Dribble the water into her mouth. Slowly!

As much as she could swallow. Then a cup for herself. Then dribble another past Órlaith's lips. Her body grew heavier and heavier while she worked. Then she turned and collapsed backward. Sunlight dappled through the leaves above, and there was a hint of dampness soaking through from the ground into her hair, and the hat slowly came forward and rested over her face. Silence. Oddly, she could feel her willpower physically, the thing she used to make herself do that which was beyond her: it was like a ball of tight-bound string in her chest. Now it was unravelling, spreading out through her body with the water. Like a faithful servant dismissed to rest with a smile and gesture.

Rest.

Reiko snatched at her *tessen*; or at least she would have, if her hand had obeyed her instead of twitching and swaying and falling back.

"Easy, Reiko-chan, easy," Órlaith said; her voice was hoarse, but no longer a grinding croak. "Easy there."

She pushed the hat off her face and bit back a whimper as she moved. Every muscle in her body seemed to have *shrunk*, turning in on itself and trying to pull her into an immovable knot. Órlaith's face looked ghastly as she tried to smile, with shreds of skin loose around her lips and her eyes sunken in her head.

"And how would you be feeling?"

"Terrible. Wonderful," Reiko said, and winced a little at the pain of attempting to smile herself.

"I think I've you to thank for not drowning," Órlaith said cheerfully despite the skull-like look of her face. "Which would be too ironic for words, drowning in this desert, would it not?"

"We are past the point of counting who has saved whose life most, I think, Orrey-chan!" Reiko said.

Very carefully she pushed herself up until her back was braced against a cottonwood stump and looked around. It was evening, and felt . . . not exactly cool, but not *hot* either. A cliff loomed northward; between it and them was a line of pools. Water trickled down the rock, amid the travertine it had deposited. Reeds and trees and odd-looking bushy palms grew thick, and there was a smell of *life* in the air that was inexpressible joy. A small fire crackled, and Órlaith lifted a cup off it. The infinitely familiar aroma of miso greeted her, and she took it and sipped.

"Ahhh," she said.

Her spirit was still unstable, and she felt a prickle of tears at the homely taste. And at the sight of Órlaith, and at the terror of what being alone here would have meant.

This is what it is to have a friend, a true comrade, she thought, and looked aside until she had composed herself.

"Indeed, and I'm less hostile to the stuff now," Órlaith said, sipping at her own cup. "I've been up for a pair of hours—got the camp set up, such as it is. And had to pee, the which is deeply reassuring."

Reiko nodded soberly; that meant lasting kidney damage from near-death by thirst was less likely. That—and the sound of trickling water—made her aware of a similar urgency. She stood cautiously, and took step by step until she found a suitable spot; the flow was thick and ill-smelling, but she felt the better for it. When she returned and washed her face and hands Órlaith had soaked some biscuit in the reconstituted soup and set out some of the dried apricots and figs. They both ate cautiously, nibble by nibble, ceasing at the first protests from stomachs just coming to life, and sipping slowly but frequently at water. Reiko could even taste it now; it was rather . . . not quite warm but un-cool, and with a mineral tang. She looked about as she did; the little stretch of vegetation extended some hundreds of yards either way along the base of the cliff, but it was narrow, barely a third of that wide.

There was also a bunch of grapes, small and thick-skinned; she took one and let it burst between her teeth, joyfully soothing to the sore interior of her mouth.

"Where are we?" she asked. "Though everything is very nice compared to where we were. If we had some tea, nearly perfect!"

"'Tis a place called Grapevine Springs . . . or Grapevine Canyon . . . by the maps. And living up to its name; there are a few wild vines. And some birds and small game about, and from the prints some sort of antelope visit here. And human kind, but not many and not that often. Bare feet; the same ones each time, I'd say. No outsiders since the Change, I'd venture, or very few. Whatever was keeping us out, we're either inside it, or it's gone . . . and I'm thinking it's gone. But for as long as it stood, it kept whoever and whatever was here inside, as well. I think it might have been possible for a few to enter, but much harder to leave."

"And the castle?" Reiko said; her head still felt a little thick.

"About a mile and a half from here," Órlaith said. "I haven't been prancing about, you'll understand!"

Her head dropped forward, and Reiko smiled again, despite the cracked lips. "I also could sleep, Orrey-chan," she said. "And if nothing has killed us yet . . ."

"Extraordinary," Reiko said a day and a night later as they approached the complex of buildings.

She was moving well now, rebounding with the resilience of someone young and immensely fit; so was her companion.

Moving well compared to yesterday, she thought.

She chuckled at the thought, and Órlaith voiced it: "Sure, and I only feel a few years past sixty the now, rather than a hundred and six come Yule, and three days dead besides."

The structure they studied was a castle, in the sense that there were exterior walls with crenellations in some parts; others had arched entryway doors, a set of three of them to either side of the main entrance they faced. One tower to their right was round and looked like those of a Western-style castle . . . in miniature, only two stories tall.

There had been gardens of some sort around it, and the skeletons of dead trees still stood, hacked and haggled for firewood. Equally dead vehicles stood before the entrance, and a clutch of bicycles that looked to have been there about as long. And a curious cart-like machine, with two bicycles in front. Several of them, in fact; they had the look of something improvised in a hurry.

"I've seen ranch headquarters that looked a little like this, in some parts of the country over the Cascades, on some of the bigger spreads," Órlaith said meditatively. "And in the Commonwealth of the San Luis, that time we visited for the Charter signing. Red tile like that and this layout, around a courtyard. But with more serious exterior walls . . . this is as big physically, but like a plaything compared to those, as if someone were toying with the thought of it. Toying with the thought of a castle, and of a manor-house at the center of an estate."

Walking closer in the growing red light of dawn they saw a firepit before the courtyard entrance. It had been crudely built up above the pavement with chunks of this and that and rocks, three or so feet deep, and then used repeatedly with little attempt to clear away ashes. There was a stale smell about it, of ancient grease gone bad, and crusted grills and spits lay about it. Reiko looked around, her hand on the hilt of *Kotegiri*, while Órlaith squatted and poked with a stick.

I feel . . . observed, she thought.

"Bones," Órlaith said as she investigated. "Birds, rabbit, small beasts of some sort. Antelope, this is a hoof. Whoever was doing the cooking wasn't much at breaking game."

She dug a little more, and exhibited a human tooth on the end of the stick. "This on the bottom layer," she said grimly.

As the light grew they could see that the stucco that covered the rambling buildings was mostly intact; it looked very much as it had in the ancient photographs. Except that something had been written on it—scored into the material, in fact, scratched deep into its substance over the doors. The writing was in the Roman alphabet, and in English:

Cody Biltmore is dead and damned, it said. Then below, the letters larger and wilder: *Damned— Damned—Damned . . .*

Órlaith took a step forward, then hesitated and stopped. "I have a feeling I'm not welcome," she said seriously, her palm resting on the crystal hilt of the Sword of the Lady.

Reiko nodded. "It was your part to bring me here, Orrey-chan," she said, and took a deep breath. "Through you your land grants me leave. But the next . . . that is mine. Give me a day and a night."

At the arched entrance she turned and bowed; Órlaith returned the gesture. Then she faced the doors and laid her hand on the hilt of her father's sword; another deep breath, and she stepped past the sagging gates of bolted timbers and wrought-iron and into the courtyard within.

"Many clouds arise:
The clouds which come forth as a manifold fence:
For the husband and wife to retire within
They have formed a manifold fence:
Ai! A fence!"

Reiko murmured the words as she walked, feeling them welling up from within. A dry wind whispered through the courtyard, louder than the sliding of cloth upon cloth as she moved, and a sound seemed to come upon it.

That is a child crying, she thought; the thought slid through a consciousness wholly focused on its purpose.

A thin bitter sobbing, lost and hopeless. She waited, absolutely still, by the entrance, letting her awareness spread outwards. The courtyard was a paved rectangle, with buildings on three sides; two stories to left and right, with an open balcony atop the one to her right and a covered one to her left with the roof supported by square pillars. A low section blocked the north side. Nothing moved, and she heard nothing but the wind, and the whimpering.

Follow the sound, then.

Quickly to the left, and along the arcade. More large doors, solid carved wood this time, but they yielded to a nudge with her foot. She waited. Nothing . . .

The door swung back as she kicked and spun into the room, the katana hissing free and her back to a solid wall. The room within was a great hall, hammer-beams above, with a gallery surrounding it and a great hooded fireplace. Her nose wrinkled at a hard stink of human filth. The floor was mostly bare, and from the pile of charcoal and ashes in the fireplace the furniture had been burned at one time or another. There were bones there too. Some light penetrated from high windows, but they were caked with decades of dust and sandblasted by windstorms.

The weeping came from an overturned sofa near the hearth. Her back prickled as she crossed the room, staying close to the wall. Someone with a bow on that gallery would be a problem without a solution save flight. She felt a little relief when she reached the massive overturned piece of furniture and knelt by it, a little sheltered and close enough to the gallery that anyone on it would have to lean far over to bear on her.

Eyes peered at her from beneath it, and then a figure crept out. It was a small spider-thin child of about two, obviously a girl-child, for she wore nothing but caked filth and a chain around her ankle, running to a massive iron fixture beside the fireplace. Huge green eyes looked at her with awed curiosity below a tangled mass of hair that was probably ginger-red when it wasn't so dirty; that turned to a ferocious focus when she held out her canteen and showed it held water. Though she spilled not a drop as she drank.

At least I do not see any lice on her, Reiko thought.

That was oddly chilling; the only way she could think someone this innocent of cleanliness could *not* be lousy was an isolation so total that there had been no opportunity for humanity's old, old companions to reach this spot.

The girl cried again after she drank. When Reiko extended a biscuit she stared at it with no recognition until the Nihonjin woman bit off a corner and ate it; then she snatched it and gobbled and drank again.

"Hada birdie," the child said; what she spoke was English but slurred by more than her age. "S'm bugs. S'm quickie-crawlies. S'gon. Hongry bad."

Reiko's eyes dipped back to her and then up to the gallery and the darkened corners of the hall again. A great iron chandelier overhead showed how it had once been lit, but shadows moved in every corner.

"Who are you, little one?" she asked softly.

"'m *Kid*," the girl replied, obviously finding it incomprehensible that someone should *not* know who she was. Again, with more emphasis: "'m thuh *Kid*."

The answer left her blank for a moment, until she remembered that was a slang term for *child* in some dialects of English.

I am the child *is what is meant*, she thought. *The* only *child, I think; she has never seen another or imagined one.*

"Where are your parents?" Reiko asked softly. Then, when there was no understanding in the odd green cat-like gaze: "Father? Mother? Dad? Mom? Mama?"

"Mama. Bad Auntie took 'er," she said, lip trembling. "Wanna mama!"

No idea of a father. Probably never knew him, Reiko thought.

She felt pity for the wretched feral thing dwelling amid horrors, but it was detached and abstract now. Someone had obviously put that chain on her ankle. That someone was almost certainly of her kin and they were probably somewhere in this darkened maze.

"Bad Auntie?" she said, handing the child another biscuit and some of the dried fruit.

The fruit puzzled her until she shoved some of it into her mouth experimentally; then she gobbled with an expression of wonder at the sweetness.

"Took 'er. Down-down."

She bared her teeth and growled and made clawing gestures and then shrieked; it took Reiko an instant to realize she was playacting something beyond her capacity to express in words.

"Dark, dark, down-down *bad*."

Reiko set the canteen down on its base after she took a long drink herself, and the packet of rations. The child promptly lost interest in her as she clutched the food and drink; she evidently hadn't even had enough of a concept of *outsider* to be much afraid of one.

Probably she saves fear for the ones she knows, Reiko thought. *Two, perhaps three . . . at that age children can still live as an animal does, wholly in the moment, accepting anything.*

The girl made an inarticulate sound and crawled back under the sofa as Reiko ghosted away; as she did she drew the *wakizashi* with her left hand, walking with a springy tensile lightness.

Into another room, also large, but full of counters and sinks and pans, covered in once-bright tiles and darker still. A woman's body hung from an overhead hook sunk into her armpit, her arms bound behind her and her feet just above the floor . . .

No, one foot.

The other leg ended above the knee, in a crusted tourniquet. Reiko swallowed, but she had seen things as bad before, in the wake of *jinniku-kaburi* raids.

The body's eyes opened, and the mouth. The tongue was gone, the stump cauterized. She held up the blade, and the dangling figure nodded, once, slowly. Reiko lunged, trying to be as accurate as possible. That was easier because the body had a terrible scar running from just below the breastbone to about the navel, old and dusty-white and healed . . . which was very strange, because she could not imagine that wound not killing.

I will end this.

There was a single convulsive jerk as the steel went home, the feeling in the hilt the familiar soft heavy resistance . . . until the point grated on something. Not bone, on *steel*. And—

Fire.

It ran through her; every vein, every nerve, and she felt the hair rising on her head, writhing and fighting against the braids and pins. The steel within the body flowed, flowed down the sword, into it, towards her. She thought she flung her arms wide and screamed . . .

And she was elsewhere, watching, and it was a man screaming. A very old man, but she knew him; it was the pillager of the Atsuta Shrine, gone bald and fat and wrinkled as if half a century had passed—half a very long lifetime, half the time between that moment and now. Enough to be in the year of the Change. Screaming as he was dragged out of the very gate she had entered a few minutes before. Less worn, less sagging from its hinges, some of the damage she had seen happening before her eyes as he clung to it and wept and one of those pulling at him hit his fingers with a blade, a katana of classic lines that must have been part of his plunder.

There were half a dozen of them, from middle-age to their teenage years, and they all had a look of him, beneath bruises and gauntness and staring eyes. As fugitives might look, who found themselves imprisoned in what they had thought to be a refuge from the madness that swept over the world. Imprisoned in a stretch of barren desert that city-dwellers had no skill to use in any event, like a cyst of sand and rock and heat . . .

The old man's screams grew louder at the sight of the firepit's glowing coals, and the knives and cauldrons.

Suddenly she was back in the defiled room, kneeling. The hook swung empty before her, and ash drifted on the still foul air. *Kotegiri* was stretched out—

No, she thought. *Not quite* Kotegiri.

The blade was different. Slightly longer, perhaps a hair broader, though with the same pure curve and no heavier in her hand. She stared with fascination as thin traceries of fire curled up along the steel, filaments far finer than a human hair, that she was not sure she saw with the eyes of the body. Yellow and ruddy and white, crawling somehow through the very substance of the katana. Weaving through the thirty thousand layers of the jewel steel the ancient master-smith had hammered, permeating it as his will and skill had done. Remaking not only what it *was*, but what it *had been*.

Full consciousness returned, and she started to her feet. Eyes probing the darkness where *anything* might lurk, alerted by the noise that had been torn from her.

But it is not so dark.

There was a wash of light; light that cast no shadow. Light that might not be light as humans thought of it. Perhaps it was the essence of which physical light was merely a reflection, the shadow cast on the wall of a cave.

A door stood open across the kitchens. Within it she could glimpse stairs, descending. *Down-down,* she thought, echoing the child's terror. *Dark, dark.*

Her sandals were soundless on the tile of the floor as she walked towards it. She was conscious of all movement, of a cockroach scuttling behind a stove, of the spider that waited for it. The room and the stairs ahead were *full* of waiting. Past the door without touching it, foot on the stairs, stair, stair, stair . . .

A rush of cloven air above her, and she twisted like a cat with the katana for a claw. A glimpse of a wild figure with blades in both hands, dropping down from above with a snaggle-toothed snarl and a mane of wild graying hair, down towards Reiko's rising steel.

Fire.

This time she *was* the fire as the sword struck the metal within the body, a wash of light and heat, energy pouring into darkness with prodigal generosity. Feeding life itself, keeping at bay the hostile cold that would freeze the worlds without it. Potential pouring into nothingness, structuring it with warmth and order, making nothing of the self-consuming sacrifice at its burning heart.

The vision that came next was merely a woman crouching in darkness. She held a shard of rusting metal in her hands, like a fragment of a sword. Pressing it against her flesh, cutting, cutting, whimpering as she pressed it and murmuring over and over:

"Mine, mine, *mine.*"

When Reiko came to herself hoarse sounds were coming from her throat. There was no pain; this was a sensation beyond pain, a suffusion that threatened every instant to scatter the very particles of her being in a blaze of infinite energy, as if she was being torn to pieces instantly, in an instant that went on forever.

"I . . . cannot," she whispered, shaking. Nothing could, nothing human could contain this. "I cannot! Cannot!"

A voice that was memory rang through her mind: *Subdue your soul. It is your* giri, *and your karma, daughter of the Empire, daughter of the Sun.*

And a thought; callused hands thrusting a shoot of rice into the mud of a paddy, and the next and the next and the next, bent back and dogged will and never ceasing.

Shaking, she thrust the shortsword back into its sheath and gripped what was no longer a thing of human craft in both her hands. Light and fire and power, flowing through her, swirling in her substance and remaking her, then channeled back into the thing she grasped.

The tunnel would have been utter blackness, but it was not. She went down it, sword poised.

Memory shredded as she did, until she was not sure if she was experiencing or recalling; or if there was a difference. A figure that wriggled on its belly towards her, teeth wet, reaching for her ankles, and the blade slashed and the flame swept through her. Two that rushed towards her back, gripping a long pole with a knife lashed to its end. She leapt over that, running *up* the wall, and the sword slashed twice and the world exploded in suffering that was almost ecstasy. Two gibbering shapes that lurched towards her, their ankles fused into a creature with three legs and four arms waving club and hatchet and knife and sharpened shovel, and she cut diagonally, and the shock was faster and faster as if she were plunging through endless depths even as she walked on her own feet.

A last one that crouched laughing in the ultimate crevice of the tunnels, holding a gnawed skull out to her in both hands as if offering a cup of tea. From somewhere there was a hint that the ancient bone was somehow *aware*.

"Cody Biltmore is dead," she said as she stroked the skull. "Dead and damned . . . damned . . . damned . . ."

It is mercy, she thought, and cut; the bone shattered and then the screeching figure flung herself onto the blade. *This must end.*

Images flashed; she was not sure if she saw them, or lived them, or traveled through them. The ginger-haired *gaijin* in a vast shed with others uniformed as he was, and an envelope passing unseen between him and another who slashed a chalk-mark on to his duffel bag. The same man older, in a crowded room where machines spun in circles and women in abbreviated costumes tossed balls upon them. Older still, gray in his hair and sagging pouches under his eyes, and pushing a katana across a table in a small room, and counting the bills handed to him.

Then he was the ancient who would be dragged out by his descendants to meet an unclean death, sleeping rolled in a blanket as the others pedaled with him through the night towards the place of his long waiting.

Then she was back in the great hall, unsure if she walked or *flowed* through it. The thing in her hand hummed, hummed with a potential beyond even the understanding she possessed now. As if it trembled on the edge of a precipice, and yearned to fall *upward*. The fabric of things strained and creaked about it.

Huge green eyes peered out at her from beneath the sofa again, and some part of her wondered how much of what she felt was visible to them. Then the girl-child shrieked, shrieked and pointed.

"Bad auntie! *Bad auntie!*"

Reiko whirled. A sword was raised, already descending, one that might have been a twin to the one she had carried into this place. The figure wielding it was a swirl of darkness to her sight now, the human within withered and slight as if it had eaten itself. She stepped in and cut with a snapping twist. The sword that had been raised to kill her clattered on the ground, but within the body was something that drew her edge towards it like a lodestone of swirling light.

This time there was no scream, as the eighth part merged with the thing, the thing in the process of becoming that was her and the Grass-Cutting Sword and neither and a combination greater than both. No sensation of almost-dissolution; instead she *was* destroyed, and yet completed. Arcs of flame rose and fell in a world where matter itself twisted and fused; something massive beyond conception, but inherent with a delicate structure that made a snowflake seem like a smear of chaos. Then she fell, fell inward, fell into herself down eons and leagues. Fire exploded from her, from every pore and particle. Beam and wall erupted, and she stood swaying as the savage heat beat upon her—entirely physical heat, as every scrap of wood and paint and the very lime mortar between the stones began to burn.

"*Seinaru hono!*" she whispered. "Divine flame!"

It was the girl's screaming that brought her back to herself. Her hand reached out to touch the point of . . .

That which I have found. That which is remade, as I am, as I have been on this voyage. Ame-no-Murakumo-no-Tsurugi, *the Sword of the Gathering Clouds of Heaven.*

. . . to the chain that bound the child's ankle. The metal dropped away, and she snatched the girl into the crook of her arm as she sheathed the Grasscutter Sword and snatched up the stolen blade that had nearly killed her.

Most terribly avenged, she thought.

As she turned and raced for the courtyard and the entrance to the castle of damnation, the girl buried her face in the fabric of her kimono, even as it smoked with the heat.

But your curse ends here, man of the Shrine. The Divine Flame burns it away, with all dross. There has been atonement. Let the child stand for rebirth.

She staggered past the burning timber of the courtyard gate, where the iron strapping turned red and then white. Órlaith waited for her, relief and joy flashing across her face as she extended an arm.

The other hand held the bared Sword of the Lady. Around them was a circle of points, and voices in a harsh unfamiliar language.

CHAPTER THIRTY-ONE

ERETZ BNEI YAAKOV
(MOJAVE DESERT)
CROWN PROVINCE OF WESTRIA
(FORMERLY CALIFORNIA)
HIGH KINGDOM OF MONTIVAL
(FORMERLY WESTERN NORTH AMERICA)
AUGUST 16TH/HAOCHIZUKI 16TH/AV 23RD
CHANGE YEAR 46/SHŌHEI 1/5084TH YEAR OF THE WORLD/2044 AD

Órlaith shivered a little as Reiko walked through the gate. Such a simple action . . .

"Oh, now this is hard," she murmured to herself. "It's easier to be brave than watch another who you care for be brave without you. Yet in all respect, I can do no other. For what are we, we two, if not our work?"

She set herself to wait. The feel of the Sword under her palm was strange . . . though *that* did not surprise her. It was as if she stood on the edge not of a building, but a hole in the fabric that was Montival. An absence of structure and connection. Not an empty hole; one that contained a bottomless whirl of energy. A maelstrom without a barrier now, threatening to spread . . . and *she* was what contained it; she and what she bore.

A *jolt* ran through the fabric of things, and her hand clenched on the hilt of the Sword as she gasped. Something was happening in there . . .

"And did I expect nothing to happen?" she said, and sought a spot of shade.

There she sat, and cradled the sheathed Sword of the Lady in her arms, sipping occasionally at the canteen; the desert's arid death still hovered at the back of her mind. There was a rightness to the dry lands now, but it was not one which paid much heed to the wants and needs of human kind. There was little of the dance of hands and nature and Otherworld that you sensed in the Mackenzie dúthchas say, or a Protectorate manor. The *aes dana* here were hard and stark and . . .

Not hostile, but hard *indeed,* she thought.

They glowed like the merciless sun, blew like the scouring sand-laden wind, rustled like the dry brush in the night-winds. She sensed creatures of feather and scale and venom, pressing inward now as this place struggled to assume its shape again.

The day passed, and an odd contentment came with it. She ate of her iron rations and considered the odd bicycle contraptions that lay scattered about what had probably been what the ancients called a *parking lot*; they were really quite ingenious, the sort of thing someone good with his hands could do quickly with a hacksaw and hand-drill.

A little later she walked out to the edge of the pavement, watching the nearby hills for a while. A herd of a dozen antelope passed by, large tan-colored beasts with lighter patches on their rumps and long black tails and a black stripe along the junction of leg and body and white socks about their hooves. The big male looked at her with liquid dark eyes and tossed its long saber-shaped horns, and then they all moved off at a gliding trot, fading until they were simply a plume of light dust against the blue-brown hills.

Gemsbok, she thought.

There had been a herd of them down here in the desert lands even before the Change, farther east, and they'd spread explosively. They were African originally, from the Kalahari; they liked heat, they liked dry—they liked it so much they didn't really have to drink water all their lives long, though they did when they got the opportunity—and probably, no, certainly, the lions liked them.

They don't even feel foreign, she thought.

The Sword gave her a grasp of things like that. Tumbleweeds *did* feel foreign, and buffelgrass; as if they were still settling in, a slow vegetable wrestling with the bunchgrasses and sage and greasewood and mesquite. The antelope . . . and the lions . . . felt more like an absence removed, a hole gaping empty being filled. Long, long ago there had been lions here, and antelope of a dozen kinds, and swarms of other beasts. That had been in an age so distant that the first of human kind were just entering, her own first ancestors in this continent.

The land remembered, and it grieved for the plenitude and magnificence it had once born. Sometimes she dreamed of it, of coach-sized beaver, of hairy elephants, of great cats with scimitar fangs and sloths the size of a small building cropping the tops of trees. Once or twice of her remote ancestors hunting them, and the beasts waiting uncomprehending for the stone-tipped spears, their eyes holding only a mild dim wonder.

She went back to the shade. Nothing much moved after that, but the feeling of things *happening* grew too, thought for once it wasn't her responsibility. Her task was to be here, and to stand between her land and something that had been eating away at it since long before she was born.

The final jolt came not long before the late summer sunset. The sun painted the bleak hills around with implausible crimsons and pinks and turned the western horizon into a band of molten copper. The burst of *something* from within rolled over her and brought her upright from a half-doze, her eyes wide, feeling as if her hair was bristling like a horse's mane. As she watched the building began to *smoke,* as if it were heated from within throughout its whole substance. And then flame burst from every window, from the timbers of the gate, seemingly from the stone itself. She threw up a hand in shock as the unnatural swiftness of the blaze towered upward. Órlaith had seen prairie fires in the far eastern borderlands moving faster than a galloping horse, but that was quietude itself compared to this.

Reiko staggered through the gate, dodging the flames, a small skinny naked child clasped against her chest. The fabric of her kimono and *hakama* seemed to smoke with the radiated heat of the conflagration, and though the sword in her hand was steel, sheathed at her waist was the very spirit of fire. Órlaith flung out an arm to support her.

And as she did she heard a multiple thudding at her back and spun around, the Sword leaping into her hand. The sound had been the feet of animals; not the hard clopping of horses, but soft tough pads striking the pavement and the sand and dirt drifted over it. A dozen camels approached in a closing semi-circle, single-humped Arabian dromedaries rather than the two-humped Bactrian breed you saw occasionally in the northeastern borderlands. They bore riders, robed figures silhouetted against the dying light. Some had long slender lances in their hands, the honed metal of the heads glinting as they swung down to the level; several held recurved antelope-horn bows with arrows on their strings, and all had shamshir-sabers and daggers at their waists. It wasn't an attack, but it was a very pointed warning.

"Tō'ēḇā!" one of them said, loathing in the tone. That meant *abomination* in a language she suddenly spoke.

"Tō'ēḇā . . . tō'ēḇā . . ."

Abomination, abomination, in a rising whisper. She decided a stop had to be put to that; it wasn't something you wanted people thinking as they pointed edged metal at you. She raised the Sword of the Lady and it caught the sunset, light breaking off the edge. Silence rammed down for a moment.

"HaRosh Mistovev," one muttered, and she knew what that meant too: *My head is spinning!*

"Who are you?" demanded a man's voice in the same choppy guttural tongue. "What do you do here? We saw your tracks heading in. This is a forbidden place!"

Meaning cascaded through her; a language whose words glowed like compacted nuggets, ready to spring into mutating forms while always remaining themselves. There was a rugged straightforwardness to it. And it was a splendid tool in her mind for fine shades of meaning, for poetry and prophecy and perhaps for inspired madness. Not born of this land, but it fit the place well.

Reiko was coughing in the curve of her arm; the child she carried seemed unharmed—if uncommonly filthy—but had her eyes squeezed shut as she trembled in a paralysis of terror. Órlaith forced her wits into operation, stood erect, sheathed the Sword and held up a hand in greeting as the man began to repeat his words in English.

"Ani medaberet Ivrit," she said: "I speak Hebrew. Peace be upon you, warriors."

"B'emet?" another asked, a woman's voice this time, shocked surprise in her tone. "In truth?"

Instead of replying aloud Órlaith reached into her sporran, and pulled out the token Moishe Feldman had given her. It glittered on her palm in the dying sunlight and rising firelight, and there was a hiss of indrawn breath; she could feel the savage rising heat of the fire on her back, and one of the camels tossed its head and uttered a groaning, blubbering moan of complaint as it tried to retreat. All of them backed and shifted a little, wanting no part of the blaze.

"I am Crown Princess Órlaith Arminger Mackenzie, of House Artos and the High Kingdom of Montival. This is Her Majesty of Japan. Are we welcome?" she asked.

There was a ringing pause; someone started to speak and another said *silence* in a furious hiss; the crackle of the building behind them was the loudest sound, and something crashed down to send a shower of sparks skyward.

The voice spoke again; a man let fall the tail of the headdress he had drawn across his hard bearded face. He looked to be thirty, or perhaps a few years less in this land of scourging sun and wind.

"Yes, for now you are welcome. And my name is Meshek ben-Raanan, *seren* of this company. We wish you no harm."

Truth, rang through her; he meant what he said, and she relaxed slightly. *Seren* meant captain, or commander more generally.

"We will take you to my father the Judge; what has happened here is a thing of importance. Too many have died in this spot over the years."

The lances swung upright and their lower thirds were dropped into tubular scabbards attached to the right rear of the big complex saddles;

the bows pointed down, which was not as good as having the arrows back in the quivers, but better than nothing.

"Can you ride a camel?" the man named Meshek asked.

"Do I have a choice?" Órlaith replied dryly, and the man chuckled.

"No, *nisicah*," he said; the term meant *woman of high rank*. "No choice at all, unless you are a very good runner."

Two riderless but saddled camels were brought up. One of the warriors leaned over and tapped them lightly on the forward elbow-joints with a long thin stick he carried and said sharply:

"Ai, hoosh-hoosh-hoosh!"

Órlaith blinked a little even then at the way they folded down from the front, like some sort of jointed ladder. The first one cocked its head at Órlaith as she came forward a little dubiously; she'd never ridden one before, or even seen one of this variety. The Sword had some lesser benefits. She guessed from the grumbling moan it was thinking of spitting at her as it writhed its lips amid a flow of gummy green saliva.

"Not even in your dreams, camel," she said firmly.

One of the riders chuckled, a welcome break in the tension. "Ben Zona there earns his name."

It wasn't particularly reassuring that they'd given her a mount named *Son of a Whore*, but she wasn't in a position to be picky.

She straddled the saddle of wood and aluminum tubing and stuffed leather cushions. It was deep before and behind, cradling her thighs and backside, and it put you just ahead of the hump, with a pack arrangement for cargo to the rear. Part of that cargo was leather waterskins that gurgled reassuringly as the animal rose, hindquarters lurching up first and forcing her to an undignified grab for the frame. Reiko followed suit on the other animal, settling the child before her after she squeaked in alarm; one of the riders frowned and handed her a shawl to wrap around the girl's nakedness. Warriors snapped long leading reins to the beasts they rode, and there were burbling, gurgling sounds as the whole party turned and padded away at a rapid swinging trot to cries of *hut-hut-hut*.

For a moment the differences from riding a horse froze her, and then she struck the rhythm with the beast, smoother than what she was used to and with a more undulating motion. Stars were appearing overhead, and the desert night cooled quickly.

Camels could cover ground; the pace was never faster than a horse, but the course they set would have been hard tasking for a Lakota or a Crown Courier with a string of remounts, and that in somewhere less hot and dry. When they reached the encampment halfway through the next afternoon Órlaith estimated that they had traveled fifty miles at least, eating cheese and flatbread and dried dates and figs and raisins in the saddle and passing around waterskins, halting only three times for calls of nature, and speaking very little. She also felt as if she'd been beaten with clubs and fell onto the mattress in the tent as if struck behind the ear as soon as she'd drunk some water. Noise awoke her, voices and the clatter and thump of people going about their lives.

"*Ohayou*, Orrey-chan!"

She blinked and groaned a little as she rose, touching the hilt of the Sword where it lay by her side. Reiko was sitting cross-legged on a low bedroll not far away; they were in a tent of some size made of beige camel-hair fabric, its floor covered with bright soft mohair rugs woven in vivid geometric patterns and furnished with cushions, chests and folding tables and stands of laminated wood for gear, or leather in a dozen forms, or light skillfully-worked metal. At second glance she thought this was probably someone's family dwelling hastily pressed into service for guests; the belongings included a chess set beautifully carved from reddish-brown mesquite and some pale smooth stone, and several musical instruments including a good pre-Change violin.

The interior was mostly dim; there were gauze windows, but the flaps over them were down, and what light there was leaked through the curtain covering the entrance; from the angle it was about two hours to sunset. Besides sun-heated cloth and leather and not-quite-familiar livestock, there was a strong smell of cooking in the air that made her stomach grumble. Meat grilling, and the even more intoxicating scent of bread baking, and scents of herbs and spices.

The child Reiko had carried out of the burning castle was sitting nearby. Someone had cropped her hair close and wrapped a cloth about her head, and dressed her in a loose shift; they seemed to have cleaned her up a good deal at the same time, which would have been quite a task. She was quite a pretty toddler if rather underfed and huge-eyed, and her face looked lively now that she wasn't utterly terrified. As Órlaith glanced her way she started to pull up the shift and rise to a squat. Reiko caught the movement, pointed and said imperiously in Nihonjin:

"Not there! Where I took you before!"

The little one looked abashed as she stood and jigged from foot to foot, darting glances out of the tent and making urgent beckoning gestures with one hand. Reiko sighed and led the girl off with the hand in hers; Órlaith used the time to drink several cupfuls of water from a goatskin bag with a tap instead of a stopper, then pour some into a basin and splash her face. By Reiko's bedroll was the blade of a naked katana, disassembled for maintenance, and gleaming with a very light coat of choji oil; a water stone lay beside it, the type used for sharpening and polishing. For a moment Órlaith thought it was *Kotegiri*, but there were slight differences—it showed harder use, for one thing.

But from the same hand, she thought; for a moment she was content to enjoy the sheer artistry of the thing, the equal of any painting or porcelain or sculpture in her grandmother Sandra's collection.

When the pair returned the child curled up and went to sleep with the limp animal finality of a puppy or kitten.

"She was raised in an entirely uncivilized fashion," the Nihonjin said. "I had to ask for a bucket of water and a brush and clippers when we got here, and you would think I was skinning her rather than washing her, from the struggle."

I'll have to find out more about that later, Órlaith thought.

"Kusanagi-no-Tsurugi?" she asked aloud in Nihongo, nodding towards the sword thrust through Reiko's sash. "I thought so, but . . ."

There hadn't been much opportunity for private speech on the headlong trip here; even their escort . . . or possibly very courteous captors . . . had spoken only for essentials. Reiko nodded, smiling slightly but with joy dancing in her eyes. She pulled the sheathed katana from her sash and laid it down, looking at it with a wondering delight, as if she still had some difficulty believing what lay beneath her hand.

"Yes," she said. "But not as it was lost. Remade from fragments as I recovered it, reforged. Given to us again, as it first was from my Ancestress so very long ago."

A finger traced the air above the other sword Órlaith had noted. "This is . . . I think it was stolen at the same time as *Kusanagi-no-Tsurugi*, and by the same man. One who knew at least that our ancient blades were things of great value. It is the *Honjo Masamune*, a very famous sword, and I know on whom I will bestow it. But this, this—"

She stilled herself, laid her hand on the hilt of the sheathed blade, and then slowly drew it and laid it on the rugs that made the floor of the tent. Órlaith inhaled sharply at the sight. The contrast with the blade that was merely steel was vivid, more so than if she had seen it by itself. The sensation was less primal than that when the Sword of the Lady was unsheathed, perhaps because this *was* Montival and not Nihon, but she could sense the might locked within. The hairs on her forearms prickled at it, like the feeling of lightning close-by.

"At first I thought this was a *horimono*," Reiko said, her finger tracing the curve of the blade without quite touching it.

The word meant carving, literally, and referred to engraving and inlay work done on some Nihonto swords. This looked much like the Masamune masterpiece Reiko had inherited from her father and borne into the hidden castle, but a second glance showed the differences. It was a little broader, a little longer—perhaps thirty inches or a fraction more. A shape writhed down the blade for three-quarters of its length, as if the steel had been chiseled and then inlaid with the thinnest film of burnished gold, and the *tsuka-ito* silk cords binding the wood and ray-skin of the hilt were of a deep yellow instead of black. The inlay on the blade was an abstract pattern, seeming at one moment to be curling leaves of fire, another an elongated form dancing, then nothing that human eyes could interpret at all. When you looked more closely you could tell . . . somehow . . . that it was not gold in the form of flame. It *was* flame, in some entirely non-physical way.

"I feel . . . potential," Reiko said seriously, sheathing the sword and laying it before her as she sat cross-legged with her hands on her thighs, contemplating it. "When I touch it. Images form, things which cannot be said in words . . . though it does not seem to teach me languages!"

"I'm not surprised," Órlaith said.

This was one of a triad of sacred treasures, after all.

"Yes, that would be the *Yato na Kagami*, The Eight Hand Mirror," Reiko said. "But that is another task."

Órlaith extended a hand towards the sheathed blade, and Reiko tensed slightly as she spread her fingers over it. And . . .

"No, that wouldn't be advisable at all, now would it?" Órlaith said, withdrawing her hand and working the fingers to get the warning tingling out of them; they were still speaking in Reiko's language, for privacy. "Just as I expected. These are not my mysteries."

"Hai," Reiko said.

As so often the simple word carried a freight of meanings; softly she murmured:

"I have accomplished the task fate set us and your visions saw. Be at peace, Father."

Even the scabbard seemed different now. It was still a lacquered black . . . but there were flecks of gold in it, as in a vast translucent space. And they moved, very slowly, so slowly that you couldn't be quite sure . . . possibly they moved, or she was seeing great depths . . .

Reiko began a halting account of what had happened. It was skeletal; as much because there was really no way to describe the experiences to another as anything else, but there was reluctance there as well. Órlaith nodded. The spiral of recurring horrors she described was well out of the world. *Better off dead* was a phrase used far more often than it should be, but there were some occasions it was precisely true.

Órlaith made a seated bow of acknowledgment and sober respect when the story ended with the flight out of the burning castle. She ducked her head slightly before she spoke:

"Omedetou . . . omedetou gozaimasu! Yoku dekimashita! Congratulations! Very well done indeed!"

Reiko returned the gesture, then frowned. "I was there a whole day, you say? It seemed more as if it were an hour, two at the most, to me."

"We both know time is mutable; it can be warped and turned upon itself. And you were very right, my friend. That which you bear now *is* perilous. Perilous beyond common conception. I'm glad that place was purified by fire, and that an end was made of what began so long ago. Let Cody Biltmore and all his find peace too."

Then Órlaith glanced at the girl lying sleeping with an arm over her eyes and mouth open and raised an eyebrow. "Not quite all," she corrected herself.

The Nihonjin tilted her head. "I found I could not leave her. Not leave her to burn; still less if she did not. It was . . . it was a very bad place," Reiko said seriously. "Saving her . . . closed a cycle. Her . . . ancestor, I do not know how many times removed . . . did that which he should not, and it cascaded through the years. Perhaps if I do what I should, it will likewise—but in a fortunate direction."

Órlaith nodded approvingly. "Threefold return for good or ill, is the way we put it," she said.

Reiko smiled wryly. "Though honestly I don't have the slightest idea what I'm going to *do* with her. She doesn't seem to be evil or an imbecile. Quite intelligent, in fact, and she has learned some speech, even picked up a few Nihongo words in the last day, but she has no more conception of how to be a human being than a dog does. Less. One that has to be housebroken. And now she doesn't like to be separated from me, which is awkward."

"I'm not surprised, though," Órlaith said. "What's her name?"

"As far as I can tell, she has none," Reiko said. "She was very startled to see men, and even more to see children when we arrived here. I do not think she ever knew her father; he must have died not long after she was born . . . or even before it, and she has no understanding of the word. Probably she had never seen a male before yesterday. And other children surprised her as well, and frightened her; she has no idea that children grow into adults, perhaps, and imagined herself a being of a completely different sort, the only one in the world. I do not really like to imagine what her life has been, though her mother seems to have protected her as much as she could while she lived."

"She's young enough to forget," Órlaith said. "What do you or I remember of our first or second years? Perhaps she was on the borderline for that, though."

"Ah!" Reiko said. "Excellent! I will call her Kiwako."

Órlaith chuckled and nodded; that meant *born on a border.* "For that she was also born on the borderline between the world of common day and the Otherworld, as well," she said.

"Hai, honto desu," Reiko said thoughtfully.

"Not Kitsune, though?" Órlaith teased; that was the Nihongo for fox . . . or for the fox spirits that scampered and shimmered changefully through their folklore.

Reiko shook her head. "No, though she will be called that by any Nihonjin children she meets. Best not to encourage it, though, teasing can be painful enough anyway."

"And now it's time to see our hosts," Órlaith said.

"Indeed. Most of them speak English, but it must be a dialect form; I have trouble understanding them. They are not hostile, but . . . stiff . . . around me. I do not think they know what to make of us. I would be surprised if they are not arguing sharply over what we are and what to do with us."

Órlaith nodded. "They seem to speak Ivrit for everyday . . . Hebrew . . . as they do in Degania Dalet . . . that's a clutch of villages near Eugene, a little federation of its own."

Reiko frowned. "Hebrew? Isn't that a tongue part of the Christian bible is written in?" she said.

As she spoke she reassembled the *Honjo Masamune* and wrapped it in a long length of cloth, then bound it with cord. It needed the protection . . . and Kiwako was of an age entirely unsafe around something so very, very sharp.

Órlaith chuckled. "It's a bit more complex than that, and I wouldn't use exactly that phrasing with them, it might be misinterpreted."

She rose, straightened her kilt and beat a little dust out of it, then combed her hair before tying it back; everything was no worse than you'd expect, and at least a good stout comb was always there in the sporran. There were two men standing guard at the entrance to the tent, where a long flap on poles created an area of shade before the entrance, paved with smooth stones. One was leaning on a lance with a round hide shield on his arm marked by the two interlocking triangles of the Mogen David.

The other she recognized as Meshek ben-Raanan; he had a bola hanging from his belt beside his curved slashing-sword and a bow in his hand and quiver across his back. It was a little odd that a *seren*, a captain, was standing outside her tent . . . but then again, if they recognized that she was who she claimed to be, perhaps not.

They both wore cuirasses of some supple but grain-surfaced brownish-gray leather that looked light and tough, reinforced by strips of carefully browned steel riveted on at vulnerable points, though they had folded and pinned head-cloths rather than helms, with tails that could be drawn across the face.

"Peace be upon you," she said to them when they turned to look at her. "We'd like to consult with your leader or leaders, please. It's a matter of some urgency."

They looked at each other; they still seemed a little disconcerted that she spoke their language without an accent. Meshek bowed slightly and touched his forehead and lips and heart with his right hand in a graceful gesture.

"And upon you, peace, *nisicah*. I shall see what can be done, and return here. My brother Dov will stay with you."

Dov nodded and grunted; he seemed the silent sort, and two or three years younger than his brother, nearer her own age. His name meant *Bear*, and he looked a bit like one, being thicker-built than was common here, with an abundant fuzzy black beard growing up his cheeks. His brother hurried off with the rolling gait of someone who spent a lot of the time in the saddle, towards a much larger tent, one flying a flag with the Shield of David in its center, blue on white and flanked by more stripes of blue.

That bit about Dov had been a hint to stay put until they figured out what to do with two very unexpected guests. And a *courteous* hint, which went with the fact that no attempt had been made to disarm them.

Moishe Feldman has helped me yet again; I think that token made a real difference. Hmmm. Moishe is truly an asset to the realm; he deserves reward . . . he's the type you reward with opportunities, I think. And the realm needs me to give him more work, for that he does it so well. I'll need able ministers . . . I'll have to think on that.

She used the wait to look about at the camp. It was located on a benchland with a good view of a broad desert valley, not quite so skeletally arid as that around the lost castle, with spindly-armed Joshua trees and a temperature that was merely *very hot* showing that they were at a considerably higher elevation too. Green creosote bush and gray-green burro sage and cholla cactus surrounded them with the white-gray soil showing between them, and faded into a dun-colored distance broken by rocky blue hills. A dry riverbed ran down the center of it, marked by denser vegetation including mesquite trees, and a dozen busy pairs of hands were erecting a wind-pump there on a stone base that looked permanent.

As she watched, the metal vanes began to spin around in the hot breeze and spill water into troughs and a tank atop a wagon. Herders controlled a few horses and cattle, large flocks of goats and sheep, and what appeared to be substantial blocks of domesticated antelope, probably gemsbok, farther out. They would need the water less.

"How do you make the antelope so tame?" she asked curiously; they were moving slowly, with mounted herders chivvying them along, but without any of the panic flight a wild herd would have shown.

Dov blinked and thought. "If they run, eat them. If they fight, eat them. If they don't, breed them," he said, and went back to leaning on his lance.

She supposed that would work, if you kept it up long enough; it was good practical genetics. More herds waited their turn, and flocks of some very large flightless bird, brownish creatures that stood man-tall; as each group was watered, it was led off to a corral of stone posts and salvaged barbed wire where it could be guarded against predators in the night.

No, not ostriches, emu, she thought, looking at the birds; both were common throughout the warmer, drier parts of the kingdom.

One of the emu made a break for it, running very fast indeed. A herder whirled something around his head, unclear at this distance but almost certainly a bola, an arrangement of three weights at the end of linked cords. He cast, and an instant later the emu went over in a thud that raised a puff of dust, the cords wrapped tightly around its legs by the centrifugal action of the weights.

The camels were mostly in the middle distance; apparently it wasn't considered wise to try to water them with the rest of the livestock, something she agreed with from brief acquaintance with the quarrelsome beasts.

They have about the same disposition as seagulls, but they're a good deal bigger and smell much worse, she thought. *Or perhaps Son of a Whore isn't typical.*

There were about thirty tents in the whole camp, mostly modestly sized. Apparently they'd been set up recently; a few more were being erected as she watched, chores being done on the order of releasing chickens from traveling cages into wicker pens, and there were a dozen big six-wheeled wagons parked herringbone fashion as well as smaller vehicles. A quick experienced eye estimated the people at about ten-score, better than a third of them children below the age of puberty, which was typical of most places.

Every adult was armed at least with a long curved knife, and many carried swords at their belts as well unless they were doing something that made it severely inconvenient, broad-bladed and sharp-curved slashing weapons. Racks before each family tent held bows made from two shaped Oryx horns joined by a carved riser of mesquite root, quivers, long slender lances, slings, bolas, helmets, light armor and shields, all prudently secured against toddlers. There was a pleasant buzz of conversation, often accompanied by lively gestures, punctuated by occasional yelling which often dissolved in laughter. Though Órlaith and Reiko attracted plenty of curious looks and she knew they were being discussed, even the children kept their distance. Or were herded away by elder siblings, in some cases.

This isn't the first time they've been here. Those firepits are well kept but they've been there a good long while, the tents are all pitched on a rammed earth pad—

She craned her head to check; yes, each was edged with a fieldstone border too.

—and have a cobbled area in front, and those adobe sheds down nearer the well are in good condition but at least a decade old and the sheet-metal roofing was salvaged from somewhere else. At a guess they have a regular route they follow with the seasons, or several, to rest and stretch the pastures, and access things like date groves around springs. A moveable village, so it is.

The people of it were ordinary enough folk, work-worn but well-fed and tough-looking. And many had something of a family resemblance, strong-boned narrow faces with full lips, olive-skinned naturally and brown where the sun struck; mostly black or brown-haired, with a minority of blonds and the occasional frizzy redhead. Men wore a cloth headdress that fell to their shoulders over shaggy hair sometimes caught up in a bun, baggy pantaloons tucked into their boots, shirts and a loose belted calf-length robe divided for riding. Women either had the same basic clothing, or sometimes long dresses and shawls, and tended to brighter colors and jewelry. All the men she could see wore beards if they were old enough, and women past their early teens had long hair covered in a snood-like arrangement often bound with a chain of ornaments.

And . . . wait a minute! she thought. *That cord binding the headdress . . .*

It was leather, wrapped twice around the head just above the brows and secured with a slip-knot, the ends dangling down on the right side. She glanced over at Dov ben-Raanan, and confirmed her suspicions; there was a loop on one end of the cord, a tab on the other, and a soft leather pocket in the middle. It was a sling, and it could be stripped off and into use with a single motion. Some of the women wore it too, around the head and then looped around their snoods.

"Would you be using lead shot for the slings?" she asked Dov, and tapped her right temple to show what she meant.

He looked at her, blinked again, then said: "Lead or ball-bearings for serious work, *nisicah*. Stones for hunting."

"Now wearing them so is clever indeed," she said, and got a wordless, embarrassed grunt in reply; his seemed to be a voluble people, but Dov was obviously an exception.

Another wagon arrived while she watched, pulled by eight camels in pairs along a draught chain. When the team had been led off burbling and complaining a beautifully decorated wooden chest draped in embroidered cloth was unloaded by a man with a blue-and-white shawl over his head and ceremoniously carried by four more into a large tent set aside from the others, to the accompaniment of chanting and blasts from a curled ram's-horn trumpet.

The first guard came back after only a few minutes, with a young woman in her late teens beside him bearing a large bundle in her arms, her black eyes bright with curiosity. The burden seemed to be mostly folded clothing and two pairs of the soft pull-on boots these folk wore, but there were towels and combs, fiber scrubbing pads and bars of soap on the top. A younger girl of twelve or so tagged along behind her, with her dark curls loose under a floppy hat woven of the same coarse fiber; that seemed to be about the age girl-children switched over to the snood-like thing.

The warrior spoke: "The Judge invites the great ladies who are the honored guests of the *bnei Yaakov*—"

Which meant *sons of Jacob* literally, but had the ring of a tribal ethnonym in her mind. And the term he used for Judge was *Shofet*, which implied rulership as well as deciding cases according to law.

"—to the evening meal. This maiden is Shulamit bat-Raanan, who will, ah, see to your needs."

At a guess . . .

"If those needs include hot water, soap and clean clothing, we are most profoundly grateful to your sister, Meshek son of Raanan, and to you, and to your father. We've had little opportunity for such of late, and it's been very sorely missed."

He'd been rather serious, but he grinned at that, and at Reiko's nod and slight bow of thanks. She also thought he was somewhat relieved that they *wanted* to bathe and change their rather dirty, dusty, smelly, sweat-stained garments. That meant he didn't have to be blunt about telling them to make themselves fit for civil company.

"I know what it's like to come in to camp after a long time lying out, ladies," he said. "The imp of the wastelands at Shulamit's heels is Aviva bat-Raanan, who will watch the child."

"I had better wake Kiwako and tell her to mind Aviva," Reiko said dubiously.

And did, which took a few minutes; the lost child was intelligent enough . . . except when she didn't *want* to understand what you were saying.

Shulamit led them away after the introductions, almost skipping with eagerness, her complex earrings of silver strands flipping as she turned from one to the other.

"Are you really from the far north?" she said. "From Montival? Are you a *princess?*"

She spoke in good if strongly accented, old-fashioned and slightly formal English; it was obvious that she'd learned it as a second language and didn't use it all that often. Mastering *Órlaith* had made her hesitate and shape the sound several times.

"I am Montivallan, and from the north, and yes, my father was High King and I am his heir," Órlaith replied, treading delicately between rudeness and revealing too much. "This is . . . ah, my comrade is usually addressed as *Heika,* which is her title, and she's from Japan. Japan is—"

"A country on islands across the ocean!" Shulamit said, almost bristling with excitement; Órlaith thought she would have clapped her hands if they weren't full. "Oh, marvelous! We learned about it in the House of Books—"

School, Órlaith translated; the words were English but the phrasing was Ivrit.

"—but I never thought . . . Oh, nothing this wonderful has happened in . . . in . . . ever!"

Wistfully: "I'd like to see the ocean, sometime. It must be marvelous, even bigger than Lake Mead! And salty like Lake Owens—I saw that once when we were trading there, oh, what is the ocean like?"

Well, it's nice to be welcome, even if it's the way a caravan of tinerants with a fortuneteller and a juggler and a dancing dog is welcome in a village after a long dull winter, Órlaith thought, amused.

"This is an unfortunate diversion," Reiko said . . . in Nihongo . . . after they'd tried to convey the sea to someone who knew it only as ancient pictures.

"Not necessarily," Órlaith said in the same tongue, smiling like a cat. "Not necessarily at all."

They got more glances as they walked through the camp, and some of her own age waved to Shulamit with every appearance of envy. Otherwise people were busy about finishing the work of the day, or winding it down as day merged into evening; some of the children were playing soccer, while others a bit older and on into adulthood were shooting the bow at marks or practicing a violently practical-looking style of unarmed combat or other martial skills, including hitting targets at alarming ranges with the sling—often while running forward or back or leaping side to side. Chess games seemed to be popular as well, often with onlookers, and there was a pleasant trickle of music—violin and mandolin, hand-drum and flute—from somewhere.

Cooking was in full swing, and there was a smell of grilling and stewing meat and things baking and one rotisserie held chickens roasting. For a moment she was puzzled by the lack of smoke, though fuel would be a severe problem in this land. Then she recognized the shining paraboloid shapes focusing on pots and stovetops, turned to take maximum advantage of the last rays of the sun. Solar cookers of that type were used as supplements in many of the drier parts of Montival, but they'd be more efficient still here in this land of constant sunshine. Since the alternatives were fires of the medicinal-smelling creosote bush and dried dung, she was thankful as well as impressed.

Reiko took a little longer to realize what she was seeing, being from a land of much cloud and heavy rain and dense forests providing plenty of firewood. Not very much longer, since she was both learned in the mechanical arts and very quick.

"How clever!" she said, delighted as she always was by a well-wrought contrivance. "This is very ingenious."

Shulamit beamed with pride at the praise from the glamorous outsider, mentioned the mathematical formula used to calculate the curvature, and started explaining things as they passed.

Her people were obviously mainly herders, but Órlaith recognized a fair number of crafts as she walked down towards the baths, often with tools set up in a covered enclosure next to the family tent; there was a smithy that also had light machine tools including a treadle-worked lathe and drillpress and doubled as a carpenter's shop, several leatherworkers, and most of the households seemed to have a light knock-down loom and a multi-spindle jenny to spin thread for it. One raised tent-flap showed a woman listening to a child's chest with a stethoscope, the toddler's mother helping to keep the thermometer in his mouth. Another had low tables and collapsible bookshelves that folded into boxes for carrying; a group of teenage boys and girls—sitting cross-legged, separately—were finishing up and comparing notes on slates as an older man closed a volume on a wire stand that she thought was titled *Desert Ecologies of the Southwest*.

Other trades could be deduced: she could hear the hum of a sewing machine from somewhere, the clothes needed vegetable dyes, there must be fletchers and bowyers. There was surely a press about the place; a small hand model could be kept in any of the wagons, and together with its type wouldn't make more than one load for a camel. Doubtless cars and trucks and any number of abandoned towns provided raw salvage materials.

The flat roof of the adobe baths had a larger version of the solar heaters she'd seen cooking food and boiling water, involving black pipes and a system Órlaith recognized used convection to move the water through the heating cycle.

"This is just the ordinary baths," Shulamit said. "That's the *mikvah*, the ritual baths over there, but that's just for, ah, us."

Órlaith nodded in understanding. The girl went on: "This is so exciting—we have other guests here now too, that's why we're at this camp so early, and have all of this company together this time of year. Guests from the Friends, but that happens four times every year at least."

"Friends? And they would be?"

"The *Pipa Aha Macav*," she said, after a bewildered pause. "Our *Friends*."

The word for *friends* she used was in her tongue, and could have meant *allies* as well. Except that was a little too detached; it had moral overtones, something like *righteous foreign people*.

And she's lively and intelligent enough I forgot she's a backcountry dweller, unused to those who don't know what's common knowledge to her, as a fish doesn't see water. The which is why your stomach drops when someone in the outlands gives you directions and then says you can't miss it, *for you can and you likely will*.

The name of the Friends was simply sounds for a moment, and then there was a sensation of *expansion*. Her step checked a little; learning a language in a moment was still not something she was entirely easy with. Then she knew that that *Pipa Aha Macav* meant *People By the River*, the river being the Colorado; what others called the Mojave tribe, who had dwelt in these lands when the first of the incomers had set foot here, the *Españoles* riding up from the south in the long ago. She supposed that they were where these folk got their grain and their cotton, which she'd noticed was surprisingly common—the cotton underdrawers and knit bra she'd been given would be a luxury in the north. She made a mental note to drop a suggestion to Moishe Feldman when time and circumstance allowed that there was probably a market for the sort of colorful, well-woven work she'd seen here. Probably the rugs too, and possibly much else.

The hot water in the baths was plentiful and truly *hot*; Órlaith would have enjoyed washing even more if her skin hadn't been rasped by sun and sand in sensitive places, but she did enjoy it, and the local girl provided sympathy and an herbal cream that soothed the injuries. That was based on jojoba oil, a local plant that apparently also provided the base of the soap and was used in lamps.

The clothes were comfortable for this climate and what Shulamit called *active*, meaning that they included pants and the overrobe rather than a dress; she showed them how to wrap the snood-things, which they called something that translated as *veil of glory*. Evidently it mattered to some taboo that the clothes were somewhat different in cut from the ones men wore, mostly a matter of fastenings and where the buttons went and the robe being a little longer, but nothing that an outsider would have noticed. They weren't new, but they were sound and both sets fit well. Which couldn't have been easy when Órlaith was taller than most of the men she'd seen here, and had several inches on every woman she'd seen closely enough to notice; there were signs of hasty alterations.

And they were very clean. In fact, they were so clean that Shulamit wrinkled her nose a bit and looked dubiously at the clothes Órlaith and Reiko handed over for washing in what sounded like an interesting wind-powered system. Then she examined them more carefully.

"They *really need* the laundry but this is beautiful work," she enthused over Reiko's kimono and *hakama*. "What is this material?"

"Silk, for that part," Reiko said. "The rest is cotton."

"Ah, I've read of silk but only seen scraps. So pretty! It would make lovely embroidery thread." A slight tug. "Strong, too."

Then she frowned a little at the kilt and plaid, dropping back into *Ivrit*. "This is well-woven wool and the dyes are bright and fast, but does it contain linen?"

Órlaith blinked—linsey-woolsey was far and away the commonest single type of cloth in Montival—but while her line might be High Kings, local custom was everywhere king in its own house, after all.

"No. Most Mackenzie kilts do, at least linen for the thread, but as it happens that one is pure wool sewn with cotton. The *lèine* . . . the shirt . . . is linen with cotton sewing thread. Both gifts from my grandmother Juniper's loom, made and sewn with her own hands."

"That is good. And she is a very fine weaver, as good as my own mother! Separate garments of linen and wool are permitted to us, but the Law says that we may not mix them in the same one."

Órlaith judged that Shulamit was bright and no bumpkin—she read two languages in different scripts fluently, for starters, and seemed well-educated generally—but she was a chatterbox and entranced with the exotic visitors. Órlaith had no doubt that if she'd been point-blank asked for things like numbers of warriors she'd have shut up, but the same innocent underlying assumption that everyone knew what everyone knew . . . what everyone *she* knew had in their general background . . . made her perfectly ready to let drop things which enabled the Montivallan to make some estimates.

There are about as many of them as there are of the Topangans, the Princess thought. *Perhaps a bit more, say three thousand or so.*

Apparently this was one of about ten groups called companies who followed the same customs and faith and acknowledged her father as their *Shofet.* They were scattered over a vast range, at least thousands of square miles and possibly tens of thousands, usually in multiple camps smaller than this, and came together at various festivals or for annual assemblies that doubled as fairs and markets or when emergencies like war or other disasters required it.

And they're better organized and armed than the Topangans and I think better-off. And more important for our purposes . . .

"What do you think they can do for us?" Reiko asked, as they walked back.

"Reiko-chan, we need to get back to our ship as fast as possible. With a little luck we can sail straight back north, confront my mother with a *fait accompli* . . . success has a thousand fathers, defeat is an orphan . . . and get on with the war. Which means we must cross the desert quickly. These people are experts at crossing deserts, and sure, it's crossing a desert we need to do."

"It is extraordinary, but they are truly at home here."

"As we are not," Órlaith said. "We're hardy enough, you and I, and I've seen deserts before, but traveling here, and in high summer . . ."

"Perhaps their skills and their beasts are enough to more than make up for going out of our way with them?"

"I think so, if we can persuade them. It's not just getting back to our main party—and remember how much joy we had of the trip from the last camp to the castle?"

Reiko shuddered very slightly, and nodded. "Without the *kami* of this place against us . . . with only . . . how do you say it . . . things in the light of common day to deal with it would not have been as difficult, but you are right, I was not looking forward to it. Especially weakened as we were, and with no supplies. It would be a cruel irony to come so far and then die with . . ."

She didn't speak *Kusanagi*'s name, but they both knew what she meant when she touched the hilt.

"Ironic, yes," Órlaith said. "Also fatal."

Reiko nodded and chuckled. "And when we reach the others, we will still be far from where we wish to be; and as to supplies, we were over-optimistic in our planning. Though it was important not to carry too much weight."

"We need to get *them* back across the desert too, as quickly as we can. I'm not comfortable with what may be happening in our absence."

Reiko nodded gravely, then smiled a little. "Egawa will be frantic. Though he will show nothing, of course."

"Not to mention Herry and John and others." She smiled wryly. "Even nearly dying, it was a bit of a relief to be away on our own, wasn't it? Nobody to be responsible for."

"For a while," Reiko said with a sigh, and a glance back at the tent that held the child she'd named Kiwako. "For a little while."

"And . . . I have a feeling our return may not be as simple a thing as we wish. My skin prickles at the thought."

Reiko nodded. "I too." She smiled. "When has anything gone smoothly on this questing? It never does, in the epics . . . save when the heroes are being lulled and a disaster is about to happen!"

Órlaith snorted. "Well, be glad the epic hasn't been written yet, and we may have boring peacefulness all the way back to Portland! Then the bards can throw in a disaster or too, spicing the stew so to say."

The tent of the *Shofet* was the largest in the encampment, more like three rectangular tents defining a courtyard that could be covered by a moveable awning; it probably did duty as courthouse and meeting-place and for other public purposes as well as a family home, and two warriors with shield and lance stood guard outside. One of them was a woman, Órlaith noted, and neither of them were Dov or Meshek ben-Raanan. Having the *Shofet*'s sons guarding her tent earlier now looked rather significant, as a gesture to her.

They didn't keep up the custom of standing to attention, though, she thought; both of these looked alert, but they didn't bother not looking bored as well. Probably they don't have guards here when there are no outsiders about; everyone who can be here is a warrior at need, as among Mackenzies, but no standing force. This too is for ceremony.

There was a rack for shoes and a brace for pulling off riding-boots at the threshold, and an assortment of sandals—made from the fibers of the Joshua tree like much else here—for guests to slip on. It was an arrangement Órlaith heartily approved of, since this was a camp of herdsmen and their animals. Reiko accepted it as a lifelong habit; she didn't say anything, but where such wasn't the custom she found people walking into dwelling-places in their street shoes repulsively uncouth.

Raanan ben-Yaakov met them at the entrance; she noticed again that the handshake had evidently fallen out of use here. He was a balding man in his forties, hard and strong but a little more heavy-set than most of his people, with a bold nose, thick bushy eyebrows and gray streaks in the original black of his full, curly beard. A dark robe with embroidery down the front panels and around the collar looked quietly sumptuous, and the loose sleeves slid back occasionally to reveal tanned forearms covered in corded muscle and seamed with scars. An elaborately tooled and studded belt bore a sharp-curved saber whose sweat-stained leather grip had seen a lot of use. Evidently local etiquette was for men to take off their head-coverings inside a tent, except for the kippah skullcap, but for women to keep theirs on.

"You are most welcome . . . Crown Princess," he said in a deep gravelly voice, bowing and making that graceful gesture of touching brow, lips and heart; the title was in English. "Peace be upon you, Your Highness."

"And upon you peace, Raanan ben-Yaakov, Judge of the Children of Yaakov," Órlaith said in Ivrit, and then thought *very formal greeting*. Words came to her: "Peace and the blessings of haShem upon all the tents of your people, their children and lands and their flocks and herds."

To Reiko he added, switching back to English with another courtly bow: "And you are most welcome as well, Your Majesty."

He spoke with only a trace of the harsh guttural accent his children bore more strongly. He ushered them into a chamber with a lamp hanging from the center pole, casting a fine steady yellow light and burning with an unfamiliar fruity scent; Órlaith hesitated slightly and then racked the Sword of the Lady at the entrance along with everyone else's long weapons, and after a slightly longer hesitation Reiko did likewise with *Kusanagi*. Neither would be very far away. Everyone sat cross-legged on flattish cushions, with a section of low folding table before them; Shulamit and a boy who looked like her sister Aviva's twin brother, and probably was, bore an ewer and basin and towels around so that everyone could wash their hands. A murmur went with them:

"Blessed art Thou, O Lord our God, King of the universe, who has sanctified us with Thy commandments and has commanded us concerning the washing of the hands," and then the one she was familiar with from the *Tarshish Queen*, much the same start but ending *who brings forth bread from the earth* instead.

The food was simple but honestly prepared and she felt sharp-set. A very tasty chicken soup with ball-shaped dumplings was followed by skewers of grilled lamb and emu seasoned with garlic and chilies on steamed semolina, round loaves of risen wheat bread shaped much like the cushions they were all sitting on, a mush of mesquite bean flour and maize-meal and beans enlivened with caramelized onions and herbs, and a number of spicy sauces and oily pastes of things like ground chickpeas for dipping the bread. There were refreshing sweet peeled prickly-pear fruit and small honey-sweetened cakes rich with dates and piñon nuts for dessert. A hot acrid herb tea of some sort and water cooled in a porous earthenware jug accompanied the food, and tiny glasses of some sweet fruit liqueur followed it.

There were about a dozen participants, with women sitting to the left and the rather more numerous men to the right of the Judge. All were adults and with an average age north of thirty years, so this was obviously not a family dinner though it included the *Shofet*'s wife, a comfortable-looking woman of about his own age who Órlaith judged was shrewd but quiet. She noted that while Dov wasn't here Meshek was, probably because he was the heir. The introductions went quickly, and everyone was speaking English reasonably fluently. She'd always been good at remembering names and faces, even before the Sword, and now she was faultless at it.

Two of the guests weren't of the *bnei Yaakov*; a man and a woman of middle years, in tunic-like shirts and pants of coarse bleached cotton, the man's long black hair braided and wound around his head, the woman's worn shoulder-length and cut square over the forehead. He wore a black sleeveless vest over the shirt, and the woman a colorful shawl worked with beads; there was more beadwork on their knife-belts and sheaths.

The other reason besides Reiko that they're using English, Órlaith thought. *Hmmm. I think they're just as happy when outsiders don't speak their language. I've seen myself it can be an advantage to have one that others can't follow.*

Both of them had ruddy-brown complexions and high cheekbones and tattoos of crisscross and vertical bars on their faces, and the sort of build that could easily turn plump if food was abundant and hard work unnecessary, which it was obvious wasn't the case with either of them. They had blocky farmer's muscles, and looked strong in a rather different way from the *bnei Yaakov.*

"Greetings," she said in their language, when they'd been introduced as Henry and Jackie of the ruling Council of the Pipa Aha Macav. "I'm pleased to meet some of the People By the River. And very pleased to see that they flourish in their ancient land."

That got her astonished smiles. It turned out she spoke the Mojave language better than either of them did, since only a small group of mostly elderly people had used it before the Change, and she switched back to English after the greeting. Though the dialect of English they spoke now after generations of seeing few outsiders was heavily salted with loanwords from the old tongue, and you could detect the influence of the way it was put together on the grammar too.

One advantage of the Sword was that intelligent people who'd heard of it rarely mistook it, or its bearer. Raanan was both, and he'd convinced everyone else he'd included in this meeting; the subdued glances they gave it where it lay on the rack of polished dark red-brown wood by the doorway showed that, as well as the effect it always had.

That didn't mean his concerns were hers, or that the outside world mattered to him the way his own people's affairs did, and still less for his followers. At least one of the men was trying to pretend she wasn't there, and looking either frightened or hostile when he couldn't, and he sat at the *Shofet*'s right hand. From what she picked up she gathered he was their religious leader, though one who also did duty in related fields like teaching.

"Frankly, Your Highness," Raanan said, when they'd exchanged news, spun the news as best they could, and filled one another in with details, also spun, "we're doing quite well, we and our Friends. That was my father's vision—a land of our own for our own people, where we could live at peace among our own and wouldn't be dependent on outsiders. Many of whom . . . again frankly . . . sometimes hated us for no good reason."

Órlaith nodded. "And your father was obviously a great man," she said . . . also sincerely. "I didn't know him, but we can be judged by the legacy of our deeds."

A brilliant man, in fact, if somewhat crazed, she added to herself. *But then, plenty of my own near relations in the past few generations were insane in one way or another . . . and often in ways much more unpleasant. It was a time of madness. And the rest were mostly . . . eccentric . . . at least.*

Solid, sensible, reasonable people had been much more likely to simply die back then waiting for things to return to normal. Oak Barstow Mackenzie's father Chuck had said something right after the Change which had become a proverb among Mackenzies: *When the going gets weird, the weird get going.* The details differed, but that had been true nearly everywhere.

Raanan stroked his abundant gray-shot beard; he'd have been born around the time of the Change, give or take.

"We fought off the Eaters and Rovers and bandits," he said. "We took in many of the desperate. We learned how to live decently in this land, though that was hard, hard—I remember hungry times when we were far closer to the edge than we are now. There was knowledge in books, but learning to apply it in the real world is a different thing. We're not hostile to anyone who respects our borders, but why should we want closer relations with the likes of the Delgados?"

"For starters, because you can't avoid it," Órlaith said. "The day of utter isolation is passing . . . at least in these lands. Topanga has signed the Great Charter. So have the House of Delgado."

Which produced surprise and alarm, only slightly lessened when she told them where the frontier line would run. Their latest news from the west was several weeks old.

"That means the realms on your western border will have more trade and more contact with the outside world, for good and ill, which will strengthen them. And the Delgado lands nearly fell into the hands of the enemies of human kind . . . and that would have been a disaster for your people in the long run."

The dark-clad rabbi on Raanan's other side leaned close and whispered in his ear. The *Shofet* listened, nodded, and then made a gentle but firm gesture for silence when he tried to go on.

"Your ways are not ours," he said to Órlaith. "That could create problems."

"Yes, it will," Órlaith said, made a gesture of assent and then raised her eyebrows. "Is there a time or place without problems?"

Everyone chuckled. More seriously:

"The time of isolation total and complete is passing, but the old world isn't going to return, either. Your lands here . . . which I and the Crown freely recognize as yours forever . . . are never going to house great cities or attract throngs of outsiders."

She tactfully didn't mention the obvious reason; that the lands of the *bnei Yaakov* were a howling wilderness of dry death where a two-day walk could kill you without elaborate precautions in the way of specialist knowledge and gear, something she'd just very nearly demonstrated personally. There was a grim spare beauty to this country, but she couldn't imagine more than the odd scholar or eccentric coming here just for that. Or possibly a mystic.

"The outside world is coming to you willy-nilly, but you can control that traffic, if you use good judgment. So that there will be enough of it to enliven and enrich your lives, without threatening your way of life. If you—eventually—choose to sign the Great Charter and become formally part of Montival, you get substantial control of who settles here."

"But not of who passes though," Raanan said shrewdly. "From what I've heard there is a free-passage and free-trade clause in this Great Charter?"

Órlaith made a gesture that indicated the desolation around them, where the encampment of the *bnei Yaakov* was a single dot of wavering yellow light in the darkness.

"Would many want to?"

The *Shofet* chuckled at that, and his son did too. She went on:

"In fact, with your skill with camels and the advantage of being on the spot, I imagine you'll dominate what long-distance trade there is around here."

"Something to consider," Raanan said. "But to consider at length."

"Exactly. I wouldn't ask you to, mmmm, make such a decision offhand, without sending your own folk to see the truth of the outside world and bring you detailed reports."

The male of the Mojave pair spoke: "*Shofet*, I think it is worth sending envoys. *Ka'avak!* Listen! We have raids from the *Dilzhę'́é*—"

Her Sword-assisted mind translated that as Apache.

"—and the Navajo, and sometimes from the Chino Valley Federation, those bandit chiefs in Sonora, and even from the Trans-Pecos. From outlaws in those places, at least, and their bosses don't care or don't have the heft to stop it."

Meshek spoke: "We fight by the side of our Friends against all such threats!"

The Mojave chieftain nodded. "You do, *Seren*. We couldn't have done nearly so well, without our Friends and their camel-fighters. And we value your trade."

He grinned. "Camel is tasty, too," he said. "If you stew it long enough."

There was a general laugh; evidently the *bnei Yaakov* got around the ban on the flesh of their beasts by swapping them for cattle raised by their neighbors.

He went on seriously: "But it would be much better to end the fighting. We are farmers and hunters, not crazy men who live to prove themselves in battle, and all we wish is to live as we choose in peace."

He looked at Órlaith again. "Would your High Kingdom give us that, if it came here?"

She thought for a moment, sighed, and spread her hands.

"We would try to stop raiding and disorder, so we would," she said. "And eventually we would succeed, or at least keep it down; but it would be a matter of sending you help, not doing it all ourselves. To be honest with you, Councillor Henry, one reason you haven't seen anyone from Montival before this is that you are very, very far away from the heartlands of the Realm, and we have many calls on our resources and are reluctant to shoulder more responsibilities and spread ourselves too thin. That's changing, to be sure it is, but . . . slowly."

Unexpectedly the dark man smiled, and the woman beside him nodded and spoke: "If someone promises you the moon in a bowl for a light, they're lying. Loaning you a lamp and warning you the jojoba oil's short, that may be the truth."

He looked at the *Shofet*. "News does travel. We heard of how Montival sent food to the coastal people, when they were in a bad way four years ago."

Raanan stroked his beard again, then looked at her. "We heard, yes. That was well-done, and you asked no return for it."

Órlaith smiled and spread her hands. "But when I arrived there, I did receive a return, a return of friendship, trust and help. I think your holy books have a phrase, cast your bread upon the waters, it shall return to you many times? In my religion, we say deeds will return to you threefold, for good or ill."

There were nods at that. The Mojave councillor went on: "I told you of what we'd heard of the San Luis, and the Land of the Honeybee, *Shofet*."

New Deseret, she thought; its flag had a beehive, and its thinly held southwestern-most territories were only most of a thousand miles of deserts and mountains away.

And we admitted the Federated Districts of the San Luis, which is about the same distance, up in what used to be southern Colorado . . .

"We're certainly not eager to extend the Great Charter to these lands," Órlaith said. "Even the areas on the coast right west of here might have waited a generation or two, if it hadn't been for the . . . special circumstances. If you don't want to become member-realms . . . we certainly aren't going to try to force you, as long as you don't become a wanton trouble to those of your neighbors who have, which from all indications you don't want to do anyway. There will be plenty in Dún na Síochána just as happy to use you as a useful buffer for our new members, a shield that will take blows for us and to which we don't have legal obligations."

Plenty including my mother, who's a wee bit conservative as a strategist, Órlaith thought but did not say. *She'll accept the Topangans and Chatsworth Lancers because the Charter itself says we have to recognize anyone within the borders who wants to join, and we defined the borders broadly at the start. But she won't be over-happy to be hurried into it, especially with this war brewing across the Mother Ocean. And sure, there are real arguments favoring a slow approach, not least that it spares the burden of taxes, which always rest on the shoulders of the common folk in the end. But some things just need doing.*

Órlaith also didn't mention that ambitious and restless youngsters would undoubtedly filter out of this country for greener—literally—pastures, once that became possible. It would probably never be a real problem for the *bnei Yaakov* as a whole, though it might for individual families. In fact life could be easier for the rest of them, or at least more tranquil, because of it.

"But for the present, Judge Raanan, what I would ask of you is much simpler. I and my party at—"

She described the place where she'd left her companions. Raanan nodded to his son, who produced a rolled-up map from a pocket in the cloth wall of the tent and spread it. It was quite large, hand-drawn on densely-woven cotton, and included things like notes on the seasonal availability of water at various places.

"If you read our script—"

She nodded.

"That's here. At haNakik Oleh," he said, using his curved dagger as a pointer. "There is water, but not much this time of year."

She nodded. "Yes, Emigrant Canyon," which was exactly what haNakik Oleh meant. "We need transport back to the seaward side of the San Bernadino Mountains. The faster the better. I assure you this will be regarded as a gesture of goodwill, and will be remembered."

Even by my mother, in fact. I say absolutely nothing of how refusing it would be remembered; one of the pleasant things about dealing with smart people is that you don't have to be blunt about such matters.

"Sixty-four of you, and none used to handling camels," Raanan said.

His eyes narrowed in calculation, juggling time and space and carrying capacity, watering holes and available animals.

"Say twenty escorts . . . better than a hundred camels and their gear."

"We could get help quickly from Arik and Tuvyah's companies," Meshek pointed out.

Unexpectedly, the Rabbi leaned forward. He was a man of about his ruler's age, but thinner-faced and with more white in his beard, and he'd been avoiding talking to her directly during the meal. Now he spoke harshly.

"But that leaves the question . . . Princess . . . of what you were doing in that place. The *tō'ēḇā*."

Órlaith nodded gravely, and obviously surprised the man. "The abomination, yes; that is an excellent term for the evil thing. We were cleansing it, learned *rav*," she said.

Rav was an Ivrit term that literally meant master and in the *bnei Yaakov*'s dialect of the language was the precise, if somewhat formal and very respectful, term for a religious specialist. His use of *tō'ēḇā* was completely sincere; she could sense the freight of loathing and unacknowledged fear.

To be sure, simply denying it is often the best way to deal with fear.

He blinked. Whatever he'd been expecting, it wasn't that immediate agreement.

She went on: "You found it impenetrable, and sensed peril and great evil, am I right?"

He nodded reflexively. "I performed the ritual of Rabbi Gershon, with prayer and the blowing of the shofar. That helped to contain the wickedness."

Órlaith nodded sincerely; it probably had. The *rav* didn't seem to be a particularly nice man, but the sincerity of his belief was like a banked fire, and vaguely behind him she sensed Power—less a person than the glowing might of an absolute WORD. The *Shofet* spoke:

"Ever since the Change, I think; my father passed by that way in the early days. The books say there are a clutch of buildings and a consistent spring with a substantial flow. That would have been useful—it's scorched this time of year but there's good winter and spring grazing around there if you have a watering-point. The secret to herding in this country is to keep your beasts moving with the seasons and the ground cover, never the same place for too long and rarely the same area for two years in a row. But we found we couldn't . . . approach it. We send patrols periodically around the perimeter of the . . . effect."

"That's what I was doing. Sometimes we'd find tracks heading in," his son Meshek said. "Once they came out again, but he was a babbling madman who soon died in his sleep, in the middle of a screaming nightmare. And listening to what he was babbling . . . not a good idea. An abode of Lilit."

His father nodded. "Or like an ant lion trap."

Órlaith grimaced; that metaphor hadn't occurred to her, but it was unpleasantly apt. That type of insect was more common in dry sandy places. It dug a pit and waited at the bottom. Once past its edge, no matter how the prey scrabbled it circled down and down towards the waiting jaws.

"So it was declared forbidden," the Rabbi said, and glared at her. "But you chose to violate that ban."

"With respect, *rav*, no," she said. "It was not a matter of choice. I would have avoided that place of horrors my life long, were it not necessary."

Reiko nodded vigorously, and Órlaith went on: "Your war-captain Meshek ben-Raanan will have told you that the barrier about it no longer holds, and that there was a great fire. If you go there again, you'll find nothing but a burned ruin no more dangerous than any other. The spring is open for your use."

Which avoids the question of what terms we use for things like abominations. This is a man to quibble over the naming of things, I think.

"That . . . remains to be seen," he said.

"Indeed, and I advise you to send to the place yourselves," she added calmly. "Judge for yourselves; I'm a stranger, and I don't mind if you verify what I say, that's only reasonable, sure and it is. Go yourself, *rav*."

Meshek spread his hands palm-up. "There was a . . . a breaking. Suddenly we could enter; though we were afraid, of course. And we found the buildings burning, and the two ladies and the child. Leaving was . . . was normal. The shadow of fear no longer lies over that place. If that is right, we can use it. The buildings are gone, and I'm glad of that, but the water is good even now in summer, we filled our skins. That is no small thing."

"And the child of that evil?" the Rabbi asked.

Reiko had been mostly silent: these were not her people in the sense that they were Órlaith's. Now she leaned forward with her hands on her knees and spoke, slowly and clearly:

"I freed Kiwako from that . . . place. And she is under my protection, and that of the Empire of Dai-Nippon . . . of Great Japan. Does this create any problems, good sir?"

He looked aside. "No. If she goes with you."

"She does."

Órlaith turned to the *Shofet*. "Whatever you decide, Judge Raanan, we must return to our friends, and soon."

She smiled and spread her hands and turned them palm-up. "Duty calls. If we must walk, we will."

CHAPTER THIRTY-TWO

ERETZ BNEI YAAKOV/PARTICIPATORY DEMOCRACY OF TOPANGA
(MOJAVE DESERT/TOPANGA CANYON)
CROWN PROVINCE OF WESTRIA
(FORMERLY CALIFORNIA)
HIGH KINGDOM OF MONTIVAL
(FORMERLY WESTERN NORTH AMERICA)
AUGUST 22ND/HAOCHIZUKI 22ND/AV 29TH
CHANGE YEAR 46/SHŌHEI 1/5084TH YEAR OF THE WORLD/2044 AD

Meshek ben-Raanan pulled up his camel and the others followed suit; the animals didn't wear bits, but instead a hackamore bridle with the reins linked to nose-plugs. His head went up as he looked at either side of the canyon ahead of them, silent and dark in the dense heat of midafternoon, and Órlaith saw his eyes narrow thoughtfully.

"Your friends are watchful, *nisicah*," he said, amusement and respect in his tone. "It's well-done for them to be so ready for us, though we certainly left a plume of dust getting here."

Órlaith chuckled, and pulled back the *bnei Yaakov*–style headcloth she was wearing to show her face and hair.

"Watchful they are, *seren*," she said, feeling relief like a cramp unwinding in her gut. "Also alive, which is often the same thing. I'll tell them the good news."

Then she tapped the long thin stick on her mount's rump and gave a *hut-hut*; she was still riding Son of a Whore most of the time, and the animal regarded her as a nuisance . . . but by now as *his* nuisance. It would be a long time if ever before she had the instinctive command on one of these beasts as she did on a horse, but a few days had made her competent enough that her escorts weren't hovering near in fear of a disaster. Now she and Reiko drew in a little way ahead of the main body, halted again—prompting a peevish *make-up-your-mind-bitch* burble from Son of a Whore—and stood in the saddle and waved.

"All's well and better than well!" she called, the agreed signal that she was acting un-coerced; Reiko simply gave a brief order in her own language.

What looked like a pile of dirt and waxy shrubs stood up, and turned out to be Morfind Vogeler with her bow in hand. She shook back the camouflage cape and turned to wave to someone on the rim of the split in the rock, grinning enormously as she did. Two samurai rose from behind a rock, one with a *naginata* and the other holding a *higoyumi*; they both bowed deeply.

The grin had an unfortunate effect on Morfind's scar, but the *bnei Yaakov* coming up looked at it with knowledgeable and sober respect; they all knew what the mark of an ax looked like.

"Not bad," Meshek said, looking around their camp. "Not bad at all, for wetlanders."

He managed to convey surprise that outsiders hadn't stood in the full sun sucking on their thumbs until their brains fried, and the irony was so subtle she wasn't altogether sure whether he was joking or not, even with the Sword by her side.

There were twenty-one of the nomads in this party, a considerable commitment of their resources, and she'd been impressed anew with their efficiency. The *Shofet* had judged that a score were enough to handle the great train of camels necessary to move all of Órlaith's party, along with baggage animals and spares. The twenty-first was Shulamit bat-Raanan, who'd turned up riding one camel and leading another after trailing them unobtrusively for days.

Órlaith grinned again at the memory of the volcanoes-and-earthquakes family quarrel that had followed, with Meshek and Dov and

Shulamit all face-to-face and windmilling their arms as they shouted commands, imprecations, invocations of filial duty and citations of previous outrages, eventually going back to the time *someone* had dumped a roadrunner into a chicken coop and before that propped up an—admittedly dead—rattlesnake just where you were going to be suddenly face-to-face with it when you sat down in the jakes. Their tribesfolk had all looked elsewhere, some a little shocked, others trying very hard not to snigger.

In the end her brothers had relied on age and family authority, and Shulamit had countered with the simple fact that they could either let her come along or spend much time and several men sending her back tied to a saddle and constantly trying to escape.

Meshek's eventual quietly ominous *Father will deal with this* had left his sister unwontedly silent for most of a day, but she'd pitched in with the chores without a word, and had helped with Kiwako as well. Right now she was not far behind her brothers, virtually squirming in her saddle with excited happiness as the exotic foreigners showed themselves.

Egawa Noboru came trotting forward. When Reiko looked at him and gave a single slight nod and touched the hilt of the sword that was no longer *Kotegiri* his usual stoic self-control split for a moment in a grin, and he pounded his fist into his thigh. Then he went to one knee with his right fist to the ground and ducked his head for an instant of proud delight.

Órlaith tapped Son of a Whore's knee with the camel-stick.

"Ai, hoosh-hoosh-hoosh," she said, and the beast knelt and went to its belly in the usual jerky front-first manner.

She dismounted in time to touch the stick to his nose and say a firm *no* as he looked around with idle anticipation for someone—best of all, someone who smelled strange—to bite, and/or shower with smelly green mucus. Somewhat sulkily he settled in to chew his cud instead, his huge dark eyes a guileless statement of innocence.

Heuradys hit her like a blizzard and they hugged and pounded each other on the back, the knight's ironic reserve vanished for the moment. Greetings ran down from there through the grins and back-slaps of the clansfolk to the fist-to-chest salutes of the Associates to Macmac crawling on his belly to beg forgiveness for whatever sin had made her leave him behind, and then throwing himself into the air like a hairy wiggling porpoise in a dance of joy before trying to sniff inappropriate places to make sure she was all right.

John gave her a salute too, though he was grinning hard and looked a bit haggard. Thora and Deor were behind him. A clansman she recognized as Ruan Chu Mackenzie of Dun Fairfax was holding hands with the bard.

"Are we ready to move out?" Órlaith asked, looking up at the sun for an instant; it was around six, and about three hours to twilight. "After a quick meal—we've got plenty of supplies with us. These beasts can carry better than three hundred pounds each, and we've got scores."

"Though I prefer a bit less weight," Meshek said, as he came up with his siblings. "For a long trip. Peace be upon you all, warriors of the High Kingdom, and of Dai-Nippon."

The introductions were polite but brisk, and matters soon went to technicalities despite several of her party bursting with curiosity; Meshek wanted to see what he'd be putting on his packsaddles personally.

Thora Garwood added some specifics—the main task would be taking down the tarpaulins, if they decided to bother—and went on:

"And it'll be a pleasure as well as a relief to leave. The sand here gets into *everything*."

Slightly to her surprise John blushed up to his earlobes, and Heuradys snorted amusement. Órlaith made a mental note to tease her brother later. The slightly leathery Bearkiller was very handsome in an austere way, but she wasn't at all like the dewy-eyed beauties he usually tried for, and that was apart from being a decade and change older. Then again, Thora Garwood struck her as a woman accustomed to getting what she wanted.

"We can leave the bicycles," she said instead. "With the *bnei Yaakov* and their camels we'll go cross-country and save a fair bit of time not sticking to the old roads. But the horses . . ."

They trooped over to the picket line set up in the shade. The *seren* walked along it thoughtfully, gentle but firm with the four mounts when they shied at the smell of camel on his robe.

"These are fine horses, and in better condition than I would have thought," Meshek said, straightening up from feeling the fetlocks of Morfind's dappled Arab. "Nevertheless, if you try to take them with us, they will die; this land is not kind to their breed. And they would slow us before then."

Morfind's teeth ground. As they did, Susan Mica stepped up behind her and laid a gentle hand on her arm.

"*Lirimaer,* he's right," she said.

It carried conviction; her horse-lord people regarded their mounts as dear companions as well as wealth and symbols of position. Faramir sighed wordlessly from her other side. Her shoulders slumped. Probably nobody but Faramir and Órlaith understood when she muttered in Sindarin:

"Or he just wants to get his sand-thief hands on some good horses."

The beasts had already lost some condition; they were also rolling their eyes and snorting and occasionally pulling at the picket line at the unfamiliar scent. Órlaith had heard that camels frightened horses unaccustomed to them, and evidently it was true.

"He *is* right," Thora Garwood said.

She cocked an eye at the mass of *bnei Yaakov.* "Not the first time Deor or I have ridden a camel, either. For this sort of country, they're better."

Meshek nodded, glanced at Órlaith, and spoke: "I'll have a reliable man bring the horses on slowly. There are enough water-holes for that, if you know where. Sachar, you're good with horses, you see to it."

He cocked a sardonic eye at his sister. "And we have someone to do your share of the camp chores as well as her own."

"*Ken, seren,*" the man replied, roughly *as you command, captain.*

The *bnei Yaakov* loved to argue, but she'd noticed that when it came to military matters they obeyed with discipline that even Bearkillers would have approved.

Órlaith uncrossed her arms. "And now, time's wasting. Let's grab a bite and go!"

Reiko lowered and sheathed the Grass-Cutting Sword. "Raise your heads," she said to her followers' deep bows as they knelt before her.

Many of them were frankly awestruck, despite the self-control that governed their lives; they were mostly very young, after all.

Though no younger than I, she reminded herself. *The effect of* Kusanagi-no-Tsurugi *is more . . . more subtle when it is at rest than that of the Sword of the Lady; we are a more subtle people, and older. Still, it is strong. How strong I can only sense, as if the flow of great rivers or the fall of mountains awaits my command. No wonder it was hidden away at the Shrine in the ancient times! Carrying this always at your side would tempt a God, and I am the descendant of Amaterasu, not the Immortal One Shining in Heaven Herself.*

Ishikawa Goru was looking at her—when he dared to raise his eyes at all—as if she *was* one of the Great Kami come to Earth. Egawa was—if you knew him well—struggling against the smile that kept trying to break out.

She looked from one face to another in the fading alien light of this strange desert.

"You have followed me a very long way, my warriors," she said as they knelt facing her.

Her eyes rose to the sunset, lurid copper and jade-green and midnight blue in the west. Beyond lay home . . .

"Through storm and battle, across oceans and this strange wasteland of thirst and rock. None of you turned back, none flinched. Those who met death met it gladly, falling with their faces to the enemy and their swords in their hands. Through their courage and discipline, and yours, the Sacred Treasure has been restored to us. I know you all, as you know me. You will not be forgotten, not by me, and not by Dai-Nippon so long as our people and our nation endure. As the names of the Seventy Loyal Men and their commander will be spoken for centuries to come, so will yours."

Egawa flung his arms in the air. *"Tennō Heika banzai!"* he barked.

She knew he had always measured himself against his famous father, and driven himself to meet that standard. It was probably just dawning on him that he had now displayed equal merit. With an inner smile, she knew his sons would feel the same pride and the same burden.

"To the Heavenly Sovereign Majesty, *ten thousand years!*"

The samurai and the surviving sailors took it up in a crashing chorus: "Banzai! Banzai! *Banzai!*"

And now they are mine, she thought. *Mine in my own person, not simply by the right of the title I bear. Whatever happens, I think that will endure.*

"Now you are dismissed to prepare for our departure," she said with a snap in her tone. "The road home will be as long and as hard as the one we have traveled!"

She could feel Egawa's energy crackling from him as he came forward and went to one knee briefly.

"You have secured us the transport, even, Majesty," he said, looking at the herd of camels farther down the canyon.

"The Montivallan Princess arranged it."

"These are not much like the camels I saw in Korea, they have only one hump, but I assume they will serve."

"They are of another breed, more suited to hot deserts," Reiko said. "They can carry far more weight than a horse; even with a rider they bear over a hundred and fifty pounds on that packsaddle behind the one where the rider sits, and we have some just for baggage."

"So we are freed from supply worries even in this desolation," Egawa said, nodding with a professional's appreciation of logistics.

"And over any substantial distance in this type of terrain they are faster than horses as well—more enduring. They can go for up to three days without water and they will eat anything that grows."

Egawa began to reply, then halted as Kiwako scampered up and hid behind her, holding Reiko by the sash and peering at him dubiously around her body with a pouting lower lip. His gaze was equally pawky.

"The *gaijin* infant looks like a fox spirit, with those eyes and that hair," he grumbled. "What does the Majesty intend with her?"

"I am not sure, General," Reiko said honestly. "But she was . . . was essential to what I accomplished. Indeed, without her warning at a crucial instant in the place where the Grass-Cutting Sword lay, I might well have died. She will return with us; I will see that she receives a civilized upbringing and education, and provide for her future. She is still a wild thing, and very young; allowances must be made for her behavior until she learns better. She is to be guarded from all harm, and treated gently with no more firmness than is absolutely necessary; I strictly charge you with this and you will so inform your subordinates."

"Hai, wakarimashita, Heika," Egawa said, bowing.

He understood the concept of a debt of honor perfectly, of course, and that it didn't matter if you liked the one you owed it to.

"It will be done, Majesty."

Since several of them including his second-in-command were right behind him, it certainly would be. She smiled as she stroked the child's head, and at his slight expression of enquiry went on:

"I was thinking of debts of honor," she said, and turned to bring out a long wrapped bundle from her kit. "Kneel, General Egawa."

He did, his eyes widening as she extended it horizontally in her right hand.

"Receive this. *Kotegiri* is no more; now and forever it is part of something greater. But it is fitting that one of our party at least should carry a Masamune sword, here in this foreign land. Bear it as it deserves, and hand it on to your descendants in their time!"

His hands trembled slightly as he undid the wrapping. That stopped when he saw the blade within. She had had time to give it some care, and its stay in the dry desert had done it little harm. The few small chips in the edge and slight etching where salt blood had lain had been incurred long ago, in Japan. Very long ago.

"Yes," Reiko said to his unspoken question. "It is the *Honjo Masamune*."

Receiving a blade from the *Tennō*'s own hands was a signal honor. This one was a product of the great master-smith, each surviving one of which had its own name and history. Even in that select company the *Honjo* was unusual. For many centuries it had been in the possession of the Tokugawa Shoguns, the Generalissimos who had been puppetmasters to so many Emperors. To give it to a general in *her* service was a public statement of unconditional trust.

"But, Majesty, the *Honjo Masamune* was lost when . . ."

It had been lost at the end of the Pacific War, taken like many others of the famous *nihontō* blades by a mysterious American soldier known only by variations on his name—Cody Biltmore, or something which had sounded vaguely like that to Japanese officials as ignorant of English as he was of Japanese. Egawa's eyes flashed to the sword by her side. Then he raised the gift wordlessly across his palms as he bowed his head.

"Mountain," Reiko said, pointing past the child towards a single peak.

"Yama," Kiwako repeated, from her perch in the front saddle; they were using a two-seat model, one before and one behind the hump.

"Mountain range," Reiko said, running her finger from east to west along the line of peaks before them, the mountains that separated the Valley from the inland deserts.

"Sanmyaku," Kiwako echoed.

Then Reiko took up the slate she had borrowed from Shulamit and wrote with the chalk: 山脈, accurate despite the swaying pacing gait of the camel. Kiwako giggled, repeated the word, and then made an awkward attempt to duplicate the characters with her tongue sticking out one corner of her mouth.

"Motto tango, Heika!" she said. "More words, *Heika*!"

"Enough for now, little fox," Reiko said, putting away the slate.

"Kiwako!" the girl said sharply, pointing to herself. "Not *kitsune*, *Kiwako*. No, no, no!"

Never having had a name, Kiwako was immensely proud of hers now that she realized it was unique and uniquely her own, and would sometimes say it over and over again; she'd also learned how to say *no* in three languages. They'd been at the vocabulary lesson for several hours, and now that she wasn't hungry and terrified the girl absorbed words the way the desert sands did spilled water, and had even grasped the concept that the characters *represented* words, which made her a little doubtful of her first estimate of the girl's age. But now they were coming up to the Valley's northern checkpost, a small adobe fort flying the running horse sigil of the Delgado family.

Órlaith's retainer Droyn Jones de Molalla waited there. Surprisingly, the lord of the Chatsworth Lancers and his wife were present too. They needn't have waited in this spot—lookouts with telescopes on the heights would have spotted so numerous a party some time ago, and could have flashed messages with mirrors or smoke-signals. A little closer, and she saw two of the leaders of the Topangans as well; she congratulated herself on being able to recognize the *gaijin* faces immediately.

Still, this is ominous. Something has gone wrong.

"Not re-enamored of your former friends, Lord Mark?" Órlaith asked.

"No," he said shortly. "Your Highness. And I didn't think they were friends, even then. I thought they were allies and we could be mutually useful . . . and OK, I was wrong about that, too."

Truth, she thought; the Sword was by her side, and she knew he believed what he said.

And she knew from his sideways glance he knew that she knew; her crooked brow told him that she knew he knew she knew. Then he laughed.

"I wanted to lead the Chatsworth Lancers south through the Canyon to the sea," he said. "And by God, I've finally done it!"

Jared Tillman and Kwame Curtis both looked as if they thought the joke in very poor taste. The Chatsworth Lancers *were* here at the southern end of Topanga Canyon Boulevard, about a hundred and twenty of them, each with a couple of armed followers on foot; plus the Topangan levy, her own followers, Reiko's, and the score of *bnei Yaakov* riders. Delgado's eyes slid their way; they were off southwestward, downwind, to keep their camels from spooking the horses. One of the beasts raised its long neck and gave a blubbering moan, and several of the equines shied anyway.

"A lot more of those crazy Jews out there than I thought, evidently," he murmured. "Tough-looking bastards, and they've got good gear for that type of country."

"Yes, there are, and yes, they do," Órlaith said. "And if I were you, Lord Mark, I would accommodate their desire to be quiet neighbors."

He shrugged. "Yeah, fighting them would be like trying to hunt birds with a hammer, right? Nothing in the Mojave worth having anyway," he said. "Glad to have them here *now*, I'll tell you."

Many of the desert tribesmen were staring in blank astonishment at the sea; this position gave a good view of the Pacific. Shulamit was entranced, and she was far from the only one.

And would that I was simply looking at the Mother Ocean in gladness, Órlaith thought. *Nothing as simple as just returning victorious from my own Quest . . . or to be more precise, from helping with Reiko's. But then, Da and Mother didn't either—when they came back with the Sword of the Lady, the whole last half of the Prophet's War lay ahead, years of grinding-hard bloody work, and building the Kingdom during that and after it.*

The little harbor that the Topangans had made was much more crowded than usual. The *Virgen de las Esmeraldas* and the Astorian merchantman had been gone for days, but four ships were anchored in line a hundred yards from the shore, within easy catapult range. All of them were three-masters, all with the squared-off bow that she recognized from the naval battle in the Glorannon, and all were flying the same flag. One with a broad red stripe running the length of it, with a white circle and a red star in its midst, and narrow strips of white and then blue above and below.

"*Bakachon,*" Reiko said grimly. "The reason the *jinnikukaburi* did not pursue us into the desert was that they planned to intercept us on our return if their first efforts failed."

Órlaith nodded. "My father was fond of saying that the enemy, those dirty dogs, have a plan of their own . . . which is why we call them *the enemy.*"

Egawa gave a slight snort at that, amused even in this situation. He seemed calmly confident, doubtless because his *Tennō* now bore the Grass-Cutting Sword. Órlaith was less so. The Sword of the Lady was a terrible thing to confront in battle, but it didn't make her invincible or immortal; to be a weapon in the common sense was not its primary role. When she grasped it and closed herself off from the world of common day, the thing that Reiko now bore at her side seemed to shine with a radiance of sheer power, but how decisive an aid it would be in a fight . . .

That we do not know yet. I'd rather not depend on an unknown when so much is at stake.

The comforting thing was that the Korean ships were not alone in the water. The *Tarshish Queen* was standing to a little farther out, her sails half-furled, beating slowly back and forth in the wind from the northwest. And farther out still, the long dark shape of RMN *Stormrider* waited, coming about slowly as she worked back and forth too; the portlids of her broadside were pointedly open and her boarding and splinter-netting rigged.

The locals had a telescope longer than a man was tall mounted on a complex tripod, some pre-Change amateur astronomer's pride and joy salvaged later; rather ironically, its labels proclaimed it was made by *Nihon Seiko*. Delgado and the Topangan Brains were using it to examine the *Stormrider* carefully.

"That frigate is one impressive piece of ship, Your Highness," Delgado said, and Kwame nodded agreement.

"I gather that's the state of the art up north?" Kwame said.

Heuradys nodded. "Pride of the fleet, Captain Curtis. I just wish we had two of them here now. That would make things much more . . . controllable."

"We have the pair of trebuchets," Kwame said thoughtfully.

Sir Droyn looked between the ships and the berm that hid the Topangan weapon. "I suspect they could saturate that area with napalm shell before you did serious damage," he said. "Unless your artillery got lucky, of course. Trebuchets are best against large stationary targets."

Órlaith handed her knight her helm and stepped up to the telescope. She adjusted the aiming knobs and scanned the enemy ships. The powerful instrument put her vision right on top of them, which wasn't entirely positive. She could have done without the memory of an armored man looking back at her with a pair of binoculars while nibbling on what was obviously a salted, smoked human hand and occasionally spitting out a small bone. More important . . .

"They've got Eaters on board," she said. "Local ones, I mean. Though I could swear I recognize one from the action in the Bay, or at least his ax, but they must have gotten the most of them from the LA tribes. A hundred or so on each of the ships, besides their usual complements."

Jared Tillman whistled softly. "That's . . . a lot of the bastards."

"More than I've ever seen," Delgado said. "They sneak in by ones and twos and small groups sometimes and we have to hunt them down, but nothing like this."

"We can hold the Canyon, and I think they know it," Kwame said. "They haven't attacked yet, and they've been here two days now."

"They haven't attacked because they haven't had the targets they desire within striking distance," Órlaith said. "Which is to say, myself and the Majesty."

She nodded to the frigate and Feldman's ship. "And if they send their fighters ashore, they make themselves vulnerable . . . more vulnerable . . . to those. With the Eaters, they may have enough for a ship action and one on land, though."

Decision firmed. "Reiko, can I borrow your Captain Ishikawa, and his men?" she said.

The Nihonjin nodded decisively, and spoke a word of command to her followers.

"Johnnie," she went on.

Her brother was in full plate. They were all in complete war-harness now, back to the smell of rancid canola and the bake-oven feel, though after the Valley of Death she was never going to complain of ordinary heat again. His fist-to-chest salute made a martial clank.

"Take the Nihonjin sailors, and go there." She pointed west, past the giant old-world wreck. "There are some longboats at the saltworks. Take them, and . . . the crossbowmen from the Protector's Guard, and a few others, say four, pick them yourself. Feldman's shorthanded for a full-scale action; you reinforce him. And tell him to cooperate fully with Captain Russ of the *Stormrider*."

He shot her a swift look of surprise, and she stepped closer and spoke softly; there was no need to let the Topangans or Delgado in on the full details of her little disagreement with the High Queen Regnant.

"Johnnie, Reiko *has* her Grass-Cutting Sword the now. We've done what we set out to do. Now we go back to Mother, roll on our backs, wave our paws in the air and whimper for forgiveness. She'll recognize a magic sword when she sees one! So will anyone with the least bit of the Sight, without Reiko having to do anything too . . . dramatic."

Deor Godulfson was standing close. He nodded. "It *burns*," he said. "Like carrying the very sun in your hand. . . ."

John nodded himself, giving it a glance. "Why not just have everyone go out to the *Tarshish Queen* and show them our heels?" he said.

She shook her head. "They've some on those ships who could sense Reiko and me moving, given what we bear," she said. "They'd be waiting for us on the water, that they would. For you, not so much. We pin their attention here."

Deor made a soft sound of agreement at that, too; and John obviously remembered how he'd tracked the Haida shaman at the battle in the Bay.

"Also I'm not inclined to leave our new subjects in the lurch," she said, and tapped her sabaton-armored foot on the dusty faded asphalt with a clank.

For this part she let her voice ring. It was the truth, and the truth of her heart, but kingship always included an element of show. Symbol and performance were of its essence; you just had to remember to truly be what you wished to seem to be.

"This is Montivallan soil now, and by Macha Red-Locks and Nemain of the Blood-Shout and Badb Catha of the Crows, these are our folk, every one of them, and House Artos stands with them! The Shadow Queen bear witness!"

He nodded, saluted again, and collected the crossbowmen; Deor went with him, and Thora. Ruan Chu Mackenzie spoke a word to Karl, who looked at her. Órlaith wasn't surprised, though an outsider might have been; folk tended to underestimate Mackenzie discipline. She wasn't exactly a clanswoman herself, but she wasn't exactly not one either, and she understood them inside the skin. She nodded, Karl grinned and thumped his comrade on the shoulder, Mathun tossed him a spare bundle of arrows, and the young archer-healer from Dun Fairfax pelted after John's party with his bow pumping in his hand. When he caught up he and Deor exchanged an instant's brief fierce embrace.

A fleeting memory went through Órlaith's mind at the sight, some ancient sage she'd read: *Indeed, an army of lovers would be invincible, for under the eyes of the beloved the lover fears nothing but shame, and each is driven to noble deeds.*

"Though to be sure the same applies to comrades and true friends," she murmured, though she still felt a little envious.

No life is complete without friendship. On the other hand, it isn't complete without love, either.

Heuradys chuckled, following the byplay and the thought. Then her head nodded to the enemy ships. "They're moving," she said.

They were; at least, one longboat was rowing towards the shore. Órlaith stepped up to the telescope and adjusted it. One large boat of the sort most substantial ships towed or carried on davits, with six oars to a side. The first look through the eyepiece showed her a close view of a naked, muscular back seamed with whip-scars that seemed to ripple with the flexing effort. Then she focused on the bows, and frowned.

"That's odd," she said, with a sinking feeling in her stomach. "They've got a truce-flag on a stick, but there's a man in Nihonjin armor in that boat . . . two . . . and one's carrying the *Hinomaru*."

They both had their hair dressed in the samurai way, with the pate shaved back to the topknot. One was a man of no great years, perhaps a decade older than she or Reiko, though oddly his hair and sparse chin-beard were speckled with white. The other . . . it was impossible to judge from his face.

Mainly because parts of it were missing, including most of the lips.

Reiko gasped aloud. That itself a sign of something desperately wrong. Órlaith stepped aside, and the Nihonjin ruler stepped up to the telescope.

Her face went gray-white beneath its usual pale honey tint. "Yoshihito," she whispered. "My brother."

"If this is Prince Yoshihito, will you draw the Grass-Cutting Sword against him, Majesty?" Egawa asked.

It was a little over a thousand yards to the little group waiting by the boat drawn up on the shore, and the Japanese were keeping to a steady, slightly slow pace. Reiko concentrated on her breathing for a moment, until the dizziness passed. The noonday sun was blinking on the rippled surface of the water ahead, turning the figures of the men on the beach to black silhouettes against brightness.

"If I do, will you be with me?" she asked.

His speech gave a strong hint; in strict law, Yoshihito was the *Tennō*, and she the Princess. Her elevation had been on the assumption that he had perished. And perhaps he had, even if he still breathed.

"Yes, Majesty," he said; quietly, but without hesitation. "To the death."

The four samurai at her back echoed that with a soft-voiced *hai!* Reiko nodded.

"I shall proceed as seems best under the circumstances," she said. "I do not wish to have my brother's blood on my hands."

Her left hand was resting on the scabbard of the reborn *Kusanagi-no-Tsurugi*, and a feeling of warmth spread from it. Warmth, life, *power.*

The situation makes me feel helpless, but I am not, she thought. *I have cherished my memories of him, of watching him in the dojo or at ceremonies or playing go with me in the private quarters. I have seen him teasing a kitten with a feather, and playing his flute, and winning a line-capping game, and making little Yōko laugh by making faces at her. I sat with him and ate sweet dango as we watched the waxing harvest moon. I have grieved for Yoshihito, and lit incense at his grave marker for Obon. Let that remain.*

There were two men in Japanese armor . . . armor that looked old and not particularly well maintained, as if it had been sitting in a storeroom for years and just recently taken out. One was Yoshihito . . . but aged a decade beyond his true tally of years. The one with him was a ruined horror, with only the twitching of the eyes to show that it was a living man. Egawa grunted and then spoke a name softly; not one she knew, but probably one of the guards who had been on her brother's ship when it sailed and never returned. Behind them were half a dozen Korean warriors in their mail-and-plates shirts and spired helmets. And another man, in motley, shaggy clothing.

Kangshinmu, she thought, her left hand clamping harder on *Kusanagi*. *Sorcerer.*

"Where is Kiwako?" Shulamit said suddenly, and frantically.

"*What?*" Meshek asked, tearing his eyes away from the drama below.

"She was right here!" his sister said, looking about and doing everything but patting her pockets. "She was right in the rear saddle—"

Suddenly she pointed downslope, towards the sea. "She's running after the *Heika*! *Come back, you little idiot!*"

Shulamit threw herself out of the saddle, landed like a bouncing ball and dashed off. Meshek leaned far over and began to snatch desperately at her as she passed, but she was as lithe as a snake as she swayed aside . . . and he didn't complete the motion anyway. As he knew from painful experience in practice sessions, she was as good in the art of *krav maga* as anyone her age and weight could be, so he couldn't just clutch her hair unless he wanted a dislocated thumb for his pains. When she focused on doing something, she gave it everything she had, and she was fiercely protective of the feral toddler.

"Ha-matzav khara!" he swore desperately, and flung up his hands to halt the onward surge of the *bnei Yaakov* riders after the daughter of the *Shofet*. "No! If we all go it will seem like an attack!"

The camels were groaning and burbling, catching their masters' building alarm. "Dov, keep them in order. Everyone, quiet, and leave this to me! *Now!*"

He slapped his bow back into the case on his saddle, leapt down, threw the reins to a man who made a surprised but successful grab at them, and took off after his sister with his left hand gripping the scabbard of his *shamshir* to keep it from flapping. He ran crouched over, instinctively using folds in the ground to stay as invisible as possible to anyone looking up from the beach, a skill learned in long training. And by experience even more savage, ground into him stalking and being stalked by Apache raiders with death by torture as the price of failure. With a little luck, using the ground and the neutral earth color of his robe would keep eyes off him until he could . . .

"Do *something*!" he said desperately to himself.

He could see the weird little child too now, scampering along with her shift fluttering around her calves. Shulamit was gaining rapidly on the girl, even an active two-year-old just didn't have the length of leg to run very quickly, but the child could creep about like a cat, soundlessly and low to the ground. She'd managed to get a good head-start before Shulamit noticed, and they were only a thousand yards or so from the shore to begin with. He didn't bother to call after his sister the way she was yelling herself. The probability of her just coming back and leaving the child to her fate was about as great as the chance of him giving up and letting her run into whatever deadly peril was shaping down by the sea.

Meshek pulled the bola from his waist, the three round stone weights and their connecting cords of thin supple braided camel-hide. His thick wrist flicked them into motion about his head, and they whirred through the air like the blades of an ancient helicopter. It was a dangerous weapon, and using it was a desperation move . . .

But I'm desperate.

"*Watakushi no imouto,*" Yoshihito said, smiling in a way that made her want to weep. "My sister. Make obeisance to your sovereign."

Reiko stood, with her hand on the scabbard, looking at him as the sand rutched under her sandals. His eyes were familiar . . . save that they drew you inward. There was a feeling there, a lassitude beyond mere weariness as the thirst she had felt in the desert of the Valley of Death was beyond being a little ready for a draught of water. A craving for death stronger than the heartbeat, controlled only by a fear unnamed. Then because that hurt too much she looked at the enemy ships. They swarmed with the Eater horde, and *jinnikukaburi* officers were marshaling them, shoving them down ropes into waiting boats. She made a wordless prayer, closed her eyes for a heartbeat, then opened them.

And . . .

"This is the sword of the *Tennō*," she said steadily. "Bestowed by Amaterasu-ōmikami, our Ancestress."

Reiko went to her knees. Droplets of seawater blew off the waves that hissed up the beach behind the other party's heels, and gulls screeched with hurtful obliviousness. Egawa gave a shocked gasp. She pulled the scabbarded blade from her sash and held it in the posture of presentation, across her raised palms with her head bowed.

"Take it, and draw it, my brother," she said. "You are of the Imperial

House, eldest child of the Emperor of Rebirth, heir to the Chrysanthemum Throne."

The smile grew harder to bear; she had to suppress an impulse to take handfuls of sand and grind them into her eyes. But somewhere, there was her brother.

Perhaps it could purify him, she thought desperately. *Oh, perhaps!*

He reached out and took the sword. Warrior's reflex deeper than thought settled his hand on the hilt, and began to slide the not-steel out. Suddenly the *kangshinmu* screamed in rough pidgin Nihongo:

"No! Slave-dog-fool, do not draw it! Hold only!"

"Egawa, *kill him,*" she shouted, pointing to the magus.

Her eyes remained on her brother. Sweat beaded on his brow; as he frowned she could see the lines beside his eyes, lines of long torment. Steel clashed, but it seemed incredibly distant, a tale told in another age.

A child's treble sounded from behind her, piercing the noise of battle and the shouts of the warriors as no common sound could:

"Bad auntie! *Bad auntie!*"

Reiko spun in place as she rose. Her hand plucked her *tessen* from her sash and snapped it open as she moved, fluid and sure, every part of her body following paths as prescribed and inevitable as geometry. It was not necessary to see, but she did. The *kangshinmu* moved through the sudden battle like a man moving at normal speed among those for whom the air had turned to amber honey. Egawa was falling, blood spouting from the stump of his left wrist. And the razor edge of the war-fan moved as she whirled, in and under the sorcerer's rising sword. It struck below his ear, into the flesh, across and down in a diagonal drawing slash that ended below the Adam's apple. Blood spouted as steel parted the carotid, and the depthless eyes grew wide. Knees buckled and the sword wavered, but she continued her whirl without slowing.

That had spurred her brother. The flash of steel, and the feel of a sword-hilt in his hand; and instinct fostered since their father placed the first small *bokken* in his chubby child's paws so long ago. *Kusanagi-no-Tsurugi* swept free, the scabbard dropping as he raised the blade two-handed in the pear-splitter, aiming for the crown of her helmeted head.

Yoshihito's eyes flew wide. For an instant there was only wonder in them, and his lips moved, forming words:

"Namu . . . Amida . . . Butsu . . ."

Then he screamed, a sound that echoed in her mind as if it would never leave. And he *burned*. As fire had threaded through the steel of the katana, now it wound through his flesh. It did not sizzle or stink; the process was far too swift for that. The sword of the Sun tumbled free through a fall of black ash that scattered on the wind. Some of it blew onto her lips, bitter and salt. The hilt slapped into her hand, with a feeling as if continents were colliding.

And they are, here, she knew with a sudden certainty, feeling the colossal masses striving beneath her feet. *And I could break them!*

On the hillside above her, Órlaith knelt and thrust the Sword of the Lady into the earth. Something crystalline, something not of matter, spread out. Like a protective shell forged in the heart of an ancient star, shielding the soil of Montival. But that was good, was *right*. The power of the thing in her hands was of the sky, of air and winds and fire and a dance of particles between the stars. . . .

She stood with her arms outstretched, a fixed point about which worlds turned. She could feel the negation that drove the *kangshinmu*'s body on past the point where the natural fire within faltered and ceased, as there was not enough blood to sustain it or movement of the lungs to drive the elements of breath into the fluid. It reached for her, dropping its blade, beyond such things, grinning with wet teeth and eyes vanished in pools of tar. One arm batted Kiwako aside with a squeal of pain.

Shulamit tore the sling loose from her snood as she ran, dropped a two-ounce lead egg into the pouch, whirled the camel-hide thong once around her head and cast with a snapping flex of the whole body and a hawk-shriek of:

"Mi chamocha ba'elim haShem!"

The shot whirred through the air too fast to really see, a blur as it traveled seventy yards downslope, and the back of the *kangshinmu*'s head burst with a *crack* and a spray of blood and bone-splinters and gray-pink tissue . . . and through it writhed a net of black thread, infinitely fine, as threads of light and fire did through the steel of *Kusanagi*. And still he walked. Meshek's bola struck the dead thing's thighs and instantly wound itself around them a dozen times, the stone weights thudding into the obscenely moving flesh. Then the *kangshinmu* fell at last, bloody teeth snapping at the sand before he went limp.

Reiko moved beyond him in a wheeling movement, slow and stately. It was not necessary to see more of him, or of Shulamit tenderly raising Kiwako and checking for injuries, or the last of the Korean swordsmen falling to the skilled fury of her samurai.

I thought this could move mountains. Mountains of air! some part of her mind that was still her realized.

The mountains of air were there, sliding currents smoother than glass, huge masses always hanging above her. Light and fire streamed down upon them, drew the tears of Ocean upward, slid around the whirling surface of the globe. And when she called, they answered: answered her, answered the great glowing figure that she could sense danced above her. Reiko danced now too, a thing of swift steps and slow, stately and serene. Clouds gathered above, unfolding with a majesty that only seemed deliberate.

Ame-no-Murakumo-no-Tsurugi.

That had been the first name of what had become the Grass-Cutting Sword, in a time more ancient than legend. The Sword of the Gathering Clouds of Heaven.

Air fell down the mountains of rock behind her. Air struck the water. Storm hissed and blossomed and grew, and the sky darkened in a turning gyre of black cloud laced with the actinic white of lightning-bolts. Órlaith still knelt, her hands clenched around the long hilt of something that Reiko now realized *was* a symbol that could be touched, face blank with concentration as it bowed over the crystal pommel. The wind still scourged the shore and made the people above cover their eyes and crouch, but the most of it slid over that protection. Over it, down, gathering strength and weight and speed, and . . .

Her dance turned quicker, building, raising, holding the titanic forces in check as they grew and grew and strained. Fire raced through her, consuming and welcome. Then she turned and *Kusanagi-no-Tsurugi* slashed outward. Struck as Yamato Takeru had used it in the age of legends, in his own time of desperate need, as a whip of fire and air.

The winds raced out, and lashed the ocean to froth before them. The edge of the waters receded a dozen yards in a rush and boiled as gravity warred with the spirits of air. The enemy ships beyond heeled far over. One swung around its anchor and capsized, the terrified shrieks of its crew mere shapes of open mouths lost in the elemental roar that blew past Reiko. The others desperately cut their anchors and skidded through seas grown heaving and mountainous and meeting in chaotic collisions, their voice a tiger's snarl larger than worlds. The two Montivallan ships ran ahead of them.

A voice in her own language was shouting as well, triumphantly: "God-Storm! *Divine wind!*"

The dance ended in a long slow motion of dismissal. The mountains of air collapsed away, the strong subtle patterns of the natural world taking control of them once more. Reiko felt her being collapsing inward as well, falling back *into* her very self; and at the edge of awareness there was a smile like her mother's.

Daughter of the Empire, it whispered, warm with love and pride. *Daughter of the Sun. My beloved child.*

She staggered, panting; none of the samurai dared do other than kneel and press their foreheads to the ground. She found the scabbard and sheathed the Grass-Cutting Sword, and the *click* as the *tsuba* met the *koiguchi* shattered the last of the protection around her. Her whole being quivered as she took one deep breath, retained it, exhaled, another. Each seemed to make her more herself, but that self was not what she had been.

Reiko knelt by Egawa's side. The tourniquet around his left wrist was crude, a lacing cord from his armor twisted with the hilt of his *tantō*-dagger, but it would serve for now; his eyelids fluttered, but he was conscious.

"You are . . . the Immortal One Shining in Heaven," he said, his voice a thread.

"No, Egawa Noboru," she said. "But for a moment I was. And in that moment, Her blood was renewed in my line."

Kiwako crept up and pressed against her side, shivering. An arm went around the thin shoulders.

Poor little fox, she thought. *The world is so wide and so terrible.*

"In our line," she said, smiling down at the man who had been her second father. It took a moment for that to bring his brows up.

"Your son Ryōma is a young man of good character and much promise," she said. "And eventually I will need a consort. The grandchildren of your grandchildren may rule a Dai-Nippon once more great and at peace. To build that day, you need only serve me as you have before."

His injured arm stirred. "I will serve my *Tennō* as well as a one-handed swordsman may."

Reiko made a *tsk* sound.

"You will serve me with what is here . . ."

Her fan moved to touch his right hand.

". . . and what is here . . ."

Then it rested on his brow for a moment.

". . . and most of all, with what is *here,*" and the fan touched over his heart.

"I . . ." his voice grew slower. "I do not know what I would do with myself in a time of peace, but it is a worthy dream, Majesty. And until then . . ."

She looked up. The clouds were long white streamers now. Her retainers were tending to their wounded, and behind them Órlaith and her band were picking their way down a slope where much had been uprooted or washed away. Westward her homeland waited, still unknowing.

"Until then? Deeds like skies full of storm, my *bushi*. Like skies full of storm."